Ladies'
Night

ALSO BY MARY KAY ANDREWS

Spring Fever

Summer Rental

The Fixer Upper

Deep Dish

Savannah Breeze

Blue Christmas

Hissy Fit

Little Bitty Lies

Savannah Blues

Ladies' Night

Mary Kay Andrews

St. Martin's Press
New York

This is a work of fiction. All of the characters, organizations, and events portrayed in this novel are either products of the author's imagination or are used fictitiously.

www.stmartins.com

LIBRARY OF CONGRESS CATALOGING-IN-PUBLICATION DATA

Andrews, Mary Kay, 1954–
   Ladies' night / Mary Kay Andrews.—1st ed.
      p. cm.
   ISBN 978-1-250-01967-7 (hardcover)
   ISBN 978-1-250-01965-3 (e-book)
   1. Divorced women—Fiction. 2. Friendship—Fiction.
  3. Psychological fiction. I. Title.

   PS3570.R587L34 2013
   813'.54—dc23

                          2013009101

St. Martin's Press books may be purchased for educational, business, or promotional use. For information on bulk purchases, please contact Macmillan Corporate and Premium Sales Department at 1-800-221-7945 extension 5442 or write specialmarkets@macmillan.com.

First Edition: June 2013

10 9 8 7 6 5 4 3 2 1

In memory of my brother, John Joseph Hogan,
who left this world too soon.
Miss you, Johnny.

1

If Grace Stanton had known the world as she knew it was going to end that uneventful evening in May, she might have been better prepared. She certainly would have packed more underwear and a decent bra, not to mention moisturizer and her iPhone charger.

But as far as Grace knew, she was just doing her job, writing and photographing Gracenotes, a blog designed to make her own lifestyle look so glamorous, enticing, and delicious it made perfectly normal women (and gay men) want to rip up the script for their own lives and rebuild one exactly like hers.

She peered through the lens finder of her Nikon D7000 and frowned, but only for a moment, because, as Ben had told her countless times, a frown was forever. She made a conscious effort to smooth the burgeoning wrinkles in her forehead, then concentrated anew on her composition.

She'd polished the old pine table to a dull sheen, and the available light streaming in from the dining room window glinted off the worn boards. With her right hand, she made a minute adjustment to one of the two deliberately mismatched white ironstone platters she'd placed on a rumpled—but not wrinkled—antique French grain-sack table runner. She replaced the oversized sterling forks, tines pointed down, at the edge of the platters. Should she add knives? Maybe spoons? She thought not. Spare. The look she was going for was spare.

Edit, edit, edit, she thought, nodding almost imperceptibly. Less was more. Or that's what Ben always claimed.

Now. About that centerpiece. She'd cut three small palmetto fronds from the newly landscaped driveway . . . No, she corrected herself. The builder's Web site referred to it as a motor court. The palmettos were giving her fits. She'd arranged them in a mottled, barnacle-crusted pale aqua bottle she'd plucked from a pile of random junk at the flea market the weekend before. They should have looked great. But no. They were too stiff. Too awkward. Too vertical.

Grace replaced the palmettos with a cardboard carton of lush red heirloom tomatoes. Hmm. The vibrant color was a good contrast against the nubby linen of the runner, and she loved the lumpy forms and brilliant green and yellow stripes on some of the irregularly shaped fruits. Maybe, if she placed the container on its side, with the tomatoes spilling out? Yes. Much better.

She grabbed a knife from the sideboard and sawed one of the tomatoes in half, squeezing it slightly, until seeds and juices dribbled out onto the tabletop.

Perfect. She inhaled and clicked the trigger on her motor-driven shutter. Click. Click. Click. She adjusted the focus so the pale gel-covered seeds were in the foreground. Now, she zoomed out, leaving the tomatoes as red blurs, so that the old ironstone platters were in focus, their age-crazed crackles and brown spots coming into sharp relief.

"Very pretty," a voice breathed in her ear.

Grace jumped.

Ben rested a hand lightly on her shoulder and studied the vignette.

"Is that for tomorrow's 'Friday Favorites' post?" he asked.

"Mm-hmm," Grace said. "I tried the palmetto fronds and, before that, a basket of seashells, and then some green mangoes, but I think the tomatoes work best, don't you?"

He shrugged. "I guess."

"What?" Grace studied his face, as always, craving his approval. "The tomatoes don't work for you?"

"They're nice. In an artsy-fartsy kind of way," he said.

She pushed a strand of light brown hair off her forehead and took a step back from the table. She'd spent an hour putting the table together, and she'd been fairly pleased with the effect she'd achieved. But Ben didn't like it.

"Too country-cutesy?" she asked, glancing at her husband. Ben's trained eyes missed nothing. He'd been in the ad business forever, and no detail was too small or too insignificant. It was why they made such a great team.

"It's your blog," he reminded her. "And your name is on it. I don't want business stuff to impinge on your editorial freedom. But . . ."

"But what? Come on. I'm a big girl. I can take it."

"The Aviento folks sent us a big crateful of pieces of their new fall line," Ben said, hesitating. "Treasures of Tuscany, the new pattern is called. It's for the giveaway you're doing on Monday. I was thinking maybe you could put the tomatoes in one of those bowls they sent."

Grace wrinkled her nose. "That is seriously the ugliest pottery I have ever seen, and it looks about as Italian as a can of Chef Boyardee."

"You don't have to set the whole table with it. Just maybe put some of the tomatoes in one of the bowls. They *are* spending a lot of money advertising with us now, and it would be good if they could see their product . . . you know."

"Stinkin' up my 'Friday Favorites' tablescapes," Grace said, finishing the sentence for him. "Did you promise them I would use it editorially? Tell me the truth, Ben."

"No!" he said sharply. "I would never try to influence you that way. But would it hurt to maybe try a couple shots with one of the bowls. Or a plate?"

"I'll try it out. But if it looks as crappy as I think it will, I'm not going to run it. Right? I mean, you promised when we monetized the blog, we wouldn't be whoring me out by using the advertisers' product in a way that would compromise my aesthetic."

"It's your call," Ben said, picking up one of the tomatoes and examining it. "These are weird looking. What kind are they?"

"Don't know," Grace said, gently taking the tomato from him and replacing it on the table. "J'Aimee picked them up at the farmer's market."

"Kid's got a good eye," Ben said. He glanced back at the table. "How long before you're done here?"

"Maybe an hour? I guess I'll try some shots with the Aviento stuff. Then I need to edit, and I've still got to actually write the piece." She glanced down at her watch. "Good Lord! It's after six. I've been piddling around with this tabletop for hours now. Why didn't you say something?"

"Didn't want to interrupt the genius while she was at work," he said. "But since you brought it up, is there any actual food to go on these pretty plates?"

"Nada," she said apologetically. "I'm sorry. I completely lost track of the time. Look, I'll just take a couple more shots with the Tuscan Turds, then I'll run down to Publix and pick up some sushi. Or maybe a nice piece of fish to grill. I can have supper on the table by seven. Right?"

"Finish your shots," Ben said easily. "J'Aimee can pick up supper."

"No, I'll go. I've had J'Aimee out running errands all afternoon."

Ben dropped a kiss on her forehead. "That's what assistants are for, Grace."

"But I hate to bother her," she protested. "She just went back over to the apartment an hour ago."

Grace gestured in the general direction of the garage, which was at the back of the "motor court." J'Aimee, her twenty-six-year-old assistant, had been living in the apartment above the garage since she was hired three months earlier. Her battered white Honda Accord was parked in the third bay, beside Ben's black Audi convertible.

Their builder had referred to the apartment as a mother-in-law suite, or even a nanny suite. But Grace's mom lived only a few miles away on Cortez and she wouldn't have moved to this "faux chateau," as she called it, at gunpoint. Ben's mother lived quite happily down in Coconut Grove. And since the fertility specialist still couldn't figure out just exactly why Grace couldn't get pregnant, the apartment, for now, was the perfect place to stash an assistant.

"Finish your shoot," Ben said, settling the matter. "I'll walk over there and roust J'Aimee. In fact, I'll ride to Publix with her."

"Thanks," Grace said, going back to her camera. "You're the best."

Ben gave her a gentle pat on the butt. "That's my girl," he said.

Grace went into the kitchen and found the heavy wooden crate with the Aviento shipping label sitting on the polished black granite countertop, pausing, as she always did, to flick a crumb into the sink. She hated the black granite. Even the tiniest fleck of sea salt showed up on it, and she seemed to go through a gallon of Windex every week, keeping it shiny.

But Ben and the builder had ganged up on her to agree to use it, after the granite company offered the countertops at cost in exchange for a small ad on Gracenotes.

She was soon immersed again in her work, barely registering the familiar roar of Ben's car as it backed out of the garage. Grace looked up in time to see that he'd put the Audi's top down. He did a neat three-point turn and gave her a carefree wave before he sped down the driveway, his forearm casually thrown across the back of the passenger seat, and J'Aimee's long red hair flowing gracefully in the wind.

Ben reminded her of Cary Grant in *To Catch a Thief,* a golden boy, elegant, aloof, mysterious, maybe even a little dangerous? She reflected briefly on how unfair life really was. At forty-four, Ben was six years older, but you'd never know it from looking at him. He never gained weight and never seemed to age. He kept his tennis tan year-round. His gloriously glossy dark brown hair still didn't show a speck of gray, and the faint crow's-feet around his eyes lent him the look of wisdom, not imminent geezerdom.

Grace, on the other hand, was beginning to spend what she thought of as an alarming amount of time on maintenance. At five-four, even five extra pounds seemed to go right to her butt or her belly, and she'd begun coloring her sandy-brown hair two years earlier, at the suggestion of Ruthanne, her hairdresser. Her face was heart-shaped, and only thirty minutes in the Florida sun left her round cheeks beet-colored, giving her even more of the look of a little Dutch girl when Ruthanne got carried away with the blond highlights. Ben insisted she was still as pretty as the day they'd met six years earlier, but they both knew that with Grace's blogging career about to take off, she would have to be that much more vigilant about her appearance.

Blogging? A career?

If anybody had told her two years ago that she'd make a living out of journaling her quest for a more beautiful life, she would have laughed in their face. And if anybody told her that she would become enough of a success that Ben would quit his career to run hers? Well, she would have politely written that person off as a nutcase.

But it was all true. She and Ben were on the very verge of the big time. This house, a 6,500-square-foot Spanish colonial located in a gated golf-course community had been one of the subdivision's model homes, and the builder, whose wife was an avid Gracenotes reader, had given them an incredible deal on it in exchange for a banner ad across the top of the blog. Most of the expensive upgrades on the property—the landscaping, the pool and spa, their amazing master bath—had also been trade-offs for advertising.

She'd always loved writing, and had tinkered with photography for years, but once the blog took off, it had somehow caught the eye of magazine editors and television producers. In addition to having their own house featured in half a dozen magazines, writing, photography, and decorating assignments had begun coming her way. She'd become a contributing regional editor for *Country Living* and *Bay Life* magazines, and next month, they were going to start working with a production company out of California to shoot a pilot television show of Gracenotes for HGTV.

All because of her silly little blog.

She couldn't say why she awoke so suddenly. Normally, Grace fell asleep the moment her head hit the pillow, and she slept so soundly Ben often reminded her of the time she'd slept through Hurricane Elise, not even stirring when the wind tore the roof totally off the screened porch of their old house in a slightly run-down Bradenton neighborhood.

That night was no exception. She'd retreated to her office after dinner, writing and rewriting her Gracenotes post and fussing over the photographs before, finally, shortly before eleven, pushing the SEND button and crawling into bed beside her already-slumbering husband.

For whatever reason, she sat straight up in bed now. It was after 1:00 A.M. Her heart was racing, and her mouth was dry. A bad dream? She couldn't say. She glanced over at Ben's side of the bed. Empty.

She rubbed her eyes. Ben was probably downstairs, in the media room, watching a tournament on Golf TV, or maybe he was in the kitchen, looking for a late-night snack. Grace yawned and padded downstairs, already planning her own snack.

But the downstairs was dark, the media room deserted. She went out to the kitchen. No sign of him there, either. The kitchen was as spotless as she'd left it three hours earlier, after finishing up the last of the dinner dishes and packing up the faux-Tuscan pottery. Not even a cup or a spoon in the sink.

Grace frowned, and this time she didn't bother to worry about wrinkles. She checked the downstairs powder room, but the door was open and there was no sign of her husband. She ran back upstairs and peeked inside the two guest suites, but they were empty and undisturbed. She walked slowly back to the bedroom, thinking to call Ben's cell phone. But when she saw his cell phone on his dresser, along with his billfold, she relaxed a little. And then she noticed the keys to the Audi were missing, and her heart seemed to miss a beat. She went to the window and peered out, but saw nothing. There was only a quarter moon that night, but it was obscured by a heavy bank of clouds. The backyard was wreathed in darkness. She couldn't even see the garage.

"It's nothing," she told herself, surprised to realize that she was talking out loud. She shrugged out of her nightgown, pulling on a pair of shorts and a T-shirt, slipping her feet into a pair of rubber flip-flops. "He's fine. Maybe he's out by the pool, sneaking a midnight cigar."

The sandals slapped noisily on the marble stairs, the sound echoing in the high-ceilinged stairway. She ditched them by the back door, carefully switching off the burglar alarm before stepping out onto the back patio. She paused, put her hand to her chest, and could have sworn it was about to jump out of her body.

"Ben?" She kept her voice low. It was pitch black, except for the pale turquoise surface of the pool and the eerie green uplights on the date-palm clusters at the back of the garden. Cicadas thrummed, and in the far distance, she heard a truck rumbling down the street. She crept forward, her hands extended, edging past the pair of chaise lounges perched at the edge of the patio, feeling the rough-textured coral rock beneath her feet.

Gradually, her eyes adjusted to the dark. There was no glowing cigar tip anywhere on the patio or the garden. She glanced toward the garage. No lights were on in J'Aimee's upstairs apartment, and the garage doors were closed. Was Ben's car there?

For a moment, a train of scenarios unspooled through her imagination. Ben, passed out, or even dead, at the wheel of his car, an unknown assailant lurking nearby. Should she retreat to the house, find some kind of weapon, even call the police?

"Don't be an idiot," she murmured to herself. "You're a big girl. Just go look in the garage. You live in a gated community, for God's sake. The only crime here is dogs pooping on the grass."

She tiptoed toward the garage, skirting the electronically controlled metal doors, heading toward the side door, trying to remember whether or not it would be unlocked.

Luckily, it was. The knob turned easily in her hand, and she stepped inside the darkened space, her hand groping the wall for the light switch.

And then she heard . . . heavy breathing. She froze. A man's voice. The words were unintelligible, but the voice was Ben's. Her hand scrabbled the wall for the switch. She found it, and the garage was flooded with light.

A woman squealed.

Grace blinked in the bright lights. She saw Ben, sitting in the driver's seat of the Audi. He was bare-chested, his right hand shielding his eyes from the light. His hair was mussed, and his cheeks were flushed bright red.

"Grace?" He looked wild-eyed.

And that's when she realized he wasn't alone in the car. Her first instinct was to turn and run away, but she was drawn, like a bug to a lightbulb, to the side of that gleaming black sports car. The top was retracted. She looked down and saw that distinctive mane of flame-red hair.

J'Aimee, her loyal, invaluable assistant, was cowering, naked, making a valiant effort to disappear into the floorboards of the car.

"What the hell?" Grace screeched as she yanked open the passenger-side door.

"I'm sorry, Grace, I'm so sorry," J'Aimee blurted, her eyes the size of saucers.

J'Aimee's clothes were scattered on the floor of the garage, and, come to think of it, that was Ben's shirt—his expensive, pale-blue, custom-tailored, monogrammed, Egyptian cotton shirt that Grace had given him as a birthday gift—that was flung over the Audi's windshield.

With the passenger-side door open, Grace saw, at a glance, that her husband was nearly naked, too—if you counted having your jeans puddled down around your ankles as naked.

For a moment, Grace wondered if this was some bad dream she was having. Hadn't she just been asleep a moment earlier? This couldn't be happening. Not Ben. Ben loved her. He would never cheat. She shook her head violently, closed her eyes, and reopened them.

But this was no nightmare. And there was no mistaking what she'd just interrupted. Suddenly, she felt a surge of boiling hot rage.

"Bitch!" Grace cried. She clamped a hand around J'Aimee's upper arm and yanked her out of the car in one fluid, frenzied motion.

"Ow," J'Aimee whimpered.

Grace flung her against the side of the car.

"Stop it," J'Aimee cried. Her face was pale, with every freckle standing out in contrast to the milky whiteness of her skin. For some reason, Grace, in an insane corner of her mind, noted with satisfaction that J'Aimee's breasts were oddly pendulous for such a young woman. Also? Not a real redhead.

"You stop it!" Grace said, drawing back her hand.

"Jesus!" J'Aimee screamed. She raised her arms to cover her face, and for a moment Grace faltered. She had never hit anybody in her life. She dropped her hand and glared at the girl.

"Now, Grace," Ben started. He was wriggling around in his seat, trying in vain to surreptitiously pull up his pants. "Don't get the wrong idea. Don't . . ."

"Shut up, just shut up!" Grace shouted, her eyes blazing. For a moment, she forgot about J'Aimee. She flew around to his side of the car, but before she could get there, Ben had managed to slide out from under the steering wheel, zipping up his pants as he stood.

"How could you?" she cried, raining ineffective punches around his head and shoulders. She was aware that her high-pitched shrieks sounded like the howls of a lunatic, but she was helpless to stop herself. "You? And J'Aimee? My assistant? You were screwing her? Under my own roof?"

He easily caught her fists and held them tight in his own. "No!" Ben lied. "It's not what you think. Look, if you would just calm down, let's talk about this. Okay? I know this looks bad, but there's a logical explanation."

"Like what? The two of you snuck out here to the garage while I was asleep and you decided to have a business meeting in your car? A clothing-optional meeting? And suddenly, J'Aimee decided to give you mouth-to-penis resuscitation? Is that the logical explanation for this?"

"Calm down," Ben repeated. "You're getting yourself all worked up . . ."

Grace saw a flash of movement out of the corner of her eye and looked over just in time to see J'Aimee scoop up her clothing and make a run for it.

"Oh, no," Grace said. "You're not getting away from this." J'Aimee darted out the door, and Grace went right after her.

"Stay away from me," J'Aimee cried, running in the direction of the house. "I'll call the police if you come near me . . . It's aggravated assault."

"You don't know the meaning of aggravated," Grace shouted. She flinched when her bare feet hit the lawn, damp from the automatic sprinklers, but ran after J'Aimee, who was surprisingly slow for a young woman unencumbered by clothing. She picked up her speed until she was only a few yards behind her former assistant. She reached out to try to snatch a handful of J'Aimee's hair, but her prey danced out of reach.

"Don't you touch me," J'Aimee cried, backing away. "I mean it."

But Grace was quicker than even she expected. She managed to grab J'Aimee's arm, and the girl screamed like a stuck pig.

Lights snapped on at the house next door. A dog began barking from the back of the property.

"Get away," the young woman screeched, dropping her clothing onto the grass and windmilling her arms in Grace's general vicinity. "Get away."

Now they heard the low hum and metallic clang of the garage door opening. Grace glanced over her shoulder to see Ben come sprinting out of the garage. "Are you insane?" he called. "For God's sake, Grace, let her go."

In her fury, Grace turned toward her husband, and in that moment J'Aimee slipped out of her grasp. While Grace watched, speechless, J'Aimee scampered, naked, around the patio. A moment later, she'd disappeared behind the thick hedge of hibiscus that separated the Stantons' property from their nearest neighbor.

"Go ahead and run, bitch!" Grace screamed. "You're fired. You hear me? Your ass is fired!"

Ben was walking slowly across the grass, his hands raised in a cautious peace gesture. "Okay, Grace," he said, making low, soothing sounds at the back of his throat, the kind you'd make to coax a cat out of a treetop. "Oh-kay, I know. You're upset. I get that. Can we take this inside now? You're making a spectacle of yourself. Let's take it inside, all right? I'll make us some coffee and we can sort this out . . ."

"We are *not* going inside," Grace snapped. "Coffee? Are you kidding me? You think a dose of Starbucks Extra Bold is going to fix this? We are going to stay right here. Do you hear me?"

"The whole neighborhood can hear you. Could you lower your voice, please? Just dial it down a little?"

"I will not!" His calmness made her even crazier than she already felt. Grace megaphoned her hands. "Hey, people. Neighbors—wake up! This is Grace Stanton. I just caught my husband, Ben Stanton, screwing my assistant!"

"Stop it," Ben hissed. "I was *not* screwing her."

"Correction," Grace hollered, lifting her voice to the sky. "She was blowing him. My mistake, neighbors."

"You're insane," he snapped. "I'm not staying around listening to this." He turned and stomped off toward the house. "We'll talk when you've calmed down."

"One question, Ben," Grace called, running after him. She grabbed him by the shoulder to stop his progress. "You owe me that."

"What?" He spun around, rigid with anger. She noticed three small love bites on his collarbone. Hickies? Her forty-four-year-old husband had hickies? A wave of nausea swelled up from her belly. She swallowed hard.

"How long? How long have you been fucking her?"

"I'm not . . ." He shrugged. "Come inside. All right?"

"How long?" Grace felt hot tears springing to her eyes. "Tell me, damn it. This wasn't the first time, was it? So tell me the truth. How long?"

"No matter what I say, you won't believe me," Ben said quietly.

"Tell me the truth and I'll believe you," Grace said.

"No," he said softly. "Not the first time. But we can fix this, Grace."

"Fix it?" Grace exploded with pure, white-hot rage.

"Fix it," she said, lifting her voice to the heavens. "He's been screwing her for a while now, and he thinks we can fix it."

"That's it," Ben said. "I won't stand here and let you humiliate me like this."

"Don't you dare walk away from me," Grace called.

"I'm gone," Ben said. True to his word, he stalked away toward the house. She raced to the back door, to discover that he'd locked her out.

"Let me in, damn it," she screamed, pounding on the kitchen door.

Nothing. She kicked the door. Still nothing.

She looked around for something, anything, to break the glass in the door. Just then she spied the heap of clothing J'Aimee had discarded in her hasty escape.

Grace scooped up the clothes and returned to the back patio. She craned her neck in the direction of the hibiscus hedge, hoping she might spot J'Aimee's bony white ass back there, hiding in the foliage or, better yet, being gnawed on by the neighbor's dog, a vicious-tempered chow mix named Peaches. But nothing moved in the shrubbery.

She had an idea. She stepped onto the patio and found the light switch for the outdoor kitchen, with its granite counters and six-burner gas-fired barbecue.

Earlier in May, her Gracenotes blog had dealt with barbecues.

Mr. Grace and I are fortunate to live in Florida, where grilling season never ends. But just because we're dining outdoors doesn't mean I serve burnt hot dogs on spindly white paper plates. I love to spread a white matelassé bedspread diagonally across our glass-topped patio table and anchor it with a pair of heavy black wrought-iron candelabras,

*or, if it's a windy day, I'll place votive candles in old Mason jars an-
chored with a layer of bleached-out seashells. Especially for casual occasions like this, you do not have to have a set of matched plastic dishes.
I'll let you in on a secret: I hate matchy-matchy! Instead, I have an assortment of mismatched Fiestaware plates picked up at junk shops and
yard sales over the years, in bold shades of turquoise, green, pink, yellow, and orange. Paired with silverware with ivory-colored Bakelite
handles, and oversized plain white flour-sack dish towels bought cheap
from Ikea, and a bouquet of brilliant zinnias cut from the garden, they
telegraph the message to guests: the fun is about to begin!*

Speaking of fun, Grace chortled as she tossed J'Aimee's clothes—a T-shirt,
pair of shorts, bra, and pink thong panties—onto the counter and then reached
into the stainless steel bar fridge and found herself a perfectly chilled bottle of
Corona. She didn't really like beer all that much, and there were no lime slices
handy, but she'd just have to make do. She uncapped the bottle and took a long,
deep swig, and then another. She pushed the IGNITE button on the front burner
and the blue flame came on with a satisfying whoosh.

The beer wasn't bad at all. She took another sip and tossed the panties onto
the burner. The tiny scrap of synthetic silk went up in flames and was gone in
a second or two, which was a disappointment. The shorts made a nicer display,
and she watched the blaze for two or three minutes, reluctantly adding the
T-shirt and then, after another five minutes, the bra. The bra, which had heavy
padding, smoldered for several minutes, sending up a stinky black fog of smoke.

She looked around for something else to add to the fire, and remembered
Ben's shirt, still draped over the windshield of his Audi.

Ben loved expensive things. But Grace, raised above her parent's working-
class bar in the nearby fishing hamlet of Cortez, could never quite get comfortable with the luxury goods that her husband had grown up with as the pampered
only son of a Miami bank executive. The day she'd bought the shirt at Neiman-
Marcus, for $350, she'd walked away from it twice, finally forcing herself to pull
the trigger and buy the damned thing.

Grace stood in the open doorway of the garage, scowling at the Audi. If the
shirt was Ben's favorite, the Audi, a 2013 Spyder R8 convertible, was beyond his
favorite. It was his obsession. He'd bought the Audi without consulting Grace,
right after they signed the pilot deal with HGTV. Ben wouldn't disclose what

he'd paid for the car, saying only that he'd "worked a deal" on it, but when she checked the prices online, she'd discovered that the thing retailed for $175,000! She'd somehow managed to swallow her resentment over not being included in the decision to buy the new car, telling herself that if Ben, who handled all the family finances, thought they could afford the car, then she shouldn't worry.

She walked around to the driver's side, snatching the shirt off the windshield. Looking down, she noticed the keys were still in the ignition.

The next thing she knew, she was using the shirt to wipe down the bucket seat's leather upholstery—just in case. She slid beneath the wheel and turned the key in the ignition, smiling as the powerful engine roared to life.

Ben didn't exactly prohibit her from driving the Audi, but he didn't encourage it either, telling her it was "a lot of car" for a woman and pointing out that her experience driving a stick shift was limited, although she'd learned to drive on her father's beat-up manual-transmission Chevy pickup.

Maybe, Grace thought, she'd just take the Audi for a spin around the neighborhood. Wouldn't that just fire Ben's rockets? She hoped he was watching from one of the upstairs windows. He'd have a stroke when he saw her behind the wheel. She eased the car into reverse, carefully backing it out of the garage.

Maneuvering an expert three-point turn, she was about to head down the driveway when the kitchen door flew open.

"Grace!" Ben yelled. "What do you think you're doing?"

"Going for a drive," she said cheerfully, raising the Corona in a jaunty salute.

"The hell you are," he barked, walking toward her. "You've been drinking and you're in no shape to be driving. Get out of my car."

"Your car?" she raised an eyebrow.

"You know what I mean," he said. "You've had your fun. This is taking things too far."

Too far? Grace revved the Audi's engine and slammed the car in first, screeching past Ben, who was a shouting, raving blur. Now she was at the edge of the patio, knocking over chaise lounges and the wrought-iron table with its jaunty green umbrella. The limpid turquoise surface of the pool was straight ahead. She closed her eyes, held her nose, and stomped the accelerator. The shock of the water was a final reminder. This was no nightmare. She was awake.

2

G race had grown up living above a marina, but she was only an okay swimmer. Still, she could dog-paddle and manage a serviceable backstroke when the occasion demanded. The shock of the cold water disoriented her momentarily, but seconds later she managed to kick herself free of the Audi and power up to the surface, blinking and gasping for air.

As soon as she surfaced, the enormity of what she'd just done came crashing down. She pushed her hair from her eyes and saw Ben, standing at the side of the pool, staring down at her, wild-eyed and more agitated than she'd ever seen him. "Jesus, Grace!" he shouted. "My car! What have you done to my car?"

He wasn't alone. A uniformed police officer stood at his side, training a large flashlight over the pool. Grace wished she could dive back down to the bottom, maybe hide in the Audi's trunk. Just until things got a little less crazy.

"Ma'am?" The cop was young, with close-shorn hair and a look of concern that was noticeably absent from her husband's face. "Are you all right?"

Grace coughed and brushed a strand of hair from her face, dog-paddling to stay afloat. "I'm all right," she said cautiously, flexing her toes and examining her hands just to make sure. Not a scratch, she thought, which pleased her. After all, she was homicidal, not suicidal.

"You're not all right," Ben snapped. "You're fuckin' nuts."

"Ma'am, could you come out of the water now?" the cop asked.

Grace looked around the backyard. "Where's the slut?" she called.

The cop looked confused. "Who?"

"J'Aimee. The slut. I'm not coming out if she's still here."

"Who's Jamie?"

Grace jutted her chin in Ben's direction. "Ask him." Her legs were getting a little weary from all the dog-paddling, so she floated onto her back and stared up at the sky. It was a gorgeous evening. The clouds had cleared, and the stars sprinkled in the deep blue heavens looked so close she felt she might just reach out and pluck one. It was too bad she couldn't just float here for a long time, enjoying this view.

"Sir?" she heard the cop say.

"It's not Jamie, it's J'Aimee," Ben said. "And she's our assistant. The woman my wife assaulted earlier this evening. Grace chased her off. I don't know where she's gone."

"Our assistant?" Grace said. "I thought she was my assistant. Of course, that was before I found her assisting you earlier this evening." She turned to face the cop. "I caught them, doing it, right there in the garage. In the front seat of the Audi. So you see why I want to make sure she's gone, can't you?"

The cop was blushing now, which made him look even younger. He coughed and crossed his arms and looked over at Ben. "Is that correct?"

"No, it's not correct," Ben said. "My wife thinks she saw something she didn't, and now she's blown everything completely out of proportion."

"Blown!" Grace called, her legs pumping underwater, her voice abnormally gleeful. "You got that right, buddy. Only I wasn't the one doing the blowing, was I?"

"You're disgusting," Ben said. He turned to the cop. "She's been drinking, obviously."

The cop gave Grace a stern look. "Ma'am, have you been drinking?"

"I had half a beer," Grace said. "You want me to take a Breathalyzer? Want to draw some blood?" She held her arm above water, as though he might tap a vein right there and then.

While he was considering that, the radio clipped to his shoulder began to crackle. He turned his back to her, spoke into it briefly and then turned around again.

"I think you need to come out of that pool now," he told Grace. He turned to

Ben. "You told the dispatcher you were afraid she might get hurt. Or hurt somebody else. Are you still concerned about that?"

Ben shrugged. "I suppose not."

"What about you?" the cop asked Grace. "Did your husband strike you, or threaten to harm you in any way?"

"Not really," Grace admitted.

"What about this J'Aimee person? Do I need to get a statement from her?"

Grace swam to the shallow end of the pool and pulled herself up on the coral rock patio. The May night was warm, but she shivered as the water streamed off her body.

Ben's voice was low. "That won't be necessary."

"I want to get a statement from her," Grace called, standing up. She pointed toward the hibiscus hedge. "She went that-a-way."

Her teeth were chattering and she hugged her arms around her torso. "Excuse me," she told the cop. "I'm just going to get a towel to dry off."

Grace found a thick yellow and green striped beach towel in the cabinet at the edge of the patio and wrapped it around herself. She took another towel and wound it around her head, turban-style. Suddenly, her legs felt weak. She sat, abruptly, on the edge of the only chaise lounge she hadn't mowed down on her way to the pool.

The young police officer looked down at her with an expression of unspeakable pity. "Are you sure you're all right? You didn't hit your head or anything?"

"My head is fine," Grace said, tears springing to her eyes. She couldn't say the same of her heart. Her chest felt like it might explode.

"What happens now?" Ben said, his voice gruff. He was standing ten yards away, keeping his distance so her craziness didn't rub off.

"Unless one of you wants to file a complaint, nothing happens," the cop said. "I'd suggest you take your wife inside and get her some dry clothes."

"She can get her own clothes," Ben said.

"Also, considering the, um, circumstances, I think it would be best if you did not both spend the rest of the night here," the cop went on. He looked over at Ben. "Maybe you could call a friend? Or get a motel room?"

"I'm not going anywhere!" Ben said, outraged. "This is my home." He looked over at Grace. "Besides, I can't exactly leave, since my car is currently resting on the bottom of the pool."

"Don't worry, I'm going," Grace said, struggling to her feet. She glanced in the direction of the house. She could see the lights she'd left on in their bedroom, and the kitchen light, too. The house looked enormous, like something she'd seen in a magazine layout. Or a real estate ad. It didn't look real to her. Not like a home. Nothing like a home.

The cop looked from Ben to Grace. His radio crackled again. "Are we done here?"

"We're done," Grace said wearily.

Ben stomped off in the direction of the house. A moment later, he switched off the exterior lights, throwing the yard into sudden darkness. The cop gave a nervous cough, but he didn't leave. He switched on his flashlight, but held it down at his side.

"Um," he said, and she could see that he was blushing again.

"I swear, I'm not going to do anything violent," Grace said. "I'd just like to tell you that, for whatever it's worth, I'm really a very normal, peace-loving person. I've never, ever done anything like this before."

She peered at his face, to see if he believed her.

"Look," he said hesitantly. "I didn't want to say this in front of your husband. But I'm a big fan of your blog."

"You read Gracenotes?" Grace wasn't sure if she should be embarrassed or flattered. "Really?"

"Oh yeah. I even subscribe. My girlfriend and I just moved in together, and we're fixing up our place, and we both really enjoy Gracenotes. Next weekend, we're even going to paint our bathroom ceiling the same color you painted your powder room."

"Waterfall? That is so sweet!"

"Well, we're going to cut the strength fifty percent, like you suggested in your blog," he said. "But Amy, that's my girlfriend, she's already painted the walls Cloud Cover. How do you think that will look?"

"It'll be great," Grace assured him. "That's one of my favorite whites. And Benjamin Moore is an excellent paint. I use it all the time."

Am I really discussing paint colors with a cop? Within an hour of my life imploding?

"Great," the cop said. He reached into his pocket and brought out a business card. "Hey, uh, I'm sorry about tonight. Don't quote me, but I kinda don't blame you for what you did with his car. I mean, what kind of douche bag does something like that?"

"The kind I'm married to, apparently," Grace told him. She took the card, and he held up his flashlight so she could read it. "Officer Strivecky."

"Pete," he said. "My cell phone number is on there, if you need me again tonight. I'm on shift until seven, okay?"

"Okay," she said, touched by his kindness. "Thanks for not arresting me."

"You've got a place to go?" he asked. "It's really not a good idea for you to stay here."

"Don't worry," she said, feeling a shiver run down her spine. "I'm just going to throw some things in a bag, and then I'm gone. My mom lives over on Cortez. I'll head over to her place. You couldn't pay me to spend another night here, now that I know what's been going on right under my own nose."

"I could hang around," Pete Strivecky said, gesturing in the direction of the house. "Make sure he doesn't try anything tricky."

"He won't," Grace said. "He's a douche bag, like you said, but he's not a dangerous douche bag."

He turned to go.

"Officer Strivecky? Pete?"

"Yeah?" he said, pausing at the edge of the pool, glancing down at the submerged Audi.

"Do you mind if I ask how old you are? You look too young to be a police officer."

He laughed. "I get that all the time. It's the red hair and freckles. I'm twenty-six. Been on the force for three years now."

"Twenty-six," Grace said wistfully. "So young . . ." She nodded her head in the direction of the house. "Seems like a long, long time ago."

"Yes ma'am," he said.

She had an idea. "Hey. Send me a photo of your bathroom after you're done, will you? For the blog? I'd love to see how it turns out."

"I'll do that," he said. "And you take care."

An open bottle of Chivas Regal stood on the kitchen counter. She could hear the sound of the television coming from the media room. The door was firmly closed, but he'd turned up the volume on the surround sound, and she recognized Bruce Willis's voice. He was watching one of the *Die Hard* movies again.

For Ben, watching the bad guys blow up buildings and try to shoot down airliners just never got old.

She ran up the back staircase to their bedroom. On her side of the his-and-hers bathroom suite, she peeled out of her sopping wet shorts and T-shirt, stopping only to drape them neatly over the towel bar beside her Jacuzzi. She grabbed a cosmetic bag from a drawer in her dressing table and swept in some random toiletries: her shampoo and conditioner, deodorant, and her vitamins. Her hand hovered over the Clomid pill bottle. She'd been scheduled to start her second round of the fertility drug at the start of her next period, in two weeks.

It had taken Grace two years to talk Ben into seeing a fertility specialist. An only child herself, she'd always wanted children. Ben claimed to want them, too, although he didn't see why they couldn't just "wait and see" if she'd get pregnant what he called "the natural way." Finally, two months ago, he'd relented. "Now or never," was the way Ben looked at it.

"Never," Grace said now, tossing the pills into the trash. She wondered if he'd already started sleeping with J'Aimee when she'd begun taking the Clomid. But she couldn't think about that right now. What was done was done. And she—and Ben—were done.

Standing in her walk-in closet, she dressed quickly in a pair of white jeans and a favorite navy-blue knit top. She slid her feet into a pair of Jack Rogers sandals. Opening a suitcase on the top of the island that housed her folded clothes, she dumped a handful of random things: panties and bras, some shorts and tops, and a pair of jeans. She threw her running shoes and socks on top of the clothes, then zipped the suitcase.

Grace stepped into the bedroom and looked around. One last time, she told herself. At the silver framed photos of her and Ben in happier times, at the paintings she'd collected and hung on the walls, at the gorgeous custom-made linen drapes. It was the nicest room she'd ever owned, and she was getting ready to walk right out of it.

She found her purse on the tufted velvet bench at the foot of the bed and slipped the strap over her shoulder. Picking her suitcase up, she made her way back down the stairs. She stopped in her office, shoving her laptop computer and a handful of file folders into an oversized tote bag. She dumped her camera bag on top, hefted the tote onto her other shoulder, and made her way awkwardly to the kitchen door.

The Chivas bottle was gone from the kitchen counter and the door to the media room was still closed. From within, Bruce Willis was kicking ass and taking names.

Grace paused by the door. She raised her hand to knock, but changed her mind. She went out the kitchen door, walked to the garage, and got into her own car, a four-year-old Subaru. "Now or never," she whispered aloud.

3

Grace was idly switching channels on the big wall-mounted television at the Sandbox, her mother's bar on Cortez, a spot only seven miles, but light years, away from Grace's house on Sand Dollar Lane.

"Leave it on channel four," Rochelle said. "Please."

Grace gave her a look. "You know I always watch the morning news on four," Rochelle said. "I hate that weather guy's hair on channel eight."

Grace gave a martyred sigh and did as she was told, turning back to her mother's favorite channel, just in time to see a reporter standing in front of her very own front yard.

"Holy crap," Rochelle whispered. "Is this what I think it is?"

"Good morning," said the reporter, a black woman who'd been a local television mainstay for as long as Grace could remember. Camryn Nobles. Grace stared at the television. How the hell had Camryn Nobles gotten past security?

"I'm at the exclusive gated community of Gulf Vista on Siesta Key, where police were summoned this morning to what they termed an escalating case of domestic disturbance. But what makes this story newsworthy, in fact, fascinating, is that the principals involved in the incident are a nationally known domestic goddess—and her husband—or is it safe to say, soon to be ex-husband?"

The camera panned to show a pale-pink stucco two-story Spanish colonial revival mansion with red tile roof sprawling across a swath of emerald green lawn dotted with colorful beds of tropical flowers and half a dozen black-and-white Sarasota County sheriff's deputy cars, as well as a fire truck, an emergency rescue ambulance, and a large black tow truck. A traffic helicopter from the Tampa CBS affiliate droned overhead.

"You're a media event," Rochelle said, and Grace shot her another look.

"If this palatial house and grounds look familiar to many of you," Camryn Nobles said, her voice lowering to a confidential tone, "it's because this is the home of lifestyle blogger Grace Stanton, who writes the wildly popular Grace-notes blog. The house has been featured in numerous national publications, and Ms. Stanton has been a frequent guest on network shows like *Oprah, Ellen,* and, yes, even the *Today* show, and of course our own *Suncoast Morning!* where she's been practically a fixture over the past two years, as a lifestyle expert."

Now Camryn was talking again, strolling around to the side of the house, down a long coral-rock driveway toward the rear of the Stanton mansion.

"Grace Stanton is a successful interior designer and a hometown girl who grew up in modest circumstances in nearby Cortez," Camryn said. "After moving to South Florida and marrying, she had a thriving design practice before moving back here to the Suncoast in 2009. Husband Ben, forty-four, was an advertising executive who gave up his career two years ago in order to devote all his energies to maximizing his wife's burgeoning lifestyle business. Grace and Ben Stanton are fixtures on the local social scene; in fact, they hosted a charity party for the local children's shelter right here in this lovely poolside setting back in October. But authorities say this bucolic scene turned ugly sometime after midnight. Here's the tape police have released, of the panicky 911 phone call they received at one fifteen A.M. from Ben Stanton. And we want to apologize to our viewers, in advance, for the somewhat graphic language in this tape."

"Yeah, I'm gonna need some assistance here. My, uh, my wife, she's out of control."

The female 911 operator sounded bored. *"Sir, are you in physical danger?"*

"What? I don't know. She went crazy on me. I've never seen her like this. Look, I think you better get an officer over here before she does hurt somebody."

Shrieks were clearly audible in the background. And then came Ben Stanton's muffled voice.

"Grace, what are you doing? This isn't funny. Are you crazy? What the . . . Get the hell away from there!"

In the background came the sound of a car door slamming, then a high-powered motor revving, tires squealing across pavement. And then, a loud splash.

"Christ! Grace, what the hell have you done? Jesus H! . . ."

"Sir? Do you have a life-threatening situation there?"

Stanton's voice, when he came back on the line, was grim. *"If she hasn't already drowned, I'll kill the bitch myself."*

"Turn it off, please," Grace said, turning her back to the television.

Rochelle dialed down the volume, but she kept watching.

Camryn was back on camera, walking toward a patio area lined with a lush hedge of sea grapes. Graceful coconut palms and hibiscus shrubs were scattered about the patio, which included a fully outfitted kitchen and thatch-roofed tiki bar.

The reporter gestured in the direction of a two-story, three-bay garage. "The police won't say what sparked the altercation between Grace and Ben Stanton last night, but I spoke off camera to a neighbor who claims to have overheard what she termed 'a spirited exchange' between the married couple last night. That neighbor says the source of the problem was Mrs. Stanton's stunning twenty-six-year-old female assistant, who has been living in a garage apartment on this property for some months now. The neighbor also says that in the early morning hours before dawn today, that assistant, whose name we aren't divulging, fled in terror through that hedge," Camryn pointed to the sea grapes, "wrapped only in a beach towel."

"Neither of the Stantons were available for comment at airtime," Camryn went on, still walking toward the patio, "But despite the lack of witness statements, or cooperation from the parties involved, there are some simply inescapable conclusions we can draw about what went down here last night."

The camera pulled back to show a three-car garage, with all three parking bays empty, and then panned over toward the swimming pool, a shimmering free-form turquoise oasis set on a patio of more coral rock. The shallow end of the pool had coral rock steps that descended into a separate, enclosed whirlpool spa. And the deep end?

Camryn Nobles stood at the edge of the pool and looked down, the camera following her gaze. A lime-green canvas beach umbrella floated tranquilly on the surface of the water, as did four chartreuse vinyl lounge cushions. Totally submerged and barely visible beneath the water was an ominous-looking oblong black form.

"And that," Camryn said, her voice somber, "appears to be Ben Stanton's 2013 Audi Spyder convertible, which retails for approximately 175,000 dollars."

Rochelle Davenport pointed the remote control and finally, mercifully, clicked it off.

"You really drove a car worth 175,000 dollars into the pool?" Rochelle asked her daughter.

Grace shrugged. "I doubt he paid that much for it. Knowing Ben, he worked some kind of advertising trade-off with the dealer."

"This is just so unlike you," Rochelle said. "I mean, I don't blame you for what you did, but it's just so not you."

"Temporary insanity," Grace said. "That's the only explanation I can think of."

"You could have drowned," Rochelle said. "Did you think of that? You'd have left me a childless widow."

"And then Ben could have collected on that two-million-dollar life insurance policy we bought last year," Grace muttered. "I gotta change that."

"It was a dumb thing to do," Rochelle insisted. "Seriously."

"I couldn't have drowned. The top was still down," Grace said, suddenly returning to her normal, logical self. "I guess it got kind of hot in that garage, while she was . . ."

"Giving him a blow job?" Rochelle said helpfully.

"Yeah. In the front seat of the Audi."

"I also can't believe Ben just let you drive it into the pool," Rochelle said. "How exactly did that happen?"

"I can't discuss that right now," Grace said, staring moodily into her iced tea glass. "It makes my head hurt."

Rochelle reached behind the bar for the industrial-sized bottle of ibuprofen she kept there, shook two into her hand, and handed them to her daughter.

"Thanks," Grace said, swallowing the pills. "Have you got any food around here? I've always heard that heartbreak kills your appetite, but I haven't eaten in twelve hours, and, I swear, I could gnaw my arm off right now."

Rochelle pushed one of the plastic laminated menus across the bar.

Grace looked down at the Sandbox menu, which, as far as she knew, hadn't changed in at least fifteen years. "Buffalo wings. Stuffed potato skins. Stuffed potato skins with Buffalo-wing sauce. Onion rings. Fried oysters. Fried shrimp." She looked up at her mother. "Seriously? How are you still alive, eating this stuff all this time?"

"I don't eat this crap," Rochelle said, nonplussed. "You kidding me? I'd be big as a damned house."

She allowed herself a satisfying glance in the mirror over the back bar. At fifty-nine, Rochelle was proud of her still-trim figure. She took good care of herself, slathered herself with sunscreen before taking her two-mile walk along Bradenton Beach every morning, colored her hair a soft brown at home, and allowed herself a single glass of heart-healthy red wine or the occasional beer most evenings. She'd quit her pack-a-day smoking when Grace was still a baby, and her doctor said she had the bone density of an eighteen-year-old.

"I microwave myself a nice Lean Cuisine for dinner, usually. And for breakfast, I juice."

"You juice? As a verb?"

"Don't get snotty with me," Rochelle said. She nodded at the oversized Oster blender on the back bar. "Felipe, this real nice Mexican guy, comes in here with his soccer team on Sundays, his mom runs a produce stand at the Red Barn, and he brings me all kinds of fresh produce. Spinach, kale, chayote, strawberries, pineapples, mangoes. Herbs, too. I like mint and ginger. I put it in with everything."

"That doesn't sound too bad, actually," Grace admitted. "You got anything like that you could fix up for me? Not kale," she said, wrinkling her nose. "But any of that other stuff?"

"Sorry," Rochelle said. "I used up the last of the fresh stuff this morning. I could maybe make you a sandwich. Would a BLT offend your delicate sensibilities?"

"That'd be great," Grace said, resting her cheek against the bar and folding her arms over her head. Her shoulders heaved, and she let out a muffled sob. It was the first time Rochelle had seen her cry since she was a teenager, and it wrenched her heart just as it had back then.

Rochelle hesitated, but then reached over and smoothed her daughter's mussed hair. "Don't worry, sweetie. We'll fix this. We'll figure it out."

Grace raised her head and looked at Rochelle, tears streaming down her cheeks. "Fix it? That's exactly what Ben said, 'we can fix this.' And then he admitted it wasn't the first time. How do we figure this out, Mom? I loved him. I thought he loved me. But it was all a lie. Everything was a lie. What do I do now?"

Rochelle handed her a paper towel. "Blow your nose. Dry your tears. Eat something. And then we'll call your Uncle Dennis and take the bastard to the cleaners."

"Uncle Dennis is a real estate lawyer," Grace said, sniffling. "He doesn't do divorces."

"No, but he's been divorced twice himself, so he'll know who we should call, and who we should avoid."

Grace took a gulp of tea. "I'm not even sure I want a divorce."

"You're kidding," Rochelle said. "You caught Ben having sex in your garage with your assistant, who he's surely been screwing at your house all these months, and you're not sure it's over?"

"I don't know," Grace wailed. "This is not the way I thought my life would go. I don't understand any of this. I thought I would have a forever marriage, like yours and Daddy's."

Rochelle considered this, started to say something, then changed her mind. Now was not the time.

"Have you talked to Ben since last night?"

"No."

"Any plans to talk to him?"

Grace shrugged. "I've got to go over there and pick up some more clothes pretty soon. And I'll have to figure out what to do about the blog, and the HGTV pilot and all the rest of it."

Rochelle busied herself putting together her daughter's sandwich. She popped two slices of bread into the toaster, slapped some bacon on the griddle, and picked up a fat red Ruskin tomato from a bowl on the back bar. She had the knife poised to slice it when Grace spoke up.

"Could you peel that, please?"

Her mother shot her a look of annoyance. "I fixed you a million BLTs in your childhood, and now, suddenly, you have to have your tomatoes peeled? La-de-damn-da."

Grace stood up and came around the bar. "Never mind. I'll make it myself if it's that big a deal."

"It's not a big deal. I just don't get why it's necessary. The peel has the most vitamins."

"That's not true," Grace said flatly, taking the knife from her mother and proceeding to pare the skin from the tomato.

Rochelle stood back with her hands on her hips. "Who says it's not true? It's absolutely true."

"According to who?"

"I forget," Rochelle said stubbornly. "Maybe I heard it on one of those cooking shows."

Grace shook her head and reached into the refrigerator for a head of lettuce. She peeled a leaf from the head and gave a martyred sigh.

"What now? You don't like my lettuce?"

"I'm just not crazy about iceberg," Grace said. "Romaine is so much tastier. And prettier, not to mention better for you, since we're talking about vitamins."

"I like iceberg," Rochelle said, her tone frosty. "It's what I've always bought. It was always good enough for you up until now."

Grace fixed her with a look. "Are we going to get into this again? I'm sorry, Mom, if I like nice things. Sorry if it somehow offends you that I outgrew my childhood taste for Kraft macaroni and cheese and frozen Tater Tots and casseroles made with cream of mushroom soup and canned onions rings. And Asti Spumante." She shuddered involuntarily at this last listing.

"That chicken casserole used to be your favorite," Rochelle said. "You insisted I make it for your birthday dinner every year."

"I was a kid," Grace said. "I grew up and my tastes changed. Refined, if you will."

Rochelle rolled her eyes and built the sandwich. She placed it on a plate, deftly cut it in half on the diagonal, and handed it to Grace.

"Thanks," Grace said. She took the sandwich and moved back to her barstool, chewing slowly.

Rochelle wiped the bread crumbs from the cutting board. "This split-up could get pretty messy, pretty fast, you know. Ben is involved in every aspect of your business. You can walk away from him, but can you walk away from everything you've built up in the business? Not to mention the house?"

Grace shrugged to indicate she had no answers, and kept chewing.

"Counseling?" Rochelle offered. Grace shook her head violently and took another bite of her sandwich, and then a sip of her iced tea.

"All right," her mother said, glancing meaningfully at the neon Budweiser sign that hung over the mirrored bar back. "It's after eleven now. My lunch trade is gonna start trickling in here pretty soon."

"I can take a hint," Grace said, finishing off the last of her sandwich. She pushed the empty plate aside and stood. "I'm gonna go upstairs to my old room and try to get some work done. I'm doing a giveaway of this hideous Tuscan pottery on Monday, and I've got to write that blog post and figure out what I'm writing about tomorrow."

She picked up her laptop case. "You've got Wi-Fi, right?"

Rochelle wrinkled her brow. "I guess. They hooked up some kind of Internet doohickey when I changed cable providers back in the spring."

"Password?"

"Who knows?"

"Never mind, I'll figure it out myself," Grace said. She headed for the stairway that led to the family's upstairs living area, and then stopped and poked her head around the doorway. "If Ben calls here looking for me, you haven't seen me and don't know where I am."

"Gotcha," Rochelle said. "I hope he does call. I'll give the son of a bitch an earful."

"Thanks," Grace said, offering a wan smile. "It's good to know you've got my back."

"I do," Rochelle assured her. "I'm your wingman, right?"

Grace pushed the bedroom door open with her hip. She'd decorated the room herself, at the age of fourteen, and not one single thing had changed in all these years.

She'd been in her Laura Ashley phase then. She'd longed for the pink and white striped wallpaper she'd seen in a *House Beautiful* layout, but with no money to spend, she'd laboriously taped and painted pink stripes over the cheap knotty pine-paneled walls that her mother had previously slathered with white paint. Grace found a crappy $9.99 faux-mahogany four-poster bed at the Salvation Army and painted it white, then stenciled a sappy design of green vines, pink daisies, and blue ribbons across the headboard.

Grace kicked at the worn and stained beige wall-to-wall carpet on the floor. She'd begged and pleaded with her father to let her rip up that carpet—the same stuff that covered every surface in their apartment, but Butch had been adamant. "Do you know how much money I spent on this stuff?"

She settled onto the faded pink chintz bedspread and opened her laptop, clicking onto the logo for Gracenotes. She reread the post she'd written the previous evening, which seemed like something from a previous life. There were already forty-seven comments posted. Had any of her readers seen the news about the flamboyant scene at her house? She decided against reading the comments. Maybe later.

Instead, she concentrated on writing Monday's post, going ahead with the topic she'd already settled on a week ago: how and where to find great deals on discounted designer home fabrics. Soon she was typing away, copying and pasting images of favorite fabrics and room settings, copying Web site links, losing herself in the process of creation.

When she looked up from her work, she realized that two hours had passed. Her cell phone, lying on the nightstand, had not rung, and no beeps had signaled an incoming text message. She'd halfway expected Ben to call, either downcast and contrite, or furious and full of threats. The silence seemed ominous. No matter. She glared at the phone, daring it to ring. She would not call him. Not ever. Let the swine call and beg her to come crawling back.

Grace went back to her work. She checked for typos, misspellings, links that didn't work, pictures that were improperly sized. Finally satisfied with her work, she pulled up the Gracenotes blog page, and clicked on the sign-in and password buttons.

A red highlighted italicized sentence flashed on the screen.

Invalid password. Try again?

She frowned and winced as she retyped the password. *GracenBen4ever.*

Invalid password. Check for misspellings?

Not possible. She typed the word again, with the same results.

Reset password?

She checked her e-mail, waiting for the message to alert her that her new password had been sent. But when she opened the e-mail, she stared down at the message in disbelief.

New password may not be reset. Invalid user name. Please contact technical support if you believe this message has been sent in error.

She fumed and dialed the number provided, waiting on hold for ten minutes. Finally, a young man who identified himself as Hans came on the line.

"Hello," she said briskly. "My name is Grace Stanton, and I write a blog called Gracenotes. I've just spent half an hour trying to get access to my dashboard so I can write a new post, but I keep getting error messages, and, finally, I got a message telling me that I can't set a new password, because I have an invalid user name. But it's not invalid. I've been writing this blog for three years under the same name. So I can't understand what is happening."

"Let me just check that," Hans said. She could hear his fingertips flying over a keyboard. "Just a moment," he said, putting her on hold.

A moment later he was back on the line. "Mrs. Stanton?"

"Ms. Stanton," Grace said pointedly.

"Right. Um. The thing is, you don't have access to the blog dashboard."

"I know that," she said sharply. "That's why I'm calling you. Because I need access. It's my blog."

"Wellll," he said. "From what I can tell, the domain owner has changed the user sign-on and password. That would explain why you're locked out."

"That can't be," Grace said, feeling her face get hot. "I'm the domain owner. The blog is Gracenotes. I'm Grace Stanton."

There was a long meaningful silence on the other end of the line. "Actually," Hans said, "according to our records, the domain owner is Ben Stanton. And apparently, he's changed the access."

"He can't do that," Grace cried. "Change it back. It's my blog. I started it, I write it, I own it. And I want you to change it so I can have access to my own blog."

"I'm sorry, Ms. Stanton, but I don't have the authority to do that," Hans said. "Now, is there anything else I can help you with?"

Downstairs, in the bar, Rochelle was pouring a longneck Sweetwater Pale when she heard an unearthly shriek coming from the direction of upstairs.

Frank, a mailman who'd just come off his shift, gave her a questioning look.

"My daughter," Rochelle said apologetically. "She's having some marital issues."

4

Three days had passed since Grace had walked out of the house on Sand Dollar Lane.

They were three of the longest, most miserable days of her life. During the days, she tried to help out around the Sandbox, working behind the bar, waiting tables, even doing a brief stint as a short-order cook, until her mother unceremoniously fired her from that job after she caught Grace substituting ground turkey for ground chuck in the bar's signature Sandbox burger.

"I know you mean well," Rochelle said, ordering her out of the kitchen. "But my customers don't care about saturated fats or sodium or antioxidants. They just want a big, greasy, salty burger on a puffy, white, highly processed white bun. With maybe a slab of gooey yellow cheese on top. And they definitely don't want a side order of smug advice about healthy dining."

Evenings, Grace locked herself up in her bedroom, spending hours writing blog entries she couldn't even post. When she finished writing and editing, she slipped out to the second-story deck overlooking the Cortez marina. Growing up, she'd hated that marina. She hated the stink of the diesel fuel burned by the boats and the shrill cries of seagulls wheeling overhead as the shrimpers and commercial fishermen returned to the docks with their catch. She'd hated the greasy water lapping against the seawall, and the constant ebb and flow of fishermen and regulars who regarded the Sandbox as their home away from home.

Most of all, Grace hated the fact of where she lived. In high school, the guys she dated thought it was awesome that she lived right on the water, and above a bar! But she didn't want to live on a marina. She wanted a regular suburban house, with a grassy green lawn, and although she loved her parents, she longed for a father who worked in an office and wore a necktie, with a mother who stayed home and played bridge and got her hair done every Thursday.

The only ties Butch Davenport owned were bolo ties, which he wore with his ever-present violently colored Hawaiian shirts. As for Rochelle, who cut her own hair, Grace was fairly sure she didn't even know how to play bridge, although she was a demon at pinochle.

For some reason, the sights and sounds of the marina, and the bay that flowed beneath the weathered gray boards of the docks, were now oddly comforting. When sleep wouldn't come, and it rarely did, she crept out to the deck, in her night-gown, and sat for hours, her knees tucked to her chest, staring off at the sparkling black water and the shadowy hulks of the fishing vessels tied up at the dock.

That first morning Grace had moved home, Rochelle found her like that when she arose at seven to make coffee.

Her mother sank into the chair next to her, wordlessly handing her a steam-ing mug. Grace nodded her thanks and sipped.

"Gonna be another hot day," Rochelle said finally, looking at the pink-tinged sky.

"Hotter than the hinges of hell," Grace agreed, repeating one of Butch's fa-vorite sayings.

"You sleep any?" Rochelle asked.

"A little," Grace lied.

"I've got some Ambien, if you want," her mother offered.

Grace stared at her, shocked. The only drugs she'd ever known her mother to take were baby aspirin.

"Don't look at me like that," Rochelle said. "The doctor gave 'em to me, after your daddy died. I only took the one. Slept for fourteen hours straight, and when I finally did wake up, I'd eaten most of a pecan pie somebody brought to the house after the funeral. I looked it up on the computer. It's a real thing. Sleep eating, they call it. Hell's bells, I eat enough when I'm awake. I don't need a pill that makes you eat a whole pie without even remembering it."

Grace was forced to smile.

"You hear anything from the asshole?" Rochelle asked.

"Not a word," Grace said.

"Are you okay for money?" Rochelle asked.

"For now," Grace lied.

Rochelle knew it for the lie it was, but didn't call her daughter out on it. Instead, she sighed and gave Grace a sideways glance. "I think you better give your Uncle Dennis a call."

When she couldn't access her blog, Grace reluctantly called Ben, leaving a voice mail when he didn't pick up. Three days later, Ben still wasn't returning Grace's phone calls. But he'd been a busy little worker bee during that time. He'd changed the PINs for their joint checking and savings accounts, and although she'd gone to the bank in person, twice, and argued with the branch manager, she still couldn't make them understand that her estranged husband was freezing her out of her own hard-earned money. He'd canceled her AmEx and Visa cards. And when she'd gone to her gym to try to work out some of her frustrations in a Zumba class, she'd been greeted with the unwelcome news that her membership had been terminated, since the gym was no longer able to debit her checking account for her fees.

"Call Dickie Murphree," her Uncle Dennis said, when she finally got him on the phone. "I finally got smart and hired him the second time around. He's the best divorce lawyer in town. Didn't the two of you go to high school together?"

"Dickie! Of course," Grace said, her black mood lifting, just a little. "That's a great idea. Dickie took me on my first real car date. I haven't seen him in a couple years."

"Give him my best when you call," Dennis said. "And tell him I hope I never have to see him again. No offense."

She called the law offices of Murphree-Baggett-Hopkins twice a day, for two days in a row, each time asking the receptionist to please have Dickie call her about an urgent matter.

"He's in court," the receptionist told her. "I know, but I'm an old friend," she said, giving the woman her maiden name. Might as well start getting used to it again, she thought glumly.

Things really were getting pretty dire.

As much as she dreaded another confrontation, she had to talk to Ben. Aside from business matters that had to be settled, she needed more clothes, her treasured interior design books and magazine files, and the macro lens for her camera. Also panties.

Finally, she decided on an ambush. Grace dressed carefully for the outing, as carefully as she could considering the fact that her hastily packed suitcase contained three faded T-shirts, two pairs of yoga pants, her jogging shorts, and a pair of skinny white jeans that she hadn't actually been able to fit into in two years.

Now though, the jeans zipped with ease. Heartache, she thought ruefully, was the ultimate diet aid.

She tried calling Ben one more time, and when her message went directly to voice mail, she resolutely got behind the wheel of the Subaru and drove the ten miles to Siesta Key, her stomach roiling so badly that once, a mile from the house, she had to pull off onto the side of the road to barf on a white oleander bush.

On the way over, Grace rehearsed her lines.

"Hello, Ben. I know you've been avoiding me, and you're probably still furious about me driving the Audi into the pool, but hey! I'm still furious about finding you and J'Aimee doing the nasty in the front seat, so why don't we just call it a tie and figure out a way to get through all this with some courtesy and civility?"

She thought that was an excellent opener. And she would follow it up by letting him know that he would absolutely HAVE to unfreeze the bank accounts and credit cards and restore her access to the blog.

"It's my business, Ben. It's called Gracenotes, for God's sake. Your preventing me from participating in it is foolish and shortsighted."

That would get him. Ben was *all* about business. Since he dealt with all the blog's advertisers, he would certainly want to keep them happy to keep the ad dollars flowing. Right? Surely he would be reasonable, now that he'd had some time to think things over rationally. Right?

Up ahead, Grace spotted the thick emerald green embankment that meant she was approaching Gulf Vista, their subdivision. A stately row of royal palms, underplanted with thick beds of asparagus ferns, lined both sides of the road, and a classic arched white stucco bridge crossed over a canal. A hundred yards ahead, she spotted the security gate and felt a sharp, unexpected wave of panic so strong that she had to clutch the steering wheel to keep from turning around and fleeing in the opposite direction.

Stop this! She told herself sternly. This is a business transaction. No need for emotion. Be strong.

She pulled the car alongside the electronic card reader and swiped her plastic key card through it, waiting patiently for the heavy iron gates to slide open.

Nothing. The gate didn't move. She wiped the card on the leg of her jeans, a trick she'd used many times when the finicky card reader refused to open sesame.

Grace tried three more times with the same results. Despite the fact that she had the Subaru's air-conditioner thermostat on the subarctic setting, she could already feel sweat beading up on her forehead. Her mouth was dry, but her hands as they gripped the key card were clammy.

The driver of the black Lexus behind her car tapped his horn impatiently, but Grace had no place to go. The gate wouldn't open, and there were two more cars behind the Lexus.

The driver tapped his horn again. Finally, near tears, Grace rolled the window down and leaned out to address the situation. "I'm sorry," she called, waving her key card. "It's not working. Can you back up so that I can back up?"

The driver, an older man with silver hair, gestured impatiently. Finally, all three cars backed up so that Grace could get out of the line. She parked her car on the shoulder of the road and went to the guard shack, whose dark tinted windows obscured those inside. She felt limp and defeated, and she hadn't even gotten to the house yet, a destination she was already dreading.

She tapped on the guard-shack window, and finally a uniformed security guard, a middle-aged guy with a graying military crew cut, opened the door. She was grateful for the cold blast of air-conditioning. The guard stepped outside and Grace recognized him at once.

"Oh, hi, Sheldon," she said, favoring him with a smile. "I'm so glad you're on duty." She held up her key card. "I'm Grace Stanton. My key card won't work. Can you fix it for me?"

He frowned slightly, taking the card, turning it over and over to examine it closer. "Looks okay."

"I know, but it won't work," Grace said.

"Hang on a minute," Sheldon said. He stepped back into the guard booth and closed the door. A mosquito buzzed around her face, and she swatted it away. The sun beat down on her head, and she was sure she was about to melt.

The door opened, but only an inch or two. The security guard's friendly smile had vanished. Now he glowered at her. "Sorry. I can't help you."

"What?" Grace said, startled. "Why not?"

"I can't discuss it," Sheldon said, and he started to close the door again, but before he could, Grace grabbed the doorknob.

"Wait a minute," she said, feeling her face growing redder by the moment. "What's going on here? Why won't you fix my key card?"

He glanced around, to make sure he couldn't be overheard. As if!

"I can't help you because your card has been deactivated."

"That's ridiculous!" Grace said. "Is this because of . . . my marital situation? Did my husband call up here and tell you people to keep me out? He has no right! I live here. At 27 Sand Dollar Lane."

"I don't make the rules, ma'am," Sheldon said. "All's I know is, according to the computer, you are no longer listed as a resident of Gulf Vista."

"He can't do that," Grace said, her teeth gritted. "Please! Look, I don't want to make a scene . . ."

"Then don't," Sheldon said. He held up a walkie-talkie. "My supervisor told me to tell you that if you have a problem with the card situation, you should contact an attorney. Until we have some kind of a legal document stating otherwise, I can't let you in." He reached around and gently removed Grace's hand from the doorknob. "Sorry."

Grace heard a light beep of a car horn. A white Lincoln rolled up beside her and the passenger-side window slid down. Anita McKenna, an older woman she knew slightly from the country club, gave her a friendly smile. "Hi! It's Grace, right? Are you having car problems? Anything I can do to help?"

"Anita! Hello," Grace said eagerly, stepping closer to the car. "Actually, I am having a little issue . . ."

There was a tap on her shoulder. She turned to find Sheldon standing directly beside her. "Mrs. Stanton? My supervisor thinks it would be a good idea if you would just move along now." He held up his walkie-talkie again.

Grace felt her spine stiffen. "I was just . . ."

Anita McKenna looked from Sheldon to Grace. "Oh," she said. "My goodness. I didn't realize." The window slid up again, and the Lincoln breezed through the gate.

She called Dickie Murphree's office twice more on her way to back to Cortez. Finally, his receptionist allowed her to leave a voice mail message.

"Dickie," she said, fighting back tears. "It's Grace Davenport. I've been calling and calling. I really need to talk to you. I've left Ben. Maybe you saw it on the news? Now he's frozen our bank accounts, cut off my credit cards—he's even fixed it so I can't get back to our house to pick up my clothes and things. Please, Dickie. Please call me."

Grace was pulling into the crushed-shell parking lot at the Sandbox when her cell phone rang. She saw that the caller was Murphree-Baggett-Hopkins.

"Hello?"

"Hiya, Gracie," Dickie said. "I just got your message. Sorry it took me so long to call you back. I'm in trial this week, and the damned judge just now cut us loose for a lunch break. How's your Uncle Dennis?"

"He's fine," Grace said. "He sends his best. Look, Dickie, if you listened to my message, you know I'm in big trouble. When can I come see you? To talk about my situation?"

"Welllll," Dickie drawled. "I'm not sure that's a good idea."

"Why not?" Grace asked, stunned. "Uncle Dennis said you're the best divorce lawyer in town."

"Hell of a guy, your uncle," Dickie said, chuckling. "He sure gets himself in some damned interesting jams, doesn't he?"

"Why isn't it a good idea for me to come see you?"

"Awwww, Grace," Dickie drawled. "You know I think the world of you, don't you? We had some good times, way back there in high school, didn't we? You broke my heart when you threw me over for that basketball player, sophomore year. What was that guy's name? He went on to play college ball at FSU, didn't he? It was years before I got over you."

"That's sweet, Dickie," she said impatiently. "His name was Calvin Becker. Could we discuss current affairs? Like my divorce?"

"The thing is, we can't talk, Grace," Dickie said. "It ain't even really proper for me to be talking to you right now, but I figured I owe you an explanation."

"What are you explaining?" Grace asked.

"That I can't represent you. Because I already agreed to represent Ben."

Grace put the phone down in her lap. She closed her eyes and rested her head against the steering wheel, utterly defeated.

"Grace?" Dickie's voice rose faintly from the phone. "Grace? Are you there?"

She pushed the disconnect button.

5

I take it things didn't go well with the asshole," Rochelle said, pouring her a large glass of iced tea and pushing it across the bar. "Drink that. It's sweetened. You're losing weight so fast it's starting to scare me."

Grace took a sip of the tea and sucked on an ice cube. "I never got to see Ben. I couldn't get through the security gate. He had my key card deactivated."

"Bastard," Rochelle said, pouring her own glass of iced tea. The lunch-time rush hour was over, and only two people remained at opposite ends of the bar, one watching the Rays game on the TV, the other staring intently down at his smartphone.

"Did your uncle's lawyer ever call you back?" Rochelle asked.

Grace stirred her tea with a straw. "Dickie Murphree. Yeah, he called. But I can't hire him."

"Why not? Just because you dated years ago?"

"I can't hire him because Ben beat me to it," Grace said, lifting her eyes to meet her mother's. "Yeah. Ben has already hired the best divorce lawyer in town. Face it, Mom. I'm screwed."

"No, you're not," Rochelle said. "The Yellow Pages are full of divorce lawyers. You can't swing a dead cat in this town without hitting a lawyer. We just need to find you the right one." She drummed her fingers on the bar's scarred wooden surface. A minute later, she disappeared into the kitchen.

When she reemerged, she handed her daughter a well-worn business card.

"Mitzi Stillwell, Attorney at Law?" Grace asked, lifting one eyebrow. "Who's she?"

"A lawyer I know," Rochelle said. "Give her a call."

Mitzi Stillwell didn't waste much time with niceties. She'd been practicing domestic law for a dozen years, and she generally believed her clients needed the truth more than they needed coddling.

She listened for fifteen minutes while Grace recounted her tale of what she now thought of as the meltdown, nodding and occasionally jotting some words onto a legal yellow pad.

"So," Grace said, when she'd finished. "What do you think? Can you help me?"

Mitzi tapped the pen against the legal pad. "You walked away from your own home—even though your husband was the one screwing around on you?"

"Yes," Grace said.

Mitzi cocked her head and a strand of gray-flecked dark hair fell across one eye. She was in her early fifties now, but when her hair started graying twenty years earlier, she'd chosen not to color it—just to give herself the look of an older, more experienced jurist. At home, she favored bright colors and clothes designed to show off the figure she worked hard at maintaining, but in the courtroom, Mitzi mostly chose expensively tailored business suits in neutral colors, with just enough feminine detailing to remind her clients—and prospective jurors—that she was a woman in charge.

"You know, Grace, it's supposed to work the other way around. You're supposed to kick his butt out of the house."

"Sorry," Grace said. "I'm new at all this. It never occurred to me to ask him to leave. Anyway, after I sank his car, I'd pretty much made the statement I needed to."

Mitzi laughed. "I've handled hundreds of divorces over the years, but you're my first client to drown a car." She half stood and bowed in Grace's direction. "Awesome. Although probably not prudent."

She sat down again and looked at her notes. "How are you for money?"

"I'm broke," Grace admitted. "Ben froze our bank accounts. He canceled my credit cards. I had to borrow money from my mom to buy gas to drive over here today."

The lawyer nodded. "Nothing unusual about that. We'll have to try to get the court to order your husband to come to a temporary financial agreement between the two of you."

Mitzi doodled something on her legal pad, then considered whether or not to share some unhappy news with her client. She hesitated to pile more bad news on Grace Stanton, whose life had taken an ugly turn for the worse ever since she'd drowned her husband's sports car two weeks earlier.

Grace caught the meaning of her lawyer's pitying glance.

"What?" Grace said, tucking a lock of hair behind one ear. "You're giving me that look."

"What look?" Mitzi asked.

"It's the look doctors give their patients before they tell them they've got an incurable disease. The look my college professor gave me right before he announced I'd pulled a D in statistics. The look that Ben gave me right before he admitted that night with J'Aimee wasn't the first. Come on, Mitzi. Spit it out."

Mitzi sighed. "Your divorce case has been assigned a judge, and we've got a date for an initial hearing."

"But that's good news, right? The faster we get things settled, the faster I can get my life back on track."

"It would be good news," Mitzi agreed. "Except that you drew Stackpole."

"Who's he? One of Ben's old drinking buddies?"

"If only," Mitzi said. "If we could prove he had some kind of association with your ex, that would be grounds for recusal, which would be great. But I doubt Ben and Cedric Stackpole have ever met."

"Then, why is he bad news?"

"Because," Mitzi said, "Cedric N. Stackpole Jr. is unofficial head of the He-Man Woman Hater Club."

"Why?"

"Nobody knows. Stackpole just hates women in general and women plaintiffs specifically."

"But, he's a judge. I mean, judges are impartial, right?"

"Supposed to be," Mitzi said. "Only Stackpole never got that memo. He's a notorious misogynist. I've been lucky. I've only had one other divorce in front of him in the past."

"How did that go?"

Mitzi's eyes strayed to the row of framed diplomas on the wall opposite her desk. "Hmm? Don't ask. My client got shafted. Her husband abandoned her and her two small children, left them basically penniless while he lived it up, funneling their marital assets into a dummy corporation. We had clear proof that he'd hidden assets, but Stackpole refused to hear a word of it. But because she finally had to go out and get a job to support herself and the children and eventually hooked up with a decent guy and allowed him to move in with her and the kids before the divorce was final, Stackpole decided she was an unfit mother. Gave the ex custody of the kids, forced her to move out of the house and sell it and split the proceeds with the ex, who was already a millionaire several times over."

Mitzi shook her head at the memory. "The ex didn't even want the kids. He just didn't want to pay her child support. It was brutal."

"How can a judge get away with that kind of thing?" Grace asked, horrified. "Can't you report him or something?"

"That's not how it works, unfortunately," Mitzi said. "We're just going to have to hope for the best. We'll lay out the facts; Gracenotes is your business, carries your name, and is written and photographed solely by you. By locking you out of your own Web site, Ben has essentially hijacked your name, which is trademarked, right?"

Grace shook her head. "I was *going* to trademark it, but I just never got around to it. I guess I assumed Ben would take care of that."

"Unfortunate," Mitzi said. She scribbled a note to herself. "All right, the good news is, at least we know what we're dealing with."

"If that's the good news, I don't want to hear the bad stuff," Grace said. She gathered her papers and went home to figure out her next move.

6

They'd gotten there early. The courtroom was half-full, and another hearing was still under way. Mitzi Stillwell led her up the right-side aisle and gestured at a vacant seat toward the front third of the room.

Grace studied the judge, who sat erect in his high-backed chair, listening intently. He looked to be in his late forties, with receding strawberry-blond hair combed straight back from a high forehead, steel-rimmed glasses, and a long, narrow, unsmiling face. "Is that our judge?"

"That's Stackpole, in the flesh," Mitzi said.

"I thought he'd be older," Grace said.

"He was two years behind me in law school at UF," Mitzi said. "And he was a pain in the ass, even then. But a politically connected pain. He was appointed to the bench at forty."

A uniformed bailiff, a young black woman with startling platinum marcelled hair who was standing at the side door to the courtroom, caught Mitzi's eye and gave her a very slight shake of the head.

"We gotta keep quiet," Mitzi murmured. "Or he'll have that bailiff toss us out."

A lawyer standing at the table on the left front side of the room stood and spoke into a microphone. "Judge, we'd like the court to view this video my client shot of her husband, while he was terrorizing my client." Grace couldn't see the lawyer's face, just the back of his balding head, and his neat, dark suit.

An older woman sitting at the opposite table stood. "Your honor, we have not seen that video, so we're going to oppose that being introduced into evidence."

The judge gave her a mirthless smile. "We'll all see it together right now, shall we, Ms. Entwhistle?"

"My client was deliberately goaded into an altercation by Mrs. Keeler's boyfriend. For months now, she and Luke Grigsby have repeatedly violated the terms of their custody agreement by either delivering Bo hours late, or not at all, at times when my client was scheduled to have Bo."

"Well, Ms. Entwhistle, I don't see where you've notified the court about that," Stackpole said evenly.

"No sir," Ms. Entwhistle said. "My client was trying to keep things amicable and civil, for the sake of the child. On the day that video was shot, Bo was to have been dropped off at his father's house before lunch. Mrs. Keeler was aware that Bo had a T-ball game at four that afternoon. My client even sent her a text message reminding her of that fact. But she was a no-show. She never notified my client of Bo's whereabouts, instead dropping him off at the park half an hour after the start of the game, and without his team uniform or his glove. The child was distraught, in fact, in tears, because he thought he'd let his team down."

The opposing lawyer stood up. "Judge, if you watch our video, you'll see that if there were indeed any tears, which my client states there weren't, it was probably only because Bo was afraid that Wyatt Keeler, who also happens to be his coach, and who obviously has a volatile temper, might be angry at *him*."

The man who'd been sitting at the table beside the female lawyer shot to his feet. He was coatless, but dressed in a pale yellow long-sleeved dress shirt and a blue necktie. He looked to be in his late thirties or early forties. His clean-shaven head was deeply tanned and gleamed in the glow of the courtroom lights. "That's not true," Wyatt Keeler called out, his voice cracking with emotion. "My son has never been afraid of me. He was crying because it was a big game, and Callie and Luke couldn't be bothered to get him there in time to play."

"That's enough, Mr. Keeler," the judge snapped. "Anything else, and I'll have the bailiff remove you from this courtroom." He closed his eyes for a moment and pinched the bridge of his nose. "All right," he said, gesturing to the same bailiff who'd already shushed Grace and Mitzi. "We're about to be running late. I want to see this video right now."

A moment later, a projection screen had been set up at the front of the room and the overhead lights dimmed. The video, grainy and depicting jerky movements, obviously shot from a cell phone.

As Grace and the other observers in the court watched, they saw Wyatt Keeler, dressed in a bright turquoise T-shirt with MARASOTA MAULERS in script lettering across the front, come storming toward the camera, his eyes narrowed, jaw set angrily, fists clenched.

"Hey, man," he called. *"I'm not done with you."*

Now the camera showed a second man, with dark, slicked-back hair, wearing khaki slacks and a red polo shirt, walking hurriedly toward the camera. He wore dark sunglasses. *"Make sure you get all this, Callie,"* he called, glancing over his shoulder. An unseen female voice said. *"I got it."*

Now Wyatt Keeler charged toward the other man, grabbing him from behind by the shoulders and spinning him around. It looked like he was saying something, but their voices were muffled.

The woman's voice rang out. *"Get your hands off him, Wyatt."*

Sunglasses man easily shook himself free of Wyatt Keeler's grasp and went jogging away with Wyatt Keeler following at a steady clip.

"Back away, Wyatt," the woman's voice called. *"If you put your hands on Luke one more time, I am calling the cops. I mean it, too."*

Wyatt Keeler looked right at the camera, stricken. His pace slowed and his facial expression softened, slightly. The camera moved back a little, now showing a gleaming white Trans-Am in the foreground.

"Don't do this, Callie," Keeler pleaded. *"Bo needs me. You can't just take him away like this. I won't let you. This is his home."*

"Not anymore it ain't," Luke Grigsby taunted. He was almost at the driver's side of the Trans-Am. *"You call living in a double-wide trailer a home? The kid doesn't even have his own room. He's coming with us to Birmingham, and there's nothing you can do to stop us."*

"Fuck you, Luke," Wyatt Keeler's voice rang out crystal clear. He was advancing again, his face menacing.

"Get in the car, Callie," Luke said loudly. *"Come on, before this maniac hurts somebody."*

Luke opened the driver-side door and started to slide onto the seat. The camera was moving now, so the footage was even jerkier and out of focus. Even with that, Grace watched, appalled. Grigsby's head popped up above the car door. *"See you later, alligator,"* he said, smirking, just before he closed the door.

Wyatt Keeler lunged toward the car. *"The hell you say,"* he bellowed, smashing his fist into the rolled-up car window.

"Stop it, Wyatt," the woman yelled. Her shrill scream pierced the cool courthouse air. The video stopped abruptly, and a moment later, the lights in the courtroom were turned on again.

Grace stared, wide-eyed with horror at the now-white screen.

"Ms. Entwhistle?" Judge Stackpole's face was deadpan. "I can see why you didn't want the court to view that video." He turned toward Wyatt Keeler. "You, sir, are lucky that gentleman did not file assault charges against you. Frankly, what I've just seen here turns my stomach."

Wyatt Keeler bowed his head and buried his face in his hands.

His wife's lawyer saw an opening and dove right in. "Judge, as you can see, Wyatt Keeler is not a fit father or role model for a young child. We'd ask the court to grant my client's application to go ahead with her planned move to Alabama with her fiancé, Mr. Grigsby, and of course, we want to have the previously agreed-to custody settlement amended to reflect that. Mrs. Keeler would be willing to allow Bo to visit his father for monthly supervised weekend visits, and she'd also be open to discussions about alternating holidays and, possibly, summer visits of up to a week. Again, to be supervised by a neutral party."

Wyatt Keeler raised his head. "One weekend a month? This is my son we're talking about."

"Quiet, Mr. Keeler!" Stackpole boomed.

Betsy Entwhistle stood and placed a warning hand on her client's shoulder. "I apologize for my client's outburst. He won't do it again. And I'll add that he is not proud of his behavior that day. But judge, that video was choreographed and shot by Mrs. Keeler and Mr. Grigsby. It's just as important to note what you don't see as what you do. For instance, that video doesn't show Mr. Grigsby deliberately baiting my client . . ."

"I saw all I needed to see," Stackpole interrupted, waving his hand dismissively. "Mr. Keeler?"

Betsy Entwhistle gave a brief nod and her client stood.

Stackpole's eyes drilled into the hapless Wyatt Keeler. "Regardless of what that video did or did not show, I find the actions shown there to be alarming, bordering on criminal." He looked over at the opposing lawyer. "When do Mrs. Keeler and Mr. Grigsby intend to relocate to Birmingham?"

After a brief whispered conference, the other lawyer cleared his throat. "Early August, Judge. Although Mr. Grigsby will move there immediately, Mrs. Keeler needs time to settle things here. But we'd ask that your custody order become effective immediately."

Stackpole thought it over. "I don't see any need for a rush. I'm going to take this under advisement. I have some thoughts, and I'll issue a ruling, probably by the end of business today." He glared at Wyatt Keeler. "And you, sir, are to stay away from Mr. Grigsby. If this court hears of even a hint of any more aggression from you, I'll issue a temporary restraining order. Is that understood?"

"Understood," Betsy Entwhistle said.

"Understood," her client echoed.

Stackpole flicked his eyes over at Callie Keeler, who was dressed in a demure pale-blue, long-sleeved dress. "Mrs. Keeler, if there are any more incidents, you're free to take that back up with the court again."

"Oh, I will Judge," Callie said, her high-pitched voice sounding defiant. "You better believe I will."

Stackpole jerked his head at the bailiff. "Ten-minute recess. Then I'll hear my next case."

Mitzi touched Grace's arm. "Let's make a bathroom run before they call us." Grace followed her lawyer out of the courtroom and down a long, narrow hallway.

As they walked, Grace spotted Wyatt Keeler. He was sitting on a wooden bench, focused on conversation with his lawyer. He was deeply tanned, and from here Grace could see that his dress shirt was ill-fitting, the collar too big, the sleeves too long. The shirt had obviously just come from a package, as the factory fold marks were still visible.

The other lawyer looked up just as they were passing. "Hey, Betsy," Mitzi murmured, nodding. "Looks like Stackpole is in rare form today."

Betsy Entwhistle rolled her eyes. Her client turned, noticing the two women who'd been in the courtroom earlier, and blushed, then looked down at his hands. For the first time, Grace noticed that his right hand was heavily bandaged.

"He's a peach, isn't he?" Betsy said. "I saw you sitting in the courtroom. Are you on his docket today?"

"Unfortunately," Mitzi said. She gestured toward Grace. "This is my client, Grace Stanton."

"And this is my nephew, Wyatt Keeler," Betsy said.

Wyatt Keeler offered them a solemn smile, revealing choirboy dimples. His eyes were a deep chocolate brown, framed with stubby dark lashes. He was seated, but he had the lean, lanky look of somebody who spent a lot of time outdoors. "I hope you fare better with that guy than I did," he said quietly.

Up close, Grace thought, he didn't look quite as much like the deranged goon he seemed in the video shot by his wife. Up close, he looked sad. Defeated.

"I was just telling Wyatt he's lucky Stackpole didn't order him to be castrated," Betsy said.

"He did seem pretty worked up today," Mitzi agreed. "I was kind of surprised, since it's usually the wives he's antagonistic towards."

"That damned video didn't help us any," Betsy said bluntly.

Mitzi glanced down at her watch. "Whoops. Sorry, but we've got to make a pit stop before Stackpole readjourns."

"Good luck in there," Wyatt said.

They slid into their seats at the front of the courtroom just as the bailiff at the rear of the room was closing the doors.

Mitzi Stillwell shot Grace a sideways glance. "You okay?"

Grace nodded. "As good as I'm gonna get." She turned halfway in her chair and looked around the courtroom. There was no sign yet of Ben and his lawyer. She didn't know whether to be glad or mad.

"What happens now?" she asked, turning back to her attorney.

"It should be pretty cut-and-dried," Mitzi said. "We've asked the judge to order Ben to mediation for a financial settlement, since he's so far resisted all our efforts in that direction. We've produced plenty of documentation that the business is yours and that he's put you in an untenable situation. Even Stackpole should agree that you are arguably the rainmaker for Gracenotes."

"And then?"

"Then we figure out a way to divide up the marital assets, seek a final decree for you, and Stackpole pronounces you unmarried."

"You make it sound easy," Grace said.

Mitzi shrugged. "Not easy. The statutes don't want to make it too easy to get a divorce. But if Stackpole makes Ben play by the rules and divvy up the goods, this shouldn't be too terribly complicated from hereon out."

Grace heard footsteps coming up the center aisle of the courtroom and turned slightly before swiveling violently back toward Mitzi. "He's here," she whispered. "Oh, God. I don't think I can breathe."

She still hadn't laid eyes on Ben since the night she'd driven his Audi into the pool on Sand Dollar Lane. He strode past her, eyes front, and sat at a table directly to the right of the one where she sat. He was dressed in a conservative charcoal suit, sharply pressed white dress shirt, and a purple silk tie. His glossy hair looked freshly cut, his black Gucci loafers were polished to perfection. He was carrying a briefcase Grace hadn't seen in years, and he busied himself now, snapping it open and sorting through file folders.

Grace felt something tighten in her chest. "Breathe," Mitzi instructed quietly. "In. Out. You can do this, Grace. Don't let the bastard get you rattled."

"I *am* rattled," Grace said, feeling her face flush. She felt a hand clasp her shoulder and looked up.

Dickie Murphree smiled down at her. "Gracie," he said, his hand lingering on her shoulder. "It's great to see you."

Dickie looked much as he had the last time she'd seen him, at an expensive restaurant on St. Armand's Circle, not long after she and Ben had moved back to town. Had it been three years ago? His thinning brown hair was a little too long in the back and he had a rakish mustache and that same impish smile he'd used so effectively to get his way all through high school.

"No hard feelings, right, Grace? This is just one of these things. You'll get past this, and you'll be fine. Right?"

No hard feelings? Grace felt her jaw drop. With Dickie's help, Ben had effectively impoverished her. Right this very minute, she was wearing the dressiest clothing she possessed, a pair of her mother's cast-off sandals, and an ill-fitting rayon knit dress she'd picked up for $3.60 at a thrift shop near the hospital. No hard feelings? Not long ago, Grace wouldn't have used this dress as a dishrag. Dickie didn't wait for her reply. He nodded now at Mitzi, flashing his easy smile. "Hey there, Ms. Stillwell."

"Dickie." Mitzi gave him a curt, dismissive nod.

He finally removed his grasp of her shoulder and slid onto the chair next to Ben's.

Ben was still busily sorting file folders, avoiding meeting her eyes.

"Exhale," Mitzi said quietly. "Think about a happy place. Picture yourself there."

"I don't have a happy place anymore," Grace whispered. "Ben got custody of it."

"Then try this. Picture your ex with his dick caught in a rattrap."

Implausibly, Grace began to smile. As the image formed in her mind, she began to giggle. Horrified, she clamped her hands over her mouth, but not before the giggle became a guffaw. Ben's head turned sharply. His eyes narrowed and he looked, briefly, disgusted. He glanced at the back of the courtroom and gave an almost imperceptible shrug before returning to his paper shuffling.

"Feel better?" Mitzi asked, a smile playing at the edge of her lips.

"Much," Grace said. Her eyes followed Ben's gaze toward the back of the room. Sitting in the last row, wearing a form-fitting chartreuse dress and dark sunglasses, a raven-haired woman was staring down at her cell phone, her fingertips racing over the keyboard. Probably sexting Ben, Grace thought.

"I don't believe it," Grace said, her mirth short-lived. "She's here. Right in this courtroom. She's wearing sunglasses, and I think she's dyed her hair, but that's definitely J'Aimee. I can't believe he had the nerve to bring her here."

Mitzi turned all the way around in her chair to have a look, not bothering to hide what she was doing. "Oh. The green dress, right? What is she, about thirteen? Did he have to sign her out of homeroom?"

Just then, the blond-haired bailiff strode past them to the front of the room. "All rise for the Honorable Cedric N. Stackpole," she intoned.

7

Mitzi laid out the case neatly before the judge, letting him know that Ben had locked Grace out of their home, canceled her credit cards, and denied her access to their joint checking and savings accounts.

"Your Honor," Mitzi said, gesturing toward Grace, who was sitting straight in her chair, eyes forward, like an obedient schoolgirl on her first day of class, "Mr. Stanton has effectively impoverished my client. She has no funds, no home, and no way to make a living, thanks to him."

"No way to work?" Stackpole looked startled. "Now how is that possible? Didn't you tell me Ms. Stanton was some kind of professional writer?"

"Yes sir," Mitzi said. "Ms. Stanton is—or she was before all this happened—one of the most successful lifestyle bloggers in the country."

"A blogger?" Stackpole's high forehead wrinkled and his lips thinned in distaste. He waved his hands in the direction of the neat printouts Grace had made of six months' worth of Gracenotes. "Do you mean to tell me Ms. Stanton here makes a living writing this material?" He picked up one of the sheets and skimmed its contents.

"Recipes? Pictures of sofas? Directions for painting an old table? This looks like some kind of hobby to me, Ms. Stillwell."

Grace's heart sank. Mitzi had warned her that Stackpole might not take her work seriously.

"No sir," Mitzi said sharply. "Not a hobby in any way. Ms. Stanton's blog has 450,000 followers. That's just people who have subscribed to her RSS feed. Her blog receives 1.3 million unique visits each month. Since Gracenotes was monetized, which means Ms. Stanton started accepting paid advertisers, the site has consistently generated twenty thousand dollars a month in revenues."

"Impressive," the judge admitted.

Mitzi beamed. "We think so. Judge, Gracenotes is named for Grace Stanton. It was conceived by her and it is written and photographed solely by her. There are no other outside contributors. In other words, this blog is intellectual property, and, as such, it belongs to her. But Ms. Stanton's estranged husband, Ben Stanton, is deliberately blocking her from access to her blog."

"I see," Stackpole said. He swung his head to the left, smiling at Dickie Murphree.

"What do you say to that, Mr. Murphree?"

Dickie thrust his hands in his pockets and gave an exaggerated shrug. "Obviously, Judge, we'd refute just about everything Ms. Stillwell has just said. Grace Stanton is free to write whatever she wants, whenever she wants, and, as far as I know, there's nobody stopping her from doing that. The Internet is a big ol' marketplace, and there's plenty of room in it for everybody, last I heard."

"Mm-hmm," Stackpole said. "And what do you have to say about the dire financial situation of your client's estranged wife? Ms. Stillwell makes a convincing case that your client has effectively cut off her access to all the couple's marital assets."

Dickie's face registered what passed for genuine shock. Grace wondered if Dickie had ever done anything in his life that was genuine.

"Judge, I would just point out to you that Ms. Stanton is the one who initiated all the turmoil in this marriage. It was she who abandoned my client, moving out of their home, of her own accord, after a violent outburst. And, I would add, she did so in a manner that was calculated to humiliate and embarrass my client—not just in front of this couple's immediate neighbors, but in front of everybody in this community, and across the country, for that matter. If her business has been damaged, that is Ms. Stanton's own doing."

"He went there," Mitzi muttered under his breath. "I should have known."

"I'm afraid I don't understand," Stackpole said.

The lawyer clapped a reassuring hand on Ben's shoulder. "Your Honor, I deeply regret having to trot this out again. My client certainly didn't want me to drag all this out in the open again, but sometimes, sir, you have to get these things out in the open."

"What things?" Stackpole asked, leaning back in his chair.

Dickie let out a long, anguished sigh. "Well, ahhh, it's a long story, Judge."

Mitzi stood up. "Your Honor? If Mr. Murphree is referring to the matter I think he is, that matter has no direct bearing on the issue of my client's right to her share of this couple's marital assets. And I strongly object to his trying to introduce it here today."

"What matter?" Stackpole asked, looking peevish.

Dickie shrugged. "The matter of Ms. Stanton intentionally driving my client's 175,000 dollar Audi convertible into the swimming pool of their home on Sand Dollar Lane, thus destroying it. The matter of her assaulting and slandering my client's employee."

"What?" Stackpole's eyebrows shot up. "When was this?"

"The night of May eighth," Dickie said. "Ms. Stanton misunderstood some communication between my client and his employee and flew into a rage. My client eventually began to fear for his life and locked himself into his home and called the police, who, unfortunately, arrived on the scene after Ms. Stanton destroyed the Audi."

Stackpole gave Grace a stern look. "Is this true?"

Grace's voice came out in a squeak. "It's true that I drove the car into the pool, yes sir. But it's not true that I assaulted J'Aimee. I would have, but I couldn't catch her. And anyway, she was my assistant, not Ben's. And it's a joke to think that Ben would be afraid of me. But Your Honor, you haven't heard the whole story."

"That's right, Judge," Dickie said quickly. "You haven't heard how Ms. Stanton raised such a ruckus that their entire neighborhood could listen in on this private marital spat. And I'm assuming you didn't see the network news footage of the aftermath—including footage showing Mr. Stanton's personal vehicle sitting at the bottom of his pool?"

Stackpole's eyebrows shot up. "It was on the news?"

"I had nothing to do with that," Grace offered.

"Enough!" Stackpole glared over the top of his glasses at her.

Dickie held up a small plastic rectangle. "I have the news footage right here on a flash drive, if Your Honor would like to see it."

"I don't intend to do any such thing," Stackpole said. "Let's get back to the matter of finances. Mr. Murphree, I want your client to come to some kind of equitable agreement with Ms. Stanton." He flipped through the files before him.

"Ms. Stanton? Your attorney has asked for what seems like an exorbitant amount of money to pay your monthly expenses. I find it hard to believe a resourceful woman like yourself can't live on $2,000 a month. My own wife manages quite nicely on that amount."

"But Judge," Mitzi sputtered. "Ms. Stanton is entitled to much more than that. She has business expenses involved in writing and producing her blog. And she'll need to find a place to live. She can't continue to live in her mother's very small quarters. And furnishings . . . Besides, it's really immaterial how much allowance you give your wife. Ms. Stanton was the primary breadwinner in this marriage . . ."

Dickie shot to his feet. "That's not true! Mr. Stanton incorporated Gracenotes. He managed the business, sold advertising, dealt with every aspect of the business, and built it up from a small-potatoes hobby to the entity it is today. He, in fact, is the CEO of Gracenotes, Inc., and the owner of the domain name, among other things. It was Ms. Stanton's choice to be paid a weekly salary on a work-for-hire agreement, because she did not want to be troubled with the business of running a business."

"What?" Grace shrieked, then quickly covered her mouth with her hands. She tugged urgently on Mitzi's hand. "I never agreed to any kind of a weekly salary," she whispered. "Ben just drew money out of the corporate account and put it in our personal checking account. I left all of that up to him and the accountant."

"Judge," Mitzi began, but Stackpole wasn't listening.

"Two thousand a month," he said firmly. "It was apparently Ms. Stanton's decision to leave this marriage, so I'm afraid she'll have to deal with the repercussions of that."

"Thank you, Judge," Dickie said quickly.

"That's not all," Stackpole said. He took his glasses off and rubbed the bridge of his nose. "Ms. Stanton, I find myself at a loss for words as far as your behavior in this matter goes. This is the second instance today of parties to a divorce acting in dangerous, violent, even criminal behavior. I'm troubled by that. Deeply troubled."

"Judge, if you'd just listen to what provoked my client," Mitzi began, but Stackpole held up a hand to stop her.

"There can be no justification for the wanton destruction of property or for harassment or assault on a third party. This is just the kind of thing that escalates, until we have domestic violence, armed stand-offs, and God knows what."

"It won't happen again," Grace said in her meekest voice.

"It certainly won't," Stackpole agreed. "We'll see how you do with this new financial settlement, while the two of you work out the other details of your divorce settlement. But in the meantime, Ms. Stanton, I want you to begin seeing a therapist who is an expert in divorce, uh, counseling. Immediately. Dr. Talbott-Sinclair does excellent work, as you'll see." He glanced down at his calendar. "I believe she has a group meeting on Wednesday. If she can fit you into her group meeting tomorrow night, that will give you six weeks."

Mitzi stared at the judge. "Your Honor, are you also ordering *Mr.* Stanton to attend these group sessions?"

"No," he snapped. "Mr. Stanton seems to have his anger issues under control. Now, Ms. Stanton, if Dr. Talbott-Sinclair signs off on your rehabilitation, then I'll take that into consideration when I see you later this summer. Understood?"

Grace could do nothing but nod. Inside was another story. Inside she was screaming.

But Mitzi wasn't done. "Judge, we still need you to rule on the matter of ownership of Ms. Stanton's business. As it stands right now, Ms. Stanton has been deprived of access to her blog, which in effect deprives her of making a living."

"Why can't she just start another blog?" Stackpole asked, gathering up his papers and shutting the file in front of him. "Nobody's keeping her from writing, are they?"

"Mr. Stanton is keeping her from writing," Mitzi said, sounding weary and out of patience. "He is in effect hijacking her intellectual property."

"Talk to me in six weeks after your counseling," Stackpole said. He jerked his head in the bailiff's direction. "I can feel my blood sugar getting low. Let's break for lunch."

Mitzi was stuffing papers into her briefcase. Ben stood and began to stride past, but Grace reached out and grabbed his sleeve.

Ben looked down at her with a blank expression. "Don't do this," he said, his voice chilly.

She jumped up. "Do what? Ask you to answer my lawyer's phone calls? Ask you to treat me with some kind of fairness, some kind of decency, even if our marriage is over? Why are you doing this? If I can't write my blog, neither of us makes any money. You realize that, right?"

Dickie was at Ben's side now. "Now, Gracie. This is very inappropriate. You heard what Judge Stackpole just told you. You need to get your issues under control. If you have something to say to Ben, you need to have your lawyer bring it up with me."

Ben looked her in the eye. "That means no more phone calls. No more showing up at the gates at Gulf Vista, embarrassing the security guards. You wanted it over, Grace, so that's what you've got. It's over. You get on with your life, and I'll get on with mine."

He carefully pried her fingers from the fine fabric of his suit coat, then picked up his briefcase and strolled toward the door, where J'Aimee was already standing, waiting for him. She grasped his arm and, just before walking out, turned and shot Grace a triumphant smile.

8

It was four o'clock on a steamy Tuesday afternoon and Jungle Jerry's Olde Florida Family Fun Park was nearly deserted. There were no families present, and not much fun in evidence.

A quartet of blue-haired tourists from Michigan were taking advantage of the "buy one, get one" coupon they'd found in that day's newspaper. They were having a nice enough time, wandering the crushed-shell footpaths, admiring the unusual flora and fauna, especially the wading pool full of preening pink flamingos.

If they noticed that the temperatures were in the high nineties, and the humidity at 2,000 percent, they didn't remark upon it. Instead, they fanned themselves with the yellowing cardboard Jungle Jerry's Fan Club fans they'd bought for $1.99 in the gift shop and inhaled the heady fragrance of frangipani and ginger lily.

The four paused in their leisurely tour to stare up at the gnarled crimson boughs of a particularly eye-catching tree. "What the heck is this?" asked the only man in the group, a spry seventy-six-year-old who was actually the youngster of the crowd.

Wyatt Keeler happened to be nearby, trimming dead branches from an oleander bush that seemed particularly stressed by the summer's dry spell.

He was dressed as he always was at the park, in a khaki shirt bristling with epaulets and with flap pockets and embroidered Jungle Jerry patches, matching khaki cargo shorts, lace-up work boots, and, of course, his ever-present safari hat.

Wyatt walked up to the group and gave them a welcoming smile, flashing his dimples. Old ladies were crazy for the dimples. He gave the tree trunk a loving pat, as though it were a beloved family pet, which, to Wyatt, it essentially was.

"This is a gumbo-limbo tree," he volunteered. "It's one of the more unusual species we have in the park. It's Latin name is *Bursera simaruba*, and it's a native of tropical regions like Florida, of course, as well as Mexico, the Caribbean, Brazil, and Venezuela. Some people call it the 'tourist tree,' because the bark is red and peeling—like a lot of tourists we see down here in the wintertime."

The Michiganders laughed at this and themselves by association.

"Interesting," murmured one of the women, a sturdily built eighty-five-year-old widow in a pink sun visor.

Wyatt felt himself suddenly cheered by his own speech, and by the interested comments from these tourists.

The very oldest member of the group, a spindly legged ninety-year-old in a thin cotton housedress, stepped closer and peered at Wyatt's Jungle Jerry's name patch, which had faded into obscurity from years of laundering.

"You're not Jungle Jerry," she said sharply. "You'd be too young."

"No ma'am. I'm Wyatt Keeler," he offered her his hand. "Jungle Jerry was my grandfather. He bought this place in 1961, when it was still a commercial orange grove."

One of the women did a little full-circle turn. "You don't see a lot of orange trees here now."

"That's right," Wyatt said. "My grandfather, Jerry Brennan, bought six hundred acres here on County Line Road, back in the day when this was considered way out in the boonies, and he thought he'd become the orange king of Manatee County. And he might have done it, too, except that this area experienced a record-breaking frost in 1963. Temperatures dipped into the low teens and stayed there for three days. My granddad didn't know enough about citrus growing back then to know that he needed to fire up the smudge pots. He lost most of his orange trees in that freeze, and most of the family money, too."

"Too bad," the man muttered.

"Fortunately," Wyatt went on, "he met my grandmother, Winnie, not long after that. And *her* family still had some money. Granddad's family had once owned a little amusement park back home in Tulsa, and, since tourism was going great guns in Florida then, he decided maybe he could take the old orange grove and convert it into what he called a kiddie park."

Wyatt gestured to a rusty jungle gym partially obscured by a hedge of orange-flowering shrubs. "He put in all kinds of rides and playground equipment, and because my grandmother Winnie loved flowers, the two of them also started planting new trees and shrubs as they took out the dead orange trees."

"It's lovely now," the ninety-year-old said. "We used to bring our grandchildren here when we all came down every spring. Whatever happened to all your wild animals? I was just telling my friends, there used to be lions and a tiger, and do I remember a zebra?"

"Yes ma'am," Wyatt said with a laugh. "We had all that and more. My granddad watched a lot of those old Tarzan movies in his younger days. He bought the animals from a traveling circus that had gone bust. A lot of circus outfits used to winter down in this area, you know. He'd always loved animals anyway. So he named himself Jungle Jerry, and he got a retired lion tamer to teach him a few tricks of the trade."

"I thought I remembered a lion show," the woman crowed. "So that was the real Jungle Jerry?"

"The one and only," Wyatt said. "We had the big cats, plus Zoey, that was the zebra, and an elephant, and even a Florida black bear, right up until the late seventies. After my granddad retired, my dad took over, and he phased out most of the large animals."

The woman in the sun visor glared at Wyatt. "They didn't . . . kill them. Tell me they didn't."

"Not at all," Wyatt assured her. "Those animals were like my grandfather's own kids. Boo-Boo, he was the bear, he died of natural causes the same year granddad retired. Monty, the lion, and Tonga, that was the tiger, they retired to an exotic animal shelter in Ocala. Daphne, our elephant, was donated to the Lowry Park Zoo over in Tampa."

The four tourists all seemed relieved. "I love all the tropical birds you have around here," said the woman in the baggy shorts.

Wyatt put his fingers to his lips and gave a long, shrill whistle. They heard a flapping, and suddenly a huge gray parrot flew down from the top of a nearby poinciana tree and perched on Wyatt's shoulder.

"Oh!" one of the women said, clapping her hands in glee.

The bird nuzzled Wyatt's ear, then dipped its neck and poked her head into the right breast pocket for a treat.

"This is Cookie," Wyatt said. "She's an African gray, a total diva, and the star of the parrot show. I can't take any credit for her, though. The birds were my mom's idea."

"Weren't there monkeys, too?" the ninety-year-old inquired.

"You've got a good memory," Wyatt said. "The monkeys were here when I was a little kid. But when this neighborhood started going residential, with all the subdivisions closing in, we were getting a lot of complaints, especially since the little boogers were too clever and kept getting out of their pens and frightening the neighbors. Eventually, all of them were adopted out."

Cookie found a parrot pellet in Wyatt's pocket and began chewing contentedly.

"That was certainly interesting," the old man said, pumping Wyatt's hand again. "This is a grand place you've got here. We're a little surprised to have it all to ourselves today."

Wyatt was not surprised. But he made a valiant effort to keep up a good front.

"You just happened to catch us on our slow day," he lied. "But you come back later in the week, and the crowds will be here, I guarantee."

That was a lie, too. They hadn't had what you could call a real "crowd" at Jungle Jerry's in months and years. Okay, decades, if you wanted to be brutally honest. In this post-Disney era, families got their kicks in air-conditioned comfort, with audio-animatronics and movie-quality special effects. Animal rights advocates didn't approve of exotic birds performing quaint tricks like riding a tiny bicycle on a high wire, and kids were bored silly just looking at a bunch of plants and trees.

Jungle Jerry's had shrunken significantly over the years. Right now, they were at around a hundred acres, since Jungle Jerry's son-in-law, Wyatt's father, Nelson, had been forced to sell off a chunk of land to pay inheritance taxes after Jerry's death.

Wyatt had never intended to work in the family business. He'd been a horticulture major in college and had gone to graduate school at Clemson for a degree in landscape architecture, which was where he'd met Callie Parker, a twenty-two-year-old graphic arts major from Orangeburg, South Carolina. He and Callie had been in a fever to get married, such a fever that he'd canned the idea of getting his master's and dropped out of grad school to get a job working for a mail-order nursery in Greenville.

He'd worked there for four years when his mother called to beg him to come home to run Jungle Jerry's. Nelson had suffered his first heart attack, and Peggy, his mother, had just been diagnosed with breast cancer, although she didn't tell him that until after he and Callie moved back to Bradenton.

Peggy lived just long enough to hold Bo, christened Nelson William Keeler II, before succumbing to the cancer.

The first few years at the park, Wyatt had worked furiously to try to turn the tide at Jungle Jerry's. He'd advertised, joined civic associations, networked like crazy. He'd phased out the old kiddie rides, which were rusting safety hazards anyway, and had begun emphasizing ecology and the botanical aspect of the park. And at first, things seemed to be working. Attendance crept up. Callie came to work at the park, designing posters and ads. Bo took his first steps chasing after Beezus, a gold-capped conure. They weren't getting rich, but they were young and happy. And dumb, Wyatt reflected now. At least, he was.

They'd bought their first house in one of the newer subdivisions nearby and enrolled Bo in the neighborhood school, one of the best in the school district. Wyatt was working crazy long hours at Jungle Jerry's, and Callie was doing some sporadic freelance work. Most of the other families on their block were like them, young marrieds with one or two kids. They cooked out together, took the kids en masse to Holmes Beach—all the things you did when you were young with not much money.

The one bachelor on the block, Luke Grigsby, was a salesman with a chemical company. Luke was the neighborhood fun guy. He wore cool clothes and drove a sharp white Trans-Am. His home was the biggest, newest house on the block, and since he had a pool, he entertained frequently.

Every year Luke threw a big, crazy Halloween party. Everybody competed to come up with the most outrageous costume. Wyatt wasn't a big one for parties, but Callie loved dressing up. That year, she decided they should go as Aladdin and Jasmine, the characters from the Disney movie.

Wyatt reluctantly allowed himself to be talked into wearing a turban, idiotic-looking billowy pants, and, worst of all, a short embroidered vest over his bare chest. For her own costume, Callie outdid herself. She took one of her old bikinis and covered the top and bottoms with hot-glued gold sequins, then attached some kind of filmy fabric to the bottoms to make harem pants. She bought a felt fez, cut a hole in the top, and pulled her blond ponytail through, then made herself a veil with more of the filmy fabric.

Callie refused to let Wyatt see her in her costume until the night of the party. When she stepped out of the bedroom, he couldn't believe this was his wife.

She'd swept glittering blue eye shadow on her eyelids and outlined them in black liner. Her breasts jutted out of the skimpy sequined bikini top, and her harem pants skimmed right above her pubic bone. She wore half a dozen jangly gold bracelets on each arm, huge earrings, and little gold sandals. As a final touch, she'd somehow attached a huge plastic rhinestone in her belly button.

Callie's eyes danced from above the veil obscuring the lower half of her face. She did a little pirouette followed by a suggestive hip grind that sent her bracelets jingling.

"What do you think?"

"Where's the rest of it?" Wyatt asked.

She pouted. "What's that supposed to mean? You don't like it?"

He looked over his shoulder, toward the kitchen, where the teenage babysitter was trying to con Bo into eating his dinner. "I like it just fine if we're staying home tonight—just the two of us," he said in a low voice, running a finger down her bare arm. "But don't you think it's a little, uh, I don't know, risqué for a neighborhood party?"

"No, I do not," Callie snapped. "I've been working on this costume for weeks. Yours, too. And that's all you can say? I look risqué?"

He shrugged. "You asked."

"Well I don't care what you think. I think I look hot. And cute." She grabbed a gold beaded clutch purse and opened the front door. "Are you coming?"

He went to the party, had a couple beers, talked football with a couple of the guys, and watched glumly from across the room while his wife knocked back half a dozen wine coolers and then proceeded to strut and shimmy and flirt with every guy in the room.

Callie was doing a tipsy but highly suggestive belly dance with Luke out on the patio when Wyatt tapped her on the shoulder. She whirled around, then frowned when she saw it was her husband. "What?"

"It's eleven thirty," he said pointedly. "We promised we'd get Melanie home by midnight."

"It's Friday night. There's no school tomorrow! Just call her and tell her we're going to stay later," Callie said. "It's no big deal."

"It actually is a big deal," Wyatt replied. "She's got to get up early because she's taking the SATs tomorrow."

"Oh, for God's sake," Callie said. "Just when the party is starting to crank up." She looked over at Luke and gestured at Wyatt. "Meet Aladdin—he traded his magic carpet for a wet blanket."

"You don't have to leave," Wyatt said stiffly. "I'll go, since she drove herself over to the house."

"You mean it?" Callie's face lit up, her pout forgotten. "I won't stay that much longer. I just want to hang around long enough to see who wins the costume contest."

Luke laughed and wrapped an arm around Callie's shoulder. "You already know who won—lady." He gave Wyatt a wink. "Don't worry about her. I'll walk her home myself. Okay?"

What could Wyatt say? Callie planted a perfunctory kiss on his forehead. He walked the two blocks home, paid the babysitter, and walked her out to her car. He looked in on Bo, who was fast asleep, then went to bed. Alone. He woke up at 3:30 A.M., glanced at the clock, and then back at Callie's side of the bed. She wasn't there.

He couldn't sleep. Finally, Wyatt got up. He peered out the front window, just in time to see Luke and Callie stroll slowly up the sidewalk. The window was open, and the curtains billowed in a faint breeze. Callie's giggle floated on the night air, and Luke said something in a low voice. She leaned heavily on the arm Luke had around her waist. As Wyatt watched, they stopped just short of the driveway. Luke pulled her from the sidewalk into the shadow of their neighbor's Florida holly tree. Wyatt's heart stopped. His hand clutched the curtain fabric as he watched his wife wrap her arms around Luke's neck, press herself up against his chest, and pull the neighborhood fun guy into a long, deep kiss.

As he walked back to their bedroom, Wyatt checked the dial on the clock radio on his side of their bed. He made a note of the time. 3:47 A.M. It was the moment time stopped in what he thought had been a perfectly happy marriage.

9

Callie never did come to bed that night. She was asleep on the living room sofa in the morning. Her fez was on the floor, her hair mussed and spilling over the sofa cushion. The blue eye shadow and black liner were smeared into raccoon circles under her eyes. One breast peeked all the way out of the bikini top.

"What happened to Mommy?" He hadn't heard their barefoot son pad into the room. Bo stood looking down in horror at Callie.

Wyatt pulled an afghan over Callie's shoulders and scooped Bo up into his arms. "She didn't feel so good last night when she came home from the party, so she slept out here. Come on, sport, let's get you some breakfast."

Months later, after the trial separation, after the tears and accusations and denials, Wyatt knew, in retrospect, he should have said something the night of the Halloween party. Maybe if he'd let Callie know what he'd seen, told her he loved her and didn't want to lose her, maybe things would have turned out differently. Or maybe he might have admitted he didn't love her enough. Not enough to fight Luke for her.

But things didn't turn out that way. Eventually, Callie admitted that she and Luke were in love. Eventually, she told him the marriage had been in trouble for a long time. And so Wyatt did the decent thing. They agreed it was important for Bo's life to retain some degree of normalcy. Callie would keep the house so that Bo could stay in his school. Wyatt was thirty-eight years old, with a failed marriage and an ailing business.

Wyatt moved out of their little house and into a battered double-wide trailer at Jungle Jerry's that had once been the living quarters for a security guard—from back in the day when they actually had the funds and the need for a security guard.

When it came time to start divorce proceedings, his Aunt Betsy offered to handle his side, pro bono. They somehow worked out a time-sharing agreement, with Bo splitting his time between the two of them. Wyatt's dad, Nelson, moved into the second bedroom of the double-wide to help out with child care for Bo on the weekends and after school on the days Bo stayed with Wyatt.

Wyatt was shocked at how fast his marriage unraveled and dumbfounded at the changes in Callie once she and Luke moved in together.

Or had she been somebody else all along? Wyatt would never be sure.

Their temporary custody-sharing arrangement got off to a rocky start. On the first weekend Bo was to spend with Wyatt, he got a tearful call from his son on Friday night, hours after Callie was to have dropped him off at Jungle Jerry's.

"Daddy?"

"Hey, Bo," Wyatt said, relieved to hear his son's voice. "Grandpa and I are waiting on you. We're having your favorite, mac 'n' cheese."

Bo sniffed, and then, in a thin, wobbly voice, "Mom says if you want me, you gotta come pick me up."

Wyatt frowned. That had not been the agreement.

"Sure thing," he said. "I'll be right over."

Now Bo was crying. "But, I'm not at Mom's house. I'm at Luke's friend's house, and it's way far away."

He heard Callie's voice in the background. "Just tell him you'll see him in the morning. Your dad will understand."

"But I wanna see Daddy," he heard Bo wailing, and his heart sank.

"Oh, for Pete's sake," he heard Callie say.

And then she was on the phone, her voice crisp and unapologetic.

"Look, Wy, we've had a little change of plans. We went over to St. Pete Beach with Luke for a work thing, and with Friday traffic and everything, we're just not gonna make it back in time tonight. You understand, right? I'll drop him off first thing in the morning."

"This is crap, Callie," Wyatt protested. "You were supposed to bring Bo here as soon as school was out, four hours ago. Now you call me and tell me you took him all the way to St. Pete? And I'm supposed to be okay with that?"

"You're supposed to be okay with doing what's good for your son," Callie snapped. "Luke's friends live right on the beach here, and they have a pool, and Bo was having a blast until he all of a sudden decided he needed to talk to you. The next thing I know, he's blubbering and saying he wants to leave. And if we leave now, with traffic and everything, he'll be asleep by the time we get him there anyway. So what's the difference if you get him tonight or tomorrow morning?"

"The difference is, I haven't seen him in three days," Wyatt said, feeling his chest tighten with anger. "I made plans for tonight, with Dad and Bo."

"Whoop-dee-shit," she said. "Fine. Whatever. I'll pack his ass up now, and we'll get in the car and drive him all the way back over there so you can see him. Asleep."

Wyatt took a deep breath. "I wish you wouldn't cuss in front of him. But all right, he can stay. As long as you have him here first thing in the morning. And since you've got him tonight, I want him to spend Sunday night with me."

"Great." She hung up without another word.

10

Gracenotes

Despite what you might think, I am definitely not a neat freak. My desk is frequently a disaster area, and dust bunnies are not an endangered species at my house. But truthfully, I get deep personal satisfaction out of making my surroundings beautiful—and comfortable.

I've learned a few tricks that make housekeeping less drudgery and more delight. For one thing, I try and tidy up every night before bedtime. Dishes always get put in the dishwasher—is there anything more depressing in the morning than a sinkful of greasy crockery? I spritz the sink and kitchen counters with my favorite all-purpose organic cleanser, watered-down white vinegar.

In the morning, after I've showered, I use more of my diluted vinegar-water spray to freshen up the tub and shower surfaces, and I keep a special "squeegee" under my bathroom sink to allow me to wipe down the glass shower door before it gets any annoying water spots or streaks.

On the Wednesday after her court appearance, Grace flipped the last of the heavy wooden chairs onto the tabletop. She dipped the mop in the bucketful of scalding soapy water, then, with rubber gloved hands, wrung out the excess soap. She swished the mop back and forth across the Sandbox's gritty linoleum floor, halfheartedly listening to the morning news roundup of traffic accidents, taxpayer revolts, and local political skullduggery.

The smell of coffee somehow managed to waft through the biting aroma of Pine-Sol. Her mother was standing at the bar, holding out a freshly brewed pot.

"Come on, hon," Rochelle urged. "It's early. You can stop for one cup. That floor ain't going nowhere."

It was barely eight o'clock. Grace had been up since six, taking a run along the quiet predawn streets of Cortez while it was still relatively cool, then starting in on her new ritual of swabbing down the restaurant, from floor to ceiling.

Out of boredom and desperation, in the weeks since she'd moved in, Grace had been waging a one-woman war on the Sandbox's decades-old accumulation of grease, grime, and clutter.

She'd started in the storeroom, clearing out an entire Dumpster's worth of antiquated equipment, a deep fryer her father had always meant to fix, an ice machine that had stopped working ten years earlier, boxes and crates of old business records, food service catalogs, and broken chairs and tables.

From there she'd moved on to the kitchen, ruthlessly tossing anything and everything that wasn't essential to their food-service operation. She'd inspected every glass, dish, and piece of cutlery, consigning anything chipped, bent, or discolored to a crate she'd allocated for the local homeless shelter's soup kitchen.

Along the way, she'd had to abandon all her old, genteel ideas about housecleaning. Diluted vinegar and baking soda were useless in her dust-busting efforts here. Now, her weapons of choice included every industrial-strength, commercial-grade cleaner she could find at the local janitorial supply house.

Grace set her mop aside, peeled off the rubber gloves, and sipped her coffee. She gestured around the room. "I feel like I'm finally making some headway, don't you?"

Her mother shrugged. "Place doesn't even smell like a bar anymore. You've scrubbed away every last trace of the Sandbox ambiance."

"Mom, that wasn't ambiance, it was crud. Years' and years' worth of baked-on, smoked-in, ground-down crud. This place was gross. Can't you just admit you like it better clean?"

Rochelle rested a hand on the old mahogany bar. "I liked it the way it was," she said pointedly. "We were shabby before shabby got cool. Now it's like a hospital operating room, for God's sake. Who wants to grab a beer and a burger in a hospital?"

"There's a difference between shabby gentility and run-down and decrepit, and it's really not so fine a line," Grace said. "Our regulars may grouse at first, but you wait, they're gonna appreciate pouring beer from a pitcher without a busted spout or eating with a fork without bent tines."

"*My* regulars don't know what a fork tine is," Rochelle said.

Maybe, Grace wanted to tell her, if we clean this place up, change the menu, and raise our standards a little, maybe we'll attract a clientele that actually will pay $15 for a decent dinner entrée.

But before she could lob another useless argument into Rochelle's court, she happened to glance up at the television and stopped, midsentence.

Rochelle followed her gaze. "Aw shit. Here we go again."

The morning news hour had segued into *Sunrise Sarasota,* one of those chatty, morning-magazine-format shows. The cohosts, an unbearably perky husband-and-wife team named Charley and Joe, were doing an "In the Kitchen" segment that had the wife, Charley, attempting to crack a Florida lobster shell while the husband, Joe, was being tutored in the finer points of crafting a table setting.

When Grace heard an all-too-familiar voice, a high-pitched nasal twang, she turned around to stare at the wall-mounted television above the bar.

The guest coaching Charley and Joe through their cooking segment was none other than J'Aimee. Her J'Aimee, or rather, Ben's J'Aimee.

Rochelle grabbed for the remote to change the channel, but Grace was faster, snatching it up from beneath her mother's fingers, then staring, dumbfounded, at the television.

"Don't go away!" Charley was saying. "We'll be right back with Gracenotes-style blogger J'Aimee."

"What?" Grace shrieked. "Gracenotes-style blogger? Seriously?"

"Just turn it off," Rochelle said soothingly. "Tune it out. This means nothing. You're just going to get yourself all worked up for nothing."

"It's not for nothing," Grace said, still staring up at the television. "This is all Ben's doing." She scrabbled around on the bar, looking for her phone.

"I'm calling my lawyer," Grace said, scrolling through the numbers on her contact list. "He can't do this. He can't promote her as a Gracenotes blogger. He can't turn her into me!"

"Looks like he already did," Rochelle said, under her breath.

Grace got Mitzi Stillwell's voice mail. "Mitzi! This is Grace. Turn on *Sunrise Sarasota* right now! Ben has J'Aimee on there, promoting herself as the Gracenotes-style blogger. You've got to do something, Mitzi. Call the judge, get an injunction or something. Call me back, okay?"

The commercial break was over, and Charley and Joe were back with their guest.

"Look at that whore!" Grace ranted. "See how good she looks? I swear, Ben's gotten her a makeover. She looks almost classy."

J'Aimee was wearing a sleeveless hot-pink dress, her newly dyed dark locks worn in a simple upsweep.

"They must have put some kind of concealer on that barbed-wire tattoo she has on her right bicep," Grace muttered. "And I think maybe she got Botox on her lips. You see how full they are now?"

Rochelle shrugged. "I never paid that much attention to the girl, to tell you the truth."

J'Aimee was now openly flirting with Joe, batting her artificial lashes at him, giggling and playfully flicking a dinner napkin at him . . .

"Hey! That's my damned napkin." Grace scrambled up on one of the barstools to get a closer look at the television. She pointed at the screen. "Those are my hand-blown Mexican wineglasses." She felt tears welling up in her eyes. "I carried those all the way back from Puerto Vallarta on my lap.

"And look. She's using that fugly damned pottery from my Gracenotes sponsor. That's strictly a Ben move."

She sank back down on the barstool, unable to take her eyes off the television. Now J'Aimee was placing a centerpiece in the middle of the table. It was a large, shallow glass bowl, heaped with shiny green Haas avocados.

"I always like to use fresh local fruits and vegetables in my table settings," she told Charley, adjusting one of the avocados. "It gives a party a sense of authenticity, don't you think?"

"Authenticity?" Grace howled. "She didn't know an avocado from an orange before I hired her."

Rochelle quietly removed the remote control from Grace's clutch. She aimed it at the television and clicked.

"You're getting yourself all worked up for nothing," she said. "So what if she's on television? So what if Ben has her writing a blog with your name on it?

She's not you. She's just a cheap little floozie. You are the real thing. You're butter and she's . . . she's not even Parkay. Ben will figure that out soon enough. Your readers will figure it out. Everything will work itself out."

"No, it won't," Grace said tearfully. "She's stolen everything from me. My house, my husband, my napkins. That was my wedding silver she was setting the table with. My Repoussé silver, Mom."

Rochelle sighed and folded her weeping daughter into her arms. "It'll be okay, Grace. Really it will. I know it hurts right now, but you'll get through this. You will. I'll help you."

Grace looked up at her. Tears streamed down her face. Her eyes were red-rimmed and her nose was snotty. She sniffed loudly. "How, Mom?"

"I just will," Rochelle vowed. She grabbed the bottle of spray cleaner Grace had left behind the bar. "Look. I'll let you clean the office next, okay? You can throw out whatever you want, and I won't say a word."

After the judge refused to give her back her blog, Grace promised herself she would *not* look at Gracenotes. But that afternoon, once she'd filled the Sandbox's Dumpster with dusty files and years' and years' worth of old *Sports Illustrated* and *Florida Sportsman* magazines, Grace opened her laptop and clicked on the icon for her blog.

"Oh no she didn't," she murmured, looking at the home page. Everything had changed. Including the name. It was now Gracenotes for Living, with J'Aimee! The new banner was in a nearly unreadable font, in a garish orange and teal color combination. The rails on both sides of the page were filled with tiny, one-inch squares advertising everything from *New Unbelievable Anti-Aging Serum!* to bank credit cards to cruise ship vacations to *Pet Meds by Mail!*

"Horrible," Grace said, shaking her head. "Heinous." She counted three dozen ads on the home page. Ben must have been having a field day, she decided, maximizing and monetizing to his greedy heart's content.

She read the previous day's post. It was titled "How to Buy Furniture."

"Hmm. Scintillating," Grace said. As she read, she felt sick. The entire blog was really a thinly veiled advertorial for Room in a Box, a wholesale furniture company with franchise operations all over central Florida. The same furniture company whose banner ad now took up the entire top of the home page.

Room in a Box's marketing people had been pestering Grace for more than a year to write about their furniture. They'd even had the nerve to ship a faux-leather recliner chair to the house—as an inducement/bribery for Grace to write testimonials about their product line.

"No way," Grace had said, as Ben cut the cardboard crate away from the chair—which actually came with a remote control allowing it to recline, vibrate, and even play music. "Pack that thing up and tell UPS to come back and get it. I don't even want it to stay here overnight."

Ben knew it was useless to argue with her. Obviously he'd waited until he no longer had to argue with her. Grace was gone, and with her had gone any hint of editorial standards.

She couldn't read any more of this drivel. She closed out the blog, opened a file, and began to type, her fingers flying over the keyboard.

By four that afternoon, she'd registered a new domain name for herself, TrueGrace. Maybe not the most original name, she admitted, but it would serve its purpose, hopefully letting her readers know this blog was the real thing.

This time around, she promised herself, the blog would be all hers. And for her first post, she decided to go public with what had happened in her life and to her old world.

No more prettying things up, Grace decided. She was still writing, deleting, revising, when she looked down at her watch and realized it was nearly 7:00 P.M. She hit the SAVE button, closed her laptop, and reluctantly went downstairs.

Rochelle was behind the bar, pouring a beer for an older woman Grace didn't recognize. She looked up in time to see Grace heading for the Sandbox's front door.

"Where are you headed?" Rochelle called.

Grace grimaced. "To my so-called therapy group."

"Looking like that?"

Grace looked down at herself. She was wearing a faded lime-green Sandbox T-shirt, white shorts, and flip-flops, the same outfit she'd changed into after her morning run. Her hair was knotted in a limp ponytail and she wore no makeup.

"The judge said I had to go," she said, her chin jutting out defiantly. "He didn't say I had to dress to impress."

Rochelle handed the beer to her customer and hurried around the bar to her daughter's side. "Honey, you don't want to go in there with an attitude," she said, her voice low. "Maybe these sessions will actually be helpful. Maybe you should keep an open mind. Or at least do something about your hair."

Grace sighed. She reached into the glass display case where they kept the Sandbox-branded merchandise, the koozies, tees, bumper stickers, and key chains. She grabbed a baseball cap with the Sandbox logo embroidered on the bill, jammed it on her head, and looped her ponytail through the opening in the back of the hatband.

"Better?" She didn't wait to hear Rochelle's answer.

11

G race had to check the street address on the therapist's door to make sure she'd arrived at the right place. This was a shrink's office? It was a drab one-story stucco storefront occupying the end slot in a strip shopping center that also boasted a Vietnamese nail salon, a hearing aid salesroom, a business called the Diaper Depot, and a tattoo parlor. The dusty plate glass window was boldly lettered in gilt-edged black letters; PAULA TALBOTT-SINCLAIR, L.S.W. FAMILY AND MARITAL COACHING, DIVORCE DIVERSION, EMOTIONAL HEALING.

"Emotional healing," she muttered to herself, taking a last sip of lukewarm coffee before getting out of her car. "Right. Like that's going to happen." There were four other cars in the otherwise empty parking lot. One of them, a shiny black VW bug, boasted a yellow smiley-face bumper sticker with the motto "Change Happens." Had to be the therapist's car, she decided, hating her on the spot.

Paula Talbott-Sinclair's reception area wasn't much more impressive than her storefront. Worn and faded brown indoor-outdoor carpet, a low-slung olive-green pleather sofa, and a couple of armless chairs. There was a receptionist's desk, with a computer terminal and telephone, but no sign of a receptionist. Only a clipboard with a hand-lettered sign on the desktop: DIVORCE RECOVERY GROUP MEMBERS, PLEASE SIGN IN HERE. There were three other names on the sign-in sheet, all women, Grace noted.

The door on the wall opposite the front door was slightly ajar, and Grace heard the low hum of voices. She wrote her name on the sign-in sheet, hesitating a moment, before jotting down Grace Davenport.

"Hello?" she said softly, approaching the door. A woman popped her head out. Grace guessed she must be in her midforties. Her heart-shaped face was framed with a cascade of sandy-blond curls, and she had startlingly blue eyes behind wire-rimmed glasses. She was dressed in a figure-hugging sleeveless black tank top and tight black yoga pants, with a gauzy black shawl draped around her bony shoulders. And she was barefoot.

"Oh hi," she said brightly, looking Grace up and down. She grasped both of Grace's hands in hers and squeezed. "I'm Dr. Talbott-Sinclair, although in group, we all just use first names. So I'm Paula. And you must be Grace Stanton?"

"Actually, it's Davenport," Grace said. "If you don't mind."

"I see," Paula said, pursing her lips. "Well, that's something we're going to want to talk about, isn't it?"

"Taking back my maiden name?" Grace asked. "Does the judge have a problem with that?"

Paula cocked her head and blinked. "The question is, Grace, do you have a problem with it? Is this something you're doing out of anger? Because we can't have a healing when our hearts and minds are full of bitterness. You'll come to see that, I think, eventually, in group."

"It's *my* name," Grace said, feeling unusually obstinate. "I was a Davenport for way longer than I was in Stanton."

"All right," Paula said, pushing the door open. "Let's hold that thought. For now, come on in and meet the other members of group."

The inner office consisted of a large glass-topped desk and a swivel chair, in the corner of the room. It had the same brown carpet as the outer office and a pair of smallish windows that were covered with a set of shiny bronze drapes in a cheesy sheer fabric. Five folding chairs were arranged in a semicircle around a high-backed brown leather chair. A row of framed diplomas was stretched across the wall above the desk, and three women, all of them looking ill at ease, were clustered around a small wooden table that held a coffeepot and a stack of Styrofoam cups, talking in subdued voices.

"Ladies," Paula said, her voice rising to let them know she had an important announcement. "Ladies!"

The women turned their attention to the newcomer. If Grace had any expectations about what her divorce recovery group would look like, this wasn't it.

"Don't I know you?" A tall, elegantly dressed black woman approached Grace, hands on her hips, studying the newcomer intently. She wore her hair in a sleek bobbed cut, and the first thing Grace noticed about her were her almond-shaped eyes and her luxuriously thick fringe of eyelashes. Fakes?

"I, I'm not sure," Grace said, stuttering a little. Wasn't group therapy supposed to be anonymous? Wasn't Paula Talbott-Sinclair supposed to protect her identity?

"Wait, I've got it," the woman snapped her fingers. "Gracenotes! Am I right? You're the lifestyle blogger who drowned her husband's 175,000-dollar ride. Damn! I covered that story, and it got picked up by all the networks." She patted Grace's shoulder. "Nice goin', girlfriend."

Grace felt her face flame with embarrassment. So much for anonymity.

"You! You're that reporter! Camryn. Camryn . . . something. You snuck into our subdivision, trespassed, talked to all my neighbors." She lowered her voice. "Did you follow me here today? Don't you people have any sense of decency?" She looked around for the therapist, ready to chew her out.

"Relax," Camryn said, chuckling. "Me, follow you here? Don't flatter yourself. I'm here for the same reason you are."

Grace narrowed her eyes. "You drove your husband's car into a pool?"

"Not quite," Camryn said. "Let's just say what I did do didn't set well with some parties."

Another woman walked up to join them. She was younger than Camryn Nobles but older than Grace, petite and slender, with sun-streaked shoulder-length blond hair pushed back from her forehead by a pair of designer sunglasses. Her skin was flawless, and she was dressed casually, in white capris and a flowery pink and orange tunic top and gold sandals. She wore a fine gold chain around her neck, and dangling from it was a whopper of a diamond, three carats, at least, Grace estimated.

"Hey, y'all," she said, in a honey-dipped drawl. She glanced over her shoulder at Paula Talbott-Sinclair, who had seated herself in the swivel chair and was looking expectantly at the door. "Are you thinkin' what I'm thinkin'?"

"What's that?" Camryn said.

"Well, I'm just wondering what kind of dog-and-pony show we've lucked into here. I mean, did you get a look at this shopping center? I've been living in Sarasota all my life, and I have never, and I mean ever, stepped foot in a place like this. What kind of a therapist has her offices between a tattoo artist and a diaper store?"

"The kind who charges three hundred dollars a session," Camryn said. "Obviously she's not spending what she makes on overhead."

"For real," the blonde said. "And the thing is, my lawyer says I probably can't make my ex pay for these sessions. Even though I'm not the one who was fuckin' around on the side. I'll tell you, that damned Stackpole has my lawyer runnin' scared."

"Stackpole!" Camryn said with a snort. "He's the judge hearing your divorce?"

"That's the one," the blonde said. "You too?"

"Unfortunately," Camryn said. She looked at Grace. "How about you?"

"Afraid so," Grace said. "My lawyer says he hates women. Especially women lawyers."

"My lawyer's a man, and I still got the shaft," Camryn pointed out.

"Me too," the blonde said. "Well, I guess we're in this together, huh? By the way, I'm Ashleigh. Hartounian."

"I don't think we're supposed to tell our last names," Grace said.

"Why not?" Camryn shot. "I got nuthin' to hide. Anyway, y'all both know my name, so why shouldn't I know yours?"

Grace sighed. "Whatever. I'm Grace Davenport."

"I thought your name was Stanton," Camryn said.

"It was. I'm taking back my maiden name."

Camryn rolled her eyes. "I'll bet the judge is gonna love that." She turned toward Ashleigh. "So, is your ex Boyce Hartounian? The plastic surgeon?"

"You know him?"

"Only his reputation," Camryn said. "He did an eye lift for one of my girlfriends at the station. I swear, she looks ten years younger."

"Boyce is good, all right," Ashleigh admitted.

Camryn took a step closer and examined the younger woman's face. "How 'bout you? Did he do some work on you?"

"Some," Ashleigh admitted. She lifted her shoulders. "He gave me these boobs, not long after we started dating. And for our first anniversary, he gave me Reese Witherspoon's nose."

"Damn," Camryn said. "Those boobs are fine."

The fourth woman in the room wandered up, looking distinctly uneasy. She was older than all of them, in her early fifties. Her dark brown hair was streaked with gray, and a thin network of crow's-feet radiated out from her eyes. She was neatly dressed in a pale gray linen blouse and gray slacks.

"Hello," she said quietly. "I guess I should introduce myself? I'm Suzanne."

"Ashleigh."

"Grace."

"I'm Camryn. Look here, is the judge hearing your divorce named Stackpole?"

Suzanne looked startled. "As a matter of fact, yes."

"Uh-huh," Camryn said, nudging Grace. "And did you do something ugly to your ex? Maybe act out a little bit, something like that?"

Suzanne's face paled. "I can't . . . I don't . . . I won't . . ."

"Never mind," Grace said. "Whatever you did, I'm sure your husband deserved it."

Suzanne bit her lip. "I still can't believe I went through with it. And I can't believe I'm here, tonight. It all seems so surreal."

"What's surreal is the fact that this group is all women," Camryn said. "This isn't group therapy. It's ladies' night."

"A really, really, expensive ladies night," Grace put in.

"Ladies . . ." Paula called from her seat at the front of the room. "Let's get started, shall we? I'm expecting one more member to join us, but I think we'll go ahead and get started. So take a seat, if you will."

Grace sat down on one of the folding chairs and crossed her legs. The other three women did the same.

"Well," Paula said, giving them a bright smile. "I take it you've all introduced yourselves to each other. Ashleigh, Grace, Camryn, and Suzanne. Tonight is an important night for all of you. Right? It's the night you all start the healing. And the forgiving."

"No way," Camryn muttered under her breath.

"Excuse me?" Paula said sharply.

"I said, no way," Camryn said defiantly. "That judge can order me to come to these bullshit counseling sessions. And he can order me to pay through the nose for the privilege of coming here. But he cannot make me forgive what Dexter Nobles did to me."

She crossed her arms over her chest. "And neither can you."

"I see," Paula said. She nodded at Ashleigh. "What about you, Ashleigh? Did you come here with an open mind tonight?"

"I came with an open checkbook," Ashleigh said. "That's the best I can do right now."

Camryn guffawed and Grace managed to stifle her own laugh.

"Grace?" Paula's look was expectant.

"My husband has locked me out of my own home," Grace said, feeling her throat constrict. "He's frozen my bank accounts. Canceled my credit cards. I have no way to support myself. I'm living with my mother, tending bar to pay for gas money. He's living in a two-million-dollar home, shacking up with my twenty-six-year-old former assistant. So no, right now, I'm really not ready for what you call a healing."

Paula frowned. "All this negativity. I find it very sad. Very disappointing."

Too damn bad, Grace thought. She glanced over at Camryn Nobles, and then at Ashleigh Hartounian. Their faces were impassive. Suzanne's face was scrunched in concentration.

"We've got a lot of work ahead of us," Paula said after a moment. She went over to her desk, picked up a stack of old-fashioned black-and-white-spattered composition books, and handed one to each of the women.

"This," she said. "Is your divorce journal. I want all of you to get in the habit of writing in it, at least once a day, although several times a day would be most helpful."

"Write what?" Ashleigh demanded.

"Everything. Anything. We're going to be doing some visualization exercises that I think will be helpful. And I'd like you to search, really search your souls, for the truthful answers to some questions I'm going to pose to all of you. Because, in here, honesty is everything."

Paula waved toward the windows. "Out there, with your family and friends, you can hide your pain. You can cover it up, sanitize it, deny it. But in here—with group—I expect nothing less than absolute honesty."

She opened the bottom drawer of her desk and brought out a boxy Polaroid camera. She walked briskly to the semicircle of chairs and snapped a photo of Grace, before Grace had time to object. When the photo ejected from the camera, the therapist handed it to Grace and moved on, pictures of Camryn and Suzanne, then Ashleigh, handing each woman her photo.

Grace stared down at the Polaroid, watching as the pale gray of the film disappeared and a grainy image of herself came into focus. She was shocked at what she saw. Her formerly full, round face looked gaunt. Her hair hung limply from a center part that emphasized her dark roots. She hadn't bothered with makeup that day, hadn't actually bothered with it at all since the day she'd been turned away from the security gate at Gulf Vista. There were dark circles under her eyes and deeply etched grooves at the corners of her mouth. It struck Grace that she couldn't remember smiling, not in days. She looked sad. Sad and old, and defeated.

She glanced at the other women. Camryn and Ashleigh didn't look any more pleased with their photos. In fact, Ashleigh had pulled a compact from her Louis Vuitton satchel and was busily applying more lipstick. Suzanne stared at her photograph as though she'd never seen a picture of herself before.

Now Paula handed Grace a stapler. "I want you to staple the Polaroid to page one of your divorce journal. This is your before picture. Now, turn the page and describe what you see in yourself in this photo. Tell me where you are, today. What you're feeling about the place you're in, right now, emotionally. If you like, you can write about this experience you're having, your first night in group. Be honest. I know you all resent me, resent being here. I expect that." She looked down at her watch. "I'm going to give you fifteen minutes to write. And when I come back, I want you all to be ready to share what you wrote with the rest of the group."

"What if I don't feel like sharing?" Ashleigh asked, tossing her hair behind her shoulder. "What if I don't feel like writing anything?"

Paula's smile was tight. "Oh, Ashleigh. You know Judge Stackpole made your attendance at group mandatory as a condition for granting your divorce, right?"

"How could I forget?" Ashleigh asked.

"It's not as simple as just showing up," Paula said. "Judge Stackpole knows some people will just go through the motions, simply so they can get that divorce decree. Despite what you all think, I must tell you, Cedric Stackpole is really a very wise man. So he's asked me to be very clear about his expectations for all of you." She smiled.

"Each week, I'll be reporting in to Judge Stackpole about your progress in group. And if I feel that you're only coasting, just giving group therapy lip service, I won't be able to sign off on your attendance report."

"Attendance report?" Ashleigh asked. "Like in kindergarten? Are you serious?"

"Very serious," Paula said. "You have fifteen minutes to write. Starting now." She walked out into the reception area, closing the door firmly behind.

Grace began scribbling on the second page of the journal.

I can't believe I have been "sentenced" to group therapy. I have nothing in common with these other women. I don't see how hearing their pathetic stories is going to help me get over what was done to me. I don't need therapy. I need a divorce. I was betrayed by my lying, cheating, dirtbag husband. You want to know how I feel? I feel different ways, different days. Most nights, I can't sleep. I don't know what's happening with my life. How will I make a living for myself? Where will I live? I can't keep living with my mother, but right now I don't have a choice. I have no choices at all. That's what I think I resent the most about all this. The feeling of powerlessness, of being helpless. It's so damned unfair. And I'm supposed to get over all of this? I'm supposed to reach a point where I don't feel this rage, bubbling up inside me, threatening to boil over at any moment? Most of the time, I am CONSUMED with anger. And when I'm not, I'm just sad. So damned sad. And lonely. Everything I had is gone. I'm thirty-eight. And alone.

"This is bullshit," Camryn Nobles was saying, as she made bold, looping lines of script on the open page of her journal. "My lawyer didn't tell me anything about having to write in a journal, or having to report to therapy, like a high school kid to study hall. I'm calling him tonight, just as soon as I get out of here. That bullshit judge can't make us do this shit."

"Shh," Ashleigh whispered, jerking her head in the direction of the door. "She'll hear you and tell the judge what you called him."

"I don't care what she tells that damned judge," Camryn said fiercely. "I'm not in his courtroom now. This is America. Not some damned banana republic, where he gets to lay down the law and make us salute every time he farts."

Grace laughed despite herself. "Maybe you could do an exposé of the judge for your television station."

"Maybe I will," Camryn shot back. "Just as soon as I get my divorce from Dexter Nobles, I might just do that."

The room was quiet then, with only the scratching sounds of their pens as they scrawled their thoughts across the cheap notebooks.

After she'd filled two pages of her journal, Grace looked at her watch. "It's been thirty minutes. Where do you think Paula went?"

"Who cares?" Camryn said. "This whole thing is a charade."

"I'm gonna go check on her," Grace said. "I've had a long day. I just want to get out of here."

She walked across the room, opened the door, and peeked out into the reception area. Paula Talbott-Sinclair was slumped down in the chair behind the reception desk, her chin resting on her chest. She was snoring softly.

Grace stood there for a moment, uncertain what her next move should be. Then she heard the front door behind her open.

A man stepped inside the reception area, looking uncertainly around the room.

He was tall and lanky, and sunburned. He was about Grace's age, she guessed, and at first she thought he was completely bald, until a closer look revealed a fine dark stubble of hair covering his scalp. He was dressed like a workman, in baggy khaki cargo shorts, a grimy-looking faded khaki safari hat, and high-topped lace-up work boots. His eyes were dark, nearly black, with an astonishing fringe of thick, luxuriant lashes. And dimples. It was the dimples that reminded Grace that she'd seen this guy before, and recently.

"Hey," Wyatt Keller said, scowling at her. "I'm looking for Dr. Talbott-Sinclair?"

Grace nodded in the direction of the slumbering therapist. "You just found her."

12

Is this a joke?" Wyatt asked, narrowing his eyes. He pulled a slip of paper from his pocket and reread the card the judge had forced him to take. Then he took a closer look at Grace.

"Didn't we meet . . ." he hesitated. "In court?"

"That's right," Grace said.

"I'm supposed to be here for the, uh, divorce recovery group," he said.

"Well, you're late," Grace snapped. "It started thirty minutes ago. Not that you missed much."

"Damn," Wyatt said. "The bridge was up. I've got a sick bird, and I had to run her to the vet's office, and the asshole vet tech wouldn't wait for me to get there, and the office was closed by the time I got there, and I had to stop at a drugstore and buy some meds . . ."

"Really?" Grace sniffed. "That's the best you can do? The dog ate your homework?"

Wyatt bridled. "It's true. Anyway, what do you care?"

Grace shrugged. "I don't. I just care about getting out of here. Right now. I've had enough 'sharing.'"

Wyatt nodded in the direction of Paula, who hadn't stirred despite their odd conversation.

"What's wrong with her?"

"Don't know, don't care," Grace said. "It's eight o'clock. My time's up."

She marched over to the desk and shook the therapist's shoulder. "Paula," she said loudly. "Hey, Paula. Wake up."

Nothing.

"Is she sick or something?" Wyatt asked, taking a step closer. He reached out and touched the side of her neck, looking for a pulse.

"Who's that?" Paula's eyes flew open and she swatted his hand away. She looked wildly around the room. "What's happening?"

"You told us to write for fifteen minutes, but it's now been more than thirty minutes," Grace said. "I came out here to check on you, and found you dead asleep. Or passed out."

"Ridiculous!" Paula said. She stood, fluffed her hair, and straightened her clothing, looking like Stevie Nicks after an epic bender. "I was meditating, waiting on the group to complete their visualization exercise."

"Who are you?" she asked, looking Wyatt up and down.

"I'm Wyatt," he said. "Judge Stackpole said I had to come see you. For divorce recovery group."

He said the words with such distaste, that Grace almost laughed out loud.

"Didn't the judge tell you our sessions start promptly at seven?"

"He told me," Wyatt said. "But I had a family emergency. And the bridge was up. But I'm here. I've been here for . . ." he looked down at his watch, and then at Grace, his dark eyes pleading.

"Twenty minutes," Grace volunteered. "We weren't sure whether or not to wake you."

Paula studied Grace's face carefully. "Really?"

"It's true," Grace said, with a shrug. "You can ask the others. We were all waiting for you to come back and take a look at our journals, to see if we did what you asked."

Paula waved her hand distractedly. "Never mind that. It's late. I'll read them next week."

"So . . . we can go now?" Grace asked. "All of us?"

"Didn't I just say that?" Paula asked.

She went into the inner office and clapped her hands for attention. "All right. That's the session for tonight. I'll see everybody next Wednesday, at seven o'clock. Remember to bring your journals."

She turned and handed Wyatt a notebook. "And next week, please be on time."

Camryn and Ashleigh stood quickly and headed for the door, while Suzanne was still jotting in her notebook. "Ladies," Paula said, gesturing toward the newcomer. "Before you go? This is Wyatt. He'll be a part of group for the next few weeks. I'd like you to welcome him to our little circle of healing. Wyatt, this is Ashleigh, Camryn, and Suzanne. And you already met Grace."

Suzanne looked distressed. "Uh, Paula, no offense to him, but I thought this was just a women's group? Nobody said anything about men being part of it."

"We welcome anybody with an open, willing heart to group, Suzanne," Paula said.

"Hey," Wyatt mumbled, blushing slightly as the women carefully looked him over.

"Hmm," Ashleigh purred.

"What's your story?" Camryn wanted to know. "Did Stackpole sentence you, too? I thought he only hated women."

"Never mind that," Paula said. She grabbed her camera and snapped a picture of the startled Wyatt. When the photo had developed, she handed it to him.

"What's this?" he asked, gazing down at the picture. It was not what you'd call a flattering image. The harsh overhead lights cast his face in deep shadows. He needed a shave, he noted, and there was a distinct sweat ring around the collar of his shirt. Also? There was a tell-tale white dribble on the shoulder of the shirt. Parrot poop, from Cookie, who'd insisted on riding on his shoulder the whole way to the vet's office.

"That's your before picture," Paula told him. "Staple it in the book. And the journal is your homework assignment. I want you to write in it at least once a day, every day, more often if you can. Tonight's assignment is to write about how you feel about where you are in your emotional journey."

"Ohh-kay," Wyatt said slowly.

"And Wyatt? As the ladies can tell you, the one thing I insist upon in group, besides punctuality, is absolute honesty. No whitewashing. No lies. Understand?"

Camryn snorted. "He's a man. They're genetically programmed to lie."

"Telling a man not to lie is like asking him to pee sitting down," Ashleigh agreed.

"Ladies?" Paula said wearily.

Wyatt had had more than enough. He could feel the hostility radiating out of every woman in this room. Man-hating ball busters, every one of them.

"Also?" Paula held out her hand. "Your counseling fees must be paid in full, in advance of each session. Did your attorney explain my fee structure? You understand I don't accept personal checks? Credit cards, although no American Express, or a cashier's check."

"She told me," Wyatt said. He reached into the pocket of his shorts and pulled out a tightly rolled bundle of money. The bills were faded and creased, and as he counted off each of the six fifty-dollar bills he thought of what that money should be going to. Groceries. New tennis shoes for Bo, and, now, payment on his ever-growing vet bill.

He pressed the money into Paula's hand.

"Cash?" She looked down at the bills as though he'd just handed her one of Cookie's bird turds.

"Yeah," he said. "Can I get a receipt for that? My lawyer told me to make sure and get one. To prove to the judge that I was here."

When he finally got outside the therapist's office, he took a deep breath of the hot, humid night air. May, and it was already sweltering. Well, that was Florida. Anyway, it felt good to be outside. It had been freezing in that damned office. And all those women, staring at him, like he was some kind of spawn of Satan.

Just because he was a man. Betsy had warned him it would probably be like this. "It's a divorce recovery group, honey," she'd said. "A bunch of sad, mad, depressed, repressed women. All of 'em blaming all their problems on some man who done them wrong. Just sit there and take it, and with any luck, six weeks from now, Judge Stackpole will sign off on your divorce and you and Bo can get back to living your lives."

He'd parked at the far end of the parking lot, mostly because he didn't want anybody riding by to know he was going to see a shrink. As he approached the truck now, he saw a woman standing beside it, bending down, looking in the open window.

It was that woman from group. What was her name? Grace, yeah. Grace.

He quickened his step until he was right beside her.

"Is there a problem?" he asked gruffly.

She looked up, puzzled. She had nice eyes, Wyatt thought, when she wasn't pissed off.

"You really do have a bird in your truck," she said, wonderingly.

"That's what I tried to tell you," Wyatt said. "What? You think every man is a liar?"

She ignored that, concentrating on Cookie, who was roosting on the steering wheel, her head tucked under her wing, eyes closed.

"It's a parrot, right? What kind?"

"African gray."

"Aren't you afraid he'll fly away, leaving the window open like that?"

Wyatt laughed. "Cookie? Nah."

"You said he's sick? What's wrong with him?"

"She. Same old thing," Wyatt said. "Cookie will eat any damned thing she can get her beak around. One of the kids at the park fed her something today. A gummy worm, probably. It, uh, didn't agree with her digestive system."

Grace looked closer at the slumbering bird. "Looks like she pooped all over your steering wheel."

"Yeah," Wyatt said with a sigh. "She's bad to do that."

She turned and pointed at his right shoulder. "I think she got your shirt, too."

"I would make a joke about getting shit on by everybody, but I wouldn't want you to think I'm bitter," Wyatt said.

Grace straightened. "Are you?"

"Oh yeah," he said easily. "Isn't everybody bitter about something?"

She thought about it. "I'd hate to think so, but yeah, it seems that way to me these days. Although maybe my mom isn't. God knows why, but I really think she doesn't have a bitter bone in her body."

"I've got enough bitter for both of us," Wyatt said.

Grace was looking at Cookie again. "You said something about a park. Do you work for the city or the county?"

"Hell, no," he said emphatically. "I work for myself. At Jungle Jerry's."

Her face lit up. "Jungle Jerry's," she said delightedly. "I remember that place! We used to go there every year on field trips for school. I used to love the parrots and the little Key deer. They were so adorable. Do you still have the parrot show? Where they ride the little toy bike on the high wire?"

"Yeah," Wyatt said, feeling himself thaw a little. "Cookie here is the star of the show. When she isn't eating Popsicle sticks and Happy Meal toys."

"Jungle Jerry's," Grace said wistfully. "I haven't been there in years and years. In fact, I didn't even know it was still there."

"You and everybody else in Florida," Wyatt said. "But we are definitely still there, right where we've always been.

He hesitated, then reached in the pocket of his shorts and pulled out a bright orange card. "That's a free pass. If you're not doing anything some day, you get in free with that. Bring your kids, if you want. It's good for the whole family."

"No kids," Grace said lightly. "Just me."

"Guess that's just as well," Wyatt said. "Since you're getting a divorce, right?"

"Yeah," Grace said. "Just as well. Since he turned out to be a scumbag."

Her mouth hardened and her eyes narrowed, and she looked like she had earlier in the evening, when he'd first walked into the therapist's office. Wyatt found himself missing her smile already, and wishing he could do something to bring it back.

"Guess I'd better go," he said, unlocking the truck.

"Me too," Grace said. "Gotta go home and write in my divorce journal."

"Yeah." Wyatt opened the driver's door and slid onto the seat. "Hey, uh, thanks," he said.

"For what?"

"Covering for me with the therapist," Wyatt said. "I can't afford to get crossways with her, or that damned judge."

"It's okay," Grace said. "Sounds like we're all in the same boat. Divorce-wise," she added.

"Yeah, divorce-wise."

She gestured at Cookie, who was awake now, and hopping up and down on the steering wheel.

"Will your parrot be okay?"

"She'll be fine," Wyatt said. "I'm gonna pick up some Pepto-Bismol at the Seven-Eleven, and see if that settles her down any."

"Hey. Does she talk?"

He laughed. "When she wants. If she likes you."

Grace leaned into the car, and Wyatt caught the scent of her, faintly soft and sweet, like the flowers in the park after a spring rain. She held her hand out, and Cookie happily stepped onto her outstretched index finger.

"Ohhh," Grace breathed. "Is this okay? She won't bite, will she?"

"Not usually," he said.

"Hi, Cookie," she said.

The bird cocked her head and blinked. "Wassup?"

Grace giggled just like one of the kids at Jungle Jerry's. "Cookie want a cookie?" She looked over at Wyatt. "Dumb, right?"

The parrot inched her way up Grace's forearm, until she was perched on the crook of her elbow.

Now Grace was getting nervous. "She won't try to fly away, will she?"

"No such luck," Wyatt said. "She knows where her bread is buttered. Literally."

"Gimme a beer," Cookie demanded. "Gimme a shot of whiskey. Gimme some peanuts."

"You don't really give her beer and whiskey, do you?"

"Nah," Wyatt said. "She just says that for the shock value. But she really does love peanuts."

Grace smiled again, and Wyatt found himself smiling back. "I better get going. It's trivia night."

"You play trivia?"

"Not really. I'm terrible at it. Actually, it's trivia night at the bar where I work, and it gets pretty busy about this time."

"You work at a bar?"

She bristled. "Anything wrong with that?"

"No," he said hastily. "Not at all. Which bar?"

"It's just a hole in the wall. Over in Cortez. You never heard of it."

"Try me."

"The Sandbox."

He grinned. "I know that place. My whole softball team used to go there after games. So it's still there? I heard the owner died a while back. What was his name? Butch?"

"Butch Davenport," Grace said. "Yeah, he's been gone a couple years now."

"You knew him?"

"He was my dad," Grace said. "My mom runs the place now. I moved in with her, after the split with my ex." She held her arm out straight and laughed as the bird waddled down her forearm and back into the truck.

"Good night, Cookie." She looked in at the bird's owner and was surprised to see him smiling at her, flashing those choirboy dimples.

"Good night, Wyatt."

"See you next week," he said.

13

Wyatt found his father asleep in the battered leather recliner in the tiny living room, the remote control still clutched in his hand, the television turned to the Cooking Channel.

"Pop." He shook the older man gently. "Hey, Pop. C'mon. Why don't you go on to bed now?"

Nelson yawned and stretched. "I'm waitin' for Rachel Ray to come on. I like those quickie recipes of hers."

"You like that cute ass of hers," Wyatt retorted. "Anyway, her show just went off. Go on to bed, okay?"

Nelson pulled himself out of the chair with effort. He was only seventy-four, but a lifetime of physical labor around the park had left him feeling every ache and pain this time of night. "I gotta make Bo's lunch and put a load of clothes in the dryer."

"I'll do it," Wyatt said, giving his father a gentle push in the direction of his room. "Everything go okay around here tonight?"

"Sure thing," Nelson said. "Bo and me, we had some hot dogs and coleslaw for dinner. He ate up every scrap I fed him. That kid's got a hollow leg for sure."

"Don't I know it," Wyatt said ruefully. "He's already outgrown the pants I bought him at Easter. And his toes are coming out of the top of his sneakers."

"How's Cookie?" Nelson asked. "The vet fix her up?"

"The damned vet tech closed up before I got there," Wyatt said. "Anyway, I think she'll be all right. I just put her up for the night. Anything else going on in the park?"

"Slow," Nelson said. "Like all week. No sense in staying open when there's nobody around. I locked up the gates around seven thirty." He brightened. "We got that Brownie troop coming tomorrow. Fourteen little girls, and the troop leaders and some mamas. I put some sodas in the snack-bar fridge, and I thought I'd go pick up some candy to sell in the morning."

"Skip the candy," Wyatt advised. "Just get some fruit—maybe some grapes and apples and stuff. These scout leaders don't let the kids eat the kind of junk we used to eat."

"It never killed you," Nelson pointed out. He started toward his room, then turned around.

"Callie called."

Wyatt sighed. "What now?"

"I don't know," Nelson admitted. "She wouldn't talk to me. Just ordered me to put Bo on the phone. I did, and when he hung up the phone from talking to her, he burst out crying. I should've told her he was outside playing and couldn't come to the phone. That's what I get for being honest. And stupid."

"Did he say why he was so upset?" Wyatt asked, his heart sinking. Callie knew damned well he'd be out of the house tonight, at his so-called divorce recovery group. She'd been sitting right there in the courtroom when the judge ordered him to attend.

"Oh yeah," Nelson said. "Callie told Bo she and the asshole are picking him up right after school on Friday, because they're going to Birmingham this weekend, to look for a new place to live."

"Dammit," Wyatt said. "I told her it's Scout's birthday party Friday. Anna's taking all the kids to that new water park, and then they're going out for pizza afterwards. Bo's been talking about it for two weeks now, ever since he got the invitation in the mail."

"Remind me who Scout is?"

"She's Bo's best friend, and she's our shortstop on the T-ball team. Anna is her mom."

"That's right," Nelson said. "Bo's had his bathing suit laid out on his dresser since Saturday. Poor kid. Now he'll have to miss it. All because Callie can't stand to see him have a good time unless it's something she engineered. Isn't there anything you can do?"

"I doubt it," Wyatt said, his jaw tensing. "It's her weekend. Technically, it starts as soon as he gets out of school on Friday. Never mind that most Fridays she calls me at the last minute and has me pick him up because 'something's come up'—like she wants to get her nails done, or she and the asshole are slugging down margaritas at The Salty Dog."

"Damned shame," Nelson muttered.

"And I can't call her anyway," Wyatt said. "Since she got the judge to forbid me to contact her, unless it's in writing."

"I know she's a woman, but she oughtta be horsewhipped," Nelson said angrily. "And that's my opinion on the subject."

Wyatt opened the bedroom door and undressed in the dark. He heard the soft rustle of sheets.

"Dad?"

He went over to the narrow twin bed and sat on the edge. He ruffled his son's light brown hair. "Hey, buddy," he said. "What are you doing awake?"

"I tried to wait up for you, but I fell asleep," Bo said.

"You're supposed to be asleep," Wyatt chided. "You're a little kid. You need a lot of sleep so's you can grow another six inches before tomorrow morning."

"I'm really mad at Mom," Bo said. "She says we have to go to dumb old Birmingham this weekend, and I have to miss Scout's birthday party."

"I know," Wyatt said. "Granddad told me, and I'm so sorry. I know how much you wanted to go to that water park."

The little boy sniffed. "Cory went there for his cousin's birthday. He says they have a killer wave machine that'll make you pee your pants just looking at it. And water cannons. They have water cannons so strong you could knock a kid down with 'em. I told Mom I didn't want to go to Birmingham. I told her I don't want to move there, and I don't want to live with you know who."

"Oh, Bo-Bo," Wyatt said. He rubbed his son's back, feeling the warmth of his skin through the thin fabric of his Lightning McQueen pajama top.

"Dad?"

"What, buddy?"

"I got so mad at Mom, I called her a bad name. Did Granddad tell you that?"

Wyatt had to stifle a laugh. "He didn't mention it. What kind of bad name did you call your mom?"

The child hesitated. "Granddad told me if I said it again, he might have to wash my mouth out with soap like he did when you were a kid."

Now Wyatt did laugh. "I'll tell you a secret on your granddad, Bo. He's all hat and no cattle."

"Huh?"

"That means he just talks a good game. He never washed my mouth out with soap. Not ever. Now, what kind of name did you call your mom? Just between us guys?"

Bo dropped his voice to a whisper. "I called her a shit."

Wyatt was glad for the cover of darkness, because his grin split his face in two. Then he forced himself to sound stern.

"Well, son, that's not a very nice thing to call your own mother."

"I was very, very, very mad at her."

"I know you were. But you can't go around calling people a shit, just because they made you mad."

"She called me a shit first," Bo said.

"When was this?" Wyatt asked, surprised.

"Right after I told her I wanted to stay with you this weekend and go to Scout's birthday party. She said, 'listen, you little shit. I am picking you up Friday right after school and that's final.'"

Wyatt tried to choose his words carefully. Betsy had warned him that he was on thin ice with Callie, now more than ever.

"I don't think your mom should have called you that, Bo," he said finally. "But that doesn't make it right for you to use bad words. Right now, your mom is really mad at me, too, because I don't want her to take you so far away from me. So, she might say some stuff to you that she doesn't really mean, because she's actually just mad at me. But, Bo, even if she says mean things sometimes, your mom really loves you. We both do. Right?"

"I guess so. But I still don't want to go to stinkin' Birmingham."

Wyatt leaned over and kissed his son's cheek. "Sleep now."

He climbed into the matching twin bed and pulled the worn sheet over his chest. The old walls in the mobile home were paper-thin, and he could hear his father snoring in the room right next door. A moment later, he heard the soft in and out of his son's drowsy breathing. For once, he was glad of the cramped quarters in their makeshift house. He reached out his hand and let it rest lightly on Bo's wrist. For tonight, anyway, Callie could not pull them apart.

14

On only their second night of what she'd begun to think of as divorce camp, their counselor, Paula Talbott-Sinclair, looked, Grace decided, a hot mess. Her eyes were red-rimmed, her thick black mascara smeared. She seemed not to notice that her haphazard topknot of blond curls was coming undone or that a fine sprinkling of crumbs adorned one strap of her turquoise tank top.

She'd lit a stick of incense, and the pungent white smoke drifting through the room made Grace's eyes water and her nose itch.

"Everybody here?" Paula asked, looking around the room. She gave Wyatt Keeler a droopy-eyed wink. "Wyatt, I see you made it on time this week. That's good. Verrrry good."

She was slurring her words, Grace thought. Was she drunk, stoned? She looked around the therapist's office. Nobody else seemed to notice Paula's condition. Maybe it was just her imagination.

"Now," Paula said, giving her hands a clap that sent her half dozen bracelets a-jingle. "Who wants to read from their recovery journal?"

Silence.

"Nobody?" Paula frowned. "Friends, we have to share here. It's part of our healing process. So who will break the ice? Am I going to have to call on somebody, or will you volunteer?"

"I'll go," Camryn said. She was dressed in gym clothes tonight, a snug-fitting fuschia Nike shirt, black bike shorts, hot pink running shoes. She'd wrapped a hot-pink scarf around her hair and had ditched the false eyelashes.

Camryn opened her black-and-white notebook and cleared her throat. "Okay," she said hesitantly. "Here goes."

She traced a line of writing with her fingertip, took a deep breath, and began reading.

"I feel like a victim. It's my job as a journalist to interview people, to tell their stories, convey their experiences. So here is my experience, and I am going to tell you exactly how it happened and how it makes me feel, and the hell with anybody who wants me to say I am sorry, because I am not sorry.

"My husband, Dexter Nobles, is scum. He lied to me, he lied to our daughter, he lied to all our friends. Bad enough he cheated on me, but no, he had to do it with our daughter's best friend. A twenty-year-old! So how do you think that makes me feel when I look in the mirror? When I look at this picture of myself, I'm reminded of the victims I interview at a crime scene. Like the old lady who gets pistol-whipped by a thug on a street corner, or the guy whose car is jacked at a gas station. I used to wonder, what was that old lady doing out that time of night? Or why did that guy drive through that part of town in a new Mercedes? Were they that clueless? But now I know, a victim isn't asking to be jacked or pistol-whipped, or cheated on by somebody they used to love. I know it because I'm a victim. I'm somehow less than I used to be. And I don't like it worth a damn."

Camryn paused and looked up at the others, and then at Dr. Paula Talbott-Sinclair. "There's a lot more, but you get the idea."

Paula's eyelids drooped, then fluttered. "Very . . . revealing." She was quiet for a moment, her blond topknot resting against the leather armchair's headrest, her eyes closed.

"Are we supposed to talk about what Camryn wrote?" This from Ashleigh, who was leaning forward, her hands clamped on her knees.

Paula's eyes remained closed. She waved her hand. "Go ahead."

"Your ex actually did that? Screwed your daughter's best friend? Like, even in your house?"

"Repeatedly," Camryn said. "In my house, my bed, my living room. In motels, and in the apartment she shared with my daughter. Did I mention this girl is our daughter's roommate?"

"Ooh," Ashleigh said, wide-eyed. "That is cold."

"Stone cold," Camryn agreed, her smile evil. "But I dealt with the bitch."

"What? More talk of revenge?" Paula's eyes flew open and she seemed to rally for a moment. "None of that," she warned. "No revenge talk. That's regressive behavior."

Ashleigh rolled her eyes.

"Whoosh next?" Paula asked, blinking rapidly. "Audrey?"

"It's Ashleigh. And yes, I can share."

Paula tilted her swivel chair backward, then around, so that her back was facing the group.

What the hell? Grace looked wordlessly at Camryn, then at Wyatt, who shrugged.

Ashleigh opened her notebook with a flourish and began reading, her voice breathy, dramatic.

"I look good. I mean, why should I let the fact that Boyce mistakenly believes he is in love with somebody else give me an excuse to let myself go? Working for a plastic surgeon, I see all kinds of women. I see middle-aged women who are trying too hard, desperately trying to stay young, and I see young girls who think a smaller nose or higher cheekbones or a tighter ass will change their lives, make them something they're not. But I'm not like that. Boyce fell in love with me—the real me. I am the same person he fell in love with, just a few years older. That whore he's with now? I know where she lives. I watch her come home—sometimes he's with her. I want to call her up, laugh in her face, tell her, 'just you wait. You think he's in love? Think he'll stay with you? Hah! What you don't know is this: you're just like a carton of yogurt at Publix. You've got an expiration date, only you can't see it, cuz it's stamped on your ass. You won't even know it, until one morning Boyce Hartounian locks you out of your condo and stops payment on your new Benz.'"

Ashleigh closed her notebook, looking expectantly at the others. "Well?"

Suzanne Beamon cleared her throat, and all heads turned to stare at her. She'd barely said a word since the group started, hadn't even looked any of them in the eye yet.

"That's an interesting metaphor for marriage, the thing about the expiration date," Suzanne said. "I'm an English teacher," she added apologetically.

"You're really watching your husband's new girlfriend?" Grace asked Ashleigh. "Isn't that a little creepy?"

"Isn't it actually stalking?" Camryn put in. "The judge finds out about that, he's not gonna like it."

"He won't find out," Ashleigh said. "What goes on in group, stays in group, right, Paula? Everything we say here is confidential, that's what you told us."

No answer.

Camryn got up and gently swiveled the therapist's chair around so that it was now facing the group. Paula's head rested at an awkward angle on her shoulder, her mouth was slack-jawed with a tiny thread of spittle trailing down her chin, but her eyes were closed.

"Passed out cold again!" Camryn stepped back so the others could see for themselves.

Suzanne knelt on the floor beside Paula Talbott-Sinclair and pressed two fingers lightly to the pulse point on her throat, relieved to find an even, steady beat. Her dark brown eyes were intent behind the tortoiseshell frames of her glasses.

"She's not dead, thank heavens. So, what do we do now?" she asked, looking to the others for guidance. "Should we call somebody, make sure she gets home okay?"

"Who would we call?" Grace asked, looking around the office. "We don't even know if she's married. Or where she lives or anything else."

Camryn walked to the desk in the corner, sat down, and boldly began searching through the desk drawers, a journalist to the last.

"Here's her purse," she said, drawing a small multicolored crocheted handbag from the bottom desk drawer.

Suzanne frowned. "Is that really necessary? It's such an invasion of privacy." She shuddered. "I'd hate for a bunch of strangers to go pawing through my purse."

"We're not strangers. We're her 'friends,'" Camryn said, making air quote marks. She unknotted the drawstring closure and pulled out a small leather billfold. She flipped it open to the driver's license.

"According to this, she lives over on Anna Maria Island," Camryn said, lifting one eyebrow. "Obviously, she spends her money on a mortgage, not on the rent on this dump." She dumped the rest of the pocketbook's contents on the desktop, taking inventory as she examined each object.

"Lipstick, just some cheap drugstore crap. Hand sanitizer. Car keys." Camryn held up the key. "Big surprise, granola girl drives that VW Bug out front." She put the key back in the bag. "Cell phone."

She tapped the phone's screen, looking, in vain, for a call history. "Cheap-ass phone, too," she complained.

"Hello!" she said brightly, holding up a small brown plastic pill bottle. "Here's something interesting."

She squinted down at the tiny print on the bottle's label. "Why do they make the writing so small? Melasophenol?"

Ashleigh snatched the bottle away. "Here, let me. I was married to a doctor."

Camryn calmly reclaimed the pill bottle. "And I was married to a lawyer, but that doesn't make me Perry Mason." She opened the bottle and spilled two different colored capsules into the palm of her hand. "These are all that's left. Sleeping pills, I bet."

Ashleigh picked up one of the capsules. "Believe me, honey, they haven't made a sleeping pill I haven't sampled. Well, the label says melasophenol, which is a fairly mild tranquilizer, but this blue one here"—she held it up—"isn't melassophenol, which is actually a pale yellow tablet." She held up the other pill, which was pale yellow. "She's mixing tranqs with something else. Which might be the reason she's so out of it."

She leaned over and lightly ran a finger down the sleeping therapist's cheek. "Paula? Yoo-hoo. Anybody home?"

The woman didn't stir, didn't flinch.

"Clinically speaking, I'd say she's out for the night," Ashleigh concluded. "I say we blow this place. It's so depressing, I'm tempted to borrow one of these babies. And I would, but I've got plenty better stuff at home."

Grace wanted to leave as badly as anybody else. But. "You really think we should just leave her like this? I mean, what if she has like, respiratory failure or something? Or chokes on her vomit or something? You read about that with celebrities."

"You want to take her home with you, be my guest," Ashleigh said, heading for the door. "But I bet she won't be happy when she wakes up and figures out you people went through her purse and dragged her out of her office, unconscious."

Camryn hurriedly stuffed the pill bottle and the billfold back in the pocketbook. "She's got a point, you guys," she said. "Right now, I do not need to piss

Paula off and get the judge pissed off at me." She placed the purse back in the desk drawer and quietly closed it.

"I say we leave her like she is and just go. And I don't know about you guys, but I could definitely use a drink. Who's in?"

"A drink sounds fabulous," Ashleigh said, nodding vigorously. "Grace? Wyatt?" At the last minute, she included the quietest member of the group. "Suzanne?"

"I wouldn't mind a drink," Grace admitted. "But let's at least put her on the sofa in the reception area, make her comfortable. If she stays like this much longer, she's going to have a hell of a headache when she finally wakes up."

Without saying a word, Wyatt leaned down, scooped Paula into his arms, and carried her to the outer office. He set her carefully down on the sofa cushions, placing a pillow beneath her head. She snored loudly.

Ashleigh followed him out to the reception area, watching Wyatt with an appreciative eye. "Good work," she purred. She sat down on the edge of the sofa and unceremoniously lifted one of Paula's eyelids. The therapist did not stir.

"Out like a trout," Ashleigh proclaimed. "Wyatt? What about that drink?"

"I don't know," he said uneasily. "My day starts pretty early. And I've got my son tonight."

"It's just barely eight," Camryn said, coming up behind him. She turned to Grace. "What about you?"

Grace did not intend to spend any more time with these people than necessary. Still, a long night stretched before her. And she was getting sick of her own company.

"Tell you what," she said, wondering if she'd lost her mind. "We can go to my mom's bar. The Sandbox? Do you know it? Over in Cortez?"

"Cortez?" Ashleigh wrinkled her pretty little nose. "Isn't that kind of a dive bar?"

"Exactly," Grace said.

"Perfect," Camryn said. "I love a dive bar. Let's roll." She turned to Suzanne. "Are you coming?"

"Well . . ." she said, her brow furrowed. "I told my daughter, Darby, I wouldn't be late."

"You won't be," Camryn said. "One drink. Think of it as group therapy."

"I guess one wouldn't hurt," Suzanne said finally. "I don't think I've ever been to Cortez. Is it very far?"

"Ten minutes," Camryn said. "I did a story over there a couple months ago. You can follow me. I'm in the white BMW sedan."

"What do we do about locking up?" Grace asked, glancing around the room.

"Nothing," Ashleigh declared. "What self-respecting thief would want any of this crap? Look, Paula will probably wake up in a couple hours and either sleep it off here or take herself on home. Either way, it's her problem, not ours."

15

It was a slow night at the Sandbox. Rochelle was seated on her stool behind the bar, halfheartedly watching *Dancing with the Stars*, when Grace walked in, followed by three women she'd never seen before.

Grace gestured toward a table in a darkened corner of the bar, and they all slid into the booth and gave her their drink orders.

"Margarita for me," Ashleigh said. "On the rocks. No salt."

"Vodka tonic, double lime," Camryn said. "I don't suppose you have Grey Goose?"

"Nope," Grace said calmly.

"Stoli?"

"Nope. We've got any kind of vodka you want, as long as you want Smirnoff." It was one of Butch's favorite lame jokes, and Grace was surprised to hear herself using it.

"Suzanne?" Grace was also surprised that Suzanne Beamon had actually come along. She was seated at the far edge of the booth, anxiously checking out her surroundings, as though she'd never been in a bar before.

"Oh. Uh, just club soda, if you don't mind."

"Club soda?" Ashleigh gave Suzanne a playful tap on the shoulder. "Come on, Suzanne, chill out a little."

Suzanne's nose turned pink. "I have to drive home tonight, and I live over in

Bradenton. I don't dare risk giving my ex any more ammunition with which to torture me."

"Good point," Grace agreed. "Be right back."

Rochelle raised an eyebrow as Grace approached where she was seated.

"My divorce recovery group. Paula passed out again, halfway through the session, so we decided to come over here for a drink."

"Interesting," Rochelle said, looking over her daughter's head at the group arrayed around the table. "Didn't you tell me there's a guy in your group? Where's he?"

"At home with his little boy," Grace said. "Just us girls tonight."

The drinks came. Ashleigh took a long sip of her margarita. "So . . . who's going to go first?"

"First with what?" Grace asked.

"You know. The dish. What really happened with all of y'all's marriages. How everybody ended up in 'divorce recovery' with all of us outlaws."

"It's not that interesting," Suzanne said, her voice low. "We were betrayed. End of story."

"Oh, I disagree," Camryn said quickly. "Grace, for example, has a fascinating story."

"You should know," Grace put in. "Anyway, everybody already knows what I did and how I ended up as one of Paula's people. Everybody in Florida knows, thanks to you, 'girlfriend.'"

"Not me," Suzanne said. When the others voiced their disbelief, she added. "I don't watch much television. Anyway . . . I guess I've been caught up in my own drama."

"Come on, tell it," Ashleigh urged Grace. "We want to hear your side of the story."

Grace gave a condensed version of the swimming pool story. "Afterwards, when I was driving over here, thinking about it, I couldn't believe that was me. Grace Stanton? Well, Davenport, now. I didn't plan to do it. I'm not a person who acts out like that. But I guess you never know what you're capable of until you're put in a situation like that."

Camryn snorted. "It was just a car. And you know he had insurance on the damned thing. As for planning something? Oh, hell yeah, I'm big on planning. Especially when it comes to that kind of thing. You know that quote, 'revenge is a dish best served cold'? I am all about that."

Suzanne leaned across the table. The small candle lit her face, giving it a greenish glow. "Did you catch your husband and that girl?"

Camryn's expression changed, hardened. "No. And that's what makes this whole thing so nasty. Our daughter, Jana, caught her daddy, in bed, with her best friend and roommate."

"Oh no." Suzanne looked sickened.

The other women at the table were silent.

"Awful," Suzanne mumbled.

Grace blotted the tabletop with a paper napkin. "Did you confront him?"

"Oh yes."

"Did he admit it?"

Camryn shrugged. "What was he gonna do, call his baby girl a liar? And then I found that little DVD of his."

She turned to Grace, rattling the ice cubes in her now-drained glass. "You think I could get another one of these?"

Grace turned toward the bar, caught her mother's eye and held up Camryn's glass. Rochelle nodded and a moment later arrived at the table. She didn't seem in a hurry to leave, either. So Grace introduced her to the other women, Rochelle went to refill everybody's glass, and before Grace knew it, Rochelle had pulled a chair up to the edge of the booth.

"You mentioned a DVD?" Ashleigh asked, after the introductions had been completed.

"Uh-huh. The fool hid it inside the family Bible. I guess he thought Jesus loves a liar and was counting on forgiveness. But not from me." Camryn shook her head. "Not after what I saw."

"Porn?" Suzanne's nose wrinkled in distaste.

"You could say that," Camryn said. "Dexter had been a busy little boy, filming his very own self. Getting ready for his 'dates.' And yeah, he lied about that, too, Treena wasn't his only 'Forever Your Girl.' Uh-huh, yes. That was the theme song for his date nights. Paula Abdul's 'Forever Your Girl' was his turn-on tune. But what really turned him on was the sight of himself in the mirror, prancing around in his red satin thong."

"Eeewww," Grace said. She shuddered. "Just . . . eewwww."

"I used to really like that song," Ashleigh said sadly.

"You'll have a whole new appreciation for it if you see that video," Camryn said tartly. "You got a smartphone?" She held out her hand. "Give it here and I'll show you how to find it on YouTube."

"No thanks."

"So . . ." Rochelle interrupted. "How did the video get on YouTube?"

"I put it there," Camryn said. "Oh, yes I did. Dexter Nobles, in the flesh—a whole lotta flesh! Getting dressed in his lil panties, getting ready for business meetings, lunches. County Commission meetings. Oh, he loved the feel of that satin under his suit when he was doing county business."

"You really did that?" Ashleigh asked, glancing down at her phone.

"Sure did. And it's gotten over twelve thousand hits," Camryn said.

"And that's what got Judge Stackpole on your case," Grace said. "Right?"

"His lawyer got the video taken down, but as soon as he did, other people put it right back up there. It's gone viral."

"Does your daughter know you put it on YouTube?" Suzanne asked.

Camryn sighed. "I didn't tell her. But she found out. She's furious. Not speaking to me." She looked around the group. "Does that seem fair to you? Dexter's the one who cheated, the dirty pervert. But she's mad at *me*—for outing him."

"Kids don't want to know bad stuff about their parents," Rochelle said.

"Dexter and I? We'd been living separate lives for a long time now," Camryn admitted. "I guess we stayed together for Jana. I don't miss his sorry ass. Not a bit. But I miss my little girl."

"She'll just have to get over herself," Ashleigh said. "Like you said, he's the pervert. The cheater. I bet she'll come around."

Camryn managed a wry smile. "Hope so. Now what about you, Miss Ashleigh? What did you do to earn yourself a spot in divorce recovery?"

"It's really not that big a deal," Ashleigh protested. "Nothing like what you guys did. I mean, it's a paint job, okay? The whole thing got blown way out of proportion."

"Why don't you just go ahead and tell us everything that happened?" Grace asked. "After all, you heard what happened with us."

Ashleigh pulled her compact from her satchel, checked her makeup, fixed her lipstick, and flipped her hair behind her shoulders.

"So . . . you already know who my husband is. Boyce Hartounian. We met when I was working as an insurance billing clerk in his office." She looked over at Rochelle. "Boyce is one of the top plastic surgeons in Florida. He is *the* man for boobs, in case you're ever interested. And, of course, he was married at the time, but honestly, Beverly, that *cow,* was totally a joke. So that happened."

"Wait," Grace interrupted. "What happened? Did we miss something?"

"They split up," Ashleigh said. "She hired this weasel of an investigator, and there were some unfortunate photographs, and what with that, well, Beverly did very, very well for herself in the settlement."

Suzanne interrupted. "I'm sorry, but I'm going to have to go." She opened her pocketbook and placed a five-dollar bill on the table. "Will this be enough?"

"More than enough," Grace assured her. "Are you sure you can't stay?"

"I really can't," Suzanne said, looking flustered. "My daughter, Darby, still isn't used to the idea of her father being gone. She gets anxious if she's alone at night."

"How old is she?" Camryn asked.

"She'll be eighteen in October," Suzanne said. "A senior this fall. This split-up has been very hard on her."

She looked around the table. "Good night, everybody. Thanks for including me."

Camryn watched Suzanne leave the bar. She turned to Grace. "There's something very odd about that woman. Afraid to leave an eighteen-year-old at home alone? And she still hasn't told us a thing about herself."

"I think she's probably just very shy," Grace said. "An introvert."

"I don't know about you guys, but I am *dying* to know what she did to her ex," Ashleigh said. "It's those quiet ones who always surprise you with something outrageous."

"Speaking of outrageous," Camryn said pointedly.

"Okay, sooooo. Boyce and I have been married, what, four years now? And it was amazing."

"And then?" Grace asked.

"My biggest mistake was quitting my job. Boyce told me he didn't want me working so hard." She shook her head ruefully. "I never even saw it coming."

"Hello?" A man's voice bellowed. "Rochelle? Where the hell are you?"

Their heads swiveled. A grizzled, shirtless old man wearing baggy shorts that hung below his kneecaps stood at the bar, banging the wooden surface with his glass.

"Pipe down, Milo," Rochelle hollered back. She stood. "Hang on. I want to hear this. I'll be right back."

Rochelle scurried behind the bar, scolding her regular as she drew him a beer.

"Your mom seems nice," Ashleigh told Grace. "Did you say you're living together? Where?"

Grace pointed her index finger upward.

"Here? You live above a bar?"

"I grew up here," Grace told her. "There's an apartment upstairs, two bedrooms, living room, dining room, kitchen. It's not fancy, but I guess you get used to it. At least it's close to the beach."

"I'm back," Rochelle slid back onto her chair. "You were saying?"

"Long story short, Boyce wanted me out of the office because he was having a fling with this slutty little drug rep named Suchita." Ashleigh laughed bitterly. "He even took her to the same suite at the Ritz where he used to take me, back when he was married to Beverly."

"That's just plain tacky," Rochelle said. "But how'd you find out?"

Ashleigh flipped her hair over her shoulder. "One of the girls in the office spilled the beans that he was getting friendly with the Juvenesse rep. I knew it was this Suchita chick right away. I parked across the street from his office and followed them to the Ritz."

Tears welled up in her eyes. "That was *our* place! Afterwards, I followed her back to her house, and when I saw the neighborhood she was living in, I knew it was true. No drug rep can afford to live in Newtown. So I decided to fix her little red wagon. Teach her a lesson."

"There was a Home Depot a couple miles away," Ashleigh continued. "I went home and changed into my guerrilla warfare outfit: black T-shirt, black Theory slacks, black Tory Burch flats. Then I went back after midnight. I painted HE'S MARRIED in these big, scary red letters all across the front of her house. Oh yeah, and on the front of her Beemer."

"You wore Tory Burch on a covert mission?" Camryn looked offended.

"They were last season, and I'd worn them to death," Ashleigh said. "So that's it. See?" She glanced around the table. "The whole thing just got blown way out of proportion."

"I'll bet," Rochelle said, helping herself to a sip of Grace's pinot.

"I know, right?' She turned to Grace. "Apparently in this state it's considered some kind of capital offense or something if you paint all over your husband's mistress's house. And then there was some crap about defacing private property . . . I let my lawyer deal with all that. I paid some fine. But then!" She paused for effect. "Stackpole found out. And he literally blew his stack!"

"And that's how you ended up at Ladies' Night," Rochelle said. She picked up Ashleigh's empty glass. "Anybody ready for another?"

Camryn frowned. "Better not. The station put me on 'probation' after they found out about the YouTube video. My lawyer says the only reason they didn't fire me is because I'm a community institution. I'm not but forty-two. And they act like I'm friggin' Betty White or something. Plus, I have 26,345 Facebook fans."

"You're only forty-two?" Ashleigh leaned way across the table to study Camryn's face. "Have you ever thought of Botox?" She traced a finger over Camryn's forehead, and down to her upper lip. "Because I could totally hook you up. Boyce showed me how to inject myself. It's really easy-peasy."

Camryn drew back. "Uh, thanks just the same. I don't think I'm up for any DIY Botox sessions at this time."

Ashleigh sighed and looked at her watch. "Guess I'd better get on home, too." She fumbled around in her billfold, finally finding a twenty-dollar bill, which she laid on the tabletop. "Thanks, ladies. It's been fun."

Grace hung around downstairs, long enough to help count out the cash register, wash the last of the dirty glasses and dishes, and turn off the neon WE'RE OPEN sign on the front door.

"That's a fascinating group of women you've got going there," Rochelle said, as she trudged up the stairs to the apartment.

"I don't know that I'd call them fascinating," Grace said, three steps ahead. "Bat-shit crazy is more the word that comes to my mind. I was a little worried about Ashleigh. She was slamming those margaritas pretty seriously."

"No worries," Rochelle said. "They were actually fakearitas. I just barely passed the tequila bottle over 'em."

"Good thinking," Grace said. "And I will admit it's just a little bit comforting to put things in perspective and find out there are people who've done worse things than me."

"Yeah . . ." Rochelle agreed. "I might need you to show me how to look at that

YouTube video that Camryn was talking about. You know," she added hastily, "just to help you put things in perspective."

"I keep thinking about Paula, the therapist," Grace said, when they got up to the living room. "She was really zonked. I don't feel so good about leaving her all alone like that."

"What else could you do?"

"I could have made sure she got home okay," Grace said finally. She turned around and headed for the door.

"You're going back to check on her?" Rochelle asked.

"Yup."

16

The strip shopping center looked even gloomier after midnight. Empty beer bottles and discarded fast-food wrappers littered the asphalt pavement. Blue lights flickered from behind the tattoo parlor storefront, and she could see a burly, bare-chested man inside, reading something on a computer screen. There were only three vehicles left in the parking lot, and neither of them was the shiny yellow VW. But one was a pickup truck.

Grace pulled along beside it and rolled her window down. "I thought you had to get home to your little boy."

"I did," Wyatt said. "He's asleep. My dad's there, so it's cool."

"You came back to check on her too, right?"

Wyatt Keeler got out of the truck and walked over. "Paula's gone," he said sheepishly. "I looked in the windows of the office, and I could see the sofa, so she's definitely not there. I checked around back, too, just to make sure her car wasn't there."

Grace let out a long breath. "That's a relief."

"Yeah," Wyatt said. He thumped the roof of her car. "Guess I'll head back home. See ya."

Grace didn't start her car just then. "You're not such a bad guy after all, are you?"

He raised an eyebrow. "Who said I was?"

"I was in the courtroom the day your ex's lawyer showed that video, remember? You put a fist through that guy's car window. It looked pretty scary from where I was sitting."

He sighed. "If I had it to do over again, I'd have turned around and walked away. Next time I will. What if I told you my side of the story?"

"What? Here?" Grace looked at the clock on her dashboard and considered. "Can we go someplace else? This place gives me the creeps. Gus's is just down the road."

She followed him in her own car to a brightly lit doughnut shop a few miles away. Seated at the counter, just a few stools away from a couple of goth-looking teenagers, Wyatt ordered coffee and two apple crullers while Grace ordered an iced tea—and a chocolate-iced cake doughnut.

He looked surprised.

"I usually don't eat a lot of sweets, she explained. "But I've been losing weight, since, you know, and anyway, their chocolate doughnuts are the best. Ever."

"You know this place?" He looked around. The dull green linoleum floor tiles were chipped and cracked, the red leather booths were held together with duct tape, and the white tiled walls were lined with yellowing framed newspaper clippings and faded family photos.

"Yeah, we used to come to Gus's all the time when I was a kid," Grace said. "It was a big treat."

"So, you really grew up here? Living above the Sandbox?"

She nodded. "How about you?"

"Sarasota. Kinda like you. We didn't exactly live above the company store, but we did have a house right around the corner from Jungle Jerry's."

"Right," Grace said. "I almost forgot."

The waitress brought their food, and Wyatt took a huge bite of his cruller. "Sorry," he said, in between chews. "I missed dinner tonight. I'm starved."

He washed down the first doughnut with coffee. "You've lived here, always? Never moved away?"

"I went to college at Florida State, which is where I got my interior design degree, and after college, I moved down to Miami. We moved back here a few years ago."

"Miami. Is that where you met your husband?"

"Afraid so. What about you? Where did you meet . . . what's her name?"

"Callie. We met while I was in grad school at Clemson. But for some reason, I thought it was more important to get married than finish my master's. I was working for a seed company in South Carolina, and Callie was pregnant with Bo. Jungle Jerry's was in rough shape, and my dad really wanted to retire, and my mom was begging me to come back down here to run it. She'd been diagnosed with cancer then, but she didn't want that to influence my decision. Anyway, we came back, Bo was born, and my mom died just a few months later."

"I'm sorry," Grace said.

"She got to hold him right after he was born, babysit him a few times, before she got really sick," Wyatt said. "And we named him after her father, which really tickled her."

"How old is Bo?"

"Six," Wyatt said. "Just finished first grade." He reached for his cell phone, scrolled through his photos, and held it out for her to see.

A sturdy freckle-faced boy with soft brown bangs and his father's dimples grinned into the camera, showing off two missing front teeth. He wore a baseball cap set back on his head and had an aluminum bat resting on his right shoulder.

Wyatt touched the screen with his fingertip. "Kid lives and breathes baseball. He's as crazy about it as I was at that age."

"Very cute," Grace said, taking the phone to study the little boy better. "What position does he play?"

"He's a catcher. Like I was. I tried to get him to play shortstop, told him he didn't want to be crawling in the dirt like I did the whole time I played ball, but he was determined to catch. He's not bad, either, even if I am his dad. And his coach."

She handed his phone back.

"So. I know you said you don't have kids. Ever want them?"

Her face colored, and he instantly knew he'd made a misstep.

"Sorry," he said. "That's a pretty personal question. Forget I asked."

Grace picked at the chocolate frosting with her fingernail. "That's okay," she said finally. "I do want kids. Well, I did. I'd started seeing a fertility specialist . . ." She blushed again. "I guess it's a good thing it never got that far." She gave him a sideways glance. "I don't know that I'm cut out to be a single parent."

"Sometimes, you don't have a choice," Wyatt said grimly. "I never thought I'd be a single dad, that's for sure. But I'm not sorry we had Bo. He's the best thing that's ever happened to me."

She broke off a piece of the doughnut and chewed. "You asked me if I wanted to hear your side of the story. About why you busted out that car window. I would like to hear it, if it's not too painful."

Wyatt held up his hand. The bruises were still a vivid greenish-black. "Pain? Me? Nah."

"Callie and Luke were gaming me, for months. That day at the ball park was the last straw. I coach Bo's T-ball team. Callie had the game schedule. I gave it to her myself. But all spring, she'd drop him off late for the games half the time, without his glove or his shoes, or even his uniform shirt. It got so I bought extras of everything and kept 'em with me. But I'd sent him home with the spares the week before. That day? They didn't bring him until the second inning—and again, with no equipment. Poor Bo was so upset, he was in tears. Luke acted like it was nothing, just blew me off. Told me if I didn't like it, too damn bad."

Wyatt flexed his right hand and winced. "You saw how I reacted. Not my finest moment."

He'd finished his doughnuts and his coffee. Grace broke off half her doughnut and placed it on his empty plate.

"Really?"

"Yeah, I think I just wanted a taste. To remind me of old times here. You know how that is?"

He gobbled the doughnut. "I'll tell you a secret. I feel the same way about Krystal's sliders."

"Ick," Grace said. "Not the same thing at all."

"Krystal was where my granddad would take me on Saturdays, for lunch, when I was a kid," Wyatt said. "Just the two of us. He'd order me two sliders, and he'd eat four. Right out of the paper sack, in the front seat of his old tan Buick Regal. Every once in a while, not that often, but sometimes, if I have Bo on a Saturday, we ride through the Krystal, get ourselves a bag of sliders, take 'em out to Holmes Beach, sit on the sand, and scarf 'em down."

"Sweet sentiment, but still, ick," Grace said. "Does your ex know you do that?"

"If she did, she'd probably sic the Department of Child Welfare on me."

"Not to mention Judge Stackpole," she added.

"You saw how he treated me," Wyatt said, leaning back on his stool, "How did you do?"

"Let's put it this way," Grace said. "Not great. Mitzi—she's my lawyer—is trying her best, but we still can't get his lawyer to respond to us, and I'm still essentially locked out of my business. He's supposed to be 'giving' me two thousand dollars a month, but I haven't seen a dime yet. And, oh yes, that money he's 'giving' me? It's mine anyway. All this while he transforms his new girlfriend into Grace 2.0." She fluttered her eyelashes. "Does that make me sound bitter?"

"Kind of," Wyatt said. "But then, I'm on a first-name basis with bitter these days. Right now, it looks like Bo's going to be moving to Birmingham by the end of summer, and so far, there's not a damned thing I can do about it. Yeah, technically I can see him weekends, but how do I pull that off when he's living nine hours away? I can't afford to buy a plane ticket every weekend, and anyway I've got a business to run. Or what's left of a business."

"That's really rotten," Grace said. "I can't believe any mother would deliberately deny a child the chance to see his father. It's just cruel."

"Callie's into cruel these days," Wyatt said. "She'll do anything she can to punish me. And the weird thing is, I can't figure out what I did to make her hate me like this. She wanted out of the marriage, I let her out. She wanted the house, I gave it to her." He shook his head and yawned.

"Yeah," Grace said, standing up and stretching. "It's pretty late for me, too."

"Thanks for listening to me vent," Wyatt said. He hesitated. "I got the feeling, back there at Paula's office, all of y'all were ready to tar and feather me. Just for being a guy."

Grace shrugged. "Everybody in that room is there because a man dumped on her."

"Hey, a guy dumped on me, too," Wyatt said. "Remember?"

"Right."

They paid at the cash register and walked out to their cars. Wyatt looked back at the old-timey neon GUS'S DONUTS sign. "I gotta remember this place. Bo would love it."

"If you feed that child Krystal sliders and Gus's for the same meal, I'll report you to Stackpole myself," Grace threatened.

"Hey," Wyatt said. "Thanks for listening to me tonight."

"You're welcome," Grace said, meaning it. "See you next week."

"If Paula's conscious. Do you think she's really on drugs?"

"She's definitely on something," Grace said. "My mom would say she's one ant short of a picnic."

Wyatt laughed. "One brick shy of a load. I can't believe I have to come up with three hundred dollars a session for this crap, on top of all the child support I'm paying Callie."

"Do you think it would do any good to report her?" Grace asked, fumbling for her car keys.

"Report to who?" Wyatt asked. "Stackpole? I'll mention what's going on to Betsy, but I already know what she'll say. 'Shut up and turn up.'"

17

G race sat cross-legged on her bed, her laptop balanced on her lap, tapping
away at the keyboard.

*Lately, I've gotten interested in the farm-to-table movement. Here on
Florida's Gulf Coast, where I live, there's the tendency to think farms
are all in the Midwest, or up north. But that's not true. We have amazing small farms all around us. Citrus growers, of course, and small
avocado groves, but once I started looking around, I was surprised to
find honey producers, organic chicken and egg farmers, and even small
family "row-crop" farms producing gorgeous lettuces, tomatoes, peppers, cucumbers, corn, and, of course, strawberries. In addition, we're
lucky here to have local seafood brought to port by fishermen who keep
us supplied with fish, crabs, and shrimp caught right in the gulf and
bay, and beef from the cattle farms that have been in the interior parts
of this area since I was a little girl.*

*My mother's generous friend Felipe brought us a bushel of white
corn on Sunday. Picked that morning, it had the sweetest taste you can
imagine. We feasted on it for dinner, but then I started thinking of new
ways to combine it with other locally produced goodness, and I came up
with this corn-crab chowder recipe. It utilizes the corn, plus sweet blue*

crabs, which are being harvested here right now, not to mention red bell peppers and jalapeño peppers, readily available anywhere. I hope you'll try this at home, and let me know what you think.

She glanced over at the notes she'd scrawled in the kitchen earlier in the day. The corn-crab chowder really had been a triumph. She'd diced sweet yellow onions, jalapeños and red peppers, and some garlic, then sautéed them in bacon drippings in the cast-iron Dutch oven. Rochelle had grumbled about what a pain in the ass it was to cut all the corn off the cobs, but once she'd dumped them in the bacon drippings, along with diced tiny new potatoes and added chicken broth, the aroma wafting through the Sandbox kitchen had been irresistible. After the corn had simmered for twenty minutes or so, Grace had dumped in the crab. It was just back-fin crab, because Rochelle insisted you really didn't need lump claw meat for a soup, and, although crab was in season, her supplier still charged her $6.99 a pound.

Half-and-half was carefully added to the corn and crab mixture, along with a generous sprinkling of Old Bay seasoning—at Rochelle's insistence. As that simmered another five minutes, Grace diced up the crisp bacon she'd set aside from the pan drippings.

She'd gone outside to snip chives from the pots of herbs she'd started growing by the Sandbox front entrance, and when she reentered the kitchen, she caught her mother, standing over the stove, the Old Bay tin poised over the pot of chowder.

"Hey!" Grace protested, snatching the can from Rochelle's hand.

"I was just adjusting the seasoning." Rochelle dropped a wooden spoon into the big stainless steel sink.

"It doesn't *need* any more adjustment," Grace said, through gritted teeth. "Do you know how much salt is in that stuff? Not to mention the sodium in the bacon?"

"I don't need to know. I just know you can't make soup—especially soup with corn and crab, without a good douse of Old Bay," Rochelle retorted. "I've been making soup for way longer than you've been alive, young lady, so don't go lecturing me on salt. Or on cooking."

Grace bit her lip. She wanted to remind her mother that she was already on medication for high blood pressure and that her doctor had been urging her to cut back on sodium. Instead, she began snipping the chives into a milk-glass custard cup. "If you want more Old Bay in your soup, you can keep the shaker by your bowl. But please don't add it to the pot. Please?"

"Hmmph." Rochelle began tossing dirty dishes into the sink, a sure sign that she was miffed.

Ignoring her mother's tantrum, Grace found two old ice cream sundae glasses and placed each on a white plate. She started for the bar, to grab the sherry bottle, then, quietly, picked up the Old Bay can and took it with her. Just in case.

She turned the burner down to low and added a splash of sherry to the soup. Tasted, then added another splash.

A few minutes later, she made diagonal slices in the loaf of Cuban bread that had been delivered to the restaurant that morning, dribbled olive oil over the slices, and ran them under the broiler just long enough to toast them a light brown.

She placed a slice of bread on each plate, then dipped a ladle into the Dutch oven, carefully spooning the chowder into each sundae glass. A sprinkling of chives and diced bacon topped each glass.

Grace grabbed her camera and began snapping photos.

"Who serves crab chowder in a sundae glass?" Rochelle asked.

"I just like the way it looks," Grace said, snapping away. "Eccentric."

"Weird," Rochelle muttered, watching from the sink. "Are we eating or shooting?"

"Eating," Grace said, setting the camera down. "But if the finished product tastes as good as it looks, I think this will make a terrific blog post."

She grabbed two blue and white striped dish towels from the stack on the stainless steel prep counter and draped them over her arm before picking up the soup dishes and pushing her way through the swinging door into the bar.

Grace unfolded the dish towels and spread them out as a placemat on the bar. She grabbed a couple of wineglasses, poured in some white wine, and stood back to look. Finally, she added a paper-thin slice of lemon to the side of each plate for a shot of color. Pleased with the effect, she went back for her camera and took a couple more exposures. "Let's eat," she called, over her shoulder.

Rochelle eyed the place settings at the bar. "Pretty fancy, just for Saturday lunch for the two of us."

"You eat with your eyes, as well as your tastebuds, you know," Grace said, refusing to let her mother bait her.

"Hmmph," Rochelle said. But she dipped her spoon into the soup, tasted, and closed her eyes.

"Well?"

Rochelle took another bite of the soup. "Not bad. Not bad at all." With a fingertip, she fished a small limp green fragment from her soup and held it up for Grace to see.

"What's this?"

"Sorry," Grace said. "It's just a sprig of tarragon. I was supposed to remove it before I served the soup, but I got distracted. So . . . you really like it?"

"I do," Rochelle said. She dipped a piece of toasted bread into the soup and chewed.

Grace ate slowly, pausing to make notes on her ever-present yellow legal pad. Next time, she thought, she might do cheese toasts to go along with the soup, maybe adding slivers of goat cheese to the bread before broiling. She pondered the soup's consistency, finally deciding she'd need to add an immersion mixer to the kitchen equipment at the Sandbox, so that in the future she could puree part of the soup. Her own immersion mixer was back in the kitchen at the house on Sand Dollar Lane. Ben's house.

When Rochelle finished her soup, she got up from her seat, found a piece of chalk, and began writing on the blackboard on the wall by the cash register.

Today's SPECIAL—CORN CRAB CHOWDER à la GRACE. $10.

"You really think the customers will like it?" Grace asked, secretly pleased. She'd been living with Rochelle for nearly two months, and it seemed like the first time she'd done something in the kitchen or the bar that Rochelle approved of. "And more importantly, that they'll pay ten dollars for a bowl of soup?"

"They'll lap it up," Rochelle predicted. "We just won't tell 'em how healthy it is. And if anybody gripes about the price, I'll show 'em my bill from the seafood wholesale house."

They'd had a busy evening. One of the local softball leagues was having a tournament, and word had apparently gone out that the Sandbox was the place to meet after the games.

The first batch of soup was gone by 7:00 P.M., and Grace made another gallon, using up all the crab in the big walk-in cooler. At 9:30, she had to tell Rochelle to "eighty-six" that night's special.

A loud groan rose up in the bar as Rochelle crossed the special off on the blackboard.

They were both exhausted by the time Rochelle's late-night shift, consisting of Almina, a young Latin woman, and her husband, Carlos, showed up to take over at 10:00.

While Rochelle showered in the apartment's only bathroom, Grace settled down to write her blog post, referring to her notes and editing and refining the photos she'd shot earlier before uploading to her blog, accompanied by a list of local farms, complete with their links.

It was after midnight when she tapped the PUBLISH button. She viewed the blog in its final form and smiled. "Take that J'Aimee," she muttered, right before padding off to take her own shower.

Sunday morning, Grace was still sleeping when she heard the cell phone on her nightstand ding softly, signaling an incoming message.

She sat up and yawned, looking out the window. It was barely daylight. But the message on her phone woke her in a hurry.

HAVE U SEEN YR OLD BLOG TODAY?

The text message on her phone was from ShadeeLadee, one of her earliest Gracenotes followers and another lifestyle blogger based in Miami. Over the years they'd met at various blogger meet-ups and gotten friendly, and, although ShadeeLadee had a real name, which was Claire King, Grace always just called her Shadee.

Grace clicked over to what she thought of as Faux Gracenotes, and swore. Loudly.

The photo was the exact one Grace had posted on her own blog, but with the headline Grab Some Crab.

Beneath it was Grace's corn-crab chowder, which J'Aimee (or more likely Ben, Grace decided) had rechristened Crab-Corn Bisque. She'd cleverly changed the recipe in the slightest ways, calling for a sprig of rosemary instead of tarragon and decreasing the amount of half-and-half. But otherwise, it was Grace's recipe. And it was definitely Grace's photo.

"Oh, hell no!" Grace exclaimed. She scrolled down to see the number of comments J'Aimee's post had garnered. There were seventy-six, and it was barely 7:30 A.M. on a Sunday, usually her slowest day for blog traffic.

She quickly typed in a comment of her own. "THIS RECIPE AND PHOTO WERE HIJACKED FROM TrueGrace.com. To see the original, much better, recipe, click over to here." And she added a link to her own blog.

Most likely, Ben, whom she assumed was the blog's administrator, would delete Grace's comment and block her from trying to comment again, but Grace didn't care.

She opened her own blog. Nothing. Her new banner was there, but the only thing beneath it was a vaguely worded link. She instinctively clicked on it, and immediately regretted it. The link took her to the vilest, most sickening display of pornography she could have imagined.

Grace stared at the screen in stunned silence. How? She didn't have to ask who had done this, who'd not just erased her blog post, but sabotaged her entire blog. It was Ben, that she knew. She just didn't know how.

How could he have infiltrated her blog? She had a new protected password; he couldn't have accessed it, or could he?

Fuming, she left the blog and went to check her e-mail. Her in-box showed she had eighty-eight new messages.

She read the first one, from another lifestyle blogger, Shana, of Design or Die, and cringed.

Grace, what's going on with you? Your blog has been hacked, and it's not only got a porn link, it's infecting anybody who opens it with a virus. Love ya, girl, but for the sake of my readers, I'm removing you from my blogroll until you get your act together.

The next e-mail was from Nathan Woods, an influential interior design blogger with nearly half a million followers. Grace had been on cloud nine the day Nate had e-mailed to tell her how much he loved her post "Window Treatments That Ought to be Outlawed," which he'd privately called "Swags for Hags." He'd done two cross-promotions with Grace that had gained her a slew of new followers, and had even given her invaluable business advice about which advertisers to avoid on her own blog.

Nathan's e-mail was terse and to the point.

What the fuck is this??? It was followed by a link, which took her to an infamous online forum called SnarkSauce, where contributers posted venomous items about Internet celebrities.

I HATE NATE was the post's headline.

Closet queen Nathan Woods's tenuous hold on the title of "Biggest Boozer" has never been challenged, but recently the Manhattan-based designer and blogger was knocked down a rung when textile giant F. Shumacher & Company ended their five-year contract with Woods, whose lame-ass line of botanical-based fabrics never quite lived up to its early promise. Apparently the only person in the tightly knit New York design community who was surprised by the move was Woods himself. Insiders tell me Woods is also about to be asked to leave his post as contributing editor at Architectural Digest. Also? We hear Woods's love interest, boy-about-town Marc Klein has moved out of Nate's East Village love nest. Stay tuned y'all!

Although the posts on SnarkSauce were usually anonymous, the Nate item was signed. *Grace from Gracenotes.*

Her fingers flew over the keypad. "I never wrote any such thing. This is all Ben, my soon-to-be ex. You have to believe me, Nathan, I would never, ever write anything like this. Ben has hijacked my blog, and he's sabotaging me every way he can. I don't know why he's decided to do this, but I'm going to get this post taken down, and make SnarkSauce print a retraction. I swear."

A moment later, she saw that Nathan had replied. His message was succinct. "You are dead to me."

Grace was devastated. She closed the laptop and put it on the floor, like a diseased thing, best avoided.

18

G race stormed downstairs to find Rochelle sipping coffee at the bar. "I'm going to kill Ben, so help me. Right after I tear that little bitch J'Aimee limb from limb."

"What've they done now?"

She poured a mug of coffee for herself and plopped onto the barstool next to her mother's. "I spent hours yesterday making that crab soup, photographing it, editing, then writing and posting my blog. Hours!"

"So? If you're still fishing for compliments, I'll say it again. The soup was damned good."

"The soup was amazing," Grace cried. "And the photos were amazing. So amazing that Ben lifted the recipe, nearly word for word, and the photos, my photos, and put them on J'Aimee's blog. And, somehow, he managed to erase my blog post. In its place, he put a link to the foulest, most degrading porn site on the planet. A site that, if you were to click the link, would give your computer a virus."

"You're sure it was Ben?" Rochelle asked.

"Who else? It had to be him. I can't figure out how it's possible, how he could figure out the password to the new blog, but somehow he did."

Rochelle rolled her eyes. "What a slimy bastard. It's a damned shame Ben wasn't locked in the trunk of that car when you drove it into the pool."

"And that's not all he did," Grace said. "When he was done hijacking my blog post, he hopped all around the Internet, poisoning people against me. He left nasty comments on my friends' blogs signed with my name, and he wrote this incredibly bitchy piece on SnarkSauce about Nathan Woods and signed my name to that, too."

"Who's Nathan Woods? And what's SnarkSauce?" Rochelle asked. She could never keep all this Internet stuff straight.

"Oh, Mom, you've seen his show on Saturday mornings. He's probably the best-known interior design blogger in the country. His blog has like, I don't know, probably seven hundred thousand followers. He did a cross-promotion with me back in February, and my analytics took a crazy jump, just because of my exposure on his blog."

"You still haven't explained SnarkSauce," Rochelle reminded her daughter.

"I don't know if anybody can explain SnarkSauce. I guess you'd say it's hater central for lifestyle bloggers. People post these vicious remarks about well-known bloggers. I never read it, but Ben always did. He thought it was hilarious. That's how I know it must have been Ben that wrote that crap. Now Nathan is furious with me. He says I'm dead to him. And all my other blog buddies hate me, too, all because of Ben."

Grace banged her head on the bar top. "Why me? Why?"

"Did you let these people know it wasn't you that wrote the stuff? That it was Ben, trying to get even with you?"

"Of course! But I don't think anybody believes me. People are dropping me from their blog rolls and defriending me on Facebook. At this rate, I won't have a single friend in the business." Grace jumped up and paced back and forth in front of the bar, close to tears.

"Grace?" Rochelle's voice was stern. "Sit down and listen to me." She caught her daughter by the elbow. "Sit."

"What?" Grace knew she sounded like a spoiled brat, but she couldn't help herself.

"Anybody who thinks that you would be capable of doing something like that doesn't really know you. And if you tell them you didn't do this stuff, and they still don't believe you, well, screw 'em. They were never your real friends at all."

"But they were," Grace insisted. "You don't know what the blog world is like. We read each other's blogs and comment and cross-post and guest blog. And we see each other at meet-ups, once or twice a year. I care about these people, and they care about me."

Rochelle shook her head. "No, they don't. Did any of these so-called friends call you after your big breakup with Ben was all over the news? Did any of them drive over here, take you out to lunch, or just give you a shoulder to cry on when you needed it most?"

"That's not how it works in my world," Grace said stubbornly.

"Then your world is seriously screwed up. You've gone through a lot in the past two months, but as far as I can tell, not a single friend has stepped up. And not just these so-called blogger buddies of yours. Where are your old girl-friends? The couples who used to come to all those dinner parties you used to throw all the time?"

Grace clutched her coffee mug so tightly she thought it might crush. "I don't know," she whispered. "A couple left me messages on my phone. But I was just too embarrassed to call them back. After a while . . ."

"They quit calling," Rochelle finished her sentence. "Fair-weather friends, every last one of 'em."

"I guess Ben got custody of all our old friends." Grace blinked back tears, and wondered if her tear ducts would ever dry up. "And that hurts, too. I try to keep busy, to keep from dwelling on everything, but everyday, it's like some-thing else happens, another slap in the face. My blog? I know it seems silly to you, but, Mom, this is my work. If I don't have a marriage, and I don't have any friends, and then, somehow, I can't even make a living, what the hell else do I have? What kind of life is this?"

Rochelle handed her a paper towel. "Dry your eyes, honey. This is the life you've got, so put on your big-girl panties and make it what you want it to be. All your old friends are gone? Find some new ones. Ben's attacking you. Coun-terattack. Stay on the offensive. The best way to do that, from where I'm sitting, is to figure out a way to do what only you can do, and then get on with it. Every-thing else will take care of itself."

"How?" Grace's voice quivered with emotion.

Rochelle threw up her hands in surrender. "I don't know, Grace. I'm not Dr. Phil. But you can't just give up and sit around and whine. That's not how we raised you."

She leaned closer to Grace, rested her forehead against her daughter's. "Fig-ure out what you want. And then go get it."

. . .

She hadn't had all that much contact with the Gracenotes advertisers. That had been Ben's department. But she'd had some correspondence with the bigger, most important ones: Home Depot, Levolor, Benjamin Moore, Viking, a big carpet manufacturer, and DeWalt, a power tool manufacturer.

Now Grace scrolled through the contacts on her laptop, searching them out, mentally composing the message she'd send.

Dear Sir: Just wanted to take the time to thank you for your past support of Gracenotes. Unfortunately, a situation has arisen that I wanted to make you aware of. I am currently in the middle of an unpleasant split from my husband, Ben. The result is that although Gracenotes.com is still online, I am no longer authoring or associated with those posts. I've started a new blog, TrueGrace.com, and I hope you'll take a look at it. In the meantime, you should know that Ben is actually lifting my intellectual property—my writing, my recipes, and my photographs—and publishing them on Gracenotes, representing them as original. I also believe he's actually engaging in sabotaging my career as a blogger, by posting potentially libelous, scurrilous, negative comments and material on other lifestyle blogs and signing my name to them. I know your company values your brand and identity too much to underwrite these kinds of activities, and I hope you will take the appropriate steps to ensure that your company is not associated with individuals who rely on devious, underhanded, negative activities. All best, Grace Davenport (formerly Stanton), the True Grace.

She pushed the SEND button and, for the first time in weeks, felt like herself. The real Grace.

19

Grace had never been what you would call athletic. She'd been a book nerd as a kid, always happier inside with a book than outside with a racket or a club or playing a sport that made her sweaty.

It was only after her sophomore year of college, when she'd gained not just the freshman fifteen but a whole twenty pounds, that she'd reluctantly taken up running. She'd kept it up, off and on, since then. Running to keep her weight down or the stress of daily life at bay.

Lately, she'd started running for sanity. Since the split with Ben and moving into the apartment above the Sandbox, she'd taken to waking before dawn. Sometimes she read; sometimes she worked on her blog; sometimes she laced up her running shoes and hit the road.

Reading again through all the e-mails in her in-box left her feeling infuriated and helpless, even a day later. Ben—or somebody—had done a thorough job of poisoning her Internet presence. Using her name, he'd posted inflammatory blog comments on every single blog from her old blog roll. She knew this because nearly all of the bloggers had e-mailed to tell her that she was dead to them, too.

She had to get away. It was still dark when she slipped down the stairs and let herself out the Sandbox's side door.

Grace wasn't fast, and her running form left much to be desired. She popped her earbuds in, pressed the PLAY button on her iPod, and loped down the street. The route she'd developed took her along the winding roads that paralleled the Gulf of Mexico. If she looked to her left, she could see blue skies, sometimes catch patches of blue-green surf through the tree line of shaggy Australian pines and palm trees.

After crossing the bridge from Cortez, she ran through Bradenton Beach, on to Holmes, and Anna Maria. After an hour, her nylon tank top was drenched with sweat, her gym shorts plastered to her butt. Even her ponytail dripped sweat onto her shoulders.

The last mile of her run was actually more of a cool-down walk. She did a run-walk on the beach for a half mile or so, keeping her eyes on the surf line, scanning for any shells, watching the seagulls and sandpipers. At one point, she stopped and stared at a huge gray heron, poised, motionless at water's edge. The bird never flinched as Grace approached and stood, marveling at its elegant blue-gray plumage. Eventually, she moved on, but the heron did not.

It was early Monday morning, so the streets of Anna Maria were quiet. She loped up one sandy, narrow street after another, walking, fuming. Every once in a while, she felt a faint breeze coming through the tree line. The houses on these streets were cottages, many of them bearing real estate signs indicating they were vacation rentals.

This was a new neighborhood to Grace. She slowed to a stroll, appreciating the modest concrete block or frame structures, so unlike the rambling, over-blown megamansions on Gulf Vista. She wished she had her camera to capture the early morning sun, the tropical gardens of palms, bromeliads, crotons, bougainvillea, and hibiscus.

Grass was sparse here. Instead, the small yards seemed to consist of dense plantings of vines and ferns and flowers. Lizards darted across the narrow sand-strewn road, and she saw hummingbirds hovering over the thick hedges of ixora with their star-shaped coral blossoms.

It seemed the whole world was still slumbering, until she came across a house that stood out like a sore thumb on this block of neatly maintained homes. The curb was heaped high with trash, the yard weedy and strewn with dead palm fronds and fallen limbs. Barely visible, behind an overgrown hedge of ficus, she could see a glimpse of faded white siding.

Also blocking her view was the mountain of refuse. Two big city-issued receptacles were spilling over with plastic bags of garbage. Alongside these were sodden cardboard boxes overflowing with old clothes and shoes and more. A stained king-sized mattress leaned against the receptacles and was propped up by two cheap fiberboard nightstands.

Grace heard a screen door slam, and, as she watched, an old man muscled a long rattan couch through the doorway and into the yard. He cursed softly as he pushed and shoved the sofa to the curb.

"Hey," he said, barely noticing Grace. He dumped the sofa, wheeled, and went back into the house.

Something about that sofa caught her eye. She glanced at the house, to see if the man was watching, but he'd disappeared.

The rest of the discards at the curb were junk, cheap, soiled, ruined junk. But this sofa . . . Grace squatted to get a better look.

The rattan arms formed huge pretzel-like shapes. It was a three-seater, and it looked, she thought, like it could be by Paul McCobb. The rattan wrappings were in surprisingly good shape, and all the seat supports looked intact.

A moment later, the screen door slammed and the man reappeared, this time with a wheelbarrow heaped with thick cushions covered in a hideous orange and rust synthetic plaid fabric. He dumped the cushions without comment and wheeled back inside.

Grace was intrigued. She walked across the street, down the block, and then doubled back again. It was like a floor show whose second act she couldn't bring herself to miss.

By now, an armchair had joined its matching sofa. And the man with the wheelbarrow was back, this time bringing a low-slung, boomerang-shaped rattan coffee table with a yellow pine top, which he unceremoniously dumped on end. The table's top, Grace saw, was marred with cigarette burns and water rings, but the legs and the rattan wrappings were in fairly decent condition.

The man looked annoyed at having a spectator. He was tall and thin, with a high forehead and thinning gray hair and a lit cigarette dangling from one corner of his mouth. He wore a pair of loose-fitting khaki slacks and a shapeless gray T-shirt.

"Can I help you?" he asked.

Grace blushed. "Did somebody die?" she blurted out.

"I wish," he said. His voice was gravelly. He set the wheelbarrow down, took a wrinkled handkerchief from his back pocket, and mopped his face.

"My damned tenants moved out and left me with this mess," he said, removing his eyeglasses and wiping them down.

"That's awful," Grace sympathized.

"You don't even know," he agreed. "Three months back rent owing, not to mention they trashed the house so bad, I don't know how long it'll take me to get it into shape to rent again."

He was gazing at her, taking in her sweaty, disheveled appearance. "Don't I know you?" He gestured at her ball cap, with the Sandbox logo. "Maybe from the bar?"

Now that he mentioned it, she did think he looked familiar. "Maybe. I'm Grace Davenport. Rochelle's daughter."

"Riiight," he said, wiping his hands on his pants and shaking her hand. "And I'm Arthur Cater. I knew your daddy. Took him fishing a couple times. Butch was a great guy. How's your mama gettin' along?"

"She's good," Grace said. "We miss him, but if you know Rochelle, you know she's a tough old bird."

"She is that," he said with a laugh.

Now he gestured toward the mountain of trash. "Should have trusted my gut instinct. But they were a young couple, and my wife felt sorry for 'em. Famous last words."

Grace gestured toward the mound of trash. "You're throwing all of this out? Not even calling Goodwill to come pick it up?"

He snorted. "Goodwill wouldn't take this mess. Would you? Mildewed, pee-stained. They had dogs, even though the lease specifically forbids pets, and they swore they didn't have any. So everything is crawling with fleas."

Grace shuddered and took a tiny step backward.

He flicked his handkerchief at the rattan sofa. "This was my grandmother's. She left me the house, and this was always in it, as long as I could remember. We've been renting this house, furnished, with no problems for fifteen years, and then these bums move in, and now it's not fit for the dump."

He was mopping his neck. "You see anything here you want, be my guest."

"The rattan furniture is actually very pretty," Grace ventured. "Probably from the forties. You're sure you don't want to keep it? Maybe have the cushions redone?"

"Nah," he said dismissively. "We got a house full of furniture. And my wife doesn't like this old grandma stuff." He studied her. "There's an end table and another armchair inside, that goes with this set, if you think you might want it. Course, you'd have to haul it off yourself."

"I just might want it," Grace said, surprising herself. And then she had an idea.

"Would it be all right if I came inside, took a look at the furniture?"

"You got a clothespin for your nose? And if you get bit up by fleas, don't blame me."

The walkway to the front door was brick, but it was barely visible beneath the tendrils of vines and weeds that grew up in the sandy yard. The house was raised up from ground level on concrete block piers. It had a steep gabled roof with slatted wooden air vents near the V-shaped peak and a half-shed tin-roofed porch with large wooden brackets supporting the overhanging porch eaves. The siding was aluminum, and it was pulling away from the house in several spots.

Arthur Cater yanked open the screened door, and she followed him inside.

It took a moment for her eyes to adjust to the dim light. She was on a screened porch, or what was left of it. Most of the rusty screens were torn, and in some cases, they were missing entirely. Two cheap plastic armchairs were overturned, and the painted wooden floor was littered by overflowing trash bags.

Her new friend pushed open the front door. "After you," he said with a flourish. She was greeted with a pungent smell—a mixture of urine, mildew, and stale cigarette smoke.

"Oh my," she gasped, forcing herself to breathe through her mouth.

"Now you see what I'm dealing with," he said.

The front of the cottage was basically one room. They were standing in the living room. Its windows were cloudy and smeared with dirt. Venetian blinds hung crazily from one hook on a long window that looked out on the porch. The rattan armchair was pushed up against the wall, heaped with an old sleeping bag and pillow, and a matching end table rested, upside down, atop it.

"That's it, right there," the man said. "And I warn you, it's heavier than it looks."

Grace upended the table, setting it on the filthy avocado-green shag carpeting. Its top had more water rings and cigarette burns, but she loved its rounded-off triangular shape. She gingerly removed the bedding from the armchair and concluded that it, too, was in sound shape, although the cushion was ruined.

"You really don't want these?" she asked Arthur, who'd walked to the other end of the room. Which was a dining room, from the looks of it. The only furniture here was a flimsy card table and a pair of old-timey folding aluminum beach chairs with rotting plastic webbing. A cheap brass chandelier dangled over the table, but only one of its candle arms was lit.

"What?" He turned around. "Nah. But I would have liked the dining room furniture that used to be here."

Grace went over to join him. "They stole your furniture?"

"Yup," he said. "Mahogany table and chairs, and a buffet kind of thing. Those were my mama's. I thought about taking 'em out of here, but we didn't have room at the house, and I thought they'd get ruined if I left them in the garage." He shrugged. "I'd love to know how they got that heavy stuff out of here. They didn't have but one car, and that was a crappy little Kia."

"Mm-hmm." Grace wasn't really listening. She was taking a good look at the house itself now.

It was a typical Florida cracker house, she thought. These walls were board and batten, probably old pine under the multiple layers of paint and dirt. The ceilings were quite tall, also board and batten, although they'd never been painted. Through a tall doorway, she could see into the tiny galley kitchen.

"Okay if I look around, Arthur?" she asked.

"Just watch your step," he advised, heading back toward the porch with another load of trash.

A single grungy window over the kitchen sink let in feeble light. Grace found a light switch, and as the ceiling fixture flickered on, half a dozen cockroaches skittered for the shadows. She shuddered, but was not surprised. Roaches were as much a part of living in Florida as palm trees and sunshine. Her least favorite part.

The kitchen was something of a time warp. The countertops were speckled gray formica. The cabinets were wooden, with gummy-looking chipped white enamel paint. There were two wooden upper cabinets, one on either side of the sink, and two lower ones, each topped by a drawer. The cabinet doors were all ajar, and she could see a sad assortment of mismatched pots and pans, some cloudy glasses, chipped plates. An old avocado-green stove sat at the far end of the counter, its surface spattered with grease and food particles. A small sauce-pan with an unspeakable layer of burnt...something...sat on the front burner. The oven door was open, and when Grace closed it she saw another scattering of roaches.

Turning around, she saw the refrigerator. It was a somewhat newer model than the stove, but its white surface was freckled with rust. To the left of the fridge was another counter, with a pair of wall-mounted upper cabinets. Be-neath the counter there was nothing but an open space, where an evil-smelling plastic trash can was tipped on its side.

Through a second doorway was a short hall. An open door showed the bath-room. The black-and-white penny-tile floor was now a grimy gray. The sink, commode, and bathtub were pale pink, which meant, Grace knew, that they probably dated from the early fifties.

There were two more doors, both closed. Grace was about to open one when she heard a faint scratching sound coming from inside the room.

She took a step back. Rats? She took another step back.

Arthur poked his head inside the hall. "I wouldn't open that door unless you wanna get attacked," he warned.

Grace decided she'd seen enough of the house.

"Bad enough those lowlifes trashed the house like this," he said. "They went off and left their damned dog behind. I ask you, who moves out and leaves a dog behind?"

"No," Grace said, appalled. "There's a dog in that bedroom? Can I see it?"

"Look all you want," Arthur said. "I penned her up in there because with me coming and going outside, I was afraid she'd run out and get hit by a car. I'm no dog lover, but even I couldn't stand that."

20

As she and Arthur talked, the scratching grew more intense, and now it was accompanied by a series of high-pitched yips.

She put her hand on the doorknob. "Don't say I didn't warn you," Arthur said.

Grace pushed the door open and stepped inside the bedroom, where a small brown bundle of fur began leaping at her knees in a frenzy of barking and yipping.

"Heyyyy," Grace said softly, bending down to get a closer look. The dog leapt into her arms and began lavishing her chin with a soft pink tongue.

"Oh my God," Grace said, holding the reeking animal at arm's length. "You poor thing."

Her best guess was that she was some kind of poodle mix. But it was hard to tell because the dog's fur was filthy and matted. Its liquid brown eyes were cloudy and tinged with some milky substance, and there were speckles of dried blood on its muzzle.

She set the dog down gingerly and wiped her hands on the seat of her shorts. The dog sat back on its haunches and looked at her expectantly.

"Pathetic, ain't it?" Arthur asked, standing behind her in the hallway. "She'd been locked up in this room, I don't know how long, when I got over here this morning." He jerked his head in the direction of the bedroom. "You can see the mess she's made. Not that you could blame her."

The room was, as Arthur said, a disaster. Even mouth-breathing could not contain the stench.

Grace picked the dog up again and stepped into the hallway, closing the door to the horrors within.

"What will you do with her?" Grace asked, still holding her at arm's length.

Arthur reached into the bathroom and found a threadbare bath towel. "Here. Wrap her in this. She's got fleas pretty bad."

As Grace wrapped the towel around the dog, she felt it shivering violently.

"I think she's sick, too," she said, looking up at Arthur.

"Gotta be," he agreed. "I give her a bowl of water when I found her this morning, and what was left of the sausage biscuit I had out in my truck, but there's no telling how long it had been since she'd been fed."

"Those people should be tracked down and put in jail for something like this," Grace said fiercely. She swallowed hard, feeling nauseous.

"I've filed a report with the sheriff's department, but there's no telling how long they've been gone. I know the wife, well, I guess she was his wife, I don't really know, but she did mention at one point that they had family in Alabama."

He looked down at the shivering bundle of fur in Grace's arms. "I was gonna take her to the animal shelter. Later on. But if you'd take her, that'd be a whole lot better." He reached out and scratched under the dog's chin, and she wriggled in delight. "She's kinda cute, in a homely sort of way."

Grace looked down at the dog and sighed. "She seems like a sweetheart. But I'm living with my mom, above the bar. And if you know Rochelle, you know she doesn't believe in having inside pets."

"And my wife has got three big ol' tomcats, and they don't like dogs any more than I do," Arthur said. He took the dog from Grace's arms, opened the bedroom door, and set her back inside before firmly closing the door.

The dog's plaintive whines tore at Grace's heart.

Arthur knew how to deal with such a thing. He stalked out to the living room and began loading his wheelbarrow with more trash.

Grace wanted not to hear the dog's cries. "How long do you think it'll take to get this place cleaned up?" she asked.

"Who knows? However much time it takes, it's more than I can spare,"

Arthur said. "We usually spend the summer up in North Carolina. Fixing to leave next week, until this happened."

"I have an idea," Grace said slowly. "It's kind of crazy."

"Crazier than me letting these folks do me out of three months' back rent?" Arthur asked.

She took a deep breath. "What would you think of letting me fix the place up for you?"

"Why would you want to do something like that?" Arthur asked, his eyes narrow with suspicion.

"I'm an interior designer, and I write a blog about home design and home improvement," Grace said. She gestured at the dank room they were standing in. "This little house actually has good bones. It's small, but it could be terrific. I could make it terrific. And I could photograph it and write about the process. If you'd let me."

She was already writing the blog posts in her mind, picturing the rooms, stripped of their filth, the cottage returned to its old Florida vernacular architecture. Let J'Aimee try to copy that!

Arthur shook another cigarette out of the pack in his breast pocket. "I don't know . . ."

"Okay," Grace said easily. "As I said, it was just an idea."

He lit the cigarette and inhaled. The smoke smell was actually an improvement. "What would you charge for something like that?"

"Uh, nothing," Grace said. And then she hurriedly backed up. "That is, you'd need to pay for the materials." She did a 360-degree turn around the room. "Paint, new light fixtures."

"Carpet, for sure," he added.

Grace stubbed her toe into the shag carpet. "What's under here, do you know?"

"Wood floors, best I remember," he said. "God knows what kinda shape they're in. We've had carpet down, ever since I can remember."

"Best-case scenario, rip up this carpet and refinish the wood floors," Grace said. "It's way cheaper than buying new carpet, and if you put down a good finish, your next tenants shouldn't be able to ruin it."

She walked out to the kitchen. "I'm thinking you'll need new appliances in here." She knelt down and peeled at an edge of the vinyl-roll flooring. "This stuff would have to come up, too. So either refinish if there's wood or put down new vinyl."

He nodded. "I was gonna have the stove and fridge hauled off, probably tomorrow."

"How much were *you* thinking it would cost to get it ready to rent again?" Grace asked.

Arthur pursed his lips and flicked his cigarette ash onto the carpet. "With appliances—there's a washer and dryer on the back porch, and they're ruined, too, I'm thinking a couple thousand."

"With appliances? I'm thinking at least five thousand," Grace shot back. She'd walked out to the porch and was staring out at the overgrown yard. "The screens out here are all shot and you've got rotten framing, too."

She turned around. "How about the air-conditioning? Does it work?"

"Window units," he said, pointing to a rusting brown hulk that stuck out of the front living room window. "Couple smaller ones in the bedrooms. They do the job. Or they did, up until now."

Grace put her hands on her hips. "What do you charge for rent? If you don't mind my asking?"

"Four-fifty a month," he said. "And we pay utilities."

"Oh, Arthur," she said with a knowing smile. "This house has such potential. And you're only, what? A block from the bay? If we fixed this place up—I mean, really fixed it up, cleaned up the yard, got it landscaped, maybe put in a little central air unit . . ."

"No central air," he growled. "Think I'm made of money?"

"It couldn't cost that much," Grace said. "How many square feet here?"

"A little under a thousand," he said.

"If you're paying for the electric, you're spending way more money now with three old window units," Grace said. "I bet if you put in a new efficient central unit, you'd save enough to pay for it after just a couple years. Plus, once I've got it fixed up and looking great, you're gonna get more rent anyway, and definitely attract a better-quality tenant."

"You make it sound so easy," Arthur said. "You have any experience fixing up houses? Or handling investment properties, for that matter?"

"I've fixed up three old houses," Grace said. "And my ex-husband and I had a little two-bedroom, two-bath in Bradenton that I did this very same thing with. That one, I gutted to the studs. By the time we sold it, a year ago, we were getting $1,200 a month. Unfurnished."

"Ex-husband?"

"About to be," Grace said casually. "We split a couple months ago. That's why I'm living with my mom right now."

"Sorry to hear it," Arthur said.

"I'm not," Grace said, lifting her chin. "So? What do you think?"

"Have to run it by my wife," he said. "Five thousand. You're talking about a lot of money."

She decided to push her luck. "Five thousand, more or less. I haven't even seen those bedrooms. And we don't know what shape the floors are in."

He chewed on that for a minute or two. "All right. Assuming my wife doesn't hate the idea, you've got a deal."

"Great!" Grace beamed. "What about the rattan furniture? It's really good stuff, Arthur. I love it, but I don't actually have a place I can use it right now. Once I get this house cleaned up, it'll be perfect in the living room. Is there a place we can store it until then?"

He yanked his head in the direction of the back of the house. "There's a garage out back. Guess I could lock it up out there for now."

She couldn't believe what she'd just done. Gone out for a run, found a set of cool old furniture, and ended up with a new decorating gig and several months' worth of potentially fabulous, totally original blog posts. This was a nonpaying gig, sure, but she couldn't wait to dig in, turning this toxic-waste dump into a treasure.

"When can I get started?" she asked, trying not to sound too anxious.

"As soon as you like," Arthur said. "I'll get the worst of this crap hauled off tomorrow. Meet me over here then, and I'll give you a key."

"How will we work out paying for the materials?" Grace asked. "I'm, uh, kind of tight on funds while I wait for my divorce to play out."

"I'll set up a draw for you at the hardware store," Arthur said. "Just keep the receipts. Oh, and there's just one more thing. Part of the deal, you might say."

"Yesss?" Grace felt her throat tighten. She knew it was too good to be true.

He walked toward the hallway. A moment later, he thrust the stinking, shivering bundle of fur into her arms. "You keep the dog."

21

She didn't dare tell her mother what she was up to. It was nearly 9:00 A.M. by the time she'd walked home with her bundle tucked under her arm. She thanked every holy force she could think of that it was Monday, and Rochelle had gone out do the week's grocery shopping.

Grace dragged a washtub from the carport and filled it with water from the garden hose.

"It's okay, sweetie," she cooed, keeping one hand on the dog's back for reassurance. "We're gonna get you cleaned up a little. This won't hurt, and you'll feel a lot better afterward." She squeezed a little of her own shampoo into her hand and gently rubbed it into the dog's fur.

The animal whimpered a little, but Grace rubbed and cooed and breathed through her mouth as a vile stream of brown water surged off the quivering animal.

When finally the water had turned clear, and she could see no more crust in the dog's fur, Grace wrapped her in a beach towel. Upstairs in her bedroom, she set the beach towel on her bed and turned her blow-dryer to cool, running it back and forth over the little dog's damp fur.

Even though she was now semiclean, the poor little thing still looked so pitiful, Grace could have wept.

"Okay, sweetie," she said, ruffling the dog's ears. "There's a vet over on

Anna Maria. I think we'll just run over there to see if they'll take a look at you."

It was Grace's first time in a vet's office. The receptionist looked up at her with a blank expression.

"So . . . you don't know anything about this dog?"

"No. Basically, she'd been abandoned, in a house. Locked in a bedroom, and I don't know for how long. When I got her, she was kind of bloody. I think she'd tried to scratch her way out. I gave her a bath, but I think there's probably something else wrong with her. Because she keeps shivering."

Grace looked down at the little brown dog, huddled under the swaddling of beach towel. "But you're a good girl, aren't you, sweetie?"

The girl had been typing on the computer. She looked up. "That's her name, Sweetie?"

"Uh, sure," Grace agreed. It was as good a name as any.

"It's slow right now," the girl said, clicking over to another page of her computer. "I think Dr. Katz can see her pretty soon. Can you wait?"

"The vet's name is Dr. Katz?" Grace suppressed a giggle. "Really?"

The girl rolled her eyes. She'd heard it all before. "Really. How did you want to pay today?"

Grace hesitated. "Cash, I guess."

"You can sit over there," the receptionist said, pointing to a chair. She held out her arms and Grace handed the dog over, towel and all. "It's okay now, Sweetie," the girl said softly. She reached into a glass jar on the counter and gave the dog a biscuit, which she eagerly snapped up. Then she disappeared behind a swinging door.

Grace sat in a hard vinyl chair and read a magazine about schnauzers. She hadn't realized there was so much to say about schnauzers, but apparently there was. On the opposite side of the waiting room, an elderly lady cradled a pet carrier in her lap. A huge tabby cat nearly filled the thing, its tail sticking out through the wire-mesh door.

Thirty minutes later, the receptionist was back at the desk. "Sweetie Davenport?" she called.

Grace suppressed a giggle. It was as though she'd acquired a new baby sister. "Yes?" she said, standing.

"Dr. Katz is back with Sweetie, in examining room one," she said. "You can go back and talk to her."

The veterinarian was a compact blond woman, in her late forties. She wore a short white lab coat that had silk-screened cartoon images of dogs and cats on it.

Sweetie was lying on a stainless steel examining table, and the vet held one hand on her back, slowly stroking her fur. When the dog spotted Grace, her stubby brown tail beat a tattoo on the table.

"Hi there," the vet said, nodding at Grace. "You've got a very good little girl here. She let me examine her, and she didn't make as much as a squeak."

"Is she okay?" Grace asked.

"A little deyhydrated," Dr. Katz said. "And she's got an intestinal parasite, and some wounds on her paws, which are infected."

Grace felt her throat tighten with anger. "The people who owned her, they just left her, locked in a bedroom of the house they'd been renting, and took off. She'd apparently been trying to dig her way out. We don't know how long she'd been there when the landlord found her today."

"It happens," Dr. Katz said, ruffling Sweetie's fur. "I'm sorry to tell you we see all kinds of cruelty to animals. It's upsetting, but not unusual."

"What can you do for her?"

"I'd like to keep her overnight. Put her on some IV fluids and get her started on antibiotics," the vet said. "We don't have any idea of her medical history, but given the fact that she was abandoned in this condition, I think we should assume she's never had any shots. We'll give her parvo and rabies shots, and start her on worm meds. And," she added, "give her a good flea dip."

"Right," Grace said. She hesitated. "Look," she said, her cheeks flaming with shame. "I'm in the middle of a divorce, and right now I just don't have a lot of money. I'm living with my mother, and getting a dog was the last thing I'd planned. How much will all this cost?"

Dr. Katz put a hand on her sleeve. "Don't worry too much about that. Let us work on Sweetie a couple days. We'll call you Wednesday and let you know what time you can pick her up. We do have a special rate for people rescuing strays, and we can always work out a payment plan, if need be. Does that sound all right?"

"Yes," Grace said. "Thank you! I'll be honest with you. I've never owned a dog, and wasn't looking for one. But I couldn't just leave her there and let her be dropped off at the dog pound."

"Good for you," Dr. Katz said.

"Can you tell me anything about her?" Grace asked. "Like what breed she is, or how old?"

Dr. Katz continued to stroke Sweetie's head. "She's no puppy. Judging by her teeth, I'd say she's probably at least four years old. It's hard to tell without doing DNA testing, but I feel confident that she's got a good bit of toy poodle in her, maybe some cocker spaniel, too. Considering what she's been through, she's surprisingly calm and docile. Once we get her feeling better, she'll make you a loyal, adoring little buddy."

Grace's eyes rested on Sweetie's big brown ones. She could have sworn the dog was grinning at her.

"And Grace?"

"Yes?"

"I think she's housebroken! I was examining her, and she started to whimper, so we took her out to the dog run, and she did her business right away."

Now Grace returned Sweetie's smile. "Thanks, Dr. Katz. That's the first good news I've heard today."

22

She spent Tuesday working in the bar and fuming over Ben's sabotage of her blog. But early Wednesday morning, Grace bounded down the stairs to the bar, her camera bag in hand.

Rochelle had the blender going, whipping up an evil-looking green concoction. She shut it off, poured the sludge in a glass, and sipped, all the while taking in Grace's work ensemble, which consisted of a pair of thrift-store jeans, oversized T-shirt, and cheap tennis shoes. "No run this morning?"

"Nope," Grace said, unable to suppress a grin. "I've got an actual job." She poured herself a mug of coffee and snagged a banana from the fruit bowl on the bar back.

"Is that so?"

"Yup."

"How'd you get this job? Where is it? What's it pay?"

Grace couldn't remember when she'd been this excited at the prospect of working for free.

"You won't believe it, Mom," she said. "When I was out for my run Monday I passed this really rundown house over on Anna Maria. There was a huge pile of junk at the curb. Obviously, somebody was doing a clean out. I stopped to look, because this guy had just dumped a great old midcentury rattan sofa. And then he added more pieces, and I kind of struck up a conversation with him. The house had been a rental, but the tenants trashed the place and skipped out on the rent, and the guy I met was the landlord. The rattan was really good stuff. Very collectible, so I asked him if I could have it, although God knows where I'd put it. He invited me inside the house—which was a disaster area, but it could be really wonderful."

"Slow down," Rochelle ordered. "You went into a house with a strange man? Are you nuts? What if he'd been some kind of deviate or something?"

"He wasn't a deviate; he actually knew Dad," Grace said. "So he was complaining about how long it was going to take him to get the place fixed up to rent again, and I asked him if he'd let me do it. You know, as a before-and-after story for the blog. And he said yes!" Grace was practically jumping up and down.

"How much?" Rochelle asked.

"I finally got him to agree to a minimum budget of five thousand dollars, although I think it'll probably run more than that," she said.

"He's paying you five thousand? Honey, that's great," Rochelle said. "I'm so proud of you."

Grace shook her head. "No. He's not paying me anything. The budget to fix up the house is five thousand. Or more. I'm doing the work for free. So I can do a before-and-after series for my blog. Wait 'til you see this place, Mom. It's over on Mandevilla, on Anna Maria, about a block from the bay. It's a real old-timey Florida cracker house, with the pitched roof and the screened porch. All the inside walls are the original pine. Right now, there's some skanky carpet on the floors, but I'm sure there's hardwood under there. It's got a tiny little galley kitchen, again with the original cabinets. I'm thinking I'll take the doors off the upper cabinets . . ."

"Wait," Rochelle said. "You're going to do all this work? Without getting paid? How is this a good thing?"

"Because it's design work," Grace said. "I'll be rehabbing a historic old cottage. It's what I love to do! And I can photograph it from every stage and blog about it. And that is something that not even Ben and J'Aimee can rip off."

She dug into her camera bag and brought out some Benjamin Moore paint chips, rifling through the colored cards until she found the one she wanted. "Here. Dove White. I'm thinking of using it for all the interior walls. The house is kind of dark inside, because of the porch overhang, so I want to brighten it up, make it look crisp and clean. Have you ever seen a prettier white?"

"You know all white paint looks the same to me," Rochelle said. "But if you say it's the best white ever, I believe it."

"I might do the kitchen another color, maybe a soft aqua, something like that," Grace mused. "But I want to get it all defunked, have a clean slate, before I make too many design decisions."

"What's the owner going to say about all those design decisions? And who is it? You said it's somebody who knew Butch?"

"He doesn't care what I do, as long as I get it presentable and ready to rent again," Grace said. "He'll be the perfect client—especially since he's leaving soon to spend the summer in North Carolina. I won't have him breathing down my neck, second-guessing everything I do. Oh yeah. His name is Arthur Cater. He said he used to take Dad fishing on his boat."

"Arthur Cater? He's your client?" Rochelle rolled her eyes.

"What's that supposed to mean? No, never mind. I don't want to hear it. I am not going to let you rain on my parade. Whatever you know about him, keep it to yourself."

"I wasn't gonna rain on your parade," Rochelle said. "Arthur's an okay guy. He used to come in here a lot, when they lived on the island, back before he got fancy and moved over to Longboat Key. There's just one thing I want you to know about him."

"Whatever," Grace said, packing up her paint chips impatient to get started on her new project. "Can I have the key to the shed? Thank God I didn't get around to cleaning out Dad's tools. All my stuff is still back at Sand Dollar Lane. I don't even have a hammer or a pair of pliers to my own name now. And I want to get that nasty carpet pulled up this morning. First thing."

Rochelle went into the kitchen and came back with a key ring, which she handed to her daughter. "Just know this about Arthur. He is the world's biggest cheapskate. He's got tons of money, but he didn't get that way throwing it around. He will nickel and dime you to death. Your dad used to say Arthur was so tight he squeaked when he walked."

"I don't care," Grace said, cramming her sweat-stained Sandbox ball cap on her head. "I've dealt with cheap and I've dealt with difficult. I'm just happy to have a job again."

Arthur Cater was standing in the driveway of the house on Mandevilla, directing two Hispanic day laborers as they loaded the avocado-green stove into the back of an ancient rust bucket of a pickup truck.

"Hey, Arthur," Grace greeted him.

"So you didn't have a change of heart, huh?" He took in her work clothes and toolbox.

"No way," Grace said. "Did your wife give us the thumbs-up?"

Arthur mopped his face with his handkerchief. "She says you're a big-deal interior designer. She's all excited now. Says she reads your blog and she can't believe I could trick you into working for nothin'."

Grace laughed. "She doesn't know I'm the one who tricked you, does she?"

He gestured toward the house. "I got over here right at sunup this morning and set off a couple of flea bombs in there. I just opened up all the windows, so you should be all right to go in now." He reached in the pocket of his own faded blue jeans. "Here's the keys. Front and back doors, and the garage." He nodded at his workers, who were bringing the washing machine out on a furniture dolly. "I had the fellas put all that furniture in the garage, and put a tarp over it. There's some other odds and ends out there you can maybe use."

"All right," Grace said. She took her camera from around her neck and stepped into the street, clicking off a few frames.

"Stand right there by the mailbox, will you Arthur," she called. "I like to document everything, right from the beginning."

Arthur stood awkwardly by the curb, his hands thrust in his pockets. "You don't want pictures of this ugly old mug," he growled. "It'll break your camera."

"Let me be the judge of that," Grace said, stepping backward to shoot. "Arthur, do you have any idea when this house was built?"

"Let me see. Well, I'm seventy-three, and we've got old family pictures of my grandma, standing out front of this house with me in her arms. I know my grandpa bought the house, probably sometime in the thirties. It looked a lot different back then. There was no front porch, no real trees, just some scrub palmettos and sand, and where the kitchen is now, was a porch they used to cook on. There was an old wood cookstove out there. My grandpa used to fry mullet on it Friday nights. Hard to believe they raised seven kids in this little bitty place, isn't it?"

It was just a little after nine, but the sun was already high in the sky, the summer heat relentless. Grace walked all the way around the house, photographing it from every conceivable angle, swatting at mosquitoes and stopping to pick off the sandspurs clinging to her ankles. She prayed no snakes were lurking in the thick underbrush. Despite that, the more she saw of the house, the more she liked. Virtually nothing had been done to change the house in the years since the porch had been added. In a way, she decided, it was a very good thing that Arthur Cater was a cheapskate.

When she got back to the front of the house, Arthur was standing by the truck, waiting on her. He handed her a slip of paper. "Here's my phone number. You call me if there's a problem, hear? I set up a draw for you at the hardware store. And my wife said I should tell you she'd like it if you'd e-mail us some pictures as you go. She's all jazzed up about this project of yours. Good thing we're leaving town, or she'd be over here all the time, sidewalk superintending."

Grace stood on her tiptoes and planted a kiss on Arthur's grizzled cheek. He looked surprised, but not displeased. "All right then, get to work," he ordered. He drove off with the two laborers in the back of the truck, wedged in among the rusted appliances. A moment later, he was backing down the street toward where she stood at the curb.

He hung his head out the open window. "Meant to ask you about that little dog," he said, failing miserably at pretending he didn't care. "How's she doing? Did you find somebody to take her in?"

"Sweetie is going to be just fine," Grace said. "They kept her overnight at the vet's office, giving her some IV fluids and some antibiotics. I'm going to pick her up this afternoon. And I'm going to keep her myself, until I figure out something else."

"Sweetie, huh? Dumb name for a dog."

Grace paced every inch of the cottage interior, snapping photos and making notes. She found an old broom in a tiny utility closet off the kitchen and swept up an entire village of dead insects. Then she cranked up the music she'd downloaded onto her iPod, adjusted the tiny little speakers, pulled on her work gloves, and got down to business.

A veteran of the remodeling wars, Grace donned a paper face mask before tackling the carpet. It was a hot, filthy job. The carpet was so old and brittle, hunks of it tore apart in her hands as she pried it from the nail strips along the baseboards. But when she pulled up the thin foam padding and got the first glimpse of the intact oak floors, she got a new burst of energy. By noon, when she took her lunch break with a sandwich and a bottle of water she'd brought from home, she'd pulled up all the carpet in the bedrooms, rolled it up, and dragged it out to the curb.

She was buzzed with adrenaline, dancing around the smaller of the two bedrooms doing a creditable accompaniment to Adele's "Rolling in the Deep," using the broom as a makeshift microphone. The music echoed in the high-ceilinged empty rooms, and she whipped her sweat-dampened hair from side to side as she cataloged the all-too-familiar misery of a lover done wrong.

Grace didn't hear the front door open. Didn't hear anything except the music, until she happened to turn around and see Ben, standing in the doorway, arms folded over his chest, watching her performance with no trace of amusement.

Her face flamed. She grabbed for the iPod and shut it off.

For a moment, she couldn't think of anything to say. Her throat went dry, and all she could think of was how idiotic she must have looked to him, dancing around a filthy house, in her filthy clothes, playing air guitar with a broom.

Then she got mad and found her voice again. "What are you doing here?" she asked, clutching the broom, because she needed to clutch something. It was the first time she'd seen him since their day in court.

He was dressed for golf, in a spotless white polo shirt, crisp black shorts, golf shoes, his aviator sunglasses pushed back off his forehead.

"I came to see the floor show," Ben said. "Good thing it's free."

"How'd you know where to find me?" Was he following her?

"Your mother told me you were working at a house over on Mandevilla. You're not that hard to find. She really, really doesn't like me, you know."

"That makes two of us," Grace snapped. "I'm surprised she actually spoke to you at all. But then, probably you lied to her. Lying seems to be your good thing."

He smiled. His orthodontics were a thing of beauty. "I told Rochelle I had something to give you. I guess she assumed it was money."

"But it's not."

"No," Ben said. And his smile dissolved, like Alice in Wonderland's Cheshire cat. "No money. Just some advice."

He took a step into the room. "I got a call this morning, from Anna Stribling, at Home Depot. It seems she had some 'concerns,' as she called them, about the originality of our material on Gracenotes."

"Oh?" Grace wondered if he could see her hands shaking as she clutched the broom.

"Yes. She was specifically wondering if J'Aimee's corn-crab chowder recipe was original. Because, she said, she'd had a disturbing e-mail from you, accusing us of stealing your material."

"Which you did. A blatant rip-off," Grace said. "My photos, my recipe, my everything. And that's what I told her."

"But you don't have any proof of that, do you?" Ben raised one eyebrow, amused.

"Because you hacked into my Web site and erased it. And put that filthy porn link on there," Grace fairly spat the words at him.

"And you don't have any proof of that, either."

Ben took a step closer. She could smell his elegant cologne. The Clive Christian 1872 that sold for $310 a bottle at Saks. Everything about Ben was elegant. "What I told Anna during our chat today is this. I told her that you're delusional. That you're bitter and jealous and emotionally fragile. I mentioned that you're in court-ordered counseling. I think she felt a lot better after our conversation. In fact, I know she felt better, because Home Depot just agreed to take a bigger Gracenotes banner ad starting next month."

Grace clamped her lips together to keep her jaw from dropping. She hoped Ben wasn't close enough to detect the sense of defeat that swept over her, threatened to knock her off her feet and destroy her hard-won equilibrium.

Ben towered over her—intimidation through proximity was his motto. "Don't fuck with me, Grace," he said, his voice light and even. "You'll get mowed down every time. Know this. If you send out any more of those incendiary e-mails, I'll haul your ass back to court in a New York second. And that judge will be only too happy to shut you down for good."

She took two steps backward, nearly tripping over the damned broom. "Get out," she said, recovering quickly. She poked the broom at his spotless two-toned golf shoes. "OUT!"

He stood his ground. She jabbed at his ankles. "I said out!" He chuckled, shook his head, and strolled for the door, with Grace right on his heels. He'd left the door open, and now she saw an unfamiliar car in the driveway, a gleaming ebony Porsche Pantera.

"Nice car," she spat.

He gave her a mock bow. "Glad you like it, since I have you to thank for it.

And you know? I actually like this one much better. It handles so much smoother."

She finished ripping out the rest of the carpet, without the music, now that Ben had managed to poison that source of joy. Slowly, she swept the living room and dining room floors, taking grim satisfaction from the cockroach body count.

Grace retrieved her cleaning supplies—bucket, mop, sponge, and spray cleaners—from her car and attacked the filthy windows, using an entire roll of paper towels on the front room. Logistically, it made no sense to spend so much time cleaning a house that still had so far to go in the rehab process, but she did it anyway, inhaling the scent of the strong pine cleaner as she filled her bucket with hot water.

When she found herself humming as she mopped, she got her iPod and turned it on again. The music filled her head and helped erase, temporarily, the image of Ben, smug, self-important, all-powerful Ben. "Gonna wash that man right out of my hair," she muttered, dumping the gray mop water down the toilet and flushing it with a flourish.

Finally, satisfied that the surface layers of crud had been eradicated, along with Ben's overpowering cologne, she set down her mop and picked up her camera again.

She photographed the front rooms, pleased with the way the afternoon sunlight slanted in, leaving atmospheric shadows on the old oak floors. She was so absorbed in her work she was startled at the sudden rattle of rain on the tin roof of the porch.

Time to go, she thought. She had to pick up Sweetie at the vet's office, get cleaned up before her Wednesday-night "therapy" session, and, in the meantime, figure out how to hide a dog from her mother.

23

Wyatt Keeler stood in front of the tiny closet he shared with Bo, barefoot and dressed only in his cotton boxers, and felt gloom. He walked over to the closet, opened the door, and his mood did not improve. He hadn't thought about clothes in months, not since the breakup with Callie. Okay, maybe even before that. His style guidelines in adulthood had gotten simple; he liked clean, and he liked cool. As in temperature, not trendiness.

At one time, he'd prided himself on being a sharp dresser. Just the right label jeans, good-quality classic shirts, ties and jackets. Nothing too flashy or outrageous. He'd learned a lot from his fraternity brothers in college. He'd been, like the ZZ Top song, a sharp-dressed man.

No more. Now, he idly plucked at the meager assortment of shirts and pants hanging limply on the wire hangers. "Dude," he muttered under his breath, "you are really, really lame." Finally, he found a pair of presentable navy blue Dockers and a short-sleeved plaid dress shirt that had been a Father's Day gift from Callie. The J.C. Penney price tag still hung from the sleeve.

The pants fit reasonably well, but they were wrinkled. He put on the shirt, then padded out to the living area, where Nelson was eating a chicken potpie at the dinette and reading the sports section. "Dad, do we own an iron?"

"Dunno," Nelson mumbled, his fingers poised over the box scores. "Your mother always handled that." He glanced up, looked surprised. "Since when do you iron?"

"Since now," Wyatt said. He checked under the kitchen sink, then on the top shelf of the hall closet, to no avail. "Screw it," he said, tossing the pants into the dryer.

While he was waiting for his pants, Wyatt went back to the bathroom. Feeling foolish, but somehow lighthearted, he brushed his teeth, again, and flossed. Back in the bedroom, with the door closed, he checked himself out in the cloudy mirror on the back of the closet door.

He wasn't a bad-looking guy. His teeth were straight, he was clean-shaven. After that crack Callie had made about his baldness he'd thought about letting his hair grow out again, just to prove he had plenty, but later he'd changed his mind. Screw Callie. He worked outside in the blazing Florida sun all day, and it was just much cooler without hair. Obviously, she liked a guy with hair. Luke wore his hair deliberately shaggy, like a surfer dude, although the guy had clearly never been anywhere near a surfboard. And Wyatt had always secretly suspected Luke of being a bottle blond.

Luke, Wyatt thought, had a body like the Pillsbury Doughboy. Big, pillowy hips, blobby butt. He was a desk jockey and looked it. But a successful desk jockey.

Now Wyatt turned and surveyed his own body, sucking in his gut—okay, just a little. He had wide shoulders, and all those years of hard labor at the park left him with the pects and abs to prove it. He was just a shade over six feet tall.

Callie'd always claimed his eyes were what made her start flirting with him at that bar back in Clemson, all those years ago. That and the dimples. His eyes were a mud color, he'd always thought, but he had his mother's eyelashes, thick, black, Bambi lashes, as she called them.

A lot of good they'd done him lately.

What the hell. He fetched the pants, got dressed, put on his grandfather's gold watch. For maybe the millionth time, he looked at the plain gold wedding band on the ring finger of his left hand. He'd taken it off dozens of times, put it back on again the same number of times. He couldn't say why. Callie had replaced her wedding rings with the flashy diamond "engagement" ring Luke had bought her. Was it technically possible to be engaged while you were still married? Maybe he'd remove his own ring once the divorce was final. He only knew it wasn't time. Yet. Probably this made him a double loser. He took a deep breath and picked up the truck keys from the dresser.

"You goin' to church?" Nelson asked. He'd moved to the recliner in front of the television and found the Braves game. He was dressed in an old T-shirt and a pair of faded pajama bottoms. *Geezus H.*, Wyatt thought. *Save me from ever wearing pajama bottoms.*

"Church? No. Remember, Dad? I told you. I've got to go to that divorce therapy session."

"Oh, right," Nelson said vaguely. "And Bo's at his mom's?"

"Yes," Wyatt said patiently. "Bo is with Callie tonight. "I'll pick him up Thursday. Remember?"

Every night he replayed this same scene. Nelson would ask where Bo was, and Wyatt would tell him. Most of the time, his father seemed perfectly with it, lucid, same old Nelson. But in the evenings, he got . . . vague. Wyatt told himself his father was fine. He was still physically fit, strong as an ox. He ran the concession stand in the park, took tickets, helped out with the never-ending landscaping and maintenance. But in the past year, Nelson had begun a slow, almost indefinable slide. Sometimes, he needed help with the bank deposits. He got aggravated if there was even the slightest deviation in his carefully mapped daily routine.

Wyatt worried. But hell, he worried about everything. Like now. He doubled back to the bedroom, hung up the dress pants and the plaid shirt. He rolled up the sleeves of the white dress shirt he'd worn to court and put on his nicest pair of shorts. And what he thought of as his dress shoes, a pair of leather flip-flops. At least he felt like some version of himself.

Paula Talbott-Sinclair greeted them all in the reception area. Her usually flyaway hair had been tamed and twisted into a sleek, artful chignon. She wore a long wispy yellow and green flowered dress with bell sleeves that made her look like a butterfly, bright coral lipstick, and her usual dozen or so bracelets. She wore gold gladiator-style sandals, and tonight she seemed lucid and bright-eyed. She was, Grace thought, a woman transformed. Which made Grace immediately suspicious.

"Hello, friends," she said, grasping the hand of each group member as they arrived at the office. She made a show of having them all sign in, inviting them to have coffee, asking them how their week had gone.

Grace was surprised when the first person she saw was Wyatt. He'd obviously taken pains with his appearance tonight. "Hey," she said, sidling over to him at the coffee machine. "You look nice tonight."

"No parrot poop, right?" He looked embarrassed. "You look nice, too. But unlike me, you always look good."

"You wouldn't say that if you'd seen me a couple hours ago," Grace assured him. But she was glad he'd noticed. On her last thrifting excursion, she'd found a pair of nearly new black DKNY capris at the Junior League for three dollars and a simple acid-green polished cotton wrap blouse, which set her back ninety-nine cents at the hospice shop. The blouse was sleeveless, and she thought it was flattering to the new tan she'd acquired from all that running. With the black ballet flats from Target and a wide gold bangle bracelet she'd borrowed from Rochelle, this was the nicest outfit she owned, and she'd spent less buying it than she had a tube of lipstick in her old life.

Wyatt nodded his head in Paula's direction. "Obviously, she found her way home last week."

"Look. She's even wearing shoes. Maybe she's got a hot date afterward," Grace murmured.

At the stroke of 7:00 P.M., Paula began herding them to their seats. "Please be seated," she said, clapping her hands. Paula looked around the room, taking a silent body count. Grace prayed she would overlook the oversized totebag she'd stowed under her folding chair.

"So," Paula began, her voice in a slightly higher-than-normal pitch. "We've completed two weeks of recovery therapy. At this stage of your process, I hope you're beginning to feel a little more comfortable in your own skin. We've talked a little bit about how you see yourselves, following the breakup of your marriage. And I'd like to continue that discussion this week, with having you share from your journals."

Paula's cell phone was in her lap, and while she spoke, her eyes continually watched it.

She gazed around the room. "Who haven't we heard from?"

Wyatt and Suzanne slumped down in their chairs, ducked their heads, hoping they wouldn't be noticed. It was painfully clear the therapist had no memory of what had transpired in their previous session.

"I don't think Suzanne has shared with us yet," Ashleigh volunteered.

"I'll just bet you were that kid in elementary school who always reminded the teacher she hadn't assigned homework, just before the bell rang," Camyrn said, giving Ashleigh the evil eye.

Suzanne's olive skin flushed.

"That's right," Paula said. "Thank you, Ashleigh. Suzanne?"

Grace felt a sharp pang of sympathy for Suzanne, hunched down in her chair, eyes glued to her journal. Her face was pale, with two bright spots of pink on her cheeks, but her face was beaded with a fine sheen of perspiration.

Suzanne was dressed in a dull, unflattering beige dress and scuffed brown leather sandals. It was as if she was wearing her own brand of camouflage, to blend into the surroundings.

"Uh, well," Suzanne stuttered and blinked rapidly. Grace noticed that the damp palms of her hands had begun to make the ink on Suzanne's journal run.

Suzanne's voice was low.

"Once, I was a wife," she began, reading in a stilted monotone.

"I was a lover, a mother, a teacher, a mentor. I had value, to others as well as myself. And then I discovered my husband's treachery. He was cheating on me, with one of my coworkers. I didn't confront him. I kept telling myself it might not be true. I became obsessed with checking on him, on her, confirming my worst suspicions. I figured out where they were having their trysts. I followed him. I checked into the same cheap motel room after they'd left, and I told myself I would take some pills and kill myself, in that same bed, and it would be the perfect, poetic justice. Just another Shakespearean tragedy. But I couldn't even do that. Even after I knew, I did nothing. I was paralyzed. He loved someone else. She was younger, prettier, cleverer, sexier. How could I compete with her? I was a failure, at everything, especially marriage. If I couldn't keep Eric, how could I be a success at my job? How could I be a good mother to my daughter Darby? So I have stopped trying, because if I don't try, I can't fail. Every day I shrink a little more. Soon I'll be invisible. Will anybody notice? Will Eric?"

Suzanne closed her notebook, but didn't look up.

"Oh, wow," Ashleigh breathed, breaking the silence. "You actually slept in the same motel room they'd just screwed in? That is all kinds of crazy."

"Ashleigh!" Camyrn's eyes blazed. "Will you please shut the *fuck* up?"

Paula didn't appear to have heard Ashleigh's comment. She was staring down at her cell phone, reading something on the screen.

Now, she looked up, realized the group was expecting some comment from their therapist.

"That was very powerful, Suzanne," she said, beaming, and then looking around at the others. "Any comments? Thoughts?"

Wyatt twisted his wedding band. "I've been there," he said, finally. "I couldn't put it in words like you just did, Suzanne. But yeah, every day, when I think about it, letting some other guy just take my wife, just stepping aside and letting her leave? What a loser I am. So who could blame her for leaving me for him?"

"You're not a loser," Grace said fiercely. "None of us are losers. Just because my husband didn't value me—all the things I am? That doesn't change who I am. But it changes who he is. Somebody who lies. Somebody who cheats." She sat up. "My ex came to see me today. And I finally saw him for what he is."

"Oooh, girl," Camryn said. "Was he begging you to take him back?"

"No." Grace thought about it for a moment. "He just wanted to grind his heel in my face. Punish me some more, make me feel like crap. Let me know he'll always have power over me."

Suddenly, Paula stood up. "Very nice, Wyatt and Grace. Excellent work, sharing with our friends. Let's take a little ten-minute break, and then we'll come back and, um, I have a surprise for all of you. Also? Who haven't we heard from yet?"

"Me," Wyatt said reluctantly.

The others shot out of the room like first graders at recess. All except Suzanne, who sat demurely in her chair, ankles crossed, hands in her lap.

Grace slid into the chair beside hers. "Suzanne? That was really wonderful, what you wrote. I think all of us saw something of ourselves in what you've gone through."

Suzanne brightened, just a little. "So, you don't think I'm the queen of crazy-pants?"

"You? Nah. That title belongs to Ashleigh," Grace said. Out of the corner of her eye, she saw a small pink nose pop out of the top of her tote bag. "Oh, Lord," she breathed. "I've gotta go outside for a minute. So—will you come to the Sandbox tonight, after? Just for a little while? At least so we can discuss what's up with Paula?"

Suzanne brightened. "So, it's not just me? There is definitely something weird about her. Weirder than usual tonight, because she's actually acting normal!

About the Sandbox, I'd come, but it's just such a long way there and then home again."

"If you like, you can leave your car here and ride over there with me," Grace offered. "I'm sure one of the others will give you a ride back afterward."

"Maybe," Suzanne said. "Let me think about it, okay?"

"Friends," Paula began, once their break was over, her face flushed with excitement. "I didn't want to announce this earlier, because, well, I wasn't sure it was going to happen. But I got a message just before our break, and it appears that we are going to have a guest joining us tonight. I, for one, am incredibly honored that he's taking time out from his very busy life to be with us." She glanced down at her watch and, then again, at her cell phone.

She took a deep breath. "I'm sure he'll be along shortly. In the meantime, I'd like us to think about options." She looked around the room. "From what you've told me, all of you feel you've been badly hurt by your spouses. Of course, since we don't have your partners here with us, I only have your version of events that led to your breakups."

Camryn snorted. "We're the ones got ordered to be here, Paula. If you want Dexter Nobles's version of what happened, feel free to drag his ass in here."

"Camryn?" Paula frowned at her. "Sharing time is over. Now. All of you have spoken of your feelings of powerlessness and inferiority. Now, I'd like you to explore what options you have, going forward with your lives."

A man cleared his throat. All heads swung in the direction of the reception-room door. "Er, hello?"

Paula jumped up from her chair and clapped her hands in glee. "Judge Stackpole! Your Honor, we're so glad you could be here!"

24

Judge Cedric N. Stackpole Jr. was dressed in his version of business casual and Grace's idea of what not to wear to divorce therapy. A black short-sleeved knit shirt with the top button fastened—although Grace saw the glimmer of a thick gold chain resting amidst a tuft of chest hair sticking out over the top button. Very shiny, very faux-distressed, very obviously brand-new jeans, belted and worn navel-high. Highly polished black slip-ons, no socks.

His thinning reddish hair was slicked back with some type of hair product that he'd obviously bought in bulk in the eighties.

He nodded curtly at the group, and cracked something similar to a smile at Paula.

"Hello, hello," he said briskly, his hands thrust awkwardly in his jeans pockets. "Uh, Dr. Talbott-Sinclair invited me to drop in tonight, just to see how everybody is doing. Er, uh, I hope you are all listening closely to her message. Because, uh, if more people like you all came to sessions with therapists like Dr. Talbott-Sinclair, there'd be lots less work for judges like me." He seemed to think this was a hysterically funny line. "Right?" he asked. "Judges might not have jobs. Right?"

Paula's laughter trilled up and down the musical scales. "That's right!" she said, clasping her hands. "Very intuitive, Your Honor."

Grace didn't dare cut her eyes sideways to the left to see Camryn's reaction to this. Instead, she pretended to study the journal on her lap. Through lowered eyelashes, she could see Wyatt, on her right, his arms folded across his chest, glaring directly at the judge, barely disguised hostility emanating from every pore.

"Well," Stackpole said, "please don't let me interrupt. I'll just sit here in the back of the room, and you all go on as though I weren't here."

Like that's gonna happen, Grace thought. She glanced nervously down at her tote bag, but for now it was very still.

Paula stood and faced the group. Her hair was neatly combed, and Grace noticed she'd reapplied her lipstick and powdered her nose during the break. And was the neckline of her dress tugged just a little lower? Showing just a hint of cleavage that hadn't been visible before?

"Most of you are here because in the heat of the moment or, perhaps, after some very deliberate but ill-thought-out reasoning, you decided to strike out— violently, publicly, even *criminally,* against your spouse. Probably, you reasoned, 'this person has hurt me, and my only option is to strike back.'" She nodded at Grace.

"Isn't that right, Grace?"

"No," Grace heard herself say. "That isn't what happened at all."

Paula gave her a patronizing smile. "We'll come back to that."

"What I'm trying to say," Paula went on, "is that whether you know it or not, you had options at the time you acted out, and you have options now. Do you stay, or do you leave? Forgive? Forget? Neither?"

"Huh." Wyatt shook his head. "That ship has sailed, Paula."

"Yeah," Camryn put in. "I already left, or rather, I kicked his butt out the door. You want me to forget? How do I erase the image of him in bed with my twenty-two-year-old daughter's best friend? I wish I could forget it," she said, throwing up her hands in surrender. "What's that drug they used to give women during childbirth? Scopolamine, yeah, the twilight drug. You feel the labor pains, but after, you have no memory of the pain. You tell me how to find the equivalent of Scopolamine for what he did to me and my family."

Grace's mind flashed again to the scene of Ben and J'Aimee in the darkened garage. She closed her eyes and willed the scene to disappear, the same way she had nearly every night since it had occurred.

"That's right," Suzanne murmured, pressing her fingertips to her forehead.

"I don't have any drugs to give you," Paula said, her face flushing. She was looking past Camryn and the others, directly at the back of the room, where Stackpole sat.

Grace heard a little gasp at this, but then, at almost the same time, she felt the tote bag at her feet move. She dropped her journal to the floor as a cover, reached in, and scratched the warm furry head there, felt a tiny pink tongue rasp against the palm of her hand. She stole a backward glance at the judge, who was staring down at his watch, pointedly tapping the crystal. She sat back up again.

"I can tell you, though," Paula said, her voice rising, "that until you spend time figuring out what went wrong with your marriage, until you stop blaming yourself, your partner, the other lover, you will never move past those scenes like the one Camryn describes. Even if your marriage is irretrievably, undeniably finished now, there was a time when you had hope. You had love. Whatever your version of love is. Next session, I want you to try really hard to get past your bitterness and write down one quality, perhaps one anecdote, that might explain what drew you to your partner. What about that person made you happy?"

"That's easy. It was the big ol' honkin' ring he gave me," Ashleigh whispered, with a giggle, fingering the bauble she wore around her neck.

Paula hadn't heard, as usual. "I'll see you all next week."

Grace looked at her watch. It was barely 7:30 P.M. Why was Paula suddenly in such a hurry to end the session? When she looked up again, she saw Stackpole speeding toward the door with the look of a man with a mission.

25

Sandbox?" Camryn murmured, as the group drifted out to the parking lot.

"I'm in," Ashleigh nodded vigorously. She turned to Suzanne. "You coming?"

"Well, I guess I could. I did tell my daughter I might be a little late," Suzanne said.

Grace looked at Wyatt. "How about you?"

He hesitated. Camryn tugged at his arm. "Oh, come on. You can't hold out forever."

"I thought this was a girls-only thing," he said. "No boys in the tree fort?"

Ashleigh gave him a wink. "For you, we'll lower the rope ladder. Right, ladies?"

A hastily scribbled RESERVED sign was taped to the booth in the corner. Rochelle hurried over to the table when Grace pushed through the front door. "They're coming tonight, right?"

"Yeesss," Grace found herself slightly annoyed at her mother's eagerness, but she couldn't say why. While Rochelle returned to her post behind the bar, she slipped outside with the tote bag, and when she returned five minutes later, the rest of the group were arranged around the table, each with a drink in front of them. She slid into the booth beside Wyatt, who was sipping a beer.

"What was going on with Paula tonight?" Ashleigh asked.

"Here you go," Rochelle said, as she placed a glass of white wine in front of Grace and a big basket of freshly made popcorn in the center of the table. She plunked herself down beside Camryn at the opposite end of the booth.

"Why?" Rochelle wanted to know. "What was Paula doing?"

"She was, like, sober," Ashleigh said. "All dressed up. With shoes and everything. She actually kind of looked like what I pictured a professional therapist would look like. It was kind of crazy."

"Mm-hmm. Mama was definitely on some new meds tonight," Camryn agreed. "There were a couple times tonight she managed to almost sound coherent. Not that I agree with any of that forgiveness crap she was selling," she added hastily.

"I couldn't get over how changed she was. And when Judge Stackpole came in, I was really struck by the transformation," Suzanne said. "It was like she was hoping for his approval. Dying for it."

"The judge showed up?" Rochelle asked, her eyes widening.

"Asshole," Wyatt muttered, staring down at his beer.

All the women turned to look at him at once. "Can't help it," he said defensively. "He's gonna ruin my son's life, letting Callie drag him off to Birmingham. How often will I be able to get to Birmingham to see him? Every other month? Probably not even that. Even if I could forgive her, I'll never forgive him, if I lose my kid."

Ashleigh waved the straw from her half-empty margarita glass in the air. "I think Paula's got a big ol' school-girl crush on Stackhole."

"Stackhole, that's good!" Rochelle said. "What do you think, Grace?"

Grace had been surreptitiously slipping a handful of popcorn in the direction of the tote bag, which was between her feet. She was distracted by the soft snuffing sounds and hoped the din of the bar would drown them out.

"Well...I agree, Paula was definitely on her best behavior tonight. And I did wonder about Stackpole's appearance. Why was he there? Paula told us she reports to him on our progress. Doesn't he have anything better to do than sit in on our sad little sessions?" She turned to Suzanne. "Do you think maybe there's something going on between them?"

"Maybe," Suzanne said, her voice tentative.

"Eeew," Ashleigh said, wrinkling her nose. "Paula and that... old man? And isn't he married or something?"

"He's not all that old. My lawyer, Mitzi, was in law school with him. When he was appointed to the bench, he was the youngest judge in Florida. But, yes, he's definitely married," Grace said. "During our hearing he made a point of telling my lawyer that his own wife has no problems running his household with two thousand dollars a month."

"Which pays for what?" Rochelle asked. "I'll bet he doesn't expect her to pay a mortgage or utilities or insurance for that."

While they batted ideas around, Camryn was busily typing away on her iPhone. "I've got the Florida judiciary Web site here," she announced, thumbing down the page. "Gimme a minute. Okay, here it is. Cedric Norris Stackpole, age fifty-one. B.A., University of Florida, 1980. J.D., University of Florida, 1983. Appointed to the bar, 2000." She looked up. "Wow, a judge at forty. That's impressive, even if he isn't." She scrolled a little more. "Married, 1999, to the former Eileen Bolther of Kissimmee."

"Bolther? Why is that name familiar?" Suzanne asked.

"If she's a Bolther and she's from Kissimmee, she must be related to Sawyer Bolther. As in Bolther Groves and Bolther Beef. Two of the biggest cattle and citrus growers in Florida. Not to mention Bolther Bank and Trust," Camryn said.

"How do you know all this stuff?" Ashleigh asked.

"I'm a reporter. I don't know it off the top of my head, but I get paid to know how to find it out," Camryn said. "I covered the last three governor's races, and, as I recall, Sawyer Bolther was one of the biggest campaign contributors to that last joker we elected. So that gives you an idea how ol' Cedric got named a judge at the ripe old age of forty. His wife's family is politically connected."

"What about Paula?" Suzanne asked. "I'm a little curious about her, I have to admit. She's such an enigma. After those first two sessions, I'd written her off as a total fraud, or at least a deeply troubled person with some kind of substance-abuse issues. But tonight?" She looked around the table for consensus. "She actually said a couple things that I thought made sense."

"Like what?" Wyatt asked. "I mean, I'm not disagreeing."

"I can't quote her directly," Suzanne said, flustered. "It was something about taking the time to figure out what went wrong with our marriages, putting blame aside, and just, you know, taking a look at what the problems really were."

"Wasn't the fact that everybody's husband or wife cheated on them the big, overriding problem?" Rochelle asked.

"A problem? Or maybe a symptom?"

All heads turned toward Grace. She shrugged. "I don't know anything. I probably know the least about marriage of anybody here. I thought my marriage was just peachy, until it all went up in flames. I'm not saying I want Ben back. If I ever did before, the things he's done since I left have opened my eyes to the kind of person he is. I keep wondering how I didn't see the real him."

"Sometimes, maybe we do see the real person, but we convince ourselves that we can live with him, or somehow change him, just by loving him enough," Rochelle said.

Grace stared. Where had this come from? And why did Rochelle keep hanging around?

"Dexter changed, once he had a taste of success, once he got into politics," Camryn said. "In college, when he was at Morehouse, and I was at Spelman, he wrote poetry! Yes, he did. He was this shy, skinny, geeky mama's boy. Not anybody I ever would have taken a second look at. But one of my sorority sisters was dating his roommate, and she begged me to go out with him, as a favor so the two of them could get some privacy on a Friday night. I asked him to a mixer, and it turned out the guy could dance. I mean, dance! Later on, he admitted he'd been watching Michael Jackson videos for years, learning his moves. I thought that was so sweet. You know? That's the Dexter I fell in love with. He had ideals. He wanted to change the world."

Camryn sipped her drink. "I don't know him now. Obviously."

"Would any of you take your husbands—or wives—back, if they wanted to come back?" Ashleigh asked.

The table got very quiet. "I'd take Boyce back," Ashleigh volunteered. "But, I mean, there'd have to be some changes. For one thing, I'd go back to managing his practice. Some men you just have to keep on a short leash. I know he doesn't love that tramp he's seeing. She's not even his type! I've learned my lesson, I'll tell you that." She grinned mischieviously and leaned forward. "I'll tell you something else, too. When he comes back—I'll be a lot more adventurous. In the bedroom, you know? Keep him guessing."

Grace felt herself blushing. She'd just met these people. There was no way she'd ever talk about her and Ben's love life—especially with her mother sitting right there!

Ashleigh pointed at Camryn. "How about you? If Dexter wanted you back—would you do it?"

"Oh, hell to the no," Camryn said. "How could I respect myself if I took him back? I know what a sleaze he is. Jana's sad about us breaking up, but I want her to know, as a black woman, she needs to have some standards. I don't want her settling for second-rate, or thinking it's okay for some brother to cheat on her and degrade her. Besides? He's been dipping his pen in a lot of ink. And I know Dexter. I know he wasn't wearing a condom for any of those close encounters. Who knows what kind of diseases he might be carrying around?" She shuddered. "We hadn't been sleeping together for months anyway, but just to be sure I got myself tested as soon as I saw that little DVD of his. Somehow, I got lucky. Everything tested negative."

"How about you, Wyatt?" Camryn asked pointedly. "You've been pretty quiet all these sessions."

"Yeah," Ashleigh agreed. "I'd just *looove* to know how it feels when the shoe is on the other foot."

Wyatt's face colored. "You don't think women cheat on their husbands? Look, it's different with me."

"Because you've got a penis? And choices?" Camryn asked.

"Because I've got a six-year-old son to raise," Wyatt half stood, obviously roused. "I've got to put my kid first, and myself second."

"What if you didn't have a kid? Or what if she broke up with the other guy?" Ashleigh persisted.

Wyatt glared at her. "Can we just drop it?"

"No, we can't," Camryn snapped. "Can you quit being macho man long enough to answer an honest question?"

He eased back into his chair, some of the fight gone out of him. With his thumb, he twisted his wedding band around and around. "You read all these statistics about the children of divorce. They don't do as well in school, have emotional problems. I don't want that for Bo."

"Listen, Wyatt," Rochelle said, reaching down the length of the table and grabbing his hand. "Shrinks can come up with all kinds of statistics to make people feel guilty. What kind of home will you be raising Bo in if he knows you and Callie hate each other? Kids aren't dumb. They can sense things. And what happens if you take her back and she decides to go off with some other guy?"

Wyatt's face contorted and Grace wished she could kick her mother under the table. Instead, she spirited some more popcorn into her tote bag.

"Suzanne?" Now Rochelle was concentrating on the least forthcoming member of the group.

"What about you? Would you take your husband back?"

Suzanne seemed to shrink into her chair. "Our situation . . . is unique," Suzanne said. "I'm sorry. You've all been so open and honest. I feel like a voyeur, sitting here, contributing nothing. I'm still . . . still trying to sort out my feelings." She took a deep breath and started again.

"Let me try to explain. I come from a very religious Catholic family. My father dragged us to Mass every Sunday. My mother was very pious. From the outside, we looked like the ideal family. Inside?" She shrugged. "He cheated on her. Always. Made her life miserable. She'd never worked outside the home, what was she going to do? Leave him? Besides, we Catholics don't divorce, right? So she stayed, a martyr to the end. Why did she put up with his crap? My two sisters and I swore a pact that we would never, ever fall into the same trap she did.

"Damned if we didn't. Tricia's husband is a closet drinker. Eileen? We think he abuses her, but we don't have any proof, and even if we did, she has kidney disease, and she needs his medical benefits. And me? Eric and I lived together off and on for eight years. When I was thirty, and still working on my Ph.D., I got pregnant with Darby." Suzanne's small, sad face suddenly lit up. "It was a huge surprise. I'd had ovarian cysts in my twenties, and my doctor told me I probably wouldn't have children."

Suzanne took several deep breaths, sucking in more oxygen to fuel her narrative. The others waited, willing her to continue. "Even then, I waited until Darby was two, just to be absolutely sure, before I agreed to marry Eric. I thought we had something good, you know? Not perfect, but a much better marriage than my parents'."

"You poor thing," Rochelle said. She stood quickly. "Don't say another word, okay? I need to see if everything's all right in the kitchen. Can I get anything for anybody?"

Ashleigh raised her nearly empty margarita glass. "I could use a freshie."

Grace could feel her jaw tightening. Did she dare suggest that Rochelle stick to bartending instead of marriage counseling? Probably not.

"Listen, Suzanne," Grace said gently, "don't feel like you have to talk, if you don't feel like it. We all understand."

"No!" Suzanne said, taking a gulp of her tea. "I think this is probably good for me. I've never discussed my family's . . . marriage issues, to anybody. Ever. Not even with my best friend. Not even with my sisters. So thanks, for listening. And not judging."

"Oh, you are just so welcome," Ashleigh said, looking around the table for consensus. "Isn't this awesome? I mean, I feel soooo much better, hearing what you guys have been through. If I didn't hate the whole idea of paying three hundred dollars an hour to Paula, I would think just being with you all was totally worth it."

Camryn had her chin propped on her hands. "Yeah. I can't believe Stackpole is making us pay Paula that much money for the privilege of watching her fall asleep and drool on herself once a week." She grimaced. "Speaking of sleep, I've got to be at the studio at six, to tape an interview with some exercise diva, and if I don't want to have king-sized bags under my eyes, I better get out of here right now." She stood, pulled money from her billfold, and placed it on the tabletop.

"Grace, tell Rochelle I said 'bye. See y'all next week!"

Ashleigh yawned widely. "I can't believe it's not even ten o'clock and I'm this sleepy. Guess I need to take off, too." She stood up and slapped her backside. "My new trainer is making me do this really intensive booty camp, starting tomorrow." She added some bills to the pile on the table. "I'll just run by and tell Rochelle never mind on the drink," she added. "I probably don't need the calories anyway."

"I hate to ask," Suzanne said, turning to Grace. "But is it too much trouble for somebody to give me a ride back to Paula's office?"

"I'd be happy to take you, but the front seat of the pickup is loaded with sacks of bird feed and crap for the park," Wyatt said apologetically. "Didn't want the chance of it getting rained on."

"I can take you," Grace said. She was painfully aware that that the tote bag at her feet was starting to wriggle, and every once in a while a small brown muzzle would pop out. "Be back in a minute."

By the time she got back to the table, Suzanne and Rochelle were deep in conversation. Wyatt was standing, looking around, unsure of his next move.

"If you're going to take Suzanne back to Paula's office, why don't you let me ride with you?" He was trying to sound casual, cool even. "It's not that great a neighborhood."

26

There were now a dozen cars in the shopping center parking lot. The lights were on in the tattoo parlor, heavy metal music blaring from within, and a trio of imposing black Harleys were parked on the sidewalk in front of it. Suzanne leaned over the front seat console. "Here's my car." She pointed to a silver Prius. "Thanks again, Grace. Wyatt. See you next week."

Grace pulled alongside Suzanne's car and waited until she'd started the car and eased out of her parking spot.

"Hey, look." Wyatt pointed at the very end of the parking, where a black Lexus had just pulled into the space nearest the end. As they watched, Paula emerged from the passenger's side of the sedan. She slammed the car door, and then, while they watched, she kicked the tires. Next, she ran around to the driver's side. She was screaming something, slapping at the car windows, pounding, but the driver never cut the engine, instead throwing the car into reverse. Its tires screeched and skidded as the driver slammed it into drive and sped out of the parking lot, turning left onto Manatee Avenue.

Paula stood, hands on hips, watching it go. Then, she walked back, unlocked her office door, and disappeared.

"Oh my God," Grace said. "Do you think that's Stackpole in the black car? Looks like they were having a knock-down, drag-out fight, huh?"

"Only one way to find out," Wyatt said, leaning forward to keep his eyes on the car.

"I'm on it," Grace said, pulling out of the shopping center. Traffic was light that time of night, and she could see the Lexus's red taillights only half a block ahead of them.

"Good of him to be such a safe driver," Grace said.

"If it's Stackpole, the last thing he wants is to get pulled over by a cop," Wyatt pointed out.

Grace followed the Lexus west on Manatee, for five blocks. It stopped at the light at West 75th and put on its blinker to turn left. Grace pulled behind the Lexus and did the same. "You think this is really a good idea? Following Stackpole—or whoever is in that car?"

"We're just two people out for a drive. No big deal. You're not speeding and you didn't even drink all your wine, right?"

"That's right."

"And I had a beer, over the course of two hours," he said. He glanced toward the backseat. "How's the dog?"

She grinned sheepishly. "How'd you know?"

Instead of answering, he reached around and pulled the wriggling dog out of the bag, setting her carefully on his lap.

"She popped her head out of there a couple times, back at group," Wyatt said. "It was all I could do to keep a straight face. Every time she heard your voice, the whole bag would move—she was wagging her tail so hard." The dog stretched its neck and rewarded Wyatt by licking his chin.

He held it at arm's length, checking its undercarriage. "Hello, little girl," Wyatt said, rubbing the top of the dog's head, then scratching its belly. "What's your name?"

"Meet Sweetie," Grace said. "The new kid on the block."

Sweetie put her front paws on the passenger window, straining to see out the window.

"Where'd you get her?" Wyatt asked.

"Sweetie has kind of a sad story." While she recounted the tale of the dog's rescue, her adoptee climbed over the console, wriggling its way under Grace's arms. "But she's feeling better now. The vet fixed her up, gave her some IV meds, kept her overnight."

"And you got yourself a dog," Wyatt said. "What's Rochelle think about that?"

"She doesn't know," Grace admitted. "My mom is not really what you'd call a pet person. You can't really blame her, I mean, we live above a bar. So I'm guessing I'll try to keep her a secret, until I figure something out."

"Do you think you'll be getting your own place pretty soon?"

"I hope so," she said fervently. "I'm too old to be moving back in with the folks. You've seen what Rochelle's like. I love her, but she's . . . got an opinion about everything. If my asshole husband will start making the payments the judge has ordered him to make, and if I can get my blog up and generating income, I hope I can move out, sooner rather than later."

"What are you going to do with Sweetie until then?" Wyatt asked. "You can't keep hiding her in a purse."

"I know. She does seem pretty laid back. She's house-trained, so that's a big plus. The vet said she was amazingly calm while they treated her, and she's been so good all night tonight, not making a peep, just sleeping in my tote bag."

Grace scratched the dog's ears affectionately. "She's really a very chill little girl. My plan is to keep her in my room with me at night and sneak her down the back steps first thing in the morning, for a potty break."

"What about during the days?"

"That house where I found Sweetie? It's on Anna Maria. I was out for a run and spotted this cool old rattan sofa in a pile of junk on the curb. I struck up a conversation with the landlord, this old guy named Arthur, who, it turns out, used to be kind of fishing buddies with my dad. He invited me in to see the house. It's a wreck right now, but it's got wonderful potential, and it's in a great location—a block from the bay. I'm going to be working on it, fixing it up, redecorating it for Arthur, getting it ready to rent again. I'll be photographing and writing about it for my blog. Sweetie can stay there with me during the day while I work on it. In fact, I'm thinking I'll write her into the story, too. It was her house, after all."

"Look, he's turning up ahead," Wyatt said, pointing at the Lexus. "He's headed back out to the beach. I bet he lives out there."

"Not at Cortez, for sure," Grace said. "We're not fancy enough. I bet he lives at Longboat Key."

"You're probably right." Wyatt said.

Grace stayed back a few car lengths but made the same turn. She kept on Cortez Drive, passing the turnoff for the Sandbox in the fishing village, crossing the bridge over the Intracoastal Waterway and into Bradenton Beach. At the light at Gulf Drive, the Lexus signaled to make a left turn.

"Well, he's definitely not going to Anna Maria," she said, following as the black car turned south.

The moon was nearly full, and as they followed the road paralleling the ocean, they could catch occasional glimpses of silvery water through the thick fringe of Australian pines and sea grapes lining the road in the intermittent patches of undeveloped land.

Grace smiled, as she always did when passing the sign for Coquina Beach. "That was our beach, growing up," she said. "How about you, which beach did your family go to?"

"Holmes Beach, mostly," Wyatt said. "Once I could drive, though, I was too cool for school. A bunch of us used to hang out at Siesta Key, where the rich girls were—or so we thought."

As they drove, the landscape changed from sparsely developed to the manicured civility of Longboat Key. High-rise condo complexes hugged the shores of the gulf on the right and the bay on the left, and imposing stucco homes painted in sherbet hues were set back behind hedges and gates. Grace slowed when she saw the Lexus's brake lights and then turn signal.

She waited until it made the left turn into a sprawling development called Lido Bay. "Should I keep following him, you think?" She glanced over at Wyatt. "If it's Stackpole, I really don't want him to notice us."

"Up to you," Wyatt said. "I don't want to get us in trouble either, but I'd like to know if it really is Stackpole."

He looked out the window at the homes lining the neatly landscaped street. All the homes were done in a similar hybrid Tuscan/Spanish-mission style, with stucco walls painted in pinks, peach, apricot, and buff, with red barrel-tile roofs. "Nice real estate," Wyatt said. "Wonder what these homes sell for?"

"Hmm, four or five years ago they were probably selling for seven hundred to eight hundred thousand dollars," Grace said. "The ones on canals or directly on the bay used to go for over a million. Now? You could probably move in here to a perfectly lovely home for under three hundred thousand."

"If I had three hundred thousand, I wouldn't want to live here," Wyatt said. "Too cookie cutter for my taste. Huge houses all jammed in here together on these little-bitty lots. Anyway, that's never gonna happen."

The Lexus made a wide left turn, and, as Grace started to follow, its brake lights went on. "Better slow down," Wyatt said. "Maybe turn off your lights. We don't want him to see us."

Grace pulled to the curb four houses down from the driveway where the Lexus turned in and, as suggested, cut her headlights.

"Come on, Cedric," Wyatt quietly urged. "Get out of the car and let us see your pretty face."

"Damn!"

As they watched, the garage door slowly, soundlessly rolled up, and the Lexus pulled in, with the garage door rolling down right behind it.

Grace burst out laughing, and after a moment Wyatt laughed, too. "Well, that was certainly anticlimatic," she said, turning around and driving out of the subdivision.

He was still sizing up the real estate. "Even with the real estate market in the toilet, that subdivision was pretty high cotton," he mused. "Wonder what kind of money a judge makes in Florida?"

"Don't know," Grace said. "But remember, Camryn said his wife's family is loaded. So maybe it's her money. Or maybe he does well in the stock market. Or he's cornered the market for black-market Oxycodone."

He gave her a startled look.

"Just kidding," she said. "Remember, we don't even know if that really was Stackpole. It could be anybody. It could even be Paula's husband, if she has one."

"Don't think so," Wyatt said. "Remember, we checked her driver's license. Paula lives on Anna Maria. Not Longboat."

"I'd love to know what that fight was about," Grace said, after a moment. "Paula seemed so different tonight, and then, wham, something really upset her apple cart."

She reached down and scratched Sweetie's silky brown ears. The dog hopped across the console to Wyatt's lap and scratched at his door, whining.

"Uh-oh," Grace said. "I think somebody needs a pit stop."

"Why don't you pull over up here at Coquina Beach," he suggested. "It's a nice night, and I haven't been to the beach since all this crap started with Callie. We can take her for a walk, if you want."

She raised an eyebrow. "You know dogs aren't allowed on the beach, right?"

"I won't tell if you won't," he said. "Besides, Sweetie's been such a good girl, she deserves a little treat, right Sweetie?"

The dog's tail beat a tattoo on the window.

"I swear she knows her name already," Grace said.

She parked the car beneath one of the towering Australian pines and clipped a leash to Sweetie's new pink collar, extracting a plastic bag from her tote bag.

Grace slipped off her shoes and Wyatt did the same with his flip-flops, and they left them, side by side, in the soft white sand at the parking-lot edge. After Sweetie had taken care of business and Grace had disposed of the plastic bag, they took the boardwalk over the dunes, past gently waving fronds of sea oats.

The tide was out, and the moon bathed the beach with a silvered pearlescent sheen. The ocean surface was as calm as a puddle after a summer storm, lapping gently at the edge of the shore. Only the faint breeze rippled the water.

Sweetie paused and looked startled when her feet first touched the damp sand, then sat on her rump and gave Grace a quizzical look.

"Come on, girl," Grace said, tugging gently at the leash. "Let's walk."

"I'll bet she's never been to the beach before," Wyatt said.

Grace tugged again, and finally the little dog stood and began trotting toward the water. She got all the way to the surf line, stopped, and looked back at her mistress.

"It's okay," Grace coaxed. "You can get your feet wet. Give it a try."

To demonstrate, Grace waded in, letting the warm ocean water lap against her ankles. "It's like bathwater," she told Wyatt, who followed her in.

The dog edged in and immediately scampered back onto the dryer sand, barking as the wavelets edged toward her.

"Okay," Grace agreed. "You walk on the sand; we'll walk in the water."

"Can I take her?" Wyatt asked. Grace handed over the leash.

"Come on Sweetie," Wyatt called, veering onto the beach. "Let's run!"

He broke into a trot, and the dog obediently followed behind. After less than a hundred yards, though, Sweetie ran toward the shell line, where mounds of crushed seashells and seaweed marked the high-tide line.

Sweetie sat, barked, and began nosing in the shells, digging frantically and occasionally stopping to give an excited yip.

"What's she doing?" Grace asked, when she caught up to the pair.

"She smells something" Wyatt said. "I think she must have some terrier in her, the way she's going after it."

Suddenly, the little dog yelped. She backed away slightly and gave a menacing growl, barked again, crouched, and growled again.

"It's a ghost crab," Grace laughed, as the pale creature scuttled away. She bent down and picked up the dog. "Stay away from crabs, Sweetie. Crabs are not your friend!"

They walked down the beach in companionable silence, with Sweetie meandering along, sniffing the air and occasionally stopping to growl at imagined threats to her security. After half a mile or so, by unspoken agreement, they turned and walked back toward where the car was parked.

A concrete picnic bench was perched under the shadows of one of the big old pines. "Let's sit for a little bit," Grace suggested. She sat on the tabletop and placed Sweetie in her lap. Wyatt sat beside her.

"We used to come out here and go 'parking' in high school," she said, with a sigh. "Seems like a long time ago."

"When I was in high school, we liked someplace a little more secluded," Wyatt said. "There was this dead-end street over on Holmes Beach. You could pull your car way up under the trees, and it was on a little bit of a rise, with a perfect view of the water. Although"—he laughed ruefully—"I don't remember being that interested in actually looking at the water back then. I was a horny little bastard, back in the day."

"And now?" Grace turned to look at him, her gray eyes teasing.

He hesitated, but stood abruptly, brushing sand from the seat of his pants. "I don't remember."

She felt her face aflame with embarrassment, jumping to her feet and startling the dog, who yipped her reaction. "We should probably go."

"Look. I'm not divorced yet. You're not divorced yet. I'm pretty sure this is against every divorce-recovery-group rule Paula ever thought of."

"This?"

He sighed. "You know. Us getting together. Gotta be against the rules."

Something inside her rebelled. Against rules, and best intentions and common sense. That mischievous smile of hers was back. "I won't tell if you won't." She tilted her face up, waiting to be kissed.

And then . . . he coughed politely. She opened her eyes and saw that he was putting on his shoes.

. . .

Ever since they'd pulled over to the Coquina Beach parking area, Grace had been anticipating this moment. Wondering what she would do if Wyatt tried to kiss her. Or even touch her.

Okay, maybe she'd been wondering all of the above since the minute he'd walked into Paula's office earlier in the evening. Not that he hadn't been kinda hot the other times, unshowered, dressed in his Jungle Jerry's safari work clothes. She didn't usually go for all that down-and-dirty muscley, manly type, but somehow, on Wyatt, it worked. Then, tonight, he'd obviously made an effort to look good. Was it for her? And had he noticed that she'd dressed up tonight, too? She hadn't anticipated how crazy all of this was making her feel.

It had never occurred to her that they would come this close—and he would so totally and completely shut her down. Dammit, she was no good at flirting after all this time.

But maybe Wyatt didn't know that.

Grace cursed all that stinking moonlight. She gathered her keys, her shoes, and her dog and stomped off toward the car.

"Jesus!" Wyatt's voice was hoarse. He grabbed her arm as she was unlocking the car. "Don't think I don't want this, Grace. I do. More than I can tell you, I want it. But where do we go from here? It makes no sense."

She spun around to face him. "I don't care. I don't want to make sense. I just want to be held, and be kissed." She raised her eyes. "By you. Does that make me a criminal? Or some kind of a slut?"

"No! Of course not. Don't call yourself that."

She felt her jaw clench. "That's how you're making me feel."

She placed Sweetie on the backseat, brushed the sand from her feet, and sat in the driver's seat, with the engine running. A moment later, he got into the car.

"Grace?"

She didn't answer, just pulled the car out of the lot and onto the beach road, keeping her eyes straight ahead. Sensing the tension in the air, Sweetie whined from the backseat, but Grace kept her back stiff.

"Look," he said, running his hand over his gleaming head. "I'm playing way out of my league here. You know?"

"No, I don't know."

He closed his hand over her shoulder, but she wrenched it away. He tried again. "You are incredibly beautiful, smart, and sane, and nice."

"Sane?" She raised one eyebrow. "Nice? What kind of left-handed compliment is that?"

"I don't know!" he shouted. "I don't know anything. I haven't been with another woman in eight years. Okay? I have no idea what I am saying or doing tonight. My instincts say go for it, but I'm afraid, all right? What happens if you and I . . . start something? Where does it go?" You say you'd never take your husband back, but maybe you'll change your mind. How do I know?"

"How do I know you won't take Callie back?" she retorted. "Right now? I just don't care. I really don't. I'm tired of worrying about what might happen. I've got no control over anything: your marriage, what's left of my marriage, that asshole judge, my career. From now on, I'm going to do just what everybody else in this world does. I'm going to do what feels good. And the *hell* with the what-ifs."

"I don't have that luxury," he said quietly.

27

It was the most erotic sensation she could ever remember having. She was having smoking-hot, crazy sex—under a Hawaiian waterfall of all places. Or she guessed it was a Hawaiian waterfall, from the profusion of flowering orchids and waving palms surrounding them. She couldn't see her lover's face, but my God, his body was sleek and hard and muscled and tan all over, and he had magic hands that did the most amazing things, and it seemed to go on forever and ever, until he had her body humming like a concert violin. And then, just as she was about to climax, a gigantic parrot swooped in and landed on his shoulder. "Gimme shots, gimme beer," the parrot called. Her lover turned his head. It was the honorable Cedric N. Stackpole Jr.

The horror made Grace sit straight up in bed so abruptly that Sweetie, who'd been nuzzled on the pillow next to hers, yelped.

"Shhh!" Grace bundled the dog into her arms and hugged her close. "It was just a dream, Sweetie. No, not a dream, a terrible, terrible nightmare." She shuddered at the memory of it. Looked over at the nightstand to realize it was five in the morning. "Stupid men," she said, pounding the bed with her fist. "Stupid, stupid men!"

Sweetie hopped off the bed and made a beeline for the bedroom door. "Okay," Grace said wearily. "Let me put some shoes on."

. . .

The only good thing about waking up early from a nightmare was getting to work early, Grace decided. It was still dark outside when she unlocked the door of the house on Mandevilla and switched on the lights.

Dark outside, but sweltering inside. She set Sweetie down on the floor, then ran from room to room opening all the windows she'd closed the previous day. She sniffed the air. The house reeked of Pine-Sol, in a good way, but there were still strong undernotes of mildew and pet smells, not to mention more dead bugs.

It took two more trips to retrieve the rest of the day's supplies, which included a pair of old box fans she'd found in the shed back at the bar. She set one fan in the window of the living room and another in the back bedroom where Sweetie had been imprisoned and switched them both to the HIGH setting.

The little dog apparently hadn't been totally traumatized by her time living in the house. She trotted from room to room, her nails clicking on the wooden floors, and had a high old time in the kitchen, barking and growling at a cockroach in the death throes.

Her plan for the day had been to carefully assess the house and work out a list of priorities and a timetable. But her mood, following the previous evening's disastrous encounter with Wyatt, and the revolting sex dream that had followed, left her in no mood for assessments.

"Right," she said briskly. She wheeled in the huge plastic trash can she'd borrowed from the shed, lined it with a black contractor's bag, snapped on her rubber gloves, and began emptying the kitchen cabinets of their contents.

She'd considered trying to salvage the pots and pans and dishes left behind, but one glance at their cracked and battered status convinced her to discard them, too. When the house was done, she'd bully Arthur into letting her buy new cookware.

With the cabinets empty, Grace took another look. In a perfect world, she'd rip out all the upper and lower cupboards and fit the kitchen with inexpensive Ikea cabinets, ones with Shaker-style door panels, with matching drawers. She'd outfitted their little rental house in Bradenton with the exact same ones, spending less than seven thousand dollars for everything, including hardware and countertops. She didn't have that kind of budget here.

Instead, she got out her cordless electric screwdriver and removed all the upper-cabinet doors, setting them aside, just in case she found another use for them down the line. The kitchen immediately looked better.

The gray aluminum-edged Formica countertops were funky but age-appropriate for the house, and the deep porcelain-over-cast-iron sink was filthy, but she knew a good cleaning with Bar Keepers Friend would make it shine again.

Grace gazed out the kitchen window and saw the first orange streaks of daylight at the edge of the overgrown yard.

On an impulse, she clipped a leash to Sweetie's collar and walked out the kitchen door, drawn to the glorious glow. They walked the block to a sandy lot that overlooked the bay, and the two of them stood there, basking in a Technicolor Florida sunrise. Whoever ended up renting the little house on Mandevilla would have the privilege of watching that same sunrise whenever they liked. Maybe she would have to make it a habit to get over here every morning in time to do the same thing. It wasn't a bad way to start the day.

She turned to go back to the house, resolving to start ripping up that revolting vinyl kitchen floor. It would feel good to jab something inanimate with a knife, a pry-bar, a chisel, or anything sharp she could put her hands on.

For months now, Wyatt had been meaning to take down the sprawling thirty-foot-tall Brazilian pepper tree that had taken over the area near his grandmother's old orchid slat-house. As he set out on his golf cart with his weapons of battle—chain saw, ax, and ladder—he grimly decided that today, Wednesday, was as good a day as any.

The Florida Department of Agriculture had placed the Brazilian pepper, a nonnative invasive "shrub," on its hit list of noxious plants. It was definitely a pushy interloper—with its massive crown of branches, it shaded out anything else in its path, and it grew so rapidly he hadn't noticed it had sprung up and taken over the old orchid-house area.

Though it was a typical summer day, with temperatures promising to rise to the nineties, he knew enough about the Brazilian pepper's near-poisonous sap to take precautions, outfitting himself in long pants, a long-sleeved shirt, work gloves, and blue bandanna on his head. He set up the ladder next to the trunk, fastened a rope to the chain-saw handle, and began climbing into the canopy. When he'd gone as high as he could, he steadied himself against the main trunk, hauled the chain saw up from below, and fired it up.

The roar and the whine of the saw as it chewed its way through the brittle wood made a huge din, and the gas fumes filled his nostrils.

For two hours, Wyatt hacked away at the tree, dropping the limbs to the ground, steadily moving downward as he decimated the upper canopy.

Twenty feet aboveground, with a buzzing chain saw in hand, he was focused only on the tree, the chain saw, and avoiding falling out of the tree.

By noon, his clothes were sweat-soaked, his face was itchy from the pepper-tree fumes, and the tree itself was looking like a grotesque, defoliated skeleton. He considered going back to the house to shower, change clothes, and grab lunch but went back to work instead. The pepper tree, like Callie and Luke and their lawyer and Judge Stackpole, was his nemesis. And this one he intended to cut right down to the ground.

"Jesus, son!" Nelson recoiled at the sight of Wyatt when he came tramping into the house. "What the hell did you do to yourself?"

"To me? Nothing. It took me all day, but I cut down the pepper tree, sprayed the stump with the legal equivalent of napalm, then raked up every limb, leaf, and seedpod I could find and hauled it all off to the dump."

Wyatt collapsed onto one of the wooden kitchen chairs. "I'm whipped. What's for dinner?"

"Beanie-weenies, Tater Tots, cornbread, coleslaw. Doesn't your face hurt?"

Wyatt stripped off his gloves and put a finger to his cheek, which, come to think of it, did feel kind of hot and swollen to the touch. The backs of his hands were covered in a nasty red rash, too.

"Guess I better hit the shower," he said. "I might be having a slight reaction to the pepper-tree sap."

"If that's slight, I don't want to know severe," Nelson said.

The face of a monster stared back at Wyatt in the bathroom mirror. His entire face was mottled red and swollen, his nose a puffy red blob, his eyes rimmed in pink. Dime-sized welts ran down his neck and to the V of where his shirt collar had been open.

When he took off his shirt he saw that his chest was also streaked with angry crimson slashes. He unzipped his pants and stepped out of them, as well as his boxers, and looked down.

Holy shit! His crotch was covered in blisters. *Everything* was red and inflamed—and not in a good way. He turned on the shower full force and jumped in, letting the cool water sluice over his head and chest. He grabbed a bar of soap, lathered up, but the first touch of the soap to his chest felt like a splash of acid.

Wyatt dropped the soap and looked down again. Not good. How the hell had this happened? He'd been so careful, with the long pants and shirt, high socks, work boots, gloves. And then he remembered and would have smacked himself in the face if that face hadn't felt like an open wound just then.

He'd had to pee. And who could unzip and do all the rest wearing work gloves? He must have gotten some of the sap on his hands, and then, well, his boys. Which were now itching like a son of a bitch.

He tried to think back to a college class he'd taken on noxious plants. They'd studied poison ivy, oak, sumac, and a few others, and, of course, over the years, working in landscaping and now running Jungle Jerry's, he'd run into all of the above. But he couldn't remember anything about the hazards of Brazilian pepper.

After gingerly toweling off the inflamed skin, he found a bottle of Calamine lotion in the medicine cabinet and slathered it all over himself. Within a few seconds, the thick pink goo had dried and started to cake and crack. And he itched, God how he itched.

Wrapped in nothing more than a towel, he carefully stepped over the clothes he'd just discarded. In his bedroom he donned the loosest pair of cotton shorts he could find and an old, threadbare cotton T-shirt.

Wyatt sat down at the kitchen table as his father was taking a pan of corn-bread from the oven. "Does it feel as bad as it looks?" Nelson inquired, after he'd served his son a plate heaped high with food.

"Worse," Wyatt said, pointing toward his crotch. "It's . . . everywhere."

"Ow," Nelson grimaced and poured him a glass of iced tea. "I think we've got some Benadryl around here somewhere. That might help some."

"Maybe after dinner," Wyatt said. "I'll fall asleep with my head in the plate if I take it now, and I've got some stuff I need to do tonight."

They cleaned up the kitchen, and Nelson retired to his recliner to watch his nightly roundup; *Wheel of Fortune, Jeopardy,* and the Rays game.

Wyatt sank onto the old sofa and tried not to think of his inflamed privates while he leafed through the paper, but he was so acutely uncomfortable he gave in shortly after eight and went looking for the bottle of Benadryl.

"Okay, Dad," he said, poking his head out from the hallway. "I'm turning in."

"Hmm?"

"I'm going to bed," Wyatt repeated.

"Did you ever talk to your Aunt Betsy?" Nelson asked, his eyes glued to the television.

"No. Why would I?"

"She called here looking for you. Guess you must have had your phone turned off."

Wyatt came around and stood directly in front of the television, the only way he knew to get his father's attention this time of night. "Dad? What did Betsy say?"

"Hey! Come on now, it's the bottom of the inning, two outs, and we've got the bases loaded."

"What did Betsy say? Did she have news? Come on, Dad, this could be important."

Nelson waved his hand in irritation. "How'm I supposed to know what she wanted? She just said to call her. Not tonight, she had something goin' on. Now, can I watch my game?"

Wyatt called her anyway and left a message on his aunt's phone. The itching was driving him nuts, but he resisted taking the Benadryl. At 9:30 he called and left another message for her, and at ten, in desperation, he texted. *WHAT'S UP? DAD SAID YOU CALLED.*

Thirty minutes later, his phone dinged and he lunged for it. Betsy's message was clear as mud. *CAN'T TALK, CALL U IN A.M.*

Finally, sometime after ten, he popped some Benadryl and fell into an uneasy sleep, imagining all the bad news his attorney might be saving up for the next morning.

28

Betsy Entwhistle was sitting at a table near the window of Eat Here, her favorite breakfast spot in Holmes Beach, when she spotted her nephew making his way through the parking lot, a baseball cap pulled down low over his face, sunglasses covering his eyes.

She sighed. She hated the bruising Callie was giving Wyatt. He'd been a good husband and a loving father, and the little idiot thought she could do better with that punk Luke? She'd known Callie was trouble from the start, and she'd told her sister, Wyatt's mom, that, in confidence. In confidence, Peggy had agreed wholeheartedly. But Wyatt was in love, and they both hoped things would work out.

"Hey," Wyatt was almost out of breath. He dropped into the chair opposite hers. "What's going on? What couldn't you tell me last night?"

"Good Lord, what have you done to your face?" Betsy reached over and tipped back the bill of his cap, removed the sunglasses. Wyatt's handsome face was a crimson, contorted mess. His eyes were nearly swollen shut, his nose and cheeks covered with red blisters that crawled down his neck to his chest. His hands were covered with a similar eruption.

"I took down a tree at the park yesterday, and I've had some kind of reaction to the sap," Wyatt said. "Just tell me what's going on, would you? Have you heard from the judge?"

"Honey, that's not just a reaction," Betsy said. "Your eyes are nearly swollen shut. Have you seen a doctor?"

"I don't need a doctor," he insisted. "It's like poison ivy. I put some Calamine on it and it's some better."

She pressed her lips in disapproval. "I'll tell you what's going on, but then I'm taking you to see my dermatologist. Wyatt, that stuff is in your eyes. What if you lose your eyesight?"

"Okay, whatever," he said. "Would you please talk to me now?"

Betsy took a sip of her coffee. "Don't you want some breakfast? I ordered you some pancakes and bacon."

"Betsy!"

"Okay. Here it is. I got a call from Stackpole's clerk yesterday. It seems Callie is claiming you've been interfering with her time with Bo. He wants to see you in his office this afternoon."

"Me?" Wyatt was incredulous. "I haven't done a damned thing. I don't even call Bo anymore when he's with her. Whatever she's telling the judge, it's total bullshit, Betsy."

"I know it is, but Stackpole doesn't," Betsy said.

"Did the clerk give you any details about this so-called interference?"

"Something about a birthday party Bo was supposed to go to this past weekend?"

"Yeah? What about it? Callie deliberately planned a trip to Birmingham with Fatso, supposedly to look at houses. She knew last weekend was his best friend Scout's birthday party at that new water park, but she planned the trip anyway and insisted Bo had to go. Bo was furious with her." He laughed. "He confessed to me that he called her a shit."

"It's not funny, Wyatt," Betsy said.

Wyatt slapped his hat on the table in disgust. "I didn't tell him to call her that. In fact, I told him it wasn't nice to call his mother names, although, privately, I can think of lots worse names to call her. And incidentally, he says Callie called him a shit first, and I happen to believe him. So that's what this is about? Some name-calling? Seriously?"

"It's worse than that," Betsy said. "When Callie went to pick him up at school on Friday, Bo wasn't there. She claims she called you, but you never answered her phone call."

"Wait? Are you telling me Bo went missing? And this is the first I'm hearing of it?"

"Calm down," Betsy said. "I did some checking. Apparently, Bo never had any intention of going on that trip to Birmingham. He told Scout's mom, Anna, his mom wanted him to spend the night with her and go to the party, and Anna, not knowing any better, took him home from school with her, and on to the party."

"That little con artist," Wyatt said. "I don't know whether I want to pat him on the back or whack him on his butt. But I still don't see how Callie can say any of this is my fault. It was her weekend to have Bo. I didn't call him, didn't pick him up, didn't hide him from his mom."

Betsy shrugged. "Don't kill the messenger, okay? Callie's made a serious charge, and Stackpole, in his totally random way, seems to find her story believable. So we're going to see the judge this afternoon." She looked over his shoulder and saw the waiter approaching with a tray of food. "Right after we get you your pancakes. And see my dermatologist."

"Sir, remove those sunglasses and that hat," the Honorable Cedric N. Stackpole said, as soon as Wyatt and Betsy were seated in his office.

Wyatt shrugged, took off the glasses and the baseball hat. Stackpole cringed. "Are you having some medical issues?" he asked brusquely.

"An allergic reaction to some underbrush he was clearing," Betsy said. "He's gotten a cortisone shot and he has some steroid cream. He'll be fine."

Callie was sitting in a chair on the judge's left side. She was dressed in a short pink skirt and a tight-fitting black tank top that displayed yet another tattoo, and glimpses of her abdomen whenever she moved. She leaned forward and grimaced. "You look like something out of a horror movie." She glanced over at her lawyer. "I don't want my son to see him like that. It's upsetting."

"I'm fine," Wyatt said, clenching and unclenching his fists. "The swelling has already started to go down. It's not contagious. Bo has seen me with poison ivy before."

"Let's stick to the subject at hand, shall we?" Stackpole said. He looked down at a file on his desk. "Mrs. Keeler, you're alleging that Mr. Keeler is interfering with your son's visits with you? Something about a birthday party?"

"Bo knew we'd been planning this trip to Birmingham, to look at houses,"

Callie said. "Wyatt knew it, too. We'd been planning the trip for weeks, and then suddenly, Bo was having a fit over going, because of some little party a friend was having. When I went to pick him up from school on Friday, he wasn't there!"

She leaned across her lawyer and glared at Wyatt. "You put him up to this. And I know it."

"Put him up to what?" Wyatt demanded. Betsy gave her client a small head-shake, warning him not to be baited.

"Bo deliberately lied to his friend's mother, told her I wanted him to spend the night with them that night, so he could go to the party! He even packed a bathing suit and pajamas and hid them in his school backpack," Callie said. "He never would have done that on his own, not without his father giving him the idea."

The judge eased back in his leather desk chair. "Mr. Keeler, did you suggest to your son that he disobey and lie to his mother?"

"Absolutely not," Wyatt said. "This is the first I'm hearing about any of this. Bo did tell me his mother had scheduled a trip out of town, and he was upset over having to miss his friend's party that he'd been looking forward to for weeks. He even admitted he called his mother a bad name. But when I told him that wasn't acceptable behavior, he told me his mother called him that name first."

Stackpole raised an eyebrow. "What kind of bad name?"

"Bo told me his mother called him a little shit," Wyatt said calmly.

"Ridiculous," Callie snapped.

Stackpole's head swung in her direction. "Do you deny calling your son that name?"

Her face reddened. "Bo's been hostile to me for the last few months. He acts out, talks back. Whenever he comes back from a visit with his father, he's belligerent and defiant. And he's openly disrespectful to my fiancé."

"Mrs. Keeler, did you call your six-year-old a 'little shit'? Yes or no?"

Callie burst into tears. "He's my little boy! How would you like it if your son told you he hated you? How would you like it if you went to pick up your son and he refused to get in the car? I may have called him that, in the heat of the moment, but I never meant it."

Wyatt folded his arms across his chest and looked away. Callie loved to turn on the waterworks whenever she was backed into a corner. It was her go-to tactic. He wondered if Stackpole would fall for it. Betsy claimed the judge hated women, but Callie seemed to be the exception to that rule.

Betsy saw an opening and went for it. "Judge, Mr. Keeler is also concerned about his son's behavior. If Bo is unhappy after returning from a visit with my client, it's because he is uncomfortable seeing his mother living with a man other than his father. Bo is upset over the breakup of his parents' marriage, which is totally understandable, and I want to address that in a minute. But in the meantime, Mr. Keeler would like to know more about this past weekend. If Bo wasn't at school when Callie went to pick him up, why didn't she notify my client?"

"I left him a voice mail!" Callie said. "He never returns my calls. I basically assumed Wyatt had Bo."

"But she didn't know that," Betsy said calmly. "Did she do anything else to check up on her son's whereabouts? Question the teachers at the school? Go over to my client's home to see if Bo was there? Did she call his friend's homes to see if he'd gone home with one of them?"

"I just told you, I figured Bo was with Wyatt." Callie glared at Betsy.

Stackpole frowned. "Mrs. Keeler, did you leave town for the weekend without knowing your son's exact location?"

"We had to get on the road," Callie said, her voice shriller by the minute. "We had dinner reservations. It's a long drive to Birmingham, and I was positive Bo was with his father. I never would have left Bo home alone. And it turned out fine! He was with Anna."

Betsy went in for the kill. "He could have been abducted, Judge. My client relied on Mrs. Keeler's representation that his son was in her custody for the weekend. He had no knowledge that Bo wasn't where he should have been. And we find that very disturbing."

"As do I," Stackpole agreed. He looked Wyatt up and down. "Mr. Keeler, Dr. Talbott-Sinclair tells me you've been attending her divorce-recovery sessions, and I, ah, noted your presence there this week when I stopped by. She seems pleased with your progress."

He swung around in his chair and considered Callie, who was dabbing at her crocodile tears with a Kleenex in a valiant effort to look brave and vulnerable.

"Mrs. Keeler?"

"Yes?" she whispered, her lower lip trembling.

"If you and your son are having relationship issues, perhaps you'd better spend more time working on your relationship with him, and less on your fiancé."

Stackpole said the word "fiancé" as though it were some revolting sexual practice. Wyatt felt his spirits start to brighten.

"A young, impressionable boy needs a father in his life. Mr. Keeler had that regrettable episode at the baseball park, but he seems to be making some progress handling his anger and hostility. I'm starting to rethink the wisdom of allowing you to move your son so far away from his father."

Yes! Wyatt wanted to jump up, fist-bump Betsy, maybe even hug Stackpole. Nah, not that. But still.

"Now, Judge," began Callie's lawyer, who'd been noticeably silent until now. "Mrs. Keeler's fiancé has already accepted a job in Birmingham and put his home on the market. It's going to work a real hardship on them if you prevent them from moving . . ."

"I'm not preventing anybody from doing anything, yet," Stackpole interrupted. "I'm just saying I'm rethinking. I still want to wait a few more weeks to make sure that Mr. Keeler completes his therapy, and I want to hear reassurances from Dr. Talbott-Sinclair that there won't be any more episodes of violence before I rule on this custody issue."

"Thank you," Wyatt said fervently. "Thanks very much, Judge."

Stackpole was staring at Callie, eyes narrowed.

"And Mrs. Keeler?"

Callie blew her nose on the tissue. "Yes, Your Honor?"

"The next time you are in my presence, I do not want to be assaulted with the vision of your body piercings. Is that clear?"

Callie looked down and yanked her top over the diamond-studded navel ring winking from her abdomen.

Wyatt waited until they were in the elevator to gather his aunt into a bear hug. "You did it!" he exclaimed. "Finally, a win for our side."

"Not a win, necessarily, but at least a point for our team," Betsy conceded. "I can't believe that little . . ."

"Shit?" Wyatt grinned.

"Shit works, although I *was* going to call her an ignorant slut," Betsy said, returning her nephew's smile. "No offense."

"None taken," Wyatt said. "You were awesome in there, the way you kept on about how Callie just left town, not knowing where Bo was."

"I wasn't just grandstanding. It really is appalling that she was so focused on her little trip she didn't even care enough to make sure Bo was somewhere safe. In the past, I just thought Callie was a selfish, stupid, self-involved little twit. But now I'm starting to wonder how fit a mother she is."

Sobered, Wyatt nodded in agreement. "I keep telling myself she really does love Bo, but since she hooked up with Fatso, Callie's changed. It's like she's turned into this eighteen-year-old party animal overnight. She wasn't always like this. She was a good mom. She wouldn't even let Bo sleep in his nursery until he was, like, eighteen months old, because she'd read all this crap about Sudden Infant Death Syndrome. He slept in a bassinette in our bedroom or in bed with us, until I finally convinced her he'd be okay in his own room. Maybe we got married too young. Maybe she's just immature. Maybe this, the tattoos, the piercings, the clothes, maybe it's all just a phase."

"I hope you're not making excuses for her," Betsy said. "She's thirty-six. It's a little late for her to be in a 'phase.'"

"Hell no, I'm not making excuses for her." Wyatt pulled his baseball cap on again. "Maybe I'm making excuses for me, for letting her go without putting up a fight."

"Don't beat yourself up," Betsy said. "Callie and her lawyer are doing enough of that. You're a good guy. Remember that, okay? And don't go getting soft on me." She made a fist and thrust it into his face. "And if you start thinking about taking her back, I'll punch out *your* car window."

"No worries there," Wyatt said.

"Listen," Betsy said suddenly. "Did I understand Stackpole right? Did he actually sit in on your therapy session the other night?"

"Yep," Wyatt said.

"So weird. What was he doing there?"

"Paula said she invited him," Wyatt said. "But there's something definitely . . . kinky going on between the two of them."

"Kinky and Stackpole are not two words you necessarily think of together," Betsy said. "Kinky how?"

"There's a vibe between them. And everybody in the group noticed it. Paula was positively giddy that he showed up. In fact, she was stone-cold sober, which is a major change."

"Your therapist? You mean she's not usually sober? Wyatt, what's going on with this group?"

The elevator dinged, and the doors opened. They emerged into the courthouse lobby. Betsy pulled Wyatt by the arm, gesturing for him to sit on a bench.

"Talk," she ordered.

"Paula's stoned out of her gourd during most of our sessions," Wyatt said. "The first one, I got there a little late, and she was passed out cold. I had to wake her up to make sure she realized I was there. On a good night, she's just vague and glassy-eyed. During our second session, the light was getting dimmer, if you know what I mean, and then after we got back from break, she zoned out again. We actually left her on the sofa in the reception area. But before we left, just to make sure she hadn't overdosed or something, we checked her purse and figured out she's mixing tranquilizers and sleeping pills."

"Don't you think that's something you might have mentioned to your lawyer?" Betsy scolded.

"Wouldn't do any good," he said. "Like I was telling you, Stackpole showed up at our last session. Paula was on her best behavior, all dressed up and proper and professional. She actually ran the session."

"She doesn't usually?"

"Not really," Wyatt said. "But this week was different. She had her act together, and was so excited about him being there, it was kind of pathetic. He made a stupid little speech, about what a good thing it was we were all doing, blah, blah, blah. And it was going good, and all of a sudden Paula just ended the session. We're supposed to be there an hour, and it wasn't even thirty minutes."

Betsy was shaking her head. "How on earth did he find this woman? And if she's obviously on drugs, like you say, why would he refer people to her?"

Wyatt glanced around the lobby and lowered his voice. "I'll tell you why, but you're not gonna believe it. Because he's in her pants."

"Shhh!" Betsy yanked him up by the arm and hustled him out of the courthouse.

"Oww," Wyatt winced and she loosened her clutch.

"In my car," she said, making a beeline for the parking lot.

. . .

When they were in Betsy's car, with the air conditioner blowing at full blast, he gave her the whole story. Or as much of it as his pride would allow.

"Wednesday night, after Paula let us leave early, we all went over to the Sandbox, like we always do."

She gave him a fishy look. "Tell me that's not a strip joint."

"All those women? You know I'm the only guy, right? The Sandbox is a bar. In Cortez."

"That dumpy little fishing village?"

"It's not all that dumpy," Wyatt said. "Anyway, the Sandbox is a classic dive bar. It's even got an original Ms. Pac-Man. One of the women in the group, Grace, her mother owns it, which is why we go there."

"Who's we?"

"Everybody in the group. Me, Grace, Camryn, Ashleigh, and Suzanne. Like I said, I'm the only guy. At first I thought they were gonna scratch my eyes out, because they've all been shafted by their husbands, and they all hate men, but we're cool now."

"You were telling me about Stackpole being, as you indelicately put it, in your therapist's pants? What makes you think that?"

"For one thing, you had to see them in the same room together. Paula was all giggly and flirty. And then, well, there was this other thing."

"Tell me." Betsy dug in her pocketbook, pulled out a stick of gum, offered it to her nephew, then took one for herself.

"Okay, but you're not gonna like it," he warned.

When he'd finished recounting his story, Betsy sighed. "You're right. I reallllly don't like what you guys did."

"Do you happen to know where Stackpole lives?" Wyatt asked eagerly.

"I have no idea. But I would imagine he probably lives somewhere over on Longboat."

"How about his car? Do you know what kind of car he drives? Like I said, this was a Lexus."

"Stackpole is as conservative as it comes, so whatever he drives, I'd be willing to bet it's a big American-made land yacht."

"Hey!" A light came into Wyatt's eyes. "Do judges have assigned parking spaces? Here at the courthouse?"

"Probably," Betsy said. "God forbid a judge might have to drive around and hunt for a parking spot like the average Joe."

She sighed. "I suppose you want me to swing through the county parking deck to check this out?"

Wyatt leaned over and pecked her on the cheek. "Did I ever mention that you're my favorite aunt?"

"I'm your only aunt," Betsy said. But she started the car and went on the prowl.

29

Transformations and Dirty Laundry

Dear Readers: If you've managed to follow me over here to my new blog, TrueGrace, from my former blog, you know that my personal life has been dealt some, uh, "challenges" lately. My marriage came off the rails in a fairly spectacular way, I've left my husband and lost my home, and now my former blog has been co-opted by my estranged husband and my former assistant. It sounds like it should be a funny story, but unfortunately there's no punch line.

Somebody—and I have a good guess who that is—has been sabotaging me professionally, wiping out my blog posts, leaving nasty comments falsely attributed to me on other blogs, and just generally smearing my good name in the blogosphere. I won't make any accusations, but I would like to assure all my readers, and other bloggers, that I have never and would never engage in such scurrilous behavior.

On a positive note, my life these days is a clean slate. And I have an exciting new project to share with you! Over these next few weeks and months I hope you'll follow along as I rehab, restore, and redecorate a wonderful original 1920s cottage.

Mandevilla Manor, as I call it, is a classic example of a vernacular

Florida cracker cottage. Built of heart pine on a raised cinderblock foundation, it has the original pine board and batten walls, oak floors, and an airy screened porch.

I discovered this diamond in the rough when I was out for a morning run recently. I noticed a huge pile of trash sitting on a curb, which meant a house was being cleaned out. As I watched, a gentleman dragged a fabulous 1940s rattan sofa to the curb. When I struck up a conversation with Arthur, who turned out to be the landlord, I learned that his deadbeat tenants had vacated the house after thoroughly trashing it.

The house has been in Arthur's family for three generations, and he was disheartened by all the work it would take to make it habitable again.

At Arthur's invitation, I toured the house, and, although it was filthy and in terrible disrepair, I could easily see all the charm just waiting to be rediscovered. So Arthur and I worked out a deal. He has provided a tiny budget, and I will provide the vision—and the sweat—to bring Mandevilla Manor back to life.

This will be a true shoestring operation. I'll be shopping at discount centers, thrift stores, and yard sales, and, yes, I'll probably be doing some Dumpster diving and curb cruising. Since my budget is so small, I'll be providing most of the girl power myself. As you can see from this first batch of before and "in process" photos, I've already torn down all the yellowing venetian blinds and ripped up all the nasty old carpet. The kitchen cabinet doors have been removed, and that ugly vinyl flooring is currently under attack. Watch this space for frequent updates!

One other thing. Meet my new BFF, Sweetie. She is an adorable poodle mix who was cruelly locked in a bedroom at the cottage and abandoned by her former owners. Can you believe she is the first dog I have ever owned? Sweetie is an expert at watch-dogging and cockroach wrangling, and she works cheap—just a little kibble and a lot of love. Life is full of twists and turns, dead ends and detours, isn't it? Lose a husband, gain a dog, take a run, find a house to transform.

I can't wait to see what the next chapter of my life will bring.

Grace uploaded all the before photos she'd taken of the little cottage, resizing and writing captions as she went. The last photo she posted was her favorite,

Sweetie, posing on the front steps of the cottage, ears pricked up, tongue lolling, as though to say, "Hey, check me out!"

She held her breath and clicked the PUBLISH toggle on her new blog's dashboard.

"Just try and hack me now, Ben," she muttered to herself. She'd knocked off work on the cottage at noon, just so she could come home and re-create her blog. One more time. She'd chosen a new, easier platform, WordPress, and gone through every security move she could think of to foil any other attack on her blog, including running a malware program that would pinpoint and hopefully eliminate whatever method Ben had used to sabotage TrueGrace.com.

"Everything new" was her motto this time around. She didn't have the graphics knowledge Ben had, and she sure didn't have any of her former advertisers. But her new platform was clean and simple. The writing was brutally honest, and from the heart. The photos of Mandevilla Manor were clear, and Grace felt certain this project would resonate with all the homeowners, thrifters, and DIY-ers in the world, in a way her old blog never had. How many people, after all, could relate to a three-hundred-dollar Belgian linen tablecloth like the one that had adorned the dining room table at Sand Dollar Lane? Were there really all that many hostesses who wanted recipes calling for black truffle oil and imported pink sea salt?

After she published the blog post, she copied the URL and e-mailed it to every lifestyle blogger she'd ever read, explaining to them that Gracenotes had been taken over by Ben and apologizing, again, for any spurious negative comments they might have seen floating around on the Internet.

I've reinvented myself, and my blog. I'm TrueGrace now, and I would love it if you'd drop by and check out my new project. And since I'm starting from scratch, I'd be humbled if you saw fit to add me to your blog roll.

Grace lolled back on her bed pillows and closed her eyes. It was nearly six. She'd been hunched over her laptop for hours. She was tired and sore from being down on her hands and knees hacking away at the kitchen floor. She told herself she was in no mood for divorce-recovery group. And she really dreaded seeing Wyatt Keeler again after her clumsy and humiliating encounter with him after their last session.

She was surprised to find that she was looking forward to seeing the others. Camryn's wisecracks and brutal honesty never failed to entertain her. Suzanne, quiet, vulnerable Suzanne, seemed close to revealing whatever secrets were tormenting her, and even that gold-plated gold digger Ashleigh was at least good for comic relief.

And yes, she was definitely curious about Paula after witnessing her encounter with the mystery Lexus driver. She got dressed and slipped Sweetie into her now-familiar tote bag, giving her a doggie treat to chew on and keep quiet.

A hastily scrawled note on the back of an envelope was taped to Dr. Paula Talbott-Sinclair's office door.

DUE TO FAMILY EMERGENCY NO GROUP SESSION TONIGHT—PTS

"What's going on?" Ashleigh Hartounian stuck her head out the window of her red BMW and called to Camryn Nobles, who was standing in front of the office door, fuming.

"No session tonight," Camryn said.

"Whaaat?" Ashleigh scrambled out of her car and joined Camryn on the sidewalk in front of the office. She peered into the office window, but there was nothing to see.

"What are we looking at?" Grace asked, as she walked up to the two women.

"See for yourself." Camryn gestured toward the note taped to the door.

"Huhh," Grace said, frowning. "And there's no sign of life inside the office?"

"None that we could see," Ashleigh said. "So what do we do now?"

"We don't spend three hundred dollars on Paula's bullshit, at least tonight," Camryn said.

"Oooh, that's exactly how much the pair of shoes I've been stalking at Saks are," Ashleigh said, rubbing her hands together in glee. She bowed in the direction of the door. "Thanks, Paula."

Camryn adjusted the strap of her pocketbook on her shoulder. "Since I had to clear my calendar anyway, should we go somewhere and grab dinner?"

"Absolutely! I know this adorable new bistro at Saint Armand's Key," Ashleigh said. "If we hurry, we can still get in on happy hour martinis."

Grace glanced at her watch. "What about Suzanne? Shouldn't we wait for her? I'd feel bad if she came all the way over here just to turn around and go home again. She's always so quiet, but I get the feeling we're the only ones she can really talk to."

"Although she hasn't really told us anything at all," Ashleigh pointed out. "I'm thinking whatever she did to get Stackpole to order her to therapy must have been really, really radical. And scary."

"Scarier than writing on her husband's mistress's house and car with blood?" Camryn asked.

"I told you, it wasn't blood. It was only red paint," Ashleigh said. "Although now I kind of wish it had been blood, which would wash off, because I was in such a hurry when I did it, I grabbed oil-based paint. And since my lawyer is making me pay to have the bitch's house and car repainted, it's costing me a fortune."

As they talked, a Prius rolled up to the office.

"Oh good, here's Suzanne now," Grace said. "Looks like the gang's all here."

"What about Wyatt?" Ashleigh asked. "We can't leave him behind."

"It's five after," Grace said. "Maybe he's ditching us tonight."

"Who's ditching us?" Suzanne asked as she joined the group. "And why are we all standing out here on the sidewalk?"

"Paula's got some kind of family emergency," Grace said, pointing at the note on the door.

"Allegedly," Camryn added. "We're just talking about going out to dinner, since we're all here anyway. Care to join us?"

Suzanne hesitated. "Well, since I'm here anyway . . . but what about Wyatt?"

Grace made a show of checking her watch again. "He's probably not even coming tonight. Look, we better get going if we're going to Saint Armand's. You know how crowded it gets there."

"Saint Armand's?" Suzanne's face fell. "I, well, never mind. You all go on without me. I'll get something to eat on the way home."

"No, Suzanne," Grace protested. "We don't have to go to Saint Armand's, if you have a problem with that. We could go anywhere."

"What's your problem with Saint Armand's?" Ashleigh asked. She was promptly given a not-so-subtle elbow in the ribs from Camryn.

"Why don't we just go over to the Sandbox, like we usually do?" Camryn said. "I'm not really in the mood for a twelve-dollar martini tonight anyway. Your mom serves food, right, Grace?"

"Sure, anything you want, as long as it's fried."

"Then it's settled," Camryn said. "Suzanne, do you need a ride? I can drop you back here afterward."

As they headed for their cars, Grace took a quick look around, mentally crossing her fingers and hoping Wyatt would not drive up as they were leaving.

When she got home, she bounded up the outside stairs at the Sandbox, unlocked her bedroom door, and opened the top of the tote bag. Sweetie climbed out, yawned widely, then hopped onto the bed.

"Good girl," Grace laughed. "I'll be back in a couple hours or so, and we'll take a quick walk before bedtime." She scratched the dog's ears and earned a generous tail wag for her efforts.

"You're early," Rochelle said when Grace strolled into the bar. "But I already reserved your table. Where are the rest?"

"They'll be along," Grace said, moving toward the table. "Could you bring some menus when they get here? We're going to have dinner."

A few minutes later, Rochelle appeared with menus, a glass of wine for Grace, and a basket of popcorn for the middle of the table. "Did your therapist pass out on you again?"

"She wasn't there," Grace said, helping herself to a handful of popcorn. "There was a note on the door saying she'd had some kind of family emergency. Very cryptic. Very mysterious."

"Does anybody really believe Paula had an emergency tonight?" Ashleigh speared a french fry with the tip of her fork and chewed slowly. "I mean, I find it hard to believe Paula even has a family. She's just so . . . spacey. I mean, can you imagine having her for a mom? Or a wife?"

"It might not be something with a child or a husband," Suzanne said timidly. "Maybe she has elderly parents. A friend I teach with has to use up every day of her sick leave and vacation time caring for her mother and her aunt, who both have dementia."

Grace tore off a piece of her patty melt and chewed slowly. "I was thinking it could have something to do with Paula's behavior last Wednesday night. She was definitely on edge."

"Family emergency, my ass," Camryn said. She squirted ketchup on her burger. "I knew all along there was something odd about that woman . . ." She broke off her sentence.

"Oh, my precious baby Jesus! Will you look at that boy's poor face?"

They all turned to see what she was talking about. And that's when they spotted a familiar-looking figure, threading his way through the maze of tables and chairs in their direction.

He was still dressed in the neatly pressed navy slacks and dress shirt he'd worn to court earlier in the day, and the bill of the baseball cap was still tilted low over his eyes, but he'd removed the sunglasses.

"How'd he find us?" Grace muttered, but as he got closer to the table and she saw his face, she gasped aloud.

"Hey, ladies," Wyatt said. He pulled a chair from a nearby table and sat down. He nodded curtly at Grace. Before he could say anything else, Rochelle arrived with a pitcher of beer and two glasses. She poured one and handed it to him, then sat down and poured a glass for herself. Rochelle reached out and gently touched Wyatt's cheek. "Your face! Did you fall into a fire-ant hill?"

"Not exactly. I did something even stupider. I purposely cut down a Brazilian pepper tree."

"That's bad?" Camryn asked.

"It is if you're allergic to the sap, which I apparently am," Wyatt said. He tried to smile, but his stiff, swollen lips were nearly immobile. "I know it looks pretty gnarly, but this is actually an improvement. My aunt dragged me to a doctor, and he gave me a cortisone shot and some steroid cream, so I'm starting to feel semihuman again, even if my face does look like a piece of raw meat."

Ashleigh leaned her body across Suzanne's to get a closer examination, and to give her pseudo-professional opinion. "Hmm. It looks like the eruptions haven't scabbed over. That's a good thing. I'd hate for you to have scars all over that pretty face of yours."

Wyatt ducked his head, obviously embarrassed by all the attention.

"What can I get you to eat?" Rochelle asked. "Hamburger? Wings? Loaded potato skins?"

"Nothing, thanks," he said. "I had a late lunch after my date with Stackpole."

"Stackpole?" Grace stared, wondering what he'd been up to, halfway dreading the answer.

"Yeahhh," he said slowly. "It's kind of a long story." And then his face cracked painfully, but he smiled anyway.

"Well, since Paula called off our session, we've got all night," Camryn said. "So don't keep us in suspense."

He filled them in on Callie's efforts to get him into hot water with the judge, and how his lawyer had instead managed to turn the tables on her.

"Wyatt, that's huge!" Suzanne said, beaming. "I'm so happy for you." She looked at the other faces around the table. "We're all happy for you."

Grace saw Wyatt watching for her reaction. "It's great, really," she said. "For once, the good guy comes out ahead with that clown Stackpole."

"Thanks, Grace," he said. "Maybe he'll change his mind about you and Ben, too."

"I wouldn't count on that," Grace said. "I'm a woman, remember? I'm the gender he loves to hate."

"Did you, uh, tell everybody about last week?"

Grace blushed at the memory.

"What?" Ashleigh demanded. "Did something happen after we left here?"

"You might say that," Wyatt said. Had Grace imagined it, or had he actually winked at her? She'd hoped to avoid any mention of their late-night chase the previous week.

"We don't actually know for sure that the car was Stackpole's," she put in, when he was done.

"Although . . ." Wyatt was trying his best not to look smug, but it was a hard-fought battle. "Today, while I was at the courthouse, my aunt and I took a drive through the county parking deck. Did you guys know judges get assigned parking spaces?"

"They probably don't even have to pay for 'em, either," Camryn said. And then she perked up. "Stackpole drives a Lexus?"

"A black one," Wyatt said, "with a little Florida gator decal in the lower left corner of his rear window."

Grace grinned despite herself. "So, it was Stackpole!"

"Maybe," Camryn cautioned. "Half the judges in this state probably have a UF Gator sticker on their car. And of those, there's probably a whole bunch of them who drive a black Lexus."

"But there's only one judge in Manatee County who drives a black Lexus with a UF sticker *and* who resides at 4462 Alcazar Trace, Longboat Key. And that is the Honorable Judge Cedric N. Stackpole Jr." Wyatt said.

"You're sure?" Grace asked.

"Yup. Betsy did an online search. It's him."

"Well, I'll be damned," Rochelle said. "What do you think that means?"

"I knew it!" Ashleigh said. "You can always tell with those straitlaced types. They're the biggest horn-dogs on the block. And, of course, they're *always* married."

"It might not mean anything," Grace cautioned, although she hoped against hope it did. "Maybe they were just having a professional meeting, and he told her he didn't like the way she was conducting our group session."

Camryn was drumming her long acrylic fingertips on the tabletop. "Okay, y'all, I'll tell you what I think it means. I think it means a hard-nosed piece of investigative journalism will unveil a web of intrigue and paybacks between a respected local circuit court judge and a disgraced therapist. And I think, maybe, just maybe, it might mean a daytime Emmy for a certain hard-hitting member of the News Four You I-Team."

She held up her iPhone. "I've been doing a little dirt digging on my own."

30

P aula Talbott-Sinclair," Camryn said, pausing for dramatic effect, "used to live in Oregon. But three years ago, the state revoked her professional license. She moved to Florida sometime after that and set up an office here, but she's not licensed by the state of Florida to be a clinical therapist. So how does she get away with charging three hundred dollars an hour for a group session? And more importantly, when the phone book is full of marriage counselors, why does Stackpole insist people like us attend counseling sessions with her?"

"Do we know why they revoked her license in Oregon?" Suzanne asked. "And does the state of Florida require her to be licensed in order to be a therapist here?"

"This is Florida, honey," Camryn told her. "Just like we attract every kind of poisonous reptile, bug, or plant, every whacked-out criminal, huckster, or con artist, we also get every loony-toon variety of self-appointed therapist on the planet. Even though Florida seems to have pretty strict licensing requirements for therapists, there's always a loophole. So you could still call yourself something else, hell, you could call yourself a divorce whisperer, and as long as you have a business license from the county, you're good to go. Paula does have that. I checked. As for why Oregon took away her professional accreditation, I'm working on it, but it's slowgoing. All these state licensing boards have layers and layers of confidentiality rules. I've got an intern at the station working on trying to dig up the particulars, but so far we're getting sandbagged."

"I wonder if her losing her license had anything to do with drugs?" The others at the table turned to look at Grace.

"She's obviously impaired, at least some of the time. And we did find those sleeping pills and tranquilizers in her purse," Grace reasoned. "Camryn, can your intern check to see if she's had any drug arrests, or something like that?"

"I can ask," Camryn said. "But this kid's no rocket scientist."

"I don't care what she's done or how she lost her license," Suzanne spoke up. "Paula is obviously troubled, but I honestly believe she cares about us. I don't know about you guys, but she's helped me. A lot. I feel sorry for her. Can't we help her, instead of making her part of an exposé?"

Ashleigh laughed. "You think she's helped you? I mean, no offense, Suzanne, but you've never said one thing in group about what happened in your marriage. All we know is that your husband's name is Eric and he cheated on you with another teacher at your school."

"Ashleigh!" Grace chided.

"I don't care," Ashleigh tossed her honey-colored tresses. "We've all opened up our innermost secrets, and she just sits there, every week, with her lips zipped."

"Something you might try once in a while," Camryn said.

"No, Ashleigh's right," Suzanne said. "I haven't been open. And that's not fair to you or me. That's one reason I was so disappointed our session with Paula was canceled tonight. That question she asked us Wednesday night—the one about a moment with our spouse when we were happy?" She gave a sheepish smile and pulled her journal out of her pocketbook. "I wrote ten pages! Which is hard for me to believe right now, but I did."

"Well? Are you gonna read it?" Ashleigh asked, daring the others to shut her up.

Suzanne glanced at the table directly behind them, where two grizzled fishermen sporting three-day beards and sweat-stained T-shirts lolled backward in their chairs, obviously interested in their conversations. "It's sort of private," she whispered.

"Let me handle this," Rochelle said. She stood, hands on hips and faced the table. "Miller, Bud, you guys need to pay up and move on." She jerked her head in the direction of the door. The men scowled but pulled some rumpled bills from their pockets, threw them on the table, and ambled toward the bar.

"Nuh-uh," Rochelle called, following in their wake. "You two are done for the night. Unless you plan to actually buy a drink or some food."

"Oh no, Grace, make her stop," Suzanne blurted. "I don't want your mom to chase off paying customers for me, especially your regulars."

Grace rolled her eyes. "They're her regular deadbeats. That's not even their real names. She just calls them that because that's what they order. A Bud and a Miller. But only one. They eat a boatload of popcorn and generally annoy all our paying customers. Plus, they stink to high heavens. And they're crappy tippers. Believe me, they'll be back tomorrow. They're shameless barflies."

Rochelle shooed the men out the front door, then returned to the table. "What were you saying, Suzanne?"

Suzanne took another deep breath. "If you guys really want to hear it, I think I'm ready. Don't worry," she added hastily. "I won't read all ten pages. I'll give you the abridged version."

She took a gulp of wine and laughed nervously. "Liquid courage, right?"

"It was a Saturday night, and our daughter Darby was playing in an out-of-town soccer tournament. I guess I am the ultimate soccer mom. Usually Darby and I share a room during the tournaments, because Eric rarely goes, and I love giggling and gossiping with her. We are so much closer than most moms and daughters. But this time, Darby specifically asked me not to go because she wanted to room with her two best friends, so I stayed home.

"At first, Eric and I didn't know what to do with ourselves on a Saturday night alone! We talked about going out to a nice restaurant, but it was raining out, so instead we stayed home. Eric did something he hadn't done since the years when we first moved in together. He fixed me my favorite dish and cleaned up the kitchen, too. After dinner, we opened a good bottle of wine, and we sat on the sofa together and dialed up a movie on Netflix, a silly little chick flick. But it made us laugh, and parts of it were so romantic. I was stretched out on one end of the sofa, with my shoes off, and Eric was giving me a foot massage. And it was just . . . so sweet, and tender. I just, I don't know, got really turned on."

Suzanne stopped reading. "I can't . . . I can't believe I am reading this out loud. My heart is pounding so hard right now, it feels like it might jump out of my chest."

"You're doing great," Rochelle said, patting Suzanne's hand.

"Thanks," Suzanne said, her voice sounding wobbly. "I think I'll be okay if I just don't look at your faces while I read. Dumb, huh?"

She stared down at the notebook. "Uh, I'm going to skip over this part." She blushed furiously, flipping the notebook pages. "And this. Nobody wants to hear this."

Ashleigh's hand shot up. "I do."

"Damn, Suzanne," Camryn drawled. "Ashleigh's right for once. Don't be such a scaredy-cat. You had relations with your husband? Why is that such a big deal? We're all grown folk here. You said you were going to read, so read already and quit making us beg for the good stuff."

"Sorry, sorry, sorry," Suzanne said, fanning her face with her hands. She turned back to her starting point and began to read again.

"Eric couldn't believe I was actually initiating sex with him. And I couldn't either. But I did. I undressed him, right there on the sofa, and he undressed me, and we . . ."

She bit her lip.

"We did it! We had sex in the family room, on the same sofa where Darby does her homework every night. Eric made me leave the lights on and everything. I don't know what came over me that night, but it was all different. I did all the things he's been begging me to do for years. Tried different positions. I talked dirty to him. He loved it."

Suzanne whispered, without looking up at the others. "I loved it."

"We were different people that night. We were who we used to be, before life reshaped us. Mutated us. I can't remember ever achieving that sense of intimacy before, even when we were dating. I thought maybe that night would change our marriage. I thought the next morning, I would get up and make us a late breakfast in bed, and we would make love again and everything would be different. But it wasn't. Still, that was the happiest I've ever been with Eric. It made me remember how we used to be."

Suzanne closed the notebook and folded her hands on the cover.

"Wow," Grace breathed. "Just, wow. The next morning, after your night of grand passion. What happened?"

"Nothing. I woke up, and Eric had gone for his ten-mile run," Suzanne said, her shoulders slumped. "When he got back, he disappeared into his office for the rest of the afternoon. Then, Darby got home from the tournament, and, well, things went right back to the way they'd been."

"Did you ever talk about that night?" Wyatt asked. "Did you tell Eric how much you enjoyed it? Or try doing the same thing again?"

"No," Suzanne said, her voice small. "The time just never seemed right. And not long afterward, I . . . discovered he was cheating on me. So there wasn't any point to any of this, was there?"

"You had fabulous sex! There's always a point to that," Ashleigh said.

After the laughter died down, Grace brought up something that had been on her mind since the first night she'd met Suzanne.

"Suzanne, you say you and Darby are really, really close. And it sounds like you're pretty wrapped up in her life and her soccer and everything. I'm wondering if maybe you're too involved."

"Yeah, maybe you're one of those helicopter parents I hear about," Ashleigh said. "Why do they always call them that, I wonder?"

"Because those are the parents who're always hovering right over their kids' shoulders, doing their work for them, or interfering with teachers or coaches, or whatever," Camryn said. "I did a story about it. It's a real problem."

"Helicopter parents? That's ridiculous," Rochelle scoffed. "You've never had kids, Grace or Ashleigh, so you don't understand. Suzanne is a great mom. Darby's a senior this year, right, Suzanne? So this is will be her last year at home before going off to college. It's totally understandable that you want to be part of her life. When Grace was in school, I never missed a class play or one of her tennis matches."

"Maybe," Wyatt said, carefully choosing his words, "you got so wrapped up in your daughter's life, you forgot to pay enough attention to your husband. Maybe Eric felt, I don't know, neglected?"

"Spoken just like a man!" Rochelle snapped. "Honest to Pete, I am so tired of hearing men make excuses for their own bad behavior. If her husband was feeling neglected, maybe he should have gone to those soccer tournaments with them, instead of sleeping with any woman who caught his eye. Right, Suzanne?"

"Maybe," Suzanne said quietly. "Maybe if Eric was feeling abandoned, he could have told me that. Or maybe I should have made more of a point of including him. I just don't know anything."

"You knew enough to kick his cheating butt to the curb," Rochelle said. She glanced over her shoulder and saw a tall black man with a gleaming bald head standing pointedly in front of the cash register at the bar. She jumped up. "Oh, Lord. There's Garland, from the health department. Hold that thought," she told Suzanne. "I'll be right back."

Five minutes later, Rochelle returned to the table, grim-faced, with Sweetie clutched firmly under her arm.

She glared at Grace. "Of all the dumb luck. Garland drops in for a beer, and this little mutt comes scampering down the back staircase and into the kitchen." She thrust the dog at Grace. "You know anything about this?"

Grace sighed and held the wriggling dog against her chest. "This is Sweetie. She was left behind at Mandevilla Manor. I know you don't like dogs, but . . ."

"But you decided you'd bring her here to the Sandbox. Are you crazy? We can't have a dog in a restaurant. You want the health department on my ass? I could lose my license, if Garland decided to report this."

Grace glanced over her shoulder. Garland gave her a stern look and waggled a finger at her. "I'm really sorry. I thought I'd closed my door tight. I don't know how she got out. I'll take her back upstairs."

"And then find her a new home, tomorrow," Rochelle said firmly.

Grace carried Sweetie to her bedroom and examined the door where the dog had scratched and clawed to escape.

She carried Sweetie into the bathroom and set her down on the floor. Sweetie gave her a quizzical look. Grace sat on the edge of the bathtub, to lecture the dog at eye level.

"I know you don't like being penned up, but you just can't go downstairs, or you'll get me kicked out of my mom's house. And then we'll both be homeless." She pulled a treat from her pocket and tossed it to Sweetie, who caught it and retreated beneath the pedestal sink to savor it.

"Stay here for now, and we'll figure something out tomorrow," she promised, giving her a final, reassuring head scratch.

. . .

When Grace got back to the bar, the group was still having a spirited discussion and Rochelle was back behind the bar. She set a fresh basket of popcorn on the table and tried to avoid her mother's disapproving stare from across the room.

"What did I miss?" she asked.

"Just a lot more man bashing," Wyatt said, helping himself to a handful of popcorn. "The usual."

Camryn rolled her eyes. "It seems like Suzanne's husband was jealous of all the time she spent with their daughter, so that's his excuse for having an affair?"

"Affairs. Plural," Suzanne said quietly. "But I wouldn't really characterize them as affairs. More like one-night stands, from what I could find out."

"Oh, no." Grace blurted. "That's so awful."

"Like my asshole husband," Camryn said disgustedly. "Men really are such shits."

"Thanks," Wyatt said. He stood up and pulled some money from his pockets. "On that note, I think I'll just take my sorry, shitty man self on home and let you girls continue the vagina monologues." He did a little half bow. "Ladies?"

Camryn reached out and caught him by the elbow as he started to walk out. "Don't be such a wuss, Wyatt. You know I wasn't talking about you."

"Don't go!" Ashleigh pleaded. "We really don't hate all men. Well, I don't. I don't know about the others." She turned to Suzanne. "You tell him."

"Please stay," Suzanne echoed. "We want to hear a man's point of view. Right, Grace?"

She could feel Wyatt watching her, one eyebrow cocked expectantly.

"Right," she said finally, looking anywhere but directly at him.

Camryn tugged impatiently at his arm. "Come on, dude. Sit back down. Don't make us beg."

"It's getting late," Wyatt said, his resolve ebbing a little.

"It's not even nine o'clock yet," Ashleigh pointed out. "And didn't you tell us your little boy stays with your wife on weeknights?"

"We alternate days. I pick him up after school tomorrow," Wyatt admitted.

Camryn was steering him back toward the table. "What about you?" she asked, after he'd sat down again. "You've got a kid. Did you ever resent your wife spending more time with your son than with you?"

Wyatt took a sip of his beer. "Maybe when Bo was just a baby, yeah, I probably felt a little left out, especially when Callie was nursing him. Things got better after the pediatrician convinced her she could pump breast milk and let me take the early-morning feedings so she could get some sleep."

"You did that?" Grace turned to him in surprise.

"Sure," Wyatt said, shrugging. "It was kind of cool. I'd take Bo out to the living room, give him his bottle, and we'd watch cartoons until we both fell back asleep. I swear, he loved *Phineas and Ferb* when he was only six weeks old. He'd laugh his little ass off."

Camryn shook her head. "Dexter Nobles used to sleep right through those midnight feedings. And I don't remember him changing all that many diapers either."

"Eric changed a lot of diapers, and sometimes he'd sit up and read aloud to me while I nursed Darby," Suzanne said wistfully. "I kind of miss those days."

"He read to you? That's so sweet," Ashleigh said. "What did he read?"

"*Harry Potter,* actually," Suzanne said. "A college classmate who was living in the U.K. sent us the first book as a baby gift for Darby. Another nice memory I'd completely forgotten about."

"How about you all? Suzanne asked, polling the others. "Did anybody else come up with any deeply repressed happy moments?"

Ashleigh wrinkled her nose. "I didn't really get that question when Paula asked it. See, I was happy right up until Boyce started up with that Suchita chick."

"Any one, particular memory?" Suzanne queried.

"Oh yeah," Ashleigh said, dreamy-eyed. "One of the drug companies had a 'seminar' for plastic surgeons in the Napa Valley back in the fall. They put us up in this fabulous old inn in the wine country. Boyce and I drove over to Calistoga and did a couples-only mud bath and massage . . ." She giggled. "We got pretty naughty. I ended up with mud in the most *interesting* places . . ."

"Spare us any more smutty details," Camryn said drily. "We get the picture."

"Your turn," Ashleigh said, pointing right back at her. "And don't try telling us you were never happy. You were married longer than any of us, right? There must be some reason you stayed with your husband all those years."

Camryn sighed. "The last really happy time? I'd have to say it was that first

Christmas Jana was old enough to understand about Santa Claus. Dexter bought her this ridiculously expensive Victorian dollhouse with about a million itty-bitty pieces to it. That night, after we put her to bed, we put on my Johnny Mathis CD, and he popped a bottle of champagne he'd been saving for a special occasion. We stayed up drinking and laughing and dancing to Johnny Mathis. "I Saw Mommy Kissing Santa Claus" came on, and the next thing you know, we'd forgotten all about that dollhouse . . ." She blushed. "I sound like Ashleigh now, spilling about our sex life. Of course, that was fifteen years ago."

"You've really been that unhappy all this time?" Grace asked.

Camryn rested her elbows on the table and propped her chin on her hands while she thought about it.

"I guess I was going with the flow. At one point, when Jana was about eight, I realized things weren't great. But then Dexter made partner at his law firm, and I finally got hired on at News Four. We bought the new house with the pool and we put Jana in private school at Saint Stephen's, which was not cheap. And I thought, why rock the boat? Things will get better. But they never did. I should've ended it a long time ago. Before things turned ugly like this."

"Graaaaccce?" Ashleigh tilted her nearly empty glass. "Is your mom coming back? 'Cause I could use another of her 'ritas."

"I'll get it," Grace stood.

"And then it's your turn to share," Camryn said, making quote marks with the fingertips of both hands. "So don't think we're going to forget."

Rochelle deliberately turned her back to Grace when she walked behind the bar. "I'm fixing Ashleigh another fake margarita," she told her mother. "Could you add it to our tab?"

"Is the dog locked up?" she asked pointedly.

"She's in the bathroom, taking a nap," Grace assured her. "It won't happen again."

"We're waiting," Wyatt said pointedly, when Grace returned to the table with Ashleigh's drink.

She stuck her tongue out at him. "I notice you haven't read from your journal tonight."

"But I shared. And it was honest and it was meaningful," he taunted. "Right, ladies?"

"Come on, Grace. Your turn." Ashleigh noisily sipped her fakearita.

"Okay, okay," Grace grumbled. She pulled her notebook from her bag and skimmed what she'd written.

"I'd never lived in a real house, until Ben and I bought our first little place in Bradenton. It was the worst house on the street. Concrete-block and less than a thousand square feet. Two tiny bedrooms, one miserable bath that didn't even have a shower, a galley kitchen so narrow that when you opened the oven door it almost touched the cabinet on the opposite wall. The counter-tops were plywood covered with plastic tile."

"Sounds dreamy," Camryn said.

"I knew we could make it dreamy. But we had zero money to work with."

Ashleigh waved her hand in the air. "Excuse me, Grace, but when does the happy-memory part come in? Because, so far, this is all sounding pretty grim to me."

"That was just the setup. The prologue," Grace said. She flipped through the pages of her notebook and began reading.

"I was working for a big developer in Sarasota, designing their model-home interiors. This was before the economy tanked, when condos were selling as fast as they could put them up. Ben was an account executive with an advertising and marketing company. We'd work all day, then go straight to the house, change clothes, and work 'til one or two in the morning, go back to the condo we were renting, fall into bed, then get up and do the same thing the next day. For six months, we worked every weekend. Some nights we were too tired to even drive home, so we'd just crash on a mattress on the living room floor. Neither Ben nor I had any real do-it-yourself skills. So we taught ourselves. It was all a huge adventure, and we were in it together. We just figured if we messed up, we'd rip it out and start over. We were absolutely fearless. One night, I wanted to put up this ten-inch cove-ceiling molding in the living room. We had exactly enough to do that one room, and I knew it would be fabulous. Ben bet me I couldn't do it. And of course, I totally messed it up and ended up in tears. He took pity on me, took over, and somehow made it work. But it took hours. It was close to midnight by the time we ate our dinner of Chinese takeout and cheap jug wine, sitting on overturned plastic joint-compound buckets. We got silly drunk and ended up naked, hosing each other off in the backyard. And Ben won the bet, so you can probably figure out what happened next. I can't remember a happier time in our life together."

Grace closed the notebook. She heard a soft exhalation of breath from some-where behind and turned just in time to see Rochelle, scurrying back toward the kitchen.

"Good night," Grace said, walking out into the Sandbox parking lot with the others. They'd discussed what to do about Paula but hadn't come to any kind of consensus. "Let's see what happens next Wednesday," Suzanne had suggested, and short of any other brilliant ideas, they'd agreed to do just that.

She'd turned to go back inside. "Hey, Grace?" She turned and saw Wyatt, standing in the shadow of a clump of palm trees.

"Hi," she said.

"Can I talk to you?"

"Okay." She leaned up against the bumper of his truck and squinted to see his face in the flickering green and red light cast by the bar's neon sign.

"Wow. That rash or whatever it is on your face really looks painful," she said.

"The stuff on my face isn't the worst of it," Wyatt said, grimacing and jerk-ing his chin downward, toward his belt line.

"Oh." She caught his meaning and grimaced, too. "Sorry."

"I'll be okay. As soon as I get home, I'll, uh, apply the cortisone cream. And take some Benadryl and drift off to la-la land."

"I hope you feel better," she said, sounding cold and insincere, even to her-self.

"I hope you mean that," Wyatt said. "I know I screwed up at Coquina Beach."

Grace stepped sideways in order to escape the flash of the neon, to hide her confusion and embarrassment.

Wyatt cleared his throat. "Look. I'm not good at this crap. I wasn't good at it when I was a teenager, and I sure as hell haven't gained any momentum with age. I just wanted to tell you . . . don't write me off. Okay? I really, really like you. The other night? That was great. Really, really great. I wanted to kick myself in the ass afterward."

Grace just looked at him.

"Is any of this making any sense to you?"

"Not really."

He sighed. "Instead of divorce recovery, they should have dating-reentry therapy. For dweebs like me who never figured this stuff out."

She had to laugh then. "Dating reentry. Not a bad idea. Maybe you should suggest that to Paula. If we ever see her again."

"The point is, I think maybe I had a breakthrough when I was at Stackpole's office with Callie today."

"Oh?"

"She hates me. My wife, soon to be ex, hates me. I don't exactly know why, but she does. And to tell you the truth, I'm not so crazy about her, either. Maybe your mom is right. Maybe Bo is better off if we just split up and get on with our lives."

"And if Callie gets her way and moves to Birmingham and takes Bo with her?"

"Right now, Stackpole seems like he's switched sides. But whatever he decides to do, I'm gonna fight that as hard as I can, to keep them from taking him away," he said, his jaw tightening. "Not just because I'd miss my son, but because I know those two aren't fit to raise him. He's an afterthought to them. A bargaining chip."

Grace did what she'd been wanting to do all evening. She reached out and brushed his face with the palm of her hand. He caught her hand in his and kissed the back of it.

"For a guy, you're not so bad," she said.

He pulled her closer, wrapping his arms around her waist. "And for a man-hating ball buster, you're not so bad yourself."

She leaned in and closed her eyes.

The screened door from the kitchen flew open, and Rochelle stuck her head out. Her voice echoed in the still evening air. "Grace? Your goddamn dog was upstairs whining to get out."

Sweetie scampered out into the crushed-shell lot, looked up at Grace and Wyatt for only a moment, then discreetly trotted around the palm tree to complete her toilette in private.

31

Grace scooped the little brown dog up into her arms. Sweetie squirmed in ecstasy, covering her chin and neck with kibble-flavored kisses. "Poor little girl," Grace said. She looked at Wyatt over the dog's ears. "Sweetie hates being locked up. I think she has the doggie version of post-traumatic stress disorder. So that's that. I've got to figure out something else."

"She really won't let you keep a dog? Not even after you explain the circumstances?"

"She's not a dog person. And anyway, it's against all kinds of health codes," Grace said. "Guess I'd better start looking for an apartment."

"Can you afford that?"

"Not really."

He hesitated. "Look, I was going to suggest this anyway. Why don't you let me keep Sweetie at my place?"

"Oh no," Grace interrupted. "I found her and adopted her. She's my responsibility."

"Just hear me out. You could keep Sweetie with you during the day while you're working at the house on Mandevilla, and she could stay with me over at Jungle Jerry's, nights, and any other time you need her to. She'd love it there. The whole place is fenced in, so there's no way she could run off and get hurt. She can sleep in the house with us at night. I'll fix her a bed right beside Bo's.

He'll be crazy for her. He's been bugging me to get him a dog, and I was going to, but then Callie started busting my chops about that, claiming I'd just be doing it to get back at her."

"I don't understand how your having a dog affects her," Grace said.

"Luke's allergic. Or so he claims. Funny, though. He has this huge Siamese cat, and that doesn't seem to bother his allergies. The cat hates Bo, scratches him every time it gets a chance."

"I don't know . . ." Grace hugged Sweetie to her chest. "It's crazy, but I'm already so attached to her. She sleeps on the pillow next to me. And she's such good company."

"It'd just be 'til you get your own place," Wyatt promised. "Think of it as temporary joint custody. But I swear, I won't pull any of Callie's custody crap."

Grace scratched Sweetie's chin. "No alienation of affection? No bribing her with special dog treats?"

He held up his hand in the Boy Scout pledge. "I'll never drop her off late for visitation or forget to bring her leash."

"Well . . ." Grace sighed. "I guess that will work. If you're really sure she won't be an imposition."

"She won't be. I can take her home right now, if you want."

"I'll just run upstairs and get her stuff," Grace said. Wyatt held out his arms, and she reluctantly handed Sweetie over.

Five minutes later she was back, having hauled an overflowing black trash bag down the outside stairway from her room.

"All of that? You haven't even had her a week and she already has more stuff than I do." Wyatt took the bag and set it on the front seat of the truck.

Grace edged around him and began showing him Sweetie's belongings. "Her bed is in the bottom here. But, like I said, she likes to sleep with me."

"Who wouldn't?"

She frowned. "Is that a line? Somehow it doesn't sound right, coming from you."

"I got lines," Wyatt said. "I've got moves, too. I'm a little rusty from lack of practice, that's all."

She lifted two stainless steel bowls from the bag and set them on the seat. "Here's her water bowl, and here's her food bowl. I put the dog food in here, too. I give her a cup in the morning and a cup in late afternoon."

"Got it."

Grace handed him a pink leopard-print leash with lime-green banding. "Here's her leash. I let her out first thing in the morning. But she won't go right away. You have to walk her around a little bit, let her sniff things out before she picks her spot."

He handed the leash right back to Grace. "You keep this one. I'll get her one that's a little less, uh, girly."

"Nothing too butch," she warned him. "And no camo. Sweetie has standards." She went on unloading the bag.

"Here's her Greenies. I give her one last thing at night."

He wrinkled his nose. "Greenies?"

"They're supposed to promote healthy teeth and gums. And help with the whole doggie-breath thing."

"You're kidding."

She raised one eyebrow, which shut him up, then continued with her inventory. "Brush."

"Brush," he repeated.

"Pillowcase."

He held up the pink and white striped case with a questioning look.

"It's the one I usually sleep on," Grace admitted. "I read that dogs can get separation anxiety. This one smells like me. So she won't feel like she's in a strange place. Just put it in her bed, okay?"

"Okay."

She went back to unloading the bag. "Flea and tick medicine. She gets it once a month."

"Once a month."

"Heartworm meds. Again, once a month. I put it in the middle of a little peanut butter sandwich, so she won't figure out it's good for her."

"Peanut butter," he repeated dutifully, putting the meds back into the trash bag. "Is that it?"

"One last thing," she promised. "Chew toy." She reached in the bag and pulled out a nude Ken doll.

Wyatt held the doll up to the light and examined the teeth marks ringing Ken's overly tanned buttocks.

"Is this supposed to be symbolic?"

"Not at all," Grace said. "The first night I brought her home, Sweetie was rooting around in the closet in my bedroom and she found it in a box of my old toys and dolls. She loves Ken. It's the cutest thing, the way she carries him around in her mouth."

"You couldn't let her chew up a Barbie doll?" He handed the doll back to her.

"She likes Ken," Grace said, with a shrug.

He handed the doll back to her. "If it's just the same to you, I'll get her a ball or a squeaky cat or something else to chew on while she's at my place."

Grace looked down at the Ken doll. "I'll take this over to Mandevilla and keep it there for her."

"Good." Wyatt propped the little dog on his forearm. "Say good night, Sweetie."

Grace caressed the dog's ears and gave her one more head scratch, then looked up at Wyatt.

"Call me if you need me. Really. Like, if she won't sleep or she starts that scratching-at-the-door-and-whining thing, I could come over and calm her down."

Wyatt cupped Grace's chin in his hand. "She'll be fine. Stop worrying. I'll bring her over to you at Mandevilla first thing in the morning." He set the dog down gently on the passenger seat and closed the door.

"I'm there by eight," Grace said, following him around to the driver's side. "You won't forget to give her the pillowcase, right?"

He got into the truck and leaned out the open window. "Stop being such a helicopter parent."

She opened her mouth to protest, but she didn't have a chance, because suddenly he was kissing her. Both his hands were tangled in her hair, and he pulled her right up against the door and teased her lips open with his tongue. The kiss lasted another minute or so, and left Grace breathless and dazed. And hot. When a car pulled alongside the truck, she reluctantly pulled away.

"See?" Wyatt said, grinning as he put the truck into reverse. "Moves."

32

The little cottage—okay, he could call it a cottage, but it was really a glorified double-wide—was ablaze with lights when he pulled the truck under the carport. Wyatt tucked Sweetie under one arm and carried her and her luggage inside.

"Home sweet trailer," he said, setting her down on the vinyl floor. She took a few tentative steps and sniffed one of Bo's discarded flip-flops before picking it up in her mouth and turning to him, as if asking permission.

"Knock yourself out," Wyatt said generously. "It's way better than a Ken doll, right?"

He could hear the television in the back room. "Dad? He called loudly. All his conversations with Nelson had to be at top volume these days. He walked toward the tiny den and poked his head around the doorway. The recliner was facing the television, but there was no tell-tale tuft of white hair poking above the headrest. "Dad?"

The chair was empty, the television turned to a *Law and Order* rerun. A plate with the remains of a chicken potpie sat on the folding TV tray beside the recliner. Wyatt felt his pulse blip. He passed the open bathroom door, knocked softly on Nelson's closed bedroom door. "Hey old man," he called. "You sleeping?" When there was no answer, he opened the door to find the room empty and the bed still made, the worn quilt folded neatly at its foot. The room smelled like his father, like Old Spice and Bengay. But where the hell had the old man gotten to?

He opened the back door and peered out into the darkness. "Dad?" Nothing. He gave a soft whistle and Sweetie dropped her flip-flop and trotted over, her nails clicking on the harvest-gold vinyl flooring. "Come on girl, let's take a walk and find Granddad." Now he wished he'd taken that ridiculous pink leash.

"Stay here," he told the dog. He went out to the carport and rummaged around until he found a length of clothesline. Back in the house, he found a flashlight and fashioned a makeshift leash from the rope.

His heart was pounding as he stepped out of the cottage. It was nearly ten. His father was usually fast asleep by now, either in his recliner or his room. Nelson's car, a gas-guzzling Olds, was parked in the carport, its hood covered in a fine haze of cobwebs and pine needles. He seldom drove it anymore, claiming his night vision was fading, but Wyatt suspected his father probably realized his driving days were mostly over. Now he noticed that the golf cart was missing. He cursed softly.

Sweetie sat on her haunches and looked up at him expectantly. What was it Timmy used to tell Lassie in those old Nick at Night reruns? "What's that girl? Granddad fell down the old well?" Only Sweetie was definitely not a collie, and as far as he knew, there were no abandoned wells at Jungle Jerry's Olde Florida Family Fun Park.

"Let's take a walk," he said in a surprisingly calm voice. Sweetie inched forward, testing the air with her nose, and then set off at a trot. For lack of a better idea, Wyatt let her take the lead, playing the flashlight over the curtains of green. It was a typical summer night in Florida, the air nearly dripping with humidity. Clouds of mosquitoes swarmed his already-inflamed face, and the smell of night-blooming jasmine blanketed the thick spongy air. Sweetie trotted on, heading past the huge old banyan tree with its sinister-looking tracery of roots draping from the elephant-gray lower limbs, and around the reflecting pool with its island rookery for herons and egrets nesting in the moss-draped cypress trees. The moon was nearly full and its reflection was a butter-yellow orb in the black water of the pool. Every hundred yards or so, the little brown dog stopped, sniffed, and then readjusted her course.

Sweetie, Wyatt thought, had a lot more hunting dog in her gene pool than he would have guessed.

They were just rounding the Nursery Rhyme Garden, with its two-story concrete Mother Hubbard shoe when a pair of sharp cracks pierced the still night air. Wyatt knew that sound. It was Nelson's double-gauge shotgun.

Sweetie pricked up her ears and took off at a surprisingly fast full run, with Wyatt following close behind, the flashlight's beam bouncing off the landscape. She was barking now, excited and on full alert. She made a sharp right turn at the stand of crimson-flowering royal poinciana trees, and Wyatt realized she was headed for the area they'd always called Birdland, because it was where all the tropical bird cages and the parrot-show amphitheater were located.

The little dog barked as she ran, and Wyatt's mind conjured up every conceivable tragedy as he sprinted through the thick tropical foliage. Maybe his father had gotten confused and wandered off into the darkness, on the golf cart, armed with his favorite old shotgun. Maybe he'd imagined an intruder and gone to investigate. None of the story lines flashing through his imagination had a happy ending.

Finally, Sweetie skidded to a stop. She sat on her haunches, her ears folded back, a deep, guttural growl rising in her throat, aimed at some unseen enemy lurking in the darkness.

Silvery moonlight revealed Nelson Keeler, sitting on one of the splintery green-painted benches ringing the amphitheater, his shotgun resting across his pajama-clad knees. In the round, chicken-wire-ringed aviary nearby, Cookie, the African gray parrot, hopped agitatedly from foot to foot. "Shots and beer, shots and beer," the bird muttered.

"Hey, son!" Nelson exclaimed, spying him. Sweetie stayed where she was, on full alert, growling menacingly.

"Dad?" Wyatt sank down onto the bench beside his father. "What's going on?" He was out of breath, bewildered. "What are you doing out here?"

Nelson pointed into a clump of ferns and bromeliads ringing the aviaries. "I got the sumbitch. One clean shot. The second for insurance."

Wyatt's heart sank. For months now, the park had been the target of petty criminals. Twice, they'd managed to break into the gift shop, stealing less than fifty dollars' worth of cash, some cases of coke, and some stale candy bars. Another time, they'd gone farther into the park and attempted to cut through the wire to steal the parrots, apparently thwarted by the hue and cry raised by Cookie and the others. Although Wyatt viewed the crimes as a nuisance, Nelson had been enraged at the idea of anybody breaching the admittedly lapse security at Jungle Jerry's.

A dozen years earlier, they'd had the park wired for an alarm system and installed motion-detector cameras. Now, though, the technology was outdated and the cameras were inoperable. And they didn't have the money to install a new security system.

For a week or so, after the last break-in, Nelson had taken to patrolling the grounds on the golf cart Wyatt used for landscaping, finally growing bored after encountering nothing more than a few errant fruit rats on his nocturnal rounds.

Had his father shot and killed some young punk? Wyatt took a deep breath. "Who'd you get, Dad? Where is he?"

"Over there," Nelson gestured. "He slunk off into the ferns. See the blood? He's dead, though. I guarantee you. I nailed the sumbitch."

Wyatt's stomach turned as he observed the fine spatter of bloodstains on the crushed-shell walkway. He stood, and Sweetie took that as a signal to advance. She crept forward, her round belly scraping the sand, her nose sweeping back and forth. Five yards from the clump of ferns, she sat straight up on her haunches and growled again.

He held his breath as he played his flashlight over the greenery. Sweetie stayed close to his side on high alert. Finally, he saw where the trail of crimson ended. At first he thought it was a clump of Spanish moss. But as he grew closer, he spied a muzzle in a ghostly shade of gray, and then what looked like the emaciated body of a dog. He turned and glanced back at his father, who'd risen on shaking legs to follow them to the spot.

"What the hell is that?" Even as he said it, he realized what the form was.

"Coyote," Nelson said grimly. He turned and pointed to an aviary at the edge of the amphitheater. The wire door was ajar and the tree-limb perch was vacant. Brilliant red and yellow scarlet macaw feathers littered the cage floor. "Sumbitch got Heckel and Jekyll. I'm sorry, son."

The two macaws were the park's most senior residents, having been bought by Wyatt's grandfather in the late sixties. At one time they'd been a featured attraction in the parrot show, but now the colorful birds were officially retired from active duty. Wyatt patted his father's shoulder. "Not your fault, Dad. I'd heard about coyote sightings in and around town, but for some reason it never occurred to me they might turn up here."

"The hell it wasn't my fault," Nelson said gruffly. "I'm the one who fed all the birds today. I guess I must have left the macaws' cage unlatched. They were so old and lazy, it probably never occurred to them to try to fly away. The damned coyote had already finished 'em both off by the time I heard Cookie screaming and got over here on the cart."

Wyatt went to Cookie's cage, unlocked it, and reached in. He extended his hand and the bird gingerly walked up his arm to his shoulder. "Hey, Cookie," he said. "You're one hell of an alarm system." The gray parrot cocked its head and seemed to wink at him. "Gimme a beer," she said. He fished in his pocket and brought out a bird treat instead. "Performance bonus," Wyatt said. When the parrot finished chewing, Wyatt placed her back in the aviary and locked and double-checked it. Then, he walked around and checked the other cages. Marilyn and Lana, the cockatoos, were huddled together in the far corner of their cage, and Elvis, the huge blue and gold macaw, improbably, seemed to be sleeping.

"Okay, everybody's safe and accounted for," he said finally. "C'mon, Dad, it's late. Let's go home. I'll come back in the morning and bury the coyote." Wyatt took the shotgun from his father and placed it in the cargo hold of the cart, then climbed behind the wheel. Sweetie hopped up onto the bench seat beside him.

Nelson lowered himself into the cart, looking down at the dog in surprise. "Who's this?"

"This is Sweetie," Wyatt said, backing the cart up and heading down the path toward the house. "She's gonna be staying with us for a while." He reached over and ruffled the dogs' ears. "I think she'll fit in nicely around here, don't you?"

The old man regarded the dog with a practiced eye. "Got a lot of poodle in her. Maybe some schnauzer or cocker spaniel. Poodles used to be great hunting dogs, before they started being bred as silly show dogs. Did you know that?"

"I didn't," Wyatt said.

"Where'd you say you got her?"

"A woman in my divorce-recovery group found her in an abandoned house. She's living with her mom right now, over in Cortez, but the health regs don't allow a dog to live in a bar, so I said Sweetie could stay with us until Grace moves into her own place."

"Cortez?"

"Yeah. Her parents own the Sandbox. You remember that place?"

"Sure. Used to take you there when you were a little kid, after we'd been over at Holmes Beach. You used to love their cheeseburgers. This Grace, is she Butch Davenport's daughter?"

"Yeah. Did you know him?"

"Everybody in Manatee County knew Butch Davenport. He was quite a character. Is he still around?"

"No, he passed away a few years ago. Rochelle, Grace's mom, runs the Sandbox now."

"And what's your connection to this Grace person?" Nelson frowned. "You going out with her? Hanging out in dive bars like the Sandbox with her? Before your divorce is final? You better hope Callie and her lawyer don't get wind of that."

"Callie is living with her boyfriend, and has been for months now, so I don't think she has anything to say about my personal life. Anyway, like I just told you, Grace is in my divorce-recovery group. The whole group goes to the Sandbox after our meetings, just to sort of unwind. I have a beer or two and come home. End of story."

"But you like this girl."

"I do," Wyatt nodded. "She's a nice person. You'd like her, too."

"You sleeping with her?"

Wyatt felt his face burn. "Jesus, Dad! No. Where'd you get an idea like that?"

Nelson shrugged but said nothing else.

Wyatt pulled the golf cart under the carport and switched it off. Nelson unfolded himself from the seat, grunting with the effort, clutching the side of the cart for balance, swaying a little as he stood, trying to catch his breath.

And it struck Wyatt again: his father was aging before his eyes. The vagueness, forgetfulness, especially in the evenings, these had crept up and even accelerated since Wyatt had moved in with him. Nelson had always been strong—even into his sixties; he was fit and used to hard physical labor. Now, though, his gait had slowed and his energy level was diminished. It was all he could do to putter around the gift shop or the office a few hours in the morning before he returned to the cottage for a nap and endless hours of television.

He followed Nelson into the cottage, making sure the old man got safely into his bed before walking around the cramped cottage, switching off the lights and the television. The thin walls seemed to close in on him, choking him with claustrophobia. Sweetie followed close on his heels, seemingly sensing Wyatt's restlessness.

He held the back door open. "Come on then, let's go for a midnight ride."

. . .

As the cart jolted along the shell pathway, the headlight picked out the shaggy, overgrown landscape. Just like his father, Jungle Jerry's was aging, and not gracefully. Even the moonlight did not become it.

In his mind, Wyatt ticked off the unending items of maintenance that needed tending to. The gift shop's roof was leaking badly. He'd patched it so many times himself that the patches outnumbered the original asphalt roofing. The crushed-shell parking lot was pocked with potholes and washouts, and half the neon in the Jungle Jerry's sign had burned out.

In the park itself, dead or half-dead trees stood, waiting to be trimmed or cut down. The flower beds were choked with weeds and vines, and the abundant rain-forest plants swallowed whole sections of the pathways. His earlier visit to the amphitheater reminded him that half the benches there were rotted or splintered and all of them needed painting or replacing. The aviaries his grandfather had built decades ago for the tropical birds were rusting and were too small by current-day standards.

And that was just the physical plant, Wyatt mused. With only three employees—him; Joyce, his bookkeeper, ticket taker, and gift-shop manager; and Eduardo, who helped out with maintenance and landscaping—there were never enough bodies or hours or funds to get everything done.

Probably, Wyatt thought, he should have been smarter about all this. Six years earlier, not long before Bo's birth, a developer had offered to buy the park from the family for what seemed like a stunning amount of money—three million. His parents had considered taking the money and making the deal, but Wyatt, young and stupid and full of plans and dreams for the family business he intended to nurture for his unborn son—had urged them not to sell. How could they let a shopping center and yet another condo complex erupt on this gorgeous garden his grandparents had worked so hard to create?

Even then, Jungle Jerry's was struggling. They weren't losing money, but they weren't making much money either. Wyatt was certain he could turn things around. He'd taken marketing classes in college, had all kinds of ideas to drag the park into the twenty-first century. Callie had been furious with him. How could he be so stupid? All that money would have set them up for life! She'd raged at him for weeks after his parents turned down all that delicious money.

And then, before he could even get a Web site designed for the park, the economy tanked. Their attendance figures plummeted, and developers quit calling. Every month, the aging park went deeper into debt.

Wyatt steered the golf cart through the empty parking lot, hanging onto Sweetie's collar to keep her from flying off as the cart jounced through the potholes.

He fought the urge to surrender to the melancholy mood of the evening. Not everything in his life was crap. Earlier in the day he'd won one tiny battle against Callie. Starting tomorrow, he would have Bo for the weekend. He glanced over at Sweetie, sitting erect on the golf cart beside him. And maybe, just maybe, he would find a way to convince the dog's real owner that he wasn't such a total jerk after all.

33

She'd set her alarm for 6:00 A.M. Her to-do list for Mandevilla was long and getting longer, and she was eager to get to work. Grace opened her laptop and clicked on the comments section of TrueGrace.

This was her favorite part of blogging. Styling, photographing, writing, editing, and coming up with new ideas fed her creative soul, but hearing from readers was what kept her motivated. When she'd first started writing Gracenotes, she would stay up for hours after publishing a post, clicking and refreshing, anxious and nervous to see if anybody out there in the darkness was reading her work.

Now, she gasped. More than three dozen readers had left remarks about her last post. She clicked over to her dashboard and saw that over two hundred readers were now subscribing to the blog feed, meaning they would be automatically notified whenever Grace posted a new article.

A typical post on Gracenotes, where she had 239,000 subscribers, would have generated a couple hundred comments. But she was starting over now, from scratch, and each and every one of these readers and commenters were like gold for TrueGrace.

"Yay," she said, in a small voice. Then, louder. "Oh hell yeah, yay!"

Scanning the comments, her smile grew wider. "Go, Grace," said Justamom32.

"Love your new blog. So much more approachable and attainable," commented Wild4Style.

Of course the naysayers showed up for the party, too. "I liked your old blog better." Or, "Why don't you take some photography classes and get yourself a decent camera?" And, "Not much new or original here. All your ideas are tired and clichéd." All of the negative comments, not to her surprise, were anonymous. Her finger hovered over the delete button for a moment, but then she read a note left by Rinquedink. "Hey, Grace, don't let those bitches get you down. Haters gonna hate, taters gonna tate."

Ben had always monitored the comments on Gracenotes, deleting anything that even smacked of criticism. No, Grace decided, she would only delete comments that were obscene, libelous, or obvious spam. She'd let her readers make up their minds themselves on what was spurious.

The final comment made her laugh out loud. "I've deleted that fraud, faux Gracenotes, from my feed. You really are the one, true Grace. Wishing blessings for you and the ex-husband genital herpes." It was signed CindyLouWhoo.

When she got out of the shower, Grace checked her e-mail and saw that she had responses from six of the bloggers she'd contacted to request a place on their blog roll. The first message she clicked on was from a lifestyle blogger who called herself Eleganza.

Eleganza's real name, as everybody in the blogosphere knew, was Kennedy Moore. She'd been a contributing editor at several of Grace's favorite, now-defunct shelter magazines, including *House and Garden* and *Southern Accents.*

Grace knew Kennedy's backstory by heart. She'd been an interior designer, like Grace, and then, in the late eighties, after her children were off to college, had gone to work in the magazine world. Along the way, she'd weathered a divorce, remarried, and, within the past five years, lost her adored second husband and then her job at *Southern Accents.*

Kennedy had reinvented herself as one of the first professional lifestyle bloggers, writing witty, original posts; posing question-and-answer sessions with big-name designers; and sharing photos of the transformation of Hedgehog Cottage, her own small farmhouse in rural Connecticut. Eleganza, which featured her very personal take on interior design, cooking, entertaining, and affordable luxury, was hugely influential in Grace's world.

Grace held her breath as she clicked on the e-mail.

Congratulations, Grace, for landing on your feet again. The little house on Mandevilla is a gem, and I can't wait to see what clever tricks you'll come up with to make it shine. I was sorry to hear of the end of your marriage, but as I know all too well from past experience, endings are really all about beginnings. I'll be happy to add you to my blog roll. As soon as you get one of your rooms furnished, please send me pics and we'll discuss you doing a guest post for Eleganza. All best, K.

If the room had been larger Grace would have turned a backflip. A guest post on Eleganza was at the top of her blogger bucket list. Kennedy Moore's blog was the biggest-drawing lifestyle blog in existence, with more than three million subscribers. Her advertisers ranged from Home Depot to Tiffany to Coke. And now, TrueGrace would be on the very short, very select Eleganza blog roll. She flopped back on her bed, kicking her legs in celebration.

Quickly, she read the other responses. All but one were warm welcomes from bloggers who'd formerly included Gracenotes on their blog rolls.

The sixth e-mail contained a sobering message.

Dear Grace. I'd be only too happy to add TrueGrace to my blog roll, but I just can't. I think you should know that certain people are out there making veiled threats to anybody who gives you a hand. Since my husband was laid off his job last year, my little blog and the money it generates is our family's sole income. Unfortunately, I can't afford to make any enemies right now. Wishing you all the best, PeanutButter&Jedi.

Grace blinked. Was Ben actually contacting other bloggers and threatening anybody who helped her? Obviously, the others who'd agreed to add her name to their rolls either hadn't been contacted by him or just didn't feel threatened.

PeanutButter&Jedi was an emerging mommy blogger from Denver whose blog had been one of the first Grace added after establishing Gracenotes. Susan, its author, was the mother of four young boys, including a set of triplets, and Grace loved reading her wry accounts of decorating their home on a budget, thrifting, and her inventive recipes.

She felt a tiny stab of fear. What, exactly, was Ben threatening? His contacts with their advertisers were extensive. Maybe he'd casually dropped a hint to those same advertisers that anybody associated with Grace was poison? Whatever he'd done, it was enough to scare off Susan at PeanutButter&Jedi. And how many others?

It didn't matter, she decided. Ben would do whatever he could do. J'Aimee could preen and poach off her blog, but she would never be anything more than a poser.

Suddenly, Grace's path seemed very clear. She thought back to that first house she and Ben had restored together. They'd had nothing but sweat and perseverance. It was a cliché, but they'd made lemons out of lemonade back then. She would do it again, she vowed. Without Ben, without his connections, without money. And without fear.

34

G race stood in the paint aisle at the hardware store on Friday morning, staring at the huge display and its thousands of one-inch color chips. What she
wouldn't do for her trusted paint fan-decks, with all the notes she'd scrawled on
the backs of the cards and the yellow Post-it notes reminding her what paint
strength and finish she favored for all her favorites. But the fan-deck, along
with all her old files and design library, in fact, all her old life, were back at
Sand Dollar Lane.

She knew she wanted the equivalent of either Farrow & Ball's White Tie or
Pointing, two very specific whites for the walls at Mandevilla. Farrow & Ball
itself was out of the question. Imported from England, it was just too expensive.
She liked Benjamin Moore, too, which was what she'd used at Sand Dollar Lane,
mostly because the Benjamin Moore paint store in Sarasota was one of her blog
sponsors. She had shelves and shelves of BM paint at her old house. Now, however, neither paint would work for her tiny budget on Mandevilla. She sighed.
Cheap paint always just looked shoddy to her eye, and using it would require at
least three coats, which would take up too much of her precious time.

She walked around to the clearance endcap and scanned the assorted cans
of "oops" paint cramming the shelves.

There was a logical reason these cans were marked down; they were mistints,
custom colors that had been rejected by the original customer. Most of the gallon

cans were in shades she deemed either truly heinous—a neon bubble-gum pink, a muddy-looking taupe, a sickly green that reminded her of gangrene—or they were just unsuitable for a simple vernacular cottage like Mandevilla.

She did, however, find six gallons of an innocuous white in Benjamin Moore's low-VOC paint, marked down to ten dollars a can. That she could afford. Grace pulled a can from the shelf and studied the dab of paint on the tin lid. This paint had been custom-tinted, so it didn't have a color name or a formula. The shade was what she'd always thought of as a "dead white." But maybe if she had it tinted?

The clerk at the paint counter was a middle-aged man in a red apron. Grace set the oops can on the counter. "Help you?" he asked.

She gave him her sweetest smile. "Hi there. I'm wondering if you can add a little something to this paint to brighten it up a bit?"

He looked puzzled. "Like what?"

"Well, I was thinking you could add a little black to tint it, to see if I like it better."

The clerk took a closer look at the paint can. "Sorry. This is an oops paint. See, the sign says all paint is "as-is." That means we don't remix or add tint."

Grace sighed dramatically. "Look, it just needs the teeniest amount of black paint. I'm trying to match it to Farrow and Ball's Pointing shade. It wouldn't take very much time, and I would be soooo grateful?"

This approach had always worked for her in the past—at furniture showrooms, fabric houses, plumbing-fixture showrooms. A sweet smile and a plea for mercy, especially with men, had always been a winning formula in the past.

The hardware store clerk, though, seemed immune to her charms. "Sorry. Store policy. Can't help you." He went back to working on a display of weed killer.

And Grace went back to the clearance counter, where she loaded up all six gallons of the dead white, along with a pint of black latex paint. She would just have to experiment with mixing her own paint. She added in two gallons of white latex enamel for the trim, a paint tray, a five-gallon plastic bucket, canvas drop cloth, and rollers and brushes, sighing, again, at the thought of her workshop back at Sand Dollar, where all of her painting equipment and tools were lined up neatly, ready for her next project. At the last minute she plucked six Benjamin Moore paint cards from the display, to give herself an idea of the shades she was trying to achieve.

When the cashier added up all her purchases and applied them to the account Arthur Cater had set up for her, she was shocked that she'd already managed to make a four-hundred-dollar dent in her five-thousand-dollar budget.

It was nearly nine by the time she pulled up to the new cottage. Wyatt's pickup was parked out front, but he and Sweetie were walking around the yard, inspecting the property.

Grace's heart skipped a little beat. She told herself it was because she was happy to see her dog. But maybe Wyatt Keeler had a little to do with it, too.

He was dressed in his khaki Jungle Jerry's safari shirt, cargo shorts, and work boots, and he was bare-headed, stooped over, examining some kind of weedy shrub near the right edge of the porch. He had, Grace reflected, a fine-looking butt, tanned, muscular calves and thighs, and an admirable set of shoulders across a nice, broad chest.

"Sweetie!" Grace called. The dog turned and looked at her and, after a moment, came bounding over. She gave an excited little yip and jumped up into Grace's outstretched arms.

Wyatt followed in her wake, but he did not jump into her arms. "I was just checking out the yard. Hope you don't mind."

"It's a disaster," Grace said, "like the inside of the house. If you've got any landscaping advice, I'd love to hear it. How'd Sweetie do last night? I hope she wasn't too much trouble."

"No trouble at all. I would have been here sooner this morning, but I had to bury a coyote."

She raised an eyebrow. "A coyote? Around here?"

"In the park. My dad heard the parrots raising a ruckus last night. Turned out to be a coyote. By the time he got to the old amphitheater, where we have the aviaries, the damned thing had already finished off two of our parrots."

"Oh no! Not Cookie. Please tell me the coyote didn't get Cookie," Grace said.

"Fortunately, no. Cookie's cage was locked up tight. But our macaws, Heckel and Jekyll, weren't so lucky," Wyatt said, his expression grim. "Dad shot the varmint before he could do any more damage."

"That's awful," Grace said, feeling a chill go down her spine. She hugged Sweetie closer and shivered, despite the ninety-degree heat. "Could a coyote attack a dog?"

"Maybe," Wyatt said. "But after what happened with the macaws, I won't let her roam around off a leash at night. She doesn't seem inclined to go very far from me anyway, which is probably a good thing."

"You're not kidding." Grace breathed. She set Sweetie down carefully in the yard. "So. What do you think of my little project?"

"Great house," Wyatt said. "I love these old Florida cracker places. Not too many of them left around here."

"I know," Grace said, warming to her subject. "Do you want to see the inside?"

He glanced at his watch. "Can I have a rain check? Dad's a little worn out from his big adventure last night. I need to stick pretty close to the park today."

"Sure," Grace said, feeling a little let down.

"This yard could be really pretty with some work," Wyatt said, gesturing at the shrub he'd just been examining. "You've got some nice specimen palms in the front here, and that hedge of gardenias by the porch is in pretty good shape. Might want to spray it for aphids and trim it a little."

"What about this pathetic yard?" Grace asked, stubbing the toe of her sneaker into what was left of the crabgrass- and sandspur-infested patch of sand. "What could I do with it that won't eat up my fix-up money?"

Instead of answering, Wyatt walked away, pacing it off. He bent down, kicked at something in a patch of crabgrass, stood, and grinned. "You've got an old sprinkler system here, did you know that?"

"No!" Grace said, bending down to look. "You think it works?"

"I'd have to take a closer look," Wyatt said. "But if the lines are intact and the system is in place, that's half the battle. You can replace the old sprinkler heads and even buy new timers if necessary, but with those in place, you'd be able to replace the lawn with something hardier and keep it watered until it's established."

"A new lawn would do wonders for the curb appeal," Grace said. "But that'd cost thousands and thousands. And I don't even have hundreds and hundreds. Maybe that's something Arthur would be interested in doing down the line."

"Arthur?"

"Arthur Cater. He's the owner. He's kind of a tightwad, but my big hope is that once he sees what I've done here, he'll loosen up give me a little more money to work with."

"This yard isn't that big," Wyatt said. "I was walking around before you got here, just kind of brainstorming. You've got a lot of planting beds and borders that are all overgrown with weeds right now, but if you weeded and mulched them and put an edging around them, you're left with just a nice little swath of green up front here and one in the back. The sides of the house are mostly shaded by those oaks, and they're underplanted with some beat-up old hostas and leather-leaf ferns and begonias, but again, get that cleaned out, separate the hostas and give them some breathing room, and it'll be fine."

"What about the backyard?" Grace asked. "Pretty disgusting, huh?"

"It needs work, yeah. But it's not impossible. I'd get rid of that old tin storage shed first thing. It's falling apart and you don't need it anyway with that big garage. You've got the start of a nice fruit grove back there."

"Really? I just thought they were a bunch of old half-dead bushes. They're all overgrown with moss and half the branches look dead."

"They need some help, for sure," Wyatt said. "But you've got a couple of tangerine trees, a ponderosa lemon, a lime, a grapefruit, and a kumquat." He laughed. "You could set up your own fruit stand."

"I might if it were my house," Grace said. "But it's Arthur's. And it's a rental house."

"Have you thought about asking him if he'd rent to you?" Wyatt asked.

"Only since the first minute I saw it," Grace said wistfully. "I could do so much with this place, if it were mine . . ."

"But?" He crossed his arms over his chest.

"I told him when I've finished with it, it should rent for at least $1,500 a month, this close to the beach and being on Anna Maria. That's more than I could afford."

"But you're doing all this work, essentially for free, right?"

"So that I can photograph and write about it for TrueGrace," she said. "It's that kind of trade-off. Essentially to get material for my new blog."

"Maybe you could work out some kind of arrangement with the guy," Wyatt said. "You don't know until you ask."

"Maybe . . ." Grace said hesitantly.

He glanced at his watch again. "Okay, gotta go. What time should I pick her up this afternoon?"

"Her?" Grace was lost in thought.

"Sweetie. Remember?"

"Oh, right." She laughed. "Just come whenever it's convenient. I'm gonna try to finish ripping up the kitchen floor today, and then I hope to get started painting. It'll be a late night. So come whenever you like. I'll be here."

35

The music boomed through the empty rooms of the old house, echoing off the wooden floors and high ceilings. Grace poured a gallon of white paint into the five-gallon bucket. Yup, too dead white. She pried the lid from the can of black paint and dipped in a plastic measuring spoon. A quarter of a teaspoon to start. It wasn't scientific, but it was the best she could do. She took the wooden paint paddle and started to swirl the black into the white. Hmm. Not bad.

She dipped her index finger into the paint and smeared a bit of it on her Benjamin Moore paint chip. Not quite enough oomph, for lack of a better word, but not a bad start either. She added another eighth of a teaspoon and repeated her test.

Better. Grace slipped one of her father's old T-shirts over the tank top she'd worn to the hardware store. Its hem touched the top of her thighs and nearly reached the ragged hem of the faded blue cutoffs she'd picked up at the animal-rescue thrift shop in Bradenton. She hesitated for a moment, then stripped off her bra. It was kinky, she knew, but for some reason, she'd never been able to paint in a bra. She knotted her hair in a ponytail and tied a bandanna over the finished coiffure. She was good to go.

She'd already taped off one wall of the living room and spread out her canvas drop cloth. Now, she dipped a trim brush in the bucket and brushed it onto the wall in a two-foot-wide square. She stood back and checked the effect. It did not suck. She moved her equipment to the long wall opposite the front door and painted a swatch there. Maybe?

She fired up the box fan she'd placed in one of the dining room windows and pried open all the rest of the windows that hadn't been painted shut. It was still hot in the house, but she was pleasantly surprised when the cross-ventilation at least kept the warm air moving. Grace still wasn't convinced that the ancient window-air-conditioning units actually worked, and, anyway, the house still needed airing out.

While her test paint swatches dried, Grace went back into the kitchen. She'd managed to pry up most of the harvest-gold vinyl flooring, but what she'd found underneath was a nasty surprise. Plywood sheeting. No heart pine, like the rest of the floors, just plywood. And it was speckled with bits of mastic that had been used to glue down the vinyl. Whatever she did with these floors, she'd have to get rid of all those gobs of goo. It made her back ache just thinking of it.

The first day she'd set up her laptop in the house, she'd been thrilled to discover she could piggyback off a neighbor's wireless Internet. Now she clicked over to her blog again and read another handful of comments, all positive, except for one from someone calling herself Freebird.

Wow, what happened to that showplace mansion you used to live in? Oh that's right, your hubsand kicked you out for a real woman. This place is a pigsty and a waist of time. Save the paint and buy a box of matches and a can of gas instead.

She was positive Freebird was really J'Aimee, who couldn't spell to save her life.

Leaving TrueGrace, she clicked over to Craigslist. She'd done some preliminary shopping and discovered that even the cheapest stoves and refrigerators at the big-box chain stores would put a worrisome dent in her budget. Maybe, she thought, she could find a bargain on Craigslist. Stainless steel would be nice, but she'd be happy with nearly-new good quality white appliances if the price was right.

She typed stoves into the search bar and came up with a list of nearly two hundred possibilities, ranging from the ridiculous—"Free stove, only one burner works, door has to be duct-taped. Must pick up today." To the sublime: "Viking 48-inch stainless steel pro series dual fuel, six burners, 12-inch steel griddle, simmer plate, convection/gas oven, electric broiler, Like new, $6,000."

"This is more like it," she muttered, reading a listing for a, "Like-new GE Profile refrigerator, and electric range, removed from model home, still in warranty, $200 must pick up." She e-mailed the owner, asking about availability, and then logged off.

Grace walked back and forth between the paint swatches, debating whether or not the white would work. Was it too cold? Too gray? She held the Benjamin Moore paint chips up against the walls for comparison. It wasn't Farrow & Ball, that was for sure. She would never be able to duplicate the depth of color or matte finish of the English paint, but this color? Yeah. She nodded. It was a happy, clean white, and a huge improvement over the current dirty taupey-pink walls.

She finished taping off all the trim, cranked up the tunes on her iPod, and went to work. Grace had always secretly enjoyed painting and had done a lot of it in her early days as a single career girl and then in the first few houses she and Ben rehabbed.

But at Sand Dollar Lane, she'd happily relinquished the job to the contractor. All those soaring cathedral ceilings and huge window walls and stairwells, not to mention the miles and miles of moldings and the window frames themselves, were too intimidating. Besides, Ben insisted it was time to have everything in the new house "first-class."

"You're going to be photographing the house all the time, and we're gonna shoot videos here, so how will it look to your readers and followers if they see streaky or chipped paint?" he'd said.

Now, she worked quickly, rolling the paint to the beat of the music. Unlike most people, she loved the smell of wet paint, especially mixed with the leftover fumes from all the Pine-Sol she'd used to get rid of the funky white-trash odors the house had absorbed.

She didn't stop for lunch until after she'd finished the living room and the dining room. Then, she took her sandwich, a bottle of water, and a ripe peach out to the front porch, where she sat in an old aluminum-and-plastic-webbed lawn chair she'd found in the toolshed. Sweetie sat at her feet while she ate, gobbling up whatever crumbs Grace tossed her, then curling up in a sunny spot near the screened door for a nap.

Grace stood up and stretched. She'd considered starting on the paint in the kitchen, but since she still didn't have a solution for the kitchen floors—and because she dreaded the thought of painting the old cabinet boxes and drawers, she decided to move on to the bedrooms.

It was no good trying not to play the "if I lived here game." She'd been trying to repress the urge since day one. So while she rolled faux Farrow & Ball on the larger of the two bedrooms, she allowed herself to daydream.

The room had two decent-sized windows that looked out to that big, deep backyard.

If I lived here, I'd replace those windows with a pair of French doors and build a big, wide stoop that ended in a little patio made of old mellow bricks. Maybe I'd have some kind of trellis partially enclosing it for privacy. I'd plant a pink climbing rose on the trellis, and I'd have a pair of lounge chairs out here. Or maybe I'd even have a fabulous outdoor shower, with one of those giant rain-shower heads.

The closet in the bedroom was nowhere near big enough to be a real master-bedroom-sized closet. The closet in the house on Sand Dollar Lane was bigger than this bedroom.

But if I lived here, I wouldn't need a huge closet. I don't need a lot of clothes anymore, so that's a blessing in disguise. Maybe I'd look for a big old armoire or a chifforobe, or even one of those oversized entertainment cupboards that are a dime a dozen now that everybody has a flat-screen. I'd paint it a dusty, weathered gray-blue, and I could look for old leather suitcases at estate sales and thrift shops, and I could store my extra clothes there and stack them on top of the armoire. And I'd find a great bed, maybe use a pair of twin head-boards, something rattan or tropical? This house seems to scream for that Old Florida/British Colonial look.

Grace dragged the drop cloth over to a new section of wall. She didn't really know why she even bothered using one. The wood floors were already spat-tered with old paint and pockmarked with nail and tack holes from the wall-to-wall carpet she'd ripped up. She'd meant to check on the price of renting a floor sander at the hardware store, but she'd been distracted by figuring out the paint situation.

If I lived here, I'd stain the floors two shades darker, and I'd use a matte-finish poly. With the soft white walls and the sunlight coming in through the French doors, they'd have a deep, natural glow. No carpets underfoot, just maybe a striped cotton runner, or possibly a worn old Oriental in pale, faded greens, blues, and browns.

Planning it all out in her head, listening to the music, Grace found her painting groove again. She was dripping with sweat and spattered head to toe with paint, but it didn't matter. She was doing just what she wanted to do, how she wanted to do it, with no interference from anyone. It was a very good day.

She was just starting to move into the second bedroom when she heard the screened door open. "Helllllooo?" A male voice echoed.

"Wyatt?" She stripped the bandanna off her head and ducked into the bathroom to survey her appearance. Disastrous. Epic, Titanic-level disastrous. Her face was flecked with white paint, her arms and legs were flecked with white paint, and she had a giant smear of dirt on her right boob.

"Grace?" His footsteps echoed in the living room. "Are you in here?"

"Be right out," she called, pulling the bathroom door shut. She found an old washcloth in the linen closet, ran the water in the bathroom sink until all traces of rust were gone, and scrubbed her face and arms with it. She sighed. It was the best she could do. Anyway, who was she trying to impress?

When she got out to the living room, Wyatt was walking around, checking her handiwork. And there was a little freckle-faced boy rolling around on the floor with Sweetie, who was engaged in a spirited tug-of-war over what looked like a rag of some sort. Until she got a closer look, and realized they were actually using her discarded bra.

"Sweetie," Grace called, her face in flames. The dog looked up, with a bra strap clenched between her teeth. Grace scooped her up, disengaged the bra, and stuffed it into the back pocket of her cutoffs.

She cut her eyes over to Wyatt, whose chest was heaving with barely suppressed laughter. He was studiously avoiding meeting her eyes.

"Well, hello," Grace said, sitting down on the floor next to the child. Sweetie jumped out of her arms and began sniffing the little boy's shoes. "I bet you're Bo."

The child ducked his head. "Yes ma'am." Sweetie put her front paws on the child's chest and sniffed his neck, wedging her head under his hand until he was forced to scratch the dog's head.

"My name's Grace," she said, extending her hand. "I hear you're going to be helping take care of Sweetie."

"Yes, ma'am," the boy said. "Does she do any tricks?"

"I don't know, Bo. I've only had her a few days. But I think she's a pretty smart little thing. Maybe you could teach her some tricks?"

Bo flopped onto his back and Sweetie dutifully stepped onto his chest and began licking his neck and face, which prompted a huge fit of giggles from the child.

Finally, he sat back up and cradled the dog in his arms. "My dad taught Cookie to ride a bike and talk. Maybe we could teach Sweetie to do that."

Wyatt laughed. "Thanks for that vote of confidence, son, but even though Sweetie is really, really smart and cool, I think bike riding and talking is probably not in her future. How about if we just work on teaching her how to fetch a stick and sit up and bark on command?"

"Cool," Bo said, tickling Sweetie's belly. "Can we start tonight?"

"In the morning, maybe," Wyatt said. He touched a fingertip to one of the newly painted walls. "Man, you work fast. I can't believe you got this whole place painted in one day."

"Not all of it," Grace said. "I was just starting on the second bedroom when you guys showed up. I've still got the bathroom and the kitchen to do, not to mention the screened porch. Those are the rooms that are going to take the most work."

"Still," Wyatt said, walking into the abbreviated hall and then into the bedroom. "When you said this morning that the place was a mess, I was picturing something much, much worse."

"You should have seen it the first day I got here," Grace said, wrinkling her nose. "If my camera had smell-a-vision, I could have totally grossed out everybody on the Internet. It was so, so, nasty. Rotting wall-to-wall carpet, skanky old appliances. Everything was filthy. And that bedroom, where they'd locked Sweetie . . ." She shuddered.

"Are you ready to knock off for the day?" Wyatt asked.

"I don't even know how late it is. I kind of lost track of time."

"It's nearly six," Wyatt said. "Bo and I are going for pizza. We were wondering if you'd like to join us?"

"Pizza?"

"There's a place just over on Holmes Beach," he said. "Arturo's. Nothing fancy, but it's good and it's cheap, and if we get there reasonably early, we can get a table on the beach and watch the sunset."

Grace glanced at Sweetie. "What about her?"

"It's pet-friendly," Wyatt promised. "As long as we get a table outside."

She glanced down at her paint-spattered, braless self. "I can't go like this."

"Sure you can," Wyatt said. "Bo and I don't care. And neither does Sweetie."

"But I do," she said gently. "Certain standards must be maintained. I'll tell you what. Why don't you guys go ahead to Arturo's. I'll get cleaned up and meet you over there in thirty minutes."

"Thirty minutes?" he scoffed. "I've never known a woman yet who could shower and change and show up someplace in that little time."

"Thirty minutes," Grace swore. "If I'm one minute late, the pizza's on me."

At precisely 6:30, Grace hurried through the door at Arturo's. She was dressed in a pair of white capris, a black tank top, and a pair of gold metallic sandals from Pay-Less. Her hair was still wet from the shower and the only makeup she wore was a bit of coral lipstick. A pair of simple gold-hoop earrings sparkled at her ears, and around her neck she wore a necklace made from a tiny nautilus shell she'd found on the beach, hanging from a long thin gold chain. She walked through the main dining room and through a set of doors onto an expansive veranda, where she spied Wyatt and Bo sitting at a table close to the beach.

Wyatt's eyes swept over her appreciatively. He scrambled to his feet and gently pulled his son to a standing position, too.

"You clean up pretty good," he told her, pulling out a chair for her.

"And fast," she reminded him. "Thirty minutes. That might be a new land record for me."

"I guess that means dinner's on me," he said.

They ordered the Arturo's special, which meant a huge pie with everything, including pepperoni, Italian sausage, onions, peppers, olives, and anchovies; a glass of milk for Bo; and a pitcher of beer for the adults.

"Anchovies?" Grace asked, glancing over at Bo, who'd devoured two slices of pizza in the time it took Grace to work her way through one. "Your kid likes anchovies?"

The boy looked up, his face smeared with enough tomato sauce to fashion another whole pie. "I love anchovies!" he exclaimed, his broad smile revealing two missing front teeth.

"I haven't found anything he doesn't love," Wyatt said ruefully. "He's eating me out of house and home. I swear, every week he's grown another two inches."

"I'm the third tallest boy in first grade," Bo reported. "Cory Benton was the second tallest, but he's not going to our school next year, so I'll be the second tallest. Unless I grow some more, and then I'd be the first tallest." He took a gulp of milk and stood up, whispering in his father's ear.

Wyatt nodded. "It's inside, near the bar. Don't forget to wash your hands, and come right back here, okay?"

When he was gone, Grace took a sip of beer. "What a nice boy. I love that he's figured out he's the third tallest."

"He's fascinated with numbers and statistics," Wyatt said, shaking his head. "I do not know where he gets it. There are no bean counters in my family, and certainly none in his mother's. I haven't had the heart to point out to him that if Callie gets her way, he won't get to be the second tallest boy in the second grade at his school, because he'll be going to a new school. In Birmingham."

"Maybe it won't come to that," Grace said.

36

Bo came bounding back to the table. "Guess what, Dad? Scout's here! She and Coach Anna and her dad are eating dinner. Can I go sit with them for a while?"

Wyatt half stood, craned his neck, and spotted Anna and her family in the dining room. Anna nodded and pointed to an empty chair at the table and Wyatt gave her the thumbs-up sign. "Okay, but are you all done with your pizza?"

He eyed the last remaining piece on the tray. His father scooped it up into a napkin and handed it to him, and Bo ran off to join his friend.

"Anna's assistant coach on Bo's T-ball team," Wyatt said casually. "Scout's our pitcher, and Bo's best friend—on days he doesn't think girls are icky."

"What about Bo's father? Does he still think girls are icky?" Grace kept her tone playful.

"No, I'm a reformed girl hater." He reached across the table and tucked a strand of her damp hair behind her ear. "Especially where present company is concerned."

"Good to know," Grace said. "I've been meaning to ask you, how's your dad doing? You said he was pretty worn out today?"

"He's okay," Wyatt said. "I'm just going to have to get used to the idea that he's not getting any younger. All my life, he was this rugged, can-do guy. He literally did everything and anything at Jungle Jerry's: he built buildings, including the gift shop; paved the parking lot; dug the reflecting pond for the bird rookery. It was nothing for him to work a twelve- or fourteen-hour day, come home and play ball with me, and then get up and do it all over again the next day. I think my mom's death kind of took the wind out of his sails. He's only seventy-four, but some days, you'd think he was twenty years older."

"Your dad's seventy-four? Wow. Rochelle is only fifty-eight. How old are you?"

"I'm thirty-eight," Wyatt said. "You wanna see my ID?"

"I trust you," Grace said.

"Dad was thirty-six when they had me, same age I was when we had Bo. Dad went in the navy when he was just eighteen and got out in the late sixties. He and my mom met at an Allman Brothers concert in St. Pete, at the old National Guard Armory there. Crazy, huh? To think about your parents grooving to the Allman Brothers back in the day? My mom was six years younger than him, so she wasn't that old when she had me."

"Rochelle always says she was just a baby when she had her baby. She was only twenty when she got pregnant with me. Of course, my dad was a good bit older, too. He was already thirty, and he'd just bought the Sandbox when she came to work as a waitress. Dad claimed he threatened to fire her if she didn't marry him."

Wyatt thought for a moment. "It still bugs me, you know? That my parents had this long, happy marriage, and I had a happy childhood, and, with all that, I'm still ending up divorced. And you're in the same boat, right?"

"I guess." Grace took a sip of her beer. "I mean, I always assumed they were happy. Lately, I'm not so sure. Little things Rochelle's says. Maybe she wasn't as happy as I always thought. Certainly, I didn't have what you'd call the average childhood, growing up in a bar, but I don't think there was any lasting psychological damage."

"You grew up in a bar; I grew up in a tourist trap, playing with monkeys and parrots. And I always thought that was totally normal. I thought all kids had to shovel zebra poop when they got home from school every day," Wyatt said. His voice turned wistful. "I always just assumed Bo would have that life, too. He really loves hanging out at the park."

Grace's eyes widened. "You mean he won't, because Callie's taking him to Birmingham?"

"Not just that," Wyatt said. "I'm really not sure how much longer we'll be able to hang on at Jungle Jerry's. People don't want to spend a half a day wandering around a park where the big attraction is a bird riding a bike. Nobody cares about a tree that's two hundred years old or an orchid that doesn't grow anywhere else in the world. We're an anachronism. And we're bleeding money."

"It's that bad?" Grace asked.

He shrugged. "This is too depressing. Let's discuss something else. Like your new project."

"It's not depressing," Grace insisted. "It's just reality. Isn't there anything you can do to turn things around?"

"I've tried everything I can think of. Billboards, social media, Groupon offers, coupons in the mail. It helps a little, just never enough. Did you know that up until nineteen seventy, there were at least a dozen roadside tourist attractions, right here in this area?" He ticked them off on his fingers, "Sunken Gardens, Sarasota Jungle Gardens, Weeki Wachee, Silver Springs, Rainbow Springs, the Aquatarium, Tiki Gardens, Six Gun Territory, and that's just the ones I can think of off the top of my head. Lots of them are long gone, but others are still limping along, like Cypress Gardens. The last I heard, most of it had been turned into Legoland."

"I remember some of those places from when I was a little girl," Grace smiled at the memory. "I guess Disney coming to Florida in the seventies probably was the kiss of death."

"That and the interstates bypassing them," Wyatt said. "And people's tastes change. So, Jungle Jerry's is a dinosaur. A really expensive, dying dinosaur."

"What'll happen to it?" Grace asked.

"I'm not sure. We had a hot offer from a developer, right before Bo was born. They wanted to build one of those new urban centers, shopping and office and multifamily housing. My mom was sick; she had cancer—although we didn't know then that it was terminal—and she wanted us to keep the place running. Her father started it. He was the original Jungle Jerry. And like the fool I was, I thought maybe I could make it work." He shook his head. "Callie never let me hear the end of it afterwards. 'We could have been rich. You should have sold out.'"

"And then the economy tanked," Grace said. "How well, I know. Since nobody could sell a new house or condo, they sure didn't need a decorator to design a fabulous model home. And developers and builders probably couldn't afford to break ground on yet another new project with all that unsold inventory sitting around."

"Six months after we turned down the deal, we heard the developer defaulted on all his bank loans," Wyatt said. "So probably, even if we had made the deal, we never would have gotten paid."

"I know housing starts are starting to inch up again. Do you think it's possible that another developer would be interested?" she asked.

"Right now, there's only one interested buyer," Wyatt said, lowering his voice, as the waitress came by their table to ask if they wanted another pitcher of beer.

"Who?"

"The state of Florida," Wyatt said.

"Really? But that's good news, right? What would they do with the park? Keep it?"

"I don't know," he said, sounding irritated. "Dealing with bureaucrats is a major pain. They say they'd turn it into a state park. They say if the state legislature approves their next budget, the money's there, if Manatee County can kick in some money, too. There's a lot of 'ifs' flying around."

"What does your dad think?"

"He says he's okay with the idea," Wyatt said. "But I'm not sure he really understands all it involves. He just knows I'm worried all the time, and that worries him."

"Hey Dad!" Bo ran toward their table with a little girl with blond braids close on his heels. "Anna says we can have ice cream for dessert if you say it's okay."

"Hi Scout," Wyatt said, reaching out and tugging one of the girl's pigtails. "How was your pizza?"

"She *hates* pizza," Bo announced. "She had 'pasketti. And I had some, too."

From the looks of it, Grace thought, Both Bo and Scout had applied as much spaghetti sauce to their faces as they had to their bellies.

"It was dee-lish!" Scout announced. She was kneeling on the patio, and Sweetie was jumping up to lick her face.

"This is Sweetie," Bo told his friend. "We get to keep her at our house at night."

"Cool!" Scout said. "Does she go to your mom's house, too?"

Bo's shoulders sagged. "No. You know who is allergic. But I get to keep her at Dad's, and he's going to teach her how to fetch and stuff."

Wyatt took a napkin and wiped the outer layer of sauce from Bo's face. "Tell Scout's mom I said it was okay for you to have ice cream." He reached in his pocket and took out two dollar bills and handed it to the little boy. "That's to pay for your dessert. Don't spend it all in one place. Right?"

"Okeydoke." The two ran back inside.

"He's the real reason I hesitate to pursue this thing with the state," Wyatt said, nodding in his son's direction. "Dad and I will be okay. Theoretically, we'd come out of the deal with a little money. Enough to pay our bills and keep a roof over our heads. But Jungle Jerry's is Bo's legacy. He's grown up with the park. He thinks Cookie is his little sister. How can I sell that out from under my son?"

Grace met his eyes. "You're asking me?"

He clasped his hand over hers. "I'm asking you."

"It seems to me that Bo's legacy is you. And his grandfather. Times change. You know that as well as I do. I think we have to be flexible to survive. Look at me. When my work as an interior designer dried up—I mean, in this economy how many people need a twelve-thousand-dollar hand-knotted silk rug or eighteen thousand dollars' worth of window treatments? I had to reinvent myself. I had to go back to my roots, making do with what I had, doing most of it myself, with a lot of creativity and not much money. You do what you have to do, right?"

"Yeah." Wyatt sighed. "I just keep thinking, if I could hold on a little longer..."

He laughed. "Like I did with my marriage. And you see how well that turned out."

"It was different for me," Grace admitted. "These months, since I walked out on Ben, I've been blaming him for everything. And he's responsible for a lot of it, truly. But I think in the last few years I changed. My belief system and my values changed. It became more about status, having the best, the most expensive everything. Even though I started out writing DIY on Gracenotes, that changed, too. We monetized, got advertisers, and I needed to make them happy in order to survive. Or so I thought."

She took a sip of her beer. "I guess I sold out. And it wasn't entirely Ben's fault. I liked all that free stuff, giving big parties, living in the big house in the gated subdivision. And I loved having what seemed like unlimited resources available for any project I dreamed up. Ultimately, along the way, that's when our marriage started to go south." She gave a wry smile. "Rochelle would tell you I got too big for my britches."

Wyatt scooted his chair over toward her and leaned down to give her an unconvincing leer. "Your britches look just fine to me."

"Wyatt?"

He turned around to see Anna Burdette standing there, with Scout and Bo holding on to her hands. Anna gave Grace a friendly, if curious smile. "Hi there."

Wyatt stood. "Anna Burdette, this is my friend Grace . . ."

"Davenport," Grace finished for him, not wanting to be introduced by her married name. She shook Anna's hand. "I hear Scout's the Babe Ruth of T-ball."

Anna's nose crinkled as she laughed. "To hear Wyatt tell it, you might think so." She was studying Grace's face. "I don't mean to keep staring at you, but I keep thinking I know you from someplace."

"She's a famous blogger," Wyatt said.

Anna snapped her fingers. "Gracenotes, right? Your blog is my guilty pleasure. I read it in the middle of the night when I can't get to sleep."

"Thanks," Grace said. "Actually, I've changed the name. My old blog got, er, co-opted by my soon-to-be ex. Check out TrueGrace, if you will."

"I definitely will," Anna said. "In the meantime, the kids have been telling me about this spectacular little dog named Sweetie. I hear she's going to learn all kinds of tricks over there at Jungle Jerry's."

"She's actually Grace's dog, but she can't keep her where she's living right now, so we're sort of sharing custody. Bo has big plans for her," Wyatt said.

"Anyway," Anna said, "the reason I came by . . . Jack had to go on to work, but I told the kids I'd take them to play putt-putt for an hour or so, if that works for you. I can drop him off back at your place around eight."

"Please, Dad, please, please, please?" Bo was hopping up and down.

"I guess that would be okay," Wyatt said. "But not too much later, right, buddy? We've got a big game tomorrow, and your granddad is making you pancakes in the morning."

"Don't worry, the assistant coach is not gonna risk letting her star catcher suffer from sleep deprivation," Anna said.

"Let me give you some money to pay for Bo's golf," Wyatt said, half standing to get to his wallet.

"Not necessary. I've got buy-one, get-one coupons," Anna said. "Grace, it was nice to meet you."

"My pleasure," Grace said.

Anna leaned over and put her head next to Wyatt's. "She's cute, dude," she said in a stage whisper. "Classy, too. Don't screw this up, 'kay?"

37

Sorry about that," Wyatt said, when they were alone again. "Anna's worried about my love life. She keeps trying to get me 'back in the game,' as she calls it. But she's about as subtle as a slap in the face."

"You haven't dated at all since your split?" Grace asked.

"Me? The only other woman in my life besides Anna right now is Joyce Barrett."

"Who's she?"

"Our eighty-year-old bookkeeper slash office manager. I love Miss Joyce to pieces, but I seriously doubt she's interested in starting a new relationship."

As the waitress passed by, he gestured to her to bring the check. "It's still another hour 'til sunset, and Bo won't be back from putt-putt 'til after eight. Would you like to go someplace else for a drink? Or just take a walk on the beach?"

"Sweetie would probably love a stroll on the beach. And so would I," she said.

Grace stepped out of her sandals and stuck them in the back pocket of her pants, and after a moment of hesitation, Wyatt tied the laces of his Top-Siders together and slung them over his shoulder. They walked through the powdery white sand to the shoreline, and Grace stood and let the mild breeze blow through her hair. They walked for a while, close, but not touching.

The bright blue sky gradually darkened to deeper layers of dark blue, violet, silver, and then ochre and pink. The wind began to whip whitecaps on the incoming waves. Families lingered on beach blankets with coolers of drinks, radios playing softly. Closer to the dunes, at every pathway from the road, knots of people stood beneath the clumps of Australian pines, sea oats, and beach myrtle, waiting for the sundown ritual to begin.

The county had an ordinance against dogs on the beach, but Sweetie stayed close to Grace's side, and, as if by tacit agreement, other law-breaking dog walkers passed by and nodded in a conspiracy of silence.

The sun dipped lower, glowing gold, and when they came to a dune walkover with an empty bench, they sat down to watch the show. Sweetie hopped up onto Grace's lap, and Wyatt stretched his arm across the back of the bench; when his hand brushed the bare skin of her shoulder, she smiled to herself.

She leaned back, resting her head against his arm, and the warmth of his skin on hers felt familiar and exciting at the same time.

"Look," Wyatt said, pointing with his free arm. Out in the waves, the graceful gray backs of a pod of dolphins curved through the water. There were four or five larger ones and three or four smaller ones. "Some moms and some calves," he said.

"I've been watching dolphins in the gulf and the bay my whole life," Grace said. "But it never gets old. I used to love it when we'd go out on my dad's boat and they'd follow us, waiting for us to throw in some bait or a too-small fish."

"Yeah," Wyatt said with a sigh. "Kind of reminds you why you live here, doesn't it?"

"Mm-hmm."

The sun was sinking lower and the clouds above growing purple and midnight blue. "You ever see the green flash?" he asked, his hand grazing her shoulder.

"You mean the thing that happens the moment the sun slips below the horizon? Yes. We used to make a big ceremony out of it when I was growing up. My dad had a cowbell he'd ring at that exact moment."

But there was no green flash tonight, just another bright yellow glow, and then striations of deepening colors.

"This is nice," Grace said, snuggling back against his arm as the air grew cooler. She leaned against his chest, inhaling his clean, woodsy scent, feeling his warmth seep into her bare shoulders.

"You cold?" He wrapped both arms around her. "We could go back to the car."

Grace shook her head. She wondered if he would ever get up the nerve to kiss her again. Or if she would have to be the one to initiate things. In the meantime, she closed her eyes and told herself to enjoy the moment.

At some point, she must have enjoyed the moment so long that she dozed off. When her eyes fluttered open, it was dark.

She sat up with a start.

"What?" Wyatt asked. "You finished your nap?"

She yawned and laughed. "I'm sorry. I've been working so hard every night, I fall asleep as soon as the sun goes down. She glanced at her watch and jumped to her feet, grabbing Wyatt's hand and pulling him up, too. "Come on, Cinderfella. I regret to remind you that at eight o'clock, you turn into a dad again."

He groaned. "I'll text Anna, tell her to play another round of putt-putt. On me. That'll give us another hour, at least."

"No way. She'll think I'm seducing you."

"Anna's a hopeless romantic. She'd probably offer to get us a room."

Grace sighed. "Bo's expecting you to be home when Anna drops him off. I don't want to be the one who causes you to break promises to your son."

"I hate it when you talk sense," Wyatt grumbled.

They walked hand in hand back down the beach, with Sweetie staying close at their heels. Wyatt stood awkwardly beside her car as she unlocked the door. She sensed his nervousness, and found it touching.

She leaned over and kissed him lightly on the cheek. "About that dating-reentry counseling you mentioned—maybe we could take a class together."

38

At exactly 8:15 A.M. Wyatt hopped out of his truck and dashed into the house on Mandevilla. He found Grace sitting on the floor in the back bedroom, taping off baseboards.

"Gotta run," he said, setting Sweetie down beside her. "I promised Bo I'd throw him some extra batting practice before the game."

"Okay," she said. "How about if I just drop Sweetie off to you at the park later? Say six?"

He was halfway out the door, but he turned around, came back, and pulled to her feet. "I thought about what you said last night. Just before you left. You're killing me. You know that, right?"

She smiled. "In a good way, right?"

"Absolutely. See you at six." And then he was off again. A minute later, she ran out to the porch, hollered at him as he was getting into the truck. "I'll bring dinner. What do you like?"

"If you bring it, I'll like it." He threw the truck into reverse and headed down the road.

She was still on the floor, barefoot, dressed in her messy, paint-spattered T-shirt and cutoffs, a bandanna tied over her hair, scooching along on her butt, painting the baseboards, when she heard footsteps in the living room. Maybe Bo's T-ball game was over early? She turned expectantly.

J'Aimee stood in the doorway, looking down at her, eyes blazing with hostility.

Grace scrambled to her feet, dusting off her butt with both hands. "What do you want?" she asked, her voice cool.

J'Aimee was dressed in all black, a sheer, sleeveless black chiffon midriff-baring top worn over a black bra, black skinny jeans, and high-heeled silver-studded black sandals with gladiator-wrapped ankles. With her jet-black dyed hair she looked like a refugee from a bondage flick.

Although J'Aimee was actually about Grace's height, today, in the heels, she glared menacingly down at Grace.

"You think you're pretty damn smart, don't you," J'Aimee said, poking Grace in the chest with her forefinger. "With those bullshit e-mails you sent my advertisers. Me, steal your content? Who the fuck do you think you are?"

J'Aimee's breath was hot on her face. Grace was tempted to take a step backward, but instead stood her ground.

"Me? I'm the person who started Gracenotes. I'm the actual Grace. I'm the person who developed, cooked, photographed, and wrote that corn-crab chowder recipe you so blatantly lifted off my blog to pass off as your own work."

"There are a million recipes for that soup floating around on the Internet," J'Aimee said with a shrug.

"Ben managed to wipe out that post on my page, so I can't prove it, of course," Grace said calmly. "But I've got a new blogging platform for TrueGrace and a new protected password, and I've installed malware now, so tell him not to bother to try to mess with it. Also? I've started watermarking my photos with my TrueGrace logo, so you won't be able to poach my photos anymore either."

"Me? Poach your shit?" J'Aimee's throaty laughter was harsh. "Who are you kidding?"

She took a step backward, her eyes sweeping disdainfully over the room. "So this is your exciting new project? This *shack*?" Abruptly, she turned and walked out of the room, her high heels clacking sharply on the wood floors.

J'Aimee walked into the kitchen, took in the beat-up, doorless cupboards; the gaping spaces where appliances should have stood; the bare, glue-spattered plywood floors. She sniffed and wrinkled her nose in disgust. Just as quickly, she walked into the hallway, peered into the bedroom and then the single bathroom with its outdated tile and filthy tub and toilet.

"You're pathetic, Grace," J'Aimee said, her eyes glittering with malice. "You are desperate and pathetic, like this house. You put yourself out there to all the world on the Internet as this all-knowing authority. Miss Know-It-All: the perfect designer, entertainer, gourmet cook . . ."

J'Aimee admired her own reflection in the bathroom mirror and then stomped out of the bathroom and into the living room. "But you're not even woman enough to keep your husband interested in you. You want to know how long it took Ben to jump my bones after you hired me? A week."

She laughed at the look of shock on Grace's face. "And don't be telling yourself that I'm the little tramp that went after him. He came on to me. Uh-huh. That's right. The first time? Oh, that was while you were out giving a speech to some fancy society women's fund-raising luncheon. I even remember the title of your talk, because I had to type it and print it out for you. 'A House Is Not a Home.' And while you were giving your lame talk, I was back at your house, fucking your husband's brains out." She paused and laughed again. "In your bed."

Grace wanted to knock J'Aimee down, shove a fist in her throat, anything to shut up the torrent of bile spewing from her mouth. But she was paralyzed, speechless.

J'Aimee's smile was mirthless. "TrueGrace? That's what you're calling yourself now? Who are you kidding? Ben was the brains behind Gracenotes. He and I did all the scut work, making it look pretty and effortless, while you took all the credit."

She took another step closer to Grace again, until she was directly in her face. "Look at you now, Grace *Davenport*. Living with Mommy above a shitty bar, hiring yourself out as nothing more than a glorified housepainter." She whipped a cell phone out of the pocket of her form-fitting jeans, and before Grace could stop her, she'd snapped a picture of Grace, standing there, covered in paint, her mouth gaping. "This'll give Ben a good laugh."

The click of the camera lens suddenly snapped Grace back to consciousness.

"Just what is it you want here, J'aimee? You want more material to leave some more snarky, barely literate comments on TrueGrace? Don't bother to deny it either. I know you're Freebird. Since you're living in Ben's pants these days, you might want to get him to explain ISP numbers to you."

Now it was Grace's turn to fight. She put her paint-spattered hand squarely in the middle of J'Aimee's chest, leaving a perfect white handprint on the black chiffon.

"Hey," J'Aimee cried angrily, swatting Grace's hand away.

"You're a fraud, *J'Aimee*," Grace said, rolling the name out with the exaggerated French pronunciation. "Oh. Wait. Even your name's a fake, *Jamie*. You've never had an original idea in your life. You're the kind of bottom-feeding parasite who has to be content with whatever crap sinks to the bottom of the cesspool. But hey, you want my old blog, take it! My house and that bed you seem to love? Help yourself. It means nothing to me now. Oh, and how about my husband?"

"He's mine now," J'Aimee purred.

"And you're welcome to him," Grace said. Suddenly, she remembered something Ashleigh Hartounian had said during their first session of divorce-recovery group, something about her husband's new mistress.

"You are more than welcome to Ben Stanton, that lying, cheating piece of garbage. But here's something you need to know, J'Aimee. You are just like a cup of Publix yogurt."

"Huh? You're crazy."

"Nope," Grace said, starting to enjoy herself. "You, J'Aimee, are just like any other garden-variety skank. You've got an expiration date stamped on your bony little ass. But you won't even know when it's past—until Ben throws you out for something sweeter and newer."

Clearly, J'Aimee had no clever response. "Screw you," she said, her teeth clenched. "Leave my advertisers alone. Quit making trouble for Ben and me, or you will live to regret it." She turned to stalk away.

"No, screw you," Grace said. "Now get out of my house." On an impulse, she managed to land a kick, leaving a perfect impression of her bare foot in faux Farrow & Ball white on J'Aimee's black-clad butt.

For the rest of the morning, Grace fumed. What, she wondered, had prompted J'Aimee to seek her out here? She was obviously worried about her advertisers. Had one of the companies she'd e-mailed dropped their support for Gracenotes? Wouldn't that be poetic justice! When she finished with all the trim in the bedroom she struggled to her feet and went to check the time.

It was nearly twelve thirty. There was a peanut butter and jelly sandwich out in the kitchen, calling her name. But as she was about to put her phone down, the screen lit up with an incoming text from a number she didn't recognize, with a Bradenton prefix.

Got some news about Paula. Meet me for lunch at Rod & Reel Pier, 1 pm?
Who is this? Grace texted.
Camryn. R we good?

She looked down at her messy clothes. She'd have time to wash her hands and face, but not much more time than that. Fortunately, the Rod and Reel was an open-air restaurant at the end of the fishing pier on Anna Maria. She could go dressed as she was.

OK!

She almost didn't recognize the woman sitting at one of the tables by the window. Most of the tables were full of families, tourists, and anglers who'd spent the morning trying their luck fishing for trout or redfish on the pier. Finally, a lone woman in a floppy straw hat and sunglasses waved her down.

"Camryn? Is that you?"

"You see any other black women loitering around here?" Camryn snapped. She fanned herself with her hands. "Lord, Jesus, I'd forgotten how hot it is out on this pier."

Grace shrugged and sat down. "You picked this place, so don't blame me."

"I'm just sayin'," Camryn said. "I come here once a year for the fried grouper sandwich. Best thing I ever put in my mouth, but I try not to eat fried food, so I generally stay away."

"Why the disguise?" Grace asked.

"I'm what they call a minor celebrity in this town," Camryn said. "When I first got in the business, I got a big kick out of having people come up to me at Dillard's or a restaurant. 'Ooh, you're the lady on TV.' Uh-huh. Then I gotta have my picture taken with 'em, maybe autograph something. And I swear, every time I step foot out of my house without makeup or my hair all looking nappy, that's when somebody spots me. You think I don't see them snapping pictures of me with their cell phones, telling their friends at work, 'I saw that Camryn Nobles on channel four at the gym, and girl! Without her TV makeup, she is looking old in the face.'"

"So on Saturdays, you leave off the makeup and wear a hat and sunglasses. Makes sense."

Camryn studied her. "If I went somewhere in this town, looking like you look right now, people would be tweeting and Facebooking my picture all over the Internet."

"I was painting a house when I got your text," Grace said, deciding not to be insulted. "There wasn't time to go home and change. So what did you find out about Paula?"

"Let's order first," Camryn said. The waitress took their orders: fried grouper sandwich for Camryn, mahimahi for Grace, unsweetened iced teas for both.

When their drinks came, Camryn sucked down half her tea. "First off, don't you think it's funny that a supposed marriage counselor is divorced?"

"Maybe not," Grace said. "After all, she's not counseling us on how to hang on to our marriages. She's helping us deal with breakups. So I guess it's not all that surprising that she's in the same boat. How'd you find out she was divorced?"

"I got tired of waiting for our silly little intern to do her job, so I made some phone calls myself. Did some googling, a little investigative journalism. To tell you the truth, I'd forgotten how much fun it is to dig up good dirt. Anyway, yeah. Dr. Paula Talbott-Sinclair has only been divorced a couple years. We already knew she'd been in practice in Oregon—Portland. I called one of the assistant producers at our network affiliate out there, and she knew all about our Paula."

Their food arrived, and Camryn picked up her sandwich, nibbled, and sighed happily. "I'll have to do an extra hour on the elliptical to pay for this, but it's worth every calorie."

Grace was surprised by how hungry she was, so they ate in silence for a while. Finally, Camryn finished her sandwich. She picked up the paper plate with the remaining curly fries and dumped them in a nearby trash bin. "I don't need the temptation," she explained.

"You said that producer knew something about Paula?" Grace prompted.

"Mm-hmm. Paula and her husband, Thorsen Sinclair, were in practice together. He was a psychiatrist; she was a therapist. Connie, the woman I talked to at KTXX, says they were pretty prominent, gave workshops all over the Pacific Northwest on 'mindful marriage,' whatever that is. They self-published a book with the same title. And everything was golden with the Sinclairs. Until he fell in love with one of their patients."

"Oh, wow." Grace breathed.

"Uh-huh. Both couples split up, and it made a nice little scandal, because the husband called the state board and filed a formal complaint against Thorsen and then leaked it to the media out there. Connie sent me a link to the story in the Portland paper. 'Mindful Marriage Melt-Down.' Long and short? Thorsen dumped Paula. After their divorce was final, he married the other woman. And Paula, apparently, fell to pieces. She 'borrowed' one of her ex's prescription pads and wrote herself a bunch of scrips for tranquilizers. But she got caught."

"Did she go to jail?" Grace asked, wide-eyed.

"It was a first offense, so the judge agreed to drop the criminal charges and allowed her to check herself into a rehab program for impaired healthcare givers," Camryn said. "She must have completed it to the court's satisfaction out there, because Connie couldn't find any record of the arrest."

"Poor Paula," Grace said. "I guess she's been through the wringer, just like all of us. But how did she end up all the way out here?"

"Probably got sick of the rain. You ever been to Portland?"

"No."

"I don't actually know what brought her to Florida," Camryn admitted. "What I do know is, she only set up this divorce and life coaching business six months ago. And it seems like it's just barely legal—as long as she doesn't call herself a therapist or a marriage counselor. Which she doesn't."

"I see," Grace said, toying with a piece of lettuce that had slid off her mahi-mahi. "So—is Paula actually qualified to do what she's doing? I mean, I thought she was a quack that first week, but honestly, I think she really is trying to help us. And she has some real insights into what goes wrong with marriages."

"When she's sober or not having a 'family emergency,'" Camryn said, still clearly not convinced. "Her credentials are for real. I checked. Her undergrad degree is from the University of Washington, and she got a master's in clinical social work from Portland State. She belonged to a bunch of professional organizations in Portland and was even on the board of a center for battered women, until her life went to shit."

Grace drummed her fingernails on the tabletop. "Obviously, she's back on the pills, self-medicating. It's such a shame."

"She's a grown-up," Camryn pointed out. "Nobody's making her take those pills. What I want to know is, how did she and Stackpole get hooked up?"

"Good question." Grace considered the woman sitting opposite her at the table. "Camryn?"

"Hmm?"

"Why are you telling me all this?"

"You're a member of the group. It affects you as much as it does me."

"There are three other people in our group. You don't even like me."

"Did I ever say I don't like you?"

"Well, it's not like we're buddy-buddy. You've never called me and asked me to go to lunch or anything."

"I don't *do* lunch, Grace. You want to know about the glamorous life of a morning anchor in a third-tier market? I get up at five in the morning, get on the elliptical, haul my ass to the station. I'm in makeup at six, on air at seven. After I get off the air, I've got meetings, I read the wires, the online editions of *The New York Times, Wall Street Journal, Washington Post, Miami Herald.* Since I still do my own enterprise stories, I've got phone calls to make and interviews to set up, and lots of times I go out on remotes with a camera crew. I eat a take-out salad at my desk, go to some more meetings, make some more phone calls. Oh yeah, and I talk to my lawyer about this freakin' divorce and brood about being single again at my age. And that's my day."

Grace still wasn't convinced. "Why me?"

Camryn considered her over the top of her sunglasses. "Because other than me, you're the only normal person in this group."

Grace started to protest.

"Stop!" Camryn took off the sunglasses. "Wyatt doesn't count. He's a guy. A white guy, and I know it's a new century and we finally have a black man in the White House. And I should be better than this, but I still consider him the man. Ashleigh? Pffft. I won't even go there. You and I? Yeah, we did some stuff to our men, but they had it coming. Ashleigh is just all kinds of flaky. I wouldn't trust her any farther than I could throw her."

"What about Suzanne? She's shy, sure, but she's also smart and compassionate, and she seems to understand people."

Camryn shook her head. "No. I can't put my finger on it, but there is something definitely off about that woman."

"She's an introvert," Grace protested.

"It's more than that," Camryn said. Suzanne is damaged goods. Like it or not, Grace, it's you and me."

"You and me—doing what?" Grace said impatiently. "We don't definitely know that Paula and Stackpole are involved. She's not breaking the law billing herself as a divorce coach. I don't see us blowing the whistle on her because she's got a problem with pills. If anything, I think we should try to get her help."

"Help her?" Camryn looked disgusted. "Who's helping us? Who's helping us pay three hundred dollars a session for a 'divorce coach' who can't keep her eyes open for an hour at a time? Who's helping all those other poor women Stackpole sends to Paula for help? You ever consider that? I have. I hung around outside her office yesterday. Yeah. I saw what looked like three different 'divorce recovery' groups filing in there. Total of fifteen people. All women. I did the math. That's 4,500 dollars. In one day. Do you make that kind of money in one day? I sure as hell don't."

It didn't take long for that to sink in. "What do you want from me?" Grace asked.

"You said your lawyer went to law school with Stackpole? You trust her?"

"Yessss?" Grace said reluctantly.

"Talk to her. Ask her to sniff around. I'd ask my lawyer, but he's a man. And he's from Miami, went to law school down there. Balls of brass, great for nego-tiating your next contract at the station, but he's definitely not in the local court-house pipeline."

Grace hesitated. "I'll ask Mitzi what she can find out, but in the meantime I've got an idea of what we can do to help Paula. But I'll need your help. The others, too."

"You bleeding-heart liberals," Camryn said. "What have you got in mind?"

"I'll e-mail everybody else in the group, let them know the plan. Wednesday night, assuming Paula shows up, we ambush her. Do an old-school Betty Ford intervention."

Camryn nodded thoughtfully. Put on her sunglasses, picked up the check. "I like it." She pulled her straw hat down so that it put her face in deepest shade. "Don't tell anybody else, but I like you, too, Grace Stanton."

"Davenport," Grace corrected. "It's Davenport now."

Grace watched while Camryn sped purposefully down the pier toward the parking lot. Had Camryn Nobles actually just befriended her? Were they in ca-hoots? Conspiring against Stackpole? Her life had just taken another unex-pected turn. For the better, she hoped.

39

G race took the outside stairs to the apartment two at a time. She let herself into her bedroom and set Sweetie on her bed. She knelt beside the bed and whispered into the dog's silky ear. "I've got to take a shower and get ready for tonight. But you have to be really, really quiet, or the bad lady downstairs will kick us both out of here."

Sweetie blinked, gave Grace's nose a lick, then settled herself on one of Grace's pillows, with her head on her paws. By the time Grace emerged from the shower, the dog was asleep. She dressed quietly, in a pair of blue and white seersucker shorts and a scoop-necked white T-shirt that she'd found for a total of five dollars at the Junior League thrift shop.

She found Rochelle downstairs, behind the bar, refereeing a hot argument about politics between two of her regulars.

"You look nice," Rochelle said, raising an eyebrow. "Going somewhere?"

"I promised Wyatt I'd take dinner when I drop Sweetie off for the night," Grace said.

Rochelle frowned. "Is that dog . . ."

"Sleeping in my room. Don't get your panties in a wad. It's just until I round up some food to take over there. He's got Bo tonight. What do little boys like to eat?"

"I never had a little boy, so I wouldn't know. But I can tell you what the big ones like. Meat. Fried things. Cheesey things. Anything with ketchup or barbe-cue sauce. Or jalapeños."

"Well, it's after five now, and I promised to have dinner there at six," Grace said. "So I don't have time to fix anything healthy from scratch. What are our specials tonight?"

"Wings. Crab burgers. Fried fish bites. Taco casserole."

"God help me, but the taco casserole hits on all the major male food groups," Grace said.

She went through the swinging doors into the kitchen and found the taco casserole on the steam table. Grace scooped up enough of the casserole to fit into a foil nine-by-twelve to-go tray and fitted it with a cardboard top. She was filling another foil tray with salad when Rochelle joined her.

"What about dessert?"

"Maybe just some fruit?"

Rochelle snorted. "If you're ever gonna land another man you've got to get over this healthy fetish of yours." She turned to one of the big walk-in coolers and lifted out a plastic-covered dish. "Never met a man or a kid yet who didn't love my brownie pie," she said, slicing off a huge slab and placing it in a large Styro-foam clamshell. Then she reached back into the cooler and handed her daughter a white can. "Whipped cream. You know what to do with this. Don't you?"

"Get your mind out of the gutter," Grace said primly. She sorted everything into a large brown paper sack. "Thanks, Mom. This will be great."

Rochelle raised one eyebrow. "Don't forget the damned dog."

Wyatt Keeler emerged from the shower to find the other male inhabitants of his home immersed in the Rays game. Nelson was stationed in his recliner command center, and Bo was sprawled on his belly on the floor, his face inches from the television. The room was a disaster. A mound of clean, unfolded laun-dry took up most of the sofa. Bo's mud-grimed T-ball uniform, underpants, socks, cleats, and sweat-soaked cap were tossed on the floor. The wood laminate coffee table was littered with three days' worth of newspapers; dirty dishes, including a half-eaten potpie; empty Coke cans; and the remains of their fast-food lunch.

"Hey, you guys," Wyatt started, but then he felt his bare foot impaled with a piece of sharp plastic. He stooped over and held up a yellow Lego. "Ow!"

"Dad!" Bo protested. "You messed up my Mega-Bot." He started to scoop up the scattered red, yellow, green, and blue blocks. "I've been working on this all day. Now I gotta start all over."

"Now you gotta clean up this mess," Wyatt told him. Nelson looked up from his chair.

"Both of you," Wyatt said firmly. "We've got company coming in fifteen minutes, so I need all hands on deck here. Bo, pick up all your Legos and stash them in their basket, where they belong. Get your uniform and put it in the laundry room, then clean up all this trash on the coffee table. Dad? Didn't you say you'd fold the laundry and put it away?"

"*You* said I'd fold the laundry," Nelson muttered, bracing his hands on the recliner's arms as he struggled to stand. "And what are you going to be doing while me and Bo slave away in here?"

"I'm going to clean up the kitchen, sweep the floor, and take out a week's worth of garbage. I already cleaned and disinfected the bathroom, so don't either of you dare go in there."

"What if I gotta pee?" Bo asked.

"Take it outside," his father said.

"Who's coming over, the queen of England?" Nelson griped. He was folding T-shirts and shorts and underpants, matching socks.

"It's Grace, Dad's new girlfriend," Bo told his grandfather.

"Who told you Grace was my girlfriend?" Wyatt said. "I never said that."

"Well, she is, isn't she?" Nelson asked.

"Anna said it's okay for Dad to have a girlfriend, since Mom already has you know who," Bo commented.

"Remind me to have a discussion with Anna about minding her own business," Wyatt said. "In the meantime, just get busy, you two. She'll be here in, like, ten minutes. And she's bringing dinner, so be nice. And whatever she brings, pretend like you like it."

"What if she brings fried liver?" Bo asked. "Or lima beans?"

"Or tofu?" Nelson said darkly. "I'm warning you right now. I don't do tofu."

"If she tries to make me eat liver and lima beans, I'll blow chow," Bo said.

"She's not bringing liver or tofu," Wyatt said. "Just remember what I told you. Nice."

"I'm always nice," Nelson said under his breath. He looked over at Bo, who was busily wadding up the newspapers and paper bags and stuffing them under the sofa. "Aren't I always nice?"

Bo gave it some thought. "Mostly. Except when my mom calls."

Wyatt sprayed the chipped Formica countertops with Windex and surveyed the kitchen. He had no idea what Grace's reaction would be to his place. He knew she'd lived in some mansion, because he'd surreptitiously looked at pictures of the place on her old blog. It was huge, with something like five bedrooms and four bathrooms, a screening room, home gym, swimming pool, pool house. Hell, from the looks of it, her pool house was bigger than his crappy little double-wide.

Still, she seemed happy enough, working over at the house on Mandevilla, even admitting she'd fantasized about living there. Maybe she wouldn't turn around and run screaming into the night after she got a look at this dump.

At least it was a fairly tidy dump now. He'd picked some zinnias from the flower bed by the back door and stuck them in an empty jelly jar. The table looked okay, set with his mother's good dishes, the ones with little sprigs of blue cornflowers and gold edges. The silverware all matched, and there were paper napkins at every place, which was a huge step up from the usual roll of paper towels he kept on the table.

But there were only three chairs. How had he missed that? At one time, the dinette set had four chairs, but just a few months ago Bo had been leaning back in his chair when one of the back legs buckled and cracked. He'd meant to try to fix that. But it was too late now. He hurried through the house, looking for an extra chair. Nothing. In desperation, he went out to the carport, found an old plastic beach chair, and dragged it inside. He frowned. It was too short. He went out to the living room, where Nelson and Bo were again wrapped up in the baseball game. He snatched a throw pillow from the sofa and tossed it onto the seat of the chair, just as he heard a knock at the door.

Wyatt wiped his sweaty palms on the seat of his shorts and went to answer the door.

As Rochelle'd predicted, the taco casserole was a hit with the Keeler men.

"Pretty good," Nelson said, scraping a last bit of hamburger, tomato sauce, and cheese from his plate. He pointed at the nearly empty Pyrex dish Grace had used to warm up the casserole. "Is that a Frito?"

"Afraid so," Grace said. "Not very healthy, I know, but . . ."

Before she could apologize further, Nelson reached across the table and scooped up the last remaining spoonful.

"Dad loves Fritos," Wyatt said. "Almost as much as chicken potpie."

"Just the Marie Callender's ones," Nelson said. "Not Swanson. The Marie Callender's are more expensive, but I can usually find a coupon in the Sunday paper."

"Dad does most of the grocery shopping," Wyatt said. "He's a fiend for those coupons. Knows where all the best deals are."

Nelson beamed at the compliment. "Do you like baked beans? Because I've got an extra BOGO for Bush's baked beans at Winn-Dixie this week."

"What's a BOGO?" Wyatt asked.

"Buy one, get-one," Grace said. "And yes, I'd love a coupon, if you've got an extra."

Dinner, she thought, had been a breeze. It was so cute, the way Wyatt had obviously gone to such pains to make a good impression. She looked down at her plate. "I know this china pattern. It's Bachelor's Button, right?"

"Uh, maybe," Wyatt said.

"That's right," Nelson volunteered. "It was our wedding china. Peggy picked it out. Blue flowers were always her favorite."

"Mine too," Grace confided. "Bachelor's buttons, or cornflowers, any shade of hydrangea, iris, those deep-blue pansies with the little clown faces . . ."

"Plumbago?" Wyatt said. "You like plumbago?"

"I love it, especially the ferny leaves," Grace said.

"I grow it in our nursery here," Wyatt said. "We could dig up some clumps and plant it at Mandevilla if you want, maybe a swath of it in front of the gardenias by the porch. The lighter green foliage would be a good contrast against the dark-green gardenia leaves."

"Great idea," Grace said. She looked around the table, beaming at the sight of all the empty plates. "I brought dessert, if anyone's interested."

"I'm interested," Bo said.

"You're interested in any kind of food," Nelson observed.

"Except liver and lima beans," the child said. "Gross."

Grace laughed. "I have to agree with you there. Totally, gag-me-with-a-spoon gross."

She'd sliced the brownie pie into generous squares and arranged them on one of the chipped white plates she'd found in the cupboard. Now, she set it in the center of the table. "My mom's brownie pie. It's her secret recipe, so I don't know what's in it, but we always sell out at the Sandbox."

Each of the males at the table immediately reached for a square. They were all munching happily.

"Bo, I meant to ask, how did your big T-ball game go today?" Grace asked.

"We lost," Bo said, spraying crumbs of chocolate over his plate.

"Not with your mouth full," Wyatt warned.

Bo chewed for a moment, then, his eyes on his father, carefully wiped his mouth with his napkin. "We lost to the stinkin' Pythons. Our archenemy."

"I'm sorry," Grace said.

"But we played great," Wyatt said. "Bo hit a triple and a double. And he hit a smokin' line drive that probably would have homered, except their third baseman, who I totally think is on growth hormones, because the kid is six and he's like six feet tall, made a diving catch."

"But then I struck out. Twice," Bo said sadly.

"Boy, you're batting four hundred," Nelson reminded him. "That ain't too shabby."

Bo eyed the last slice of pie on the plate, his hand hovering just above it, until his father nodded approval.

"Granddad, I'm four hundred for the week, three-fifty for the season. This kid on the Wolverines, he's batting six hundred. Scout's striking out, like, two kids an inning."

"Wow," Grace said admiringly. "You really do know your statistics. Your dad told me you're quite a math wizard."

"He's a freak," Wyatt said, gazing fondly at his son. "But he's our freak."

Bo looked longingly toward the other room. "The game's still on, Dad. Can I be excused?"

"After you two clear the dishes. And thank Grace for the dinner she cooked."

"Don't thank me," Grace admitted. "My mom fixed everything. I just carried it over here."

"Dinner was awesome," Bo said, gathering the dishes.

Nelson stood slowly. "Anytime you want to bring over some more of that taco casserole, please feel free."

Wyatt looked at Grace, who was starting to gather up the silverware. "That's Dad's job," he said. "It's not too hot right now. I thought maybe I'd take you on a tour of the park. If you're interested."

"I was hoping you'd ask," Grace said.

40

The golf cart bumped noiselessly along the crushed-shell pathways, an occasional limb or branch slapping harmlessly at Grace's arm. The air was thick with humidity and the scent of damp earth and tropical flowers. It was twilight, and birds and squirrels twittered from the thick tree canopy. And from somewhere off in the park came an unearthly shriek that made Grace startle, so much that she nearly fell off the cart. "What was that?" she asked, clutching Wyatt's arm for balance.

"Peacocks," Wyatt said. "The bane of my existence. If only that damned coyote had jumped a peacock . . ."

"But they're so beautiful," Grace said. "So elegant."

"So noisy and cranky and a major pain in my ass," Wyatt said firmly. "People in the neighborhood around here are always calling the cops to complain that we're torturing animals over here. We can't make 'em understand that it's just normal peacock behavior."

"Why do you have them if you don't like them?"

"Jungle Jerry's has always had peacocks," Wyatt said. "The first pair, Ike and Mamie, were my grandmother's pets. After they died, we thought we were through with peacocks, but no, somebody was always 'gifting' us with new peacocks. People get them because they think they're such a classy addition to a garden or an estate. Then they hear that ungodly banshee screeching and they can't get rid of them fast enough. They don't even ask us. They just drop the damned things off in the parking lot in the middle of the night, like stray kittens."

He pointed to a huge banyan tree a few hundred yards ahead. "They like to roost there." The path wound around the tree and a clearing came into sight. It was ringed with flowering bushes, and a tall rose-covered arch was centered in a swath of grass.

"That's the butterfly garden," Wyatt said, pointing. "And the wedding chapel, in the middle there."

"How pretty," Grace said. "Do you get many weddings here?"

"Not so many lately," Wyatt said. "Couples seem to want to get married at the beach. Anyway, we don't have the kind of upscale facilities a lot of brides want. The only bathrooms are back at the gift shop, and they're not too glamorous. And let's face it, Jungle Jerry's ain't exactly a classy destination."

"That's a shame," Grace said. "It really is a lovely setting, with all the trees and flowers around, and that sort of meadow in the middle. You could bring in a tent and those fancy port-a-potties that are on trailers, with running water and everything. A good wedding planner could pull off an amazing event here."

"Know any?" Wyatt said gloomily. "Me neither."

The path made a sharp left and suddenly they were surrounded on both sides by a dense wall of bamboo. A light rain had begun falling, so she moved away from the open sides of the cart. Grace caught a glimpse of some kind of structure through the curtain of green.

"What's that back there?"

"That's what's left of Jungle Jerry's big-cat house," Wyatt said. He explained about his grandfather's short-lived career as a lion tamer, and how all the big cats had long ago left the premises.

"From what I've heard, they used to really pack 'em in for the shows," Wyatt said. "At one time we had a 'Safari Train' that ferried people from the parking lot back in here. It was really nothing more than a glorified tractor with a bunch of open cars tacked on the back. Dad sold the train for scrap after we farmed out all the animals more than twenty years ago. But the cages and the remains of the grandstand are still back there. Mostly rust and dust. He planted bamboo to try to provide a natural barrier, but he didn't really understand back then how invasive the stuff is. It's a constant, losing battle, trying to keep it from totally taking over every inch of the park."

"I had no idea what all was involved in running a place like this," Grace said, studying Wyatt's strong, stubborn profile. "I'm amazed you've been able to keep it running after all these years."

He turned and flashed her a rueful grin. "No more amazed than me. But it's not like I really had a choice."

Her hand crept across the bench seat and gave his forearm a squeeze. They rode along for several more minutes with nothing louder than the sound of the rain lightly falling and a breeze ruffling the bamboo until the path took a sharp left.

The bamboo hedge ended abruptly in a large field. Rows of flowers and young trees were laid out in straight lines. A tin-roofed shed was off to one side, under the shade of a large tree.

"This is my favorite place in the park," Wyatt said. "My nursery."

He pulled the golf cart up to the shed and jumped out. "We can hang out here 'til the rain stops." A moment later he was back with a pair of rubber boots. "It's pretty muddy," he warned, handing them to her. "You might want to wear these."

Grace slipped out of her sandals and plunged her feet into the boots, which were four sizes too big and reached nearly to her knees. She giggled as she climbed clumsily out of the cart, lumbering forward in the oversized boots.

Wyatt offered her his arm to steady her. There was a picnic bench under the tin-roofed shed, and now he turned, reached under the seat of the cart, and produced a paper bag, which he handed to her.

Grace looked inside and found a bottle of wine and two plastic cups. "It's screw-top," he said apologetically. "But the guy at the liquor store swears it's good screw-top. You like red?"

"Sure," Grace said.

"One other thing." He picked up a can of insect repellent and sprayed his own neck, arms, and legs, and did the same for her.

Grace sat down on one side of the bench, and after a moment Wyatt sat beside her. He opened the bottle and poured a bit into the cup, handing it to her to sample.

"The guy at the liquor store was right. This is yummy." She held out her cup and he filled it, then filled his own. They sat with their backs to the table, looking out over the fields, slowly sipping the ruby-colored wine.

"What all do you grow here?" Grace asked.

"Annuals for the flower beds out front and throughout the park, some peren-
nials and shrubs. I've got some saplings going that I started from seeds or
grafts from our existing trees," Wyatt said. He nodded toward a row of palm
trees at the far edge of the field. "I've had pretty good luck with the palm trees.
Those are four years old."

"Isn't it a lot of trouble to grow all your own plants?" Grace asked. "Especially with everything else you have to do around the park?"

"It's way cheaper than buying from wholesale nurseries, and anyway, I get a
kick out of growing our own stock. It scratches my horticulture itch."

"Very impressive," Grace said, tapping her cup against his.

He fumbled in his pocket for a moment, then brought out a carefully folded
sheet of paper. "I, uh, well, when I was thinking about you last night, after I got
back home and couldn't sleep, I, uh, drew something for you."

She took the paper and unfolded it. "A landscape plan?" It was an elaborate
pencil drawing of a garden, with hand-lettered botanical names. Looking closer,
she saw "Mandevilla Manor" in neat block letters in the lower right corner of
the paper.

"Some nights my mind won't shut up," he said apologetically. "I have to get
up and draw. This isn't anything fancy. Just some ideas."

"I get like that, too," Grace admitted. "I'll wake up in the middle of the night
with an idea for a recipe I'd like to develop or some crazy scheme for a house.
Since I've been working over at Mandevilla, some nights I only sleep a few
hours, I'm so stoked. I think that's how creative people operate."

"Callie always said it was how crazy people operate," Wyatt said.

Grace was examining the sketch. "So . . . no more lawn?" She pointed to the
tightly packed rows of shrubs he'd sketched for the front yard.

"Very little grass," Wyatt said. "You could change that, if you wanted, but in
Florida it takes so much in the way of water and chemicals to keep large chunks
of grass healthy. I think it would look better to do these planting beds with native ornamentals, and maybe some seasonal annuals for color. Here," he jabbed
a finger, "I'd do a crushed-shell parking pad, and then extend it to a path that
winds through the flowers right up to your front door.

"I didn't have time to label everything, but since I know now that you like
blue flowers, I'd give you lots of blues and purples, with whites and green and
silver," he said.

"If it were my house, it would be perfect," Grace said, leaning over and giving him a peck on the cheek. "I'll keep it. Maybe eventually I'll have a house again, where I could plant something like this. Well, exactly like this."

"Why couldn't you just do it at Mandevilla Manor?" Wyatt asked.

"Arthur would never go for it," Grace said. "I'm still trying to talk him into springing for central air so I can get rid of those hideous rusting window units."

"It wouldn't be all that expensive to install this plan," Wyatt said. "Most of the plants I've drawn I grow right here in my nursery. The big cost would be in the gravel for the parking pad, the pavers, and the walkway. I get that all at wholesale cost."

"And what about the installation?"

Wyatt grinned. "I know a guy. He works cheap. Or in your case, free." He put his arm around her shoulders and drew Grace closer.

She returned her attention to the plan. "Whoa!" She placed her finger on an irregular shape on the plan. "Is this a pool? In the backyard? Are you kidding?"

"It's just a little dip pool," he said. "Nothing like you had at your last address. Nothing big enough to drown a convertible," he added impishly.

Grace gave him the side eye, and then giggled despite herself. She took another sip of wine.

"The backyard is so big at Mandevilla, it would be a shame not to take advantage of it, eventually," he said. "Everything on here could be done in phases. So, phase one is the front yard and trimming and defining the shrubbery on the sides of the house. Phase two would be getting the citrus grove in the backyard looking good. Paint that barn-slash-garage thing, plant some vines to grow on a trellis to try to minimize the scale of it. Phase three would be the dip pool. And the garage-barn is so big, you could section off part of it for a guest house. The side that faces the proposed dip pool, you'd put in French doors or maybe a cool, industrial-looking roll-up bay door to a space that becomes your pool house. At the same time, you'd probably want to put a pair of French doors in that bedroom that becomes the master, so you have access to your little private patio out to the pool courtyard."

"You are really, really good at this," Grace marveled, looking from the plan to him. "Everything you've drawn here, it just perfectly fits the scale and sensibility of that little Florida cottage. Nothing too grandiose, just right, so appropriate. I can actually picture all of it."

Wyatt's face shone with pleasure. "It's cool, you know? Creating something out of nothing? I miss the design aspect of landscaping. The rest of the park"—he gestured around—"it's pretty much a done deal. All I can do is try to keep the wheels on the bus."

Grace leaned her head back against Wyatt's arm and stared up at the deepening night sky. The rain drummed softly on the tin roof. "What if money were no object? What would you do here then?"

"If wishes were horses?" He snorted derisively. She nudged him with her elbow.

"Okay, well, I'd do more to emphasize the specimen plants my grandparents brought here from all over the world. I'd eventually phase out the bird show, but not Cookie, of course. She's part of the family. I'd maybe have a big demonstration garden, showing all the fruits and vegetables that we grow well in this climate. I'd love to work with local chefs, have an outdoor kitchen here and do cooking demonstrations using locally harvested produce and seafood and meat. I'd make the park less about tourism and more of a community resource. And, maybe, I'd even enlarge the nursery, make some of the plants we've grown here available to the public."

Grace sat up. "Those are wonderful ideas! Truly."

Wyatt shrugged. "It'll never happen. Not in my lifetime. But yeah, I've got my plans."

She gave him a level look. "Do I fit into any of those plans? Or am I just another complication?"

"You? You're not a complication. You're . . . ah, hell, Grace."

He turned and gathered her into his arms and kissed her softly.

"Mmm," she said after a while. "I do like your plans." Wyatt's arms tightened around her. His tongue tickled hers, and she wrapped her arms around his neck and flattened herself to his chest. A moment later, his warm hands slipped under her T-shirt, and then under the white camisole she wore instead of a bra. He grazed her nipples with his thumbs and she inhaled sharply and twined her hands through his hair.

"Is this okay?" he whispered in her ear. "Should I stop?"

"Never," she breathed.

His kisses grew more urgent as he pushed the fabric of her T-shirt upward. Grace let her hands slide slowly down his chest, to his waist; then, working them under his polo shirt, she flattened her palms on his bare chest, feeling the warmth, sliding her hands upward, brushing her fingertips across his nipples.

A moment later, by mutual, silent agreement, they were both shirtless. Wyatt pulled her onto his lap, kissing the nape of her neck, the hollow of her throat, cupping her breasts with both hands, teasing his tongue across her tightened nipples while she kneaded his shoulders, raking her nails across his bare back. Her breathing grew ragged as he kissed and caressed and, slowly, pushed her backward onto the picnic bench.

"Mmm," she protested, between kisses. "This isn't going to work, this bench is too skinny. We'll both end up in the mud."

He stopped what he was doing, then pulled her to her feet and, without warning, picked her up and plunked her atop the picnic table. She laughed but scooted back on her behind, and soon he was right there beside her, stretched out on top of the picnic table. He worked one thigh between hers, fumbling for the zipper of her shorts. She found his zipper easily, slid it down, and traced his erection with her thumb, while she pushed his shorts down. He was still groping with the button on the waistband of her shorts when she heard a soft buzzing and then a ringtone that sounded like "Take Me Out to the Ball Game" coming from the pocket of his shorts.

"Dammit!" he muttered.

She laughed. "Can't it wait?"

He sat up abruptly, pulling at his shorts. "That's Bo's ringtone," he said, grabbing the phone. "I gotta answer."

41

Hey, buddy, what's up?" Wyatt said softly, turning so that his back was to Grace. She rested her head on his bare shoulder.

The child whispered something incoherent.

"What's that? I can't hear you, Bo."

"I said, Mom called and she sounded really mad," Bo said, his whisper hoarse.

"Why are you whispering?" Wyatt asked.

"I don't want Granddad to hear," Bo said. "He told me not to call you, but I can tell he's all upset."

Wyatt held the phone away from his face and swore softly.

"What did your mom want?"

"She was yelling at me because she said you didn't tell her we had a big game today and she missed it."

Wyatt rolled his eyes. "We gave your mom a schedule of all the games at the beginning of the season, son. I'm sorry she yelled at you, but I'll call her later and we'll get it straightened out."

"Dad, Mom made me put Granddad on the phone when she got done talking to me. And he got super, super angry. He was yelling and saying bad words. Some of it didn't even make any sense. Now he's breathing kind of funny. Dad, can you come back? I'm kind of scared."

"I'll be right there," Wyatt said firmly. "Don't be scared. You did just the right thing to call me. We're just over at the plant nursery. We'll be back at the house in five minutes."

Wyatt stood and pulled his shirt over his head. Grace dressed hurriedly, straightening her hair, and packed the wine bottle and glasses in the brown paper sack.

"Do you want me to stay on the phone with you while we ride back?" Wyatt asked. Grace climbed onto the seat of the golf cart, and a moment later they were rocketing down the path.

"No, that's okay," Bo said.

"Where is Granddad right now?" Wyatt asked. "Is he awake? What's he doing?"

"He's just staring at the television, talking to himself," Bo said. "It's okay now. He's not dead or nothing."

Wyatt laughed, despite himself. "That's good news. I'm on the way."

"Bye."

Grace gripped Wyatt's arm. "I heard part of that. What's the problem? Is your father okay?"

"To quote my son, 'he's not dead or nothin,'" Wyatt said, his facial features taught. "Callie called to ream Bo out because she missed his game today. Then, after she'd finished making him feel like crap, she got on the phone and picked a fight with Dad. She knows just how to push his buttons. Apparently, he was yelling and ranting and raving at her, and of course Bo overheard all of it, and, naturally, it got him pretty worried. He says Dad is breathing funny, just staring at the television, talking to himself. Bo's a smart kid. I think he senses that Dad is starting to slip a little, and he's protective of his grandfather."

"Thank God for that," Grace said. "And thank God we weren't far away."

"I'll just pack up my stuff and get out of your way," Grace said, as the cart approached the double-wide.

"No! This is not how I wanted the evening to end," Wyatt said. "It's probably nothing. I'll get Dad calmed down and pack Bo off to bed. It'll be fine."

"You need to spend time with them, not worry about me," Grace said. "We can have other nights."

"Really? When? We both work all the time, and the rest of the time, my life is like this," he said, pulling the cart beneath the carport. "Just stay a few minutes, please? Just 'til I get these guys sorted out."

"I don't want to be in the way," Grace protested.

"You're not in the way. I promise," he said, squeezing her hand. "Your being there will probably make Bo feel a little better. He likes you."

"He just likes my dog," Grace said, laughing.

"Whatever works."

Bo met them at the door. He was dressed in his pajamas, and his freckled face looked worried. "Don't tell Granddad I called, okay?"

Wyatt leaned down and hugged his son. "It's a deal."

He walked into the living room, where Nelson sat rigidly in his recliner, muttering incoherently. His face was pale except for two scarlet patches on his cheeks. The television volume was turned all the way up.

Wyatt touched his father's shoulder. He found the remote control and turned the television down. "Dad? What's going on?"

Nelson didn't look up. "That woman got no right to talk to me like that. No respect. No morals. I told her that, too. Told her it looks bad for her son, her living in sin with that man. Did I cuss her out? Hell yeah, I cussed her out. Do it again, too, next time."

Wyatt sat on the sofa. "I'm sorry Callie got you so upset. I'll talk to her about that. But maybe it would be better if you just didn't speak to her at all."

"She called me!" Nelson shouted. "Didn't even know she was the one on the phone until Bo said his mom wanted to talk to me. I told Bo to tell her I was asleep, but she could hear me, and she insisted Bo give the phone to me."

"What did she want?" Wyatt asked.

"What she always wants. She wanted to raise hell with me. Wanted to know where you really were. If you were out with your new girlfriend. She claimed you didn't tell her about Bo's game because you wanted your girlfriend to go to the game instead of her. I told her if you did have a girlfriend it was none of her goddamn business. Then she wanted to know why Bo wasn't in bed, since it was after nine, which is his bedtime at her house. I told her it was Saturday night and there's no school tomorrow and I didn't give a tinker's damn what time he went to bed at her house."

Nelson's voice was rising, his breathing getting shallow. He waved his arms as he shouted, and from the corner of his eye, Wyatt saw Bo, standing, wide-eyed in the doorway. A moment later, Grace was behind him, gently shepherd-ing him into the kitchen.

He leaned forward and grasped his father's arms, forcing the old man to look at him. "Okay, Dad, calm down. I am going to have a discussion with Callie and her lawyer, and tell them that she is not to talk to you anymore. All right? This isn't your fault. But you need to settle down. Did you take your blood pres-sure meds this morning?"

"What? Hell, who remembers that long ago?" Nelson grabbed for the remote control, but Wyatt held it out of his reach.

Bo sat at the kitchen table, clutching Sweetie in his arms. Huge tears welled in his dark eyes, and he was rhythmically kicking the chrome table leg.

Grace found the foil-wrapped remains of the brownie pie. She cut a generous slice and put it on a plate and poured a glass of milk, which she set in front of the little boy.

Without a word, Bo picked up a fork and took a bite. He gulped his milk and wiped his mouth with the back of his hand. Sweetie wriggled in his lap and licked his neck. Bo giggled.

"She just wants some of your pie, but we can't give her any, because choco-late isn't good for dogs," Grace warned.

She gave Sweetie a mock-stern look. "What? Sorry, little girl. There are no leftovers when you feed three hungry single men." She looked around the room until she found the jar of dog treats she'd given Wyatt. She handed one to Bo, who offered it to Sweetie, who snapped it up without hesitation.

Bo ate a few more bites of the pie. He had a milk mustache and his ears were bright pink as he looked at Grace with open curiosity. "I think my mom is mad because I told her Dad took you out to ride around on the golf cart."

Grace nodded. "She's probably mad at me, not you. But that's understandable."

"She thinks you're Dad's new girlfriend."

"I wonder how she got that idea?" Grace said. "Your mom doesn't even know me."

Bo hung his head.

She laughed, leaned over, and ruffled his close-cut hair. "It's okay with me, but I don't know how your dad will feel about hearing that I'm his girlfriend."

"You're my new girlfriend?" Wyatt walked into the kitchen and swiped the last bite of pie from his son's plate.

"That's what Bo's mom apparently thinks," Grace said. She bustled around the kitchen, packing up the empty food containers.

"Hmm," Wyatt said, looking from Bo to Grace. He nodded at Bo. "Wonder where she got that idea?"

Bo's voice was very small. "I told her. She made me very, very mad when she yelled at me about the game. So I told her you have a new girlfriend who is really nice, and whose name is Grace, and who brought us taco casserole and chocolate pie. I told her I get to take care of her dog. And then I told her I do not want to move to stinking Birmingham."

"Okay," Wyatt said. He looked at the clock on the oven. "It's past your bedtime. How about you tell Grace good night and then go brush your teeth and hit the hay?"

Bo looked like he might put up a fight, but then thought better of it. "Is Granddad okay?"

"He's kind of tired right now, so he just went to bed," Wyatt said. "I think maybe he forgot to take his medicine this morning. Guess we'll have to do a better job of reminding him, won't we?"

"Yes, sir," Bo said. He set the dog down on the floor and stood. "Good night, Grace. Thank you for dinner." He thought for a minute, then added, "And for letting Sweetie stay here."

"I'd better get going, too," Grace said, watching the dog follow Bo down the hallway.

"I could make some coffee," Wyatt offered. "Don't run off just yet."

He poured them each a mug of coffee and sat opposite her at the kitchen table. "Sorry about all the drama," he said, taking a sip. His face hardened. "It's like Callie enjoys stirring up trouble. She hasn't been to a single one of Bo's Saturday games this season. She's always too busy with Luke. Now, suddenly, it's my fault she didn't know about today?"

"It does sound like she's deliberately trying to provoke you, and Nelson," Grace observed. "The question is, Why? What does she get out of it?"

"I'm sure she's got an ulterior motive," Wyatt agreed. "But I have no idea what it could be. And I don't feel like investing a lot of energy trying to predict what her next move will be."

"Maybe just be careful with what information Bo gives her," Grace said. She felt her face warm. "So . . . it's official? I'm your new girlfriend?"

"I hope so," Wyatt told her. "Is that weird?"

"Not weird," she decided. "Different. New. I haven't been anybody's girl-friend in a really long time."

"It's new to me, too," he admitted. "Not at all what I expected when Stack-pole ordered me to attend divorce camp."

"Speaking of," Grace said. "I had lunch with Camryn Nobles today."

"Camryn? Why? I didn't know you two were buddy-buddy."

"Neither did I. She's been doing some investigating. She found out Paula lost her therapist accreditation out in Oregon, after she got caught forging her ex-husband's name on some prescriptions for tranquilizers."

"No shit?"

"It's kind of a sad story." Grace filled him in on everything Camryn had confided in her at the Rod and Reel pier and about Paula's new career as a di-vorce coach.

"We know she's taking pills again," Wyatt said. "I wonder if they have some-thing to do with her family emergency the other night?"

"I'm thinking the same thing," Grace agreed. "Camryn wants to report her to the authorities here. But what good does that do? I think we have to help her."

"And how do we do that?"

"I think we, that is, the group, have to confront her," Grace said. "Tell her we know she's self-medicating and that we know she was in rehab for the same thing. Maybe she'll open up and talk to us."

"Or . . . maybe she'll tell us all to fuck off and then rat us out to Stackpole for spying on her," Wyatt said. "And then we're all really, really screwed with the judge who has life-or-death jurisdiction over our divorces. Have you considered that possibility?"

Grace sighed. "Stackpole's the bad guy in all of this. I really think Paula is like us, another one of his victims."

"But we can't prove they're involved or that Stackpole is doing anything il-legal, right?" Wyatt asked. "And in the meantime, it's hard for me to feel sorry for a phony therapist who's ripping us off."

"I disagree," Grace said lightly. "I just don't believe Paula is the one getting as rich as Camryn believes she must be. I'm going to call Mitzi tomorrow, just to let her know what we've found out about Paula. And I think we ought to at least let Ashleigh and Suzanne know what Camryn discovered."

She took her coffee mug and set it in the sink. "But now, I think I'd better head home. Thanks for a lovely evening, Wyatt."

He walked her outside to her car, his arm slung casually over her shoulder. "I just wish things had gone differently tonight. I wish . . ."

She turned and wrapped her arms around his neck. "I wish it, too. It was nice while it lasted, though."

He kissed her. "Nelson wanted me to apologize for him. For ruining our 'date,' as he called it. He keeps asking me if we've slept together!"

"Oh my God," Grace said with a giggle. "I should not be telling you this, but Rochelle keeps asking me the same thing."

"So why haven't we?"

Grace arched an eyebrow in response.

"I'm a slow starter," Wyatt admitted. "But once I build up steam . . . I won't lie. I've been trying to figure out how we can be alone since last week."

"We can't be together at the Sandbox, that's for sure," Grace said.

"Ditto for here," Wyatt said, resting his hands lightly on her waist. "Bo and I share a room, and even on nights he's with Callie, Dad's room is right next door, and the walls in this trailer are like toilet paper."

"Poor us," Grace said mockingly.

"I'll think of something," Wyatt said. He lifted her chin and kissed her hungrily. "Soon. Very soon."

42

The coffee shop was only two blocks from the Manatee County Courthouse in downtown Bradenton. The lunch-hour rush was over, and Grace and Mitzi Stillwell were alone at a booth near the front window, sipping watered-down iced teas while the hostess counted down the money in her cash register.

"I've got a little good news for you," Mitzi said. "After much arm twisting and hand wringing, I heard from Ben's lawyer today. You'll have your first check tomorrow."

"It's about damn time," Grace said. "How'd you manage it?"

"A combination of threats, nonstop phone calls and e-mails, and borderline harassment," Mitzi said. "It's not nearly enough, but it's a start."

"I cannot wait to buy myself a decent pair of shoes. And some new under-wear," Grace added.

Mitzi gave Grace a critical glance. "You're looking good, Grace. I think the single life must suit you."

"Thanks. I'm busy, working on a house, and that makes me happy. As for single life? Things are getting, um, interesting."

"Hmm. Interesting as in good?"

"Very good," Grace assured her.

"And how's Rochelle? Do you think she'll ever get back in the game?"

"Mom?" Grace looked puzzled. "Date? We've never discussed it. To tell you the truth, the idea of her going out never entered my mind. Why do you ask?"

"No reason," Mitzi said quickly. "She's not that old, not even sixty, right? My mom married her second husband at seventy, and when he dropped dead five years later, she picked right back up again. She's always got a guy in the wings. Rochelle's a very attractive lady, very young-thinking. I just think it would be a shame if she turned into one of those dried-up mean widow women you always see in every retirement community in Florida."

"Mom. Dating?" Grace couldn't quite seem to put the words together, in her mouth or in her mind.

"Never mind," Mitzi said. "Tell me how it's going in divorce-recovery group. Does your therapist seem to have recovered from her episode?"

"That's why I called you," Grace said eagerly. "Camryn—she's that reporter from channel four. Stackpole sentenced her to group after she put a video of her husband parading around in a pair of red satin women's thong panties up on YouTube . . ."

Mitzi coughed violently, and dabbed at her face with a paper napkin. "Oh my God! That's her husband? Camryn Nobles, News Four You? What's that song he's dancing to in the video? Have you seen it? It's hysterical!"

"No, I haven't seen it. Stackpole made her take it down," Grace said. "But listen to what Camryn found out about Paula."

"Really? I'm impressed. Camryn Nobles figured this out? I always thought she was just a pretty face. Who knew she could actually do real journalism?"

"Paula's not even a licensed therapist in this state. She gets around that by calling herself a divorce coach. Mitzi, she doesn't even have a Web site. So how did she get that successful that fast?"

"Her book?"

"It's only available as an e-book, and *Mindful Marriage*'s Amazon ranking is 367,459," Grace said.

Mitzi chewed on some ice. "Those people in the other divorce-therapy sessions, were they all women?"

"Yes."

"Well . . . if we knew that all of them were referred to Paula by Stackpole, that might be a very useful piece of information," Mitzi allowed.

"How could we find that out?"

"I guess you could ask them," Mitzi said.

"I think our group should have an intervention with Paula," Grace said. "We could confront her about the pills and her odd behavior. But Wyatt thinks if it goes wrong, it could make things even worse for all of us. With Stackpole."

"Wyatt?" Mitzi pursed her lips. "He's the guy we saw in court that day? The one who put his fist through his wife's car window? Are you two seeing each other?"

Grace blushed.

"Is it serious?"

"I hope so," Grace said quietly. "He's a good person, Mitzi. He doesn't deserve the crap his wife is handing him."

"I remember the wife from court. She was a terror."

"You don't know the half of it," Grace told her. "Wyatt is sick with worry that Stackpole will allow Callie to move to Birmingham with his son, Bo."

"About Stackpole," Mitzi said. "I've been asking around, very quietly. He and his wife used to be quite the social butterflies around town. She chaired the big Heart Fund ball last year, and they're members at the Longboat Key Club, where he plays a lot of tennis, but nobody's seen them out and about together much these past few months."

"Maybe the wife found out about Paula."

"Could be," Mitzi allowed. "Or maybe it's just that it's July. The Stackpoles have a house in the mountains in North Carolina. One of those woodsy, social places like Highlands or Flat Rock. I think she spends most of the summer up there."

"And while the cat's away, the rat will play," Grace said. "Mitzi, I just know Stackpole and Paula are having an affair. I can't prove it, but if you'd seen them that night when he showed up at group, it was just so obvious."

Mitzi stirred the dregs of her ice with her straw. "So what? You've only got two more weeks of divorce camp left, and then Stackpole will sign off on your divorce."

"I know," Grace said resignedly.

"Isn't that what we want? You—divorced? Free to get on with your life? Free to have a relationship with Wyatt or anybody else of your choosing?"

"The whole thing with Stackpole and Paula—it's wrong, Mitzi! And there's nothing I can do about it."

"You *are* doing something, Grace. You're building a new life for yourself. The financial aspect aside—I still haven't given up on that—I still think we can argue that you're entitled to your equity in the house since so much of the labor and materials were given to you as compensation for exposure on your blog . . . All that aside, you are doing what I preach to all my women clients. You are not letting this divorce define you. You're not letting bitterness defeat you. Grace, you're a rock star!"

Grace snorted. "I don't even have a place to shack up with the new man in my life! So what kind of rock star does that make me?"

Mitzi's eyes lit up. "Ohhhh. So it really is getting serious with Wyatt. Why didn't you say something earlier?" She dug a key ring from her purse and extracted a key, which she pressed into Grace's hand.

"Here. This is to my condo at Anna Maria. My long-term tenant just moved out, and I'm converting it to a vacation rental. I've bought some furniture and had it painted and recarpeted, but that's as far as I've gotten with the place. Decorating is just not my thing. I've been planning on hiring a decorator to finish it, but maybe that's something you could do?"

Grace flushed and tried to return the key. "Oh, Mitzi, no. I couldn't. I really wasn't asking for your charity. I just needed to vent for a minute."

"I'm not trying to give you charity," Mitzi exclaimed. "I'll pay you, for God's sake! You'd be doing me a huge favor. The management company that's going to handle the rentals has been after me to get the place ready to be photographed for their Web site, but I hate shopping, and I suck at decorating. You'd be doing me a huge favor if you'd agree to fluff the place. Please?" She grinned. "It's not fancy, but there's a sofa and a bed and sheets and towels and a flat-screen television. What more do you need for a romantic evening? Say you'll take the job, and I'll stock the fridge with champagne and chocolate."

"I don't know," Grace demurred, but Mitzi grabbed her hand and closed her palm over the key. "You've got a credit card again, right?"

"Yes, with a five-thousand-dollar limit," Grace said.

"Great. So that'll be your budget for the condo. Five thousand will be enough to get some curtains and some rugs and doodads, won't it?"

"Sure, as long as I don't have to buy the big-ticket items like mattresses or sofas or furniture, I should be able to fluff it for that much. When do you need it ready?"

"Like, yesterday, according to the property-management people. They wanted it done before Memorial Day, but that ship has sailed."

Grace gave it some thought. "Give me two weeks. Is that okay?"

"Works for me," Mitzi said. She reached into her purse and pulled out her checkbook. "Designers work on retainer, right? So, how much?"

"No retainer," Grace said firmly.

Mitzi's eyes narrowed. "Then give me back my key. Because I won't let you work for me for free. Listen to me, Grace. I have to remind my women clients about this all the time. Just because your spouse didn't recognize your worth doesn't mean you have no value. You're a professional interior designer, not some little dabbler who does this as a hobby. Don't devalue yourself by refusing to be fairly compensated. Now. What do you bill out at?"

Grace opened her mouth to argue, then closed it. Finally, she said, "Going rate here is about 125 dollars an hour, but since I won't actually be doing any sketches, and since it'll mostly be a matter of shopping and installing, I charge a hundred dollars an hour."

"Fine." Mitzi wrote the check and handed it to her client. "That's fifteen hundred. If you think it's going to take you more time than that after looking at the place, let me know."

Grace took the check and looked at it. It was written to Grace Davenport, her first paycheck under her born-again maiden name.

"Thanks," she said, her eyes shining with barely suppressed tears. And then she remembered the reason she'd asked for this meeting with her lawyer.

"Okay. What about Stackpole?"

"Oh, all right," Mitzi grumbled. "I'll take a look at his recent dockets to see what other attorneys I know have had cases before him. I'll ask around, to see if any of their clients have been sentenced to divorce camp with Paula Talbott-Sinclair. Satisfied?"

"Yes," Grace said. "Totally satisfied."

"In the meantime," Mitzi wagged a finger at Grace, "stay away from Wyatt Keeler's wife. That woman is trouble."

Grace shuddered. "Don't worry. I have no plans to get anywhere near Callie Keeler."

Wyatt Keeler spent the morning in his tiny office at Jungle Jerry's, staring at a mounting pile of bills. When his cell phone rang and he saw who was calling, he snatched it from his desktop.

"Betsy? Hey! How are you?"

"I'm fine. How's the rash?"

"Mostly gone, thanks to you. Guess I should listen to my elders more often."

"I'll have to remind you of that in the future," Betsy said drily. "Look, I won't beat around the bush. I just got a call from Callie's lawyer. They're asking Stackpole for an emergency hearing."

Wyatt's throat went dry. "What's the emergency?"

"Oh, Christ," Betsy said. "Promise me you will not go crazy when you hear."

"I won't go crazy," Wyatt said automatically. "Now tell me what's going on. Please."

He heard the sound of pages being turned. "Callie is now claiming that Nelson is suffering from acute dementia. Her filing says that when he is not confused and nonresponsive, he is verbally abusive and threatening, and he uses profane language in front of Bo, and he's capable of violence. In short, she's saying that as long as Nelson is living with you, your home is an unfit atmosphere for a child."

"What!" Wyatt put the phone down on the desk. He stood back and kicked his old army-surplus battleship-gray desk so viciously his work boot left a hollow impression in the bottom file drawer.

He sat back down and took several deep breaths.

"Wyatt?"

"I'm here," he said quietly.

"Do you have any idea what prompted this piece of garbage?"

"I do," he said grimly. He quickly recounted Saturday evening's events for his aunt.

"Well." Betsy sighed. "You and I know Callie deliberately provoked Nelson into a tirade. Is any of what she's claiming true? Is your Dad suffering from dementia?"

"No. Betsy, you know what Dad's like. He's slowing down, no question about it. Sometimes, usually in the evenings, he gets a little . . . foggy. And sometimes, again, usually when he's overtired, he can get a little verbally combative. But most days, he's still sharp as a tack. And he's a sweetheart, you know that. He adores Bo. Being around Bo, helping take care of him, it's given him a real sense of purpose. Of responsibility. And it's good for Bo, too. There is no way Dad is capable of violence. Ever! He might rant and rave at Callie, because as far as he's concerned, she abandoned us. But he would never act on his threats."

"That's what I think, too," Betsy said. "But this latest ploy has me worried. Stackpole really chewed her out last time around. I'm thinking she wouldn't risk annoying him again unless she thinks she really has something that will stick."

Wyatt buried his head in his hands. "Oh my God," he said softly. "This is like a nightmare that never ends. She really will stop at nothing."

"I know," Betsy agreed. "Stackpole wants to see us at eleven A.M. tomorrow. In the meantime, I went ahead and made an appointment with Margaret-Ellen Shank. She's a really well-respected geriatrician on staff at Sarasota Memorial. Fortunately for us, she had a really messy divorce a couple years ago, and I was able to help her out. Can you have your dad over there by four this afternoon? She's agreed to juggle her schedule to see him."

"I'll have him there," Wyatt said wearily. "But what do I tell him? He's gotta see a doctor to prove he's not senile so I don't lose custody of my son?"

"Tell him the truth," Betsy said. "I'll see you there."

43

Arthur Cater stood on the porch staring into the doorway at the little cottage on Mandevilla. He wore an ancient T-shirt with chopped-off sleeves; shapeless, colorless green pants; and a dubious expression. He poked his nose inside the living room. He sniffed. His craggy face scrunched into some indefinable expression that threatened to give Grace an anxiety attack.

"What?" she asked. "What's wrong?" She'd spent all day Sunday using a rented floor sander to take the dirty, scuffed finish off the oak floors. She'd worked all night, mopping every last particle of sawdust before staining the floors a rich, dark walnut color. Her arms and lower back were still throbbing from her efforts.

When Arthur Cater called to casually announce his intention to drop by and check on her progress, Grace had only managed to stall him until after her meeting with Mitzi. Her stomach had been in knots all morning, wondering what Arthur's reaction would be to her progress.

Now she had it, and judging by the look on his face, the news was not good.

Suddenly, she got angry. And defensive.

"Arthur," she exclaimed, "it's just paint. If you hate it, I can repaint. But I wanted a higher contrast between the floors and the walls, which is why I chose the dark stain for the floors."

"Hush!" Arthur turned on his heel and walked rapidly out to the porch and into the yard.

Grace stared, speechless. Was he leaving?

No. A moment later he was back, carrying a bulky leather-covered camera. It was an old 35-millimeter.

He stood in the doorway and clicked the shutter. He walked into the dining room and snapped another picture. When he got to the kitchen, he stopped in his tracks.

"Well, I'll be damned." When he turned to Grace, his face was actually wreathed in smiles.

"You did all this?"

"I did," Grace assured him.

"By yourself?"

"With a little help."

He gestured at the secondhand Craigslist range, fridge, and dishwasher. "How the hell did you get those in there?"

"Some guys I used to work with back in my model-home days. Jimmy and Eduardo. I hired them to pick up the appliances in their truck and to install them. I don't do wiring, Arthur."

He gestured at the floor, with its gleaming red-checkerboard pattern. "What's that made out of?"

She gulped. "It's marine-grade plywood. The old linoleum tiles just were not coming up. So I nailed the plywood down, primed it, then taped off the squares and painted it with deck paint. Do you hate it?" She prayed he didn't. Her knees still had bruises from all the hours she'd spent taping and painting.

"It's good," Arthur said, nodding and flashing that rare-as-diamonds smile again. "Better than good. It's great. This floor—it looks just like the tiles my grandmother used to have in here. I'd forgotten that until just this minute."

"How about the open shelves?" Grace asked, still anxious for his approval. "The old cabinet doors were warped and gummy with all those old layers of paint, and the only way to clean them up would have been to strip them all down to the bare wood, and I just didn't have the time or the patience for that."

"Hush," Arthur commanded. He snapped two more pictures of the kitchen in rapid succession. "Wait until my wife sees this." He chortled. "She's said all along that we should just get rid of the darned cupboard doors. She even showed me a picture in one of her magazines, but I told her she was crazy. Just shows you how much I know."

He walked back through the abbreviated hallway and poked his head into both bedrooms, nodding and snapping more exposures.

"I can't believe it," he said, shaking his head. He looked over at Grace, still dressed in a simple cotton sundress for her coffee date with her lawyer.

"A little bitty gal like you got all this done, just like that," he said, snapping his fingers.

If only he knew, Grace mused, the untold hours she'd spent working on the house, for which she'd never be compensated—not in money, anyway.

"So, do you like it?" she asked.

"I do," he said, patting her shoulder awkwardly.

"There's still so much more to accomplish," she cautioned. "The bathroom vanity—I know I told you all the fixtures were okay, but the sink has a leak, and that vanity is all rotted out underneath. I'd like to replace it with a pedestal sink with more of a period look. And the tub—I've scrubbed it and scrubbed it, but it's pitted and chipped, and it's going to look even nastier once I get the bathroom painted. I'd love to have it reglazed."

"Do it," Arthur said expansively. He was in a rare mood, Grace thought. Maybe now was the time to spring the rest of her wish list on him.

She followed him onto the front porch, where he gazed out at the yard. "What the hell have you done out here?" he asked wonderingly.

Grace blushed. "I have a friend, he's a landscape architect, and he gave me some suggestions about cutting things back, reshaping the beds. There's a lot more I'd like to do in the yard, eventually. This house has such incredible curb appeal now, but it could be even better."

"It looks grand," Arthur said, and he was actually beaming. "It looks better than it has in twenty years. Not just the yard, everything."

"I'm so glad you like it," Grace told him. "Once I get some poly on those floors, they'll really look sharp. And then I was thinking, I could probably start furnishing it in the next week or so."

"Fine," Arthur said. "That sounds fine."

"About the air-conditioning, Arthur," Grace began.

He scowled.

Grace picked up a wooden paint-stir stick from her stack of supplies in the corner of the front porch. She poked the outside of the air-conditioning unit protruding from the living room window. A flurry of rust chips fell to the porch floor.

"The salt air has completely rusted this unit out," Grace said. "It's on its last legs. And the other units aren't much better."

"No ma'am," he said firmly. "Why, those units aren't that old. I put them in here myself."

"In 1982. I found the owner's manual in the hall linen closet. Arthur, these units are almost as old as me. They've outlived their useful life."

"Then I'll buy some new ones," he said, his face set in a mulish expression.

"You'll need five window units, at the very least," Grace said, consulting the notes she'd scribbled on her last shopping trip. "I checked at Sears and Home Depot, for the BTUs we need in the main rooms, meaning, the living room, dining room, kitchen, and both bedrooms, that's a little over two thousand dollars."

"Nonsense," Arthur said. "I can buy those units for under a hundred bucks apiece."

She handed him the most recent sales flyer she'd picked up at Sears. "Maybe thirty years ago you could buy them for that, but not these days."

He scowled down at the flyer. "I suppose you're going to keep after me about putting in central air-conditioning?"

"Yes, I am," Grace said emphatically. She handed him another brochure. "That's an estimate I had worked up by a very reliable HVAC guy who my mom uses at the Sandbox. It'll cost less than five thousand dollars! You'll get an up-to-the-minute energy-efficient unit, and there may be tax breaks involved as well. And, since you pay the utilities, there will be a substantial savings on your electric bills."

He ran a bony finger down the printed estimate, frowning. "I never figured to put all this much money in this little house." He looked up at her. "There's hardly any sense fixing it up this grand, just so the next bunch of tenants can come in here and ruin all our hard work."

Now, Grace told herself. Ask him now.

"About the next tenants," she said, fixing him with her most winning smile. "What would you say to renting this place to me?"

"Ah-hah!" he cried. "At last the other shoe drops. I should have known you had an ulterior motive for wanting me to spend all this money."

"I want you to spend what is really a very reasonable amount of money to maintain and improve this lovely property," Grace said, willing herself to keep calm and use all the arguments she'd gone over and over in her head. "I really didn't intend to ask about renting it, but then, once I got it cleaned up and saw just what a nice place it could be, it occurred to me to inquire about renting it."

His smile grew crafty. "All this money of mine you've been spending, you realize the rent's going up, right?"

"Of course. If you'll recall, that was one of the arguments I gave you for fixing it up. You've rented it so cheaply in the past, it's no wonder you've gotten deadbeats and lowlifes as tenants. But if you rent it to me, at a fair market price, I'll be a model tenant. I'll pay on time, every month, no excuses. I'll keep the property in pristine condition. And I'll continue to make improvements, provided you pay for them."

"Like what?"

He hadn't, Grace realized, said no yet.

"The kitchen still needs more work," she pointed out. "Better lighting, especially under the cabinets. There's that big dead space by the back door; I think it could be made into a nice laundry room, with a stacked washer/dryer and a shelf for folding clothes. All the windows need caulking, which should also help make the house more energy-efficient. The garage needs paint; it's a major eyesore. And then there are tons of little things. Like replacing all the nasty old electrical outlets, maybe installing ceiling fans in the bedrooms..."

"You love spending other people's money, don't you?" Arthur complained.

She ignored him and went on with her list of improvements. "My friend drew up a wonderful landscape plan for the yard. Did you know there are half a dozen fruit trees in the backyard? Lemon, lime, grapefruit, tangerines. He'll show me how to trim them and fertilize them so they produce again. I'd plant more flowers in the front beds, maybe do away with some of that grass..."

"Get rid of grass?" he squawked. "What do you want to do, pave the yard?"

"Not at all," she said calmly. "Maintaining all that grass takes so much time and energy, water and chemicals, my friend thinks flower beds might be a better solution. Oh, and did you know there's a sprinkler system out there?"

"Of course," Arthur said. "Not much good, since it hasn't worked in years and years."

"My friend thinks he can probably get it working again without spending much money," Grace said. "This could be the beauty spot in the neighborhood."

"Not to mention my water bill would go sky-high," he muttered.

"Come on, Arthur," Grace coaxed. "Quit making excuses for why it won't work. Won't you at least consider it?"

He folded the brochures and stuffed them in his back pocket. "I'll give it some thought," he said finally. "Have to discuss it with my wife. She's the real boss, you know."

"That's all I ask," Grace said. "Show her the pictures you took today, tell her my ideas, see what she says."

"Can't promise anything," he warned. "We're busy, getting ready to head up to the mountains."

"That's fine," Grace repeated. "Just let me know. And Arthur?"

"What now?"

"Thanks for the vote of confidence. I'm really thrilled you like what I've done."

Truegrace

One of my favorite old movies is Mr. Blandings Builds His Dream House. *Poor Mr. Blandings (played by Cary Grant) is a harried advertising copywriter living with his happy nuclear family in a cramped city apartment who just wants to build a simple little cottage in the country, but when the dream starts to take on grandiose proportions, Mr. Blandings's sunny version of utopia suddenly turns cloudy. I've thought of that movie a lot lately, as my own home life was dramatically disrupted, and then destroyed. Up until three months ago, I was living in a 6,500-square-foot mansion, that I thought was my own dream house. Now, with the clarity that only hindsight can bring, I realize that dream was mostly spun of high-fructose fantasy.*

These days, I'm finding intense satisfaction in the transformation of a weather-beaten little 1,200-square-foot Florida "cracker cottage" into what I think will be a cozy jewel of a home—maybe even, eventually, my home. I feel a little like Goldilocks, who found one chair too big, another chair too small, but, finally, an exactly-perfect-fit chair that feels "just right." My work on Mandevilla Manor is far from done, but already it's feeling "just right."

44

Nelson Keeler was having one of his good days. "Goddamn it," he roared, when Wyatt told him of his impending doctor's appointment. "I do not have Alzheimer's! I'm fine! That scheming woman . . . you call up that judge, tell him I'll go to the courthouse right now. I'll recite the Declaration of Independence by heart, balance my checkbook, balance his checkbook, and then I'll drop and give him fifty, by God!"

"No, Dad, that's all right," Wyatt protested, but it was too late.

Nelson proceeded to do just that, right there in the living room of the trailer, flattening himself on the floor, doing fifty straight-arm push-ups, counting aloud in a wheezy voice, then sitting up, cross-legged, wiping his perspiring brow with the sleeve of his shirt.

"How many other seventy-four-year-olds you think can do that?"

"None." Wyatt gave his father a hand up. "I know you've got all your marbles. But we've got to prove it to the judge, and to do that, you've got to go see this doctor and get a bunch of tests done. Just remember, you're doing this for Bo, not for Callie."

"Callie!" Nelson spat the name. "Somebody should have knocked some sense into that woman years ago. When this is all over, I'm gonna . . ."

Wyatt steered his father toward the door. "When this is all over, we're gonna laugh about it, but until then, neither of us can afford to do or say anything that might make anyone believe we're a couple of dangerously violent misfits. Right, Dad?"

"If you say so," Nelson muttered.

"One more thing," Wyatt said. "If you're going to convince this doctor, and then the judge, that you're harmless, you've got to keep your temper under check. This means no debating Alex Trebek or the designated-hitter rule. And it especially means no discussion of your bowel movements. Right?"

"Unless the doctor asks," Nelson countered.

"But only if she asks."

It was after six o'clock. Nelson Keeler was sitting upright in a chair in the doctor's office, snoring.

"He's had a really long day," Wyatt told Margaret-Ellen Shank. "He gets up at six, always has, and some nights he doesn't sleep all that well. He usually has a midday nap, but he didn't get that today."

"No need to apologize," Dr. Shank said, her voice soft. "Your dad is quite a guy. I really enjoyed meeting and talking to him today. One thing. What's his diet like?"

Wyatt shrugged. "Dad has a sweet tooth. He likes Pop-Tarts or Twinkies for breakfast. He might eat some canned soup for lunch, and a lot of nights he'll have a frozen chicken potpie for dinner. Or, and I'm not proud of this, a quart of ice cream or some more Twinkies."

Dr. Stark was still making notes. "What did he have for lunch today, do you know?"

"I don't," Wyatt admitted. "I was out in the park working until right before time for his appointment with you."

She frowned and consulted her notes. "Your dad has good balance and coordination, is able to communicate clearly, and his short- and long-term memory seemed to be in an acceptable range for his age. But as the day wore on, his personality changed drastically. I'm not an endocrinologist, but I think there really is a good possibility that your dad might be suffering from diabetes."

Wyatt stared at her. "So . . . you don't think he has Alzheimer's?"

"We'll need to take a look at all the test results, but my initial impression is that he does not. Your Aunt Betsy called him cantankerous, but I'd prefer the word 'spirited.' He clearly adores you and your son and is not an admirer of the boy's mother."

"That's putting it mildly," Wyatt said. "As far as Dad is concerned, Callie is the enemy, because she wants to move to Birmingham and take Bo with her. And, of course, she's now trying to prove that he's senile."

"He's pretty adamant on that subject," Dr. Shank said, smiling. "And I can't blame him. By the way," she added, her eyes twinkling, "I don't agree with him on the subject of Alex Trebek. At all. I think he's every bit as intelligent and talented as Art Fleming."

Wyatt let out a sigh of relief. "We've got to meet with the judge at eleven tomorrow morning. Is there any way you can give us some kind of report?"

She glanced at her watch. "I'll fax over something by ten tomorrow. Will that work?"

"That would be great," Wyatt said, jumping to his feet and pumping her hand. "I can't thank you enough, Dr. Shank. For seeing Dad so quickly and, just, everything. You've been a huge help."

Margaret-Ellen Shank leaned over and tapped Nelson gently on the shoulder. "Mr. Keeler?"

Nelson yawned widely. "What's that?" he asked groggily.

"It's nearly seven o'clock," she told him. She offered her hand; he took it and stood slowly.

"I told Wyatt you need to eat more sensibly," she said, giving him a look of mock disapproval. "No more Pop-Tarts for dinner. Right?"

"Right," he agreed.

45

Grace heard the muffled pinging of an incoming text coming from somewhere beneath the towering pile of merchandise in her shopping cart. She shoved aside the quilt with its vivid orange and green chinoiserie print, the four turquoise and green quilted throw pillows, the green and blue striped dhurrie, and the stack of turquoise and white polka-dotted bath towels.

The pair of green chevron-striped shower curtains she'd bought for the condo's dining room windows slid off the top of the stack and onto the floor. Finally, burrowing deep down into her pocketbook, she brought up the phone.

The text was from Camryn Nobles.

Where r u?

HomeGoods. What's up?

While she waited for a reply, Grace studied the store's furniture selection. Mitzi Stillwell's kitchen had an island crying out for barstools. Here were a pair of barstools with a perfectly acceptable look, clean lines, and a great price, $59.99 a pair. The problem was that they were white. And that was the problem with Mitzi's condo. Every single thing in it was white.

The walls were dead white. The tile floors were white. The sectional sofa in the living room was white, the pair of armchairs facing it was white, the sheer draperies hung from the floor-to-ceiling windows looking out at the sparkling blue Gulf of Mexico were white. In the kitchen, the countertops were white Corian, with a white subway-tile backsplash. The master bedroom had a king-sized bed with an upholstered, tufted white headboard and footboard. The carpet was an off-white flat weave. The guest bedroom featured a pair of twin beds with no headboards at all, just an expanse of white quilted-cotton bedspreads.

Just thinking of all that arctic white made Grace shiver. Maybe, she thought, running a finger over the back of one of the barstools, she could paint the stools a high-gloss tangerine.

Her phone dinged again with a reply from Camryn.

Been digging into Stackpole's financials and hit paydirt. Lunch?

Grace shook her head, annoyed. She had just begun shopping for Mitzi's place. She still needed lamps, bedspreads for the guest bedroom, and a new chandelier to replace the hideous builder-brass one in the dining room—and art. And those was just the accessories. She still needed dining room furniture, dressers for both bedrooms, coffee tables and end tables . . .

Can't it wait til tonight? she typed. With her pocket calculator, she began adding up the tab for the merchandise in her cart. She frowned. She was already at $431.99, not counting the two barstools.

Another ding interrupted her mental mathematics.

Got good stuff. How 'bout meet @Sandbox @2?

Grace shrugged and typed.

See u there.

Cedric Stackpole drummed his fingers on his desktop. He looked down at the faxed report from Dr. Shank, then up at Nelson Keeler. "Mr. Keeler? I understand you are a Vietnam veteran, is that right? In what branch of the service did you serve, sir?"

Was this some kind of trick question? Nelson looked to his son for some kind of signal, but Wyatt remained expressionless.

"That's correct, Judge," Nelson said finally. "I was in the army. Fifth Infantry. Did two tours, managed to get home in one piece. How about you?"

"Er, no," Stackpole said. "I like to think that my time in the judiciary is of some small benefit to my community. But I thank you for your service to this great country."

"You're welcome," Nelson said. "I got drafted, so it wasn't like I had a choice or anything."

Stackpole looked at Nelson over the rim of his glasses. "I understand you had some kind of verbal altercation recently with your daughter-in-law?"

"Altercation's a big word for what we had," Nelson replied calmly.

"Your daughter-in-law is saying that you did use strong language in your conversation with her. In fact, she says you actually threatened her. Did your grandson hear you making threats against his mother, hear you using strong language?"

"I reckon he did," Nelson said, his chin dropping. "I'm ashamed of that, Judge. Ashamed I let her get me riled up like that. And I'm here to promise, I won't let her get my goat again. No sir."

Betsy Entwhistle cleared her voice. "Judge? If I may?"

Stackpole gave her a curt nod.

"I'd just like to point out that Mrs. Keeler is not charging that Nelson Keeler has ever neglected or in any way harmed his grandson. Because he hasn't, and he wouldn't. And if you've read Dr. Shank's report, you can see that Mrs. Keeler's assertion that Nelson is suffering from dementia or the onset of Alzheimer's disease is totally untrue."

Betsy took a deep breath. "Dr. Shank is waiting on the rest of the test results, but she believes Mr. Keeler's occasional, er, bellicosity, could be simply the result of low blood sugar. In fact, she's suggested that Nelson Keeler might be suffering from diabetes, which could be responsible for all these symptoms Mrs. Keeler seems to want to believe are Alzheimer's."

The judge glanced over at Nelson Keeler and considered the old man sitting in the armchair across from him.

Nelson's thinning gray hair was neatly trimmed and combed. He wore a pair of navy dress pants, a white dress shirt that he hadn't donned since his late wife's funeral, and a pair of well-polished black lace-up dress shoes.

"I'm not senile," Nelson volunteered. "There is nothing in the world wrong with me, except maybe a little sugar diabetes, and I told the doctor I'd get that checked out and lay off the Pop-Tarts."

"You do that," Stackpole said finally. He closed the file folder. "I'm going to tell Mrs. Keeler and her lawyer that for now, I agree with your Dr. Shank. It appears to me that you have all your mental faculties and that you pose no threat at all to your grandson."

"Good!" Nelson exclaimed. He pulled himself to a standing position and extended a hand to the judge, who took it, somewhat reluctantly.

"Judge," Betsy said hurriedly. "This is the second time in as many weeks that Mrs. Keeler and her attorney have launched one of these baseless attacks on my client and his father. I hope this will reinforce our argument that it is not in Bo's best interest for you to allow his mother to move her son out of state and away from his father's care."

"You've made your point, Ms. Entwhistle," Stackpole said. "I'll take it under advisement."

Camryn Nobles was sitting at their regular corner table at the Sandbox, with Rochelle seated right across from her, their heads nearly touching, deep in conversation.

Grace dropped down into a chair beside her mother. "I'm starved," she announced. "What's the lunch special?"

"Shrimp burger, tuna melt, gazpacho," Rochelle said.

"Gazpacho?" Grace raised one eyebrow askance.

"My produce supplier gave me a whole bushel of tomatoes with bad spots, for next to nothing," Rochelle said. "Do you have something against gazpacho?"

"I love gazpacho," Camryn said. "Unless it's got green peppers, which don't agree with me."

"This recipe is straight off Grace's Web site," Rochelle said. "No green peppers. Cucumbers, garlic, cilantro . . ."

"You read my blog?"

"When it's interesting, which I occasionally find it is," Rochelle said.

"You bought cilantro?" Grace's second interruption was a clear annoyance to her mother.

"Yes," Rochelle said. "And I peeled the cucumbers, just as your recipe specified, for your information. With, I might add, a garnish of diced avocado and shrimp. Now, is there anything else?"

"No," Grace said, somewhat meekly.

"Would you like a bowl of gazpacho?"

"Yes, please," Grace and Camryn said in unison.

When they'd spooned up the last traces of cold soup and drained their iced tea glasses, Grace and Camryn sat back in their chairs.

"That was pretty damned good," Camryn said with a sigh.

"Better than my original recipe," Grace admitted. "But she'll never tell me how she changed it."

"Mothers," Camryn said, in unspoken agreement.

"Yeah," Grace said. "Now. What kind of dirt did you dig up on Stackpole?"

Camryn reached for her Yves St. Laurent tote bag and extracted a sheaf of computer printouts.

"Judge Cedric N. Stackpole Jr." she said, with a flourish, "is in debt up to his pointy little ears."

Grace rubbed her hands together gleefully. "Oooh. Goody. Do tell."

"This is a list of bank-foreclosed properties I pulled from the county's Web site," Camryn said, tapping a fingernail on the first sheet of paper on the stack. She ran her finger down the columns of tiny print and then jabbed one line, highlighted with a yellow marker.

"See here? 1454 Altadora Way, unit C. Siesta Key." Her finger trailed down the page until it stopped at another yellow-highlighted line of print. "1454 Altadora Way, unit B." Grace's eyes skipped down to the next line, which she read aloud.

"1463 Altadora Circle, unit A. But the mortgage holder is listed as Solomon Holdings," Grace said, squinting at the fine print.

"Solomon, as in, wise King Solomon, biblical judge," Camryn said, deadpan. "I looked it up. C. N. Stackpole is the sole corporate officer of Solomon Holdings. And then I took a ride over to Altadora Commons. It's a development of new town houses not far from his address on Longboat Key. I'll tell you a funny coincidence. I didn't realize it until I pulled up in front of the complex, but I actually looked at one of those town houses with my real estate agent, right after I kicked Dexter out of the house. Prices aren't bad, for Siesta, the unit I looked at was a resale, and they only wanted 575,000 dollars, but it was still way too pricey for my budget, and besides, I didn't like the floorplan."

Camryn leafed through the pages of documents until she found one she wanted, a computer printout of a real estate listing for Altadora Commons. The picture showed a series of tasteful cream stucco two-story town houses with orange stucco barrel-tile roofs, and a not-so-tasteful billboard seemingly mushrooming from a postage-stamp-sized lawn that proclaimed, "Bank Owned. Prestige Homes at Distressed Prices!"

"Wow. And Stackpole owns three of these?"

"Judge Stackpole? Your divorce judge?" Rochelle had come up behind them while they were studying the printouts. She leaned over Camryn's shoulder, staring at the photo of Altadora Commons.

"That's right," Camryn told her. "According to my real estate agent, the original sales price, back in 2007, was between 875,000 and 1.6 million dollars for the biggest units, which were actually two town houses joined together. Then, well, you know what happened to real estate around here. You couldn't give a town house away. Stackpole bought three units from the developer, at what looked like fire-sale prices, in 2010. He paid 420,000 dollars apiece. Which would have been a great deal . . ."

"Except?" Grace asked.

"Except that the county's tax digest was reworked in 2011, and now those units are only appraised at 120,000 apiece," Camryn said, sounding absolutely elated. "He's underwater, in a major way."

"But he can't be broke," Grace objected. "He lives at Longboat Key, and you told us his wife's family has gobs of money."

"The wife's family has money. Stackpole doesn't have squat," Camryn said. "I checked. The house is in her name. And incidentally? It's apparently a lot bigger than it looks from the street. It's on the market for 3.2 million."

Rochelle had eased herself onto a chair. "Bring me up to speed here, Camryn. What does any of this mean to you and Grace?"

"It's just a wild theory we've been tossing back and forth," Grace cautioned.

"It's not a wild theory," Camryn said, tapping the documents on the table. "These printouts prove it. Stackpole's in debt. His wife has money, but he probably can't touch it. He's having an affair with Paula Talbott-Sinclair, and one of them comes up with the idea to mandate women going through his divorce court to seek counseling from Paula, his girlfriend. She gets to soak each of us three hundred dollars per session, for a total of six sessions. There are five people in our group alone, and on the one day I watched her office, I saw three other groups arriving for divorce counseling. Do the math, Grace. They're getting rich off our misery."

"You should do a story about this on the news," Rochelle said excitedly. "Blow the lid off the whole big scam."

"I intend to," Camryn said.

"Isn't it a conflict of interest for you to report on a story you're involved in?" Grace asked.

"It'd be a first-person piece," Camryn said. "And if the story's big enough, I don't see how my station manager can turn it down."

"Look, I'd love it if we could prove those two were in cahoots," Grace said.

"But I talked to Mitzi about this yesterday. Even if you did see all those people going into Paula's office, how do you know they didn't go there of their own free will?"

"Can't you just ask her other patients whether or not Stackpole ordered them to attend therapy with her?" Rochelle asked.

"I wish," Camryn said. "I told you I hung around outside Paula's office last Friday. What I didn't tell you was that she apparently saw me standing there in the parking lot. She came outside and asked me what I was doing! I made up some lame story about looking for a diamond earring I'd dropped Wednesday night but I think she realized there was something fishy going on."

"Mitzi did say she'd take a look at Stackpole's dockets and talk to any attorneys she knows that have had divorce cases before him," Grace said.

"But who knows how long that will take?" Rochelle demanded. "We need action!"

Grace gave her mother the look. "What kind of action would you suggest?"

Rochelle thought. She smiled. She walked away from the table, and when she returned, she brought a handful of flyers, which she offered to Grace.

Come play in the Sandbox. Good for one free appetizer or drink

"I remember these. Dad hired kids to put them on car windshields at the new Publix, right after it opened."

"Until I made him stop, because we were nearly run out of business, giving away all those free drinks and stuffed potato skins," Rochelle said.

"So?" Grace asked. "Am I missing something?"

"I'm not. Rochelle, if you ever get tired of running this bar, you might have a future as an investigative reporter. This," Camryn said admiringly, "is brilliant."

"I still don't get it," Grace said, looking from one woman to the other.

"It's simple," Rochelle said. "Tomorrow morning, I go over to Paula's office. I watch cars pulling up and pay attention to who goes inside. Then, I plaster these coupons all over their windshields. When they bring in the coupons for their freebies, you two swoop in and ask them what you need to know."

"And how do you know they'll use the coupons? Or when they'll use them?" Grace asked.

"I'll just write on the bottom of each coupon that the deal's good for one day only," Rochelle said. "Trust me. Nobody turns down a free drink in this town."

46

Paula Talbott-Sinclair clasped her hands together prayerfully as she stood in the front of the room. She took a deep breath and let it out so s-l-o-w-l-y that the members of the group all subconsciously held their own breaths, wondering what would happen next.

"Hi friends." Her voice was clear and unusually calm. "I want to start our session tonight by talking about personal responsibility." She looked around the room. "All of you are here, in a way, because you were forced to take personal responsibility for some action you took against your partner."

"Ashleigh, you were stalking your husband's new lover. You vandalized her home in what was a very terrifying and thoughtless act of vengeance.

"Wyatt, you punched out the window of your wife's boyfriend's car so violently that you smashed his window and injured your own hand.

"Grace, you deliberately drove your husband's car into a swimming pool and destroyed it.

"Camryn, you discovered a provocative and salacious video of your husband and put it on YouTube, thus exposing him to public ridicule and humiliation."

Paula nodded at Suzanne. "Suzanne, we've all been very patient, waiting for you to admit to us the actions you took that caused you to join this group. Because I'm such a strong believer in personal responsibility, I've been reluctant to force your hand. Up until now."

Suzanne lifted her chin. "I'm ready, Paula. I want to tell the group . . ."

"Are you sure?"

"No," Suzanne said, with a nervous laugh. "I'll never be ready. But I'm willing, and that's the best I can do."

"Did I tell you all that Eric, my husband, is also a professor at Ringling?" Suzanne didn't wait for a reply. "He's in the English department, too. Anyway, I discovered, by accident, that he was sleeping with a co-worker, a woman who'd been my grad assistant last year."

"How'd you figure it out?" Ashleigh asked.

Suzanne's smile was wry. "Modern technology. Eric had gone out for a run. I was doing the laundry and found his phone in the pocket of his pants. As I was putting it on the counter, it pinged, and I saw he'd gotten a text. Darby was at soccer practice, and she was supposed to text one of us to let us know she was on her way home. I just assumed the text would be from her, so I read it. It wasn't from Darby. It was from her."

"The other woman?" Camryn asked.

"Yup. I'll spare you the nitty-gritty. Let's just say she was suggesting a time and place for their next assignation. 'Come horny,' the text said, so that let me know I wasn't overreacting. Just to be sure, I scrolled down the other texts from her. They were all just as graphic, if not more so. And it had been going on for months."

"Did you confront him?" Grace asked.

"No." Suzanne's hands shook as she uncapped the bottle of water she'd been clutching all evening. "I . . . I guess a part of me still didn't want to believe it was true. But another part of me, the cold, analytical researcher, needed data. While I was going through his phone, reading the texts, I found texts from other people, women, but I had no idea who they were."

"He had more than one girlfriend?" Camryn asked. "Just like my cheating husband."

"It gets better, or worse," Suzanne said sadly. "I went online and found something called keystroke software. It's a program you can surreptitiously load onto somebody's computer, and once it's activated, everything that person does on their computer, every e-mail they write or receive, every Web site they visit, you have access to."

"You became your own private detective," Camryn said. "That's so smart!"

"Not really," Suzanne said. "Remember, Camryn, when you said you wished you could take Scopolamine, to forget about your daughter catching Dexter in bed with her roommate? Well, I learned so much about Eric's secret life, I wish the data bank in my head could be wiped clean. But I'm afraid now it's hard-wired into my brain."

She took a sip of water. "Those other women? He was meeting them on Craigslist! For hookups."

"Dear God," Grace muttered.

"Exactly," Suzanne said. "He was meeting strange women in sleazy motel rooms for casual sex. And when he wasn't meeting them in person, they were sexting back and forth. It had been going for years."

"That's just nasty," Ashleigh said. "At least Boyce . . ."

Camryn reached over and grabbed Ashleigh's arm. "Let Suzanne get through this without editorializing. Okay? Otherwise, I will have to pinch your head off of your scrawny little neck." Ashleigh jerked her arm away.

"Camryn?" Paula's voice had a warning note.

Camryn glared at Paula. "I am dead-dog serious. I will hurt her if you do not make her be quiet."

"And I'll help," Grace offered, glaring, in turn, at Ashleigh.

"Everybody?" Suzanne looked amused. "I'm fine. Really. I've been living with this for months and months now. Now? I don't want this slime taking up any more room in my brain. You know?"

They all nodded in unison. They all did know.

"You wouldn't think this could get worse," Suzanne said with a self-conscious laugh. "But it does! Not long after I found out about Eric, I had a regular check-up with my gynecologist, and I had an abnormal pap test."

She looked at Wyatt and blushed. "I'm sorry you have to hear such personal stuff. About my lady parts. But there's just no way to get around this."

"I'll survive," he said, his voice gruff.

Suzanne took a gulp of water. And then the words came tumbling out in an unstoppable torrent. "I had HPV. I didn't even know what it was. My doctor—the same doctor who delivered Darby, who's known me since I was a teenager, had to explain it to me. It was an STD. A sexually transmitted disease."

Grace had to clamp her hand over her mouth to keep from gasping aloud.

"Eric . . . having unprotected sex with those women. He'd given me an STD.

I thought I would die of humiliation, the day my doctor told me. Of course, he was as embarrassed as I was. Long story short, I had cervical cancer.

"I had a total hysterectomy, because my husband gave me a sexually transmitted virus. Which, incidentally, could still come back, as something like anal cancer. My doctor had been quietly urging me to tell Eric what was going on, so he could at least notify the women he'd had sex with. You know, so they could see a doctor. I was so calm on the outside, it was frightening. I scared myself. One day, a week before I was scheduled for surgery, I went on Craigslist. I posted a picture of Eric and advised that any woman who'd ever had a hookup with him should get themselves checked. Because he had an STD. And they were at risk, too."

Suzanne gulped more water. "Then I texted my colleague at the college. I told her I knew about her and Eric. But here was a piece of news she wasn't privy to. And I told her. The day I was scheduled to have my surgery, I told Eric what I'd done. And I told him I wanted him out of our house by the time I got home from the hospital."

"Does Darby know?" Camryn asked. "Why you split up?"

"No," Suzanne said. "I couldn't do that to her. It's bad enough I have this stuff in my head. She's only eighteen. I don't want her hating men for the rest of her life. I don't even want her hating her father."

"But . . ." Ashleigh sputtered. "You let Eric off the hook. He doesn't even have to take responsibility for what he did!"

"He's not off the hook," Suzanne said. "His girlfriend filed a grievance against him with the college, and he was fired. One of the women he met on Craigslist claims he gave her HPV, too, although I don't know how someone who's in the habit of having unprotected sex with strangers can ever figure out how she got an STD. She's hired a lawyer. And so it goes. I think it's safe to say his life is ruined."

"And yours isn't?" Wyatt's face was pink with indignation. "I'm sorry, Suzanne. As a man, I'm sorry. As a husband, I'm sorry." He looked at the others. "We're not all like that. I swear."

"I know you're nothing like that, Wyatt," Suzanne said. "And I don't think every man is like Eric. But you're wrong about one thing. My life isn't ruined. I'm not about to give him that power."

"Right on, sister," Camryn said fiercely.

"Thank you, Suzanne," Paula said quietly. "I can see now why you needed time to find the words to tell your story. We're all full of admiration for your honesty. Right, friends?" She started clapping her hands, slowly, until the others in the semicircle joined in. Paula motioned for Suzanne to stand, and she hugged her. One by one, the others stood and joined the group hug, awkwardly at first, and then, as the moment grew, they stood together, their first real campfire moment.

The members of the group drifted back to their chairs. Paula went on.

"We're in week five of our sessions, and we've got lots of work yet to do before we conclude next week. Tonight, I'm going to ask all of you to think about writing an action plan.

"It's a sort of manifesto for yourselves," Paula explained. "You're all starting a new chapter of your lives. I'd like you to put some thought into how you'll move forward, personally and professionally, physically and emotionally, in a really mindful way."

She glanced at her watch. "This has been pretty intense tonight. Let's take a ten-minute break, and when we come back, we'll talk. Okay?"

Camryn blew her nose. "What's Suzanne's action plan gonna be, Paula? What's she gonna do, grow a new cervix?"

47

Wyatt was the first one to arrive at their table at the Sandbox. He pulled Grace's chair out for her, letting his hand rest, just for a second, on her arm. "Thanks," she said, shooting him a quick, private smile.

Rochelle was at the table in a shot, bringing a pitcher of beer and menus. "Where are the others?"

"They're on their way," Wyatt told her. "I've got a feeling we're going to need a lot of alcohol tonight, Rochelle. In fact, why don't you go ahead and bring Suzanne whatever it is she usually orders?"

"God, yes," Grace said emphatically. "I think she drinks wine spritzers. And I'm gonna need a big old glass of wine myself."

"Why?" Rochelle asked eagerly. "Did something happen tonight? To Suzanne?"

Wyatt's voice was solemn. "Suzanne finally shared tonight. Her husband was having unprotected sex with total strangers he met through Craigslist. He gave her an STD."

"You mean, like venereal disease?"

"Something like that," Grace said. "Only this disease can't be cleared up with penicillin. Suzanne had to have a hysterectomy because of it, and it could still come back."

"Sweet Jesus, Mary, and Joseph!" Rochelle exclaimed. "This really happened to our darling Suzanne?"

"Yes. And she just pulled into the parking lot, so please don't mention it. I mean it, Mom. Not one word."

"I would never," Rochelle said indignantly. She sketched a quick cross on her chest. "So help me."

Suzanne looked from the wine spritzer sitting on the table to Grace. "Thanks." She took a sip. "I needed this."

"You were amazing in group tonight," Ashleigh said, leaning across the table.

"You're our she-roe," Camryn chimed in. "You're like a divorce superhero."

Suzanne sipped her drink. "Not at all. The rest of you spilled your guts that first awful night of group session, when we were all total strangers. It's taken me five weeks to get up the nerve. I'm the biggest wimp in the world."

"No, you're not," Wyatt said. "You're . . . an inspiration."

"Okay, enough," Suzanne said. "You're going to make me start blubbering again. Can we please talk about something else? Anything else?"

Camryn and Grace locked eyes, then looked away. But their expression didn't escape Ashleigh.

"What?" she cried. "You guys know something. Come on, spill. Is it about Paula?"

Grace shrugged. "Camryn found out some stuff about Paula's past."

Suzanne regarded Camryn carefully. "This has something to do with why Paula isn't licensed to practice therapy in Florida, doesn't it?"

"Yeah," Camryn said, surprised. "How'd you know?"

Suzanne hesitated. "Okay, one more thing I've been keeping from you guys. I swear, it's the very last secret. Or, the last one that concerns you. Here it is. Stackpole didn't send me to Paula. I came on my own."

"You mean, you came voluntarily? Why would you do that?" Ashleigh asked.

"After I found out what Eric had done, I was so angry, in such a rage, I scared even myself," Suzanne said. "I had all these awful ideas about how to get my revenge. Fantasies about physically harming him. That's when I knew I had to get help. I went online and googled divorce and therapy and Sarasota, and Paula's name popped up.

"After that first night, I knew there was something off about Paula. Her credentials are actually pretty impressive, but she's very careful not to advertise herself as a therapist or a marriage counselor. She just calls herself a divorce coach. Which got me to wondering."

"Why'd you even keep coming to group after that first night? Or even after the second night, when Paula passed out cold?" Grace asked.

Suzanne looked at the faces sitting around the table. "By then, I knew it wasn't really about her helping me. You all had shared your stories. I knew you were hurting as badly as I was, and I thought maybe you'd help me find a way to deal with this horrible sadness and bitterness that was engulfing me. Turns out, I was right."

"Awwww," Ashleigh said, beaming. "That's so sweet."

"But Paula's helped me, too," Suzanne said. "In her own way. Of course, that doesn't mean I'm not curious about what you discovered, Camryn."

"Okay," Camyrn said. "Here goes."

Rochelle brought another round of drinks, but Suzanne pushed hers away, untouched. "I did wonder if it was something like that. Paula's not a bad person, you know. Just . . . damaged. Like all of us."

Ashleigh was not convinced. "You mean, I'm paying three hundred dollars an hour to get counseling from a convicted drug addict?"

"Recovering drug addict," Grace said. "And remember, Paula doesn't call herself a counselor or a therapist. Just a divorce coach. And who better to coach people through this kind of crap than somebody who's been through it herself?"

"I still think it's a rip-off," Ashleigh insisted. But a moment later, she lowered her voice. "But I don't even care about Paula anymore. I don't even care about that stinker Judge Stackpole. I've got news, y'all. Boyce called! He wants to meet me for lunch next week. And here's the best part. We're meeting at the Ritz!"

"I've never eaten at the Ritz-Carlton," Rochelle said, alighting on an empty chair next to Ashleigh. "Is the food as good as they say?"

"Oh, Rochelle, you're so cute," Ashleigh said, with her tinkling laugh. "Do you know, I've never actually eaten there? As far as I'm concerned, lunch at the Ritz is totally not about the food."

"It's not?" Rochelle looked puzzled.

"Now you're going to make me tell all my naughty secrets," Ashleigh said. She cupped her hands and whispered in Rochelle's ear.

"Ohhh," Rochelle said knowingly. "Now I get it. The Ritz-Carlton is like a high-priced no-tell motel."

"Exactly." Ashleigh giggled.

"Did he say why he wants to have lunch?" Grace asked.

"He didn't have to," Ashleigh said. "It's perfectly clear. He wants me back! I wasn't going to tell y'all this, but since it's kind of a moot point, I will. I saw Suchita, that's his girlfriend, leaving Boyce's office the other day. She's getting fat! And Boyce does not DO fat. He's a plastic surgeon, and appearances have always been important to him." She looked around the table, pausing when she saw Camryn's face.

"And before you say one word, let me just say that I don't intend to let him wriggle off the hook that easily. I mean, please! I do have my pride. I mean to make him pay for what he put me through. Boyce doesn't know it yet, but he's going to be buying a major piece of jewelry to make it up to me."

"Ashleigh," Grace said, "have you really thought this through? You know Boyce was keeping a mistress. You know he cheated on his first wife when he started dating you. What makes you think he won't do it again?"

"Yeah, baby," Camryn said. "I'm sorry, but I do not see this tiger changing his stripes."

"It's different with us," Ashleigh said. "Boyce never loved his first wife. Ever. Their marriage was a joke. I didn't have to break it up. It was already a done deal. So yes, Boyce cheated on me. I've accepted that. Hasn't Paula been yammering for weeks now about acceptance and finding peace?"

Suzanne patted Ashleigh's hand. "We just don't want to see you get hurt again."

"I'm *not* going to get hurt," Ashleigh said. "This is a love story. Plain and simple. Happy ever after. Is that so hard for y'all to believe?"

"It's not that I don't believe it," Camryn said. "It's just that, so far, I've never experienced it."

Ashleigh tossed her hair over one shoulder. "Rochelle, you're on my side, right? And you were married a really long time to Grace's daddy, right? Will you please tell these people that there is such a thing as a happy marriage?"

Rochelle pressed her lips together. "Sorry, honey, that's one thing I wouldn't know about." She looked over Ashleigh's head, her eyes focused on the bar. "Dammit, there's Miller and Bud again, taking up space and hogging the popcorn." She stood. "Next thing you know they'll be having their welfare checks forwarded here. I've gotta go chase them off."

Grace watched her mother hurry away. What was that crack about not knowing anything about happy marriages? She thought back to all the barbed remarks Rochelle had made recently about Butch. At some point, Grace thought, she and Rochelle needed to sit down and really talk about this stuff. Butch had been dead three years now. Was there something about her parents' marriage Rochelle had been keeping from her?

"Grace?" Suzanne waved a hand in front of her face. "Earth to Grace. Come in Grace."

"What?" The others were looking at her expectantly. "Sorry, guess I zoned out for a minute there."

"I was just asking what you thought about Paula's assignment. You know—the action plan?"

"I think it's a good idea," Grace said. "I know for myself, after I walked out on Ben, I was really sort of . . . rudderless, I guess would be the word."

"Paralyzed," Camryn agreed. "After I kicked Dexter to the curb, I couldn't make the simplest decision. And y'all know that is not like me. I pulled through Starbucks one morning, and when the barista asked if I wanted extra sugars, I just burst into tears."

"I already know step one of my action plan," Ashleigh confided. "As soon as I get rid of that Suchita hag, I'm taking my old job back as Boyce's office manager. And let me tell you, I'll be the one doing the meetings with those cute little drug reps from now on."

"I'm sort of undecided," Suzanne said. "Darby's been offered a chance for early enrollment at Elon, a small liberal arts college in North Carolina. Their soccer team was NCAA runner-ups last year, and the head coach personally flew all the way here in the spring to watch Darby play. She turned it down, saying she couldn't imagine missing her senior year of high school, but I think the real reason was that she didn't want to go away and leave me alone so soon after Eric and I split."

"Your daughter sounds like a great kid," Wyatt said.

"I don't know how I got so lucky with her," Suzanne said. "The Elon coach is still calling the house, begging Darby to reconsider. They'd like her to come out right now, to start practicing with the team. Selfishly, I wish she would stay home, finish her senior year, and then go off to college. I want one more year of fixing her breakfast and washing her stinky practice clothes every night! But realistically, there's no reason why she shouldn't do early decision. Darby's a bright kid. She's taken enough Advanced Placement classes at her high school that college work won't be that much of a challenge. This is a terrific opportunity for her."

"Then let her go."

Their heads swung around in unison. Rochelle stood with her hands on the back of Suzanne's chair. "I know, it's none of my business. But it sounds to me like you already know what you should do."

Suzanne swiveled around in her chair. "Thanks, Rochelle. I guess that gives me step one of my plan. Now I just have to persuade Darby that her mother isn't as needy as she thinks."

"I hate to admit that Paula may finally have a good idea," Camryn said. "But what she said tonight does make sense. I've been thinking a lot lately about my career at the station, and where I want it to go."

"You're not thinking of moving are you?" Grace asked.

"You obviously don't know much about the television news business. Women don't move to other markets at my age. At least, not voluntarily. No, this little bit of investigative journalism I've been doing has been a real kick. I've actually been thinking this might be a good time to go off-camera. Maybe consider producing." She grinned widely. "I've always been great at telling other people what to do."

"What about you, Grace?" Ashleigh asked pointedly. "What would be your step one?"

"I've already taken it," Grace said. "I've asked Arthur, the man who owns the house I've been restoring, if he'd let me rent it. If he says yes, I could move in within a week or so."

"You're moving?" Rochelle looked stricken.

"Don't turn my bedroom into an office just yet," Grace warned. "Arthur didn't seem all that wild about the idea, but he didn't say no. He said he'd have to talk it over with his wife. But I'm hopeful."

48

Grace mopped the floor while Rochelle counted down the cash register and bundled up the money for the morning's bank deposit. She double-checked the front door to make sure it was locked and flipped the switch for the neon sign. Then, she went behind the bar, poured herself a glass of wine, and took a seat on the barstool next to Rochelle.

"It's after one," her mother said, looking up from her counting. "I don't mind the company, but you've been getting up and leaving pretty early most mornings lately."

"I'll go to bed in a little while," Grace said. "Can I ask you something?"

"Hmm?" Rochelle was jotting figures in the ledger where she always recorded each day's tally. "This divorce group of yours is good for business. Last year, this same date, we did eighteen hundred dollars. Today, we did twenty-one hundred. And the softball guys didn't even have a game tonight."

Grace closed the book. "Mom, what did you mean earlier, when you said you didn't know anything about happy marriages?"

"Nothing," Rochelle said casually. "You know me, sometimes I run my mouth without thinking."

"Sometimes you do, but I don't think that was the case tonight. Lately, you've been dropping these little...I don't know, hints? Is there something about you and Dad's marriage that I don't know?"

"Your dad's dead and buried, Grace. That's all old history."

"I don't think so," Grace said slowly. "Come on, Mom. Be honest with me."

Rochelle took off her reading glasses and buffed them on the hem of her blouse. "Your dad was a good man, Grace. He loved you beyond all reason and was so proud of you and the life you were building. That's what's important for you to know."

"Nuh-uh," Grace said, shaking her head. "There's more to it than that. Ever since I started this divorce-recovery group, you've been hanging around, super interested in everything everybody has to say . . ."

"I'm a nosy old lady," Rochelle said.

"What was going on with you and Dad? Whatever it is, I need to know."

Rochelle let out a long sigh. "Since you insist, I'll tell you. Four years ago, I was ready to divorce your dad. I'd hired a lawyer. I'd even found an apartment to move into. And then we found out he was sick. I couldn't walk out on him like that. He was dying. So I stayed. End of story."

She saw the stunned expression on Grace's face. "I'm sorry, honey. I really never meant for you to hear this, but you asked, and I just couldn't keep dancing around the truth any longer."

Grace felt like she'd had the wind knocked out of her. "Why? What did Dad do? Please don't tell me he had another woman."

Rochelle opened the ledger again. "Some things are best left unsaid, you know? And this is one of them."

"Just tell me, please? So, he had an affair? Was it somebody I knew?"

"It was nobody. A snowbird from Buffalo whose husband used to keep a boat here in the marina during the winter. Her husband died the summer before, and she was down here by herself, and I guess . . . she got lonely."

"Oh, God." Grace felt physically sick. Her father? Butch? The same guy who wore loud Hawaiian shirts and loved country music? The man who gave both Rochelle and Grace the same Whitman Sampler of chocolates every Valentine's Day? Butch had a girlfriend?

"It didn't last very long," Rochelle said quietly. "Your dad was a lousy sneak."

Grace swallowed hard. "How . . . how did you figure it out?"

"He was acting funny. Not like himself. You know how Butch was; he liked his set routine. But that January, he switched barbers. After twenty years of the same haircut, he grows sideburns, for God's sake. He started taking an extra shower, in the middle of the day. You know how I always went to the wholesale house for supplies, right? Well, suddenly, he insisted he should be the one to go pick up our order. He'd be gone two, three hours. One time, he came back without the paper napkins and take-out containers. He had some lame excuse that they were out. Of paper napkins?" She shook her head. "He never did have much of an imagination."

"I don't know what to say," Grace said. "You must have been devastated."

"Mad as hell, more like. Because he'd promised—promised on his mother's grave—he wouldn't put me through that crap again."

"Again? It wasn't the first time?" Grace found herself staring into her own image in the mirror behind the bar, and then at herself, and then at Rochelle, and at Rochelle's image. Who were these strangers?

"No. Not the first time." Rochelle's lips were set in a grim smile. "You were only three the first time he cheated. I found out then, and I left. I took you to my cousin's house in Jacksonville, and we stayed three weeks. Butch was heartbroken. He couldn't stand the idea of not having his baby girl around. He knew he'd messed up. He begged me to take him back, said he'd be a different man. And he was, for a long time."

"I just . . ." Grace swallowed hard. "I don't know what to think. You never said a word. The two of you never fought. My friends' parents were splitting up while we were in high school, and they used to tell me they envied me, because Butch and Rochelle—you know, Butch and Rochelle were solid."

Rochelle reached out and stroked Grace's hair. "Maybe I should have divorced him back then, after the first time. But where would I have gone with a little kid in tow? I had no real job skills; certainly I didn't have any money. And I was too proud to admit to my parents that I'd made a mistake. So I did the easy thing. I went back to Butch. And I stayed."

"All those years? When I thought you guys had the model marriage? That was all a lie? You only stayed together because of me?"

"It wasn't *all* a lie," Rochelle said. "We had some good times. We made a life here, had friends. Had you. I don't want you to think it was a bad life, Grace, which is why I never told any of this to you."

"You could have told me. Especially once I was an adult. I would have understood," Grace said. "It makes me sad to think that you were that unhappy, and I was just . . . oblivious."

"You weren't oblivious. You were busy, spreading your wings, starting a career. A marriage. But now I think, I wonder, if I didn't set you up for failure by giving you unrealistic expectations of your own marriage. Does it make me pathetic, how much vicarious pleasure I got seeing what an amazing woman you were becoming?"

"You've never been pathetic," Grace said. "But what made you finally decide to leave?"

Rochelle fidgeted with her glasses. "Besides Edwina? That was her name. Edwina! I'd say it was just a slow build. One morning, Butch was fussing at me, because I'd bought Chock full o'Nuts instead of Folgers without consulting him."

Grace rolled her eyes. "God. Dad and his coffee."

"I picked up the whole bag of beans and dumped it in the trash. I walked upstairs, packed a bag. When I got downstairs, he looked at me like I'd lost my mind. 'You're leaving over a bag of coffee?' So I looked at him and I said, 'It's not about coffee. It's about Edwina.'"

"Did you think about going to counseling?" Grace asked.

"I went to counseling. Your dad refused to go. He thought it was a waste of his hard-earned money."

"That sounds like Dad," Grace said with a sigh. "I still can't believe you got as far as hiring a divorce lawyer without telling me. Wait a minute. Mitzi? Mitzi was the lawyer you hired?"

Rochelle nodded. "You and Ben hadn't been married that long at the time. You were deliriously happy. I didn't want to upset you. And then, of course, we found out how sick Butch was. I wasn't even gone a week."

"Did he beg you to come back?" Grace asked, teary-eyed now, thinking about her father's last months of life, growing thinner, using a walker, and then, finally, a wheelchair.

"Butch? Never. He didn't have to ask. I knew he needed me, so I came. We never even discussed that week. It was like it never happened." Rochelle got a glint in her eye. She laughed.

"What's so funny?" Grace asked.

"Nothing. I was just thinking about the coffee. When I moved back here, that first morning, I went out to the kitchen to make coffee. There sat a brand-new bag of Chock full o'Nuts. That was Butch's idea of an apology."

Grace laughed until the tears were rolling down her cheeks. "Mom? You know what I remember that last year? When Dad was so sick? You were so strong. You kept the bar running, took him to all his doctor's appointments, to chemo. You bathed him and spoon-fed him when he was too sick to eat, fixed his bed in the living room so he could look out at the water those last few weeks."

Rochelle blinked back her own tears. "He made me promise I wouldn't let him die in the hospital. It was a small enough thing to do."

"So you forgave him?" Grace searched her mother's face for an answer.

"You know? I guess I did," Rochelle said, wonderingly. "At the time, I told myself I was doing it for you—because he was your daddy. But now, I think maybe I did it for me. I hated what Butch did—cheating on me—but I guess at the end, even after everything, I did still love him."

"I'm glad you told me," Grace said. "Thanks for that, Mom."

49

Good morning Grace. Don't know if you'll remember me, but you and I had some dealings a few years ago when I was an assistant to Lily Soo at House Beautiful. *I'm now features editor at* Veranda, *and I've been following your new blog and your new project with such delight. We think our readers would love it, too. Wondering if we might discuss having you write and photograph a monthly feature about your progress at Mandevilla Manor? Can't wait to discuss! All best, Doreen Zelen. P.S. Adore that checkerboard kitchen floor!*

Grace read the e-mail three times, just to make sure it wasn't a figment of her imagination. Then she tucked her laptop under her arm and went running downstairs to the bar.

Rochelle was directing the beer-delivery guy into the storeroom. "Mom!" Grace cried.

Her mother whirled around, knocking her cup of coffee to the floor. "What is it?"

"*Veranda!* They want to hire me to write a series about Mandevilla. Can you believe it? I've subscribed to *Veranda* since forever. And they want me!"

Rochelle grabbed a bar towel and dropped it to the floor, mopping the spilled coffee with her sneaker-clad foot. "Honey, that's fantastic!"

"I know," Grace said. She was hopping up and down with excitement. "*Veranda!* This is a dream assignment."

"How about some breakfast?" Rochelle asked. "You can tell me all the details and I'll cook you some eggs and bacon."

"Can't," Grace said. "I've got to get over to the cottage and get to work. I want to be able to move some furniture in by the end of the week so I'll have some new photographs to show Doreen; she's the *Veranda* editor who e-mailed me. I did a freelance piece for her years ago, when she was at another magazine. I was supposed to stop and pick up Sweetie, but I'm going to text Wyatt and see if he'll drop her off. Talk to you later!"

Arthur Cater was sitting on the front steps of the cottage on Mandevilla when she pulled into the driveway.

"Arthur!" Grace called, as she crossed the lawn. "I'm so glad you're here. Wait 'til I tell you my news."

As soon as she got closer, she saw by the expression on Arthur's face that something was terribly wrong. His face was streaked with what looked like soot, and he suddenly looked like a very, very old man.

"What's wrong?" she asked. "Is it your wife? Is she sick?"

"My wife is fine," Arthur said. "It's the house, Grace. Somebody tried to burn down the house last night."

Grace stood in the living room, staring down at the charred floorboards in the corner closest to the dining room. Soot marks streaked the white walls, and shards of broken glass sparkled from the shattered front windows. She clutched her laptop tightly against her chest and willed herself not to cry.

"The neighbor next door smelled something burning when he got up to let his dog out at six this morning," Arthur said sadly. "He called me, then he called the fire department, then he came over here himself. As soon as he got onto the porch, he saw the flames, right over there. It was just a small blaze, looked like a bundle of rags or something, he said. He broke the window and climbed in. He found the mop bucket you'd been using and doused the fire with water. If he hadn't done that, I don't guess this place would be standing. This house is mostly wood. Heart pine that burns like kindling."

"I don't know what to say," Grace said, her words catching in her throat.

"There's more," Arthur said grimly, jerking his head in the direction of the kitchen. Grace's footsteps echoed in the high-ceilinged empty room. She stood in the doorway of the kitchen, and now she did cry.

Black paint had been spattered all over the kitchen. It oozed down the faces of the new refrigerator and range and trickled down the cabinet faces. Paint pooled on her freshly painted checkerboard floor. "Fuck the Man" had been painted in wobbly black letters across the kitchen window.

"Kids." Arthur spat the word. He pointed at the sink, where an empty plastic half gallon of cheap vodka had been tossed, along with empty cans of Red Bull and assorted brands of beer cans.

"Oh my God." Grace breathed the words. She backed away from the doorway and into the hallway, where half an inch of water sloshed over the floorboards. Wadded up towels littered the floor.

The bathroom door was closed. She was about to open the door when Arthur closed his own gnarled hand over hers. "Don't," he warned. "It's awful bad." He swallowed. "They . . . Grace. They took a dump in the tub and smeared it all over the walls. Then they shoved a towel down the toilet, to back up the plumbing, and did the same thing with the sink. I've shut the water off now, but hadn't had time to clean everything up before you got here."

The bedroom doors were closed, too. Before he could stop her, Grace opened the door to the front bedroom. Day-glo orange paint festooned the walls. The empty paint bucket lay on its side, a river of orange paint spilling onto the newly refinished hardwood floor. More empty beer cans were scattered over the floor, and the room reeked of urine and marijuana smoke.

"Who would do this?" she whispered.

She heard the front door opening then and the sound of boots on the floorboards, and then the skittering of a dog's nails clicking across the floors. "Grace?" Wyatt's voice sounded panicky.

Sweetie came speeding around the corner, and Grace grabbed her up in her arms before the dog could go tracking across the orange paint.

"I'm back here," she called, her voice breaking. A moment later, he was there, by her side. Without another word, he wrapped his arms around both her and the dog, and held them close.

"I'm so sorry," he murmured into her hair. "Are you all right?"

Finally, she sniffed and wiped at her eyes. "I'm okay," she insisted, pulling free.

Arthur stood awkwardly in the middle of the room, brandishing a push broom.

"Wyatt, this is Arthur Cater. He owns the house. Arthur, this is my friend Wyatt, the one I told you about who had the ideas for the garden."

The two men nodded at one another. "What happened here?" Wyatt asked. "I saw the burned places in the living room."

"Somebody broke in and tried to burn it down." Arthur gestured around the bedroom. "But before they got around to that, they did all this. More in the kitchen. The bathroom's worse."

"Who?" Wyatt asked. "Do you have any idea?"

"Kids is my guess," Arthur said. "The neighbor said he noticed a car parked in the driveway last night, around ten. I'd told him about Grace working over here, and he just figured it was her, so he didn't think any more of it. He's the one that called me this morning."

"They had themselves a big ol' party," Grace said bitterly. "You can smell the weed in here. And there are beer cans and a vodka bottle in the kitchen."

"Damned kids," Arthur growled.

"I guess it's too much to hope the neighbor got a description of the car or a license number," Wyatt asked.

"Coulda been blue, coulda been green. It was dark, and he only just glimpsed the car from his own front porch," Arthur said. "Probably doesn't matter. They're long gone by now."

"And nobody heard anything over here?" Grace asked.

"It's been a rental house so long, and we've had so many tenants in and out, the neighbors just started tuning out what goes on over here," Arthur said. "The lady across the street came over this morning when she saw the fire truck to tell me she'd called the police twice on my former tenants, but the cops just issued them a warning. Wish she'd have told me."

"All your hard work," Wyatt said, squeezing Grace's hand. "You had the place looking so good."

"It looked real nice," Arthur agreed. "I'm glad I took those pictures to show my wife, before all of this happened."

Grace dabbed at her eyes with the hem of her oversized T-shirt. "I'll just have to start over, that's all." She picked up the paint can and looked at the label. "At least it's latex. I'll have to repaint the walls, but if I get some rags and get to work on these floors before the paint really hardens, it may be that I won't have to strip the floors again. Thank God this happened after I'd gotten the poly down."

"There's nothing much happening at the park today," Wyatt said. "I'll call my Dad and tell him I'm going to hang around here today and give you a hand. Bo's at his mom's, so I've got the day and the evening free, if you need me."

"Oh no," Grace started to say. Then she shrugged. "Who am I kidding? If you really can spare the time, it would be a lifesaver."

"Sorry, but I won't be much help to you," Arthur said. "I've got a doctor's appointment in an hour, and after that, I've got to take my wife to her doctor. It takes forever to get on his schedule, so I can't change it. Anyway, my bursitis has flared up again. It's hell getting old."

"We'll manage," Grace assured him.

"I'll check back with you later in the day," Arthur said. He looked around at the bedroom walls and shook his head again. "What gets into kids' heads these days? What's the fun of destroying property? Where are their parents? That's what I'd like to know."

He pulled a handkerchief from his pocket and wiped his paint-smeared hands on it. "I took more pictures before you got here," he told Grace. "And the police were here, right after the firemen left. I'll file a claim with the insurance company in between the doctors' visits."

"Thanks, Arthur," Grace said, following him onto the front porch.

He turned just before reaching the door. "You sure you want to bother with doing this all over again? Maybe I should just hire some young fella to come in and clean it up and paint it all and be done with it. Get it rented again and quit worrying."

"No!" Grace said sharply. She smiled sheepishly. "I mean, I wish you wouldn't. I've got so much invested here. I really want to see it through to completion. Besides, I'm still hoping you'll decide to let me rent it when it's done. So I really do have an ulterior motive."

"I'll tackle the kitchen if you want to concentrate on this bedroom," Wyatt offered.

Grace planted a kiss on his chin. "You're a good guy, Wyatt Keeler." Then she went back to work.

It was nearly two o'clock when he poked his head in the bedroom again. She'd managed to mop most of the orange paint off the floors. She'd scraped the dried paint from the window panes and had even put a coat of primer on the walls. The orange paint was so vivid, she was sure it would take at least two coats of primer, plus two coats of the Benjamin Moore. At some point, she'd have to make another trip to the hardware store to buy more paint.

"Looking good," Wyatt said. He held out a white paper sack. "I went and got us some lunch. You ready for a break?"

They sat cross-legged on the front porch to eat their turkey sandwiches. Grace rested her aching back against the wall and took a swig of her Diet Coke. "How's it coming in the kitchen?"

"There's good news and bad news. Which do you want first?"

She made a face. "Tell me the good stuff first."

"I managed to get all the paint off the fridge and stove. We didn't get so lucky with the cupboards. They'll all have to be repainted."

Grace sighed and pushed a strand of sweaty orange-streaked hair off her forehead. "What's the floor looking like?"

Sweetie, who'd been sitting politely on her haunches, stared hungrily at the sandwich wrappings and whined softly. Grace tore off a bit of turkey and tossed it to the dog, who caught it in midair.

"Like a really long night of repainting red and white checkerboards," Wyatt said, grimacing.

Grace groaned and rolled up the legs of her jeans to show him her bruised knees. "I'm still not recovered from the first time I painted that floor. Me and my big ideas."

"I know this is probably a silly question, but couldn't we just paint the whole thing one color?"

"We could—except that I got an e-mail from an editor at *Veranda* magazine this morning. They want me to do a series for them—story and photographs, of my redo of the cottage. And the editor very specifically mentioned that she adores that floor."

"Oh." Wyatt munched on a potato chip. "*Veranda* magazine. That's good?"

"Very good. Especially in my world. It's huge."

"I'd slide over there and give you a congratulatory hug, but I'm too tired."

She smiled. "I'll consider myself hugged. Anyway, who knows if I can get this place cleaned up enough now to even do the story?"

He chewed and thought. "Maybe you could make this"—he swept his hand, indicating the charred porch floor and broken windows—"part of the story. You know, intrepid girl rescues house from fire and paint bomb?"

She raised an eyebrow. "That's actually not a bad idea. Now I wish I'd taken some pictures of the bedroom before I started cleaning it up."

"Could you use the pictures Arthur took?"

"Maybe. I guess they'd have to be scanned or something." She finished off her sandwich and threw a last chunk of turkey to Sweetie, who'd been stealthily creeping closer to the source of the food while she talked.

Wyatt stood and helped her to her feet.

"Guess I'd better grit my teeth and check out the damage in the bathroom," Grace said, making a face. "Arthur wouldn't even let me look in there when I got here this morning. He said it was pretty gross."

"It was," Wyatt said. "Nothing I'd want you to have to deal with. I got the tub and all the walls wiped down with bleach, and I managed to unstop the toilet and mop up most of the water. All I can say is, if I ever get hold of the punks who did all this . . ." He made a fist. "Pow!"

"Yeah," Grace said. "About those punks. I'm not so sure this was the random act of vandalism that Arthur assumes it is."

"Really? Then . . . You're not saying your ex did this, are you?"

"Maybe. Although this—especially the way Arthur described the bathroom—that's not really Ben's style. J'Aimee, on the other hand? I'm not so sure it wasn't her. Or maybe she put somebody else up to it."

"I don't know, Grace," Wyatt said. "What happened here is pretty extreme— even for a pissed-off ex-husband. Besides the fact that the two of them are scum, what makes you think they're behind this?"

"For one thing, the paint. That was a brand-new can of orange paint, and a brand-new can of black paint. I didn't have either of those here in the house, so whoever did it took the trouble to go buy paint and bring it along. So not really a crime of opportunity. Same with the fire. That wasn't just a bunch of rags they used to start the fire in the living room. There were loads of old towels and sheets in the linen closet, but they didn't use them to start it. They brought what looks like a new canvas drop cloth. Because, again, whoever set that fire was quite the little planner. Does that sound like kids to you?"

He stared at her. "Are you sure you haven't been watching too much *CSI*?"

"I've had a lot of time to think while I scrubbed that floor," Grace said. "Shall I tell you what else I think is suspicious?"

"Shoot."

Grace pointed toward the house across the street. The lawn was neatly mowed, and two green recycling bins stood at the curb. "There were three or four different kinds of beer cans in the kitchen sink, plus the Red Bull, plus the vodka. I think whoever did this caper wanted us to think they had a party, so they probably just scooped up some empty bottles and cans along the way. Today was recycling day, so every house on this street had full bins sitting on the curb last night."

"Anything else?" Wyatt asked.

She walked into the living room, and he followed. She kicked at the remains of the charred thing on the floor. "I don't think J'Aimee intended to burn the house down. That's pretty scary, even for her. I think she just wanted to make a little fire. Why else just set fire to something like this? If someone really wanted a fire, they would have poured lighter fluid, or kerosene, or whatever all over the house. But it's just this one little corner of the room that's charred."

"Why would she, or Ben, do any of this?" Wyatt asked. "How do they even know you're working on this house?"

"Trust me, they read TrueGrace every day. J'Aimee steals my pictures and recipes all the time. Both of them have stopped by here. As to why, that's simple. For revenge. The last time J'Aimee lifted one of my blog posts, and the photos and posted them on Gracenotes as her own, I got fed up. It's copyright infringement, pure and simple. I e-mailed all their advertisers to let them know what was going on. I know at least one of their biggest accounts pulled their ads because of that."

"Will you tell the cops?"

"I would if I thought it would do any good," Grace said. "But all I have is a lot of theories. So I'm going to do the one thing that will piss them off the most. I'm going to start all over, and I'm going to make this house fabulous, even if it kills me."

"Okay," he said. "Count me in."

50

G race stood in the middle of the living room, her hands on her hips, and scowled. Wyatt came in just in time to catch her angry expression. "What now?"

"On top of everything else, she stole my damn iPod," Grace said. "I left it in here the other night. The thing was, like, four years old, but it had all my music; my running music, my painting music, everything. Now it's all gone. Dammit. I need my music to paint by."

"I've got my iPod out in the truck," Wyatt said cautiously. "But it's getting kind of late, isn't it?"

Grace looked out the shattered front window. The sun was hanging low in a bright orange-tinged sky. "Wow, it's almost sunset. What is it, after eight?"

"Five after eight," Wyatt said. "Are you ready to quit yet?"

"Are you?"

"I'll keep working as long as you want to. But you've been at it all day, Grace. Since nine this morning, with only a half-hour break at lunch. Do you really want to keep going?"

"No," she admitted. "As Rochelle would say, my get up and go got up and went. Maybe I'll head home."

"Good idea," Wyatt said.

"Unless . . ." A smile crept over her face.

"Unless what?"

"I was just thinking, you might like to see my other design project."

"I didn't know you had another project."

"It's Mitzi's condo over on Gulf Drive. She's turning it into a furnished vacation rental, and she's hired me to fluff it. The back of my car is actually full of towels and rugs and bedspreads and curtains for the place. I just started shopping for it yesterday."

"Sounds nice," Wyatt said, wondering where this conversation was headed. "But it's getting kind of late for a sightseeing tour. Maybe you could show it to me this weekend?"

"It sits right on the gulf," Grace told him. "The master bedroom has a balcony with a spectacular sunset view. And it has a king-sized bed. And I have the key."

Wyatt's eyes lit up. "Are you propositioning me?"

"Would you think less of me if I were?"

"Not at all," he assured her. "And I promise. I'll still respect you in the morning."

They left Wyatt's truck at Mandevilla Manor and drove to the Publix on Holmes Beach to pick up supplies. While he circled the parking lot, Grace made a sweep of the supermarket. She hummed as she careened through the aisles, tossing a bag of dog food, a bottle of wine, a six-pack of beer, a pound of boiled shrimp, some good cheese, a loaf of French bread, and some grapes into the cart. On her way to the cash register, she caught sight of herself in a mirrored display in the floral department. Ugh! She was a mess. She backtracked through the store and added a bar of scented soap and some shampoo and conditioner to the cart, and then, in a flash of genius, she added a jug of detergent because the condo had a laundry room.

"Get everything we need?" Wyatt asked, pulling alongside her at the entrance to the store.

"I think so," she said, holding up the wine.

When they got to the condo, Wyatt snapped a leash to Sweetie's collar and carried the grocery sacks, and Grace loaded her arms with the linens she'd bought. She juggled the packages while she dug in her pocket for the key. When they entered the apartment, it was already flooded with the dying light of the sunset.

Grace glanced down at her paint-spattered sneakers and kicked them off before stepping onto Mitzi's pristine white carpet, and Wyatt followed suit.

Wyatt dropped the groceries on the kitchen counter and walked back to the living room, standing in front of the sliding glass doors that led out to the balcony. The sky was streaked with brilliant layers of colors, from navy to violet to scarlet, orange, and pink. "Awesome," he breathed. Grace hurried into the bedroom and dropped her packages. By the time she got back to the living room, Wyatt had opened the wine and poured glasses for both of them, and Sweetie was curled up on the rug in front of the television.

"Come here," he said, holding out her glass. She took a sip of the wine. He put his arm around her, and she rested her head against his shoulder.

"Nice place," he said, looking around the room. "Kinda white, though, isn't it?"

"Mitzi's a great lawyer, but, as she herself admits, she sucks at decorating. She gave me a five-thousand-dollar budget and a deadline of two weeks, but otherwise no restrictions."

"Hmm." He was nuzzling her neck. "Is it okay for me to be here?"

Grace chuckled, thinking of her conversation with her lawyer. "I think she'd be okay with it."

He turned her toward him and slid his hands around her waist. "Pardon me for being forward, but didn't you say something about a king-sized bed?"

"Mm-hmm." She gave him a lingering kiss. "What about the sunset?"

"I thought you said the bedroom looked out onto the gulf."

"So I did." She kissed him again, then pulled away.

"Much as I hate to bring up the subject, I am absolutely filthy, and I smell like a goat. I'm just going to jump in the shower, and then maybe we can continue this discussion somewhere else?"

"Okay," he said, running a finger slowly down her arm. "Need anybody to scrub your back?"

"Mmmm. Hold that thought."

The master bedroom had a huge tiled walk-in shower with an adjustable rainforest shower head. Grace hummed as she lathered her entire body, scrubbing at the streaks and specks of orange paint that seemed to coat every inch of her exposed skin. The hot water sluiced down her back and over her chest and her head. She washed and rinsed her hair and wished she'd brought along a razor to shave her legs. The thought struck her that she still had two weeks to work on the condo. She'd make sure and stock the bathroom with a razor—and a toothbrush and toothpaste—after her next shopping trip.

She towel-dried her hair and finger-combed it as best she could, then wrapped herself in another one of the big fluffy towels she'd bought. Then she gathered up the clothes she'd left on the bathroom floor.

Wyatt's voice drifted in from the other room. It sounded like he was on the phone. She hesitated, then pressed her ear to the door.

"Hey Dad." His voice was low. "How're you feeling?

"That's good. Did you have dinner? Did you eat the vegetables I bought you? No Dad, Tater Tots don't count. Yeah. Salad's good. Did you take the new medicine the doctor gave you?"

He sighed. "Yeah, I know you're a grown-up, but I just want to make sure you take your pills. Is that a crime? Okay, great. Callie didn't call, did she? No, Dad, remember? You promised the judge you wouldn't call her that anymore.

"Listen, Dad, I'm, uh, probably not coming home tonight, but I'll be back first thing tomorrow to get the animals fed and open up.

"What? None of your business. I'll see you in the morning."

How sweet is it that he calls his dad to check on him? Grace thought. *This is somebody I could love.*

And then something else occurred to her. She grabbed the jeans she'd dropped on the floor and dug her cell phone out of the pocket. It was Thursday night, which was ten-dollar-pitcher night. Hopefully, Rochelle would be too busy to answer her phone. She really did not want to have a variation of the same conversation Wyatt had just had with his father.

The phone rang once and went right to voice mail. "Hi Mom. Just wanted to let you know I'm not coming home tonight. I've got so much to do, I think I'll just camp over here tonight. See you in the morning." She disconnected hurriedly.

Wyatt was standing by the sliding glass doors in the bedroom when she emerged from the bathroom dressed only in a towel and a smile.

He gave a long, low wolf whistle when he saw her and held his arms open.

Grace padded across the room to him. "Take off your clothes."

He grinned. "If this is your idea of foreplay I can't wait to see what happens next."

"Don't be smutty," Grace said primly. "I bought detergent at Publix, and I'm going to wash our clothes so we have something clean to wear after . . . dinner."

He reached out and grabbed her. "Does this mean we get to have dessert before . . . dinner?"

She kissed him lightly. "We'll see."

He set his wineglass on a table by the window and made a huge production out of stretching and yawning.

"Oh man," he said. "I am soooo tired. I think I'm so tired I'm gonna need you to undress me."

Grace wrapped her arms around his neck. "Is that so?"

"Yes," he said solemnly. "Please."

Grace blushed. "You know I haven't been with another man in a really long time, right?"

He cradled her face between his hands and kissed her again. "It'll come back to you. It's like riding a bike."

She tugged his T-shirt over his head and tossed it to the floor, then ran her hands over the flat plane of his bare chest, resting her fingertips on his nipples. She kissed his ear, then his collarbone, and worked her way to his chest. Wyatt slid his hands around her waist and kissed her hungrily.

Grace slid her hands down lower and felt him inhale sharply. She worked her fingers inside the waistband of his jeans and nimbly unfastened the metal snap before slowly easing the zipper down. She rolled the waistband of his cotton briefs over his slim hips, brushing her hand lightly over his erection.

"Oh God, Grace," he whispered in her ear. She slid her hands around to his rear, cupping her hands on the smooth, cool flesh of his butt, while he kissed her neck, the warm spot at the base of her throat, and then her lips again, parting them with his tongue, both hands entwined in her damp hair.

Grace tugged the waist of his jeans and briefs lower, past his hips, feeling the bulge of his erection pressed against her groin, lower, until she could wrap one bare leg around his and ease the jeans down to his ankles with her toes.

"Nice trick," he murmured in her ear. He released her long enough to kick free of his jeans, then, naked, pulled her to him again.

He flicked the edge of her towel and it dropped to the floor. He took a step backward and gazed at her pale body, silhouetted against the deep-purple sky outside. "You're beautiful," he said. "So beautiful." His hands roamed slowly, lingering on her butt, traveling up her spine and then around her ribs, until he cupped a breast in each hand. His head dipped, nuzzling and suckling each nipple until Grace could hear her own ragged breaths in the still of the darkening room.

She ducked her head and felt the blush starting at the roots of her hair and spreading downward. He pressed a finger under her chin and she looked at him from beneath her lowered lashes.

"I'll take it from here," he said. He took her hand and led her toward the bed.

51

G race lay on her side, gazing out the sliding glass doors at the deep-blue sky. At some point, Wyatt had opened the doors, and they could hear the waves washing ashore. He was spooned up against her back, his arm draped over her side, with his hand cupped against her breast, his thumb rhythmically brushing against her nipple. He was already aroused again. For that matter, so was she.

She rolled over to face him. "You've got to stop that, or we'll never get any dinner."

Instead, he bent his head and kissed her other nipple. "Would that be such a bad thing?"

"I'm starved," she announced. He caught at her hand, but she neatly slid out of the bed. Still self-conscious, she groped around on the floor for her forgotten bath towel, finally crawling over to where Wyatt had dropped it, several feet from the bed.

As she fastened it, she glanced over her shoulder and saw him, propped up in bed, watching her with amusement.

She gathered up their clothes and went out to the laundry room to load them into the washer. When she'd started the wash, she went to the kitchen and poured herself a glass of the chilled white wine. Through the open bedroom door she heard the sound of the shower starting.

Grace found a large bowl—white pottery, of course, in one of the kitchen cabinets. She dumped in the bag of boiled shrimp, cut up a lemon, and arranged the slices around the edge of the bowl, humming as she worked. She rinsed the green grapes and placed them on a cutting board, next to the loaf of French bread. There was no bread knife in the scarcely appointed drawer of kitchen implements, so she simply tore the bread in hunks and heaped them beside the grapes along with the cheeses she'd picked up in the deli department.

She heard the clicking of nails on the tile floor and looked down. Sweetie jumped up, her front paws scratching at Grace's bare knees.

"Ow," Grace said, leaning down to scratch the little dog's silky ears. "We've got to get you to the groomers to get your nails trimmed. In the meantime, thanks for reminding me. I actually did bring some dinner for you, too."

She poured dog food into one bowl and water into another and set them on the floor, then went back to her preparations, loading all the food, along with the wine bottle and two glasses, onto a large wicker tray.

Wyatt was just emerging from the bathroom as she walked into the bedroom. He had a towel wrapped loosely around his hips, and, with a hand towel, he was rubbing his closely shaven head. His chest was muscled and his abs were not quite male-porn-star tight, but close enough. His skin gleamed darkly tan in contrast to the white towel. She stopped dead in her tracks, forgetting what she'd been about to say.

"You're staring at me," Wyatt pointed out.

"That's not staring. That's lusting." Grace set the tray with the food on the nightstand. She wrapped her arms around his waist and backed him toward the bed.

He laughed, but offered no resistance.

When she had him right where she wanted him, she placed one hand on his chest and toppled him backward.

"You're freaking gorgeous," she said, looking down at him, spread-eagled across the bed. "I thought I liked you best dressed in your little Ranger Rick safari outfit, but that was because I'd never seen you naked. Or in a towel. I definitely like the towel best."

She leaned forward and brushed her fingertips lightly across his chest. Wyatt caught her hand and pulled her down beside him. He pinned her arms to the bed and rolled until he was on top of her.

He frowned down at her. "That is not a Ranger Rick outfit. I'll have you know it's an official Jungle Jerry uniform. My grandmother had them made for everybody who used to work at the park. The one you've seen me wearing is the last one left. The rest are all in tatters, and that one is one rip away from the trash."

She easily worked her hands free from his and ran her palms down his flanks. "You can never throw that uniform away," Grace said sternly. "It's what you were wearing the night we met."

"Minus the parrot poop," he reminded her. "But that wasn't the first time we met. The first time was that day we both went before Stackpole. Remember? I have to confess, I have no idea what you were wearing either time. You looked so angry and intimidating, I was about to flee the premises." He pointed at the tray. "Room service? I like your style."

"There's no dining room furniture yet," she said. "And I still have to buy barstools for the island in the kitchen. And I don't want to eat on that white sofa, not until I have a chance to spray it with a stain repellant. So . . . dinner in bed."

She crawled onto the bed and propped herself up against the padded headboard. Wyatt handed her a glass of wine and took his own. He lightly clinked his glass against hers. "Here's to divorce camp."

An hour later, they'd devoured every morsel of food on the tray and drained the bottle of wine. The towels were scattered about the floor, and after another longer, more leisurely session of lovemaking, they were spooned together on the big bed, Sweetie asleep on the floor beside them, moonlight pouring in through the open doors.

At some point, Grace was vaguely aware of her cell phone, which she'd left on the dresser, dinging softly to indicate an incoming voice mail, and then another, and then another. But she was still too drowsy, too warm and happy and overwhelmingly, bone-deep contented, to rouse herself and see what was going on in the rest of the world.

52

Driving back to the Sandbox the next morning, Sweetie sleeping on the front seat beside her, Grace finally took the time to check the voice mails from the night before.

The first, at 9:45 P.M., was from Rochelle.

"Grace! Those women from the other divorce camp sessions are here. They're on their second round of free drinks. You need to get back here and talk to them."

Shit! She'd totally forgotten her mother's plan to leave free-drink coupons on the windshields of Paula's other divorce campers. She couldn't believe her mother's crazy scheme had actually borne fruit.

The second call, ten minutes later, was also from her mother. "There must be seven or eight of those divorce women in here," Rochelle said, her voice cracking, either from excitement or desperation, Grace didn't know. "What the hell are you doing? Why aren't you here? These women all have hollow legs. They're drinking me broke!"

The third call was from Mitzi Stillwell, and she didn't sound happy. "Grace? It's ten fifteen in the evening. And I have a deposition at 8:00 A.M. I just got a call from your mom, insisting I get over to the Sandbox, to talk to some women she claims have some important information about Stackpole and your therapist. I have a vague idea where you might be right now, but I'm going to claim attorney-client privilege and not divulge that to Rochelle. Instead, I'm going to get out of bed, get dressed, and drive over to that bar to check this out. All I can say is, this had better be good. And he better be good, too."

Rochelle was practically beside herself by the time Grace walked into the bar, shortly before nine.

"Didn't you get any of my messages last night?" her mother demanded. "I kept calling and calling!"

"I'm sorry," Grace said. "Vandals broke into the cottage on Mandevilla some-time Wednesday night. It was a huge mess. They splattered paint all over the place and tried to burn it down. I kind of had my hands full. I had to try to get the paint off the floors and the appliances before it dried, and wash everything down. It was late by the time I got done, and I kind of just collapsed. I didn't get your messages until this morning."

"Vandals?" Rochelle asked. "Did you report it to the police?"

"Arthur did," she replied. "He's dealing with them." She walked around to the back of the bar and poured herself a mug of coffee. She took a sip and seated herself on a barstool. "Did you find out anything from the women who showed up here last night?"

Rochelle took a sip of her own coffee. "I found out a lot of stuff I didn't want to know, that's for sure. Husbands who are cross-dressers. Husbands who like to hang out in public bathrooms and expose themselves to little boys. Husbands who like to watch their wives have sex with strangers . . ."

"Eewww," Grace said. "Stop. I get the picture. I mean, did you find out any-thing about people who've been referred to Paula by Judge Stackpole?"

"Yup," Rochelle said, looking immensely pleased with herself. She turned to the bar back and pulled a spiral-bound stenographer's notebook from the drawer. "I took notes," she added.

"I must have put twenty or thirty of those coupons in the cars in that thera-pist's parking lot," she continued. "I didn't get over there 'til nearly eleven yester-day, and by that time, there were five women coming out of her office. I just handed them the coupons, and, since they were watching, I had to put them on the other cars. I got back over there after the lunch hour and hung around an hour, and another group of women, and one man, drove up and went into her office, so I put coupons on their cars. Then this big, burly, scary-looking guy came out of that tattoo place, and he wanted a coupon, so what could I do? I had to give him one. And then . . ."

"Mom," Grace said gently. "You did a great job handing out the coupons. But could you just cut to the chase? How many people actually showed up here last night who said they were in Paula's divorce camp?"

Rochelle didn't like having her story interrupted. "I was getting to that. I guess there were nine women who came in last night over the course of the evening with those free-drink coupons. I was trying not to act too nosy, just, you know, talking them up, asking how their day was going. A couple of them got kind of snotty with me. Just drank their free drink and left, without even leaving me a tip! What kind of woman stiffs a bartender who's giving her free drinks?"

"Probably one whose husband got to keep all the money in the divorce," Grace said.

"Eventually, though, four women sat right here at the bar. I think they were all in the same divorce group, because they were calling each other by their first names and kind of joking about their action plans. One of them said her action plan was to find herself a new sugar daddy. So I kept pouring the free drinks and playing dumb. Finally, I asked the chattiest one, this gal named Ginger, how they all knew each other, and she said they were in the same divorce-recovery group. I told Ginger I was going through a divorce myself, and how did she find out about something like that. And she said it wasn't her idea. The judge in her divorce case told her she *had* to go to a therapist. And not just any therapist. It had to be a therapist named Paula Talbott-Sinclair. That's when I started calling you."

She glared accusingly at her daughter. "And when you didn't call me back, I called Mitzi Stillwell. And she came right away."

"And that's when things started getting really interesting." A woman's dry voice came from behind them. Grace swiveled around on her barstool. "Mitzi! I thought you had an early deposition."

"I did, but when I got to the other attorney's office, he asked if we could re-schedule. So here I am."

Rochelle took a mug and filled it with coffee before handing it over to the lawyer.

Mitzi sat down beside Grace. "I'm seriously thinking of hiring your mother as a private investigator. She's *that* good at asking dumb questions and drawing people out without raising their suspicions."

"That's what happens after you've tended bar for thirty years," Rochelle said modestly.

"What did you find out?" Grace begged. "Give me the nitty-gritty, please. I'm dying here."

Mitzi nodded deferentially to Rochelle. "Go ahead."

"All four of those gals, Ginger, Angie, Becky and Harriett, had your judge in their divorces," Rochelle said.

"The Honorable Cedric N. Stackpole Jr." Mitzi put in.

"Right. Harriett Porter, she was the oldest one, probably around my age, her husband owns a Cadillac dealership up north in Indiana, but they live down here full-time now," Rochelle reported. "She discovered her husband was having himself a fling with a male stripper in Tampa. She waited for him outside that club, and when he came outside at two in the morning, she sort of lost her temper and accidentally ran over his Gucci loafers with her SRX Crossover." Rochelle took a sip of coffee. "I'd never heard of such a car, but Harriett says it's sort of a cross between a real Cadillac and an Escalade. Escalades are what all the rappers drive, Harriett says . . ."

"Mom!"

"Right," Rochelle said, without missing a beat. "Stackpole threatened to throw Harriett in jail for aggravated assault, which her lawyer later told her was bullshit, because her husband did not want to have it get in the papers that he'd been run over in the parking lot at Jeepers Peepers. Instead, Stackpole told her she had to attend divorce-recovery group. With Paula."

"And the rest of the women in the group?" Grace asked.

"Different stories, same endings," Rochelle said smugly.

"By the time I got here last night, dear Harriett was fairly intoxicated," Mitzi said. "Lovely lady, but I think she probably needs AA more than she needs divorce recovery. I sat with all the girls for a while; then, I volunteered to make sure Harriett got home safely." She raised an eyebrow. "While she waits for her divorce to get settled, she's living in an enormous rented mansion on Siesta Key. Before I walked her to her door, I casually asked how much she's paying for her divorce-group sessions. Grace, she's paying nine hundred dollars!"

"That's three times as much as the rest of us," Grace said.

"I know," Mitzi said. "I was as stunned as you are. It didn't seem to bother

Harriett. I think she's actually enjoying the sessions with Paula. She apparently hasn't made a lot of friends since moving here. Before I told her good night, I asked for her lawyer's name." Mitzi sighed happily. "It's Carlton Towne. He's senior partner in my old law firm, and a prince of a guy. I put in a call to him first thing this morning."

Rochelle pushed her steno notebook across the bar to Grace. "Here's the name of the other gals in Harriett's group. They even have a name for themselves. The Diva Divorcées. Cute, huh?"

Grace read the names scrawled on the notepad. "Are these their lawyers' names, too?"

"You bet," Rochelle said.

"I only know one of these lawyers personally," Mitzi said, running her finger down the list of names. "And because we have to do this very quietly, with an abundance of caution, I'm not going to call them until absolutely necessary."

Grace nodded. "Just what is it you're planning to do?"

"First, I'm going to call Betsy Entwhistle and chat with her about Wyatt's experience with Stackpole. Then, I'm hoping Carlton Towne will be as frank with me as his client was last night. Then, I think it's time we talked to the other members of your group, Grace, to see what their lawyers have to say. If that goes well, I think we'll probably have enough to file a complaint against Stackpole with the state Judicial Qualifications Committee."

"How long will all that take?" Grace asked. "After next week, we've only got one week of divorce camp left. Then, Stackpole's supposed to rule on my divorce. What if he finds out what we're up to?"

"Leave that to me," Mitzi said. "We're going to gather every bit of documentation possible, and I can be very, very discreet and low-key."

53

G race, can I speak with you privately for a minute?" Mitzi asked. Rochelle gave them a questioning look but retreated to the kitchen.

Mitzi lowered her voice. "How's the condo coming along?"

Grace blinked. "Good. I went shopping Thursday and picked up a lot of things to bring in some color, since you've got so much white. I don't want it to look too sterile. You're going to have turquoise and lime green, and pops of tangerine . . ."

"How about the bed? I paid nearly two thousand dollars for that mattress, you know."

Grace felt herself blushing and glanced toward the kitchen to make sure her mother was not within earshot. "The mattress is amazing. Totally."

Mitzi smirked. "I just like knowing I've gotten my money's worth."

"Trust me," Grace said. "You did."

Wyatt pulled up in front of Luke Grigsby's house shortly after ten. He'd averted his eyes as he passed his old house, just down the street. It pained him to see the smudged windows, the stack of yellowing plastic-wrapped newspapers at the edge of the driveway, and the forlorn tire swing hanging from a rotted rope tied to a spindly tree in the side yard. Mostly, it pained him to see the "Bank Owned: For Sale" sign in the weed-strewn front yard.

Losing the house to the bank, he realized, was probably more painful than losing Callie.

He glanced at the clock on the truck's dashboard, then at Luke's front door and, as always, felt the same familiar, simmering resentment replace his previously cheerful, even joyous, demeanor.

According to the written agreement they'd hashed out during their separation, Callie was supposed to deliver Bo to Jungle Jerry's on the days Wyatt had custody. In reality, Wyatt usually ended up going to get his son on what he thought of as "hand-off days," because Callie was rarely even remotely on time, which always made Bo anxious and agitated, afraid his mother would change her mind and refuse to allow him to see his father.

Wyatt tapped his fingers impatiently, the back of his wedding ring sounding a *ching-ching-ching* against the hard plastic of the steering wheel. He'd been sitting there for ten, then fifteen minutes. He was reluctant to tap his horn or even go to the front door, because the last person he wanted to see that day was his soon-to-be ex-wife.

He found his mind wandering back to the previous evening, and then this morning. He'd awakened early, as always, shortly after six. It was still dark outside, and Grace was sleeping on her side, faced away from him, moonlight silvering her slumbering form. The quilt had slipped from her bare shoulder. Carefully, he pulled it lower until her back was exposed. He marveled at the elegant curve of her spine, the way her soft brown hair spilled onto the pillow, the way her full hips flowed from her narrow waist. She had a tiny mole on her left shoulder; he could just barely see it. He'd pressed his lips to her shoulder, not really meaning to awaken her, but she'd turned, and seeing his face inches from hers, smiled lazily. He'd thought her beautiful the night before, but finding her like this, tousled and sleep-drunk, he decided she was the most exquisite woman he'd ever known.

The passenger-side door opened abruptly and Bo hopped onto the seat and slammed the door hard. He folded his arms across his chest and grunted. "Let's go."

His son's face was set in anger, his eyes red-rimmed.

"Hey, dude," Wyatt said cheerily. "Something wrong?"

"Mom's really upset," Bo said. "Some guy came over this morning and took her new car, and she's been on the phone hollering and yelling at you know who. Can we just go now?"

What now? Wyatt wondered. Callie's car was a flashy red Mustang convertible. Bo told him Luke had given it to her for her birthday a few months earlier, complete with a vanity tag that read HOTMAMA.

"Is your mom's car not working?"

"No. I mean, yeah, it works good. We were asleep, and then I heard something outside and it was still dark, so I snuck out to the living room window to see if was like a burglar or something, and I saw this guy breaking into Mom's car! I went in and woke her up and told her, and she went and got this like gun out of the dresser. Then she went running outside, but the guy was already inside her car. She was screaming at him to stop, but he just rolled the window down and threw a piece of paper at her, and then he peeled off down the street, going really fast."

Uh-oh. Sounds like the repo man had paid a visit this morning. Mr. Bigshot must have missed a car payment. Or two.

Wyatt would have found it comical, except that witnessing the unpleasant scene had clearly upset the child.

"Well, I'm sure your mom will get it figured out," Wyatt said for lack of anything better to say.

"She's really, really mad at him," Bo said. He gave his father a hopeful look. "Maybe she'll change her mind and they won't get married, and we won't have to move to stinkin' Alabama."

Wyatt was about to pull away from the curb when out of the corner of his eye he saw Luke's front door open. Callie stood in the doorway, dressed only in an oversized T-shirt that barely touched her thighs. Her hair was mussed and rivers of black mascara streamed down her cheeks.

"Wyatt!" she screamed. And then she came running toward the truck in her bare feet.

Bo's eyes were the size of saucers. "Stay here," Wyatt said. He jumped out of the truck and met Callie at the sidewalk. "They repossessed my Mustang," she cried. "It's gone! Luke swears he doesn't know what happened, but I know he's lying. He lied about everything."

Callie threw herself into his arms. He closed them uneasily about her shoulder, turning to see that Bo was still in the truck, his eyes riveted to the unfolding scene.

"Shh," Wyatt said, patting her shoulder. "It's probably just a misunderstanding. Maybe the car payments got posted wrong or something."

"No," she sobbed. "Luke's broke. He's been lying all along. Oh my God, Wyatt. It was all just a big lie. What am I going to do?"

"Hey," he said softly. "We'll figure it out. Look, this is upsetting Bo. Why don't you go inside and get dressed. Let me take him over to the park and get him settled with Dad; then I'll give you a call and we can talk about it. Okay?"

"A call?" Her voice was wobbly. Snot trails dribbled down her face. "Can't you come back here and talk? I could make us some coffee . . ."

"Not here," Wyatt said, his spine stiffening. There was no way he was setting foot inside Luke Grigsby's house again. Not ever.

"Oh," she said. "I get it. Okay. I could come over to the park . . ."

"God no," he replied. "You're not exactly Dad's favorite person these days, Callie."

"That was all Luke's idea," she said quickly. "I never meant anything by it . . ."

Wyatt sighed. "I'll meet you at Starbucks in an hour. Okay? But I can't stay long."

"All right," she said. "Oh my God. This is all such a nightmare."

For once, Wyatt thought bleakly, he'd have to agree with her.

54

Callie had managed a remarkable transformation in the hour since he'd last seen her. Her hair was now clean and shiny and pulled back in a ponytail, she had fresh makeup, and she was dressed in a low-cut pink top and tight white jeans. And, Wyatt noticed, as she clutched the mug of coffee he'd just brought to the table, she wasn't wearing Luke's flashy diamond engagement ring.

"Thanks for coming," she said, her voice low. "I'm sorry I got all hysterical in front of Bo. That was bad. But everything happened so fast . . . I completely lost it."

"He's a sensitive kid," Wyatt said. "I know it's hard to do, but, for his sake, we really have to try to keep things on an even keel."

"I know." Callie nodded and took a sip of coffee. She gazed out the window at the parking lot. When she turned to look at him, her eyes were brimming with fresh tears.

"It's over between me and Luke," she said, her lower lip trembling. "And not just because of the car. Everything he told me? Everything he promised me? It was all just a big fat lie. He lost his job. There is no transfer to Birmingham. He just told me that because he assumed he'd get a new one with another company there. He's known for three weeks now, and he never said a word. Just kept bullshitting me. About everything." She held up her naked left hand. "My ring?

Not real. Not even a good fake. And you know how I found out? I took it to the jewelry store in the mall yesterday, because I wanted to have it sized, and the girl behind the counter actually laughed at me when she saw it. It's a friggin' cubic zirconia."

Wyatt winced. "Did you ask Luke about that?"

"Yes. Of course, he had all these bullshit excuses. He tried to tell me he gave me a fake ring because he was having the real one custom-made, and it wasn't ready yet. He's got lies and excuses for everything."

"Geez. I'm sorry, Callie."

"Not as sorry as me," she said bitterly. "What do I do now? I can't stay with him. I won't. I told him that this morning. I can't marry a liar."

"What'll you do?" he asked.

She shrugged. "I have no idea. I just know I won't stay under the same roof with him. Not another night. I can't have Bo exposed to somebody like that."

"Well, of course, Bo can stay with Dad and me for as long as you need him to. But where will you go?"

"Good question. I don't exactly have a lot of options. Most of my girlfriends? As far as they're concerned, I'm the slut who cheated on her husband. They all made it pretty clear they couldn't stand Luke."

"What about your family?"

"Ha! My parents are barely speaking to me since our breakup. They always thought you walked on water, Wyatt. Anyway, I'm not about to move back to South Carolina. What would I do there? Get a job selling made-in-China sombreros at South of the Border? Anyway, Bo would hate it there. And the schools suck."

You didn't care what Bo thought about Birmingham when you thought you and Luke were moving there, Luke thought.

"What about Kendra?" he asked.

Her lips twisted. "My baby sister is just itching to get a chance to say, 'I told you so.' She never liked Luke, either. Guess maybe I should have polled all my friends and family before falling in love with him and ruining my life, huh?"

Funny how it didn't occur to Callie that she wasn't the only one affected by her affair with Luke Grigsby. She probably just considered her husband and son as collateral damage.

"You've always gotten along with Kendra. Surely she wouldn't turn you away, right? Until you get things figured out?"

"Maybe." Callie didn't sound convinced. She grabbed a paper napkin from the stack Wyatt had brought to the table and used it to blot her eyes.

"Oh God, Wy," she whispered. "How could this have happened? You were the best thing that ever happened to me. And I let you walk away. Can you ever forgive me?"

Wyatt twisted his own paper napkin into a tightly wound ribbon. "What's done is done." *What does she want from me?* he wondered. "You just need to figure out how to get your life back on track, with the least amount of disruption to Bo. He's had more than enough of that in the last year."

"I know, I know," Callie agreed. "I'll call Kendra right now. I can probably stay with her for tonight, at least."

"What about a car?" Wyatt asked.

"That bastard Luke traded my Civic in when he got the Mustang," Callie said. "I drove his old Jeep over here. And he's crazy if he thinks I'll give it back. He owes me. Big-time."

"At least that's something," he said. "Look, Callie. I'm sorry, but I really need to get back to the park. We've got a group of thirty kids coming in with a day camp in an hour, and they're expecting a guided tour and a performance from Cookie."

"I know you're busy," Callie said. "You don't have time for my soap opera. Go on. I'm just going to sit here for a while and try to get my wits about me before I go back to Luke's and start packing up my stuff."

He hesitated. "So . . . we'll plan on keeping Bo at the park, at least through the weekend. Is that okay with you?"

"Sure," she said, shrugging. "What are you going to tell him? About Luke and me?"

"Nothing," Wyatt said. "I'll leave that to you to figure out. You should probably call him later today, when you're calmer. You don't have to tell him the gory details yet. Just let him know you're okay."

Callie reached across the table and squeezed his hand, clinging to him. "I will. And I won't cry anymore. Not in front of him, anyway. Thanks, Wy."

"You're welcome," he said, slowly sliding his hand away from hers. "Good luck with Kendra."

. . .

On Monday, Grace was just unloading the last of her second batch of painting supplies from her car when Arthur's car pulled up to the driveway.

It took him a few minutes to emerge from the car, and when he did, Grace thought he looked tired. Tired and defeated. He walked, stiff-legged, toward where she stood, right outside the front porch.

"Hi, Arthur," she called.

"Hi there, Grace." He looked down at the buckets of paint she'd stacked on the porch steps and sighed and looked away. His shoulders slumped.

"I know, it's a hit to our budget," she said. "But hopefully the insurance will pay for it, right? Anyway, Wyatt and I managed to get all the paint off the floors and the appliances, so I'm just repainting the walls in the bedroom and the kitchen cabinets. And the kitchen floor. Again. That's a pain in the butt, for sure. We'll have to get a floor guy to take a look at the scorched floor in the living room, but maybe that can just be patched."

"Come on inside, Grace. I need to talk to you."

Theirs footsteps echoed in the high-ceilinged rooms. Arthur looked in at the kitchen, and the bedroom and bathroom.

"You've done real good work here, Grace," he said finally. "And I'm gonna pay you for everything you've done. I want to do right by you."

"But?" She dreaded what he was going to say next. It would not be good news, she knew.

"The wife and I had a long talk yesterday. My blood pressure was up pretty high by the time I got to see my doctor, and that got her all upset and worried. And the thing is, at my age, I just don't need the hassle."

"Arthur, once somebody's living here, I seriously doubt you'll have anything like this happen again," Grace said. "Even if you don't rent it to me . . ."

"If we rented it to anybody, it'd be you, Grace. But we're not going to rent it. We talked it over, and what with the money it'll take to put in that central air-conditioning you keep talking about, well, I just don't see putting that much money into the place right now. So we're going to sell it."

"Oh." Grace felt herself sag against the kitchen doorway. "I see."

He swallowed and she saw his Adam's apple bob up and down as he worked through what he was going to say.

"I hate like the dickens to let the place go," he said, running a gnarled hand over the doorframe. "The way you had it looking, just these past couple weeks, my folks would have been proud of that. This was their homeplace, and they always took pride in it. But my wife, she helped me see, the time has come to let it go to somebody else."

Grace couldn't trust herself to speak. She just nodded.

"I've got a real estate agent coming over on Saturday, to look the place over and tell me what she thinks I could sell it for," Arthur said. He looked up at her. "My wife was wondering if maybe you'd be interested in buying it. If you were, we'd try to make you a fair price, taking into consideration how much time you've already put into the house. But we'd need you to make a decision pretty quick, before we go ahead and list it with an agent."

She bit her lip. "If my divorce were final today, and I had the money, I'd love to buy this house," Grace said. "But to be honest with you, I can't say exactly when that's going to happen, or how much of a financial settlement I'm going to get from my ex. The judge in my case . . . well, let's just say he doesn't exactly see things the way my lawyer and I do."

"That's a damn shame," Arthur said. "And that fella, that friend of yours? I don't guess he's in any position . . ."

"He's in almost the same position I am, except he's also got child-support payments," Grace told him. "Anyway, Wyatt and I . . . well, he's a very nice person. But we just started seeing each other. It's way too early to know how that's going to turn out."

"I see. Well, I guess that's that then," he said. "I'm real sorry it had to end like this, Grace. I liked the idea of you fixing up this place, moving in and living here, starting all over again. Don't guess there's any need for you to do any more painting now. I feel bad enough that you put all this time into the place, for nothing."

"Not for nothing," Grace said. "I enjoyed the process. I just hope whoever buys the place will finish the job and do justice to it."

She followed the older man out to the front porch. "I meant to ask you," she said, as he fumbled in his pocket for his car keys. "Did you report the vandalism to the police?"

"Yes. I filed a report. I showed them the pictures I took with my camera. They didn't seem too interested. I guess they see a lot of that type of thing."

"I've got an idea about who might have done it," Grace said slowly. "Would it be okay if I talked to a cop I know?"

He gave her an odd look. "Grace, it's over. I appreciate your wanting to catch whoever did this, but don't you have something better to do with your time?"

"Humor me, will you Arthur? You're probably right. It'll probably come to nothing. But this is personal now. I'd like to see it all the way through, whatever happens."

Arthur patted her shoulder. "You're a stubborn little gal. Guess I should have figured you'd want to get to the bottom of things. All right. Go ahead. And if this cop friend of yours has any questions, have him give me a call."

55

In a pair of frayed jeans with holes at the knees, a Tampa Bay Rays T-shirt, and Wayfarer sunglasses, Pete Strivecky looked nothing like a cop and everything like a too-cool-for-school teenager as he stood on the doorstep of the cottage on Mandevilla, holding his motorcycle helmet under one arm.

"Awesome house," he said when Grace greeted him Tuesday morning. "I'm glad you gave me a call. I've been reading about it on your blog. I even rode my girlfriend over here last weekend so she could take a look at it in person."

"It is an awesome house, or it will be, when whoever buys it gets done," Grace said sadly.

Officer Strivecky stepped inside and immediately walked over to the scorched corner of the living room. "So, you said the fire started here? Looks like it didn't do much damage."

"They poured some kind of lighter fluid or something on a new canvas drop cloth," Grace said. "Fortunately, the neighbor saw the flames through the porch windows, and he was able to put it out before the fire spread."

"Did you happen to save the drop cloth?"

"What was left. I put it out in the garage," Grace said. "Along with the empty paint cans they used in the kitchen and living room."

"Good idea." Strivecky nodded his approval. "Like I told you on the phone,

I'm not a detective, and I'm sure not an arson investigator. But I don't think it would hurt to take a look around."

Strivecky walked through all the rooms in the house while Grace gave her running narrative on all that she'd accomplished in rehabbing the house—and what the vandal did to ruin her handiwork.

When they were done, they sat on the front porch steps, and Grace handed him a bottle of water.

"You really think it's your ex-husband's girlfriend? Why would she do something like that?" he asked.

"Revenge," Grace said succinctly. "She and Ben were blatantly ripping off material from my new blog for Gracenotes. So I e-mailed most of my old advertisers to let them know what was happening. I thought they should know they were spending money with people who have no ethics. At least a couple of them dropped their ads. J'Aimee came over here last week, and she threatened that she'd make me sorry. So yes, I think she's behind this."

"She sounds like a head case," Strivecky said. He took a swig of water. "I can talk to one of our detectives about your suspicions, but I can tell you right now he'll probably say that unless somebody catches her in the act, there's nothing he can do."

"What about if she left fingerprints? On the paint cans, or even in the bathroom, where she did the cute fingerpainting?"

"The bathroom was wiped clean," Strivecky reminded her. "And what if she did leave fingerprints? You said she came over here last week. She could claim she left fingerprints then. But it's not going to get that far, Grace. We already know there's bad blood between you and your ex and this woman. Our detective is going to say this is just another domestic dispute. Nasty, yes. Criminal? Probably not."

Grace kicked at the porch railing with the toe of her sneaker. "This day just keeps getting better and better. Because of *her,* the owner of the house has decided to just sell it, instead of renting it to me. And I can't afford to buy the place myself, because I don't have any money. And now you tell me, even if I could prove it was *her,* there's nothing the police will do."

She glared defiantly at Strivecky. "Now I know why people take the law into their own hands. I feel so powerless—it's infuriating!"

"But you won't do anything to get back at her—right?" Strivecky said. "We didn't have this conversation. Right?"

"Right," she said glumly. "No violence. I'll just have to figure out how to get back at Ben—and her—legally."

Dear Lily: Thanks for your recent e-mail and your kind words about TrueGrace and the cottage on Mandevilla. It was a dream project—while it lasted. Unfortunately, the owner notified me today that he intends to sell the cottage, as is, meaning that my work there will go unfinished. I'd be happy to send you photos of my other current project, although it is not on the same scope as Mandevilla. And I'd love the chance to land an assignment for Veranda. *Regretfully, Grace Davenport, TrueGrace.com*

When she'd sent the e-mail, Grace flopped facedown on her bed and screamed into her pillow. Then she stood up, combed her hair, and called her lawyer.

Nelson Keeler was kitted out in his Jungle Jerry's uniform, khaki safari shirt, khaki slacks (his old khaki shorts no longer fit around his thickened waist), and his battered old safari hat—the leather-lined one that had been handed down to him by his father. He was happily chatting with a half-dozen members of the Hibiscus Garden Club who'd gathered around him in the gift shop after buying their senior-citizen-discounted tickets.

"Now, ladies, we're going to start your tour with a little history of the park," he was saying.

Joyce Barrett, their only other full-time employee, was staring out the glass door leading into the gift shop and ticket area when she saw Callie Keeler briskly approaching.

She was in her eighties and had silver hair she wore in a long braid down her back, and her own Jungle Jerry's costume was immaculately pressed, as always.

"Uh-oh," she whispered under her breath. She glanced back at Nelson, who'd already briefed her on Callie's latest attempt to torpedo Wyatt's happiness. She reached for the walkie-talkie they kept under the ticket counter.

"Wyatt? Office to Wyatt. Storm on the horizon. Repeat. Storm on the horizon."

There was a burst of crackling static. "Shit. Copy that, Joyce. On my way. Be there in five."

Joyce tugged at Nelson's arm. "Er, Nelson?" He looked up, and she jerked her head in the direction of the door just as Callie pushed through it.

Nelson stopped speaking, midsentence. His expression darkened. "What's she doing here?"

"Don't know," Joyce murmured. "But Wyatt's heading back here right now."

"Ladies," Nelson said loudly, turning so that his back was to the door. "Let's head out to the garden now, and I'll fill you in on what's in bloom as we walk." He strode out the double doors to the park without a backward glance.

"Joyce," Callie cooed, when the older woman returned to the ticket counter. "How nice to see you. How are the grandkids?"

"Fine," Joyce said, stone-faced.

"Quite a few cars in the parking lot," Callie said, leaning against the counter. "Business must be picking up, huh?"

"It's all right," Joyce said, her voice a monotone. "We get by."

"Is Wyatt around?" Callie asked, craning her neck to try to see around the bookkeeper.

"He's been out with a group from summer day camp, but he's on his way back now," Joyce said. "Excuse me, Callie. I need to get the snacks ready for those kids. They're always hungry and thirsty when they come back in out of that heat."

She turned to go, but Callie placed a hand on her arm. "Oh, let me help, Joyce. I know where everything is." Callie stepped neatly under the old-fashioned wooden turnstile and bustled into the office.

Two minutes later, when Wyatt hurried into the lobby, followed by thirty clamoring children, Callie was setting juice boxes and plates full of graham crackers and apple slices on the long table in the snack bar.

Bo brought up the rear of the group. He was dressed in a faded and somewhat shrunken Jungle Jerry's T-shirt, and Cookie the parrot was perched on his shoulder. He beamed at the sight of his mother. "Mom!"

"Hey, Bo-Boy," she said, looking up from her task. She met her husband's unsmiling eyes. "Hi, Wy."

"Shots and beer!" the parrot demanded. "Gimme whiskey. Gimme beer."

Callie broke off a piece of graham cracker and held it out for Cookie, who snapped her beak around the cracker—taking with it a sizable chunk of Callie's fingertip.

"Owww," Callie screeched. "Son of a bitch!"

Startled, the parrot squawked and flew crazily around the room, while the day campers alternately screamed, giggled, ducked under tables, and covered their heads with their arms.

After circling the room a couple of times, Cookie finally settled on Wyatt's shoulder. He tried to soothe the agitated bird. "Shhh," he said, stroking the bird's head. "Quiet, Cookie. It's all right."

Callie held her bleeding finger out for inspection. "It is not all right. Look at this! I think I might need stitches."

Bo studied his mother's wound. "Awww, Mom, it's hardly a scratch. Cookie wouldn't really bite you. She just thought your finger was part of the graham cracker."

Callie frowned. Her eyes rolled back. "I think . . . I think I might faint." She looked around the room. "Wyatt! I feel faint!"

Before he could respond, Joyce Barrett swung into action. She bustled to Callie's side and looped an arm around her waist. "Come into the office and let me get you some antiseptic and a Band-Aid." She lowered her voice to a near whisper. "We don't want to upset the children or make them afraid of Cookie, do we?"

Callie scowled but reluctantly allowed herself to be led away. "That bird never did like me."

Later, after he'd loaded the children back on their day-camp bus, returned Cookie to her aviary, and settled Bo in the trailer for a late lunch, Wyatt walked into his office to find Callie seated in the chair in front of his desk.

"There you are," Callie said, holding up her bandaged finger. "See what that stupid bird of yours did to me?"

"Sorry," he said with a shrug. "I think maybe she got a little overexcited with all the kids around. She's never bit Bo or me or Dad before. Did you get yourself set up over at your sister's?"

"Sort of. Kendra's out of town, but she called her next-door neighbor to meet me over there with the key, so I dropped off a load of my stuff there before I stopped off here. At least I don't have to deal with her holier-than-thou crap right now."

"What's Luke have to say about you bailing out on him?"

"Don't know," she said. "He's been calling and texting me all day, but I've been ignoring him. To tell you the truth, I really don't care what that piece of garbage has to say."

Wyatt spread his hands out across his desktop. "What is it you want from me, Callie?"

"Who says I want anything? Can't I just drop by to visit with my son?"

"You've had Bo for the first half of the week. He was with you until a few hours ago. So you'll forgive me if I'm a little suspicious about your motives."

Callie gazed around the office. "God, this place is depressing. When was the last time you painted this room? Or had the floors mopped?"

"I don't have a lot of extra time or money for things like paint jobs these days," he said, struggling to remain civil. "What with legal fees, child support, and the three hundred dollars a week I have to pay for divorce camp."

"Three hundred dollars! Are you serious? That's crazy. That's money your family needs."

"Seriously crazy," Wyatt agreed, his face darkening. "But that's what Judge Stackpole mandated. After your lawyer showed him that video of me smashing Luke's car window. Which the two of you deliberately provoked me into doing."

Callie picked up an old plastic Jungle Jerry's snow globe from the corner of his desk and studied it, deliberately averting her eyes from his.

"That was all Luke's doing," she said, her voice low. "I never thought you'd go crazy and break your hand. I never intended things to go as far as they did."

"You filmed me with your cell phone," Wyatt said. "And then you called the cops. It's a little too convenient to blame everything on Luke, don't you think? You're thirty-six, Callie. Don't you think you bear some responsibility for what happened in our marriage?"

"Some of it," she said, shaking the snow globe, watching the glittering synthetic flakes settle over a tiny plastic replica of the Jungle Jerry's neon sign.

She looked up. "What if I told you I wished none of this had ever happened?"

"But it did happen," he reminded her. "You decided you were in love with somebody else and that you wanted to be with him more than you wanted to be married to me. You chose Luke over me. And our family. That's something I can't just forget."

She turned the snow globe over and picked at the yellowing price sticker with her fingernail. "Sixty-nine cents! How old is this thing?"

"It's ancient," he said. "As old as I feel right now."

Callie looked up. "Bo tells me you have a 'friend.' Is it serious?"

"Maybe. She's a nice woman. Look, Callie. I don't feel comfortable discussing her with you. I'm trying very hard to have a normal life now, to see to it that our son feels loved and safe."

"Is this your way of telling me you're moving on? That you're completely over me?"

Wyatt ran his hands over his head. "Over you? No. I'm trying, but I can't say I'm there yet."

She looked up at him through lowered lashes. "I hope you never get over me. I'm not over you. At all."

56

Grace was the first to arrive at Paula's office. She found the therapist sitting at the desk in the reception area, staring down at something on the computer screen and frowning. There were dark circles under her eyes that even a careful application of concealer couldn't hide.

Paula looked up and immediately clicked to close out the screen. "Hi, Grace," she said. "How's your week going?"

"My week sucks," Grace said flatly. "Thanks for asking."

Paula sighed. "Is there something you'd like to discuss with the group? Is this about your divorce?"

"It's about my life, and right now everything in my life has been screwed up by my divorce, so yeah, I think you could safely say that." Grace felt the tote bag slung over her shoulder move ever so slightly. She started to walk into the inner office.

"Grace?"

She turned to face the therapist.

"Things will get better. I know you think they won't. I know it's hard. But you have to trust me. I've been there," Paula said. "The pain, the rage, the bitterness—if you can find a way to let go of all that, a huge weight will be lifted from your soul."

Grace bit her lip. She wanted to confront Paula with everything she knew or thought she knew about her arrangement with Stackpole. But she'd promised Mitzi to stay quiet until they could absolutely prove their suspicions.

"You've been there?" She couldn't resist. "Through a divorce? Where you lost everything?"

"That's right." Paula's eyes met hers. "I moved here to Florida . . . afterwards. I started over with nothing. Well, next to nothing. It hasn't been easy."

The outer door opened, and Camryn and Suzanne came in. Their conversation came to an abrupt end.

"We'll talk later," Paula said.

"Friends?" Paula gestured around the circle. "We've got so much ground to cover before your completion ceremony next week. But first, I'd like to hear about how your life is going—recovery-wise."

She was met with five blank expressions. "Anybody?"

Nothing.

"All right. I suppose we'll just do this the-old fashioned way. I'll call on you, and you'll share. Camryn?"

"Recovery-wise? Dexter's lawyer called my lawyer this week. He wants his mother's dining room table. Claims it has happy family memories, and it's the only piece of furniture he wants."

"Did you give it to him?" Ashleigh asked.

"Umm-humm," Camryn said, looking pleased with herself. "I hope he can find a good furniture refinisher, though."

Paula looked at her over the top of her wire-framed glasses. "Did you damage the table?"

"Not me," Camryn said, feigning innocence. "But the movers I hired, they were sooooo clumsy. They must have just thrown it into their truck, because when Dexter got it, the top was all scratched up and gouged. I guess it looked pretty bad."

"How bad?" Grace couldn't resist.

Camryn held up her iPhone and scrolled through her photo roll and tapped the screen. She held up the phone for the others to see.

"What's that say?" Suzanne asked. "It looks like writing, on the tabletop, but it's kind of dark."

She handed the phone to Wyatt, who looked, squinted, and laughed. "It's writing. Looks like it says . . . 'Eat shit and die'? Is that right?" He looked to Camryn for confirmation.

"I was shocked," Camryn said, barely able to concern her merriment.

"Never mind," Paula said, annoyed. "You know, Camryn, if you keep regressing, acting out in these childish and vindictive ways, I'm not going to be able to sign off on your successful completion of these sessions. Truly, you're only hurting yourself."

Camryn muttered something under her breath.

"Ashleigh?" Paula turned to the next person.

"Recovery-wise, I am fantastic," Ashleigh said. "Really. Forgive and forget. I even went out to lunch today with one of the girls in Boyce's office, and I never asked one question about Suchita. I've quit driving by her house, too."

Paula frowned. "I'm glad to hear that, but I wasn't aware you were engaging in such unhealthy, obsessive activities. Remember, Ashleigh, the other woman wasn't the problem in your marriage. She was only a symptom."

"Whatever," Ashleigh said. "I am in a very good place right now. An awesome place."

"Happy to hear it," Paula said. "I wish everybody could move in that direction. Suzanne? Are things going better for you?"

"Maybe a little better," Suzanne admitted. "It's still too painful to talk to Eric, but I finally e-mailed him and told him that Darby has been accepted for early admission to Elon."

Paula beamed at her star patient. "Suzanne! That's a real breakthrough." She looked around the circle. "Friends? Let's give Suzanne our approval."

The others clapped politely.

"Darby's his daughter, too," Suzanne said. "I know she's conflicted—she feels loyalty to me, but she misses seeing him."

"Hmm. Maybe Darby would like to attend one of the 'Daughters of Divorce' seminars I'm going to be giving," Paula suggested. "And I've been thinking that might be helpful for your daughter, too, Camryn."

"No offense, Paula, but right now I can't afford to pay for any more of your sessions," Suzanne said. "Maybe I'll get her some books from the library."

Camryn coughed loudly and looked away.

"Grace? When you came in tonight, you seemed very down about things," Paula said. "Anything specific going on?"

"Very specific," Grace said, biting the words out. She recounted the events of the past few days in vivid detail. "Arthur's going to sell the house. And I'm back where I started."

"That's such a shame," Suzanne said. "I've been following your blog. It was such an adorable house. Do you have any idea who would do such a thing?"

"A very good idea. J'Aimee. My former assistant and my ex's new girlfriend," Grace said. "This is totally her handiwork. And, of course, now the house is out of my reach, because I can't afford to buy a house, because, so far, Judge Stackpole's idea of a property settlement is to give Ben the gold mine and me the shaft. Ben is entitled to everything, and I get nothing. Because he hates women."

"Fucker." Camryn said it quite distinctly.

Paula's face turned pink. "I'm sure that's not the case . . ."

"Not the case?" Ashleigh hooted. "Paula, get a grip! Those pills you've been taking have seriously pickled your punkin'."

The therapist's face paled. "That's very unfair."

"But it's true," Ashleigh insisted. "Nobody else wants to speak out, because they're all soooo afraid Stackpole will screw them even worse than he already has. Not me. I don't care what you or Stackpole say or do. Because after Monday, this is all a moot point anyway. I am so out of here."

She hopped out of her chair. "I'll see y'all later. At the Sandbox. Right?"

"Man, Ashleigh, you knocked Paula for a loop tonight," Camryn said later, with something akin to admiration. "After you left, she was back to her old self. Just going through the motions until eight o'clock rolled around. She didn't even have us read from our journals."

Ashleigh dipped a finger in her margarita and licked it. "I'm not going back for any completion ceremony, y'all." She looked around the table. "This has been kind of fun, in a weird way, but it's not an experience I want to repeat. But hey, if any of y'all ever want a little nip or a tuck, give me a call. I'll make sure Boyce gives you our professional discount."

"What about me?" Wyatt asked.

"What? You think men don't have plastic surgery?" Ashleigh chortled. "Eyelid lifts, chin implants, tummy tucks, breast reductions—honey, you'd be amazed how many men walk into our office. Not to mention all the prescriptions for Rogaine we write." She gazed meaningfully at Wyatt's gleaming dome.

He ran his hand over his head, immediately feeling defensive. "I'm not bald.

I've got plenty of hair. I shave my head because I work outdoors all day. It's cooler. And there's less chance of ticks hiding in my hair."

"Ticks. Eeew." Ashleigh shuddered.

At the other end of the table, Grace waited until the others were engaged in a lively conversation about the cause for Paula's demeanor. She leaned over and spoke in a low voice.

"Camryn? Remember the morning you and your cameraman came to my house? The day after I left Ben?"

"How could I forget?" Camryn said. "Best story of the year."

"I've been wondering. How'd you get past the guard gates?" Grace asked. "None of those other news crews were able to get through security. How'd you do it?"

"Mmm. Trade secret," Camryn said, sipping her drink. "Why do you care?"

"Because I want to go back to the house. And get the rest of my things. But Ben got the security guards to deactivate my key card."

"Gotcha," Camryn said. "Let me call my friend in the morning. See if she can help us out."

"We?"

"You're gonna need a wingman, right?"

Wyatt watched Grace, her head bent close to Camryn's, as they whispered and plotted. He felt an irrational stab of jealousy. All night, he'd tried to catch Grace alone, if only for a moment. He needed to reassure himself that what was between them was real and that they had a future together. But there was always somebody around. He took a sip of his beer, then pushed it aside. He yawned widely, hoping the exaggerated movement would catch her eye.

Finally, she glanced his way, smiling ruefully. He got up and made his way toward the men's bathroom. Grace followed, pausing at the door to the ladies' room. She opened the door, and in the next instant, he'd pushed his way inside, slamming the door and locking it in one fluid movement.

"What are you . . ."

He silenced her with a kiss. "This," he said, his voice muffled.

"And this." His hands slid under the back of her sleeveless cotton top, nimbly unsnapping her bra.

"Also this." He worked his knee between her thighs, her skirt riding up and baring her thighs, pinning her up against the sink vanity. Grace's body arched into his, and he lifted her effortlessly atop the vanity. She leaned back and ran her hand over his cheek. He caught her hand in his and kissed it, then yanked her top over her head in one fluid movement.

She laughed uneasily and crossed her arms over her bare chest. "We can't do this! Everybody's out there. My mother is out there. Somebody's going to notice . . ."

"I've been thinking about you all day, and I have wanted to do this all night," he whispered, cupping one of her breasts and kissing it. She let out a soft, low-pitched moan, then grabbed the waistband of his jeans and traced the zipper's path slowly with her thumb until she heard the sharp intake of his breath against her nipple.

"God, Grace," he breathed. She worked the zipper downward, stroking his erection. His hands fumbled with her skirt. "How does this damned thing come off?"

There was a sharp rap at the door. Grace froze.

"It's occupied," she croaked, hopping down from the vanity and hastily pulling on her top.

Wyatt grabbed for her, but she was too fast for him. He chuckled, despite himself, but she frantically shushed him.

Grace flushed the toilet twice, then groaned loudly and followed that with a remarkably authentic sound effect mimicking violent nausea.

"Come on, already," a girl's annoyed voice came. "I'm about to pee my pants."

"Employee bathroom near kitchen door," Grace called. "Sorry." She gagged violently, for good measure.

"Goddamned amateur," came the girl's parting shot.

When she was sure the girl was gone, Grace collapsed against Wyatt in a fit of giggles. "I'm sorry," she said, turning to the mirror to fix her disheveled clothing and hair. "But we've got to get out of here before we get busted."

She turned and gave him an appraising look, tugging at the hem of his shirt. "I had no idea that the scent of hand sanitizer could be such a turn-on." She opened the door and peeked out. "Okay, coast is clear." She shoved him out. "Go on. Go! I'll wait a minute and then come back to the table."

"Later?" Wyatt asked, kissing her neck. "We need to talk." But somehow, later never arrived that night.

57

D ad?" Bo walked into the kitchen, where Wyatt was shaping hamburger
patties. Sweetie followed close on the child's heels, sniffing the air expectantly.

"I know it's late and you're hungry, but dinner's almost ready," Wyatt assured, seasoning the burgers with salt and pepper, stopping to toss a bit of meat
to the dog.

"I'm okay." Bo plopped down at his place at the kitchen table. "Can I ask you
something?"

"Sure thing." Wyatt put the griddle pan on the burner and turned on the
heat. "You want cheese or no on your burger?"

"Cheese," Bo said. "The yellow kind, not the white."

"Got it. What did you want to ask me?"

Bo kicked the table leg. "Do you still hate Mom?"

"Hate her?" Wyatt asked cautiously. "I don't hate your mom, Bo. Is that what
you think?"

"Sometimes," the boy said. He helped himself to a handful of potato chips
from the bowl on the table and tossed one to Sweetie, who caught it midair.
"Mom thinks you hate her. She's pretty sad. Because now she's not gonna
marry you know who. And Aunt Kendra is a big bee-yotch." He shoved all the
chips in his mouth and chewed furiously.

"You probably shouldn't call your aunt that word, pal," Wyatt said. "It's kind of a bad, grown-up word. So . . . you talked to your mom today?"

"Do we have any onion dip?" Bo asked hopefully.

"Sorry, no. But we've got salad. Did your mom call you today?"

"Yeah," Bo said. "She says we're not gonna live with you know who anymore. Do you think we can get our old house back instead? I kind of miss my room there."

Wyatt sighed. "That's complicated, pal. I wish we could get the old house back, but right now we can't. So I guess you're stuck sharing a room with me. Is that so bad? I mean, I don't snore too loud, do I?"

"Not as loud as Granddad," Bo said, giggling. A moment later, he was serious again. "What about Mom? Where's she going to live?"

Wyatt got up and turned the burner on again. He waited until the eye glowed red, then added the hamburger patties to the grill pan.

Obviously, Callie had unburdened herself to their son at some point during the day. What the hell was she thinking, worrying a six-year-old with this stuff? Did she seriously think she could use Bo to guilt-trip him into taking her back?

"For now, your mom's going to stay with Aunt Kendra," Wyatt said finally. "And then she's going to find a new place to live. And you'll have a new room. Okay? Is that cool with you?"

"I guess," Bo said. He kicked the table leg rhythmically. "But it would be cooler if Mom and me could just live with you. Like we did before." He took another handful of potato chips and shoved them into his mouth and chewed furiously.

Shit. Shit. Shit. Wyatt thought. Callie was really pulling out all the stops. He should have seen this coming.

Wyatt heard the meat sizzling on the cast-iron grill pan. Smoke rose from the stove. He jumped up and flipped the burgers, his mind working furiously to find a way to be honest with the child. Finally, he sat down and reached across the table and took his son's hand in his.

"Look at me, Bo," he said calmly. "Mom and I both love you. More than anything. And that will never change. But she and I, we're probably not ever going to live together again. Not because I hate her, but because we don't love each other the way married people should love each other. I'm sad about that, and I know you're sad about it, too. But that's just the way it has to be. Okay?"

"Okay," Bo said. "Can Sweetie have a hamburger, too?"

"Afraid not," Wyatt said. "Now, go wash your hands and tell Granddad dinner is ready."

Their Friday-night routine seldom varied. Nelson took himself off to bed around nine, and then Wyatt and Bo either watched a movie or played video games, until one or both of them fell asleep. Right now, Bo was sprawled on the floor, scraping the last bit of ice cream from the carton as he watched *The Bad News Bears*—the old Walter Matthau version—for maybe the tenth time since the start of summer. Sweetie was curled up on the floor beside him, her snout resting in his lap.

It had started drizzling shortly after dinner. Now the rain fell steadily, beating a noisy tattoo on the trailer's metal roof and siding.

Wyatt had texted Grace earlier in the afternoon, proposing that they meet somewhere, but discarded that idea after realizing how anxious Bo was about his parents' marital status.

After dinner, he'd managed a furtive phone call while Bo and Nelson did the dishes. "Hey," he'd said, his voice low. "I don't think I can get away tonight after all. Bo is having some issues, and I think I'd better stick close to home."

"Everything okay?" Grace asked. "Your dad's not sick again, is he?"

"Nothing like that," Wyatt said. He knew he should tell Grace what was going on with Callie, but something held him back. All he knew was that he was tired of the tug-of-war. Callie was the past. And Grace was his future. He and Bo deserved a happy future, didn't they?

"I'll call you tomorrow," Wyatt promised. He glanced back toward the kitchen to make sure he couldn't be overheard. "I've got some stuff to tell you. Maybe we could have another sunset viewing at that condo?"

Grace laughed throatily. "I think that could probably be arranged."

He must have dozed off sometime between the end of *The Bad News Bears* and the beginning of *Field of Dreams*. Somebody was banging on the trailer's aluminum storm door. Wyatt jumped up, startled by the noise, but Bo, always a heavy sleeper, didn't move. Sweetie, on the other hand, went on instant alert, running toward the door and barking.

"Wyatt? It's me."

He cursed softly. His midnight caller was Callie. "Shush, Sweetie," Wyatt grumbled. He flipped on the porch light and opened the door.

She was barefoot and rain-soaked, dressed in a low-cut tank top and shorts so tight he could clearly see the outline of her panties. She'd been crying again. And this time, she'd brought baggage. Literally. A large wheeled suitcase rested on the porch, and next to it sat a plastic laundry basket heaped with her belongings.

"Can I come in?" She didn't wait for an answer, picking up the basket of clothes and stepping inside, out of the rain. He hesitated, then grabbed the suitcase, too.

"What's all this?" he asked, gesturing at the luggage.

"My stuff. Can you at least get me a towel so I can dry off before you start yelling at me?"

As she walked past him toward the bathroom, Wyatt detected the smell of alcohol and cigarette smoke. She took her time in the bathroom. He heard water running, and then the sound of a hair-dryer. He waited outside the bathroom door, arms folded across his chest, gathering resolve.

Finally, she emerged, her face pink from heat, hair fluffed, dressed only in his worn terrycloth bathrobe. "You don't mind, right?" Callie asked. "Just until my stuff dries out, okay?"

"You can have the bathrobe," he said, keeping his voice low, "but then you have to leave."

"And go where?" she asked, running her fingers through her hair. "My baby sister kicked me out. You believe that? It's midnight and we're in the middle of a monsoon, and she kicks me out. So for tonight, anyway, you're stuck with me. And I hate to ask, but do you have anything to eat? I didn't get dinner."

He took her by the arm and steered her toward the kitchen. "I'll fix you a sandwich. Keep your voice down," he warned. "Bo's asleep on the living room floor. I don't want him waking up and asking why you're here."

She yanked her arm from his grip and followed him into the kitchen. "We're still married, technically. So why shouldn't I be here?" She looked around the room and frowned. "Unless your new girlfriend is having a sleepover?"

Wyatt took a package of lunch meat from the fridge, along with a jar of mustard. He slapped the meat between two slices of bread, which he slathered with the yellow mustard, then slid the sandwich in front of her.

He decided not to allow Callie to bait him. "What are you doing here, Callie? What did you do to make Kendra kick you out?"

"Nothing!" she said, biting into the sandwich. "Kendra's just a bitch, okay? She resents me. Always has. She was always on your side after we split. And she hated Luke, of course."

She'd knotted the bathrobe loosely around her waist, and it gapped widely at the neck, giving him a too-generous view of her cleavage and a provocative expanse of her bare legs.

The truth was beginning to dawn on him. "Luke came over there tonight, didn't he? That's why Kendra kicked you out. Right?"

"I didn't *invite* him," she said indignantly. "He just showed up. He promised to get my car back for me. So I let him in, but then he started with the same old bullshit, and I called him on it. We were not fighting. It was a *discussion*. But all of a sudden, Kendra goes bat-shit crazy and starts threatening to call the cops on both of us."

"The two of you'd been drinking, right? And don't try to deny it, because you smell like a brewery," Wyatt said.

"What are you, my parole officer? Yes, we had a few beers," Callie said. "But I am not drunk. And anyway, what kind of sister throws somebody out in the middle of a tornado? Kendra wouldn't even listen to me. She literally grabbed my suitcase and pitched it out her window. And she lives on the second floor. I was barely able to grab the basket with the rest of my stuff before she locked me out in the rain."

Callie took another bite of her sandwich, and then another, chewing calmly. "God, I'm hungry. I bet I could eat another sandwich." She looked down at Sweetie, who was crouched on the floor, her liquid brown eyes focused on her.

"Is this the girlfriend's dog?" She tore off a bit of bread and tossed it to the little dog, who caught it in midair. "She's kind of cute, isn't she? What's her name?"

"We're not discussing the dog. And I'm not fixing you another sandwich," Wyatt said. "You can't stay here tonight, Callie."

She raised an eyebrow. "You're kicking me out? Where do you expect me to go at this hour? And don't suggest a motel. You might as well know. I'm flat broke."

"Dammit, Callie!" Wyatt whispered hoarsely. "I'm not going to let you manipulate me like this. I just sent your child-support check."

"And Bo needed new sneakers. And he's outgrown all his clothes," Callie said. "What is the big deal? It's just one night, okay? I'll sleep on the sofa. You won't even know I'm here."

"I will know. More importantly, Bo will know. You've already managed to get him freaked out about where he's going to live now that you and Luke are broken up. I don't want him any more confused than he already is."

But it was too late. They heard light footsteps in the hallway, then the sound of the bathroom door being opened, and then a toilet flushing. A moment later, the sleepy-eyed child rounded the hallway into the kitchen.

"Mom?" he said softly.

She held out her arms and the boy dutifully allowed himself to be folded into an embrace. "Hey, Bo-man," Callie said, hugging him tight. "Are you surprised to see me?"

"Yeah. I mean, no," Bo said, yawning widely. "I thought you were at Aunt Kendra's house."

Callie made a face. "Your Aunt Kendra is a big doo-doo head," she said, laughing as though it were all a joke. "So I came over here to see what you and your dad were up to."

"Are you gonna spend the night?" He shot his father a hopeful look. "Please, Dad? Mom can have my bed. I'll sleep on the sofa."

"Absolutely not!" Callie said. "If anybody gets to sleep on the sofa, it's me." She tousled her son's hair and looked defiantly at Wyatt. "Right, Dad?"

Bo's eyes were pleading. "Okay?"

Wyatt knew when he'd been beaten. "Fine," he said brusquely. "Come on, Bo," he said, holding out his hand for his son. "You're going to bed. I'll get your mom a pillow and a blanket. But this is just for tonight. Tomorrow, she's going to find a new place to live." He glared at his wife. "Right, Mom?"

Callie smiled weakly. "Right."

58

Grace pulled alongside Camryn's car in the Publix shopping center Saturday morning. She hopped into Camryn's car, and moments later the two of them were heading west toward Gulf Vista.

"Nice car," Grace said. She wiped her sweaty palms on her jeans and lightly stroked the Jaguar's sleek leather upholstery.

"It was an anniversary gift from Dexter," Camryn said. "The man does love to buy nice things. Of course, mostly it's to show all his friends how much money he makes and what a big man he is."

"Are you sure your friend is okay with doing this?" Grace asked as they approached the Gulf Vista security gate. "She's not worried Ben might find out?"

"Marissa?" Camryn laughed. "She and LaDarion think your ex is a stuck-up prick. I guess Ben sicced the homeowner's association on them because of Peaches's barking."

"Ben hated that dog," Grace said. "It barked a *lot*. Like, if anybody walked by their house. Or if it was home alone. Which it was, a lot. Plus, your friend and her husband did throw some pretty wild parties. Last year they hired MC Hammer to play at their Fourth of July barbecue. Do you know how many times we heard "Can't Touch This?" Over and over and over . . ."

"MC Hammer?" Camryn snickered. "Seriously? I did not even know that dude was still alive. How did he survive the nineties?"

"I don't know, but I can assure you, he did," Grace said.

There were three cars ahead of them at the visitor's gate to the subdivision. Grace's pulse skipped wildly as they pulled beneath the security shack's portico. "Here goes," Camryn said, under her breath. Grace pulled on a pair of oversized sunglasses.

The Jaguar's driver's-side window rolled down, and the uniformed security guard stepped forward. Grace sucked in her breath and looked away. It was Sheldon, the same guard who'd turned her away the last time she'd attempted to breach the gate at Gulf Vista.

"Morning, ma'am," Sheldon said, leaning in to look at the Jaguar's occupants.

"Good morning," Camryn said. "We're guests of Marissa and LaDarion Banks?"

Sheldon scanned a sheet of paper on his clipboard, running his finger down the lines of type.

"Ms. Nobles?" he asked, peering into the car's interior. Grace held her breath.

"That's correct," Camryn said.

The guard handed her a guest pass. "Leave that on your dashboard, if you would please, ma'am," he said, and waved her through.

"Nice digs," Camryn said admiringly, as they rolled slowly past the house on Sand Dollar Lane. "What did this place set you back, a million, million and a half?"

"I'm not sure," Grace admitted. "Ben handled all that. This was one of the model homes. He cut a deal with the developer, and then cut more deals with the contractors who put in the landscaping and the pool and the media room. A lot of the extras, we got at cost, or less, in return for advertising and editorial mention on Gracenotes."

"And you walked away from all that."

"'Ran away' would be a more accurate way to describe my departure," Grace said.

"And now you're living above a bar on Cortez," Camryn said. "Girlfriend, that is a big change, and I'm not just talking about zip codes."

"Want to know something?" Grace gestured out the window, at the velvety green lawns and lush beds of blooming tropical flowers and palm trees, behind which loomed glimpses of red barrel-tile roofs and white stucco homes. "None of this seems real to me. I lived in this neighborhood for two years. I went to parties, gave parties here, but I haven't heard from a single person since the night I put Ben's car in the pool."

"Mm-hmm," Camryn said. "You broke the rules. Acted ugly, made a mess. Got the law involved." She flipped up her own sunglasses, and grinned. "Welcome to the real world, Grace Davenport."

She turned the corner and pulled into the driveway of a house that dwarfed all the other houses in the subdivision. A wrought-iron gate with curlicued flourishes identified the mansion as Villa Marissa. Camryn opened her window, leaned out, and looked up at the small security camera mounted on the stucco gatepost. "Marissa? It's Camryn. Open sesame!"

The gates swung open noiselessly, and they followed the driveway around to the front of the mansion, an enormous, vaguely Tuscan villa, where a petite woman with long jet-black hair and a complexion the shade of caffe latte waited in a gleaming black golf cart.

"Ladies!" Marissa Banks beamed. She was dressed in a sleeveless hot-pink Nike tank top and matching pink golf shorts, along with pink and white golf cleats. She clapped her hands excitedly. "Welcome to my house."

"Marissa, this is my friend Grace, but I think you've probably already met, right?"

Grace reached out and shook the other woman's hand. "Thanks so much for doing this. You're really sure you want to get involved in my drama?"

"Of course," Marissa said. "You can only get your nails and hair done so many times in one week. I'm dying of boredom. This is going to be fun. Like old times, right, Cammie? Remember that time we snuck onto the grounds at Doral so you could try to interview Tiger Woods?"

"And you distracted the security guards with a phony wardrobe malfunction? How could I ever forget that?" Camryn asked, shaking her head at the memory. "Does LeDarion know you've flashed boob to half the men in South Florida, just to get exclusive interviews?"

"How do you think we met in the first place?" Marissa laughed. "Of course, he thinks he's the only one who ever got a sneak peek. And we're gonna keep it that way, right?"

"Just between us girls," Camryn said. She glanced at Grace. "Are you ready?"

Grace let out a long, shaky breath. "As ready as I'm gonna be. I want this over with. Marissa, are you sure the coast is clear? Ben has a standing golf game at the club Saturday mornings, but you just never know . . ."

"I've been watching the place since eight. He left about eight thirty, and his little girlfriend left maybe fifteen minutes after that." Marissa rolled her eyes. "What a skank! You know she sunbathes nude most of the time, right? Every pool guy and maintenance man in the neighborhood has had a look at her goodies."

"Let's do it," Camryn said.

After Marissa dropped them off in the golf cart, promising to return as soon as they texted her, Grace and Camryn walked briskly to the rear of the house, where Grace unlocked the kitchen door.

"Wowsers," Camryn said, eyeing the gleaming expanse of black granite countertops, the stainless steel commercial stove, and the glass-front refrigerator. "This kitchen is immaculate. She's a pretty good housekeeper."

Grace glared.

"For a skank, that is," Camryn added.

"Oh, please. J'Aimee doesn't know how to cook," Grace said. "They probably eat at the club every night—or order out for pizza or Chinese."

She went into the dining room and pulled open the top drawer of the mahogany Empire buffet, pausing to run an appreciative finger over her sterling flatware. "Looks like it's all here," she said, after doing a quick count. Grace trotted out to the laundry room and came back with a king-sized pillowcase, into which she unceremoniously dumped all the silver.

"Let's stack everything by the back door," Camryn said, holding up a heavily decorated silver teapot. "That's what professional burglars do. So they can make a quick getaway."

"We're not burglars," Grace said sharply. She took the teapot from Camryn's hand and set it back on the top of the buffet. "I'm not taking anything that isn't mine. The tea service was Ben's grandmother's. The flatware is mine."

When she'd loaded in all the silver, Camryn placed it in the kitchen, near the door.

Grace walked quickly up the back staircase with Camryn following close behind. "How many bedrooms?" Camryn asked.

"Um, six, but we only had furniture in three of them," Grace said. She breezed down the second floor hallway toward the master wing, while Camryn opened every door they passed to gaze inside.

"Enough with the sightseeing," Grace urged. "I don't want to stick around here any longer than absolutely necessary. Let's just get the rest of my stuff and go, okay?"

She pushed open the door to the master bedroom. The king-sized bed was unmade, and clothes and shoes and towels littered nearly every flat surface.

"Uh-huh." Camryn nodded, taking in the disarray. "Now we see the girl's true colors."

"Ironic," Grace said. "Ben is a total neat nut. He even colorizes his sock drawer."

"You could put my whole downstairs in this bedroom," Camryn said, slowly doing a 360-degree turn to take it all in. She sat on the bed and fingered the rumpled top sheet. "Are these Pratesi?"

"Yup," Grace said. "We did a giveaway with them."

"Think the skank would notice if I borrowed a set of 'em?"

"In here." Grace jerked her head in the direction of her home office. She opened one of the custom cabinets and began loading her photographic equipment into a black duffel bag she'd brought along for that purpose. Her Nikon camera bodies, her lenses—all of it went into the bag. She scanned the bookshelves holding the hundreds of design books she'd lovingly collected and cataloged over the years, pulling out her favorites and adding them to the duffel bag.

She dragged the duffel bag into the bedroom and dumped it before heading into her dressing room, where Camryn stood, looking bug-eyed at the clothing. She held out the sleeve of a gaudy tie-dyed dress. "This doesn't look like your style."

Grace wrinkled her nose. "None of this stuff is mine. It's all hers." She opened one of the drawers in the built-in center cupboard and, with her pinkie, held up a hot-pink scrap of lace. "Totally not mine."

She continued rifling through the clothing in the closet. "Damn! This is all J'Aimee's crap. If she threw my clothes out . . ."

"Hey!" Camryn stood in the doorway. "I think I found your stuff. It's in the room next door."

·   ·   ·

Nearly every item of clothing Grace owned had been dumped on the bedroom floor. Dresses and blouses still on hangers, folding clothes, shoes, handbags—all of it tossed in the corner. Grace stood with her hands on her hips, looking around the room, a lump rising in her throat.

"What a pretty room," Camryn said, looking around.

Grace had spent weeks choosing just the right shade of pale seafoam green for the walls of the bedroom. She'd chosen a natural linen fabric for drapes with a narrow turquoise ribbon trim. The dresser was an old one she'd found at an estate sale in Bradenton, a battered oak chest of drawers that she'd painted a soft white, distressed, then waxed. The only other furniture in the room was an antique wicker rocking chair. She'd reupholstered it herself with a turquoise gingham cushion.

"Where's the bed?" Camryn asked.

"Never got around to buying one," Grace said. Her smile was tight. "This was going to be the nursery."

"Oh." Camryn put an arm around Grace's shoulder. "You wanted kids?"

"Yeah. I had started taking fertility meds, but then . . ." She shrugged. "So it's just as well. I see the crap Wyatt is going through with his ex, and, well, a divorce is tough enough for grown-ups without putting a little kid through all that."

Grace picked out a few items of clothing, a couple pair of jeans, her favorite little black dress, and a battered leather bomber jacket she'd owned since high school days. "Let's go," she said, turning toward the door.

"That's all you're taking?" Camryn gestured at the mound of clothes and accessories. "You're just going to leave all this stuff here?" She picked up a hot-pink linen dress. "Girl, this is Tory Burch." She added a black-and-white striped patent leather purse. "And this is Kate Spade. You don't walk away from Kate and Tory."

"Take them if you want," Grace said. She looked around the room, searching for an empty suitcase, but found only a lumpy black plastic trash bag. She dumped the contents of the bag onto the floor.

But this clothing wasn't hers. There was a pair of denim shorts, two sizes smaller than Grace wore, a sleeveless black T-shirt, and a pair of new-looking tennis shoes. Everything in the bag was spattered with paint. Bright orange paint. The same memorable hue that had been splashed across the walls at Mandevilla Manor.

"I knew it," Grace said softly, picking up the T-shirt and holding it out for Camryn to see. "I knew it was her."

She heard footsteps on the stairs and froze. A moment later, Ben walked into the room. "What the hell do you think you're doing?"

The two women stared at him. Ben's face was already tanned, but now it was flushed red with anger.

Camryn looked at her in a state of panic. Grace swallowed hard, and then she recalled her mission, and her motive.

"I came to pick up some of my belongings," she said.

"You're burglarizing my home," Ben said. He held up his cell phone. "Sheldon spotted you when you came through the gate, and he called me to ask if I knew you were in the neighborhood. I've got to remember to tip him better at Christmas this year."

"It's still my home, too," Grace said, glaring at him. "And I'm not taking anything that doesn't belong to me."

He pointed at the duffel bag at her feet. "What's in there?"

"My cameras, some of my design books. Nothing of yours."

"I should call the cops on you," Ben said. He picked up the duffel bag and withdrew her macro lens. "This doesn't belong to you."

She snatched it out of his hands. "My dad gave me this for my birthday the last year he was alive. And I'll be damned if I'll let the two of you have it."

"Take it and get out then," Ben said. He glanced at Camryn. "I know you. Camryn Nobles, News Four You. Does your station manager know you're in the habit of breaking and entering?"

Grace shook the paint-spattered T-shirt at Ben. "Do your blog advertisers know you and the slut are in the habit of breaking and entering and vandalizing private property?"

Ben looked at the T-shirt with disinterest. "What's that supposed to be?"

"Your girlfriend was wearing this the other night when she trashed the house I've been working on over on Mandevilla. And don't even try to deny it. This is the same orange paint she splashed all over the kitchen walls. She read my blog posts on TrueGrace, saw that I had a new project, and decided to ruin it for me."

"Ridiculous," Ben said. But he suddenly looked uncomfortable.

"Were you there, too?" Grace asked, her voice rising. "Did you help her break in? I bet you did."

"You're crazy," Ben said. "J'Aimee doesn't even know where that house is."

"Sure she does. Anybody who reads my blog would know it's on Mandevilla. J'Aimee showed up there just last week. To warn me that if I contacted any more of your advertisers, she'd get even with me. And that's just what she did."

"I'm telling you you're wrong. J'Aimee wouldn't do anything like that," Ben insisted.

Grace shoved the T-shirt in his face. "She did it, Ben! And here's the proof. Orange paint. She got it all over her clothes."

He pushed her hand away.

"You really didn't know what she was up to, Ben, did you? She was hiding this stuff from you."

"Take your crap and get out," Ben said, sounding weary.

They heard a door slam from downstairs, and then footsteps.

"Ben?" J'Aimee's voice was shrill, panicky. "Where are you? Call the police! We've been robbed." She was practically running up the stairs.

"I'm in here," Ben called. "And it's not burglars. It's Grace."

59

"What's she doing here?" J'Aimee looked from Ben to Grace, eyes narrowed with suspicion.

"Picking up some of my belongings," Grace said. She held up the black T-shirt. "But I think you mixed up some of your stuff with mine."

J'Aimee pushed a strand of black hair behind one ear. She was dressed in chic lime-green cropped Lululemon yoga pants and a midriff-baring sports bra, and she was barefoot. She flicked the fabric of the T-shirt. "That's not mine." She gestured around the room. "All this crap is yours. You might as well take the rest of it when you go, because I'm getting ready to redecorate in here."

A shadow passed briefly over Grace's face. J'Aimee knew she'd been planning on using this room as a nursery. She'd even volunteered to help paint it, not even six months ago, shortly after she'd become Grace's assistant.

She swallowed her grief over what might have been and channeled it into anger over what had actually occurred.

"These clothes are yours and you know it," Grace said. She dropped the T-shirt and picked up the paint-spotted sneakers. "These shoes are a size six. And I wear an eight. Notice the paint? It's the exact same color as the orange you tossed all over the house on Mandevilla."

"I don't know what you're talking about," J'Aimee said, turning to leave.

"Ben? I'm gonna hit the shower. Could you make sure she doesn't take anything of mine?"

Grace reached out and snagged the stretchy shoulder strap of J'Aimee's top. The younger woman tried to tug loose of Grace's grip, but she held tight.

"Oh, don't go just yet, J'Aimee. Don't you want to tell Ben about the rest of the sweet stunts you pulled at that house? I mean, besides the paint? Don't you want to brag about how you actually pooped in the bathtub, and then wrote obscenities on the wall with your own excrement?"

"Classy," Camryn muttered.

Ben's face registered revulsion. "Come on, Grace."

"I'm betting you didn't share that happy little story," Grace said. "Fortunately, I've got pictures to prove it," She reached for her cell phone. She didn't, actually, but she knew Ben wouldn't look at them, even if she did have pictures.

"Gross," J'Aimee said, trying to inch away. But Grace pulled her back, keeping a firm hold on J'Aimee's top.

"You should know," Grace retorted. "How about the fire? Did you tell Ben you also set a fire in the living room? If it hadn't been for the neighbor, who saw the flames shortly after you tried to torch the place, it probably would have burned to the ground."

"I didn't!" J'Aimee said stubbornly. She grabbed Grace's hands and wrenched herself loose.

Camryn had been standing quietly on the sidelines, but now she stepped forward. She took one of the sneakers and sniffed it delicately.

"Yup," she said succinctly. "Lighter fluid." She carefully placed both shoes in her oversized pocketbook. "The fire marshall is going to want to take a look at these." She glanced over at Grace. "Let's take the shirt and pants, too. I'll bet they've got traces of lighter fluid, too. It doesn't even take a crime lab."

"Who the hell are you?" J'Aimee demanded.

"Just a friend," Camryn said lightly. "Who happens to be an investigative reporter."

"She's from channel four," Ben said, sounding uneasy. "The same reporter who snuck in after Grace left."

"How did they get in here today?" J'Aimee demanded. "I thought you left instructions at the gate."

Camryn struck a pose and held up the sneaker like an imaginary microphone, saying sotto voce, "News Four You has learned that a local lifestyles blogger, J'Aimee . . ."

She turned to Grace. "What's her last name?"

"Scoggins," Grace said.

"Lifestyle blogger J'Aimee Scoggins is under investigation for breaking and entering, destruction of private property, and arson after she allegedly broke into a residence on Anna Maria Island being redecorated by rival blogger Grace Davenport. Davenport, thirty-four . . ."

"I'm actually thirty-eight," Grace corrected.

"Davenport, thirty-eight, is the estranged wife of local businessman Ben Stanton. Sources tell me that J'Aimee Scoggins and Stanton are romantically involved," Camryn said.

"Very funny," Ben said. He pointed toward the door. "Now, leave. Or I will call the cops."

Grace gathered up the rest of the paint-spattered clothing and slid it into the plastic sack, which she gripped tightly.

"You still haven't asked her if she did it," she said. "But maybe you already know the answer."

Ben turned suddenly and stared at J'Aimee. "Tell me you didn't do any of this. Please."

J'Aimee took a step backward. "She's bluffing. She can't prove those clothes are mine. She probably put them here herself."

"J'Aimee?" Ben's deep voice was chilly. "Yes or no?"

"Yes! Okay?" J'Aimee said defiantly. "It was just a little joke. God! You people need to lighten up. I didn't mean to break the glass. I was opening the window, which was unlocked, and it just cracked. You can't break into a place that isn't even really locked up."

"What about the paint?" Ben asked.

"Big deal. A little orange paint. The place is a dump. Anyway, she had it coming, writing to my advertisers, telling them I was stealing from her . . . We lost our Kohler ads because of her."

Ben swore softly, under his breath. "And what she said? About the bath-room? Dear God, tell me you didn't actually . . ."

"It was just a joke!" J'Aimee exclaimed. "Okay, maybe it did get a little out of hand. I took a bunch of empty beer cans over there, to make it look like it was kids, and I had a couple of wine coolers of my own, so maybe that wasn't really a cool thing to do." She glanced at Grace. "I'm sorry, okay? Is that what you want to hear?"

"No," Grace snapped. "Sorry doesn't cut it anymore. You could have burned that house to the ground. It belongs to a sweet old man who was getting ready to rent it to me. But after you vandalized the place, he just wants to sell it and be done with it. You and I both know you weren't joking around when you went over there the other night. You wanted to send me a message. Well, you did that, all right. I got the message loud and clear."

Ben was shaking his head. "I can't believe you pulled a stupid stunt like this. Arson! Really? They put people in jail for that, J'Aimee."

"I'm sorry! I told you I was sorry," J'Aimee said, her voice pleading. "Ben . . ."

"Go take your shower," Ben said wearily. "I can't deal with you right now."

J'Aimee turned and slunk out of the room. A moment later, they heard the bedroom door slam.

Camryn edged toward the door, too. "I'll just, uh, be waiting outside. Whenever you're ready."

Ben watched her go. He sighed loudly. "Look, Grace, you have to believe me. I did not put J'Aimee up to this. I would never . . . I mean, we've had our differences." He swallowed and looked away. "The stuff with Gracenotes, that's business. It's not personal."

"It's very personal to me," Grace said. "You and J'Aimee have done your best to put me out of business. You say it wasn't your idea to have her vandalize that house, but you and I both know J'Aimee's never had an original idea in her life. She took her cues from you. Maybe you didn't light that fire, but you sure as hell showed her where the matches were."

He rubbed his jaw. "You're not serious about going to the police with this, are you? J'Aimee's just a kid. Yeah, she did it to get back at you. Because you intimidate her. No matter what, in a weird way, you're still her idol. You heard her. As far as she knew, this was just a prank that got out of hand."

"I'm her idol? That's a laugh."

"It's true," Ben insisted. "She reads every word you write, goes back over your old posts, trying to copy your style. I keep trying to tell her, she's got her own style, which she should develop, but for some reason she's fixated on you, on being bigger, better than you. I guess maybe I should have seen the potential for what happened, should have reined her in before it came to this."

"Ya think?" Grace shot back.

"I'm asking you, please. Don't make a federal case out of this. I'll have a serious talk with J'Aimee. And I'll do whatever it takes to make it right. I'll pay for all the damages, reimburse you for your lost time. I'll fix it. I promise."

"You'll fix it," Grace said, laughing bitterly. "There's that expression of yours again. You just love the idea of covering things up, of pretending they never happened, don't you, Ben?"

"I'm a pragmatist. A businessman," he said calmly. "So, do we have a deal?"

She crossed her arms and gave him a long, hard look. "It's not up to me. It's Arthur's house. I'll tell him about your offer."

"And you'll suggest we settle this without the police getting involved?" he persisted.

Grace saw an opening, and she went for it. "I'll suggest he accept your offer. On one condition."

Ben rolled his eyes. "Here it comes. The blackmail."

"You can call it whatever you like," Grace said. "Here's the deal. You tell your lawyer that you want to settle things fairly with me. I'm not looking to gouge you, Ben. But it's totally unfair that I should have to walk away from this marriage with not a dime to my name. We built a business together, and by rights half of the proceeds from it should be mine. That's what I want. No more, no less."

"And if I don't give you what you want?"

Grace held the garbage bag aloft. "There's always this. And remember, Camryn was standing right here when J'Aimee confessed. I wouldn't put it past her to have recorded the whole thing. You know how sneaky these journalism types are."

60

By the time Grace emerged from the house, Marissa and Camryn were waiting for her in the golf cart. Camryn held the pillowcase with the wedding silver in her lap. Grace placed the duffel bag with her books and camera equipment on the floor of the backseat and climbed onto the seat, tightly clutching the black garbage bag.

"Let's go," Grace said, glancing back toward the house, half expecting J'Aimee to follow in hot pursuit.

Marissa steered the cart down the driveway and around the corner toward her own house.

Camryn turned around in her seat, one eyebrow raised in question. "So?"

"Mission accomplished," Grace said. "I got what I came for. And more." Marissa turned around, too, and the three women high-fived each other.

"I'm afraid I blew it, though," Marissa said apologetically. "I just went in the house for a minute. They must have slipped right past me. But I hear you got the goods on that little bitch."

"We'll see," Grace said. "The big thing is, we managed to rattle Ben. He's really worried I might go to the cops."

"How worried?" Camryn asked.

"Worried enough that he agreed to talk financial settlement."

"That's great," Camryn said. "You must have done some major cage rattling after I hightailed it out of there."

"I might have mentioned that you were probably secretly taping J'Aimee's confession," Grace admitted.

Camryn smirked, then pulled her iPhone from her pocket, held it up, and tapped an icon. J'Aimee's high-pitched voice floated in the air. "It was a joke," she screeched. Camryn tapped the button and the phone went silent.

"Never underestimate a woman," she advised. "Especially one who's been jerked around the way you and I have."

The two high-fived each other one more time.

"Where's my father?"

Wyatt stood staring down at Callie, still half asleep on the sofa.

She stretched and yawned. "What?"

"Dad. He's not here. Where'd he go?"

Callie sat up slowly. "How should I know?"

"Did he see you here this morning?" Wyatt demanded. "Come on, Callie. This is important. Did he say anything?"

"No. Well, yeah. I mean, he came out of his room, and I heard him banging pots and pans around in the kitchen, making coffee. I went out and asked him if I could have a cup, and he just stared at me. He put the coffeepot down and walked out the door. God! I'm telling you, there is something wrong with that old man. And I'm not talking about diabetes, Wyatt. He's seriously senile."

"Shit," Wyatt said softly. "He's not senile! He can't stand the sight of you, if you want to know the truth. He probably saw you here, dressed in my robe, and got the wrong idea. Which way did he go, did you see?"

"You know how I am before I get my coffee in the morning. He left. That's all I know."

"Hey, Mom."

Callie and Wyatt turned to see their young son, standing in the doorway to the living room, dressed in his Lightning McQueen pajama bottoms.

"Good morning, Bo-Bo," Callie said, her pout turning instantly to a sunny smile. "Come give your mama some sugar."

Bo allowed himself to be cuddled, but only for a moment. Pulling away, he looked at his father's troubled countenance.

"Is Granddad missing again?"

"Not really missing," Wyatt said hastily. "He went out for a walk early this morning, and I'm a little worried, because I don't know whether he remembered to eat some breakfast or take his medicine. I'm going to hop on the cart and take a spin around the park to pick him up. You want to help me track him?"

"Sure!" Bo looked hesitantly at his mother. "I'll be right back, Mom, okay?"

"Take all the time you need," Callie said, yawning again. "I'll be around when you get back."

Grace tried calling Wyatt from the Publix parking lot, but her call went directly to voice mail. It was just as well, she thought, because she really wanted to tell him firsthand how her visit to Gulf Vista played out.

She drove around to the back entrance to Jungle Jerry's and found the nearly hidden driveway that led to Wyatt's trailer. His truck was parked under the carport, in front of a vehicle she'd never seen before, a battered and rust-spotted Jeep.

She tapped lightly at the aluminum storm door. "Wyatt?" she called, and was rewarded with the sound of Sweetie's answering bark, followed by a frantic scratching at the door. She waited another minute. Maybe he was in the shower? Or out in the park, on the golf cart? Grace tapped again, and Sweetie gave another answering bark.

She tried the door. It was unlocked. She pushed the door open and stepped inside. Sweetie threw herself joyously at Grace's ankle, yipping excitedly.

"Hi, little girl," Grace said, scooping the dog up into her arms. "Where are the guys? Huh? Are you the only one home?"

"Not quite."

Grace looked up, startled.

Callie Keeler stood in the doorway from the kitchen, eating from an oversized bowl of cereal. She was barefoot, dressed only in a short, faded bathrobe, loosely belted around her waist.

"If you're looking for my husband, you just missed him," Callie said. "He and Bo are out in the park, looking for Nelson."

"Oh."

Grace's chest constricted. She hugged Sweetie close and blinked. She felt her face growing hot.

Callie laughed at her obvious discomfort and took another bite of cereal. A bit of milk trickled down her chin, and she dabbed at it with her sleeve, revealing, in the process, that she was naked under the robe.

"Awkward moment, huh? I'm guessing you must be the girlfriend Bo's been telling me about. It's Grace, right?"

"Yes," Grace managed to say.

Callie held out the bowl. "You want some cereal? It's Cocoa Puffs. I swear, you're never too old for Cocoa Puffs."

"No thanks," Grace said. She turned and left.

"Don't go on my account," Callie called, chuckling to herself. "I'll tell Wyatt you dropped by."

"Dumb, dumb, dumb." Grace banged her head on the steering wheel with each exclamation. Sweetie whined and crawled onto her lap, licking her chin as a consolation prize.

She started the car and headed down the sandy driveway toward the street. She blinked back tears as she navigated through the thick foliage that lined both sides of the narrow one-way drive.

It was after ten o'clock in the morning, and there stood Callie Keeler, dressed only in Wyatt's robe, calmly eating cereal. Obviously, she'd spent the night there. "You just missed my husband," she'd said. Not "ex-husband," not "Wyatt," but "husband," letting Grace know she'd reclaimed him.

"You can have him," Grace muttered.

No wonder he'd begged off seeing her last night. He'd had a much better offer from his wayward wife. And why should that come as a surprise? Wyatt had made it clear right from the start that his first commitment was to his son's happiness. And like any six-year-old, Bo wanted his parents back together.

How could she have believed he wanted to start a new life with her? How could she let herself get sucked into a relationship on the rebound? Double rebound, if you wanted to be technical, since both she and Wyatt were coming out of ruined marriages. And with a guy she'd met in a divorce-recovery group!

"Stupid, stupid, stupid," she chanted, slapping the dashboard for emphasis. Sweetie looked up at her with huge, uncomprehending brown eyes.

"Never trust a man, Sweetie," Grace told the dog. "They all lie. Every damn one of them is a liar."

Her cell phone rang. She grabbed it and looked at the caller ID. It was Wyatt.

"This is the liar calling right now," Grace told Sweetie. "Can you believe it?"

She tossed the phone onto the seat, and the little dog sniffed it. The phone rang again. She knew without looking it would be him. And he'd probably keep calling. Why postpone the inevitable? She snatched up the phone and tapped the CONNECT button.

"What?"

"Grace, I just got back to the trailer. Callie told me you came by."

"How nice of her." Grace sneered. "She's a great hostess, Wyatt. She even offered me some of her Cocoa Puffs. I'm sure you two will be very happy. Again."

"Look, it's not like you think," Wyatt said. "I don't care what she told you; we are not back together. We are not getting back together."

"So, last night—was that just a one-night stand? And you think that doesn't count?"

"She slept on the sofa! She broke up with Luke last week, and she called me, hoping I'd let her stay here, but I told her there was no way. So she went to her sister's house, but Luke showed up over there, and they were drinking, so Kendra kicked her out in the middle of the night. You know what it was like last night—it was raining. And then Bo woke up and saw her, so what was I gonna do, kick her out into the rain, with my son standing there, begging me to let her stay?"

"Let me ask you a question," Grace said, her voice oddly cold. "You say this all started last week? Did it ever occur to you to mention to me that your wife was trying to move back in with you? Especially after you told me you couldn't see me last night, because of Bo?"

"That was a mistake on my part, and I know that now," he said, his words tumbling together. "But I didn't tell you because I knew you'd get the wrong idea," Wyatt said. "Which you did. I never had any intention of taking Callie back. It's over between us. And I've told her that. Repeatedly."

"And yet there she was this morning, all cozied up at your place. Was that your robe she was wearing? Or has she already started to unpack?"

"Dammit, Grace," Wyatt said hoarsely. "She slept on the sofa. And she's gone now. I told her she can't come back. And if you don't believe me, you can ask Dad. That's where I was when you came by, out looking for him. He saw

Callie asleep on the sofa this morning, and he was so pissed, he just took off, because he can't stand to be under the same roof with her. Or ask Bo. He's in the other room, sulking, because he didn't want his mother to go. But she has. Okay? It is over between Callie and me."

Grace bit her lip. She pulled out of the driveway and into traffic. "You just think it's over," she told him. "But she's not going to let you go, and Bo's not going to let her go. I can't do this, Wyatt. I can't hang around, wondering what will happen with Callie's next crisis. You need to figure all this stuff out by yourself. You're not ready for a new relationship. Not with me, anyway."

"Grace?" His voice was pleading. "I care about you Grace. Don't hang up, please. Just meet me someplace, okay, and let's talk about this. What about Gus's? That doughnut place? Can you just at least talk to me face-to-face?"

"I don't think so," she said sadly. "Not even for doughnuts."

61

Grace unlocked the door to Mitzi's condo and gently set Sweetie down on the floor. She sank down onto the white sofa and stared out the sliding glass doors at the jade-green surf below. The giddy euphoria she'd experienced earlier in the day, after finally forcing Ben to agree to a financial settlement, was forgotten. Now she felt the gray mist of depression settling over her, like a suffocating woolen blanket.

The bright, buttery-hued sunlight pouring into the apartment was a cruel intrusion. She covered her eyes with one of the colorful throw pillows she'd bought only days earlier and flounced facedown on the sofa.

She heard the muffled sound of her cell phone ringing and ignored it. She let two more calls go directly to voice mail. Time passed. Grace was vaguely aware of the warmth of Sweetie, who'd curled up on the sofa alongside her. She heard the waves rolling ashore outside, and the distant sound of seagulls, and the occasional slamming of a car door.

But the sound of a key turning in the condo's door jolted her back to consciousness. She rolled over and saw the front door swing open, but she did not bother to sit up.

"There you are," Mitzi Stillwell exclaimed. "I've been looking all over town for you. Why didn't you answer my calls? Or your mother's?"

"I just . . . didn't want to deal with anything," Grace said dully. "Why? What's going on?"

Mitzi walked over and sat on the edge of the club chair. "What's wrong with you? Are you sick?"

"I'm okay," Grace said. "Relatively speaking."

Her lawyer gave her an appraising look. "You had a fight with Wyatt, didn't you?"

"It's over," Grace said.

Mitzi groaned. "Oh no. Don't tell me. He's gone back to his wife?"

"Not yet, but he probably will," Grace said. "She broke up with her boyfriend, and she spent the night at his place last night. Which he didn't feel the need to tell me. So it's only a matter of time."

"Did he tell you he wants her back?"

"No," Grace admitted. "He says she slept on the sofa, and the only reason he let her stay was because it was raining so hard last night, and Bo begged him to. He swears they're through, but I don't believe it."

Mitzi patted her arm. "I'm sorry, Grace. I see this all the time in my line of work. Couples go through the worst kind of traumas, file for divorce, then, at some point, they begin to think maybe they ought to give it another try. You especially see it in families with young children."

"No kid wants to see his parents split up," Grace said, thinking about her own reaction to Rochelle's recent disturbing revelation about her marriage to Grace's father.

Mitzi sighed. "Well, that's not exactly true. There are kids who've seen too much—too much violence, hostility, aggression in their parents' marriage. Those kids crave normality; they crave peace. And the smart ones know that's only possible if a toxic marriage does break up."

"I'm just thankful Ben and I didn't have kids," Grace said.

"Speaking of Ben," Mitzi said, raising an eyebrow. "Dickie Murphree called me out of the blue a little while ago, to say they're ready to talk settlement."

"Good," Grace said.

"Good? That's all you can say? Come on, Grace, snap out of it! This is huge. For months now, they've totally stonewalled us. And now, suddenly, they finally want to settle. Any idea what caused this new development?"

"I went over to the house this morning, to get some of my things. And in the process, I found pretty solid proof that J'Aimee really did vandalize Mandevilla Manor."

"How the hell did you get past security?" Mitzi asked. "Please don't tell me you burglarized the place."

"Camryn—my friend from divorce-recovery group? She's friends with the woman who lives directly behind our house, Marissa. She's married to LaDarion Banks, the baseball player. Marissa called the gate and told them she was expecting Camryn as her guest. And I didn't have to break into the house. I still have my key. Easy-peasy."

"And at some point during your unauthorized visit, Ben just agreed to a fair and equitable settlement with you?"

"Ben doesn't want J'Aimee charged with the vandalism—and arson—at Mandevilla Manor. I told him I'd let Arthur know what I'd discovered but that I'd suggest Arthur allow Ben to pay for all the damages and make restitution, without getting the cops involved. Naturally, Ben was grateful," Grace said.

"Naturally," Mitzi said wryly. "I've got news on another front, too. I had a long chat yesterday with Carlton Towne concerning the experience of his client, Harriett, with Judge Stackpole."

"And?" Grace was determined not to get her hopes built up. She'd had enough of an emotional roller-coaster ride for one day. For one year, even.

"Carlton is very old-school. He's been practicing law in this county for more than forty years, and he doesn't like to rock the boat."

"So, that's that," Grace said. "It was worth a try, though."

"Would you stop being so negative! Carlton may be adverse to rocking the boat, but on the other hand, he is also a stickler on the matter of rules and ethics. And he was enraged when I told him how Stackpole has been ordering divorcing parties into therapy—and then steering those same parties to a woman with whom he's romantically involved. He agrees with me that we should file a formal complaint with the JQC."

"Remind me what the JQC actually is?" Grace said.

"Judicial Qualifications Committee. It's the state agency that governs and disciplines judges," Mitzi said. "So that's our next step. First, we document every single instance we know of where Stackpole made attending therapy mandatory for divorcing parties. Then, we assemble an exhaustingly thorough and compelling complaint and take it to the JQC. And if all goes well, they take Stackpole to the woodshed. Metaphorically speaking."

Grace scratched Sweetie's ears absentmindedly. "And you really think this JQC will believe us? And they'll do what?"

"They can do anything from a reprimand to a fine to a suspension from office to removing him from office," Mitzi said. "He could also be 'involuntarily retired due to illness,' although I doubt it would come to that."

"And what do you need from me?" Grace asked.

"We need Paula Talbott-Sinclair on our side. We need her to tell the JQC about her involvement with Judge Stackpole."

"Is that all?" Grace shook her head. "Mitzi, how am I supposed to make that happen? What makes you think I can get Paula to turn on her sugar daddy?"

Mitzi gave her an appraising look. "You're a woman of many talents, Grace, not the least of which is charm. So you do your thing, and I'll do mine. Deal?"

Grace stared out the window for a while. "I'll give it a shot," she said finally.

"Good," Mitzi said briskly. She reached out and patted Sweetie's head. "What'll you do about the dog? I mean, will you still split custody with Wyatt at night?"

"Gaaaawd," Grace said, flopping backward onto the sofa again. "I hadn't even thought about that. I won't take her back to Wyatt's. And I can't take her to my mom's place."

"Well," Mitzi said, looking around the condo. "I guess it wouldn't hurt if the two of you stayed here for a couple weeks. It's really coming along, Grace. I love the bright colors, and the lamps and things. I never would have thought of doing any of this."

"I couldn't just squat here," Grace said uneasily. "It wouldn't be right."

"Why not? You've still got more work to do here, and I'm too busy to use it for the next month or so anyway. The complex is pet-friendly." Mitzi picked up her oversized pocketbook and went to the door.

"I think you should stay," she said, her hand on the doorknob. "You've been through a rough patch. Spend some time here alone, you and Sweetie. If all goes well, Ben will cough up an equitable settlement; we'll get Stackpole out of our hair, if not off the bench; and then you can figure out the next chapter in the Grace Davenport story."

Grace gave her lawyer a rueful smile. "Next chapter? Right now, I can't even figure out the next five minutes."

62

Grace lolled on the sofa, flipping through channels with the remote control. She paused when she got to *The Real Housewives of Atlanta*. Rochelle watched the show religiously, but Grace had never really seen it. But tonight, she thought, as she dipped a plastic fork into the paper carton of take-out kung pao chicken, and only tonight, she would watch trashy TV reruns and wallow in self-pity.

Her cell phone rang. She picked it up and looked at the caller ID. It was Camryn.

"Where are you and what are you doing?" Camryn demanded.

"I'm at a client's condo, watching *The Real Housewives of Atlanta*," she said warily. "Can I ask you a question? Who are these women? Why do they have their own television show?"

"Girlfriend, I do not have the time to explain RHOA to you. Anyway, you need to turn on channel eight. Now. Because, honey, this is priceless."

Sweetie was sitting directly on top of the remote control. Grace gently slid it out from under the dog's butt and pointed the remote at Mitzi's forty-eight-inch flat screen. She was rewarded by fuzzy footage of what looked like two well-dressed women who appeared to be pelting each other with ... dinner rolls? They were both screeching at the top of their lungs.

"A food fight? On the ten o'clock news? This is why you called?" Grace asked.

"Keep watching," Camryn said, chuckling. "It gets better."

A man's deep voice cut through the shrill din. "Eileen! What the hell?"

"Did you get that?" Camryn asked. "Recognize that voice?"

Grace leaned forward and stared intently at the television, but the camera kept jerking back and forth between the two women. The older of the two, a brunette, lunged toward the other, clawing at her face. Now, a man was tugging at her arm, vainly attempting to fend her off. His back was to the camera, but, once, Grace glimpsed a vaguely familiar profile.

The younger woman, a strikingly attractive African-American woman with short, platinum-blond hair was batting away the other woman's blows. "Get her off of me," she hollered. "Cedric, do something."

Cedric?

"It can't be," Grace whispered, dropping onto the floor, crawling closer to the television until her face was only inches from the screen. The man glanced over his shoulder at the camera, then flung his hand across his face. "Are you filming this? Stop that! Get that thing away from me." He whirled around, and for a moment, just a moment, Grace saw the angry countenance of the Honorable Cedric N. Stackpole Jr.

"Hey, man," another male voice protested. "You can't do that." And then the camera jerked violently, and the footage ended.

"Oh. My. God." Grace was clutching her hand to her chest. "Did I really just see what I think I saw?"

"In living color," Camryn said. "Merry Christmas to us."

"What? I mean, how . . ." Grace sputtered. "What exactly did I just watch?"

"That, Gracie dear, was footage taken last night at a restaurant in Sarasota by an alert diner, who just happened to be talking to a friend on his cell phone, when Eileen Stackpole walked into the restaurant and caught her husband having a tête-à-tête with a pretty young thing."

"I think I've seen her before," Grace said. "The PYT, I mean."

"Mm-hmm," Camryn said. "We have all seen that girl. She's a twenty-three-year-old bailiff assigned to Stackpole's courtroom. Her name is Monique Massey. And I guarantee you the two of them were not discussing tort reform in a cozy little booth in a pricey French bistro at ten o'clock last night."

Grace could hardly take it all in. "How did this end up on the news? What's it all mean?"

"It got on the news because Stackpole flipped his shit when he realized the other diner was filming the whole thing. He knocked the cell phone out of the guy's hand and took a swing at him. One of the waiters pulled the judge off the guy, but, in the meantime, the cell-phone guy's dinner companion called the cops."

"Tell me they arrested Stackpole," Grace begged.

"No such luck," Camryn said. "Stackpole paid his bill and hustled lil Monique outta there before the po-po arrived. And Eileen took a powder, too. The restaurant manager smoothed things over by offering everybody in the place a free drink and dessert. By the time the cops arrived, all was calm. But at some point, the waiter pulled the cell-phone guy aside and whispered to him the identity of his assailant. Apparently, Stackpole is a regular there—and a lousy tipper. Now the cell-phone guy says he's going to sue Stackpole for assault and battery."

"How do you happen to know so much about all this?" Grace asked. "And why isn't this story on *your* station?"

Camryn sighed heavily. "The cell-phone guy e-mailed the footage to me first. But because of my, er, prior history with Stackpole, my news director doesn't want anything to do with the story. I begged and pleaded and threatened, but he won't budge. So I might have tipped off a friend at our rival station. Anonymously, of course. At least the story is out there, and it's hugely embarrassing to Stackpole. So for once, I don't even mind being scooped."

"What else do you know?" Grace asked. "Did Mrs. Stackpole just happen to bump into the judge and this bailiff, or did she know they'd been seeing each other? And what happens now? Will she divorce him? And what about the guy with the camera?"

Before Camryn could answer her barrage of questions, Grace's phone beeped to alert her that she had another incoming call. "Sorry," Grace said. "I better take this. It's my lawyer."

"I'm thinking this calls for a celebration," Camryn said hastily. "Tomorrow night, eight, at the Sandbox. I'll call everybody else. You're in, right?"

"Absolutely," Grace said.

. . .

"Did you just see the news on channel eight?" Mitzi asked gleefully.

"Camryn, one of the girls in my divorce group, called to tell me about it," Grace said. "I could just watch it over and over; it's so delicious."

"You totally can. It was on at six o'clock, too. They've already posted the footage on the station's Web site," Mitzi told her. "I've watched it four times, and it gets better with every viewing."

"Better for us," Grace said. "But how would you like to be Eileen Stackpole? Can you imagine the humiliation?"

"I can't imagine marrying the man in the first place. Yeechhh. What a worm! Of course, there's got to be a lot more to the story than what they put on the air tonight," Mitzi speculated. "And the rumors are already flying all over town. Right before I called you, I heard from one of the other lawyers who's tried divorces before Stackpole. She heard Eileen Stackpole didn't just stumble into that restaurant last night. She'd supposedly hired a private investigator. He's the one who let her know Stackpole was playing footsie with his bailiff."

"A twenty-three-year-old!" Grace exclaimed. "And I definitely remember her being in the courtroom that first time we went before Stackpole. Remember, she shushed us?"

"So that's where I've seen her," Mitzi said. She laughed. "Oh, my. Cedric has been a very naughty boy, hasn't he?"

"But is all of this anything that would get him in trouble with your JQC?" Grace asked. "I mean, is being a slimeball enough to get you kicked off the bench?"

"Good question," Mitzi said. "Having your wife attack your girlfriend in a very public place might not be grounds for discipline by the JQC. Although the fact that he's involved with an employee of the court seems unethical. But I wonder how it would sit with Paula? I wonder if she knows Stackpole has *another* other woman—besides her?"

"I guess I'll have to ask her how she feels about it," Grace said, wincing.

"You do that. And let me know what you find out," Mitzi said.

63

G race arrived at Paula Sinclair-Talbott's office at eight o'clock on that already-steamy Monday morning, determined that she would be Paula's first client of the day.

She watched idly as the strip shopping center slowly came to life. At nine, a woman wearing a brilliant orange silk sari unlocked the doors at the Diaper Depot. At 9:30 two middle-aged Hispanic women arrived together at the door to the hearing-aid center.

Twice, her phone rang. Both times it was Wyatt. The second time, she was tempted to answer, just to hear his voice, hear him tell her he missed her and wanted her back. She had to grip the steering wheel with both hands to keep from picking up. This was for the best, she told herself.

Finally, at ten 'til ten, she watched as the VW bug zipped into a parking space three cars away. Paula Talbott-Sinclair walked briskly to her office door, unlocked it, and disappeared inside.

Paula was standing in the reception area, staring down at the computer terminal, when Grace walked inside.

"Grace?" Paula looked up and frowned. Her blond curls were mussed and there were dark circles under her unmade-up eyes. She wore a faded, shapeless black jersey dress that hung limply on her slender frame and cheap red rubber flip-flops. There were no tinkly earrings or ankle bracelets this morning. It didn't look like she'd had a fun weekend.

That makes two of us, Grace thought.

"This is a surprise," Paula said. "Is there something urgent you need to discuss?"

Grace cleared her throat. "Uh, yes, actually, there is something kind of important I'd like to talk to you about. That's okay, right? I mean, in the beginning, you told us we could call you about anything."

"Well . . . I suppose I have time," Paula said, hesitantly. "My first group doesn't start until ten thirty. Come on inside."

Grace followed the therapist into the inner office. The heat was stifling. She watched while Paula switched on the lights and then a small window-air-conditioning unit. "Sit down," Paula said, grabbing one of the folding chairs from the semicircle and dragging it over to a position in front of her desk.

"I'm going to make some tea," Paula said. "Would you like a cup?"

What she'd like, Grace thought nervously, was a Xanax, or at least a stiff cocktail. "No thanks," she said politely.

Paula drifted around the room, putting a kettle on a hot plate, rearranging the circle of chairs, and then, finally, when the tea kettle whistled, pouring the water into a lumpy pottery mug.

"Now," she said, settling into the chair behind her desk. "What's happening in your world today, Grace?"

"Um." Grace fidgeted with the strap of her purse. She'd rehearsed her speech half a dozen times at home and in the car this morning, but there was no way she could make this an easy discussion.

"The thing is, Paula," she started. "I think there's something happening in *your* world that we need to discuss."

"Oh?" Paula cautiously sipped her tea. "And how is anything in my world relevant to you?"

Grace felt her face grow warm. "I've been attending your divorce-recovery sessions—for six weeks now—because Judge Stackpole basically made it a condition of granting my divorce. And the others in my group—Camryn, Ashleigh, and Wyatt—Judge Stackpole sent them to you, too."

"That's correct," Paula said. "The judge has been a wonderful advocate for my healing work."

"He's been your lover, too," Grace blurted. "Right?"

Paula looked like she'd been slapped. "I beg your pardon?"

Grace took a deep breath, and the words came tumbling out. "We saw you together! That night the judge dropped in on our session. Wyatt and I came back here to your office. We saw you getting out of his car. You'd obviously had a big fight. You were yelling at him, and then you got out of his car and kicked his tires. You were crying and really upset."

"You're mistaken," Paula said, her voice low.

"We both saw you, Paula," Grace insisted. "And we know it was Judge Stackpole, because after he left you, we followed him back to his house on Longboat Key."

Bright pink splotches of color bloomed on Paula's long pale face. "The judge is . . . a friend. We had a misunderstanding that night. That's all."

"I don't think so. We all noticed how you were around him that night. You were absolutely . . . giddy. Come on, Paula. You're always after all of us about honesty. Why don't you be honest with me? Admit you're having an affair with Stackpole."

Paula's hands shook so violently she had to set the mug of tea on the desktop. "Therapists never discuss their personal life with their patients. This is highly inappropriate, Grace." Her voice was stern, but Grace noticed that Paula was now clasping her hands tightly together in her lap—probably to stop the shaking.

Grace was shaking, too. But now the fear was gone, replaced by anger.

"Inappropriate? Do you want to talk about appropriate behavior, Paula? Because that's a subject I'd love to discuss with you. What would you say about a prominent judge—who, by the way, is married—having an affair with a therapist? Would you say it's appropriate for that judge to *require* parties in divorces in his court to attend therapy with his mistress?"

"Mistress!" Paula yelped. "How dare you?"

Paula's outrage only fueled Grace's refusal to back down.

"Mistress—it's a nasty word, isn't it, Paula? But that's what you are. You're sleeping with him, and in return he sends all these shell-shocked divorce disasters right here to your office, where they pay handsomely for the privilege of listening to your hypocrisy. The five people in my group are forking over fifteen hundred dollars a week for this bullshit," Grace said. "How much of that do you have to kick to Stackpole, Paula? Half? Or does he even let you keep that much?"

"You've got no right to talk to me like this," Paula said, pushing back from her desk, looking wildly around the room for an escape hatch.

"What are you gonna do, Paula? Rat me out to the judge? Flunk me out of divorce camp? I have every right to call you out. But what I want to know is, When do you call him out? Huh, Paula? When do you quit being his victim?"

Paula's eyes flared. "You don't know what you're talking about."

"Sure I do. You moved here from Oregon after your life went up in flames—a bad divorce, a nasty little pill habit, then the arrest and then rehab. You moved to Florida to start over again, right? But you can't get licensed to call yourself a therapist here, can you? And then you meet Stackpole, and the two of you cook up this little 'divorce recovery' racket."

"It's not a racket," Paula said fiercely. "I care deeply about my patients. I counsel them and do my damnedest to help them . . ." Her voice trailed off, and her shoulders slumped.

"Avoid what happened to you?" Grace finished it for her. "How are you going to help us, Paula, when you're still so messed up yourself?"

Tears welled up in the therapist's eyes. "That's not fair. I'm sober again. I had a relapse, yes, but that's over now. And it's because of all I've gone through that I can be effective with my patients. I can use my experiences to help them get through their pain and sense of loss."

"Keep telling yourself that, Paula," Grace said. "Maybe part of it's true. But what about the rest of it? You're conspiring with Stackpole. He funnels patients to you—and we don't have any choice in the matter. If we want to get on with our lives, you have to sign off on our therapy. It's fraud."

Paula clasped and unclasped her hands. "I am a *good* therapist. I can help people; I really can. But how was I going to start a new practice? Rent office space, establish myself in the therapeutic community here? Everywhere I looked, I had people slamming doors in my face. After my divorce—it was so humiliating. And unfair. He's the one who slept with a patient and violated his professional oath. But I'm the one who lost everything. He gets to start over with a new life and a new wife, and I get . . ." She looked around the room, with its worn and stained carpet, cheap furniture, and depressing, institutional green walls. "I get this."

Grace sighed. "Yeah, well, welcome to my world. The same thing happened to me—thanks to your boyfriend, the Honorable Cedric N. Stackpole."

Paula lifted her chin defiantly. "You're in a better place now because of me,

Grace. I know you don't believe it, but you are. Everybody in your group has made remarkable progress. Look at Suzanne. She's not the same person she was when she walked into this office seven weeks ago."

"Okay," Grace said. "I'll give you that one. Suzanne might be the poster girl for divorce recovery. But that doesn't give you a pass where Stackpole is concerned. He's a creep, Paula. He's a crook and a fraud and a cheater. He cheats on his wife, and he cheats on you. Did you happen to catch the news last night?"

Paula bit her lip but said nothing.

"Did you?"

"I saw," she said, her voice barely above a whisper. "Oh my God. It's all so ugly."

Grace felt sorry for Paula. She felt sorry for Eileen Stackpole, and she felt sorry for herself and everybody in her divorce group. But sorry wouldn't begin to fix what Stackpole had done.

"She's twenty-three, did you know that?" Grace asked. "That girl? The one he was cheating on you with? She's a bailiff in his courtroom. Her name is Monique Massey."

"He was mentoring her," Paula said, her chin quivering as she said it.

"Is that what he told you?" Grace asked. "What a crock! She's a county employee. He's a judge! You don't discuss your career in an expensive restaurant at ten o'clock at night. You talk about it over a cup of coffee in the break room. Or at lunch at the meat and three downtown by the courthouse. Even you couldn't believe a load of bullshit like that."

Paula sprang from her chair. "I have patients coming. You have to go, Grace."

Grace stayed seated. "It's all starting to come apart now, Paula. My lawyer and I have talked to your other patients—and their lawyers. We're going to file a complaint with the state Judicial Qualifications Committee. We can prove Stackpole's bias against women. Wyatt's your only male divorce-recovery patient—right? We know Stackpole had some kind of an unethical arrangement with you. And now we know about the affair with his bailiff."

Paula opened the door to the outer office. "You need to leave. Right now. I won't listen to any more of this."

Finally, Grace got up. "I'll leave," she said, standing just inside the doorway. "But I won't shut up. This isn't going to go away." She studied the therapist's face, looking for some opening, some sense that Paula might switch sides.

"I think you really do care about your patients, Paula. I don't know how you got mixed up with a sleazeball like Stackpole, but you have to know he's been using you. He's betrayed his oath of office, and he's betrayed you. Maybe you should take some of your own advice. Take an honest look at what's happened in your life since you hooked up with Stackpole. Come up with an action plan."

The bell on the outer office door tinkled and a middle-aged woman stepped inside. "Hello, Rachel!" Paula called out. "I'll be right with you."

She lowered her voice to a whisper. "You have to go!"

Grace touched the therapist's wrist. "Think about it, Paula. We need your help. We *are* going to file a complaint against him. There will be an investigation. Questions are going to be asked."

The door opened and another woman stepped inside. Paula looked frantically from Grace to the two women standing in her waiting room.

"Almost done here," Paula called cheerily.

"I'm going to have my lawyer call you," Grace said quietly. "Her name is Mitzi Stillwell. She's a nice person. Will you at least talk to her?"

"Go!" Paula said fiercely.

64

The members of the Lady Slipper Garden Circle asked endless questions about Jungle Jerry's unusual bromeliad and orchid collection, and Wyatt patiently answered each and every one. By noon he'd marshaled the eleven women through the park and returned them to the gift shop, where they ate their box lunches and listened to the patented garden-club talk his grandfather had written forty years earlier.

Finally, shortly after two, Joyce ushered the last garden clubber out the door and into the parking lot.

Wyatt collapsed onto his desk chair and drained the bottle of cold water Joyce brought him. "How was I?" he asked, as she sat in the chair opposite his.

"You were terrific," Joyce said. "You always are. Every single one of them wanted to adopt you and take you home and feed you. A couple of the younger ones? I think they had better plans."

Wyatt laughed and blushed.

"When is she leaving?" Joyce asked.

"Who?"

"Callie. You know I don't normally poke my nose into your business, but I have to be honest with you, Wyatt. If she's here for good, I'm leaving."

Wyatt's jaw tightened. "She leaves today. In fact, I told her this morning she had to be gone by lunchtime."

"She's still here. She took Bo over to Scout's house and she was gone for a couple hours, but now she's back again, and your dad is furious. He won't stay in your place while she's there, so he's been out cleaning the bird cages for hours now, and I don't think it's good for him to be out in the heat this time of day."

"Thanks, Joyce. I'll deal with it. Would you please lock up here, then go fetch Nelson and tell him the coast is about to be clear?"

Joyce smiled. "I'll be happy to."

He found Callie in the trailer's kitchen. She was barefoot, humming happily, and stirring something on top of the stove.

"What do you think you're doing?" he demanded.

"What's it look like I'm doing?" She didn't look up. "I'm fixing my spaghetti sauce for dinner tonight. It's Bo's favorite."

"Leave it," Wyatt said.

Now, she turned from the stove, still holding the spoon she'd been using on the sauce. "Oh, for Pete's sake, Wyatt. You know I don't have any place to stay. Why are you being such a complete dick about this?"

He pried the wooden spoon from her hand and dropped it in the sink. "We're getting divorced, Callie. That's what you wanted, and that's what you're getting. Despite your best efforts, I've managed to rebuild my life. Without you. I've tried to be nice, but nice doesn't work with you. So now, I need you to get your stuff and put it in your vehicle and leave."

"And go where?" she said, already pouting.

"I don't care where you go from here," he said, amazed at the fact that he really didn't. "Go back to your sister's, to a motel, whatever. But you're not staying here."

Wyatt reached into his pocket and peeled off four hundred-dollar bills. "This is all the cash I've got. And it's all you're getting until next month, so don't think you can come back here again for more."

She just stared at him. "You're really serious."

He took her hand, pressed the bills into her palm, and closed her fingers over them. "Serious as a heart attack."

"If Bo comes home from Scout's and I'm not here, he'll be heartbroken. I promised him spaghetti and garlic bread tonight . . ."

"Bo's used to you breaking your promises," Wyatt pointed out. "He'll get over it. You can call him after you find a place to stay."

Callie held up the crumpled bills. "And what am I supposed to do when this is gone? Sleep on a park bench? Eat at a shelter?"

Wyatt shrugged. "You might think about a job. But again, not my problem."

It took her two trips to pack her stuff into the Jeep. She banged the screen door as hard as she could both times. Finally, he heard the car's engine sputter and stall, and roar to life again. He heard the spin of her tires on the crushed-shell driveway as she sped down the road and out of his life. For now.

Monday was delivery day at the Sandbox. Grace found Rochelle standing in the dining room, clipboard in hand, as the Budweiser driver unloaded cases of beer and trundled them into the kitchen.

"I was wondering where you'd been," she said as Grace came around the bar to fix herself a cold drink.

"I've been everywhere . . . and nowhere," Grace replied. "I spent the weekend at Mitzi's condo." She gave her mother an apologetic smile. "Guess I should have called, huh?"

"Would have been nice," Rochelle said. "But you're an adult. I get that you need your privacy." She looked up from her invoices. "If you want to talk about what's going on with you, I'm happy to just listen."

"I'll give you the condensed version. Saturday, I went over to the house and found proof that J'Aimee really did vandalize and set fire to Arthur's house. Then I blackmailed Ben into agreeing to a financial settlement. I broke up with Wyatt. Did you see the news last night? Stackpole's wife caught him with another other woman at a restaurant in Sarasota, and it made the news last night. And then this morning, I dropped in on Paula and tried to convince her she should help us get Stackpole thrown off the bench. It's been a busy time, Mom."

"That's quite a list of accomplishments. Did I hear you say you broke up with Wyatt?"

"Yes," Grace said.

Rochelle sighed and patted her daughter's hand. "Oh, Gracie. Why?"

"His wife wants him back," Grace said. "Bo wants his parents back together." She shrugged. "It was probably inevitable."

"Doesn't Wyatt get a say in any of this?"

"He says he and Callie are never getting back together and that he wants to make a life with me, but . . ."

"But you're ready to give him up anyway?" Rochelle shook her head. "God, Grace. I could have sworn you were born with a backbone."

"This is not about standing up for myself! It's about reality, Mom. Callie will do whatever it takes to get her claws into Wyatt. She spent the night over there Friday, after she'd broken up with her boyfriend, and Wyatt wasn't even going to tell me. In fact, she told me—after I showed up at his place to pick up Sweetie. She met me at the door dressed in his bathrobe. And she made sure I noticed she wasn't wearing anything underneath."

"Do you actually think Wyatt slept with her? Or that he even wanted to?"

Grace took her time answering, slowly peeling the paper wrapper from a drinking straw. "No," she said finally. "But the point is . . ."

Rochelle waved her off. "The point is you don't trust the man. You don't trust his feelings for you. You don't trust his ability to see through his ex. And you don't trust yourself to work through any of this stuff in order to be with him," Rochelle said. "And that's a damned shame."

"I can't have this conversation with you," Grace said, twisting the straw wrapper into a tight spiral. "I appreciate that you like Wyatt, and you want us to be together, but I have to do what's right for me."

"And if I didn't love you so much, I would agree with you and let you alone," Rochelle said. "But I love you too much to watch while you let happiness slip right through your fingers. You walked away from Ben when you found out he was a cheater. And I supported you on that. One hundred percent. But honey, Wyatt's not Ben. Wyatt is good and loyal and true, and when I see the way he looks at you, and the way you look at him when you think nobody is watching, I know he's the one. I think you know it, too."

Grace pushed her drink away. "I don't know anything. That's the problem. Yeah, I think I love him. And I thought he loved me. But look what happened with Ben. I had no clue Ben was sleeping with J'Aimee, and they were literally doing it right under my nose. So how can I be sure Wyatt is the one? We only met two months ago."

"Just trust your feelings for him," Rochelle said gently. "And remember, nothing in this life is ever going to be one hundred percent for certain. But you can't just hide out, never risk getting hurt again. What kind of life would that be?"

"A safe one," Grace said.

"No." Rochelle shook her head vehemently. "Not safe. Boring. Sad. A total waste."

. . .

Grace sat on the bench on Coquina Beach and hugged Sweetie to her chest. The tide was out and a lone gray heron was stalking something in the calm shallow water. It was the same bench she'd sat on with Wyatt only a few days earlier. Sweetie wriggled in her arms, lifted her chin, and licked Grace's chin. She glanced down at the cell phone on the picnic table, for the tenth time in the past hour. Wyatt had called twice that morning and texted her half an hour ago.

His message was short and to the point. *She's gone. I'm not taking her back. You're what I want.*

He seemed so sure. Why couldn't she be like that?

Because, Grace thought. *Because you're the girl who painted her first apartment six different shades of white the first week you were living there. Because you dated Ben for two years and lived with him for another two before finally deciding to marry him.*

She'd waited and waffled after meeting Ben, and still she'd made a mistake. Maybe her mother was right. Maybe mistakes were inevitable. But maybe this time, she really had found *the* one. There was only one way to find out for sure.

Grace snatched up the phone and tapped the icon beside Wyatt's name. She wouldn't give herself any more time to think, wouldn't have second thoughts. This time around, she would just go with her heart.

"Grace?" Wyatt answered on the first ring.

"Don't talk," Grace said hurriedly. "Just tell me where you want to meet."

"Anywhere you want," Wyatt said. "Can it wait 'til I close up the park at five? Bo is at Scout's house. Dad can stay with him after I bring him back here. Are we all still meeting at the Sandbox tonight?"

"Yes, and yes," Grace said. "I'll be at Mitzi's condo."

65

Grace paced back and forth in the small living room, stopping every five minutes to look out the window at the parking lot, to adjust the drapes, fluff a pillow, or check her makeup in the mirror. She hadn't been this nervous about meeting a man since her first real car date at the age of fifteen. Her palms were actually sweaty.

She'd taken pains with her makeup and had actually changed outfits three times—not that she had that many changes of clothes to begin with—before settling on a pair of blue seersucker capris and a sleeveless white blouse. God help her—she'd even painted her toenails a vivid crimson shade called Sassy Lassie.

Sweetie lay on a throw pillow on the sofa, looking perplexed by Grace's nervous energy.

Grace was midway through her third circuit of the condo when her phone rang. She leapt to grab it, but paused when she saw the caller ID.

Ashleigh Hartounian. Probably, Grace thought, she was calling to ask about that night's get-together at the bar.

"Hi, Ashleigh," she said.

"Graaaace." Ashleigh was sobbing.

"Are you all right?"

"Nooooo," Ashleigh wailed. "I'm not okay. I'll never be okay."

"What is it?" Grace asked. "What's wrong?"

"It's . . . it's . . . Boyce."

Now Grace remembered: today was the day Ashleigh's ex-husband had invited her out to lunch. This was the day Ashleigh expected to win him back and return to her fairy-tale existence as the doctor's wife. Obviously, things hadn't gone as Ashleigh had anticipated.

"Do you want to talk?" Grace asked, hoping she didn't. She was standing in front of the window, craning her neck to see out to the parking lot, watching for Wyatt's car. It was after five.

"No! I'm so upset, I feel like my head is gonna explode."

"Well . . ." Grace started.

"That bitch Suchita!" Ashleigh said. "I should have expected she'd pull a stunt like this. That's all it is, a stunt, to try to trap Boyce."

"Suchita?" Grace was drawing a blank. A truck pulled into the complex's parking lot, but it wasn't Wyatt's.

"You know, Suchita. That little slut drug rep he's been sleeping with. She's the one who got me in trouble with Stackpole in the first place."

"Ohhh," Grace said. "The woman whose house you painted. Now I remember. What's she done to trap Boyce?" As soon as the words were out of her mouth, Grace had a sinking feeling she knew just what Suchita had done.

"She got herself knocked up! Or so she says. It's the oldest trick in the book, but Boyce is such a dummy he never saw it coming. Do you believe this shit?"

"Does this mean he didn't take you to lunch to get back with you?" *Dumb question,* Grace thought.

"He says they're getting married!" Ashleigh screeched. "As soon as our divorce is final. He only took me to lunch because he said he wanted to tell me himself, before one of the girls in the office spilled the beans. Do you believe that?"

Ashleigh was crying again, her wails so loud that Grace had to hold the phone a couple inches from her ear.

"That bitch!" Ashleigh said. "She's five months pregnant. That explains why she looked so fat when I saw her leaving his office last week. And it's a boy! Boyce is ecstatic. It was all he could talk about, the bastard. I wanted to slug him—I was so upset."

"I'm so sorry," Grace said.

"She's the one who's going to be sorry," Ashleigh said. "I'm not gonna let that bitch ruin my life."

"Ashleigh!" Grace said. "Get a grip. If she's pregnant and Boyce intends to marry her, there's nothing you can do."

"That's what you think. There's plenty I can do. And I will."

"Leave it alone, Ashleigh," Grace warned. "Do not do anything you'll regret. I know you're upset right now, but it's probably for the best."

"You don't know a damned thing, Grace," Ashleigh said, her voice suddenly harsh. "Just because you walked away from your marriage doesn't mean I'm ready to walk away from mine. I should have known better than to expect you to understand what I'm going through. I have no intention of letting that little home wrecker steal my husband."

Grace felt a chill go down her spine.

"Ashleigh, where are you right now?" she asked quietly. "I don't think you should be alone. Let's talk this through. I've been there, too, remember."

"Thanks anyway, but I'm not really in the mood for a chat right now," Ashleigh said.

"You're coming to the Sandbox tonight, right?"

"What's the point?" Ashleigh asked. "I told you last week I wasn't coming back to group sessions."

"Didn't you see the news the other night?" Grace asked. "Stackpole's wife caught him with another woman and raised a ruckus in a restaurant in Sarasota."

"Was the other woman Paula?" Ashleigh asked.

"No, that's what makes it all so deliciously sleazy. He was with a twenty-three-year-old woman who is one of the bailiffs in his courtroom. Highly un-ethical, of course."

"Does Paula know?" Ashleigh asked.

"Yup," Grace said. "I had a long talk with her this morning. I think she's this close to helping us file a formal complaint against Stackpole with the Judicial Qualifications Committee."

"And why would she do that?" Ashleigh asked.

"I think she knows he's been using her by referring all these divorcing women to her for therapy group and then forcing her to pay him kickbacks."

"Hah! Can you prove it?"

"Not yet," Grace admitted. "Just come hang out with us tonight at the Sand-box. I'll tell you the whole story then."

"I don't care about any of that," Ashleigh said abruptly. "That's somebody else's problem. Look, Grace, I gotta go now."

"Go where?" Grace asked. "Ashleigh, where are you? Are you at home? Is there somebody you could call to come over and stay with you for a while?"

"I'm in the car," Ashleigh said. "I've been driving around for hours. And I don't need a babysitter. I just wanted to talk to somebody. But I've made up my mind what I need to do."

"Ashleigh?"

The line went dead.

Grace cursed and tapped the redial button.

The phone rang twice.

"Leave me alone, Grace," Ashleigh said. "This is between me and her."

"Her?"

"You know exactly who I mean. Suchita. I'm gonna take care of business. Do what I should have done months ago, before things got out of hand."

"Ashleigh, stay away from that girl. You're angry and upset, but stalking her is not the answer. You'll only get yourself in more trouble."

"I don't care," Ashleigh insisted. "I don't care about anything. Except Boyce. He's all I have. He's the only thing in this world I give a damn about."

"Come on," Grace said. "That's not really true. You have family; you have friends . . ."

"What friends? You mean all those losers in group? Get real. None of y'all give a damn about me."

"We do," Grace said. "We all care about you. I care. You must know that, or you wouldn't have called me."

Silence.

"Ashleigh? Are you still there?"

"I'm here," Ashleigh said. She was crying again. "That's sweet, Grace. Really sweet. I'm sorry. I didn't mean to call you a loser. You're not like the others."

"You're upset," Grace said soothingly. She was looking out the window again, wondering what time it was.

"You said you're in the car. Where are you? Do you want to meet? We could get a cup of coffee and talk."

"I'm . . . oh, hell. I've just been driving around. I guess I'm at Bradenton Beach. But I don't want any coffee. A drink, maybe. Yeah, another margarita."

"Another? You've already had a margarita, and you're driving?"

"Just a couple. But they were little ones, and mostly ice. If you're gonna lecture me about drinking and driving, I'll hang up right now."

"No lecture," Grace said quickly. "Look, why don't you pull into the next gas station you see and call me back. I'm not far away at all. I'll come and meet you. How does that sound?"

"If you want to," Ashleigh said. "But I'm warning you. It won't change my mind."

"Call me right back," Grace said. "I'll meet you, wherever you are."

She left Sweetie napping in the condo and called Wyatt on the fly.

"Grace, hi," he said, sounding out of breath. "I know I'm late, but I had to go through the drive-through at Wendy's to get dinner for Bo. I'll only be another thirty minutes. Promise."

"Actually, that'll be fine," Grace said. "Ashleigh just called me. Today was the day her ex invited her to go to lunch. But instead of asking her to come back to him, he announced that his girlfriend is five months pregnant, and he's going to marry her as soon as their divorce is final."

"Oh, wow," Wyatt said. "And she was so sure he was going to get back with her. How'd she take the news?"

"About like you'd expect," Grace said. "She's obsessed with getting Boyce back, or at least keeping that girl from marrying him. She's been driving around, drinking margaritas, plotting some kind of revenge. I'm really worried she'll do something drastic. I'm going to go meet her and try and talk some sense into her."

"Is that a good idea?" Wyatt asked. "If she's been drinking?"

"I don't know what else to do," Grace said. "She's talking crazy. I'm afraid she might hurt herself—or somebody else."

"Please don't go meet her by yourself," Wyatt said. "Just wait thirty minutes, okay? I'll take Bo straight home, and then come by and pick you up. We can go together. She might listen if we both ganged up on her."

"Maybe," Grace said reluctantly. "But I promised I'd come right away, as soon as she pulls into a gas station. I'll try and stall her. But hurry, can you?"

"I'm ten minutes from home and another fifteen from the condo," Wyatt said. "Stay right there."

66

O kay, I'm here," Ashleigh said, without bothering with a greeting. "So, are you coming, or what?"

"Here, where?" Grace asked.

"Um, it's a Hess station on Manatee, but you better get here fast, because I do not like the looks of this place. It's definitely in the hood. The bathroom was so nasty I had to pee standing up."

"I'm trying to think where that is," Grace said slowly. "Like, what block of Manatee is that?"

"How should I know?" Ashleigh snapped. "I don't even know why I agreed to meet you. You can't change my mind, you know. That bitch Suchita is history. She's toast."

"Please don't talk like that," Grace begged. She hesitated, wondering if she should mention that Wyatt would be joining them. Stall her, he'd suggested. But that was no easy feat.

She gazed around the room and spotted Sweetie, who'd hopped off the sofa and was now sitting in front of the sliding glass doors facing the gulf.

"Look, Ashleigh, I just need to let Sweetie out for a potty break before I leave her alone," Grace said.

"Who's Sweetie?"

"My dog. She's a rescue, and I've got her over at a client's condo, but I don't dare leave her alone unless I take her out. Just give me fifteen minutes, okay?"

"You want me to hang around here for fifteen minutes? No way! You said you'd meet me right away. Hell, if I hang around here for another fifteen minutes, I could be carjacked. Shiiiiit," Ashleigh swore softly. "I knew this was a bad idea. Thanks anyway, Grace, but I gotta be moving on."

"No, don't leave there," Grace said hastily. "I'll come right now. You said you're at Manatee, but what's close by? What's the intersection and which corner? Give me a landmark, Ashleigh. I'm not really familiar with that part of town."

"For God's sake. I don't know. Let's see . . . um, yeah, there's a strip shopping center with a Bealls outlet right across from the Hess station."

"If you're worried about the gas station, drive over there," Grace suggested. "You can just go inside and wait until I pull up. Nobody's going to carjack you at a Bealls."

"Maybe." The other woman sounded unconvinced. "Or maybe I'll stay here and get a wine cooler while I wait."

"I really don't think you should have anything else to drink," Grace said.

"And I don't give a flying fuck what you think," Ashleigh retorted. "It's five forty-five right now. If you're not here by six, I'm history."

"I'm coming," Grace said hurriedly. "Stay right there."

Grace called Wyatt from her car. "Sorry, but I can't wait for you," she told him. "I'm meeting Ashleigh at the Hess station on Manatee. She's so antsy, I really couldn't stall her any longer. She's already talking about buying a wine cooler. I'll keep her there as long as I can, and hopefully you can meet us there."

Wyatt sighed loudly. "I don't like this Grace. If she's been drinking like you say she has, I don't think you're going to be able to reason with her. I think maybe you should call the cops and let them handle it."

"Ashleigh respects me. She'll listen to me," Grace said. "Don't worry. I'm just going to talk to her, calm her down, and persuade her to leave her car there and let me drive her home. She's not a maniac, Wyatt. She's upset, and she's talking smack, but I honestly don't think she's capable of really harming somebody—other than herself."

"I hope you're right," Wyatt said. "I just dropped Bo off with my dad. I'll be there in ten minutes. Okay?"

"Hurry," Grace said. And she disconnected.

She spotted the red BMW as soon as she pulled into the gas station. Ashleigh tooted her horn and waved. Grace parked in one of the slots in front of the convenience store and trotted over to Ashleigh's car.

The BMW's engine was running, and when the electric window slid down noiselessly and Grace bent down to talk to her friend, a blast of cold air hit her face. Grace's heart sank when she saw two empty wine-cooler bottles tossed in the passenger seat.

"Hey, Grace," Ashleigh said. Her face was pale and her usually flawless makeup was smeared and tear-streaked. "You know this is a waste of time, right?"

"I don't mind wasting my time," Grace said lightly. "Why don't we go over and sit in my car and talk?"

"Nuh-uh," Ashleigh said, shaking her head vigorously. "I like my car just fine." She patted the leather-upholstered passenger seat. "You can sit here." She reached down to the floor and pulled up a full key-lime-flavored wine cooler. "Look, I bought one for you. We can have a party. A pity party, right?"

"Um, I'm not really thirsty," Grace said. "Come on, Ashleigh. You've had too much to drink to be driving. Let's go sit in my car, and I'll drive you home. You can plot revenge against Suchita tomorrow."

"No effin' way," Ashleigh said. "Tonight's the night. That bitch is going down!" She tossed her blond hair defiantly over her shoulder. "And if you're gonna be such a buzzkiller, you can just go on to your divorce meeting. Because I've got stuff to do. See ya around, Grace." She rolled the window up.

"Wait!" Grace said, pounding the BMW's roof. She looked over her shoulder, hoping against hope to see Wyatt's truck. Ashleigh was definitely drunk, and in no mood to be reasoned with.

The window slid down again. "You comin' or not?" Ashleigh held up the wine cooler. Grace sighed and took it, crossing to the passenger seat.

Ashleigh popped the lock and Grace moved the empties aside before sliding into the passenger seat.

Ashleigh watched her expectantly. Grace uncapped the bottle and took a sip of the ultrasweet cooler.

"That's more like it." Ashleigh cackled. "Par-tay! Woo-hoo!" She threw the car into reverse and just as quickly into drive.

"Wait," Grace said, the back of her head slamming against the headrest. "Ashleigh, no! You're in no condition to drive."

"Don't be such a nag. I'm fine!" Ashleigh countered. She looked both ways, then zipped out of the parking lot and onto the highway, narrowly avoiding a collision with an oncoming white sedan before crossing the median into the far westbound lane.

Grace glanced over at Ashleigh, who looked back and laughed. "See? I told you. I'm fine. Those wine coolers have almost no alcohol in 'em, and anyway, I've got a really high tolerance. I can drink, like, half a dozen margaritas and not feel a thing. We're just a couple of girls, out cruisin', just like in high school. Didn't you and your girlfriends ever get a little buzzed and go cruisin'?"

"You're not fine," Grace said, groping for her seat belt. "And we're not in high school, and you're past being buzzed. Anyway, I thought we were just going to talk. Ashleigh, if you want to drive drunk, that's your decision, but I do not want to go along for the ride."

"Too bad," Ashleigh said. "I keep telling you I'm not drunk. Okay? You wanted to talk, let's talk."

Ashleigh wove the BMW in and out of traffic, twice coming so close to clipping another car, Grace finally just squeezed her eyes tightly and prayed, because she was too nervous to watch where Ashleigh was going.

"I want you to turn around and take me back to that gas station," Grace said through gritted teeth. "Or just pull over and drop me off. This isn't funny, you know."

"You're right; it's not funny. It's fuckin' tragic is what it is," Ashleigh said. Her eyes brimmed over with tears. "I tried calling Boyce while I was waiting for you. The number I had was disconnected. He just called me on it, like this morning. She did that. I just know it. One of her spies probably told her Boyce took me to lunch today. But what she doesn't know is—I've got spies of my own."

She fumbled in the center console of the car and came up with her cell phone. "Here. Grab the steering wheel," she told Grace.

Grace reached over and took the steering wheel with her left hand, grateful that the heavy flow of traffic on Manatee meant that Ashleigh was only doing about thirty miles per hour.

Ashleigh was squinting down at the list of contacts on her phone, scrolling down, looking for something.

"Who are you calling?" Grace asked.

"Here it is!" Ashleigh said triumphantly. She tapped the number and waited, and then frowned. "The bitch won't pick up. I bet Boyce told her not to talk to me."

"Suchiiiiita." Ashleigh's voice was low and spooky. "Pick up the phone, little mama. I've got a message for you. No? You don't wanna talk to me? That's okay. Cuz I'm coming for you, bitch. Remember? I know exactly where you live. And guess what? You can run, but you can't hide."

She disconnected the phone, dropped it into her lap, and took the steering wheel again.

Grace's mouth felt dry, and she felt beads of perspiration popping up on her forehead, despite the chill from the BMW's air conditioner. She glanced in the rearview mirror, but there was no sign of Wyatt's truck. She felt in the pocket of her shorts for her phone, found it, and slid it into her lap.

She had to call Wyatt, try to let him know what Ashleigh intended. Maybe he could call Boyce Hartounian and warn him that Ashleigh was on a rampage. She glanced over at Ashleigh, who seemed to be watching the road. She managed to thumb down her recent calls and tap Wyatt's number, but then the BMW suddenly swerved into the far left lane and, seconds later, without signal or warning, made a sharp left turn, crossing two lanes of oncoming traffic, earning her a blast of horns from the cars she narrowly avoided T-boning. Grace's phone flew out of her hand and slid down between the seats.

"Ashleigh!" Grace cried. "What the hell are you doing?"

The driver shrugged. "Sorry. Guess I cut it a little close, huh?"

"You nearly got me killed," Grace said angrily. "If you want to kill yourself, that's your business, but I want out of this car, right now. Pull over, dammit."

With her left hand, she tried groping the area beneath her seat, but the small phone eluded her grasp.

Ashleigh laughed. "Don't be such a chickenshit, Grace. Look, I'm barely doing thirty now."

It was true. They'd turned onto a quiet, treelined residential street. It was narrow, and cars were parked along the curbs on both sides, dictating a slower speed. Grace wondered if she'd managed to connect the call to Wyatt, wondered if he could hear them right now. She prayed it was so.

"What is this neighborhood?" she asked loudly.

"It's Newtown," Ashleigh said. "The bitch lives right around here, but I can't remember the name of the street. I'll know it when I see it, though."

She was scanning both sides of the street, looking ahead at the street signs.

They were going just slow enough, Grace realized, that she could escape the car without risking her life. She snaked her right hand over toward the passenger door, her fingers clasping the handle.

Click. Grace tugged at the handle, but it was too late.

Ashleigh laughed. "Childproof locks. Great invention, huh? Come on, Grace. Why do you wanna jump ship? I thought you were gonna be my wingman on this mission."

"I don't want anything to do with this," Grace said. "You're scaring me now, Ashleigh. Just pull over and let me out, okay? Or let me drive. You're in no condition to be behind the wheel. You're going to do something stupid and dangerous and end up in real trouble."

"Trouble?" Ashleigh glanced over at her. "What? Stackpole is gonna put me in remedial divorce counseling? Sentence me to community service again? You don't get it, Grace, do you? I don't give a rat's ass about any of that. I just want to give that bitch what she deserves. Once she's out of the picture, Boyce will realize what he's been missing."

Grace clamped her lips together. Finally, the reality of the situation dawned on her. Nothing she could say would sway Ashleigh's resolve. She glanced again in the rearview mirror. Was that a flash of red, a block back? Wyatt's truck? She said another silent prayer.

Ashleigh drove one block, turned right, drove two more blocks, and turned left. The truck sped up and seemed to be closing the gap between it and the BMW, but then it was forced to come to a halt as an enormous SUV backed slowly down a driveway and into the street, totally blocking it.

Come on, come on, come on, Grace chanted silently.

"This is her street!" Ashleigh muttered. "I knew it was around here." She made a sharp left and slowed the BMW to a crawl, craning her neck to see the numbers on the mailboxes.

If she hadn't been so thoroughly terrified, Grace might have been craning her neck, too. The street was lined with moss-draped oak trees, lawns with thick green grass, and neatly tended beds of flowers. The homes were cozy stucco and wood-frame bungalows built in the twenties and thirties, with welcoming porches and gabled roofs.

It was a storybook street, but Grace had a feeling that this story would not have a happy ending.

"Oh, yeah," Ashleigh said softly. "This is the right block." She glanced over at Grace. "You see this neighborhood? I checked—the cheapest house on this street sold for 377,000 dollars. And I'm living in a dump condo that rents for eleven hundred a month. Ask yourself how a twenty-eight-year-old drug rep affords a house here. I'll tell you how—she hooks up with a rich plastic surgeon and makes him her baby daddy."

She pointed to a house at the end of the street. "That's it. That's her place."

"What . . . what are you planning to do?" Grace checked the rearview mirror. No sign of the truck.

"I'm just going to talk to her, that's all," Ashleigh said, her voice singsongy. "Make her see that she needs to step away."

But as they were talking, they saw a silver Audi back swiftly down the driveway. They were three houses away. As soon as the Audi was on the street, it accelerated so quickly that the tires screeched on the pavement.

"That's her!" Ashleigh said. She sped up, but the Audi zipped through the next intersection without slowing down.

"She knows what my car looks like," Ashleigh muttered. She accelerated, closing the gap between the two cars.

The Audi made two quick turns, and Ashleigh stayed close, flying through stop signs. The Audi managed to stay two car lengths ahead, and never slowed down before making a left.

They were back on Manatee again, heading west. The Audi sped through the thinning traffic, darting in and out of lanes, but Ashleigh gripped the steering wheel and kept on the car's tail. They were doing sixty miles an hour now, somehow managing to make all the green lights. Grace kept looking in the rearview mirror, and when she glimpsed the red truck again, she began daring to hope. Wyatt was there, not far behind. He would think of some way to stop this crazy race.

The Audi sped up again, and Ashleigh did the same. They were only a car length behind now, and the BMW's speedometer was inching over seventy miles per hour.

The GULF BEACHES sign flashed by. "She's headed for Boyce's beach house on Anna Maria," Ashleigh said. "Like he can hide her. Dumb bitch."

Grace saw the fringe of Australian pines, white sands, and the glint of sunlight on the sparkling water of Palma Sola Bay. The Audi was still a car length ahead, but Ashleigh stomped on the accelerator, and the speedometer needle jumped. They were doing eighty-five now. The Audi wove in and out of traffic, and the BMW stayed right with it. They flew over the first causeway, and Grace held her breath, terrified Ashleigh might somehow send them both flying over the concrete bridge embankment and into the waters below. Her fears eased momentarily when they were over the bridge and into another stretch of causeway, lined on both sides by sandy beaches and the shallow waters of the bay, but not for long.

A lumbering dump truck loomed ahead of them in the right-hand lane, forcing the Audi to slow considerably. Ashleigh veered into the left lane and passed the dump truck. She slowed, waiting for the truck to pass on the right, and laughed triumphantly when she came alongside the Audi.

Grace glimpsed the driver as they pulled alongside the Audi—a long curtain of dark hair, and when the woman looked over and saw who was beside her, her face mirrored the look of shock and horror in Grace's own face.

"Gotcha!" Ashleigh screamed. She jerked the BMW's steering wheel hard to the right, but just as she did so, Grace heard the squeal of the Audi's brakes. The BMW veered off the road.

Grace had the sensation of time slowing. She heard screams—her own, Ashleigh's? She'd never be sure. She was aware of the car slamming through an expanse of corrugated metal fencing, of the windshield shattering, of the splintering of wood on metal as they glanced off a pine tree, and, moments later, of the rush of water.

And then it was quiet.

67

Wyatt pushed the old truck's accelerator all the way to the floor once he heard the one-sided conversation on Grace's call. He shuddered at the sound of Ashleigh's slurred speech. She was drunk, deranged, out of control. And Grace was strapped into the passenger seat right beside her, helpless.

As he closed the gap between the racing cars and his own, he saw Ashleigh's frenzied pursuit of the silver Audi, guessing the driver was Suchita, Ashleigh's romantic rival. He didn't have a clear idea of what he'd do if and when he caught up to the women, but he knew he would have to do something. He wondered, fleetingly, if Ashleigh had a gun. The only gun Wyatt owned was Nelson's old service pistol—but it was kept under lock and key in the file cabinet in the office. And what if he did have the gun? How would he use it? Shoot out the tires of a moving vehicle? Ridiculous.

A dozen awful scenarios flashed through his mind as he struggled to keep pace.

He wondered if the same scenarios occurred to Grace. Her voice sounded so calm, so cool on the other end of the phone. "Keep trying, Grace," he murmured.

They crossed the first bay bridge, and he managed to catch up to within two car lengths when a lumbering old dump truck forced everybody to slow down.

But in the blink of an eye, everything changed. He saw the BMW switch lanes, saw it pull alongside the Audi, and then deliberately try and sideswipe the other car.

The Audi's driver slammed on the brakes, and seconds later, to his horror, he saw the BMW veer off the road and plow through the metal fencing. He saw the cloud of sand spewed by the spinning tires, heard the crunch of metal on metal, and, worst of all, heard the hair-raising chorus of screams from inside the BMW.

And then nothing, except the pounding of his own blood in his ears, as he saw the car skimming into the jade green waters of Palma Sola Bay.

Wyatt was out of the truck almost before it stopped, with the only tool he had at hand, the heavy Maglite flashlight he kept under the front seat. He ran through the jagged opening in the fencing left by the BMW and waded into the warm, shallow water. The BMW was immersed up to its hood ornament. He cursed himself for not removing the thick-soled leather work boots that made his trek to the car take what seemed like hours.

Finally, he reached the car. The windshield was shattered, and water was seeping in. He could see that the air bags had deployed and were already deflated. He splashed over to the passenger side, and his heart leapt when he saw Grace's brown hair. He yanked furiously at the door, until he remembered that Ashleigh had locked it.

"Grace!" he shouted. "Grace. Are you all right?" She turned her head slightly to the right, and he could see a thin trickle of blood oozing down her face.

"Turn your head away," he shouted, and began hammering at the center of the window with the butt of the flashlight. He slammed it against the glass again and again, until finally the window seemed to crinkle into a million pieces and fall away.

"Give me your arms," he told her, but she stared at him, dazed or in shock; he wasn't quite sure. "Your arms!" he repeated. "I'm going to pull you out. Come on, Grace. I need to get you out of this water."

"I can't," she said, her voice weak. Wyatt grabbed her by the shoulder. "Come on, honey. You can do this."

She shook her head violently, fumbling with something in her lap. Wyatt stuck his head in the window and saw that her seat belt was still fastened and that water had reached her knees. He leaned in until his torso was in the car and, with shaking fingers, managed to unbuckle it.

"Okay," he said. "Okay. You're good now. Let's go, Gracie. Let's get you out."

Finally, she nodded, turned, and knelt on the seat, reaching her arms for him. He wrapped his own arms under hers. "Put your arms around my neck," he urged. He tugged while she wriggled, and, finally, she came free of the car, collapsing against him in the waist-deep water.

Wyatt stood there for a moment, holding her tightly against his chest, unwilling to let her go. "Are you hurt?" he asked. "Your head, legs, arms, anything?"

"I'm okay," she said shakily. And then, unbelievably, she laughed a little, whispering in his ear. "But I think maybe I peed my pants." He laughed, too, then. "Don't tell anybody, but I might have peed mine, too. Just a little, when I saw the car go airborne."

"Ashleigh," she said urgently. "Get Ashleigh out."

"I need to get you to the shore," he said, starting for the beach, but she pulled away.

"No. I can walk by myself. Get Ashleigh. Please, Wyatt."

He nodded grimly and turned back toward the BMW.

Ashleigh was slumped over in the driver's seat. He broke the window out with his flashlight, calling her name. "Ashleigh? Ashleigh? Talk to me. Come on, Ashleigh. It's Wyatt. Talk to me."

He reached in and touched the base of her neck. She was warm, and he could feel a pulse, but her breathing was shallow. Water was up to her lap and streaming in through the windshield and the passenger window. He wriggled halfway through the window and saw that, unlike Grace, Ashleigh hadn't fastened her seat belt. Which shouldn't have come as a surprise. He grasped the unmoving woman under the arms, in the same way he had grabbed Grace, but she was a dead weight. He backed out a little, trying for the door handle, already knowing it wouldn't open.

The water was still rising. It was chest-high. He grabbed Ashleigh again and tugged, inching her body in an agonizingly slow process. At some point, he was aware of the sound of sirens, of voices coming from the beach.

Finally, a rough arm grasped his. "We got this, buddy."

He turned and saw a pair of uniformed paramedics. "She's breathing, but she's unconscious."

"Thanks," one of them said. "You can step away now."

. . .

He found Grace sitting on the tailgate of the ambulance, wrapped in a blanket. A Band-Aid had been applied to the cut over her eyebrow. Sitting beside her, also wrapped in a blanket, despite the August heat, was a stunning brunette, who was shaking and crying uncontrollably.

It was Suchita, the driver of the Audi.

A female EMT had fastened a blood-pressure cuff to Suchita's upper arm. "You're all right," the woman said in a soothing voice. "Your blood pressure's a little high, but not off the charts. And your baby should be fine, too. But we can transport you to the hospital, if you'd like to get checked out."

"No!" Suchita said. "I want to wait for my fiancé. Boyce is on the way. He should be here soon. He's a doctor; he'll take care of me."

Wyatt nodded in Grace's direction, catching the EMT's eye. "Is she all right? Nothing broken?"

"She's good," the EMT said. "You're gonna want to watch her overnight, make sure she's not concussed, but otherwise the cut over her eye is the only thing. She was damned lucky."

Suchita turned and stared at Grace. "You're her friend? Why? Why did you let her come after me? She tried to kill me. She wanted to kill me and my baby."

"I didn't," Grace said, her voice a whisper. "I tried to stop her. But she'd been drinking . . ."

"She's crazy," Suchita said flatly. "I told Boyce she was dangerous. After she painted my house? I wouldn't stay there again. Not by myself. But she wouldn't leave me alone. She followed me, watched us if we went out together. And then she got my phone number, and she started leaving me messages. I told Boyce. I played him the voice mail messages she's been leaving me. He thought she was just trying to intimidate me. He said she wasn't dangerous." She shivered. "I only went home today to pick up my mail. And that's when she showed up."

Grace looked up at Wyatt. "Is Ashleigh . . . ?"

"She's breathing, but she's unconscious," Wyatt said. "She wasn't wearing her seat belt. I think maybe she hit her head."

"It all happened so fast," Grace said. "And I was so scared. I kept looking back, hoping you were there."

"I got there as quick as I could," Wyatt said. "But that damned SUV had the street blocked, and then, once she got out on Manatee and she was speeding, my old truck couldn't keep up. The whole thing starts to shimmy and rattle after I hit sixty."

"It doesn't matter," Grace said, clutching his hand. "You got here. You got me out of the car. You're here now. That's all that matters."

"I'm here, and I'm staying," Wyatt said, his voice choking with emotion. He looked over at the EMT. "Okay if I take her home now?"

Just then, a short, balding, middle-aged man came rushing up to the ambulance. Wyatt stepped back, but the EMT put out a hand to stop him from coming any closer.

"I'm a physician," he said, puffing out his chest. "Dr. Hartounian. This is my fiancée. Have you checked her vital signs? Did she tell you she's five months pregnant?"

"She checked out perfect," the EMT said. "Not a scratch on her. Physically, anyway." And she stepped aside.

"Suchita? My God! Are you all right?" Hartounian gestured toward the pair of EMTs who were bundling a stretcher into the second ambulance. "Is that really Ashleigh?"

"I'm . . . I'm . . ." Suchita's voice trailed and broke off into sobs as she threw herself into Boyce Hartounian's arms.

"It's okay, baby. I'm here. Boyce is here," he crooned tenderly, rubbing her back and arms. She was two inches taller than he, but his arms were tanned and muscular. He glanced over at Grace and his eyes narrowed.

"Who are you?" he asked, all business. "You're Ashleigh's friend? I just spoke to one of the police officers. They say the two of you had been drinking. What the hell were you thinking letting her get behind the wheel of a car? If anything happens to our child . . ."

"My name is Grace Davenport," Grace said, feeling her temper flare. "I wasn't the one who was drinking. That was all Ashleigh. And I didn't let her drive. In fact, I was trying to talk her into letting me take her home. She called me earlier, upset after your lunch with her . . ."

Suchita looked up. "You took her to *lunch*? Without telling me?"

Wyatt took Grace's arm and gently steered her away from the ambulance. He meant to take her home, get her in some dry clothes, let the shock wear off. But two uniformed police officers stood beside his truck, waiting for answers.

· · ·

An hour later, after giving her statement to the cops—and agreeing to a Breath-alyzer test to prove she hadn't been responsible for any of the half dozen empty wine-cooler bottles found in the BMW, Grace finally climbed into the front seat of Wyatt's truck.

He'd changed into the spare clothes he kept in a gym bag in the truck—his Manasota Maulers coaches' shirt, shorts, and a pair of baseball cleats.

"What do you think will happen to Ashleigh?" she asked, as Wyatt pulled slowly back onto the roadway.

Wyatt shrugged. "I know you feel sorry for her, but at this point, I hope they throw the book at her. Ashleigh very nearly killed three people today—four if you count Suchita's baby. She'll be charged with drunk driving, for sure. And it sounds like if Boyce Hartounian has his way, I guess they could add attempted homicide, or whatever you call it."

Grace grimaced at the mention of Hartounian. "What a pompous jerk!"

"He must have something the ladies love," Wyatt observed. "To have two hotties like Ashleigh and Suchita fighting over him."

"What he has is a nice big bank account," Grace countered. She closed her eyes and rested her head on the back of the seat. A moment later, she sat up again. "What time is it?"

"Nearly seven," Wyatt said. He closed his hand over hers. "Just rest, okay? I'm going to take you to the condo, let you get changed and showered. I called your mom, just to let her know what happened, so she won't be worried. And I talked to Nelson, to let him know I won't be coming home tonight. The EMTs told me you need to have somebody checking you through the night."

"No!" Grace said. "I mean, that's sweet and all that you want to take care of me. But everybody's meeting at the Sandbox tonight. Mitzi's coming, too. They're expecting me."

"Not a good idea," Wyatt said. "Why don't you just call your mom back and tell her to let everybody know you're not coming?"

"I can't call anybody. Remember? My cell phone is still in what's left of Ashleigh's car. Anyway, I have to go, and you need to be there, too. This is important, Wyatt. If we're going to file a complaint against Stackpole with the JQC, we need everybody to give Mitzi a statement. She's bringing women from Paula's other groups, too. And there's an outside chance Paula herself might show up."

"You think Paula's going to turn against her boyfriend?" Wyatt scoffed. "Now I know you've got a head injury."

Grace proceeded to fill Wyatt in on the Honorable Cedric N. Stackpole's not-so-honorable but very complicated love life.

"I told Paula about the meeting tonight, about what we're doing," Grace said. "She's really conflicted. But I think maybe she's tired of being victimized by him. I think there's an outside chance she'll show up and help us."

"Doubtful," Wyatt said, unconvinced.

"I don't care. Let's go straight to the Sandbox. I can shower and change there." She flashed a smile. "Please? I need you on my team."

He shrugged. "Team Grace? Okay. Sign me up."

68

R ochelle was carrying a tray of drinks and food to a table of softball players
at the back of the room when her bedraggled daughter came scuttling
through the side door of the Sandbox, trying not to be noticed.

She dropped the tray on the table, sloshing beer on the shortstop's cheese-
burger and sending the catcher's order of hot wings sailing off the plate and
into the second baseman's lap.

"Sorry." Rochelle tossed a dry bar towel to the coach, who was, thankfully, a
regular.

"Jesus H!" she exclaimed, hurrying over to Grace's side. She hugged her
daughter fiercely. "You look awful! Are you sure you don't need to go to the
emergency room?"

"I look worse than I feel," Grace said. "I'll be fine after I get a shower." She
looked over her mother's shoulder at the table in the corner, where a dozen
women chattered away. "Is everybody here?"

"Everybody except you two—and Ashleigh. If that girl's not dead already,
I'll kill her myself," Rochelle said.

"Did you tell the others what happened?" Grace asked.

"Just that there'd been an accident and that you were okay and Ashleigh was
taken to the hospital," Rochelle said. "I'll let you fill 'em in. If you're sure you feel
like it."

"Wyatt can do it while I get cleaned up." Grace leaned over and planted a kiss on Wyatt's cheek. He blushed, then kissed her back.

"I take it you two patched things up?" Rochelle asked as they watched Grace depart.

"I think so," Wyatt said. "I hope so. I can't go through another day like today. When I realized she was in that car with Ashleigh—the kind of danger she was in . . ."

He ducked his head and swallowed. "If something had happened to her? I honestly don't know what I'd do, Rochelle. I know it's crazy—falling in love with somebody you meet in divorce therapy? But I did. And I think she did, too. And when this is all over, I want us to get married."

Rochelle raised one eyebrow. "You're asking my permission?"

Wyatt laughed and blushed again. "I guess not. Just maybe for your approval. I know I'm not the best financial risk. She'd be going from that mansion she lived in with her ex to a trailer—literally. But I promise you, I love Grace, and I'll never hurt her. I'll spend the rest of my life taking care of her."

"Grace can actually take care of herself," Rochelle said. "Just make her laugh and smile and enjoy life like she used to. Be good to each other. The rest will work itself out."

Mitzi Stillwell dabbed at the beer rings on the tabletop with a paper napkin, then placed a thick file folder on it.

She looked at the eleven women arrayed around the two tables Rochelle had pushed together in a quiet corner of the bar. Camryn Nobles trained a small handheld video camera on Mitzi, then panned around at the other women.

Suzanne passed around the documents Mitzi had prepared: disclaimers, giving Camryn the right to film the women telling their stories and attesting that they were giving their statements of their own free will.

Harriett Porter cleared her throat nervously. Camryn gave her an encouraging nod. "Just pretend you're talking to a friend," she prompted.

Harriett licked her lips and began speaking. "We had our first hearing before Judge Stackpole back in December. I, er, did something I now regret, and Judge Stackpole was very, very angry with me."

"What exactly did you do that made him so angry?" Camryn asked.

"Well, I found out that my husband was having an affair with a stripper . . ." She looked at Camryn. "Is it okay to say it was a male stripper?"

Camryn laughed and nodded.

"Okay, so it was this guy. Named Anubis. I guess that was his stripper name. Anyway, Daryl, that's my husband, was putting tens of thousands of dollars on our American Express card at this place in Tampa called Jeepers-Peepers. I was getting our tax stuff ready for the accountant, which is how I found the AmEx bills. And, well, I, uh, um, I went over to that place one Thursday afternoon, Jeepers-Peepers, and I saw him—Daryl, that is, standing in the parking lot, and he was stuffing money into this guy's—what do you call it? Not a G-string, if it's a man, right? It was sort of a sequined jockstrap."

"Actually?" Thea, an attractive woman in her early fifties raised her hand. "Technically, it's not a jockstrap. It's called a codpiece. I know because I'm from New Orleans."

"Thanks, hon," Harriett said. "He was stuffing fifty-dollar bills into this stripper's codpiece. Right there in broad daylight! And it made me so mad, I lost it. Literally. One minute I was trying to take pictures of Daryl and his boyfriend with my phone, and the next minute I had crashed the car into a Dumpster. The police said I ran over Daryl's foot. I don't remember that part. I do remember he was wearing the four-hundred-dollar Italian loafers I bought him for Father's Day."

Camryn's chest was heaving with silent laughter, and tears were rolling down her face. Harriett was too caught up in her story to notice the reporter's reaction.

"Judge Stackpole called me a renegade!" she said angrily. "My lawyer said I should get half of Daryl's pension plan—I never worked after we married, because he wanted me to stay home with our children. But Stackpole told me I was an able-bodied woman and I should get a job and stop being a leech. And then he told me he wouldn't sign off on our divorce until I completed this divorce-recovery counseling. With a woman named Paula Talbott-Sinclair. Who I later found out isn't even licensed to practice therapy in this state!"

"Did the judge give you the option of seeking treatment with any therapist? Or did he specify Ms. Talbott-Sinclair?" Camryn asked.

"He handed me her business card, right there in the courtroom," Harriett said. "And he said she would have to notify him that I'd completed six weeks of sessions before he would grant our divorce."

Harriett's face was pink with indignation. "She charged me nine hundred dollars a session. Later, after I talked to some other women in the group and we began comparing notes, I found out they were only paying a third of that! And the thing is, I'm still pissed off at Daryl. I haven't recovered from our divorce at all. I don't know if I ever will."

"Thank you, Harriett," Camryn said soberly. She put the camera down and beamed at the women around the table.

"That was great. Who's next?"

Suzanne took a deep breath and a sip of her iced tea. She was wearing a bright orange top and a flattering new shade of lipstick, and she'd had her hair cut and colored.

"Shall I go?" she asked.

"Oh my God," Grace whispered. She was seated, facing the door, when a slender woman with unruly blond curls opened the door of the Sandbox and looked around hesitantly. She stood in the doorway, scanning the room, looking for something.

Grace jumped up and waved. "Paula! We're over here."

Conversation at the table came to an abrupt halt as Paula Talbott-Sinclair timidly approached the table. She stopped a few feet away, looking at Grace for guidance.

"What's she doing here?" one of the women said angrily, jumping up from her seat and snatching up her pocketbook. "Spying on us for Stackpole?"

Paula's already-pale face blanched.

"I invited her," Grace said, standing. She reached out a hand for the therapist. "Paula? There's an empty seat right here, beside mine."

Paula's lower lip trembled. "I don't want to intrude. Maybe it would be better if I didn't stay."

"No," Camryn said. "Stay."

"Please," Suzanne said.

When she was finally seated, Rochelle hurried over to take the newcomer's order.

"Mom?" Grace said politely. "This is Paula. Paula, this is my mom, Rochelle."

"The therapist?" Rochelle looked from Paula to Grace to Wyatt. "You're the therapist?"

"Counselor," Paula corrected. "And I'll just have iced tea, please. Green, if you have it." She lowered her voice and leaned in closer to Grace.

"How's Ashleigh? Have you heard anything?"

"You know about Ashleigh? Already? Has it been on the news?"

Paula shook her head. "Ashleigh called me this afternoon. I guess it must have been before you went to meet her. And then a detective called me just before I came over here. The police retrieved Ashleigh's cell phone, and they were following up on all her recent calls. They wouldn't tell me much—just that she'd made an attempt on another woman's life and nearly killed herself in the process."

Grace stared at the therapist. "Let me get this straight. Ashleigh called you? Today?"

"She called me at the office, and I just happened to pick up. She'd obviously been drinking. She was ranting and raving about getting revenge against— what's the other woman's name?"

"Suchita."

"Right. Suchita. Ashleigh was manic. It was hard to get a word in edgewise. I begged her to come to the office, to talk things over, but she wouldn't hear of it. She was cursing and making all kinds of wild threats. She talked about setting fire to her ex's house or somehow poisoning the woman."

Paula shook her head. "Ashleigh was in a very dark place."

"I still don't understand why she called *you*," Grace said. "No offense, Paula, but she thought you were a quack."

"I'm well aware," Paula said. "She told me that several times today. But I think Ashleigh knew she was spinning out of control. She was desperate for help." Paula looked around the table, recognizing all the faces arrayed around it.

"I failed Ashleigh. And I failed all of these women." She glanced over at Wyatt, who was sitting on the other side of Grace. "And I failed you, too."

Paula squared her shoulders and addressed Grace. "You said your lawyer would be at this meeting. Is she here?"

Mitzi raised her hand. "Mitzi Stillwell, attorney at law."

Paula motioned to Camryn. "You can turn on that camera now. I'm ready to tell my story. All of it. If you're ready to hear it."

"I met Cedric at a cocktail party, soon after I moved down here. We struck up a conversation. He seemed interested in my work—I told him about the seminars

I'd done out west and about the book. And—I guess I rattled on a little too long about the end of my marriage. He was sympathetic, and it was clear he was attracted to me . . ."

Paula looked directly into the camera. "I know this sounds incredibly lame—but at the time I had no idea he was married. If I'd known then—I would never have started an affair. Not after the way my own marriage ended. That's no excuse, I know. I should have made it my business to ask more questions, when he never wanted to meet me in public, insisted on meeting at my place. Maybe I didn't really want to know. Cedric is the first man I've been intimate with since my divorce.

"Maybe a month after we'd started seeing each other, he confessed he was married. I was shocked, tried to break it off, but he seemed committed to ending his marriage and being with me. I gave him my book and suggested he read it. Not long after that, he suggested that he should refer clients to me—clients whose divorces he was presiding over.

"It didn't occur to me that this was a breach of ethics. I was flattered and delighted that a distinguished judge thought I could assist these people."

"Oh for God's sake," Camryn said, pausing the video. "Paula, are you trying to tell us that it never occurred to you that you'd hit the motherlode with Stackpole making these counseling sessions mandatory? Come on! You were making fifteen hundred dollars a week just from the people in my little group."

Paula bit her lip and looked away. Rochelle brought her iced tea. She took a long sip. "I'll answer that on camera, if you like."

"When I moved here, I was very nearly destitute. I'd been in rehab and lost my license to practice in Oregon. When my husband and I divorced, we sold our home there at the very bottom of the market, for what amounted to pennies on the dollar, and, of course, he got half of that. I moved to Florida with my clothes, my car, and very little else. I was living in a motel room and working part-time as a social worker in a nursing home when I met Cedric.

"Cedric thought I should go into private practice again. He suggested I could get around Florida's tough licensing laws by not calling myself a therapist or a marriage counselor. He loaned me the money to rent my office space and buy a computer and some secondhand office furniture. Start-up funding, he called it.

He was hearing so many divorce cases. He said there was a real need for the kind of therapy I offer. And he said it could very lucrative."

"I'll say it was lucrative," Harriett put in. Camryn swung around in her seat and focused the camera on her. "With what I paid you alone in the past six months, you could have bought a nice midsized sedan. And yet you're still driving that dinky little toy car and operating out of that dump office. What happened to all the money? We heard you had a drug problem. Is that where it all went?"

Camryn chuckled, as did several other women at the table, although not Grace and not Suzanne.

Paula winced.

"That's a fair question, Harriett. I'm guessing by mentioning my drug problem you're referring to my arrest for forging prescriptions for tranquilizers in Oregon. I completed my court-ordered rehab out there, and I was doing reasonably well until I got involved with Cedric. And then . . . well, I can't sugarcoat it, can I? I had a relapse. Obtaining drugs is much easier in Florida. I went to a storefront clinic, got a script, and I was in business again.

"You want to know where the money went? Not to drugs. I'm clean again. Most of it went to Cedric. Right off the bat, he told me my fee schedule was a joke. He said the patients he was referring to me were screwed up and desperate to get out of their lousy marriages. Why shouldn't they pay, and why shouldn't he be compensated for all those referrals? Especially since he'd already 'loaned' me all the money to get on my feet again."

"Kickbacks," Mitzi said succinctly. "You were paying him kickbacks? How much?"

"I can't give you a precise figure," Paula said. "But I only kept roughly a third of my fees. The rest I handed over to Cedric."

"How did you pay him?" Mitzi asked. "Cash, check? Do you have any records?"

Paula looked puzzled. "You mean receipts? Don't be absurd. Remember, Cedric was a lawyer before he was a judge. He's really quite brilliant."

"Then, how did you pay him?" Camryn asked from down the table. "If we're going to be able to make charges stick against Stackpole, Mitzi here is going to need some proof."

"I understand," Paula said. "I was getting to that, Camryn, if you'll just be patient."

"Sorry." Camryn flashed a grin and started filming again.

"Cedric's wife kept all their household accounts. He said she watched every penny he earned or spent. I know she was pretty wealthy in her own right, and he resented that—she didn't work, but she controlled the purse strings. He was very careful. He set up a janitorial business called Clean Sweep. All the money I paid him, I wrote out the checks to Clean Sweep. It was supposed to be for nightly cleaning and paper supplies, things like that."

"But it was a dummy corporation?" Mitzi asked.

"As far as I know, I was Clean Sweep's only client," Paula said. "And I never got any janitorial services. I cleaned the office myself."

"Sounds like you got taken to the cleaners yourself, girlfriend," Thea chimed in.

Paula sighed. "He said he loved me. But he'd signed a prenup before marrying his wife. If he left, he'd be living on a judge's salary. Peanuts, he called it. The money I gave him, he called it our nest egg. We were going to buy a cottage on Anna Maria. I was going to work on getting my licensing back. He'd leave the bench, start his own law firm. We'd give our own version of my old divorce diversion seminars and travel all over. We'd write a book together. He even had a title: *De-Toxing After Divorce.*"

"Damn!" Camryn said. "That's a fabulous title. I'd buy a book called that. You know, if it was written by somebody other than Stackpole."

"And me," Paula said. She shrugged. "That's all I came to say, really. I'm sorry I allowed all of this to happen. Sorry I was a party to Cedric's scheme. Sorry I failed all of you. Could you turn the camera off now, please, Camryn?"

Camryn set the camera down carefully on the tabletop.

"Thank you, Paula," Grace said. "I mean it. Your coming here tonight and telling your story, that took a lot of courage. We all appreciate it, don't we, ladies?" She looked around the table, but the women returned only blank stares.

Suzanne stood up. She clapped her hands together. Slowly. Grace nodded and stood, too, and began clapping, as did Wyatt. They looked expectantly at Camryn, who nodded, stood, and joined in. Slowly, one by one, all the women at the table stood and joined in the polite applause.

69

Wyatt tiptoed into the bedroom and set the teacup on the nightstand. He hurried to the windows to draw the curtains. The EMTs had versed him in postconcussion rules—no bright sunlight, sharp noises, or too much physical activity. Plenty of sleep, plenty of fluids, plenty of watchfulness. Grace had fallen asleep in the truck the previous night, just minutes after they'd left the Sandbox.

He'd hurried her into bed, and spent the night on the armchair beside it, waking occasionally, to listen to her soft, steady breathing, gently touch her hair, and to reassure himself that she was here and she was safe.

It was nearly ten now. Sweetie trotted into the room and sat expectantly at his feet. He tossed her a treat, and she chewed noisily.

"Shh," he cautioned.

Grace turned on her side and sat up slowly. "Oh, stop tiptoeing around! I'm awake, and I'm fine." She patted the bed and Sweetie jumped up, did a quick circle, and then settled herself into a nest just under Grace's arm.

Wyatt dropped a kiss on Grace's forehead and sat down on the few inches of bed the little dog hadn't claimed.

"How's the head?"

"A little achey, but better than it felt last night." She glanced at the clock on the nightstand. "It's ten already! Why didn't you wake me?"

"You needed to sleep," he said. "And the EMTs told me you should take it easy for the next few days."

"But I don't need a babysitter. And you need to get to work. So move along, mister," she ordered.

He held four fingers in front of her face. "How many?"

"Four."

"How did you get hurt?"

She rolled her eyes.

"Humor me," Wyatt said. "I'm supposed to test your memory."

"I was in a speeding car driven by a maniac. We went off the road and into the bay. Things get a little blurry after we hit the water. I do know you pulled me out and saved my life."

"And then you promised to love me forever and be my sex slave," Wyatt prompted.

"That part I don't remember," Grace said.

He shrugged. "It was worth a shot."

Wyatt pulled a bottle of Tylenol from his pocket and gestured to the tea. "Drink that and take two of these. And then drink some more. You're supposed to stay quiet today. I've already walked Sweetie, and there's some cereal and fruit in the kitchen. I've got to get over to the park now, but your mom will be by after the lunch rush is over."

"Run along now," Grace said. "You're sweet, but I really don't need babysitting and I hate being fussed over."

"Humor me," he said. "I nearly lost you yesterday." He thumped his chest meaningfully. "I love you, Grace. Really, deeply, truly."

"I know it." She yawned and her eyelids drooped. "I think I love you, too. But I think I need another nap."

70

G race slept. And then she slept some more. Despite her protests and much to her annoyance, Wyatt and Rochelle continued to cosset her.

After a week had gone by she'd had enough. When Wyatt showed up at the condo after work that Friday afternoon, he found her fully dressed, tapping away at her laptop at the dining room table.

"Hey you," he said, unsnapping Sweetie's leash and setting down the bag of take-out Chinese. "What's that?"

"My blog. I haven't written a word in nearly two weeks. I'm afraid my readers will think I'm dead."

He tried to read over her shoulder, but she shielded the screen with both hands. "It's not ready for public consumption yet. My writing has gotten sort of . . . rusty. I'll let you read it after I've cleaned it up and edited a little."

"Okay." He opened one of the white paper sacks. "Which do you want for dinner? Kung pao or sizzling shrimp?"

"Neither, thanks," Grace told him. "I've been stuck here for what feels like forever. Let's go out. I don't care where, just as long as I'm not staring at these four walls and eating Tylenol."

Wyatt nodded at the view out the French doors. "You're bored looking at the Gulf of Mexico?"

"I don't want to *look* at it anymore," Grace said. "I want to walk in it, splash in it, get wet, sweaty, sandy—anything but safe and sleepy, which is what I've been all week long."

"You're sure you feel like that?" Wyatt looked at her anxiously. "No headaches? Funny smells?"

"I am absolutely symptom-free and bored to tears. And I am truly grateful for all the loving care you and my mom have given me this week. I know you must have been neglecting Bo and your dad, not to mention work."

"We aren't exactly swamped at Jungle Jerry's this time of year," Wyatt said. "Yesterday we did exactly sixty-two dollars in admissions. Anyway, Dad understands, and Bo's just happy he's gotten to spend so much time with Sweetie. In fact, he sent you this."

Wyatt reached into the pocket of his shorts and handed her a carefully folded sheet of paper.

"Awww," Grace said softly. It was a crayon masterpiece, vividly rendered in black and orange and green and red, with spiky objects erupting from what looked like either a garbage can or a spaceship. Written in exuberant red letters across the bottom was a caption reading, "GRACE, GET BETTER SOON. Luv, Your Freind Bo."

"We're working on the spelling thing," Wyatt said. "But you'll notice he spelled your name correctly. And his, too."

Grace outlined the drawing with her fingertip. "I love it. What's it supposed to be?"

"Silly girl," he chided her. "That's a bouquet of red roses. He wanted to buy you some from the QuikTrip, but since they were plastic, which I assumed would offend your sensibilities, I suggested he draw you some instead."

"I'm going to have this framed and keep it forever. He really is the sweetest, most thoughtful boy."

"He gets that from me," Wyatt said modestly. "And lest the son outshine the father, I brought you a present from me, too." From the other pocket he produced her cell phone.

"My iPhone!" She touched the ON button and the screen lit up. "It works! How did you manage this?"

"The cops told me where Ashleigh's car was towed, and Tuesday morning, after I left you, I bribed, er, tipped the salvage guy twenty bucks to let me retrieve it."

"But it must have gotten wet. It was ruined."

"It did get wet. But I went online and read some stuff about how to save it. Turns out, if you don't turn the thing on, which I didn't, and just put it in a plastic bag full of uncooked rice and let it sit for a couple days, to let the rice absorb the moisture, there's a good chance it might still work."

Grace turned the phone over and over. "It's ridiculous how much I missed this thing. I've felt like I was in solitary confinement without it."

Wyatt looked a little guilty. "I actually powered it up yesterday. I couldn't help but notice, you had some missed calls. And some voice messages."

Grace scrolled down her call log. Lots of missed calls. One from Paula Talbott-Sinclair, one from Arthur Cater, some out-of-area numbers she didn't recognize—and three calls from Ben, and two voice mails. She gave Wyatt a questioning look.

"I didn't listen to any of them, I swear. Although I'll admit I was tempted. If you want to listen now, or call anybody, I can come back in a little while."

Part of her was tempted to send him away, to hunker down with the phone, catch up with the world—and find out why her soon-to-be ex had called her more times in the past week than he had in the previous three months. And then she glanced out the window, at the sun sparkling on the water, at a handful of late-afternoon beach strollers.

"It can wait," she said, tucking the phone into the pocket of her shorts. She whistled for Sweetie. "Let's go."

They picked up grouper sandwiches and a couple of $1.50 beers at the Rod and Reel Pier, eating them on the lower deck, watching the fishermen, and chatting about life. Sweetie sat expectantly at their feet, waiting for her share of their dinner.

"Betsy called me today to say a new judge has been assigned to my divorce," Wyatt told her. "Charlie Davis. She says he's fairly young but has a good reputation. And he's speedy. His nickname is Rocket Docket Davis. She thinks it'll only be a matter of weeks now."

"That's good," Grace said, trying to sound noncommittal. "Mitzi dropped by earlier today. She says we finally got the luck of the draw with Catherine Chandler. She's the senior judge—and what Mitzi calls a card-carrying feminist. She expects Dickie Murphree and Ben will squawk about it, but there's not a damned thing they can do about it." While she spoke, her hand hovered unconsciously over the pocket with her cell phone.

"Go ahead and listen to your messages and voice mails," Wyatt said. "I know the suspense is killing you. I'm gonna go back upstairs and get a slice of key lime pie. Text me when you're done, and we can go for that walk I promised."

"You sure?" Grace flashed him a grateful smile.

"Grace?" Arthur Cater seemed to be shouting into the phone. "Are you there? Listen, I had a visit from your, uh, husband. I guess he's still your husband? Anyway, he straightened me out on a couple of things, and afterward, the wife and I got to talking. She's got her heart set on you finishing up your work on the house on Mandevilla. The upshot is, we'd like to sell you the place if you're still interested. You better call me quick, though, before I list it with an agent."

"Yippee!" Heads turned as Grace stood and did a modified happy dance, right there in the middle of the Rod and Reel Pier.

She took a swallow of beer and hit the call-back button.

"That you, Grace?" Arthur was still shouting. "I was beginning to think maybe you'd found another project for yourself."

"Not at all, Arthur! My phone and I were out of commission for a few days, so I just now got your message. I would absolutely love to talk to you about buying Mandevilla." Her heart was racing—she was so excited—but she knew she had to ask the hard question. "Do you have any idea how much you'd want for it?"

"What I want and what I'll take are two different matters," he said, chuckling. He named his price, and Grace's pulse blipped and her mouth went dry.

"You still there?" he hollered.

"I'm here, Arthur. But you must know, the house is worth at least fifty thousand more than that."

"It's probably worth seventy-five thousand more than that," he corrected her. "But my accountant says if we make too big a profit, I'm gonna get screwed over at tax time. More importantly, my wife swears she'll nag me into the grave unless I see to it that you finish what you started with that little old cracker house."

"I really want to meet your wife, Arthur," Grace said.

"That can be arranged. So . . . what do you say?"

She chose her words carefully. "I want to say you've got a deal. Right now. But to be honest, my divorce settlement is still up in the air. We've got a new judge, though, and my lawyer thinks everything should be settled pretty soon."

"Fair enough. You call me when it's all settled, then, will you?"

"The minute I know something, I'll call. And thanks, Arthur. Really. Thanks."

Grace took another sip of her beer and stared out at the water. A school of fingerling mullet slashed just below the surface of the green water, and a couple of screeching gulls swooped in to pick off a few.

Arthur said Ben had paid him a visit. Whatever he'd told the old man, it had been enough to change his mind about selling her the house. She wondered if her own mostly idle threats to tell the police about J'Aimee's involvement in vandalizing the house had prompted the visit to Arthur.

She turned the phone over and over in her hand. Part of her was dying of curiosity, part of her dreaded hearing Ben's voice. There was only one way to find out what he wanted. She listened to the first voice mail he'd left—which had been Monday evening.

"Hey, uh, it's me. Give me a call."

Tuesday morning, he'd left another message.

"Okay, Grace, if you're trying to be coy, it's not working. Call me, okay? I've, uh, got a proposition for you."

A proposition? Did she even want to know? Yes. She did want to know exactly what Ben was up to. Without giving it much more thought, she touched the redial.

"Grace?" Ben sounded . . . different. "Listen, I didn't know about the accident. Your lawyer just called Dickie about getting together to finalize the settlement, and she mentioned you'd had a head injury. What a hell of a thing. Are you all right?"

"I am now. Are we finalizing a financial settlement? Is that the reason you called?"

"It's one of the reasons. Uh, there have been some changes around here, and I thought I should let you know about them. Before it's final and everything."

"Oh-kayyy," she said slowly. Where was this going? Why was he being so civil? Maybe he'd been hit on the head, too?

"First off, I'm getting ready to list the house and move," he said briskly. "Dickie informs me that the new judge will probably make me split the proceeds with you, so he says I have to let you know, in case you have any interest in buying out my half."

"You're moving? Where? Why?"

"It's time," he said. "I've had a job offer from a big-time agency in New York. They're opening a new media division, and it's too good an opportunity to pass up. But they want me up and running right after Labor Day, which doesn't give me a lot of time to sell the house and find a new place."

Her mind was racing. "What about the blog? What about J'Aimee? Will she move with you?"

There was a long stretch of dead silence on the other end of the phone.

"No. J'Aimee is not part of the new package," Ben said. "If you must know, she's gone. As for the blog, well, that was another reason for my reaching out to you."

"I see."

"If you've been following it, you probably noticed that our sponsorships were down, and the numbers had stagnated. I won't get into the reasons for that."

A smile played across Grace's lips. Of course Ben wouldn't get into the reasons why Gracenotes had tanked. It had tanked because it was Graceless. Not that she'd rub that in his face.

"I still think it's a good business model," Ben was saying. "For the right person. Somebody like you. Anyway, if you want it back, it's yours. I'll send you the new passwords and the contact info for the current advertisers. We can work out a payment schedule as we go."

Was that a compliment he was sneaking in under the radar?

"Where is all this going, Ben?" she asked.

"Shit." He sighed.

"Ben?"

"What? You want me to grovel? Beg for forgiveness? Not my style, Grace, and you know it."

"You sure know how to charm a girl," Grace said, her tone acidic.

He sighed. "Sorry. This isn't easy for me. A lot's happened, Grace. Do I regret what happened? Yeah. I do. J'Aimee was a mistake. Huge mistake. And I take responsibility for that. I'd like to think I'm a better man than that."

"You used to be a better man than that," Grace said quietly. "But there's a lot I regret, too. Drowning your car was not one of my finer moments."

He laughed. "Nor mine. But I guess I probably had it coming."

"So. Where does this leave us?" she asked.

"I guess you don't want to buy out my share of the house?"

She shuddered. The fact that Ben had just given her the closest thing to an apology she'd ever get from him didn't mean she ever intended to spend another night in the house where he'd betrayed her.

"No thanks."

"Didn't think so. I'll e-mail you the listing agreement. You can let me know if you think the asking price is realistic. I'd like to get out from under it as quickly as possible."

"Whatever you want," Grace said. "The faster it sells, the faster I can buy a house for myself."

"Yeah. About that. I went to see the old man over there on Mandevilla."

"Arthur. He told me. And he offered to sell it to me for a price I can't pass up."

"Good," Ben said gruffly. "You should have a house of your own. And that place suits you, Grace."

She was touched. "Thank you, Ben. That's the nicest thing you've said to me in a really long time."

"See? I'm not a jerk one hundred percent of the time."

"I know you're not."

"You might share that thought with Rochelle. She doesn't have a very high opinion of me."

"Mom? Have you talked to her recently?"

"Saw her today, as a matter of fact. After Dickie told me you'd been in an accident, I took flowers for you over to the Sandbox. She told me you weren't there, but she wouldn't say where you were staying. I'm guessing you've moved in with the new guy?"

Was that a note of jealousy she detected?

"No, I'm not living with Wyatt," she said.

"None of my business, but are things pretty serious between the two of you?"

She couldn't resist. "I'll answer that if you'll tell me what happened to J'Aimee. You said she's gone? Did she leave before or after you accepted the new job?"

"You first," Ben said.

"Yes, things are fairly serious between us. But his divorce isn't final yet, either, and he has a young son, and there are complications with his ex. All that aside, he's a great guy, and I think we have a future together. Now, you."

"Christ," he grumbled. "J'Aimee's moved to California. End of story."

"Nuh-uh, you don't get off that easy," Grace chided. "What's she doing in California?"

"Auditioning for some crazy reality show she read about on the Internet. Look, Grace, I gotta go."

"Not before you tell me what kind of a reality show," Grace said. "You owe me at least that much, Ben."

He mumbled something incoherent.

"What's that?"

He mumbled again.

"I can't make out what you're saying, Ben."

"It's called *Homewreckers*. Got that? I came home from golf last week and she'd packed her crap and loaded up her car and announced she was going to Hollywood to get a part in a reality show about women who sleep with married men. In other words, home wreckers."

Grace laughed so hard, she couldn't catch her breath.

"Glad you're amused," Ben groused.

"Sorry," she said, gasping for air. "Very sorry. Good-bye Ben."

Wyatt came back and shared his key lime pie with her, and it was so good, she made him buy her a second slice. Then they got in the truck and drove up the beach. They didn't discuss it, but Grace had a feeling she knew where they were headed.

He parked the car at Coquina Beach. "We're still not supposed to have a dog on this beach," Grace pointed out, nodding at Sweetie, who was perched in her lap.

Wyatt opened his door and then came around and opened hers. "I won't tell if you won't tell."

They left their shoes on the soft carpet of pine needles and walked down to the water's edge. Grace stood still and let her toes sink into the pale gray sand. She looked down at the warm water swirling around her ankles, at the foam frosting the waves as they lapped at the shore. A lifetime ago, she'd felt a suffocating panic, strapped into Ashleigh's car, with the water rising around her knees. Now, with Wyatt's hand clasped in hers, she felt as light as the gull's feather that floated past.

She inhaled and exhaled. "This is good. This is what I needed."

They walked for nearly an hour, until the brilliant orange sun hovered just above the tops of the Australian pines. Then they found a picnic bench and settled in to watch the show.

"I talked to Ben," she said, with Wyatt's arm thrown casually around her shoulders.

"Oh?"

"He's ready to settle. I think his lawyer saw the handwriting on the wall. Anyway, it turns out he's accepted a new job in New York. He's moving immediately, and he wanted to know if I wanted to buy out his share of the house."

"The mansion?"

"Whatever. There's nothing there for me now."

"Is the girlfriend going with him?"

"No. She's gone to seek her fame and fortune in Hollywood. Ben didn't sound too heartbroken about it. In fact, I think he was relieved."

Wyatt turned to look at her. "How about you? Are you relieved? To have her out of the picture?"

She shrugged. "Funny you should ask. I find myself curiously apathetic about J'Aimee. Guess I've let go of the anger. I wonder what Paula would say about that."

"I think she'd say you've had a growth moment," Wyatt said, making two-fingered quote marks in the air.

"Maybe I have," Grace mused. "I'll have to write about that in my journal." She reached over and laced her fingers through his. "How 'bout you? Had any growth moments of your own lately?"

"As a matter of fact, I have. A couple of them, actually."

"Wanna share?" She kept her tone light.

"Dad and I had some long talks this week. Turns out, he's not opposed to my selling Jungle Jerry's to the state for a park."

"Really? So . . . it's a done deal?"

"We're dealing with the state of Florida, Grace. Everything works at a snail's pace with them. But it turns out they've got some kind of federal grant to develop what they call urban parklands. Smaller parks, under fifty acres, like ours, where the emphasis will be on community education rather than recreation. We'd keep the original gardens, get rid of the old playground equipment, and, in its place, develop demonstration gardens for heirloom Florida fruits, vegetables, and flowers. The guy with the state seems to think there's a good chance I'd be offered the job as park superintendent, or whatever they call them these days."

"That's great, Wyatt!" she said, beaming. "It sounds perfect for you."

"I know. If I had to write my dream-job description, this would be it."

Sweetie perked up her ears and gave a low growl. They both looked up and saw an elderly man inching slowly down the beach toward them. He was shirtless and his sun-browned skin gleamed in the dying sunlight. Baggy black shorts hung from his hips to just above mahogany-colored knobby knees. Below these he wore what looked like white surgical stockings and thick-soled black rubber sandals. He didn't appear to see or hear them—or Sweetie.

The old man wore a pair of enormous earphones connected to an unwieldy metal detector, and his eyes were glued to the sand as he waved the detector's wand back and forth over a three-foot-wide swath of sand.

Grace nodded in his direction. "You think he ever finds anything valuable? From the looks of him, he must spend hours and hours with that thing."

"He probably finds lots of bottle caps and pennies. Maybe the occasional set of keys or a piece of jewelry. Probably just enough to keep him in gas and beer," Wyatt said.

"But he never gives up. And he walks for miles. I've seen him every day this week, on the beach outside Mitzi's condo. I guess it gives him something to do," Grace said.

"You said you had a couple growth moments this week?" Grace asked idly, her eyes following the treasure seeker's progress. "What was the other one?"

"Mm-hmm," Wyatt said. He rested his lips briefly against her right temple. "Callie showed up at the park again yesterday, begging me to give her a job. And another chance."

Grace half stood and tried to pull away, but Wyatt gently tugged her back down beside him.

"I told her no," he said, placing his hand on her cheek. "Hell, no. What you said just now—that there's nothing there for you—back at your old house, with Ben. That's how it is with me and Callie. I wish her well, for Bo's sake, but that's it."

"You're sure?" Grace held her breath.

"Never surer," Wyatt said. "It's you and me now, kid, if you'll have me." Slowly, he slid off the thick gold band on his left ring finger. He stood up, cocked his throwing arm back, and made his pitch.

"This is me, letting go," he said.

The wedding band spiraled and looped, the dull gold catching glints of the fading sunlight. It landed fifty feet away, in the soft sand, maybe twenty yards in front of the old man, who seemed not to see it.

"Good arm, huh?" Wyatt said, admiring his own prowess.

Grace wrapped her arms around his neck and kissed her approval. "Good arm, good man," she murmured. "Good everything."

Epilogue

True Grace, Feb. 14

The old rules of etiquette for second marriages were stern and absolute. In her starchy 1957 Complete Book of Etiquette: A Guide to Gracious Living, *Amy Vanderbilt opined that the second-time ceremony must be small, and that the "mature" bride should never wear white or a veil, or, heaven forbid, expect wedding gifts. She cautioned, too, that many ministers would actually refuse to perform a second wedding in a church! Invitations should not be engraved, as with a formal first wedding, but a handwritten note would be acceptable.*

Thankfully, wedding rules these days have been relaxed, or sometimes, totally discarded. Although I'm a traditionalist at heart, for our own second wedding, my intended and I wanted something intimate and meaningful, with just a few close friends and family members.

We actually didn't tell our guests that they were coming to a wedding at all. Instead, we invited them to what we simply billed as a garden party. Of course, we have the good fortune to have access to one of the most beautiful settings I can imagine, Wyatt's family's small but charming botanical park, here on Florida's Gulf Coast.

The party was to be the last private family party at Jungle Jerry's, an old-timey Florida tourist attraction founded by Wyatt's grandparents shortly after World War II, before the park is turned over to the state of Florida.

Our guests arrived at the park's front gate at dusk and were ferried to the party site by golf carts. When they reached the small enclosed butterfly garden, they were greeted with glasses of pink champagne, iced tea, or locally brewed beer.

Wyatt and I mingled with our guests and enjoyed the food he and I prepared together from local farms and fishermen—stone crab "martinis," chilled shrimp and avocado gazpacho, and crab beignets with pineapple-mango salsa. All the food was set out on rustic wooden picnic tables that were hand-built years ago by Wyatt's grandfather, with centerpieces of hibiscus, lilies, orchids, and other flowers picked right from the gardens.

Shortly before sunset, a small string quartet arrived and began to play classical music. At that point, we invited everybody to be seated in a semicircle of battered vintage lawn chairs and proceeded to the surprise event of the evening—our wedding!

The minister, a family friend who happens to be a regular at my mother's bar, stepped in front of a weathered wooden trellis, which was lit by hundreds of tiny white fairy lights and blooming with pale pink New Dawn roses.

When the wedding march started, I joined Wyatt in front of the makeshift altar.

Amy Vanderbilt says that for a second-time-around wedding, the attendants should be limited to one each for the bride and groom and should be the bride and groom's age. But, since Amy's long gone, we broke the rules—just a little.

The bride (that's me!) wore a 1960s vintage lace-over-silk minidress dyed the same exact hue as the roses. My bouquet was one made for me by Wyatt, from flowers he grew at the park, including hot-pink lilies, deep-violet hydrangeas, and my favorites—heavenly white gardenias. No other flowers were necessary, since the scent of the orange blossoms from the citrus gardens blanketed the late-afternoon air.

I promised Wyatt I wouldn't ask him to get too dressed up, so he chose his own khaki slacks, a nice white dress shirt—and in a major concession to the importance of the occasion, a navy blue blazer, which he promptly ditched right after the ceremony. He also wore a bouton-niere—of rosemary and white phlox clipped from the garden at our tiny newly restored cottage.

Since my own father is deceased, Wyatt's dad, Nelson, agreed to give me away. Wyatt chose his six-year-old son Bo as his best man. Nelson wore his best (and only) good gray suit, and Bo was heartbreakingly adorable in his own khakis and blue blazer.

I'd begged my mother to be my maid of honor, but she gracefully declined with the excuse that she didn't want anybody to mistake her for a maiden. As if!

Instead, my friend Camryn agreed to be my attendant. Camryn loves fashion, so she wore a chic one-shouldered deep-violet silk dress by a designer so trendy I'd never heard of her. And spike heels—Camryn says she feels barefoot unless she's wearing at least four-inch heels—even during a garden wedding in February.

Amy Vanderbilt probably never considered the idea of including a pet in a wedding party, but since our little rescue dog, Sweetie, is such an important part of our blended family, she had to have a role in our big day. Bo was proud and happy to walk her down the aisle, although he did state loudly that he thought the pink tulle ruffle I fastened around her neck was "disgusting."

After we said our vows, my mother revealed her masterpiece—a three-tiered lemon pound cake with strawberry cream cheese frosting—topped with an ingenious bride and groom crafted by Bo—from Legos.

We cut the cake, had some toasts, and, when it got dark and chilly, we all repaired to the after party at the Sandbox, my mother's bar in nearby Cortez.

I don't know what Amy Vanderbilt would have thought of our second-time-around wedding, but I know, for us, it was definitely an affair to remember.

Grace was rushing around the bar, greeting guests, when she spotted a newcomer out of the corner of her eye. She threw her arms around the woman.

"Suzanne! You came back. I'm so happy to see you."

"There's no way I would have missed your garden party—and then to sneak in a wedding, well, what can I say? It was beautiful, unexpected, and so romantic, Grace. Like something out of a fairy tale."

"Thanks," Grace said, beaming. She gestured to the willowy young woman at Suzanne's side. "And this must be Darby."

"It is. Darby, meet our beautiful, blushing bride, Grace."

Wyatt wandered up and wrapped an arm around Suzanne's and Grace's waists. "And don't forget the blushing bridegroom."

Darby was a slender brunette, two inches taller than her mother, but with the same striking olive-green eyes. "Congratulations," she said shyly. "Mom's told me all about you, and the rest of the group."

"Look who's here," Camryn shrieked, enveloping Suzanne in a hug before standing back to critique her appearance. "You look amazing," Camryn said. "How's life in North Carolina? And the new job?"

"It's good," Suzanne said. "I'm slowly getting used to winter. And snow! I had to actually go out and buy a wool coat and boots. The job is good." She glanced at Darby, who'd drifted off and was chatting with Camryn's daughter, Jana. "Elon is a good fit. For both of us."

Camryn leaned in, her eyes dancing with a mischevious glint. "And what about men? Are you getting any action?"

Suzanne blushed violently. "I've actually had a couple real dates. The men's soccer coach. He's a good bit younger, but . . ."

"Ooh, Suzanne. You're a cougar!" Camryn linked her arm through Suzanne's and Grace's. "Look at us now, y'all. Grace and Wyatt married. Suzanne moved off and prowling around up there in North Carolina . . ."

"What about you?" Suzanne asked. "Grace says you left News Four You."

"I sure did," Camryn said. "There was a senior producer's slot open, but I got passed over, so I up and left. I'm producing the six o'clock news at channel two. The money's not quite as good, but I get to sleep in for the first time in twenty years. And I sub-in on camera when somebody's out sick or on vacation."

"Men?" Suzanne raised a quizzical eyebrow.

"I was seeing somebody, but it didn't work out," Camryn said. "That's one thing I learned from my divorce. If it's not right, it's not right. Cut your losses and move on."

"Has anybody heard from Ashleigh?" Suzanne asked, looking around the room.

"Oh, sure," Camryn said. "You can't keep that girl down. She did some work-release thing as part of her sentence for trying to kill her ex's baby mama. She's working for another plastic surgeon and living down in Naples. She has to wear one of those electronic-monitoring bracelet things, which she hates, 'cuz she says it makes her ankles look fat, so she has to wear pants and can't show off her legs anymore."

"Ashleigh would have been here today, except the idea of being around all the party stuff—you know, with liquor and everything, made her a little anxious," Grace said. "She's been clean and sober for six months now."

"Really?" Suzanne looked taken aback. "I mean, you two are on speaking terms? After everything that happened?"

"Grace has a much more forgiving heart than I do," Wyatt said. "I'm good with Ashleigh now, although Grace is banned from ever getting in a car with her again."

Grace laughed. "She's changed a lot since that day. I think it was a turning point for her."

"You'll never guess who Ashleigh's AA sponsor was," Camryn said.

"Who?" Suzanne was still scanning the room, looking for familiar faces.

"None other than Paula Talbott-Sinclair," Camryn said.

"I wondered what happened to Paula," Suzanne admitted. "I know you all might disagree, but I really think she did eventually help all of us in our group."

Wyatt pulled Grace into his arms. "I, for one, am eternally grateful to Paula. Without her, I might never have met the love of my life."

Grace rewarded her new husband with a kiss, then looked at her friends. "He's a sweet-talking fool, but he's right about Paula. If she did nothing else, she brought us all together, at the lowest point in our lives, and forced us to look at our attitudes and expectations about love."

"Don't forget what we did for *her*," Camryn chimed in. "She might still be mixed up with that parasite Cedric Stackpole if we hadn't exposed him for the scum-sucking dog he really is. I bet she never would have had the nerve to rat him out to the state if it hadn't been for us. And she damn sure wouldn't have been able to reinvent herself like she has without me."

"Paula reinvented herself?" Suzanne looked puzzled. "How? And what did you have to do with that?"

"Paula is now a certified laughter coach," Camryn said. "She works with people dealing with depression, terminal illness, and severe emotional problems. I did a feature story on her before I left News Four, and now she's got her own syndicated radio show."

"Any news about dear old Stackpole?" Suzanne asked.

"He's actually been in the news a good bit recently," Grace said, not bothering to suppress her glee. "The feds raided his new law office and seized all his tax records. My lawyer says the IRS is going after him big-time for falsifying tax records and tax evasion, among other things."

"That's one story I would have loved to have been in on," Camryn said. "What I wouldn't give to stick a live microphone in his sorry face."

"Just his face?" Wyatt asked. "And don't forget, Stackpole still has to deal with the lawsuit filed by that guy who filmed his wife and girlfriend's hair-pulling match in Sarasota. Couldn't happen to a nicer guy, huh?"

As they chatted and caught up on each other's lives, music began to filter into the room. Chairs scraped against the wooden floor as they were cleared out of the way, and guests began to edge onto the makeshift dance floor.

"You hired a DJ?" Suzanne asked, looking around the room.

"Better," Rochelle said, joining the group. "When Grace was making me clean up the place, I finally got rid of Butch's old Ms. Pac-Man game. It was broken, and I couldn't get anybody to fix it. Instead, I found an old jukebox at the flea market and had it restored. I put in all the records he and I used to dance to."

"And even some music from the last half century," Wyatt teased.

Grace tugged at his arm. "Okay, enough talk, mister. This is our wedding night, and you are going to dance with me, and that's final."

"Gladly," Wyatt said, leading her into the middle of the cramped floor.

Suzanne looked at Camryn. "Dance?"

"Damn straight," Camryn said. "But just so you know, I always lead."

The party was still in full swing at ten o'clock, when the two grizzled barflies known as Miller and Bud approached the Sandbox door. Miller pushed on the door, but it didn't move.

"Hey," he said, puzzled. "The lights are on, but it's locked. What's up with that?"

Bud pointed to a small hand-lettered note taped to the door.

CLOSED DUE TO PRIVATE PARTY

"They can't do that to us," Miller protested. "It's Sunday night. We always watch the games on Sundays."

Bud pressed his bulbous pink nose against the glass door and peered inside. "Man! They got all kind of food on the tables, and balloons and decorations and shit, and some kind of fancy pink drinks in martini glasses."

Miller shoved him aside and took a gander for himself. "They're dancing!" He turned to Bud in astonishment. "They're actually dancing in there." He frowned. "I see a couple guys—there's an old dude in a suit, and a younger guy dancing with Rochelle's daughter, and some little kid—hey, the kid is dancing with Rochelle."

"Lemme see." Bud elbowed him out of the way. He looked disgusted. "It's mostly women in there. And they're not even watching the game."

"Must be a ladies' night thing," Miller concluded sadly as he turned away from the door. "Looks like we're gonna have to find ourselves someplace new, Bud."

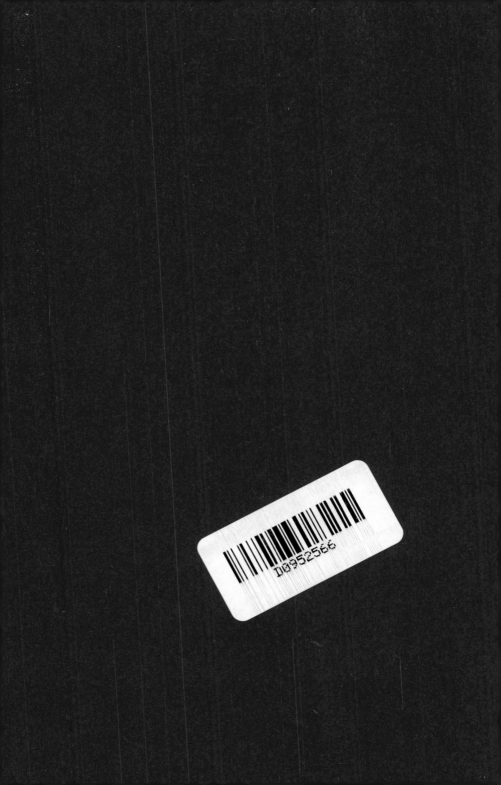

Aviary

Aviary

A Novel

DEIRDRE MCNAMER

MILKWEED EDITIONS

Published 2021 by Milkweed Editions
Printed in Canada
Cover design by Mary Austin Speaker
Cover art by Dana Boussard, "Her Whisper Saved Us"
21 22 23 24 25   5 4 3 2 1
First Edition

Milkweed Editions, an independent nonprofit publisher, gratefully acknowledges sustaining support from our Board of Directors; the Alan B. Slifka Foundation and its president, Riva Ariella Ritvo-Slifka; the Amazon Literary Partnership; the Ballard Spahr Foundation; *Copper Nickel*; the McKnight Foundation; the National Endowment for the Arts; the National Poetry Series; the Target Foundation; and other generous contributions from foundations, corporations, and individuals. Also, this activity is made possible by the voters of Minnesota through a Minnesota State Arts Board Operating Support grant, thanks to a legislative appropriation from the arts and cultural heritage fund. For a full listing of Milkweed Editions supporters, please visit milkweed.org.

Library of Congress Cataloging-in-Publication Data

Names: McNamer, Deirdre, author.
Title: Aviary / Deirdre McNamer.
Description: First edition. | Minneapolis, Minnesota : Milkweed Editions, 2021. | Summary: "Aviary explores the rich and hidden facets of human character, as illuminated by the mysterious connections among the residents of a senior residence in Montana"-- Provided by publisher.
Identifiers: LCCN 2020051026 (print) | LCCN 2020051027 (ebook) | ISBN 9781571311382 (hardback) | ISBN 9781571317384 (ebook)
Classification: LCC PS3563.C38838 A95 2021 (print) | LCC PS3563. C38838
   (ebook) | DDC 813/.54--dc23
LC record available at https://lccn.loc.gov/2020051026
LC ebook record available at https://lccn.loc.gov/2020051027

Milkweed Editions is committed to ecological stewardship. We strive to align our book production practices with this principle, and to reduce the impact of our operations in the environment. We are a member of the Green Press Initiative, a nonprofit coalition of publishers, manufacturers, and authors working to protect the world's endangered forests and conserve natural resources. *Aviary* was printed on acid-free 100% postconsumer-waste paper by Friesens Corporation.

For my luminous sisters, Megan and Kate
And again, and always, for Bryan

IT'S LIKE A LION
at the Door

1

While they slept, the sun lifted itself above the mountain surround to spread light on the little city below. Inside that city, urban deer glided across frozen November lawns to return to their hollows under backyard pines. Feline huntresses licked the blood off their paws and went home for kibbles and stomach rubs. A tied-up, shivering dog made three tight circles in the dirt and began to bark. Two joggers with lights on their shoes panted grimly and stepped up their pace. An old Falcon moved slowly, ejecting rolled newspapers onto front steps. And then a roseate calm prevailed, and the mountains moved in closer.

While they slept, in their boxes inside the bigger box of their four-story building, street sounds began: the buses, the early workers. The river moved with low-water deliberation through the center of town, carrying oblong shards of ice beneath one bridge and then another. A muttering man with crazy hair dragged a lumpy sleeping bag from a stand of tall bushes and resettled himself beneath the second bridge, up under the trusses, a few yards from the coffee place on the ground floor of the new bank.

They slept not far from the river in a neighborhood thickly planted with maples and tall old homes, in a twenty-four-unit residence for seniors called Pheasant Run.

In a normal autumn, the maples put on showy displays, fanning high into the sky, then shattering into slow red waterfalls until the branches were lattices, not crowns, and the sky was twice as large. This year, the leaves have refused to drop. They have clung, ash-colored, to the branches, inspiring general unease and several letters to the newspaper, which invited a certified arborist to weigh in. He explained that the normal separation process between leaf and twig produces a membrane that seals off the leaf and enables it to fall. Extreme cold at the wrong time, like the shocking, subzero stretch of days that happened in October, can derail that process, he said. The tree "basically clutches," and the leaves stay attached. They were strange, those gray leaves, abiding in the wrong place at the wrong time. They turned the trees to sepia-toned photographs, or remembered trees, or witnesses to some sapless aftermath.

They slept at Pheasant Run, and then they woke and prepared to move into a day with nothing, yet, about it to suggest the small and large shocks to come.

Faint, predictable smells trickled into the hallways: oatmeal, burned toast. Some televisions were turned on for talk shows or weather, and a few were loud enough, because of their owners' hearing difficulties, that the adjacent tenants began another day feeling cranky and contemplating notes of complaint.

The morning noises tended not to include conversation, as most of the residents lived alone or with an ailing, late-sleeping spouse.

At six thirty, Cassie McMackin in #412, an early riser by habit, drank her coffee and counted the pills she had accumulated during her late husband's long decline. There were relaxants that had unsuccessfully addressed his night roaming, plus several versions of painkillers, prescribed after two falls and some broken ribs, and so dizzy-making for Neil that he started giving them wary, sidelong looks whenever she urged one on him, and it soon became clear that nothing was better than something.

Now she had a couple of fistfuls in the narcotic and soporific categories, and this evening she would take them all, with antinausea medication and as much wine as she could get down. It was time. She had become tired of the world. Her blood didn't want to go anywhere anymore, and had it not been for the instructions of her bossy and indefatigable heart, it wouldn't. She didn't want to occupy some interminable waiting room where nothing was wrong and nothing was right, her motions mechanical, eyes on the tyrant clock. It was time.

At eighty-seven, she was fine-boned and straight-backed, and she tended to wear interesting clothes, like the silk robe she'd thrown on over her nightgown, a shimmering gold-toned garment with bat-wing sleeves. Her silver hair framed her face in a short pageboy. The red lipstick and frank black eyebrows of her earlier days had muted to softer shades, but it was a face that echoed unusual beauty, still.

Right this moment, what she missed was the prospect of a second cup of coffee with her friend, John Quant, who had moved, a year ago, into an apartment on the third floor of the building, directly beneath her own. Soon after they met, they had progressed from polite greetings to longer conversations, to morning coffee, to dinner in Cassie's apartment every week or so, with candles and maybe a TV movie with dessert. She had felt in his company as if she was emerging from years of emotional and physical hibernation. Her happiness shocked her.

She liked his looks—tall and sharp-shouldered, his eyes an inquiring blue—and she liked his wit, his laughter, and his combination of irreverence and courtliness. Eventually, she had felt between them a tacit acknowledgment of an alliance that could only be called romantic, in the sense that it fanned outward into whatever futures they would be granted, and it shimmered with excitement in that space.

And then, four weeks ago, there had been a sharp knock on her door, and he told her he was moving back to the little town up north where he had been a boy. For the first time since she'd known him he seemed evasive; he said only that Pheasant Run was not a good fit for him anymore, that he didn't like the feel of the place, and he particularly didn't like the new on-site manager, Herbie Bonebright. He told her he didn't feel he had a choice. He wouldn't look at her straight on. He had closed and locked the door to himself.

And he was gone, in a blink. She'd heard not another word from him, and knew she wouldn't. All she could do was add him to her list of those who'd left. John Quant, and before him her only child. And her husband of six decades. They'd flown away, leaving her craning her head skyward, aghast, as they became pinpricks and disappeared. She couldn't fully believe it, still. The flights. This final aloneness.

Down the hall in #406, Viola Six breathed out the blue vapors of a receding dream. *It is near,* the walls whispered. *It is nearly at the door.* In the dream, a man in a suit had approached her from a distance, requesting payment in full, yanking off his face to reveal something that looked exactly the same. The terror of it had shocked her awake.

Rising shakily, she gathered herself to make a cup of tea, then padded to the living room window to wait for full, dispelling daylight to arrive. A long-legged cat jumped from a tree branch to the roof of a tall house across the street. It climbed the steep slope and perched near the chimney, inky and totemic against the silvering sky. *Who do you think you are?* Viola asked it, and caught a glimpse of her young self dancing wildly with a stranger at a roadhouse near the lumber mill. Her fiancé, Ollie, leaned against the bar and looked at his shoes.

Increasingly, Viola's interrogations of her surroundings were rebounding as memories that accused or threatened her. The phenomenon gave her the panicky feeling that she lived in a sealed cavern that was nothing but Viola enclosing Viola. She was the walls; she was the interior; ongoing human life was somewhere outside. The feeling increased when she was particularly anxious about her financial circumstances, as she was today. If Captain, the man she took up with in her sixties, hadn't

7

convinced her to buy into a scam that depleted every penny of her savings, she wouldn't be living now on minimal Social Security and a small widow's pension from Ollie, three-fourths of her income going to her rent and food. The other fourth she allocated down to the penny, and if there were unforeseen expenses, as there had been this month, she had to live for a few days or a week on dry cereal and powdered milk, plus some canned goods from the food bank. She knew, in her worst moments, that she was just a few small reversals away from homelessness, that it waited for her, patient and dead-eyed, just out of her sight.

To distract herself, she sat down at her typewriter to work on her memoirs, hoping she could complete a section she'd begun a week earlier that concerned her temporary escape from Ollie in the late sixties and her subsequent month in Europe, traveling alone on meager savings accumulated over many years, ecstatic with possibility. She held her curved old fingers over the typewriter keys, but she couldn't seem to type and finally let her hands fall to her sides.

Next to her typewriter, she'd propped the photo that a flower vendor had taken of her as she leaned, insouciant, against a carved white pillar in Rome. Her long hair shone, and her face was full and smooth. She wore a wicked grin, the one she sometimes tried to recreate in the bathroom mirror as an antidote to the wrinkled mouth, the shrunken, docile eyes that met her gaze. Today, though, it was too much; the gap between her and that person in Rome was too wide. She turned the photo facedown on the desk and closed her eyes against a brief and terrible vision of herself, curled on the sidewalk under a large piece of cardboard.

"Not me," she whispered. "Not that."

In the basement of Pheasant Run, inside one of the slat-doored storage units, a boy named Clayton Spooner roused briefly from a long sleep, then sank back helplessly into the dusty quilt that held him safe. He shook off the residue of a long dream filled with sirens and flame-breathing birds that swooped down to pluck enemies from skyscraper roofs and drop them into a yellow, snake-filled lake on the next planet over.

His neck felt twisted, crooked, and sore. He had slept with a shallow cardboard box for a pillow, and he reached around in the gloom for something kinder. Powdery light sifted through the slats of the door, cutting everything inside with pale bars. One bar bent itself across something that looked like bunched material, a sloppily folded curtain perhaps, and he reached over and pulled it to him. He adjusted it under his neck and stared at the spaces between the slats and tried to think about everything that had brought him, so young, to his prison of a life. Bullied, drugged by doctors, enraged; stationed on the outside of everything calm and consolatory, peering in, until the end of time.

Most days, nothing much happened at Pheasant Run until midmorning, when the mailman arrived. They had their Facebook and their email, most of the residents, but a real letter was another thing altogether. And most still wanted any income—a pension, their Social Security—to arrive as checks, though it meant mailing them to the bank with deposit slips, or making the sometimes complicated trip downtown.

Around ten o'clock, the elevator came alive to ferry its cargo. In the lobby, a polite and faintly excited milling occurred while the mail was dropped behind the small brass doors banked on the wall. And then keys were retrieved and their owners discovered something, or nothing, or something in between, ridiculous and empty, like a flyer for a hemp festival or a brochure for oxygen systems tailored to individual lifestyles.

Anyone who got an actual, identifiable personal letter studied the envelope, studied it again, smiled in a way that was particular to the occasion because most of the recipients were all too aware that most of the people shutting the brass doors of the boxes had gotten nothing. Mostly nothing. And it was perhaps because of that fact that the mailman tended to talk in soft, respectful tones, as if he were at a memorial.

It had been the same man for several years now. He was lean and lined from the elements, and he wore logger boots through every season. He was patient with the not-infrequent requests that he take another look in his bag for an expected piece of mail. He touched the women lightly on the tops of their hands and offered the men a gruff shoulder thump from time to time. He seemed to be aware of his role as the personification of both possibility and disappointment and walked the distance between those points in a careful and deft manner.

When he was gone, the lobby felt irrelevant and somehow too bright, and so the lone elevator was summoned, and it clicked and sighed and fell and climbed again, and eventually everyone was back in his or her separate space and day.

A week ago, the mailman had come and gone as usual, but the elevator button had produced no movement, and the residents could hear, a floor or two up the shaft, the sounds of vehement banging.

It was the new manager, Herbie, once again trying to fix something he knew nothing about. The elevator had jammed shut on the second floor, trapping two residents inside, and he had arrived to hit the door's bottom with a wrench, at length, before he gave up and called the repair company, which took an hour to arrive. Herbie's theory, he said afterward, was that the door was slightly misaligned with the groove on that floor, and might be restored without recourse to expensive outsiders.

The building's residents didn't know what exactly the repair company had done, but the remedy was clearly temporary because the elevator had now acquired an ominous ticking sound. And since this potentially malfunctioning elevator was the only one in a building whose occupants had reached various stages of physical impairment—more than a few dreaded the prospect of navigating several flights of stairs—traveling in it had become a quiet terror. Think about a medical emergency. Think about fire, about howling dogs and the blocked opening of the cave.

There existed, then, a recent wariness among the residents of Pheasant Run, about the building itself and about the manager, who had been installed on the premises by the property management company that the building's condominium owners had hired recently to replace a predecessor.

Longleap Enterprises had come forward to offer its services at a much lower cost, one that seemed remarkably sensitive to the fixed incomes of the building's residents, the quiet distempers of the building itself, the erratic condominium market, and a long period of deferred maintenance. The company moved Herbie into a recently vacated second-floor apartment owned by a businessman who lived out of state.

Within days of his occupancy, several residents raised complaints about him: that he was lazy, that he lacked the barest handyman skills, that he frequently disappeared for hours at a time, that his manner could be brusque, and that the spelling on the notes he left around the building was a baboon's. (The building's water would be turned off soon for several hours of repair to the boiler, said his most recent note in the elevator. "If not fixed now, we will be playing catsup.") Worst of all, he had, within a week of moving in, caused a small grease fire in his kitchen that set off the alarms and put everyone in the building severely on edge. Though he had extinguished it in a matter of minutes, the odor of ash lingered for days.

There was also the matter of the renters moving out. Most of the condominium owners in the building also owned an apartment or two that they rented. In the six weeks since Herbie had arrived, three renters had departed abruptly, and their apartments remained vacant. Herbie, some were saying, had bullied them into leaving. But why?

His work uniform was a Hawaiian shirt, Bermuda shorts, and flip-flops. On colder days, he replaced the flip-flops with plastic clogs and added a fleece vest. On his big bald head, he wore a Steelers cap with a long brim that shaded rimless glasses embedded in a pudgy, forget-table face. The lenses looked like something a crow would want to pick up.

His impassive face, combined with his habit of wear-ing tropical clothes at all times, conferred upon him a kind of ethereal remove, as if Pheasant Run and its resi-dents were a mosquito dream he was having as he lolled in a hammock a wide world away from them all.

At seven this morning, Herbie descended to the lobby in the ticking elevator. His habit was to walk three blocks to a sports bar that served a cheap breakfast. He always left on the dot, having informed the residents that, for the next hour, he was off the grid, absolutely—no phone, no iPad—and any nonemergency problems were their own.

Today, he left the building, but he didn't go to the sports bar. Instead, he walked around the neighborhood for a while, then turned down the alley behind Pheasant Run and pulled on a rusty door that opened on stairs to the basement parking garage. He drove his car out of the garage and parked it in the alley in a spot that couldn't be seen from the building or the street. Upon reentering the basement area, he summoned the elevator.

Huffing slightly, he dry-swallowed an oblong white pill and prepared himself for the unusual demands of the day ahead. He had messages to convey in no uncer-tain terms. He had responses to imagine and missteps to avoid. He had, perhaps—this realization came to him in a toxic rush—his own life to keep safe. Unbelievably, it had come to this. They might already have him partly erased.

2

The fourth floor, this early morning, was strangely quiet. Most days, Cassie McMackin woke to the presence of Viola Six's manual typewriter clattering away at the other end of the hall, and it gave her a small boost. She'd think about how the sharp taps, the pauses, the ping of the carriage return had not a whiff of the casual or offhand. Typewriter typing always sounded like a speech. And the way a person had to sit at a typewriter—confrontational, alert—reinforced the intensity of the effort.

By contrast, the postures assumed by those composing messages on their smartphones or iPads were furtive, whispery. Their arms, their bodies, did not seem central, or even important, to the effort. The body made a cave around the device, and the digits tapped and scuffed somewhere in the interior. Watching her fellow humans' involvement with their communication tools, Cassie had the growing sense that bodies, as bodies, were becoming vestigial on a mass scale. More and more people clearly conducted their social lives, their travel, their shopping, their entertainment, and their learning in a realm that had almost nothing to do with moving their corporeal selves through space. They existed mostly in the big brain, the forest of pixels.

She felt an overwhelming tenderness at times for the younger denizens of this brave-or-not new world. They'd lived their entire lives in a glittering roar of data, images, gossip, greetings, stunts, games, polls, exhortations, lists, porn, mayhem, and ads—all of it arriving and leaving so rapidly that it couldn't form abiding constellations of persuasion or experience. How, then, could they feel assured that they had a hand in creating themselves, by selecting and evaluating what to pay attention to?

Not that she wanted to be a Luddite. She didn't. She could appreciate the liquid beauty of the new technologies and webbings, everything so small and instant. And it was undeniably innovation on a stupendous, species-altering scale. Also, at the personal level, it was sometimes comforting to her to know that bodies were becoming somewhat irrelevant to experience. Socialization had become unlinked from physical movement or physical effort. Being old, in physical decline, unable to move very far or very fast, didn't matter so much inside the communal brain.

Maybe that, the hive, was what would be shipped to another planet when this one became physically uninhabitable. Maybe bodies wouldn't even come along. And for that matter, what about vampires? Why the fixation in popular culture with vampires, bloodsuckers, exsanguinators, those emptiers of the bodily life force? Could it be an intuitive recognition on the part of the species that the individual, autonomous body was being displaced, was going away? Could visions of vampires be a way to inoculate en masse against the oncoming rupture?

Oh, stop! Cassie shook her head hard. These were the musings of either prescience or senility, and she didn't have the energy to make the distinction. They were also, she knew, her mind trying to run from itself, from the memories that could bring her to her knees and the knowledge that she was about to leave it all behind.

The pills resided inside an old printer that she'd stashed, minus its depleted cartridge, at the back of a closet. Her daughter Marian had bought the printer and a desktop computer for her, and she'd tried for some months to use them, but that was years ago. She finally got so irritated— the computer was constantly asking her if she wanted to update this or that, constantly framing her emails with ads, like an adrenalized huckster barging into a private conversation—that she reverted to longhand and stamps but kept the computer and printer on the faint chance that she'd someday change her mind. Marian had mildly reminded her that a letter took a week to reach her in Beirut, where she worked as a senior wire service report- er, but she hadn't nagged. Cassie's last letter to her, the frankest and most loving she ever wrote, arrived three days after a bomb in a vegetable market blew Marian off the face of the earth. Five years now she had been gone, outlasted only a few months by her father Neil.

Cassie never told Neil about Marian. He was in the hospital when the word came, struggling with a respi- ratory infection, and had reached the point, mentally, where he had trouble retrieving Cassie's name. He knew something was wrong that day—he kept searching her face for clues—but she said only that she had been very worried about him and nothing else was upsetting her. She couldn't bear to tell him that his daughter had been annihilated, that he would never see her again. It would have been like loading bricks on the back of a child. It would have told him that nothing about this life came out the way it was supposed to. And so she didn't. And three months later, he had moved on, or out, or over, to inhabit the same absence his daughter did.

Oh my allies, my loves, she thought. *My lost ones who, at the very end, have left me now so lost.*

She had a recorder she had bought at a yard sale. It was the kind that had been innovatively small when it came out. Now it was laughably out of date, but it worked, and it had come with a small box filled with empty microcassettes. They were exactly like the microcassettes she'd used in her first telephone answering machine. She still had those because she never erased the messages but simply replaced each cassette when it was full. In the bottom drawer of her dresser was a shoebox filled with voices leaving her messages. "Call me," they said. "Would you like me to pick you up?" they said. And because most of them were from people long dead, she had listened to them only when she could, and sometimes, listening to them, she had wept.

For the past few months, Cassie had talked into her tape recorder from time to time, saying whatever came into her mind. At times she pretended she talked to a sympathetic, imaginative human, one eager to hear anything she wanted to say, happy to listen to her talk as long as she liked. Other times she viewed the dispatches as auditory Post-it Notes. Mark this. It might be some odd snippet she'd found in the newspaper, or read on a sign, or overheard on a walk. It didn't have to be portentous. It just had to confer a delicate quiver of disruption or irony.

Her first idea was to explore what her life had added up to, what seemed worth remembering. Why had she chosen what she'd chosen? Why had she suffered in the ways she had? What had enlivened her? What would she do differently?

Smaller, odder questions then began to surface. What is most strange about the experience of life on this earth? How do our fellow creatures behave? What are the smallest components of joy? Caught enigmas. She'd heard the phrase somewhere and it seemed to apply.

On this last day, she would play back her recordings and then decide whether to destroy them or not. Who would care, really? After John Quant, the only person she considered a friend, if not a particularly close one, was Viola Six. And Viola was, quite possibly, losing her mind.

She hoped Viola's silent typewriter didn't mean she was getting ready to pay an early-morning visit and expand upon the television program she'd seen about scheming real estate developers in Spain who terrorized old people out of their apartments so they could obtain the properties cheap. Granny rattlers, the smart-alecky reporter had called them.

"One group of poor women actually sued a group of the rattlers and won," Viola had told her. "Aging Davids against corporate Goliaths. And it's not just Spain. The

UN is investigating far and wide." Her eyes, as she told the story, widened with excited fear.

This conversation had taken place yesterday in the lobby, near the mailboxes. Others were present, of course, and Cassie found herself wishing Viola would speak more softly, or at least forge some kind of context for her report.

"The point being," Viola said, "it could easily happen here." She fixed a dark look on the assembled as the mailman strode through the front door. "It's safe to say that Spain has no monopoly on granny rattlers."

Viola also had fervent theories about Herbie Bonebright and had promised to share them with Cassie very soon. Was she taking medication that made her so paranoid and voluble? And what was she writing so doggedly at her typewriter? Letters, perhaps. But to whom? She seemed basically alone, except for her son Rod, a seedy sort who came and went infrequently. *Alone, but fiercely self-contained*, Cassie thought. Her demise would be a shock to Viola, but not a lot more than that.

Viola's agitation made Cassie deeply uneasy. They had too much in common for her to be able to place Viola in some category that didn't actually or potentially include herself. They were both in their mid-eighties, both living alone. They both read books—real ones—and kept up with the real news. They both were living out their days, a few doors from each other, in a condominium building, their "fair house built upon another man's ground." The line came to her from the Shakespeare series on *Masterpiece Theater*—she couldn't remember which play it was from—and it accurately summarized a feeling she knew Viola shared: that in old age, one's presence was no longer anchored to earthly life in any reliable way. A hovering had begun, above a world that now belonged, in all substantive senses, to others.

It was a fearful thought, and fear was such a meaty, breathing thing. What was that creepy old poem, maybe a nursery rhyme?

It's like a lion at the door;
And when the door begins to crack,
It's like a stick across your back;
And when your back begins to smart,
It's like a penknife in your heart;
And when your heart begins to bleed,
You're dead, and dead, and dead indeed.

To banish it, she put on her birdsong CD and did her stretching exercises. She imagined herself as a tangerine-colored finch, stretching her wings to move swiftly through canopies of glittering leaves. Move now. Enter this last day.

"I needed someone," she said aloud. "And I had hoped for just one more person to need me."

She took some deep breaths and opened the living room curtain. Apart from the strange, furred trees, everything looked mostly as it usually did, this early-winter dawn: the pink sky, the encircling mountains, the dark cat that navigated the gambreled roof of the tallest house. All of it seemed, in some way, a map. Why, she wondered, had she never found a way to read it?

3

Viola Six's only child, Roderick, had borrowed her rent payment to go to Jackpot, Nevada, promising to repay her before it was due on the tenth. He'd told her the trip was to investigate the possibility of opening a Jack in the Box franchise, but she'd received no money and no word, and she had to assume that her $700 resided now in a casino vault.

Nothing, then, to pay her landlord, Rydell Clovis, a retired university professor who lived down the long hall in #410, one of several units in the building that he owned. She would simply have to go to him and explain. The thought made her face burn, as he was an imperious, smooth-voiced man whose manner called up a phrase from her grandmother's Psalms: *His words were softer than oil, yet they were drawn swords.*

On her desk, under the facedown photo of herself, was a letter from Mavis Krepps, the president of the condominium association, which had been distributed to both owners and renters a week ago. It was so long and complicated that Viola knew she would have to read it several more times before she understood it fully. The gist, however, was clear: condo values at Pheasant Run had steeply declined over a period of years, ever since revised borrowing regulations had drastically reduced the pool of potential buyers; renters in the building were now inexplicably moving out, which further affected those who owned the units; the owners were reluctant to raise rents because they were well aware that the financial burden would be untenable for some; deferred maintenance loomed; and there was the possibility that the association might decide to sell the entire building to an unnamed party.

If that happened, Viola and the building's other renters would have just a month before they had to vacate. "As always," Mrs. Krepps had added unnecessarily, "if a tenant is evicted for cause (felonious damage, harboring a pet, nonpayment of rent, etc.), the premises must be vacated within the week."

Mavis Krepps had long ago been a classics instructor at a small college somewhere in the Midwest and she liked to salt her communications with references to antiquity. She finished her letter with a plea for Olympian calm amid the uncertainty.

"Rumors abound, most of them without substance. Please remember that nothing regarding a potential buyout has been written in stone, or is even close to the stone-writing phase. In addition, it is simply not true that the no-pet rule applies to goldfish or small caged birds, as several renters say they have been told. In closing, I will leave you with a thought from Hesiod circa 700 BC: 'Gossip is mischievous, light and easy to raise, but grievous to bear and hard to get rid of. No gossip ever dies away entirely, if many people voice it: it too is a kind of divinity.' A thought to live by! Have a lovely weekend!"

Viola clenched her eyes. *Cast me not off in the time of old age; forsake me not when my strength faileth.* The words came to her and made her wish she weren't an atheist. What a comfort it would be to say them and believe, as her grandmother had, that they made their way to a gargantuan, sympathetic Ear.

Heavy on her mind was the documentary she had seen recently about real estate developers in Spain who were intimidating old people into moving out of their rent-controlled apartments so the properties could be renovated and sold for astronomical sums. They stopped at nothing: burglary, threats, maintenance neglect, even installing criminal elements on the premises.

And now—could it be coincidence?—Pheasant Run had this new on-site property manager, Herbie, and there was nothing about him that didn't seem suspect.

The man could put on an amiable face and talk pleasantly about lawn mowing and garbage pickup when the spirit moved him, but Viola sensed strongly that he was a gangster, essentially, and not impossibly an ex-con. Those two eyeteeth weren't missing for nothing.

At least three other tenants—all of them renters—had confided to her that Herbie had come to them with bizarre threats and accusations. He would say he smelled a dog on the premises and that the tenant's days were numbered. He would refuse to fix a wonky stove burner or a bathroom leak and tell the tenant the problem was in his or her head. He refused requests to test smoke alarms, and, pressed by courtly Leo Uberti in #402 to do so without further delay, had called him a mental case to his face.

To the building's condominium owners, on the other hand, he presented a dim but helpful face and scurried around as if he lived to be of assistance. Who was he, anyway? What was his plan? What were his orders?

She tried, now, to blink herself crisply and confidently into the day. She had to banish the specter of herself under a piece of cardboard, or in a Medicaid nursing home that breathed urine and utter exhaustion. She had to trust that her landlord, Clovis, was a reasonable man and would exhibit a degree of flexibility. And perhaps, too, the sale of the entire building was only wishful thinking on the owners' part and would never happen. There was no reason to anticipate disaster.

Perhaps Roderick would even come through with the money he owed her. She tried to banish the image of her aging only child driving off to Jackpot in his old Falcon with the drooping tailpipe, again so misguided about the course of his life that it made her light-headed. Every initiative Rod undertook—the bogus marriage to the Slovakian teenager, selling special vitamins for guard dogs, the parrot-breeding enterprise—had been idiotic and a disaster. On top of that, she didn't really like him. Never had.

She wobbled a bit as she stood. Her toes hurt more than they usually did, and her muscles, as usual, seemed to be taking a nap. How long had it been since she had been able to move with alacrity, or even with a kind of stately aged smoothness? Not since the botched knee replacement and then the procedure that was said to have unbotched it but had actually left her with so little strength that her balance was thrown off and she took a few falls, including the big one that landed her for a month in bed.

"Another crash like that, and life as you know it will be over!" said Rod, who had never been successful at masking his darkest wishes with a veneer of concern.

It had been a week of difficult letters. Two days ago, she had finished an important one to her neighbor Cassie McMackin, whom she trusted instinctively, though she wondered at her seeming unconcern about a building sale. The unsent letter was Viola's insurance against simply evaporating from the zeitgeist, in case she had to depart the building suddenly and without explanation as a result of a letter she had sent a day earlier to Longleap Enterprises. In it, she had voiced her opinion that Longleap was a front for real estate developers trying to force out the building's occupants, mostly through the efforts of the new on-site manager, Herbie Bonebright. She had a good idea what his real job was: to scare renters into leaving, which would push the condo association in the direction of selling. "Please be aware that some of us are onto you, and we ask you to cease and desist or we will alert the proper authorities," she had finished.

As soon as the note disappeared down the mail chute, she realized what she had done. She had made herself a rabbit in their headlights. All they had to do now was mow her down in some fashion and make it look like an accident.

This had made an escape plan necessary. After writing her letter to Cassie, she had put it, her phone, fifty dollars in cash, and her emergency credit card in the zippered pocket of her pink ski jacket. This afternoon, she decided now, she would take the city bus to the downtown terminal, get the next bus to the airport, and buy a one-way ticket to Los Angeles. There she would post the letter, pay cash for a bus to Santa Barbara, and begin her new life.

Rod had given her the phone in return for the Jack in the Box loan, and even taken the time to show her some of its more extravagant features before he left. She suspected he'd stolen it, and that as soon as she used it, her whereabouts would be signaled to the police and she'd be arrested for some kind of fraud. That was the sort of thing that could happen when Rod gave you a gift. So she would leave the phone, wrapped in a newspaper, on a bench at the downtown bus terminal. She liked the thought of it resting there, sending out its tiny futile signals while she boarded a long silver jet and rode it through the clouds to the Pacific.

She made another cup of tea and drank it slowly, then decided that since she was up and around, she might as well take the elevator to the basement and retrieve her gun and her Thanksgiving decorations from her storage unit. She liked to tack her crepe-paper turkey with the ruffled tail to her door at least two weeks before the holiday because November was such a grim, dark month and anything vivid and celebratory could only help. She would do that today, so no one would suspect anything was out of the usual with her. Her gun, a .22 pistol given to her by Ollie many decades ago when he was working night shift at the mill, belonged right now in her apartment, so she could use it if she had to. Though there might not be bullets. She would have to see.

It was only 7:20, and no one was likely to be up and about except Herbie, who would have left for breakfast, so she didn't change from her pajamas and bed jacket. When the elevator door opened, she was startled and embarrassed to see Leo Uberti, her neighbor down the hall. He looked just as surprised as she felt. He was breathing rapidly, as if he had a heart condition he'd kept under wraps.

Uberti was a retired insurance agent who had given himself in his golden years to his first love, oil painting. Sometime in the past few months, he had grown a thin goatee that was only slightly paler than his skin, and he had a new-looking stocking cap pulled low. He smelled faintly of turpentine, as he always did. His eyes were large and kind. Viola didn't know him well, but had always felt, in his presence, a certain calm. Maybe it had something to do with her sense that he seemed to live almost entirely in his imagination and therefore had no stake in making trouble for anyone in the flesh.

"Mrs. Six," he said, tipping his fingers to the rim of an imaginary fedora. "I was just going to tap on your door to see if a fellow early bird could spare some coffee."

"Anything wrong?" she asked, holding the door open.

"It's nothing," he said quickly, patting his sternum. "Got moving too fast." He looked at her a little more closely. "And we are arrayed in the raiment of evening, I see," he said gently.

"I'm sneaking down to get some things from my storage unit," Viola said. "I had no idea anyone would be running around yet."

"'Running' is putting it very kindly," Uberti said. He took a deep breath.

"Come get the coffee in ten minutes," she said.

"I think I'll probably lie down for a while," he said. "This day already feels a little strange on the edges, wouldn't you say?" He took a long, shaky breath and tipped his absent hat.

In the basement, Viola stared at the dim hallway of the wooden-slatted storage units. Something was wrong with hers. The padlock was gone, the hasp swung loose, and the door was fastened shut with twine. She stood frozen, a few feet away. There was a smell. It was greasy clothes and dirty hair, with an overtone of something yeasty and sweaty. There was a sound behind the door. It was small and conical, air sipped in, air blown out. It paused and something shifted. An involuntary squeak came from her throat, and she slid her slippered feet backward until she could make her body turn toward the elevator door. She battered the call button, another squeak leaping from her. How long would it take her to get up the stairs, if she managed to get up them at all? There was a click and a whir and the door opened.

Inside her apartment, she swept her gaze around the little rooms. Tears of violation and rage began to seep down her face. Someone was in her storage unit, breathing deeply in the dark, waiting his chance to sneak up the stairs and do whatever kind of unmentionable harm he could. She tried to think about what she should do.

She grabbed the blue canister that was supposed to make everything smell like linens on a clothesline by the sea and gave the room a thorough spray, then she made herself a very small gin and tonic for her nerves and tried to imagine it as an elixir, a poultice. She took deep breaths and imagined the potion making its way to her inner recesses, where her saddest thoughts beat their heads against the walls of dimly lit rooms, stunned by the world's iniquity and willingness to betray.

Here she was, living the last shard of her life, and she kept expecting a reprise of that experience she'd had two decades ago when that wealthy charlatan had convinced Captain to invest all her savings in a company that would fail—that had been *set up* to fail, for the shadowy financial advantages the con man and his cronies would enjoy. In good faith, she and others had handed over their hopes, their small insulations. As always, the memory made her light-headed and full of dread. And today, that feeling was combined with a peculiar alertness. Something was repeating. Something rapacious was on the move.

She retrieved the letter from Mavis Krepps, then put it down without reading it. She had to stop blowing embers into flames, as that way lay insanity. This she knew. She stared at the china shepherdess on her knickknack shelf and tried to envision sun and sheep and blue sashes. Her heart began to thud in her ears.

"Go!" she whispered. "Go, Viola—get out! It's time."

She walked as rapidly as she could to her bedroom, where she pawed among her clothes for something to wear. She thought of calling Cassie, but there wasn't time. She needed to move fast and she needed to move alone. She kicked off her slippers and grabbed a pair of slacks and a sweater. The inbound bus stopped on the half hour a block away. She had eight minutes. She swooped up her pills from the bathroom and sat on the bed to remove her pajamas.

Someone knocked hard on her hallway door and she twitched so violently the pill bottles flew from her hands. Someone fiddled with the knob, and inserted a key, because of course he had a key, and there it was, in the next room, her name in Herbie Bonebright's sullen tones.

From his hiding place in the storage unit, Clayton Spooner consulted his phone and saw that he'd now been there for more than fifteen hours.

Almost 7:35. His mom was going to discover pretty soon that he hadn't stayed at Steiner's last night, as he'd texted her he planned to, and that he wasn't at school. The principal's office always contacted parents about no-shows by the end of the first class, so she'd have a panic attack then and call Steiner and so on. He texted her. *No worries if school calls, mamacita. Will be in 2nd class. Xplain later.* He thought about adding a grinning emoji. Thought better of it. She wasn't going to be smiling at emojis today. *Things r fine*, he signed off. He hoped that calling her *mamacita*, rather than Carla, as he usually did, would help.

He thought about the day outside, the humans churning into motion, and put his hands over his ears.

He thought about yesterday and fought a horrible urge to weep. His teeth began to chatter and he couldn't make them stop. His hands trembled and he pressed them to his mouth, then jerked them away, disgusted at the new pimples above his lip.

First there was the battle with Carla about the pills, when he'd refused, again, to take them, and she'd completely lost it and thrown them in his face, to rattle and skitter all over the kitchen floor.

"Don't, then!" she'd shrieked. "Don't focus on anything worthwhile, God knows. Your studies, your grades. Don't give in to any kind of ambition that's going to get you down the road. Don't pay attention to anything like that."

Her eyes squeezed shut, as though the enormity of her grievances had engulfed her. She was dressed for work in her black pantsuit, which had a bunch of white dog hairs on the back. How ambitious are dog hairs on your butt? Clayton wanted to say, just to watch her go further ballistic. But he didn't dare. She was too angry and she had the circles under her eyes that meant she'd stayed up until the early-morning chat shows, writing in her journal, pacing her room, maybe even calling Clayton's father, Frank, to hiss at him about his phony life and his phony values, all of it embodied in the twenty-two-year-old he'd shacked up with across town.

She did that sometimes, and then, come daylight, blue crescents under her eyes, she pulled herself together and went off to her job as a house stager. It was a profession she'd chosen just before Frank made his first break, the one in which he said he wanted only to be alone for a while so that he could reacquaint himself with himself and come back a better husband and father. The reacquainting took place in Costa Rica, and Carla hadn't spared her son the details: that it cost half their entire savings and that in addition to Frank's singed skin, he had returned with a stupid light in his eye and an STD, one of the easier to treat.

When she loudly wished for him a brain-eroding, terminal disease, he decided his options should include a fuller investment in his autonomy, and a week later he moved in with Jailbait, as Carla referred to her.

To Clayton, his father explained that it was a sorting-things-out time that would make them all stronger and that his new friend Kaycee was wise beyond her years and someone he felt he could learn a lot from, and he thought Clayton was having some respect issues when he responded to the moving-in news by blowing a mouthful of Cheerios back into his bowl.

Carla, laid off from her office manager's job in a downsizing at T&P Motorhomes the month before Frank went to Costa Rica, had looked around at the skittish housing market, then gone to every open house she could and realized that most homeowners had silly taste and a fetish for clutter that was likely to cost them a respectable sale. A house wasn't going to sell itself. The messiness of current lives had to be stripped away in order to entice the imagining of new ones.

She'd majored in art history during her two years of college and had worked, before T&P, at a high-end furniture store under the tutelage of their resident room designer, and, quite simply, she had an eye. This she mentioned to Clayton quite often. In fact, she talked about the details of her new profession to an extent that made him want to shout and flee.

Because her house-staging philosophy relied heavily on the techniques of serenity, a phrase she had coined herself, she headed off in the mornings nearly toppling under her arsenal of room soothers: wine country coffee-table books, skinny branches in a severe black vase, a small rock fountain that splashed and babbled when you plugged it in. Foster, their schnauzer, typically experienced a frenzy of separation anxiety as she left, and he raced, yipping, in circles around her ankles until Clayton pulled him away.

"Fuck, Foster!" she'd shriek. "Why don't you just kill me and be done with it!" And then she was gone and Foster began to calm down, and Clayton could begin to breathe.

What he hated most about the whole situation, the bust-up and impending divorce, was that he felt a terrible pity for both of his parents, mixed in with the red anger. The pity wouldn't ever go entirely away, and it weakened him, and he felt that the only way he could stay upright and even make it into the next month or so was to have very little to do with either of them.

The fact that Jailbait was the half sister of one of his main tormenters at school only made everything all the more insoluble and dangerous.

From the time he could remember, Clayton had felt assaulted by the noises of his life. His volatile, overenergized parents. Everything humming and beeping and barking and yelling, until he yearned to simply push himself down to the floor of a lake and lie in the watery silence, muffled in the cool blue, ungilled.

Only once had there been a reprieve, of about a year. Then, in middle school, he slept almost normal hours and ran track, laughed sometimes with his mysteriously calmer parents, camped in the mountains with a neighbor family, got respectable grades in school. All those ordinary, quiet things.

The agitation returned when he was thirteen, just before he started to play video games with his new best friends Mack and Steiner. It found him; it lurked around, shivered all the borders, made him want to shout.

But the games, with their predictable chosen chaos and noise, actually had a soothing effect. The three of them took up their positions on the worn and puffy couch in Steiner's basement, headsets on, the Xbox at the ready. For hours at a time, they moved through urban ruins or desert war zones, shooting, trapping, torching, looting, and dying. Swarmed by yellow-eyed Nazi zombies and near death, they called on each other to bring the reviving hypodermic, and if it was too late, the screen trembled and went red and your death was blared in white letters, and then you moved back a way in the game and respawned.

Clayton liked it best when the action was fast and bloody and the kill count was high and death was avoided by individual shooting, leaping, and torching skills, certainly, but also by calling on your comrades to move through bullets and packs of mutant creatures in order to save you.

In real life, Mack and Steiner were similarly shuffling and sleepy-eyed. But put them in the game and they, like Clayton, manipulated triggers, bumpers, and joysticks with the speed and finesse of fighter pilots. They were in training for a world of endless war, endless permutations of endless enemies. And they were fearless and loyal, risking death at every turn to come to each other's aid. Grunting and cackling and whooping, they annihilated with abandon and arrived at game's end depleted and reinforced.

A kind of euphoria began to be upon him at times, and his growing success on the battlefields—with guns, against monsters, on missions, out of traps, newly heavy with loot—made him want to coax more risk and drama out of his nonscreen life. So he took a dare from Steiner and rushed up behind a cop and tapped the top of his holstered gun, so lightly the cop felt not a thing. Ha!

He found a cache of Hawaiian shirts at a thrift store, and a straw fedora, and he wore them every day for most of a summer. He became infatuated with the idea of old-time journalism where the reporter actually sat down with people for a few hours and got their whole story into his neat black notebook. And so he bought a black notebook and approached a couple of strangers at the mall, wearing his wildest Hawaiian shirt and his old-time newsman hat, and pleaded with them to sit down with him at the Orange Julius and tell him their true stories, and begged them—hold on!—not to get up and walk away.

Steiner, capable of betrayal to an extent Clayton could never have imagined, reported these escapades to his mom, who reported them to Carla and Frank, and that was the first trip to the first shrink.

He doesn't like to think much about what happened next.

Another kid at school had bought both *Call of Duty: Modern Warfare Remastered* and the multiplayer *Halo Wars 2* and had invited Mack and Steiner to his basement to play. When Mack mentioned this too casually, Clayton felt more shot than he ever had, and he doubted that he would ever respawn.

On the same day, his dad announced that he was moving into an apartment with his friend Kaycee. After that, the sounds of daily life turned into a roar as his mom tried to create a sense of purpose and bustle and multitasking. More phone calls, louder TV, Foster running around utterly batshit.

Clayton retreated to his head, where he reviewed some of the best kills and rescues he'd experienced. He lined up the enemies—zombies, turbaned soldiers, shock troops, grunts, brutes, space aliens, and mutants. He reviewed his kill chains and hammer sprees and medals. On a day he'd told Carla he was too sick to go to school, he ate breakfast, slunk to the couch, and reimagined a particularly memorable episode in which a pack of mutant dogs had, as one, leaped for his throat. Steiner's avatar, Slade, zigzagged to the rescue across a minefield littered with burning cars and pocked with sniper fire as Clayton's man tried to throw off the dogs so they could be shot or grenaded. His head felt as if it would burst. The universe was filled with snarling and barking. He could smell their saliva.

And when his eyes flew open, Foster was yipping and cowering and trying to scrape across the floor to escape another kick. Carla flew in from the next room and gave her son a look he would never forget.

"Don't you move another inch," she hissed. She yanked the old afghan off the couch and wrapped the whimpering dog in it to take to the vet. When Clayton was a small child, she used to wrap him up in the same afghan and prop him between her and Frank while they ate popcorn and watched antique reruns of *Candid Camera*, Clayton laughing so hard his stomach hurt.

The Foster that Clayton kicked so hard bore no relation to an actual dog. That animal had come from a realm of mayhem, near-death, and his yearning for the real-life friends who were drifting so rapidly away. But the fact that it had happened—Foster turned out to have a cracked rib and never again spun circles of joy when Clayton came into the house—combined with the fact that his grades had taken a nosedive and he couldn't seem to make himself pay attention to anything his mother was saying, had prompted more trips to another shrink.

That was a year and two shrinks and a bunch of drugs ago, all of it underwritten by insurance or his guilt-ridden father. Now, at fifteen, he had taken Ritalin for attention deficit hyperactivity disorder, Zoloft for oppositional defiant disorder, Risperdal for anger, Depakote and Abilify and, finally, lithium to stabilize his moods. He'd gained fifteen pounds, and he had tremors, acne, and insomnia. The two drugs he was on now seemed to clash with each other and sometimes made him want to destroy everything, wipe the earth clean, even of himself. Especially of himself. He thought of running away. He took refuge in elaborately detailed visions of himself in some heroic role, in some heroic life. Jumping out of a plane to fight a forest fire. Delivering piles of money and supplies, in his own silver yacht, to earthquake victims on an impoverished island. He wanted to instigate relief on a massive scale.

But he was just a pale, tremulous, pimpled, pudgy teenager whose old friends, Mack and Steiner, now occupied a social pod that excluded him, whose mother was an agitated, exhausted mess, whose father was in some kind of adamant trance.

His only consolation was his love for Raven Felska, the pale girl with black-rimmed eyes and tattooed sentences on her arms and hands. They sat next to each other in Spanish. She smelled faintly of tobacco and something else, maybe incense. They smoked together in the alley after school and rarely spoke, but Clayton didn't question their deep affinity, their shared sense of waiting, together, to be free from their ridiculous lives. She told him the inky words that snaked across her hands and lower arms were poem fragments. Sometimes he tried to read them when she didn't notice, and they meant nothing to him, which made him love her more.

Clayton's tormenter at school, Josh Anderson, had renamed himself Chaser and wanted everyone else to call him that. He was an angel-faced blond boy, a bit shorter than most of his friends, but fast and agile and mean as a viper. His ingratiating smile had put all the teachers in his pocket, and presumably his parents, too, if the car he drove, a new loaded Jeep, was any indication.

The only thing Clayton had ever done to Josh Anderson was to continue calling him by his given name, the name he'd known him by since grade school, no matter how upset Josh got. For his sin, Clayton had already been beaten up twice, once by Josh and once by Josh's right-hand guy, Troy. Josh had also discovered, through his half sister Kaycee, that Clayton was taking various medications. He began to go around telling anyone who would listen that Clayton was "special"—big quotation marks in the air—and should be going to a "special" school for retards. Yesterday morning he'd said it again, just as Raven passed them in the hall. Josh pointed at Clayton and lurched spastically, then turned to Raven.

"Hey," he said.

"Hey, Josh," she had murmured.

"Chaser," Josh said. "The name's Chaser."

"Hey, Chaser," she acquiesced.

Clayton felt as if she'd been captured, that she spoke from behind bars. The thought made him frantic with fury.

"Don't talk to him," he said to Raven, his voice ice.

"Josh!" he said, turning to him. "Why Chaser? Because it reminds you of someone who can run down anyone he wants? Who isn't a lame little midget with a lame little midget dick?"

And then three or four of them were on him, and when he saw an opening he hit Josh as hard as he could in the face and fled. Josh's friends bent over his prone and bloody form.

Clayton slammed through the heavy school door, almost knocking down two scrawny freshmen, and sprinted down the block. He heard shouts and veered into an alley behind the tall old people's building down the block, then realized they were probably coming at him from both directions and would engulf him at the alley's outlet. At that moment a large window opened on the ground floor and a tiny white-haired woman grabbed a rope that was attached to the lid of a big garbage bin. She stared at him.

"It's OK," he gasped. "No worries." He scrambled onto the bin and through the big sliding window so fast that the woman didn't have time to do more than step back and throw her hands up to her face. He ran down the carpeted hall, down a staircase. A door opened on a corridor of storage units the size of double closets. Most of them were padlocked, but the lock of the last one on the left had a hasp that hung at an odd angle. He jerked at it and the door swung open. Inside were boxes, blankets, lampshades, two old trunks, paint cans, turpentine, a saddle tipped on its horn. He grabbed a piece of twine from the floor and fastened the door shut behind him, then crawled behind the trunks and pulled a blanket over himself, and slept.

Fully awake now, he began to feel a kind of peace that he hadn't in a very long time. He was at the bottom of the lake, bobbing, closing his eyes, opening them to peer through the dark water. How long had it taken for him to drift to this place? What was it that had been done to him in that long sleep to leave him feeling so restored, so laser-like?

Once he heard footsteps. They weren't quick and brash like those of Josh and his friends, marching like mutants to drag him out by his hair. These were soft and deliberate. They stopped at the head of the storage room corridor and he heard light anxious breathing, and then they advanced toward him, a little slide to the feet like snakeskin, and he burrowed deeper under the blanket and tried to ignore his thumping heart. The steps stopped; the breathing grew louder. He squinted to see the vague form of a thin old lady in what looked like pajamas, and then she retreated. He was bathed in rancid sweat.

He shifted his position under the blanket and moved a box to stretch out his legs. It was a dark box, leather, with old-fashioned brass clasps, like the ones on his grandpa's ancient suitcase. As slowly and quietly as he could, he released the catches and lifted the lid. Inside, resting in indented old velvet, was a pistol. It had a dull gleam in the dim light and an eloquence that constricted Clayton's throat. Calm and beautiful and lethal, it seemed to have slid down a corridor of light from another age with the sole purpose of revealing itself to a worthy person who had suffered much and been wronged. He lifted it out and turned it this way and that, so that its intricacies of barrel and trigger and stock could show themselves to him. He rested it against his cheek.

After a while, he stood and stretched and used the blanket to wipe himself down. He was starving, he realized. Thirsty, too. He replaced the gun in its box and put the box in his backpack, then jumped back when an alarm went off somewhere above his head, as if the theft somehow had been detected. He heard running footsteps, some distant shouts and small cries. Another alarm joined the first.

Clayton hoisted his pack onto his back and scurried out of the storage unit toward the stairwell. On the first floor he ran toward the big sliding window above the garbage bin, smelling, now, a trickle of smoke. He vaulted himself out and over the bin and began to run.

Small sirens in the distance became rapidly deafening, and, in his confusion, he ran the wrong way down the alley and emerged near the front of the building, where several old people were huddled in their nightclothes. One pointed at him, and he pivoted in the other direction to run as he had never run before, the backpack hitting him hard between his shoulder blades. His breath came steadily, and he soon felt that he could run forever, that he could run forever toward Raven, in triumph, and that when he presented her with the gun, they would make their plan, together, to punish Josh and his posse into submission. Together they would do that. They would do whatever it took.

WHEN BEING HUMAN
IS FAR FROM ENOUGH

Across town, on the other side of the river, Chief Fire Inspector Lander Maki heard a humming sound coming from the living room. Rhonda was up early. He pulled on some sweats and running shoes, splashed cold water on his face, waved to her, and headed out for his early-morning slow run.

The sky was shedding its pink lights and firming up to a frank and cloudless blue, a November blue, with a desultory wafer of moon floating near the horizon. What had Rhonda told him about some Native names for the month of November? Beaver Moon, Goose Going Moon, Mad Moon. Why mad? Because a November day could seem to be caught, confused and blustering, between the falling gold of fall and the icy crawl of winter? Maybe, but not today. Today November was neither. It held the quietness of a pause. The feel of a something-before. A train whistle blew. A door slammed and a car revved up. Maki's breath smoked lightly before him.

He ran slowly through his neighborhood of small and aging houses, some with pin-neat yards, others benignly shambled. Turned-over trikes, clumped lawns, and rusty barbeques. There a tipsy pink flamingo, and over there an eave fringed with tattered prayer flags, another dangling dead flowers in a planter; a window with a Christian fish, another with a peace sign, another with a "Go Griz" banner. A neighborhood of cracked sidewalks, faded charming porches, kids, students, laborers, adjuncts, retirees, firefighters, do-gooders, DIY renovators—many of them up early with Maki, in their lighted kitchens, about to head into their days.

He rounded the last corner of his short run, slowed, then sprinted the last fifty yards toward the yellow glow from his own living room.

Inside, Rhonda was on her knees at the side of Siddhartha, their Great Dane, humming still and waving a glowing, braided stalk of sweetgrass over the dog's head. She looked up.

"Sid's exhausted from his criminal adventures," she said briskly. "It'll take a few minutes before he's clear."

The dog stretched on his huge sheepskin bed, the herby smoke moving in lazy wreaths above the odor that emanated from him. Over in the corner, their ancient turtle came out of its shell, stared around aghast, and disappeared again.

"I'm with you, pal," Maki murmured.

Sid had been missing for most of the day before, and when he finally showed up, he reeked of misadventure involving unfresh carcasses and some dairy thing that was worse. They'd managed to coax him into the shower with a piece of pizza and had tried to clean him up with Rhonda's cucumber body wash, but the smell lingered and she'd gone to bed claiming further steps were needed if the entire house wasn't going to take on a negative charge, making them all a little sad once again.

Siddhartha had all the big-boned amiability and sensory acuity you would expect in his breed, plus an extra degree of alertness that stemmed from whatever circumstances had deposited him, thin and shaking, in a glass-sharded borrow pit on the edge of town, to be discovered and rehabilitated by Rhonda. He turned out to have, as well, another trait that seemed to go beyond his breeding and history, and could only be described as a certain large kindness. It was there in the way that he tipped his heavy head to fasten a liquid look of utter empathy on his humans, in the way he had risen from his sheepskin pallet on the few occasions when Maki and Rhonda argued and placed a paw on first one person's knee and then the other's, dissipating all unease or rancor in a matter of seconds.

Rhonda had been schooled as an actuary but worked now as a seasonal tax preparer and a volunteer at the Humane Society. She was also an aspiring animal communicator and had taken, by correspondence, a course called "When Being Human is Far from Enough." It coached the student in the most successful methods of establishing superhuman channels of communication with domestic animals. This pursuit complemented a tentative investigation into certain shamanic techniques and a new interest in the cosmology and spiritual practices of her Native American forebears on her mother's side.

She was a tiny, wiry woman with a huge mop of tight black curls and, Maki thought, one of the sweetest smiles on the planet. Only her crooked eyeteeth and a sandpaper laugh rescued her from forgettable perfection.

None of her woo-woo, as Maki sometimes called it to her face, made much sense to him, but he loved her enthusiasms and general largeheartedness because they were so at odds with his baseline temperament, which was gloom and a chronic expectation of the worst. She lifted him out of that murk for minutes, for hours at a time. More and more, too, he was coming to view her unconventional practices as ritualizations or codifications of an empathy so profound that it threatened, at times, to overwhelm her. Certainly it extended to the creature that was Lander Maki in a way he'd never experienced before. Not growing up. Not in his first marriage. Not ever.

"Make sure that sweetgrass is fully extinguished before you set it down anywhere," Maki said, waving away some smoke. "Run it under some water, actually."

Rhonda gave him an indulgent look. "Listen to him," she said to Sid. "He may be our beloved, but he is also the city's fire inspector, and if we do something careless and overheated, he will come and...inspect us."

"IN-spect," the mynah bird croaked.

Sid sat up and tipped his big Dane ears toward the bird, which had long ago left its cage for the day and perched now on a curtain rod, adjusting its scabrous claws to stay upright. The deaf cat sat on the window seat, pretending to meditate.

Rhonda had named the bird Flora the day they liberated it from PetSmart because she had felt, though it was an aged male, signals from it of a longing to cross genders. And why not? Were humans the sole possessors of cravings? Was it out of the realm of possibility that animals could make their needs known in some persuasive, if whispery, fashion? Rhonda thought not. Or said as much. Maki couldn't tell sometimes if she was making fun of herself.

Her exploration of telepathic communication between humans and animals, especially dogs who had behavior problems that were distressing their owners, seemed entirely sincere on its face. An actual meeting between practitioner and pet was not required or even desirable, she told him. A photo of the animal looking directly at the camera, plus a description of the salient trouble, was enough. And then, if you heightened your awareness through meditation to permeate the membrane that protects and limits humans from unbearable perception, a conversation could begin.

Her first case was a basset hound named Pepi who had a problem with rampant lawn digging. Pepi's human companion—Rhonda preferred the term to *owner*—was a friend from her Pilates class. She offered Rhonda some details about the digging and gave her a photo of Pepi. That evening, Rhonda sat down at her laptop, searched the dog's eyes, took in the dolorous jowls. She introduced herself and explained why she was talking to him. Her fingers flew over the computer keys as she posed questions and registered his answers, assembling a transcript that she later presented to Maki and emailed to Pepi's person. The gist of it was that the dog had been an alcoholic grave digger in a previous life and had never learned to deal appropriately with unpredictable funeral schedules and feelings of inadequacy and deprivation.

When Maki read that admission, he fell back on the couch and put the transcript over his face. She tapped on the printout, and he returned it to her, then buried his face in his hands to grin some more.

She was unfazed.

"I tried to remind him that alcohol blunted growth as well as pain, so it wasn't surprising that he had never moved beyond his repeating anxieties," she said with airy detachment. "They are the reason for the holes in the lawn. We're working on it."

She told Maki now that, while he was in bed and Sid was not yet getting the sweetgrass treatment, she had tried for the first time to connect with a truant animal whose photo and history had not been presented to her by its human. Could she summon contact out of an informational void? An image had come to her of her grandparents' old Bakelite radio, so she approached it and turned the big knob. First there was just static. Then she heard a doglike voice talking in low, wise tones that were just out of range, and then, louder, a voice that had a growly little purr on the edges and was identifying itself as belonging to a female Norwegian Forest cat, age two. She said she was sitting on the very top of a big house in the university district.

"Are you afraid you will fall from that tall place?" Rhonda had inquired. "Are you afraid you'll be hurt?" Her gaze grew distant.

"And she said…" Maki waited.

"She said, 'Lady, I'm a *cat*,'" said Rhonda. Then they were both laughing, and Rhonda was making passes of the sweetgrass over Sid's head in an antic and animated fashion. She stopped abruptly and stared gravely into the dog's eyes. She nodded.

WHEN BEING HUMAN IS FAR FROM ENOUGH

"Sid wants you to make those eggs you made the other day. With extra for him."

Maki put together all the meals in the household because Rhonda was a disaster in the kitchen and because cooking calmed him. Lists, portions, methods, results—that was the ticket.

He didn't look like a person who needed calming, but how many do? In his late forties, he had a flat, rosy face and the almost lidless eyes of his Finnish ancestors. Even in suburban St. Paul, where he'd grown up and which was wall-to-wall Scandinavians, the occasional teacher or new acquaintance would be confused and ask if his name was Japanese. Maki, Skari, Talo—they were Finnish names and better sounding, Maki thought, than all those Olafsons and Offerdahls scraping their way across the endless snow. Clean clicky fish names, the Finns had, slippery and neat.

Maki spoke in low tones and moved slowly and alertly, as if his daily surroundings were as full of clues as the scenes of the mysterious fires he was so good at deciphering. In the kitchen he arranged his two cutting boards and his small glass bowl, his whisk and spices and skillet. He chopped the shiitakes he'd had soaking and sprinkled them with a little brandy, then sautéed them in walnut oil while he minced a handful of chives to add to the earthy stew. The eggs got a good whisk and a dollop of cream and were then folded into the mushrooms and chives while he turned the flame down very low. He wrapped a few pieces of thick peppered bacon in paper towels and cooked them in the microwave for six minutes while he stirred the eggs very slowly until they were coddled and creamy. When the English muffins were toasted and done, he buttered them, covered them with the crumbled bacon, added a sprinkle of malt vinegar (his special touch) and topped them with the eggs and a sprig of lemon basil. He left a sample of the eggs in the pan for Sid, who, of course, would have been just as happy with a bite of putrid rabbit skin.

Rhonda had moved from the floor to sit tailor-style on a faded velvet couch, their best estate-sale find. She'd extinguished the sweetgrass, but the smell of it lingered, and she sniffed the air as if the smoke were feeding her. Maki brought her the eggs and a strong cup of coffee on a lacquered tray.

"What a beast you are," she said. "Eggs, butter, coffee. So many sins on a single platter." She took a big bite and fell back against the sofa cushions. "I'm slain with pleasure," she whispered, impaling him with a stare.

Maki allowed himself a small smile. Because he was not an effusive or demonstrative person, he felt lucky that Rhonda supplied enough for them both, even though her growing-up years had been tempestuous and full of mistakes and terrible luck. There had been the crazy, controlling, charismatic first husband, several ill-advised friendships with out-and-out degenerates, a sporadic tequila problem, the trauma in the hypermall, all of it rife with strife and drama and tears—all of which Maki envied in a peculiar way, though he couldn't tell her that because it would seem to be discounting the pain that she felt had enhanced her talents for empathy and healing.

Six years earlier, just before they met, Rhonda was struggling through the dregs of a marriage to a man named Ridley who had begun as a set designer for a regional theater and morphed, via voracious networking and his sister's marriage to a billionaire, into a designer of hypermalls. They had moved from Seattle to Riverside, though even as she packed the last of their household goods, she knew she wasn't going to stay with Ridley, or live for any length of time in Southern California; knew with the kind of certainty that made her actions, she told Maki, seem those of a Siamese twin with entirely different priorities from her own.

But they took her as far as the new house with its whine of freeway traffic and air-conditioning always in the background, where she and Ridley ate takeout every night and she stared at all the boxes that sat around not wanting to be opened. And her Siamese shadow took her one day to the newly constructed hypermall that Ridley and the others on the design team had conceptualized and that was already drawing attention from developers with holdings all over the world, including, it would turn out, the consortium behind the construction of 1Borneo, the largest lifestyle hypermall in East Malaysia.

A prominent feature of the Riverside project was the Castle of Infinite Lavender Dreams, situated across an atrium from the Glade of Serenity, where behemoth screens displayed moving waterfalls and speakers mounted in the foliage made splashing water noises for tense and overextended shoppers who could take their ease on benches that had been molded to resemble ancient stone.

That's where Rhonda was sitting, waiting for Ridley to be done with a meeting, when a young man wearing white coveralls sat down beside her as if he were her brother and was sneaking a break. He smelled smoky. She scooted a few inches sideways to give him room—one of those ridiculous female deferences she'd been working her whole adult life to root out—and looked him in the face. It was a rather terrible face, because it talked but it was blank. Blank eyes and a blank mouth, somehow, despite his alarming words.

What he said, in a nutshell, was that he was going to march her up some back stairs to the top of the castle and hold her hostage at gunpoint until unspecified responders took him at his word and came up with a pile of money.

Rhonda had eyed the castle, seeing herself on the parapet with a gun at her back, seeing herself shot and falling—all of this in a span of seconds—and very slowly raised her arms in surrender. The man hissed, so she pretended to be adjusting her ponytail. A series of empty moments passed, a leaden, fated countdown. Rhonda kept her hands on her hair and closed her eyes. And then there were fast footsteps behind them and her companion on the bench was grabbed by two security cops who stood him up, frisked him efficiently to find what turned out to be a .22 pistol, and informed him that they had been watching him behave in an agitated manner, culminating in unmistakably threatening body language with Rhonda.

Rhonda calmly answered the questions of some other security people, gave her contact information, went straight home, wrote a brief note, bought a next-day air ticket to Montana because it was so empty and far away and she had some distant relatives there. And she never looked back.

Maki pitied her the experience, but also envied its utter outlandishness, its drama. Nothing remotely like that had ever happened to him. His childhood and young adult life, especially, had been bland and stupid to the point of idiocy. They had left him feeling, in his worst times, as if he lived in a sealed cavern of propriety and joylessness. He sometimes felt he might die from an absence of event.

There had been the inscrutable, taciturn parents, a slim, sandy-haired sister who became a stout school bus driver with no discernible relationships with anyone, and a little brother who'd grown into a gambling addict and then a sobered-up real estate salesman and then stopped calling or writing and, the last anyone had heard, was a facilitator at an upscale Christian wellness center in Costa Rica.

Their parents were now in an assisted-living facility called Forest Glen that his sister, Daphne, had found for them a few months ago near her apartment complex in a treeless commercial sprawl on the edge of St. Paul. It was owned by the behemoth ElderIntegrity chain, and Maki could only assume it was a dump, given his parents' modest resources, or that the facility's costs skyrocketed with each tick of decline in a resident's independence, and that the resident would be sent packing the minute the coffers were empty.

He tried not to think too much about the place, or about the fact that he had visited his parents only once a year since he left home.

"Bad son!" the mynah bird called, making Maki's fingertips jump.

"Matson," Rhonda mused. "There it is again. Maybe Flora once belonged to someone named Matson. Maybe he had financial reversals and had to give up everything extra, including poor Flora. Maybe he got bilked in a pyramid scheme or some kind of elder scam and had to move someplace that didn't take giant chatty birds."

"Bad son! Bad son!" the bird called.

Maki took a deep breath and released it in a purgative whoosh.

"Do you think we should cut out coffee?" he asked.

She gave it a few moments' thought. "No," she said. "That would be wrong."

She reached over and put a hand on Maki's knee, then went into their bedroom and returned with a small box, which she presented to him. Inside was a turquoise butterfly fashioned from metal and enamel that was suspended from a narrow strip of leather.

"You can figure out this situation," she said. "Right now, you can't make anything better for your parents because you feel too guilty. This will help you get past that. Wear this next to your body and it will help you feel like more things are possible. You won't feel tethered to the ground, where these people problems seem so big, so sad. You will see it all from the vantage point of something small and light, flying through the air."

Rhonda lifted it from the box and hung it around Maki's neck. While he waited to feel lighter, his phone rang, the first call of the day. He'd had the ringtone set on "Whistling Wizard" for a while, but the demented jauntiness of it was so at odds with the information he sometimes received that he'd switched it back to "Telephone."

The volume was set too high, and it sounded like something from an old detective movie.

"Eeep!" Rhonda said. "That's harsh. I don't like it. Sid doesn't, either." She touched the dog's adoring, upraised nose, and he barked happily. The cat left the realm of spirits and jumped down from the windowsill. The turtle's head emerged. The bird, Flora, made a creditable ringing sound, and Rhonda's gravelly laugh grew raucous.

I love this, Maki thought as he answered the call. *This sweet racket, I truly love.*

The dispatcher reported to Maki that a fire had broken out at the Pheasant Run senior residence over in the university district. The building had been evacuated, and the blaze was quickly extinguished. It had been limited, she said, to the second-floor apartment occupied by the building's on-site manager.

One resident fell on the stairs during the evacuation and had been transported to the ER. Another with heart problems had been treated on the scene for a slight case of smoke inhalation. A third resident, one Viola Six, had not been located, and the manager, a Mr. Bonebright, was also missing.

Maki had been called for the reason he always was: there were oddities. Though the blaze had originated and been confined to the kitchen, it didn't appear to be due to an untended stove. The firefighters thought they might have detected an accelerant. The smoke was maybe blacker than it should have been, and the burn marks suggested the kind of fast, hot fire that might have been set. There were also, notably, those two missing persons of interest.

Maki had recently bought a 1972 Volvo, cramped and army green with a wood-paneled dashboard, which he'd found on eBay for a price he still couldn't believe. Although Rhonda said it was like trying to drive an iron lung and refused to step inside it after a single trial run, Maki liked the car because it was so much more mechanical than it was helpful. It didn't worry about the driver being comfortable or about easing the efforts of window opening, brake releasing, seat adjusting, the way newer cars did. It treated you like a capable, physically competent adult.

Shortly after the dispatcher's call, Maki drove in his customary manner toward Pheasant Run, which meant that it took him quite a long time to cover the two miles. He liked to remind himself, as he drove, that the Volvo moved along the floor of an ancient lake, stupendously large, and that the mountains that began at the edge of the houses still bore the watermarks of that lake's levels during several glacial dramas that had drained and refilled the valley, time after time. Mountains as ancient shores. He found the idea oddly comforting.

Maki moved at a near-crawl because he felt that slowness, too, had become so rare as to seem almost extinct. By proceeding in a hushed and unhurried manner whenever he could, he felt like a scientist reintroducing a threatened species to its old habitat. The pace also helped him think, or rather it prepared him to think in the way that he knew he would have to in order to know what he was seeing at the fire site. Or not seeing. That was the essence of fire investigations: you had to put together a scenario from the presence of an absence. The art was in imagining what had been taken away, and how that might have happened.

Eyes half-closed, he saw everything via his inspector's antennae. There, an office building with a fire escape that looked as if it would blow away in the next wind. (He made a mental note to send a building inspector.) Over there, a handsome old house with a pair of dead cypresses that leaned against the desiccated wood of the roof. An errant bit of flame, a spark from a neighbor's grill, and the trees would ignite and torch the house in a matter of minutes. (The owners would be apprised of the danger.)

He rolled down the window and practiced his smelling. Rhonda liked to tell him that his exceptional olfactory gifts, his *hyperosmia*, made him almost a dog, and his twitching nostrils knew it to be true. Here were the cacophonous smells of a late-autumn morning in a Rocky Mountain valley populated by seventy thousand souls: evergreens, car exhaust, river water, just to record the top notes. It was several degrees warmer than normal, though the new normals made such comparisons increasingly irrelevant, and this November had the added strangeness of the leaves that had remained on the trees after that lacerating early-October freeze. Maki could smell them, too. They were crisp, but more vegetal than papery. They evoked a particular kind of dried mushroom, quite possibly enoki. There was also, in the air, the smell that was the absence of snow during what used to be snow season. It was a faint grave-like smell, chilled and dense.

He caught a whiff of something offbeat—a particular kind of smoke—and leaned out the window to inhale, almost rear-ending an elderly person driving as slowly as he was. Scolding himself, he refocused, but not before he registered the strength of the smell. Someone in the immediate area had burned very young wood the previous evening. This was woodsmoke from a sapling. Less than six months old, that sapling. And some pine cones had been added to the blaze.

His beyond-human smelling prowess was Maki's major natural advantage in his occupation. He could distinguish between fires that had been set with premium gasoline from those set with the lowest grade. He knew which smells were likely to be present in a cooking oil fire versus a blaze that had been helped along with even small amounts of a petroleum accelerant. Most rooms, to him, contained such a multitude of present and past human and animal presences, each entirely different from the others, that he sometimes became vertiginous from the sheer volume of the tracings and had to bury his face for a while in a small cotton pillow stuffed with pine needles that he kept in his briefcase.

To recall himself to his profession, he sometimes did a little mental drill in which he named as many kinds of smoke as he could and arranged them in order of personal attraction, most to least. Evergreen smoke was near the top because it was imaginary Christmases, the hearth, previous centuries, bonfires in snowy woods. Also, it was entirely uncomplicated. It was the smoke of wood, needles, and sap. Period. His next favorite was the smoke of good cannabis, and then that of burning tobacco. Powerful social, sexual, and meditative associations there, which he liked to review and think about. Down further was smoke that had a meat component—not bad if the meat was a salted rib eye grilled over a wood fire, a little worse if the grilling involved gas, or charcoal soaked with fire starter, so you got petroleum products added in. The really terrible smells involved burned fur or skin, as he knew from the aftermaths of several wretched house fires he'd investigated. And smoke that was made by burning plastics, rubber, or chemicals had its own lethality, man-made and unapologetic.

Down on the floor of the ghost lake, Maki's little city was a place where vivid bicyclists zoomed the streets, harrying winds were mostly absent, summer brought flourishing trees and flowers, independent bookstores thrived, and waitresses had master's degrees. Vigorous exercise and modest feats of physical daring were applauded. Hang gliders rose off the mountaintops and wafted like old music through the air.

Maki found himself appreciating, deeply, the salubrious qualities of the place and its surrounding physical grandeur—the encircling mountains, part forest, part scrub grass, and the way they rose into the broad sky like protectors and sentinels—but he also reminded himself to guard against enshrining it all, tempting though that was. After all, how perilously close the lively farmers' markets were to movie sets of idyllic overflowingness and goodwill! How monochromatic the handsome and tall young people! How full of misplaced zest the summer band laboring agriculturally in the river park! It was a place with such easeful surfaces that you had to work a little to see the warts, never mind the threats and the out-and-out griefs, the sort that had to play a part in the suicide rates, nearly the highest in the nation, of both the pretty valley and the grand, broad-shouldered state.

Well, there were always recumbent bicyclists as antidotes to the adamant pleasantness. A grim-faced man, in top-to-toe sweat-wicking garments in bright colors, pulled up beside the Volvo in a reclining position. These bicycles gave Maki the creeps. They were so joyless and passive-aggressive, the rider leaning back from the experience, watching his legs work. His tailbone ached just looking at the guy. The only time it ached more was when a recumbent bicyclist was attached to a baby carrier on wheels—rare, admittedly, but he'd seen it—and then the ache was combined with a certain quiet rage. There they were, adult and babe, moving two feet off the ground through tall herds of fast and heedless cars and trucks. It was the most witless embodiment of hippie-holiness and outright stupidity he'd ever seen. *No wonder I indulge modestly in pot*, Maki thought when he saw something like that. *It's the only thing that assures me I don't have to do anything. Those people just* are. However, conclusions like that were also the reason he was thinking of forgoing weed altogether. They just *are*. What a moronic rationale for bad behavior. It was the intellectual equivalent of predestination.

The sun had lifted fully over the valley, and the tawny parts of the mountainsides lit up like lions. Something about the light now made every glimpse of red take on an aspect of indelibility: the bandanna around that golden retriever's neck, its owner's hoodie, a scrim of maroon leaves on that Japanese maple, the fixed eternity of that stop sign. The redness also evoked flames, of course, and the case at hand.

Maki had a little vision, of the kind that usually came to him only in his first waking moments. Most of the time they didn't disturb him because he'd had them all his life, and they usually seemed less like missives than like helpful illuminations, as if he'd switched to the highest wattage on a three-way bulb. What he saw was something rocking like a pendulum. The moving object had no shape or color, but it had a powerful aspect of inevitability. Time was counting down, always counting down to a future still obscure. Maybe that was all it meant.

Pheasant Run, a classic sixties box construction, stood midway along a five-block corridor that ran from the high school to the campus of the university. Maki parked a block from the building, lit the first of the three cigarettes he allowed himself a day, leafed through his latest *Mother Jones* and finished reading an article in *The Nation*. His magazines relaxed him in a way that was necessary when he was about to wade into a fire scene because they identified patterns in destruction. They also confirmed that he wasn't as depressed for no reason as he sometimes thought he was. The problem wasn't necessarily his native Finn gloom; it was actual puffed-up, deal-making, happily lying, idealism-stomping operators and moguls and so-called statesmen like Little Boy at the helm, who were rapidly plunging the world into a kind of miasmic twilight lit only by the migraine shiver of dollar signs.

A group of young people walked toward the university. Others, younger still, headed toward the high school. The university-bound walkers included older sorts as well, as a number of faculty lived in the neighborhood. One of them held an unlit cigarette away from him as if offering it to invisible passersby. A man and woman with identically cut gray hair and matching briefcases and rounded shoulders looked as if they'd been lockstepping off to classes since they were five.

The high school students were adamantly underdressed, as always. And what they did wear seemed calculated to enhance their most unfortunate traits. Girls with baby-fat stomachs let them pouch and jiggle between tight T-shirts and low-rider jeans. Thin, apologetic boys, the kind who seemed to gain height as you watched them, extended their knobby knees through ripped denim. More than a few of both or multiple genders seemed to be wearing their pajamas. That one scuffed along in actual bedroom slippers. They hunched over their phones in masturbatory trances, thumbs flying.

The Pheasant Run occupants, many in nightclothes and jackets, milled uncertainly on the sidewalks. As usual, the firefighters had evacuated the entire building when such a move was entirely unnecessary. The fire had been put out quickly and thoroughly, and the smoke would have been confined to the lower floors. And still, everyone in the entire building had been rousted to make their way, the best they could, down to the lobby and out onto the sidewalk. They looked chilly and miserable and frightened.

Some were on walkers. A few firemen moved among the group answering questions.

A frigid, cantankerous breeze had come up, and it grabbed at the edges of the old people and rattled the clinging maple leaves. The sky had turned gray and clotted as some kind of new weather moved in.

Maki had a brief, mildly testy exchange with the lead firefighter, who finally agreed to move the residents back inside and reassure them that neither they nor the building was in danger. But before that was done, Maki used his phone to photograph the building's exterior and those standing outside it.

One of the residents, a lanky, silver-haired man in a tracksuit, approached him and introduced himself in a lecturer's voice as Professor Rydell Clovis, the wielder of the fire extinguisher. The hero of the day. Maki told him he'd want to talk with him at some length but needed some private time on the scene first. Clovis, excited and impatient, began to reenact his precise movements at every point after he heard the fire alarm. He sounded whipped up enough that Maki made a mental note to do a very thorough interview with the guy, and he sent him on his way. How many times had it turned out that the most enthusiastic witness to a fire had set a few of his own?

Not that this was necessarily an arson. He was going to jeopardize his own observations if he decided anything along those lines at this point.

He introduced himself to several other residents—a birdlike woman swaddled in a down coat, a bald man with an oxygen tank and a steady small cough, a stout and hearty-looking couple demanding to know how long they were to wait outside—and tried to convey a combination of reassurance and rigor. They could all expect at least a brief interview, he told them. He photographed them individually, for the record.

A stout woman with red hair in a topknot approached him and introduced herself as Mavis Krepps, the president of the condo owners' association. She had huge eyes, sad and alert, and she fixed them on him as if imploring mercy. Her voice, though, was resonant and in charge.

"I should like to set up a time in which you could speak to the residents, as a whole, about the city's protocol for fire inspections and evacuation procedures," she said. He eyed her quizzically. He rarely encountered formality in a conversation anymore.

"Yes, I know we heard from someone in your office when Herbie Bonebright gifted us with a grease fire the week he moved in," she said. "And I believe the person we talked to, at that time, raised some maintenance issues for the association to address."

Maki had two assistants who conducted inspections, and he tried to remember which one had mentioned any Pheasant Run problems to him.

"These maintenance issues have not been fully addressed," Mrs. Krepps said, "as there are several owners who think they are unnecessary expenses for the association to take on in these difficult times. That is, there was no intention to ignore the report and incur fines and so on, but simply to assess the scope of the repairs and so on, in order to proceed in a fiscally responsible fashion."

Maki had no idea what point she was trying to make. "And so…?" he prompted.

"And so, perhaps you and I should sit down in the next little while to discuss some other issues that might address the question of who is responsible, and who is not, for bringing the building fully up to code." She saw his puzzlement and looked around as if she thought the residents slowly pacing the sidewalk wore hidden microphones.

"It's possible," she said, lowering her voice, "that the building will change ownership. This is not written in stone, or is even close to the stone-writing stage, but it is a distinct possibility."

"Mrs. Krepps! Mavis!" came a voice from a knot of people just inside the open lobby door. A very pale man with electric white hair escaping from a stocking cap waved an arm for her attention.

He arrived at her side, breathing shallowly. Maki smelled turpentine, soap, recent sweat, and illness among a mélange of lesser smells. One of the fainter smells instantly conjured a memory of a terrible house fire he'd investigated out on the edge of town near the old fort, though the smell was plantlike and aromatic and had nothing to do with smoke or flames.

"Have they found Viola Six?" the man asked. Mrs. Krepps introduced him to Maki as Leo Uberti, a painter of landscapes, and said he lived on the same floor as the missing woman.

"I saw her this morning, not too long after seven," Uberti said. "She was getting into the elevator. She seemed fine, though she was wearing pajamas with some kind of jacket on top. Not so strange, really. I've seen her in that gear before, when she's going down to the lobby or

73

the storage area or someplace, and doesn't think anyone else is up and about yet. OK, a little eccentric, a little dramatic at times, but what? She just takes off without telling anyone? She just evaporates? I'm not buying it."

"I had the fire crew check her apartment again, just now, to see if she somehow got mixed up during the evacuation and went back there," Mrs. Krepps said in soothing tones. "And they checked the stairways, the parking garage, and so on. And she is not on the premises, Leo. I locked her apartment, and if she doesn't show up soon, we will bring in the police."

"And Herbie," Uberti said. "Our Mr. Bonebright. Where is he?"

"He didn't show up for his customary breakfast hour at the Den," Mrs. Krepps said. "I checked. And his car is not in the garage. So we don't know where he might be at the moment. Unfortunately, he's in for something of a shock when he comes home to find he's had a fire on his premises."

"Probably his fault," Uberti declared. "It wouldn't be the first time, would it? That popcorn grease event right after he moved in? Why wasn't he canned on the spot? He's a slob and a menace, and the owners' association is in a position to send him packing, and it doesn't."

Mrs. Krepps's mouth tightened, and she placed a hand on Uberti's forearm.

"Why don't you go talk to Cassie McMackin, Leo? She looks as if she could use a friend at the moment." She gestured toward a slim, very erect woman wearing a magenta shawl over a gold-colored robe. She'd wrapped the soft cloth around her tightly and gazed straight ahead. Her delicate face was a mask of sorrow. Her eyes were wide open, and tears ran down her cheeks. She made no effort to wipe them away. Looking at her, Maki felt a strange shock of shared grief, as if they were at a funeral for a mutual friend.

Uberti went over to her and rested a hand on her shoulder. She closed her eyes, then looked up at him and shook her head, incredulous.

"She's a friend of Viola's," Mrs. Krepps confided to Maki. "Maybe that's the trouble. She's worried."

This didn't look like straightforward worry to Maki, but he kept his thought to himself. Reviewing the photos he'd taken, he realized he didn't have Uberti or Cassie McMackin, so he summoned them over and briskly got it done, then mentioned that he'd be around quite a lot for the next few days and would want to talk with them both.

"I can tell you one thing someone should look into," Uberti said. "There has been a teenage kid on the premises who shouldn't have been here. Mrs. Rideout says he crashed in through the dumpster window when she was emptying her trash yesterday afternoon, then disappeared, then surfaced this morning outside the building during the evacuation. Ran like a shot when I called attention to him. Puffy kind of kid with a Star Wars T-shirt, carrying a sack of some kind. Could it be items that he robbed?"

Herbie Bonebright's apartment, scorched and soggy, was minimally furnished and none too clean. There was a single bedroom with a sagging, unmade bed and a plastic chair covered with dirty clothes and damp-looking towels. Some cords were tangled atop a card table but not connected to anything. Maki closed his eyes briefly and reminded himself to be on the lookout for additions and absences: anything inside that shouldn't be there and anything that should be there that wasn't.

As he always did, he identified the least affected area of the apartment—in this case the small bedroom and bath—and moved very slowly, in a counterclockwise fashion, around the spaces, taking a photo with every step. (The whispery sound of his phone made him realize again how much he missed his old Canon thirty-five millimeter with its decisive clack, its actual film. Digital photos were so easy to alter—in that way, they replicated memories—but they were the standard in fire inspections now, convenience and speed winning out, once again, over rigor.) The bathroom was filmed and stale. A toothbrush and a comb sat next to a ring of keys on the back of the toilet. Maki photographed the keys, then picked them up with gloved fingers and put them in a large Ziploc. From the bedroom closet's floor, discovered almost by accident behind a laundry hamper, he picked up an odd-looking object the size and shape of an egg. It was charcoal-colored and had a clip on the back. He put it in another bag.

The living room had a ripped faux-leather recliner, a TV table, dark-blue bedsheets for window curtains, and a large new flat-screen television, tuned to the sci-fi channel with the sound off. Tentacles the size of elephant trunks were slithering out the windows of a rusty school bus. There was a ratty old pillow on the recliner, and when Maki moved it, he found a shiny iPad partially wedged into the corner of the seat. He retrieved the largest Ziploc he'd brought and placed the iPad inside it.

The living room opened onto the galley kitchen, where the smells and scorching confirmed that he had reached the source.

Again Maki closed his eyes, this time to pay attention to his nose. The crowd of smells jostled for a few minutes, then grouped themselves into pods, some of them large and confident and familiar, others more mysterious, like the one that seemed to combine Coleman fuel and some kind of soft plastic.

The fire appeared to have started on the stove top and moved up the back wall to the ceiling and down to the floor. There was a charred pan on a back burner of the gas stove, but it had no residue in it of food or grease or anything else. The light bulb at the front of the fan had melted forward, suggesting a very hot, fast flame. He didn't touch the stove but took photos from a variety of angles and distances.

A charred area on the wall behind the stove looked blacker and deeper than it should have been. If a greasy hot pad had caught fire, or grease on the cupboard top had ignited, there would have been significant smoldering time. The mark on the wall also suggested a very hot fire. He picked at it with his knife to verify its depth.

Still, nothing he'd seen so far absolutely ruled out an accident of a slightly unconventional nature. He poked carefully through the ashes on the cupboard top, photographed them, and tweezered into a baggie a half inch of charred string and a sliver of wax.

The smell of Coleman fuel was strongest at the stove. He made another circle around the apartment, looking closely at the contents of the closets and cupboards, beneath the bed. No Coleman stove. No Coleman lantern or can of fuel. Perhaps the manager was a camper and kept those things in his car, or in the building's storage area. But why would he have brought the fuel to his apartment from somewhere else, and what would he have been using it for? Nothing about it made sense.

Maki sat in the recliner and thought about what he was smelling, seeing, feeling. The utter temporariness of the apartment's furnishings stayed front and center for some reason. The place felt like a room in a by-the-week motel. He held up the baggie with the large ring of keys in it. They had been removed from a belt loop clip, most likely, and Herbie Bonebright had left his apartment without them.

And yet what had the professor in the tracksuit told him about putting out the fire single-handedly? That he had grabbed the extinguisher and bashed in the locked door. Maki examined the door lock with some care. It was the kind that locked with a button from the inside and needed a key to unlock from the outside. And Herbie had left without his keys.

Back in the Volvo, Maki turned up the heater, rolled down the window, and smoked the day's second cigarette. Scattered debris blew down the street, and sleet ticked on the windshield. The temperature had dropped by at least fifteen degrees since early morning, and the sense of a benign November pause had given way to the first breaths of real winter.

Maki made his list: "1) Notify the police and highway patrol about the missing persons, Bonebright and

Six. See if their phones can be located and tracked. 2) Find the boy wearing the Star Wars T-shirt who was seen inside the building. 3) Get Bonebright's iPad to the geeks. 4) Get the lab work going. 5) Begin interviewing the Pheasant Run residents." He revved the Volvo a little and added a last item as an emotional nod to Rhonda and her ability to entertain the widest range of possibilities. "6) Rule nothing out."

NIGHTWALKERS'
SONG

7

Cassie McMackin opened the curtains in her living room and sat in her velvet plum-colored armchair, which faced the window. The day's half-hearted storm had blown through, leaving the night sky, also plum colored, minutely punctured with icy stars. The season had turned, however, and now it would be winter.

She made herself a cup of hot chocolate with a shot of peppermint schnapps and returned to her cradling chair. It was night now. And she was alive.

The fire and evacuation had shocked her into terror first, and then into a sweeping sadness for those among her poor neighbors who, forbidden the elevator, had been herded whimpering down so many painful steps to stand outside in the morning's deepening chill. She needed some time to think about all this. She needed to find out what had happened to Viola.

From under a magazine on the side table, she retrieved her recorder, and she inserted a new cassette. Her voice low, she began to talk to Neil, as she had many times before.

"Strange developments in the aviary, Neil. This morning we had a fire. A shout, and heavy pounding on my door and on down the hall, and then firemen in their huge yellow uniforms were yelling at us to grab coats and shoes, and they marched us down the stairs that seemed endless, and out onto the sidewalk to mill like cattle in a pen. I kept watching for Viola, not finding her, and at some point I was told that she was missing, vanished. That her apartment had been empty when the men arrived, and no one—no one—had seen her after Leo Uberti spoke with her briefly, not long before the alarm blared and all became chaos. How does this happen? There is a lively, opinionated, feisty, hoping woman, and then there is an absence. When I thought about that, as we shivered and waited on the sidewalk, I became overwhelmed again by the idea that hope seems to exist only to march us toward utter, inevitable loss. And for what? What is served?"

She paused the machine to close her eyes, to pull her shawl close. He deserved to know. She depressed the recording button again.

"Before all this, I had a plan for today. I had a plan to go to sleep a final time. Right about now, I would be embracing oblivion, so to speak. Many reasons, love. Or maybe just a few or one. I'm sorting it out. And I'm reserving the option."

She felt involved suddenly in an argument, and she clicked the machine off. The laundry room would be empty this late, and she needed something to distract her long enough for her thoughts to sort themselves out. She wheeled her wire laundry basket from the closet and added a half dozen clean handkerchiefs of Neil's that she kept folded in drawer. A man with a clean white handkerchief, always. He carried one in his pajama pocket, his

pants pocket, his ski jacket pocket. His ski jacket zipped
to the chin as he stood on the top of their favorite mountain. One more missive for the evening:

"Remember how we stood atop the white mountain
on our skis, in our woolens, and the snow made caped
creatures of the pines and settled a grand hush on it all?
How the noises that remained were small and distant,
like rumors of themselves? The miniature clang of the
T-bars as they swung around the spool at the top? The
Strauss waltzes floating from the tinny speaker outside
the warming shack?

"We were so new to each other. We anticipated so much.

"Sometimes, on the mountain, the fog rolled in
and the swaddled trees fell back into it, fainted, and the
waltzes fainted, too, and all we heard was the chatter of
our long wooden skis, the scrape of the snow, an occasional small shout or whoop somewhere far away.

"Standing at the top—you, me—there was the knowledge of difficult terrain to navigate, a spectacular fall or
two or three to prepare for, challenge and travail and the
fast heart, and always a certain kind of necessary misery to
endure—the tight boots and soaked woolens, the glassed
eyelashes and wonky knee—but we careened down the
white mountain to arrive gasping on the level and ready to
do it all again. We couldn't wait."

She let the tape roll as she fetched the kitchen cloths
for the laundry. Someone down the hall turned up a talk
show that filled the outside corridor with aggrievement
before it was turned down.

"And remember that bright white day we rode the
small bus down the mountain because our car was dead

in the lot and we had to find someone in town to fix it? That beautiful, dark-haired woman in the bus, wrapped in a mink coat, wearing beaded sealskin boots and weeping? Huge sunglasses she had, and from beneath them tears dropping off her chin. Sometimes she blotted them with a tissue. Sometimes she didn't. She seemed transported from a nineteenth-century novel, in full costume and bearing a tragedy that we were supposed to decipher from her tears. She thrilled me. Where had she come from? Where was she going? Why was she so swaddled and alone? She wore thin black leather gloves pulled tight across the bulges of her rings.

"The driver let her off at the train station, and you asked him what her trouble was. Snow blindness, he said. All that light bouncing off all that snow, and she had no idea she couldn't be out in it with bare eyes. Some people, he said. And his voice was mean."

Thumbing through a *National Geographic* in the basement laundry room, Cassie listened to the dryer's tumble and tick and imagined Neil's handkerchiefs flying like white birds through the jungle heat. Always, he needed a clean pile of them. And she had happily obliged. It was a small thing to do, to launder and iron a dozen squares of cotton a week, and it mattered to him. So odd, in its way. Who could ever predict in the early years of a six-decade marriage how small gestures of care would count, especially toward the end?

She added them to her laundry simply to comfort herself with the ritual, to be reminded of the wit that had survived almost every mental depredation in Neil.

When she snapped at him, as she sometimes had done when it all seemed too much to weather, he liked to retrieve a handkerchief from his fleece vest and wave it as a flag of surrender. Sometimes it made them both smile. Sometimes it didn't.

They were nothing less than a fixation for him. Possibly it had to do with the fact that he'd had fierce nosebleeds as a child. That information had come from his mother, who said they occurred for a few years only but were exuberantly bloody when they happened and that stanching them could be dramatic and prolonged. That would scare a child—the idea that his blood was leaking from him and who knew when it would stop? Perhaps Neil later felt that his memories had become like that blood, escaping him, unstanchable. One day, watching the news of the latest massive oil spill, the earth hemorrhaging again, he had anxiously reached for a handkerchief and held it to his nose. His eyes over the top of the cloth were stretched with fear.

Cassie looked up, suddenly aware of someone in the room. A boy, a teenager, stood panting in the doorway. He sounded as if he had been running for days. His shoulders heaved. The hand that grasped the door frame was as delicate and articulate as a girl's. His rain-soaked backpack drooped heavily from his elbow, as if it were full of rocks. He wore a Star Wars T-shirt.

She folded her arms in a reflex of self-protection. He raised his hand like a traffic cop.

"Where did you come from?" she asked. It was rare to see any young people on the premises apart from the occasional visiting grandchild. He vaguely gestured upward. His breath was so labored he couldn't speak. It squeaked on the edges. A door slammed somewhere and he jumped. Cassie knew she should suspect the worst: that the boy had been rifling through a tenant's medicine cabinet or stealing a wallet left on a counter—that someone even now was on the phone to 911 or searching the hallways for his retreating back—but he looked so stripped and scared that she couldn't seem to feel him as any kind of threat.

"Sit down," she said. He flopped into a plastic chair as she shut the door to the laundry room, though they were unlikely to be disturbed this late in the day.

She studied him. His hair was dull and stood up from his head in rampant spikes and clumps. His skin was mottled. His eyes were large and brown and they moved quickly around the room. He was puffy and underdressed—thin T-shirt, ripped jeans, sad old sneakers. His foot tapped the floor. He smelled stale and oddly metallic.

"What's the trouble?" she asked quietly. "Why are you in here? What's after you?"

He avoided her eyes. Then he yawned, a huge yawn, as if it were the only way he could get enough breath.

"Sorry. I'm not bored. I can't help it." He looked up at her. "I'm on some meds that make me do that."

"You have health problems."

Perhaps that wild look meant he was on the verge of a seizure. She tried to remember what action was called for in such a case. A pen on the tongue, so the tongue couldn't be swallowed?

"Well, if a contaminated brain and being driven nuts by everyone in the world are health problems, well I guess

I have health problems." He stressed the last two words. His foot resumed its tapping.

"That's a peculiar term, isn't it?" Cassie said. "*Health problem*. It's sort of like saying, oh...*love trouble*. How can health be a kind of problem, or love be a kind of trouble? What's meant is problems *with* one's health or *with* a love situation. The shorthand isn't always so accurate, is it?"

The boy looked at her blankly. "Totally," he said, wiping sweat off his face with the hem of his T-shirt. "Plus my girlfriend disappeared this evening. She's not answering texts or calls. I think she ran away somewhere."

"Would you like one of these?" Cassie asked, handing him a clean handkerchief.

"I'll destroy it," the boy said.

"So destroy it," Cassie said.

He scrubbed his face with the cloth. He looked ready to cry. "Her name is Raven," he said. "Like the bird."

Cassie didn't know what to say next, so she sat down on the chair next to the boy and pretended to get lost in her own thoughts. It was a method she'd discovered rather late in life for putting a stressed person at ease. You simply remove any obligation for that person to respond to you.

A few minutes passed. The dryer turned off. Cassie got up to retrieve the last of the clothes and began to fold them. The boy had tipped his head against the wall and closed his eyes.

"I just about got myself killed today," he said. "This guy at school hates me and he rounds up his friends and they come after me. They did it yesterday and I hit him and escaped. Then, today, when I went to school, I thought I was feeling, you know, up to them. I even went back to school this evening for band practice. But they cornered me and I broke away and they chased me. One other time there were six of them, and I ended up in the ER." He took a long breath. "But Josh Anderson doesn't have a clue about what I could do to him, if I really wanted to. If I just didn't care anymore, and really wanted to." His voice had taken on a peculiar lilt.

Cassie had a flashing moment in which her daughter's face, when she was embarking on a new assignment in a more dangerous region, wore the sound of the boy's new voice.

"Do your parents know that they are after you? Do they know you aren't safe at school?"

"'Safe at school'!" He shook his head as if he couldn't believe such gullibility existed. "And my parents. Well, my dad is shacked up with the half sister of the guy who wants to fucking kill me, and my mom spends most of her time trying not to go crazy from wanting to fucking kill my dad." He stood up briskly. "She goes to some kind of sweat yoga tonight." He consulted his phone, shook his head, and tapped out a brief text. "She doesn't know what to do with me.

"Sorry for the shitty language," he added as an afterthought.

"So why here?" Cassie asked. "Why this place?"

"Well, the guys who were after me aren't going to follow me into a building where people can see them jump me."

"Won't they wait outside?"

"Not if I stay here for a while."

"In the laundry room?"

"Well...somewhere," he said, gesturing vaguely. "It's pretty late for them to wait around, if they're out there. I think they'll leave pretty soon." He bent to retie a shoelace.

"You know," Cassie said, "There was a fire in the building early this morning, and one of the residents says she saw a kid in a Star Wars T-shirt enter the building yesterday afternoon—that he jumped through the garbage window when she was emptying her trash and ran down the hall. And then a man who lives on my floor says he saw that T-shirt on a kid who was outside the building right after the fire, when we were all evacuated. I'm going to guess that those people saw you."

The boy squinted at her. He shrugged.

"That fire inspector came over to the school," he said. "He already talked to me. The principal knew right away I was the one they wanted to talk to." He pointed to his T-shirt. "And he got me out of class to talk to that guy Maki."

"Well?" Cassie asked.

"He basically said I was going to have to account for my whereabouts during some certain hours. That I would need some proof of my whereabouts. He's going to talk to me again."

"And where were you?"

The boy considered this. "Not anyplace where anybody else saw me."

Cassie surprised herself with the thought that she should invite him to her apartment to eat something and gather himself. He seemed to need every kind of nourishment. She knew about needing nourishment. Then she surprised herself more.

"What if I said you were with me when that fire broke out?"

He looked at her as if she had said something embarrassing.

"Why would I be with you?" he asked so carefully that Cassie felt slapped.

"Because I went outside, early, before the fire, to see if the paperboy was in sight. And I saw you walking, and you looked very cold, or possibly injured, and I invited you to my apartment for a cup of hot chocolate."

"Oh," he said.

"And when the fire alarm went off, you ran off, down the stairs, and I didn't see you again."

She sounded crazy to herself, but she didn't care. She located the Post-it Note block that was left in the laundry room for messages among tenants ("Please remember to clean the lint catcher after every use!") and she wrote down her name and her phone number and gave them to him. He told her his name was Clayton.

"You can call this number anytime, and I'll answer it, Clayton," she said, as she placed her folded clothes in a wire basket with wheels, Neil's old handkerchiefs folded neatly on top. "Or if I don't, leave a message."

"What would I say?" he asked. His exhausted eyes made her look away.

"Anything you want to," she said as she pushed her folded clothes out of the room.

In her apartment, Cassie put away the laundry and poured herself a Gatorade. She needed the electrolytes. She needed something. The kid, Clayton, had appeared so suddenly and in such a state. It was as if the events of his day had hooked him out of home waters to leave him flopping and gasping on a riverbank. Or did he even have some equivalent of safe water, someplace that felt calm and familiar to him, someplace where he could swim and breathe? So many of the young fish seemed not to.

He had followed her from the laundry room to the elevator, waving in a stylized sort of way as the doors closed. Probably she should have made sure he was out of the building before it was locked for the night. Maybe he was quietly slipping into someone's bathroom right now, slipping past an old person napping in front of the TV and leaving with a handful of sleeping pills or painkillers. Possible. Not likely, though. She hadn't lived this long to end up with no instincts at all about another's intentions or criminal capabilities.

How utterly different, for instance, had been her visceral reaction to the boy as compared to her reaction to the lame-brained newcomer Herbie Bonebright. Why had she even listened to him when he passed her in the hall, a week ago, then turned to call her name?

He wore a pasted-on smile. His face was shiny with sweat. He put a hand on the wall and asked how everything was going for her, his tone so bored she knew it wasn't a question. And when she answered briefly, he just smiled and watched her.

"Mrs. McMackin," he said in a very low voice. "I've heard you make things up. I've heard that you and Mrs. Six tell lies, just to entertain yourselves. Is that right?" His eyes opened wider, and there was something in them that was frozen and virulent.

She felt the heat roar into her face.

"Who the hell do you think you are?" Cassie said very quietly. "You don't know anything about me. But what you should know is that some of the renters in this building have a problem with you. My friend John Quant who recently moved away, for instance."

"I'm sure he did," Herbie said, nodding gravely. He still blocked the door with his lumpy body. Down the hall, behind him, Cassie saw Viola Six standing outside her apartment door, eyes fixed on his threatening back.

Cassie raised her arm and called an adamant greeting to Viola. Herbie flinched. He turned on his heel, ignored Viola, who simply stared at him, and disappeared into the elevator.

"There is something wrong with that man," Viola called to Cassie. "There is something about him that reminds me of my old beau, Captain, who left me destitute." She thought for a moment. "Minus the charm."

Cassie put down her Gatorade, bent her head, and said a short prayer for the boy, Clayton. And then she prayed, as she did every day, for all the children, for her dead husband and her dead daughter, for John Quant, and for those she knew when she was young and had lost through time, distance, or death. She prayed for the groaning, hectically gorgeous, steaming world, which seemed, more and more often, to lurch and shudder on its planetary path, as if trying to correct its course—buildings tumbled then, oceans surged, hurricanes annihilated, wars and diseases erupted—before it resumed its ponderous spin, heavy under new layers of the innocent dead.

She prayed for surcease and hope and for the better instincts out there to triumph after she was gone. She prayed that she had lived well, by her lights as she had been able to know them. Then she prayed once more for the pale and sweaty boy who seemed to be hanging on by his fingernails.

Cassie prayed without the barest image of a deity. This was relatively recent. It was as if she had conducted, for decades, a lengthy call-and-response with an entity that, somewhere along the line, had installed a slowly evaporating hologram of itself and walked away. Or as if God had, for her, become a phantom limb, absent but extremely painful.

Part of the reason was that she had lost her faith in the Catholic Church, the institution she had embraced so long ago because of its very particular combination of texture, gravity, and practice. She had long felt that reckoning with suffering was the only credible function of religion, and that the Church took it on in a complex and artful way. How could one listen to Mozart's *Requiem*, for instance, and not hear in it the terror and rage of the dying young composer, his confusion and pity and yes, finally, a hint of his understanding of the nature of suffering and of God?

Her break, which she knew to be final, came swiftly on the heels of her realization that, theology and tradition and music quite apart, this was an institution that had protected the utterly corrupt and life-denying among its priests and nuns, that it had created suffering on a rather grand scale. And the victims were children—the innocent, the yearning, the idealistic, the vulnerable. She requested an explanation from the entity she had addressed for so many decades, and she got nothing. "This is such bad timing," she complained to the blankness. "Now when I'm old, and could have used some blind faith."

The fire, the aftermath of the fire, Herbie Bonebright's disappearance, Viola's disappearance, and now the presence of this puffy tormented boy—it was such a welter. So many unfinished stories that seemed to want her to address them, but wouldn't say how.

It wasn't yet ten p.m. She decided to check Viola's apartment, on the long shot that she had simply left the building before the fire, for her own reasons, and had decided to return. She knocked, then ducked under the yellow strips the police had placed across the door and used the key Viola had given her to let herself in, calling as she went.

The apartment was spare and tidy, as it always was. Viola had placed crocheted doilies on the arms of the two chairs that faced the ancient rabbit-eared TV on a card table. Next to the television was a framed photograph of the young President Kennedy, grinning into the sun. The door to the small balcony was closed. A plastic vase on the coffee table held a profusion of paper tulips.

In the bedroom, Cassie studied the clothes on the bed and those in Viola's closet, arranged by function and color, feeling again the sadness that seemed so much a part of old age, sadness that had something to do with the fact, the *fact*, that the simplest of undertakings—getting dressed for a day—required a level of care and planning that approached the valiant. Nothing was casual anymore.

But why were some clothes laid out on the bed, as if she'd been preparing to dress but hadn't completed the job? Had the alarm interrupted her? And then what?

A Post-it Note on the bureau directed Viola to "Find lapis necklace!" Clearly it had been an unexpected gap, so panic-producing that Cassie felt a little surge of helpfulness and opened the top drawer, the one where everyone kept their necklaces, to see if the necklace had simply been overlooked.

There was a photograph in the drawer, turned facedown. On the backing cardboard, in Viola's handwriting, was a single word. *Italy*. She turned over the photo to find a radiant, clear-eyed woman wearing a satiated smile. She leaned against a white pillar that was darkly streaked with rust or erosion. Two pigeons at her feet pecked at the ground. It was a black-and-white photo, and the light was muted. A vendor with a tray of flowers seemed to be assessing the person snapping the photo.

The woman had Viola's thick hair, but in a tawny shade, long and wavy and swept back from her forehead. Her eyes were dark and widely spaced. She seemed loose-limbed and tall, the way she had casually but artfully tilted herself against the stone, so that a pretty leg parted her coat. The smile—that I-own-the-world smile—was, yes, Viola's. The same crooked eyetooth was there, and even an expression of pleased self-deprecation that Viola sometimes wore, as if she were mimicking someone she didn't feel herself to be, and, in fact, when all was said and done, didn't want to be.

The necklace, just visible at her throat, could have been lapis lazuli. One eyebrow was very slightly cocked, in worldly complicity with the viewer. She looked ready for anything.

When had this Italy visit occurred in Viola's life? Cassie had difficulty imagining it, and, as she struggled to, she experienced a wave of shame. She hadn't actually believed Viola's stories of her adventures, especially the more risqué ones. She had thought them to be wishful thinking because she herself evidently did not possess the imagination necessary to link them to the stolid, white-haired, bespectacled, opinionated, solitary woman who was her friend.

Would the photo have been taken before she came home to marry Ollie the mill worker? That seemed impossible. Who would set off for adventures abroad, fully alert to the world and its possibilities and her own considerable beauty, and come home to marry someone she'd known most of her life, someone who would, by her own admission, always have about him the feel of a small room without air?

Maybe she had discovered she was pregnant.

But would she have embarked on the adventures she told Cassie about after she had married and had a child to care for? Not likely. Not in that era, certainly. So had she waited, perhaps, until the child, the unlikable Rod, was out of the house, at which point Ollie suffered his untimely death in a mill accident, and she began to traverse the big wide world? She would perhaps have been only forty, with half of her life still ahead of her. Could this beauty in an Italian piazza be forty? Cassie squinted as she brought the image closer. Yes, she could.

She prepared for bed, exhausted, and placed her recorder on the nightstand. She had more to tell Neil's ghost. She wanted to offer some kind of summation of their years together, in a way that didn't discount the ordinary—the raising of their daughter, her own years as a librarian and a volunteer and a close friend to half a dozen now dead, and Neil's years as a high school history teacher and his flying of small planes and his passion for secret fly-fishing spots—but in a way that made it, instead, the summary of their moments of most-aliveness, separate and together. And the words wouldn't come. She turned on the recorder and went back to the day on the mountain.

"In the hotel bar that night, we had beers and burgers and stomped around in our after-ski boots. Some big guy in a plaid wool shirt and suspendered wool pants said something at the other end of the bar that made all the men laugh. His girlfriend or wife or date slapped him on the bicep and shook her head. Her face was flushed. Big new roars of laughter.

"The men, so many of them veterans of the war, two of them survivors of the POW camps, were adamant about the possibility of normalcy. The blur, the beer, the shouts, and yet they, you, had your own scorched eyes. You grieved to be hoping boys again, so you were unapologetic about becoming, when you felt like it, extra-boys.

"In the women's bathroom, a small window was cracked to the night. I pushed it open and sucked in the sharp air. The sky was black in the old way. The town was tiny and the streetlights made pale V shapes on the street. Fields of stars in that black sky fell together into an immense vault that reached further than I had ever seen before. I felt I was looking up through an enormous bell. A train howled in the distance and a dog barked in the street. My muscles hurt.

"'Shall I?' I said aloud, testing it. 'Yes. I will have a child. She will be the freest part of me, my traveler, my joy. She will be the part of me that survives me, that moves into the future.'

"And, you know, at that moment I did see Marian as a child, and even as an adult. I saw her personality and her prospects, most of them, as strange as that may sound. I saw a lot of it, but not the end.

"Your voice made its way through the crowd sounds outside the door, jubilant, oblivious.

"The snow-blinded woman on the train in the night, speeding east, slept behind her dark glasses.

"She left me to it."

8

Leo Uberti in #402 arranged his easel and paint supplies near the curtainless window that framed the crown of a Chinese maple out on the boulevard, grateful again that he had landed a rental on the fourth floor, where his view was something better than tree trunks, parked cars, and teenagers shuffling off to school as if they had been tipped out of their beds onto a moving sidewalk, too sleepy to resist. In the early night, he could discern the tree's outlines and remember in detail how it looked in full sunlight. He removed the Emperor Concerto from its gray paper sleeve and placed the record on the hi-fi he had seen no reason to update. He liked his music with the delicious whisper of revolutions at the beginning, like a nervous performer breathing through his teeth.

He closed his eyes and ran his fingertips along the ribs of his right side. Still tender to the lightest touch. How stupid he had been to take on Herbie Bonebright over the issue of a leaking showerhead. Well, it hadn't really been about the showerhead at all, of course. It had been about Leo's right to ask whether Herbie knew anything at all about plumbing, and Herbie's refusal to answer. It had been about Leo's right to ask Herbie why

John Quant on the third floor had moved out so suddenly, after warning Leo to stay out of Herbie's way—the way Herbie had just laughed at that, bringing his wide face and his rank breath right up to Leo's face, to ignite the white rage that made Leo take a swipe at that face and get a hard chop to the ribs in exchange. White rage and such depletion afterward that he could scarcely move.

At least Herbie was off the premises now, and Pheasant Run's residents didn't have to add his presence to the stresses of the day. Didn't have to think about him at all, if they didn't want to.

The chaos around the fire in Herbie's apartment this morning had deeply unnerved Leo: the labored evacuation, the comings and goings of the engines and hoses and personnel, Mrs. Rideout's fall on the stairs and Jerry Olson's shortness of breath, the terrified eyes of his fellow tenants, a new and ominous tremor in his hands, his impending interview with the fire inspector, a raging headache, Viola Six's vanishing—all of it culminating in a state of near-panic that he hoped Beethoven might mitigate.

And that boy. Who was that boy, darting in and out of the building? What was his particular agenda?

The smudge-colored foliage this November intrigued him. He'd never seen anything like it—those clinging leaves, so far past their time to be gone. He felt they very nearly told him something important about displacement, about disparity, about a feeling that had provoked and mystified him most of his life. What was a physical entity when it became marooned from its customary location? An erratic. One of those boulders carried by white ice away from its original home. The leaves should have been mulch on the ground by now, but there they were, clinging, in the wrong place, at the wrong time. As perhaps he was, as well, and had been doing since he was a very young man.

Well, maybe those gray leaves could tell him something about the dislocations of his own life, about the incongruity of being a dark-skinned, dark-eyed Italian Jew in a white-bread college town in the American inland West. The shocking circumstances of his arrival. The slights out of nowhere, the muted disdain he'd endured all his years in the so-called land of the free. His emotional paralysis. The disjunction of being an elderly artist, a perceptive and discriminating person, in a country, an era, that wanted its elders, no matter what attributes they might possess, to be innocuous and erasable, especially if they were too poor or sick to line anyone's pockets.

He lowered his eyelids to produce a veiled gaze. Then he tried to move his mental stage lighting from the front, where he saw furred black branches against a deep evening sky, to the background, so that the scene might take on the additional depth that made it revelatory.

What he saw, when the shift occurred, was the low lights of a little city in the fog. They seemed to breathe in a shallow sort of way, their borders daintily expanding and contracting. Cristóbal. Cristóbal, Panama. Panama in the fog, every spot of light a tiny buoy, warning Leo and the other crew on the huge ship that their futures were going to be what they could never, in their wildest dreams, have imagined.

What a glitter-palace the *Conte Biancamano* had been when she carnivaled through the big waters with her several thousand passengers, her musicians, her dance floors, her champagne and swimming pools and movies. Leo had never tried to paint it, but if he did, he'd wash it all in a luminescent pink. Near dusk, the floor show singers warmed up in their cabins as the big engines thrummed, and the setting sun made the portholes rosy and excited looking, and it was easy to imagine the first-class passengers cast in that pink glow as they finished their dressing drinks and adjusted scarves, sequins, and collar studs for the evening ahead. Walking the upper deck after his shift in the kitchen, young Leo (just fifteen) liked to breathe in all the sounds: the floor show, the crooner in the first-class lounge, the spiking laughter, ruffles of clapping, the murmurs of the other deck-walkers he passed—all of it riding the deeper sound of ocean water churning and spraying as the festive little city cut its path from port to port.

And then to be interdicted in Cristóbal, Leo and the rest of the Italian crew ordered by the Allied forces to remain with the ship in that sweltering, gray place—sky gray, water gray, tempers gray and then worse. Meals became desultory affairs. Fights broke out. They felt they'd been detained on the flattened grass of a circus that had moved to the next town.

And after a year and a half of the motionless gray?

The presence of something colorless and coiled, ready to spring. Pranks, shouts, fights, booze, plots. Running feet at night in the long corridors. Talk of engine-smashing or ship-jumping. And himself, young Leo, escaping to the granular light of the ship's abandoned library to read anything he could find that had to do with gadgetry, gallantry, inventions, tricks, or Houdini.

Deeper in the ship: Wrenches banging on engine parts. Small fires springing to life. Tony, his hotheaded friend, bragging that he knew how to set one in which the ignition was delayed and he could be eight hands into a poker game when the alarm was raised.

And the color of Ellis Island after the emptying of the ship? Cement. And the barred train car that whistled across the vast and tawny American interior, taking Leo and some of the others to the internment camp somewhere in the mountains of the West? Yellow sunlight barred with black.

My striped chariot, Leo thought. *Bringing me to a former cavalry fort, just a few miles from this very room. From this room where I stand, more than seven decades off that train, to paint leaves that don't know what they are supposed to do.*

He kept his eyes squinted and dipped his brush in the cadmium white and began to make little lights on an anonymous vegetative color he'd mixed up a few days ago and laid down with a broad brush in impatient X's. Dab, dab, dab. His pinched motions made him feel small and angry. He didn't dare open his eyes fully to see how stupid and desperate the marks might look.

The fort's commander, Harold Tone, wasn't a terror. He didn't abuse anyone physically. Did he ever hit anyone? No. He was just quietly cruel. He had the ability to present one convincing face and manner to his equals, and another, entirely different, to the internees, especially the

Italians, who seemed to provoke in him a particular kind of vehemence. In that respect, he wasn't unlike Herbie Bonebright—so fawning with Pheasant Run's condo owners, such a bully with the renters. A personality split down the middle.

Tone, walking the grounds in the evenings, carrying a big Hasselblad and a tripod, taking his leisure in a way that was predatory, as if he were coercing his surroundings to deliver something to him. Leo, raking leaves, waiting for him and his obstreperous camera to move to a new place, and the way he remembers what happened next, to the very word.

"What do you want," Tone said.

"To get the last of the leaves," Leo said, pointing at the commander's feet.

Tone's face congealed. "You stupid wop," he said quietly. "Who the hell do you think you are?"

Leo felt dipped in acid. Everything burned. He ordered himself to stay silent, avoid the man's direct gaze.

Tone slowly folded up his gear and took a step toward Leo, the tripod shaft held like a weapon. Leo tightened his grip on the rake handle.

He came so close that Leo could smell his yeasty breath.

"Let me tell you something," Tone said. "You know, I could trade you off for a yellow dog."

He squinted into the distance.

"And then I could shoot the dog."

The fort and its grounds had a peaceable look with its handsome tall trees, the river flowing nearby, the mountains all round; and inside the fences were the sounds of string quartets, of hammers, of men speaking in Italian, and Japanese, and German.

Each nationality pretended the others didn't exist. So many of the Italians had been musicians aboard the ship that they staged performances most nights in the entertainment hall. *I pirati* with its slavering plunderers whipping machetes through the air. And what was the other musical in which the guy named Francisco donned a fluffy dress and played the ingenue? *Romanticismo.* What else? Leo had a brief vision of Francisco in his dress and huge booted feet ambling up the gravel path where several Japanese picked the pebbles they used to make pretty little pots. And the Germans? Leo couldn't remember what they did, the Germans, to pass the time, to move through the kind of time that made some of the men sick in the head. They flocked to the camp doctor with this strange headache, that case of the jitters, nightmares and sometimes weeping, all of it the more desperate, somehow, because the setting was so pleasant. Bella Vista, the Italians had instantly dubbed the fort.

During the church hour at Bella Vista, he liked to walk the grounds, slowing as he passed the tall house of Tone's second-in-command, Captain Whiston, because the captain's daughter, Mary, apparently a heathen like himself, was often on the porch at that hour, reading.

He called out to her once, asking if she could recommend whatever it was that seemed to absorb her so much. She called back that it was only a ladies' book and she was bored with it, and she might take a stroll around the grounds. Which she did. Which they did, keeping to a small path on the periphery where they weren't likely to be noticed. And that was the beginning, and the beginning of the end.

In his old age, the fort's cemetery was one of Leo's haunts. He liked its quietness, its smallness, the way the breezes tossed the branches of the big cottonwoods, the way the three sheep in the field next door made their timeless sheep sounds as they gobbled up the rampant knapweed. He thought then of Vasto on the Adriatic, and the sounds of bells and the sheep in the mornings as they were herded out to the hillsides.

Yesterday, pedaling his bicycle to the grocery store, he'd felt every nanosecond of his nearly ninety years. He knew they thought he shouldn't be riding his bicycle at all, the others in his building who watched him chain up his old Schwinn after an outing, his hands trembling with exhaustion. But what harm could he possibly do to anyone but himself? They were ones who thought nothing of jumping into their cars to engage their failing reflexes in fast traffic, to nick parking meters and occasionally terrorize bicyclists and pedestrians alike. He, on the other hand, did battle with nothing but the muscles in his legs, the disintegrating alveoli in his lungs. He was nothing but a potential victim, especially because he always made it a point to ride without a helmet because of his life insurance policy. If he was killed, some would find themselves showered in coin.

A few days ago in the grocery store, the background music—some kind of soft rock—had suddenly opened its curtain to admit the utterly old-fashioned sound of

"Greensleeves," and it had made him want to weep. It took the checkout girl with the metal bolt in her tongue a few throat clearings and small coughs to jolt him into handing over the money for his beans and orange juice.

He put them in his bicycle basket and pedaled slowly to the cemetery.

He and Mary were to meet behind the officers' quarters. She had said she'd give him her answer, adding teasingly that if he didn't show up, she'd know the worst. Mary. Mary of the long pale fingers. Mary of the sly laugh.

They were both eighteen, and would wait for the war to be over. They would marry, and stay in the mountain valley, and have four children, two boys and two girls. They would give all of them beautiful, antique names that could be shortened if the kids wanted something normal. Antigone. Ferdinand. They would love each other enough to erase the perfidies of the war, of all wars.

He walked toward their meeting place in the dusk under a wafer moon, and Leo knew joy, and thought it was his to keep.

There was a scrim of snow, light as talc. Warm lights glowed in the windows of the officers' houses, and smoke tendriled out of the chimneys. In the last house, a slouching shadow filled the back kitchen door, smoking a cigar.

Tone beckoned him over. He asked him what he was doing. Leo responded that he was taking a stroll before sleep, that it had been a long day and he was tired of his barracks mates and wanted just to walk and to think. He adamantly did not turn his gaze toward the small field behind the houses, the broad-crowned tree in its far corner where he knew she waited. He took a deep breath. Maybe an apology was coming from the commander.

"Take a load off your feet," Tone said, pointing to a splintery old bench next to the door.

"I will keep walking, I think," Leo said, trying to sound light, to sound genial.

"Take a load off your feet," said Tone. He patted the seat of the bench.

Leo took a few steps backward. He thought briefly about simply turning and walking away. But he could hear the soft, condensed fury in Tone's voice. Tone patted the bench again. Leo sat down. Tone gazed at a pale line of light on the horizon and took a long meditative pull on his cigar. And then they just waited. For a few minutes, for five, for perhaps fifteen. Leo made a tentative move to stand, and Tone placed the flat of his hand on Leo's head and pushed him back down.

More time. Much more time. Until it was full dark, and what had seemed a full hour or more, and suddenly Tone fixed Leo with an alert, even surprised look, and asked him what he was still doing on the bench. Didn't he have something better to do?

Leo couldn't speak past his anger. He said nothing. He pulled his sweater sleeves over his chilled hands and walked toward the barracks.

"Pleasant evening, old dog," Tone called.

When he circled back and made his way to the tree, she was not there. Could she really have decided he'd had second thoughts? He didn't think so, but he had no way to know, because in the morning word came to the barracks and flew around the entire compound that Captain Whiston's pretty daughter, the pale reader, had scarlet fever and was not expected to survive. In two days, she was gone.

For reasons still unclear to him, Leo was never able, after that, to imagine a life for himself that didn't have her at its center. He stayed in the little mountain city with the fort on its western edge. He educated himself, learned the insurance business, worked at a steady job, pursued his painting, made a few friends. He never married, never had children.

The fort grounds now housed a few offices and a museum. Its cemetery had very old graves, including that of Mary Whiston, dead at eighteen. Leo visited it weekly. He clipped the grass and weeds around it, and wiped away any dust or debris on the stone.

Leo had made a will that provided in part for ongoing upkeep of the grave and the little cemetery as a whole. He had a term life insurance policy that expired soon, and the other beneficiaries had been updated recently to include the maintenance fund of the condominium association of Pheasant Run. He wanted his old neighbors to have a safer building, and a less fearful one. He hadn't been a perfect person, a perfect neighbor. But he could do that much.

He would finish the painting he was working on, and then it would all start to happen.

9

Lander Maki lay half-awake in bed, Rhonda snoring softly at his side. As it sometimes did in his twilight states, a certain Minnesota night came back to him, as if wanting him to review it one last time before finally putting it to rest.

It is winter, a deep evening rimed with snow, the sky low and hard, like a lid. He is delivering flyers for the Lutheran church's upcoming pre-Christmas arts and crafts show, trying to do it on his bicycle, to get it over with, but the wheels keep wobbling and skidding on the ice and so he is forced to move more slowly than he would have on foot. It infuriates him, this thwarted fleetness. He feels he is wrestling with too many things at once: the bag of flyers slung across his shoulders; the treacherous dimming ice; the scarcity of streetlights on some blocks, so that he can't see any ice gleams on the ground; the stupid mission itself.

Why didn't the arts and crafts women just post the flyers in the neighborhoods, at grocery stores and on telephone poles, like everyone else did? It seems to him that all of them, his mother included, all of the quilters and crocheters, the baby-clothes makers and jewelry beaders and ski-cap knitters, that they all have such an oversize investment in fussy, colorful little comforts that they can't even tell people to come and buy them in a way that isn't fussy. They have to enlist their children to deliver the word to all those doors in person. Stuffed penguins! Embroidered hot pads!

But he is almost done. His flyer bag is almost empty. He can smell the damp canvas bottom of it. He is starving, as he has been starving, it seems, since the very day he became ten.

The light on the front of his bike isn't working. It flickered out a half hour ago. It is so cold he thinks maybe the batteries are frozen. Can batteries freeze? He can barely move his gloved fingers on the handlebars.

He has entered a neighborhood in which the houses are imposing brick, centered on huge lots behind boulevards planted thickly with maples. Four more blocks and he will be at the intersection where he can hang a right and speed the five minutes home. Golden lights glow behind curtained windows. The thick ground cover of accumulated snow forces all that solid, planted darkness into sharp relief. The maples lean their bare branches toward the street.

Now he is frightened. Because of his dead light, he can't see far ahead of him. There is no traffic moving on the streets. He feels that the big houses are saying, *Move on. You don't belong here. Our comforts are not your comforts. You live in a careful little bungalow with doilies on the chair arms, and your mother cleans and waxes the kitchen linoleum on her hands and knees, and you can't wear shoes in the house. And now you are late for warmed-over tuna casserole and a bowl of fruit cocktail. You are late, but she is more peeved than worried. She will want to know, first, if you delivered all the flyers. She will not ask if it was asking a bit too much of you, after a long school day, to embark on a chore that should have been hers.*

Without saying a word, she will manage to suggest to you that you failed to do something right. Not that you did something wrong, exactly, but that it was not quite right, either. It is what she does in order to suggest that you have placed yourself outside bounds that have never been described to you. You have no idea where they are located. Just that it's good to be inside them and bad to be outside, and you always seem to be just outside. Just beyond embrace.

At the intersection, he turns right, too fast, and his front wheel slides fast, to the left, and lays the bike and young Lander Maki flat on the icy road. The right handle grip somehow jams itself into his rib cage as he goes down, and when he stands up shakily he feels the sharp bite in a rib. He touches the bone and nothing seems out of place, but it grabs him with each breath. The big houses seem to walk backward, to retreat from this spectacle. A car approaches, slows, and the driver asks if he is all right. Yes, he says. No problem. Need to get my breath.

After the car turns out of sight, he leans to pick up his bike and nearly cries out. He can't imagine lifting his leg over the bar to get back on, the way he'd have to torque his upper body just that much. He bends over slowly and rights it, and walks it to a large bush on the boulevard where he can drop it so that it is almost out of sight, to be retrieved tomorrow. Then he starts walking toward his house.

In his mind, he runs. He flies down the street, wind in his ears, the big trees whispering encouragement, the now-visible winter moon increasing the speed of its path across the blackness to pull him on. In real, body time, he walks very slowly, trying not to move his rib cage any more than necessary. Inside, he leaps and dodges and cries out to those on the other end that he is on his way. The blocks inch past and put him in a neighborhood that he recognizes, and finally there is the filling station and the shadowed corner market, and, two long blocks farther, his street. His breath chugs. His fingers are numb. The yard light is on.

As he walks up the steps to the shallow porch, his mother's shadow appears behind the curtained glass. He takes a very small breath, trying not to move his ribs. She opens the door.

"What?" she says. "Why are you just standing there? Why are you so late? Can it take that long to deliver a few flyers?" She runs exasperated fingers through her permed hair.

He stands there. Shrugs a little. Waits for her to perceive his injury, his immense ordeal. He thinks of making up an exciting story: a speeding driver, attack dogs, a hobo who stole his bike. He wants to give her something huge. Something that will make her say, *How horrible! How worried I was about you! How completely amazing that you made it home!*

She looks distractedly over her shoulder and calls to his sister to check the stove and feed the old dog. Her housedress smells old. She reaches toward him impatiently, to pull him inside, and he backs away and puts up his hand like a traffic cop.

"Don't touch me," he says. "I'm hurt."

She narrows her eyes as if to laser through his obstinance to something he is hiding.

"I'm hurt," he repeats.

"You're not hurt," she says. "You just say things like that."

10

In the evening, after all the tumult around the fire, Professor Emeritus Rydell Clovis in #410 paced his apartment, then sat himself down, hoping for some noirish old police procedural on the classic movies channel, only to discover that a surfing musical was all he could expect. He popped his shirt cuffs and stared at the backs of his hands. Two more red splotches. Senile purpura, his toddler-faced doctor had smirked, and nothing to worry about, and, yes, well, it was an ugly-sounding name, and, yes, it could be said to be insulting, but, bottom line, the name was a lot worse than the reality, so go home and don't worry about it. The patronizing little moron.

For most of the two years since he'd retired from the English department, Clovis had been adamantly upbeat. He began each day with ten minutes of stretching and flexing to the electric hum of Tibetan monks. Then he racewalked through the halls and stairways of Pheasant Run for a half hour, making sure, via his enhanced activity tracker, that his pulse topped 65 percent of the maximum for his age. For breakfast, he brewed a mug of sencha tea and ate multigrain cereal topped with goji berries while he listened to NPR and read the ever-thinner newspaper, after which he scrubbed himself in the shower with a loofah, sometimes followed by a vigorous evocation of a hot tub experience he'd had with a pair of stoned minxes from his Chaucer workshop in the spring of 1972. And then a long final rinse and he was ready for whatever came his way.

At some point, however, the pallor of his circumstances had become unignorable. Here he was, in something not unlike a second prime, occupying a cramped apartment in a ridiculously named residence for senior citizens, and why? Because, due to a series of unfortunate investments and too many early withdrawals from his retirement fund, he couldn't afford anything better than an apartment for himself and another, in the same building, to rent out so that he could adequately supplement his modest fixed income going forward. And what a renter—the hysterical, nearly indigent Mrs. Six, who seemed now to have taken a powder. Whatever a powder might mean in the universe of Viola Six.

Still. All this—the doughty old ones, the sketchy new building manager, the pathetically earnest and hapless condominium owners' board—would be behind him very soon, if the stars lined up right. And why shouldn't they?

Clovis had been more than surprised when he was notified, a month ago, that he was one of three finalists for director of the university's proposed new Center for Ethics and the Digital Humanities. He was a literature man, but yes, he had made himself technically proficient before his not-entirely-voluntary retirement, to the point of serving on several university-wide committees aimed at bringing the institution into the twenty-first century and the digital universe on a minimal budget with lean and mean staffing. As it turned out, "lean and mean" included a 60 percent cut in English faculty, including a few modest buyouts—Clovis among them—and threats from the provost to eliminate all junior faculty if the remaining warhorses didn't gracefully retire earlier than they might have planned.

And then, it seemed, a donor had come along, and planning for the center got underway, and Clovis applied for the director's job on a whim. It seemed he hadn't been forgotten as thoroughly as he'd thought, because, to his frank surprise, he had now survived all the winnowing except the last round of it, and the job could very well be his. His prospects, and his financial future, had lit up like the opening footlights at a musical revue. And he was not even that old, physiologically, and there was time for a new life. So why was he so terrified that it might all be some cosmic joke?

He began to pace again, but when he felt his pulse rate skip ahead of his steps, he forced himself, again, to sit, and he turned on the surfing musical. As he watched the ridiculous spectacle, 95 percent bikinis to 5 percent waves, with bouts of execrable singing thrown in for laughs, he relaxed into the nonsense and began to drift.

When and if he got the job, he'd have enough money to go to high-end beach resorts and come back with a compelling tan, and, not impossibly, would cross paths with a classy, lithe woman with stilettos and a big mane of glossy auburn hair, a fellow divorced person perhaps, but no, more likely a widow. A youngish wealthy widow with pooling eyes who might want to redeem her years with a fat-cat, philandering husband by taking up with the director of an entity with a lofty name. And perhaps—again not impossible, surely—he'd hire a lovely discreet intern who was conflicted enough to be especially receptive to his mentoring for a period of time, to their mutual benefit, he thought he hoped.

It wasn't out of the realm. The other two finalists for the job were academic hipsters with blurry sexual orientations who'd been brought in from a couple of no-count campuses in the Midwest, and were so cant-ridden and vacuous in their presentations to the all-campus forum that the conclusion was, he hoped, inevitable. Because, face it, the director's main job would be to lend tone and a certain gravitas to encounters with high-minded, deep-pocketed potential donors. And if some silver-hairs with money to burn were going to support a center that explored topics like the ones he had proposed on a for-instance basis to the search committee—"The Poetics of Triggered Hedge Investing" and "Coding the Imagination"—then they were going to want to allay their nervousness by putting it in the palm of a calm, techno-savvy and seasoned guy who seemed not at all shaken in his cultural and academic foundations, attentive though he was to the cutting-edge currents at hand.

Clovis had to admit to himself that he would be hard put to explain to someone outside academia—a beer stocker at a Minute Mart, say—what exactly the center would do, day by day. But he had found, in his university career, that titles tended to create content and function. So not to worry. He genuinely felt himself to be a humanist as a result of his literary studies and his

long belief in the capacity of the human to realize himself (or herself!) via reason and historical perspective,
rather than divine or psychic lightning bolts. And then,
well, nice tension there between ethics studies and the
digital zeitgeist with its cold, rapid-fire efficiency, its
rampant rebraining of the human universe. Shove the
two ideas together and you had a big old capacious tent
with room enough inside for any number of circus animals to mill around.

The surfing musical ended in a riot of song, dance, skin,
and waves against a lurid Pacific sunset, rousing Clovis
and leaving him short of air. He threw back his living
room curtains and opened the window a few inches. He
knelt on the rug and rested his chin on the sill to breathe
in the new and wintry night. Just barely, he could make
out the creeping form of the black cat that frequented the
neighborhood rooftops, descending now, like slow ink, to
the ground. *What next for that cat?* he thought. Was this
the beginning of its day's excitements, or the end?

He tried to meditate, to clarify, to do something in
his head that would isolate and address the sources of his
unease. OK, a small one was that he had lost his activity and mindfulness tracker sometime today. The device
had simply come untethered from his waistband at some
point. Before the fire? After the fire? When he made a
quick afternoon trip to the little grocery for chai and
shaving cream?

And here came another nagging worry. Two members of the search committee, both of them professors in the School of Business, had made a point at the

post-interview reception of verifying where he lived.
Where he lived! This wasn't kosher and they knew it.
Because he was unable to think of any plausible reason
for the question, Clovis had decided that his interrogators wanted some evidence from him that he was tuned
into the economic conditions of the community, including housing availability, perhaps because they envisioned
that the center ultimately would draw faculty, students,
and visiting scholars whose decisions to relocate might be
affected by their housing options.

And so he had launched into an overly elaborate description of Pheasant Run, his very temporary dwelling
place, and its occupants and the sorts of people who lived
there. He had described the half-owner/half-renter situation, and the deferred maintenance, and the pressures on
the owners to make up for declining condo values by raising the rents of their tenants, nearly all of them on modest fixed incomes. And he also offered the information
that rumors of a mass buyout were circulating, though
he, Clovis, was skeptical that the owners would go for it.
Where would they move? Where would the renters go?

"Well, they—you—might be wise to think about it,"
one of his interrogators advised. "Speaking from a strictly
business standpoint, I'm saying you owners should be
thinking in those terms. Someone comes along and offers
a decent enough price for undermaintained property, you
might want to think about it."

"It takes leadership, though," the other chimed in.
"Any kind of group, a homeowners' association, a university center, is going to be best off when they have a real
leader piloting the ship."

Reviewing that brief conversation, Clovis could hear the gear sprockets engaging. He'd been issued an ultimatum of sorts. Certain persons connected with the university—perhaps the university itself—wanted to acquire Pheasant Run, and the directorship hinged on Clovis's willingness to help that process along. Whether the two faculty members wanted it for private real estate speculation or the university hoped to acquire a nondescript off-campus building at a bargain price, with minimum fuss and publicity—for its cybersecurity program? For animal experiments? For lucrative resale?—seemed almost beside the point. What mattered was that they were verifying that Clovis could help to make it happen. Was that what his candidacy had been all about from the beginning?

If so, he was happy to fudge his ethics a tad and try to accommodate them. At the very least, he could urge the condo association to seriously consider a buyout. Before he had second thoughts, he sat down at his computer and composed an email to Mavis Krepps and sent it with a maestro's flourish.

And now he had only to make sure the search committee knew he'd done so. A casual mention would do the trick.

But there was another problem, and he'd known what it was from the beginning of his candidacy. It concerned the Bad Old Days and the possibility they would come to light while he was still under consideration for the director's job. Would it really matter that he had, more than half a century ago, engaged in some petty thievery and a car-burning with a few other bad actors, not long before he met the inestimable public defender Bonnie Jo Archer, who kept him out of jail, got the charges expunged from his record, supported him through college, married him, and eventually pretended she'd never known him as anything other than a scholar of medieval literature? Bonnie had been out of the picture for years, and he couldn't think of any reason she'd try to do him out of the director's job—the divorce settlement had been grossly skewed in her favor—but who knew?

And now it also seemed possible that the moronic Herbie Bonebright, who very likely had his own criminal record, might have somehow uncovered some information about Clovis's mishaps back in the mists of time and be prepared to come forward with them for money.

Just two days ago, Herbie had unsuccessfully addressed a dripping kitchen faucet in Clovis's condo by doing a lot of swearing and wrench-banging, which prompted some sharp words from Clovis, maybe sharper than was strictly necessary. Herbie then said a peculiar thing.

"You should try to remember that you and I are in this together," he said. "And I know a couple of things about you that don't exactly add up to a great personal reputation, I guess I'd say. So you might want to think about the best way to get along with me. That's all."

"In what together, may I ask?" Clovis had said as icily as he could.

Herbie shrugged elaborately and ambled to the door, flip-flops slapping. He zipped up his puffy vest, then glanced down at the newspaper on the hall table. It was folded open to the second page, which had a photo of Clovis and the other finalists for the director's job. He studied it.

"Hey," he said. "There you are. You probably wish the whole thing was over, eh? Get the whole thing over and done. Get the job."

Every detail of that conversation came back as Clovis tried to recover from the exertions of putting out the fire in Herbie's apartment, the chaotic evacuation and milling around, the fire inspector's request for an interview. Herbie knew something, and he was prepared to use it against Clovis. But what, exactly? And how? And what was this "together" business? He and Herbie Bonebright had about as much in common as a jaguar and a two-toed sloth.

His exercise routine for the day was in shambles, but Clovis felt as if he had been running since dawn. To calm down, he did some hamstring stretches and drank some valerian tea. He reviewed every step he'd taken since he went out his door at dawn. Every step. He bent over because he suddenly felt light-headed. Old and light-headed and afflicted with some kind of unnamable craving.

He drank a tall glass of water, then retrieved a stale packet of Top Ramen from the back of his cupboard, yielding to a perverse craving for pure salt. As he dipped his finger in the spice packet and touched it in a contemplative way to his tongue, a cold rain pocked with sleet began to tap against his windows. Public radio was playing some kind of whining Celtic dirge. He stared down at the sidewalk, where two hunched walkers moved among the pale streaks of near-ice as if they swung among silver ropes in a slow dream.

Somewhere a violin played. Live or recorded, he couldn't tell because the sound was too faint. It was probably from an iPad. But it had, at its heart, a yearning quality that pierced him. Which of his old neighbors was listening to the violin to calm down after the day's shocks and disruptions? He couldn't begin to guess. The violin stopped and dread bloomed.

Knees splayed, he closed his eyes and rested his hands on his knees. *I am here*, he thought, *and my lives are over there*. He couldn't have said where *there* was, but it seemed to exist beyond a glass wall and it held his past life, his future life, and—the realization made his whole body clench—his current life. He leaned back in his leather chair and shook his head slowly from side to side. He dug his clenched fists into his eyes like a furious, exhausted child.

11

Viola Six stood alone under the stars at an unpeopled rest stop on the Continental Divide. She was shivering hard, partly from the cold and partly from the strain of the call she'd just made to say she'd been abandoned in her pajamas and ski jacket, high on a mountain pass, and needed help very soon.

The rest stop lot was framed with leaning halogen lights that seemed to be humming messages to each other. Or maybe not. She couldn't let her imagination run away with her, or she might become convinced that she inhabited a murmuring anteroom of the afterlife and would stand, too soon, before the monstrously whimsical judge she had managed not to believe in for most of her life.

A car, very long and low in the old way, crested the rise of the highway and followed the arrow of its headlights into the haloed lot. All that Viola could see of the driver was a nest of black hair that barely topped the steering wheel. This wasn't an officer of the law.

The car stopped and the driver got out, leaving the engine rumbling. She was a teenager, maybe fifteen, with blue-black hair, kohl-rimmed eyes, and tattooed sentences snaking across her forearms and hands. She circled the car slowly, kicked a tire, and squatted to look closely at another. Only then did she walk over to Viola and look her up and down in a way that suggested she was not unfamiliar with the bizarre. Her eyes were swollen and red. Everything about her seemed aggrieved. Now and then she glanced over her shoulder at the empty road, the sentinel pines.

Viola needed to think. Almost as soon as she had completed her call, she had realized that she could very well be in some kind of psychiatric holding pen by dawn. Who would believe her story? That it was true didn't mean it wasn't preposterous.

She made her frozen feet step carefully back from the girl as she thought about how to present herself and her situation. Her phone buzzed. It was the dispatcher she'd just spoken with, seeking more information, telling her to shelter herself in the restroom, verifying details of her physical surroundings, all with an oily patience that was worse than outright accusation.

The girl walked back to the car as if she didn't want to intrude. She opened the passenger door and stood by it.

Viola nodded. She pointed the phone at the salty stars. The miniaturized voice beeped and cheeped before Viola pressed the red icon and dropped it in a nearby dumpster.

As she got into the car, she explained that she had been the victim of an unsuccessful abduction and would now like to proceed to California. The girl sniffed and nodded. She said California was fine with her. They'd go back to Butte and take I-15 south, then cut west someplace in Utah. Viola settled her cold feet under a warm blast of air. They drove, without speaking, into the quiet black night. Near the outskirts of Butte, a garbage truck with undimmed lights pulled up behind them too fast, then lurched into the other lane, passed them, and roared down the highway, taillights scribbling.

"Nice," said the girl. "Dim your dumb lights, you drunk punk."

"I couldn't agree more," Viola said.

At a complicated and lit-up truck stop, the girl gassed up and returned to the car with moccasins, face wipes, a toothbrush, a gray T-shirt with an elk on it, and gray sweatpants printed with tiny pink dinosaurs. She handed it all to Viola. Out from behind the wheel, she looked older and more confident, and she pulled rolled money from her cowboy boot to pay for things.

She drove fast, pulling over every several hours to take the briefest of naps. Otherwise, they stopped only for fuel, gas station food, and restrooms. Viola changed into her new clothes and was pleased to find that they all fit. No one, anywhere, gave them much notice. She fell into a deep sense of relaxation and inevitability, sleeping in spurts and waking rested. The miles flew away, and there was no need to decide anything for a while. The girl clearly had her own wild troubles, but no apparent interest in sharing them, which was a re-lief. The hot dogs they consumed with stale corn chips evoked in Viola a not-unpleasant memory of a county fair with a spinning ride that pressed her child-body against a wall like a huge hand and stuck her there while the floor fell away.

The West became tweedy with snow, then seriously white in the higher reaches. She felt amazed to be on the move. And she was moving toward something she fervently wanted: a new life in a warm place by the ocean. A place where the temperature varied only ten to fifteen degrees through the seasons, and gregarious flowers spilled over rock walls, and the Franciscan mission bell on its high knoll chimed the hours, as it had done for a couple of centuries.

If Rebecca Tweet from Seniors could find a life, a niche, in Santa Barbara, so could Viola. She would count on Rebecca to help her get situated, but she wouldn't presume on her ongoing hospitality or companionship, because it wasn't company she was looking for; it was the experience of feeling intact and safe in a place she had chosen for herself. A place far away from Pheasant Run and its lurid troubles. She would miss dear Cassie McMackin, and maybe courtly Leo Uberti. Her typewriter she might miss. But that was about it.

Somewhere in northern Nevada, she and the girl began to converse in fits and starts. The girl identified herself as Raven and said she had decided, as they drove, that she would go to Los Angeles, as a first resort anyway. She said she would like to see anyone try to find her there. Viola said Santa Barbara was where she wanted to go.

They discovered that they had been living in the same small city and, in that moment, eyed each other at length, mutually relieved to experience not a glimmer of recognition.

Raven said she was escaping the place because she was afraid some big trouble was brewing that could involve her. She threw a wary glance at Viola.

"This kid I know, I just found out he's got a gun, and he's got enemies at school and thinks they insulted me. I need to get away because he might try to turn into a super-hero if I'm around. And then, last straw, some home shit I don't need. My stepdad. Toby the terrible." Her face closed. Viola noticed that she was driving with her eyes shut. For five, ten seconds she didn't open them to blink. She had done this several times before, producing in Viola some cu-riosity, but not alarm. It seemed a technique for conserving energy, if nothing else, and there weren't that many other vehicles to worry about, as they had now abandoned the interstates, where they might be easier to find.

Pheasant Run, Viola's home for the past decade, faded with each mile they covered. By the time they were climbing toward Tonopah, it seemed like a place she had only heard about. And the freedom of that distance made her want to talk about it.

She turned to Raven. "Do you find that putting a lot of miles between yourself and trouble can somehow make the trouble seem as if it belongs to someone else?"

"Nope," said Raven. "Absolutely not. Trouble catches up with you. Don't kid yourself about that. My personal goal is just to give it a run for its money."

"That sounds...would you say...a little bleak?"

Raven shrugged. "You think it doesn't?" she said. "Find you? You think you're going to get to wherever you're going and find that your troubles have stayed back in Clowntown, Montana, USA?" For the first time in the trip, she was ruffled. Viola wasn't sure if that was a good thing or a bad thing. It did seem that the climate of the car, its air, was circulating in a livelier way.

"I was abducted from my building yesterday morning," she told the girl. "I knew I was in danger, and it turned out I was."

Raven gave her a long look and pressed her lips together.

"He drove all over for a while, saying all kinds of crazy things, and I thought I was going to be killed," Viola said. "Hours and hours on various roads and back roads, like he was looking for the perfect place to do the deed, and then eventually we were back on the interstate and he let me out at the rest stop to use the restroom, and when I came out he was gone. Second thoughts, or maybe something scared him? Somebody maybe drove into the lot and gave him a curious look before driving away, and he thought he better hit the road."

Raven closed her eyes for a few seconds. "For sure," she said.

"I knew about some things that some very powerful people didn't want me to know, and they ordered my abductor to get rid of me, is my theory."

Raven lit a cigarette. "Let's not talk for a while," she suggested. "I don't think it helps anything. Maybe in a year, we'll both look around and go, *Well, hey. Things turned out OK.* But maybe not. Point is, we're moving, and it's all we can do, and all we should do, and I think we oughta just sit back and do the ride." She closed her eyes and draped her thin hand with its gnomic scribbles over the top of the steering wheel, where it made minute, automatic adjustments to the shapes of the road.

"At one point I heard whimpering just like a little hurt dog," Viola said quietly. "And I realized it was me."

—

In Santa Barbara, she'd need only a room, really. She could find a room. She would take the bus to the beach every time she felt like walking on the sand. She'd gather lemons from a small tree in the yard of the handsome house where she rented the room. She would have her morning coffee on a small terrace outside the French doors of her room, a separate terrace from the ones the homeowners used. Theirs was on the other side of the house and had a firepit and a water feature.

Her mind, in the room by the lemon tree, or outside on her terrace, would untangle itself so that the fears and worries and suspicions that had lodged themselves inside the knots would be free to float into the blank blue sky. She would wake no more in a sweat of dread about being evicted as part of a plot devised by cold-eyed capitalists to make a pile of money off a piece of real estate that needed only to be rid of its elderly occupants in order to quintuple in value.

She would be free of her role as the town crier, the Klaxon, the alarmist; free of the fear that she would be killed because of the danger she presented to the plans of the capitalists. She had tried to stop them. She had almost paid with her life. And now she was happy, more than happy, to be many miles from a place that had begun to feel hellish to her.

They turned toward the coast at Bakersfield and drove into Santa Barbara just after dawn. The water glittered. The gulls cried. The little city woke up to another perfect day.

Inside a public restroom near Stearns Wharf, Viola washed her hands and face and examined herself in the mirror. She felt oddly pleased that the dinosaurs on her new pants matched her ski jacket. She didn't need the jacket, but she decided to tie the arms around her waist because she didn't know about the evenings yet.

She thanked Raven, who was going on to Los Angeles right away. She wished her well. Raven reached into her boot and retrieved her roll of bills. She peeled off $300 in fifties and put them in Viola's hand and rolled Viola's fingers around the money with her own.

"You can thank terrible Toby," she said. "The guy who thinks the perfect ATM password is his dog's name."

"Not necessary, but thank you so much," Viola protested. "I have my emergency credit card. I also have a son who owes me some money, and maybe there will be a miracle and he'll get it to me somehow. Stranger things have happened." She retrieved an envelope from her pocket. It was addressed to Cassie McMackin in #412 at Pheasant Run.

She examined the seal as if she might open it, then quickly handed it to Raven.

"There is more I could add to this, but I will write a follow-up. Mail this when you get to the City of Angels," she said. "I'm counting on you to do that."

Raven nodded. She slid behind the wheel of the long car and lifted her scribbled hand to Viola.

"You will be pretty much OK, then," she said.

Viola nodded and the car moved away.

"I won't remember you, if you won't remember me," Raven called out the open window as she rumbled onto the road that would take her south to the metropolis.

Viola returned to the restroom to verify that she looked presentable and smelled relatively clean. Then she walked slowly along the waterfront. The November air was soft and lucid and filled with sparkles and a light breeze. A group of elders performed trancelike movements on the beach. Tall palms flanked the walking path like auditioning showgirls, and the terra-cotta roofs of the little city rose gently from the water toward low hills. All was containment and ease. At the harbor, boats in their slips looked freshly painted in the bright sunshine, and there were the fake pleadings of the gulls and sometimes small bells or the faint chatter of talk radio. A dog stood at the prow of one of the boats and barked at her in an inviting and friendly way.

She bought fried clams and coffee at a place with sidewalk tables that served seafood all day, took a long time to eat, and ordered more. She was famished. She would have to fortify herself to find Rebecca, an enterprise that suddenly felt overwhelming. In her postcards, Rebecca had never included a return address, but she had once remarked that she was in the phone book, should Viola ever decide to abandon the endless northern winters and dabble her toes in some salt water.

She asked the waitress for a phone book, which the girl had some difficulty locating, and which turned out to be three years old, so there would be no Rebecca in it. She asked if she could use the restaurant's phone, and called information, and lucked out. There was a number for an R. Tweet. Viola wrote it down and decided to wait a few hours to call, as it was still early in the day and Rebecca had often said she was basically comatose before noon.

Along the harbor street she caught the first metro bus that came along and rode it for several miles, maybe more, until she realized she was in another part of the city, thickly planted and hushed with wealth, and when two middle-aged women ahead of her got off, she did, too. They were a half block from the entrance to a parking lot, and there was a sign at the turnoff that said "Lotusland."

For the flash of a moment, Viola felt she was in a child's dream. But the two women were pragmatic, stolid-looking sorts, and they walked with purpose toward a small group of other middle-aged and older people who were gathered around a tall, broad-shouldered woman with a name tag and a mane of electrified-looking hair to her shoulders. She wore a safari hat and was checking a list. There was a low building behind her, restrooms and a gift shop. Viola reminded herself that she looked very nearly respectable and summoned the will to approach the tall woman, who informed her that tours of Lotusland were by reservation only but, since it was the very end of the season and three people hadn't showed, she was welcome to join them by paying the fee inside.

Lotusland felt like the inside of a fierce and agitated mind, all looming fronds and deep shadows, statues of twisted dwarves, giant cacti, aggressive palms. Even the peaceful interludes—the Japanese garden, the allée with its roof of winding lemon-heavy branches—had something about them of the mind instructing itself to stay within the bounds of control. Viola was sorry she had come and quickly weary to her bones. The guide told them the heiress who designed the place had imported the world's most exotic flora, but she couldn't seem to retrieve the botanical names of anything. She looked as if she had had a bad night.

When they were at long last near the end of the tour and within sight of the visitors' center, Viola slipped away from the group to rest for a few minutes on a broad rock near the blue garden. And then she must have dozed, because when she opened her eyes and rose to catch the group, it was gone.

She felt watched by eyes far back in the leafy surround. What kinds of animals might live in this sort of place? Did they go in and out of Lotusland, sunning in the late-day dappled light, napping on a gargoyle, taking their leisure in the place after the tour groups had left for the day? How did they get in? How did they get out? She sat on the rock again, to capture a little more strength so that she could proceed with her day.

She stood up quickly, suddenly afraid that the group would forget all about her and the grounds would be locked with her inside. The world tilted sideways. She flailed her arms to right herself. And all the blue plants came rushing toward her.

She surfaced to the sound of a woman explaining where they were. The day had proceeded without her. Late-afternoon light now filtered through the tall plants. The voice she heard was lovely and low, and it stayed ahead of a multitude of whispering footsteps and lesser beings asking questions. The voice seemed not to want to speak in real sentences or convey any ordinary sort of information. When someone in the inaudible distance asked another question, the guide said a number of words, but they all seemed to frame and support the best ones in the center. "Bromeliad," she said. And then "Shade palm." Every word that made its way to Viola—*topiary, succulent, aloe, pavilion, blue*—gave her a little shock of recognition and grief. How had she failed, all these years, to appreciate the tensile grace of her own language?

Her body felt crooked and inert. It was arranged on a loamy substance and curtained by the high plants. Her head was next to a large rock and was paralyzed with pain. She felt planted, as she couldn't seem to move. Only the lids of her eyes. Only the tiny rasp of her breath, as rapid and shallow as that of the small lizard that stared at her from under a drooping fern. Her voice was out of the question. It had done all of its speaking. *Pavilion.* She could only think it. *Topiary.*

Long, benign light warmed her shoulder. The people whispered into the distance, their guide's voice like a gentle gong that they carried on a litter, around some far corner, into the ongoing world. Wouldn't they miss her? Wouldn't they give her a thought?

The patron saint of gravediggers. The phrase came to her from one of Rebecca's postcards.

"Saint Barbara was a very beautiful young woman who lived in the second century AD. When she was beheaded by her father for becoming a Christian, he was instantly struck dead by lightning. She is the patron saint of gravediggers and architects, and protects against lightning, sudden death, and impenitence."

When Rebecca moved to California and wrote her post-cards, it was deep winter back in Montana. Everything felt like expired food in a refrigerator.

"A Chinese man who lived here a century ago was famous all over the country for predicting the weather. He called his forecasts 'celestial morsels.'"

The soft, towel-swaddled form of Rebecca lay on a chaise, nibbling daintily at a large shrimp that had been scooped up that very morning from the sea.

"But what the Chinese man had to forecast is a mystery to me. The weather here does not require thinking about or preparing for or guarding against or running inside from or hoping for. It is constant meteorological kindness."

In the winter in Montana, Rebecca had worn a stiff woolen jacket and fake fur hat, donations she'd confiscated from the Seniors thrift store, and stern leather laced boots to which she had attached climbers' crampons to keep her from falling on the eternal ice.

"The stations of the cross at the mission are so darkly painted, and so small and high on the wall, that it is impossible to see what kind of suffering is being shown. Only the very lightest parts are visible at all, such as a raised arm or a band of silver at the horizon beneath a black sky."

Viola wandered with Rebecca under a black sky. A smoky forest surrounded them and blocked their passage to the ocean, a silver line in the far distance. The cracking and hissing of a fire grew louder. Ash intensified the silver tones in the plants that towered above her and above the lizard, who hadn't moved. *More than anything*, she thought. *More than anything, I want the tiny living creature to stay. Aloe. 'Allo. Abide.* A trickle of liquid left her ear, slow and jammy. The lizard blinked. It had turned from a leafy green to the palest blue. It held her in its tiny stare.

THE PRESENCE

OF AN ABSENCE

12

Maki had completed his initial interviews at Pheasant Run. He had also intended to have another chat with the teenager who'd been lurking around the building, but Cassie McMackin had provided an alibi for the boy and a brief explanation of his troubled circumstances, so he'd put that one on the back burner.

There was something about Cassie that felt so familiar to him that he had found himself engaging in a conversation that went in many other directions than the fire and its complexities. They talked about Little Boy and his latest, and wondered, almost at the same time, how long the frightening nonsense would last. She asked Maki questions about his work and his life, and when he told her a bit about Rhonda and her animals, she laughed in the way you do about the propensities of a longtime and beloved friend.

Sitting in his parked Volvo, he tried to reside for a while in the part of his mind that skittered and whispered just beneath his full consciousness. His cell rang. Rhonda had news. Their limbless lizard, Roscoe, seemed to be dying. Maki trained his sights on a little boy across the street who was executing perfect figure eights on his skateboard, looking entirely unburdened by the day-to-day.

They'd rescued Roscoe the day before from PetSmart. The creature, which looked like a snake, had Morse-tapped its snaky little snout on the glass of its cage as Rhonda and Maki were walking past it toward the dog food. Rhonda felt an immediate affiliation and began to quiz a nearby clerk, who told them the reptile was a so-called glass lizard with unique self-protection abilities that she didn't specify. Ten minutes later, the clerk, Shilo, had filled them in on the reasons a snake could be technically a lizard—movable eyelids, external ear openings, and almost invisible appendages near "the rear vent"—and Roscoe was in the back of the car in a cardboard box.

"At first, I thought Roscoe was just shivering in place because Sid had fake-pounced at him like he does—that way he raises his paws in the air and brings them down hard, just close enough to make him seem serious?" Rhonda said.

"Well, you might seize up, too, if a hairy beast two hundred times your size did something like that."

"We're not talking about me," Rhonda said in her arguing voice, though what there was to argue about Maki wasn't sure. "In fact, he seemed to recover and was blinking and moving his head around. And then! I went to make some tea, and when I came back to his little pen, maybe a third of him had broken off and was in a separate part of the cage."

Maki digested this for a few moments. "Various pieces, or a single piece?" he asked.

"Various," Rhonda said. "Shilo said not a thing about this possibility."

"And I don't want to be indelicate, but do any of the pieces happen to contain the critical rear vent?"

"Oh ha ha," Rhonda snapped. "I haven't done a microscopic exam. And I haven't told you the worst part."

Tell me there is something worse than getting your ass broken off, Maki thought better of saying.

"The parts are moving," Rhonda said, glum. "And the rest of Roscoe is alive, but just looks, I don't know. Unable to proceed with his life. And Sid's pouncing at the parts. Which are definitely twitching."

Maki tried to give all this his single-minded concentration. He understood the feeling of being unable to proceed with a life. The boy on the skateboard wiped out spectacularly but regained his feet in one fluid move.

"Do you want me to come home?" he asked.

"Of course not," Rhonda said. "I just want you to know what you're facing when you do."

There goes my mulling time, Maki thought as he placed the phone in his pocket. There went his chance to repair to the backyard to his thinking shed with the space heater, where he would try to put together the pieces of the Pheasant Run fire as he could identify them at present. There went the phosphorescent particles of near-knowledge that had started to gain some steam and climb to the surface of his mind. *Gain some steam.* He felt a sharp pang of nostalgia for the idea of an era powered largely by boiling water.

Although idly cruising the internet was against his rules for himself when he was on the job, he typed in "glass lizard."

The word from Wikipedia was that glass lizards, also referred to as glass snakes, are so named because they "have the ability to deter predation by dropping off part of the tail which can break into several pieces, like glass. The tail remains mobile, distracting the predator, while the lizard becomes motionless, allowing eventual escape. This serious loss of body mass requires a considerable effort to replace, and the new tail is usually smaller in size than the original."

Maki pretended he was in his thinking shed and shut his eyes. At first he saw the panting Siddhartha jubilantly crouched over the moving tail parts. And then he saw a huge rally of some kind. The figure at the center wriggled around the stage, out there in the spotlight, shaking outstretched hands, giving the thumbs-up, engaging in high fives. And off to the side, some human figures in the shadows watched the antics, turned away, whispered among themselves in a way that chilled.

He gave his head a shake and reminded himself to cut down on the melatonin.

When he got home, Rhonda waved a weary arm in the direction of the lizard's cage without lifting her eyes from her computer screen. She told Maki she was with a client. The toes of her slippers were duck heads, and they pecked nervously as she typed. Her hair was limp and her face was drawn.

The lizard was indeed in a segmented state, the head and torso cowering frozen in the corner, the remaining parts gyrating on the other side of the cage.

"Jeez," Maki said. Siddhartha, banished to the mud-room, whined piteously.

"That cat I was conversing with the morning of the fire?" Rhonda said, head cocked, fingers flying across the computer keys. "The one on the rooftop?"

"Righto," Maki said. He really needed to go to his shed.

"She told me just now that a guy came out of Pheasant Run during the evacuation and ran off toward the high school. She said he stepped behind a tall bush and pulled a gun from his backpack and pointed it straight at her." Her fingers quit moving. "She said she felt her heart stop." Rhonda's face took on a distant, remembering aspect.

"Sweetheart," Maki said. "Why don't you take Sid for a drive? He really needs not to feel like a dog for a while. He needs to sit in the front seat and look around at the big world, and forget about pouncing at lizard parts. Don't you think?"

She searched his face, then let Sid into the room. While she got her jacket and purse, the dog leaped at the lizard cage until she pulled him out the front door by his collar, claws clattering across the floor.

"Did you eat lunch?" Maki asked as he accompanied them down the walk. She said she had, but had a headache that wouldn't seem to go away.

"I'll make something so delicious for dinner that you'll thank me in a dozen interesting ways," he said. She rolled her eyes and opened the passenger door for Sid, who took up his position, haunches to shoulders like a holy man, head tipped out the open window.

Maki watched the two of them heading into the afternoon, their valiant profiles plowing the steely day. He worried excessively on the infrequent occasions when Rhonda seemed seriously below par, then tried to talk himself out of it because he knew he was worrying as much about himself—about losing the fuel she gave him—as he was about her. It was time for him to shake off the pall and do his work.

Some kind of knowledge was waiting for him to deserve it—*it* being some real insight into what might have transpired at Pheasant Run. He knew he needed to cultivate a state in which his inner eye could move alertly among the random facts and images that presented themselves. Only then would the edges of those facts and images become portals, rather than a frame that constituted the limit of what he knew.

In his interview with Cassie McMackin, he had put it this way: "We're looking at something that was destroyed, and we have to be able to put it back together again, either in the mind or physically, to determine the origin and cause." Cassie told him, without further explanation, that she felt she was doing much the same thing in her own life.

To prepare himself for the process, he needed some food energy. Not a lot, but it had to be the right kind. There were similarities, he'd found, between really fine cooking and investigating a suspicious fire. In each, you wanted to follow an adopted method but keep your mind elastic enough that unexpected avenues of investigation could present themselves.

From the top cupboard shelf, he retrieved the pretty ceramic bowl with the vermillion glaze. He minced some scallions and leeks and quickly stir-fried the leeks in sesame oil until they were curling and crisp. He left the scallions raw because their cool grassiness so perfectly offset the hot crackle of their cousins. He was about to dice a red bell pepper when he saw that shredding it finely would open much more surface and allow it to cook just the right amount of time in the broth to come. He boiled some water, poured it into the bowl, and stirred in the shredded pepper and a dollop of miso paste. He sprinkled the top with the scallions and leeks, then ground black pepper (for acuity) over it all. Smoky, meadowy, pungent, thoughtful, ancient. He drank from the bowl and licked up the dregs.

In his shed, Maki lit a Kool and sharpened two pencils to needle points. He found a fresh legal pad and placed one pencil on either side of it. The space heater hummed away, eager to assist.

He squinted and thought about the old people in their four-story building. An early-morning fire breaks out in the manager's second-floor apartment. The manager is absent, presumably eating his customary breakfast at the sports bar. The smoke alarm in the hall goes off. Professor Emeritus Rydell Clovis, strenuously speed-walking as per his daily routine, finds himself in the area, grabs an extinguisher, gains entry, snuffs the blaze. The firefighters come sirening in and mop up. The bar reports that Herbie never arrived for his breakfast. His car is not in the Pheasant Run garage. Attempts to locate his phone are unsuccessful.

Maki had sent photographs and what little physical evidence he had to the insurance company people, to be reviewed and forwarded to the lab. He'd consulted with the detectives who were trying to locate the missing Herbie and the missing Viola, and handed off Herbie's iPad to the geeks. So there was a lot to be discovered.

The biggest development, of course, was that an elderly woman using Viola Six's phone had made a call to 911 late the day of the fire. She said she'd been abducted, and then she seemed to vanish into the ether. Her phone had been zigzagging across the state for the two days since then and still hadn't been located. By the time the highway patrol got to its most recent location, it would be gone. So how was Viola Six traveling, if the caller had indeed been Viola Six? Of her own volition? It didn't seem likely.

And what about the fire itself? His gut feeling was arson. The lab evidence, so far, was more suggestive than conclusive: a test suggesting the presence of something that could have been soft plastic, Coleman fuel traces in an apartment that didn't have a Coleman stove, too hot a blaze for a simple grease fire, and there were still a few last refinements of the tests to be run. The lab was analyzing what it could of the burned material—Professor Clovis had done a regrettably thorough job of coating it all with extinguishing foam—but there was scarcely a cinder.

For Maki, though, the strongest evidence for arson was the absence of any evidence that suggested an accidental cause. It was what he liked to think of as a black hole arson: a large absence that itself was a powerful presence. Where was the grease residue? The fragments of trash that a junk-filled apartment would have in the kitchen?

By everyone's account, Herbie was an out-and-out slob. He couldn't adjust a thermostat without making a mess. Every part of his apartment, with the exception of the kitchen, was littered with old newspapers, balled-up tissues, plates of half-eaten food, dirty socks, tattered towels, fast-food sacks and containers. French fries were embedded in the carpet near the TV-watching chair. Why, then, would the kitchen be so clean?

Where were the traces of greasy hot pads, Chicken McNuggets, paper napkins—all the stuff that would have littered the countertops of someone like Herbie? If they had been there, someone had removed them. And if someone had removed them, it meant that the person had taken pains to make sure the fire didn't get too large too fast, wanted it contained enough that it wouldn't spread to the rest of the apartment or any other part of the building. A rather sophisticated undertaking. The person in question knew the habits of fire and trusted his own skills.

Would Herbie Bonebright have a motive to set it, even if he happened to have those skills? A second fire in his place could only hurt his prospects of retaining his job. Why would he want that to happen? And if he had set it, would he have left his new iPad on the premises? Not likely. And if he'd set it to terrorize the building's residents, why take pains to make it so strictly contained?

Had one of the building's residents set the fire to take revenge on Herbie for something he'd said or done to them? It was difficult to imagine a bent, white-haired person scanning the long hall like a hawk before entering Bonebright's unit to concoct a very sophisticated, self-limiting, delayed-ignition revenge fire that would seem to have been caused by Herbie's carelessness and get him fired. But who knew? Maki had seen a lot of things in his career.

In any case, something unspoken and weighty was going on in that building. During his interviews, Maki had been struck by the residents' independence, intelligence, and lucidity. They were extraordinarily on top of it for their ages, especially given their obvious physical fragility in some cases and the fact that the majority of them lived alone.

And yet, when asked about Herbie Bonebright's general habits and his capabilities as a building manager, a number of the tenants (all of them renters) had answered in an extremely guarded manner. They looked scared, as if something had knocked and they were afraid to open the door.

And what about Professor Clovis, the hero of the moment? Both the professor and his story bothered Maki. There was the matter of the lock. In all likelihood, Herbie Bonebright had left his apartment unlocked when he went to breakfast, as was his habit, according to several tenants. If he'd locked it, he would have needed a key to unlock it upon his return, and he'd left his ring of keys in his bathroom.

So why did Clovis say the door had been locked? Maki consulted his notes. Yes, unequivocally, the apartment, according to Clovis, had been locked, and he had had to bash the door open with the extinguisher. He'd shown Maki how he had struck it like a murderer.

There was a general fishiness about the man. Nothing he said or did seemed entirely sincere. He had also taken pains to let Maki know he was about to take the reins of a new center of some sort that was being hatched over at the university—that he was a man of some considerable standing, should Maki have somehow missed that fact.

Maki tried to envision Clovis's smile again, the way it was an offering, not a response, and was therefore entirely strategic. He wanted something or he was deflecting something. Mirth was not even in the equation.

He had a strong feeling that, despite his education and credentials and tweedy manner, Clovis had been an abused child or had even done some prison time. It was that smile, partly, but also a quality of alertness that was utterly divorced from curiosity, that was purely self-protective. Or maybe many years at a university could make you that way. He'd heard stories.

The professor reminded Maki of what Sid was like when they first brought him home, and poor, declawed Rosemary the Manx, before the fatal raccoon. They'd had several rescue animals who had arrived with convict alertness, who had paused just a nanosecond in every exchange to assess the degree of threat. Most had eventually seemed to understand that their surroundings, their people, had pleasures and comfort to offer. But it could take quite a while, and in a few cases, it had never happened.

Maki closed his eyes and let it all twirl and amble in his head. He turned off the space heater and did a few stretches. His knees popped. It was time to make dinner.

He wanted something that would comfort Rhonda and make her forget her wretched first marriage, the man at the mall with his gun, the lizard falling to pieces, all the world's troubled and chatty animals. Something vegetarian and earthy, then, with a dessert that smelled like a storybook grandmother's kitchen.

Linguini with vodka sauce. Toasted sourdough baguette brushed with emulsified garlic in walnut oil. His special chopped salad with the fennel, red onion, and macadamia nuts. Pear clafouti, warm from the oven, topped with soft folds of whipped cream spiked with vanilla and a whisper of cognac. A shot of the freezer-chilled Absolut first, with chopped pickled herring and fresh dill on rye toasts. A glass or two of that rowdy Malbec with the linguini.

"A symphony of tastes and textures," he said to the cat on the windowsill. He found himself unable to check on the condition of the lizard. The cage was very quiet.

As he slowly stirred the vodka sauce and listened to The Decemberists, he examined the patched crack in the ceiling above the stove. Time for some paint touch-ups around the place. He put the lid halfway on the sauce and turned it to a very low burble. He looked again at the ceiling. Something about it was pricking at him. What was it? And then he pictured the cupboard over the stove in Herbie Bonebright's apartment. He had focused intensely on the burn pattern when he was there, but now he remembered something else. There was a small hook attached to the bottom of that cupboard, directly over the stove. A little, charred hook.

As he tried to think about why someone would put a hook in that place, a hook that was far too small to hold a pot or pan or even a cooking utensil, Rhonda blew in with the dog. They both looked as if they had engaged in some exciting minor larceny. A few leaves were caught in Rhonda's curly hair. Sid ran into the kitchen, wriggling with excitement. He had an orange balloon tied to his collar.

"Something in here smells not unlike heaven," Rhonda called from the vicinity of the coat closet.

"Hello, creatures," Maki said, pouring the icy vodka into shot glasses he'd placed on a small tray next to the herring toasts. He set the tray on the coffee table near the pellet stove, which emitted a toasty aura, stole a look at the lizard, which was still two-thirds frozen and one-third segmented and mobile, and threw a towel over the cage, leaving a little room for air. The dog seemed to have forgotten about it. He was studying the balloon as if waiting for it to leap at his throat.

"Some kids at the park were dressed up like medieval knights and having a sword fight," Rhonda said. "They had a bunch of balloons tied to the picnic table for some reason, and one of them fetched this one and presented it to me with a big knight-in-shining-armor bow." She sipped the vodka and smiled. "He had a good bow."

Sid pawed the balloon into a corner of the room, then tried to stare it down. Maki thought about kitchen ceilings and studied Sid.

"You know," he said. "It's possible to set a delayed fire with a balloon."

"Don't put felonious ideas in Sid's head," Rhonda said. "There isn't room." Sid turned to gaze at them with rapt, mouth-breathing tenderness.

"Some pissed-off person fills a balloon with fuel, knots the top with a string, and breaks into his enemy's place. He tacks the balloon to the ceiling or some other surface with a small hook and places a lit candle on the cupboard or stove directly below, with some combustibles—newspapers, telephone book, and so on—nearby. Then he sets the balloon swinging widely, exits the place, and has been in a bar down the street for almost a quarter of an hour when the fire is reported. He has calibrated it just right. It took at least ten minutes for the balloon to come to rest directly over the flame. A few moments more and…whoosh."

Outlandish as it was, he had a scenario that would account for the faint smell of soft plastic, undetected by anyone else at the scene, and for a few shards of wax among the remains.

Maki's phone did its text gurgle. Detective Hanrahan wanted a call.

Stacy Hanrahan was six feet tall and 260 pounds, a former bull-riding champion from some scraped and howling part of Wyoming. In his early forties, he still moved remarkably fast for his size. He had a reputation as a ladies' man, and when he wasn't hard on a case, he was a Saturday night regular at the Cabin out on the edge of town, where a band called the Laid-Off Cowhands played all the old schottisches in addition to a rock repertoire that stopped at about 1959. Maki and Rhonda had seen him out there a time or two, pounding Dr Peppers and escorting a sequence of lovelies around the dance floor in the side-by-side shuffle that requires such extraordinary finesse and lightness of foot, and which paradoxically seems to attract oversize men with big guts emblazoned with big buckles, who tend to execute the movements perfectly.

Detective Stacy Hanrahan seemed to know, from the first cases he and Maki had worked on together, that Maki's real interest was always in the why rather than the how of a potential arson. The how was evidence, analysis, comparisons, records, a certain kind of intuition. But the why was human yearnings, resentments, scheming, desperation, even, not infrequently, a kind of evil.

So, over time and as they came to like and trust each other, Hanrahan brought Maki in on the police end of certain investigations, confident that he wouldn't overstep his authority and sympathetic to his wish to know where the trail was leading.

Hanrahan also had a zest for his work that affected Maki in somewhat the way that Rhonda did. Basically, he felt happier in their presence. More alert. And they both made him laugh, especially, in Hanrahan's case, because he channeled the speech patterns of almost everyone he dealt with in a professional capacity. Sometimes it was almost uncanny, the way he became the ventriloquist's dummy.

"We know more about Mrs. Six's phone than we did," Hanrahan told Maki. "So OK, it was on Homestake Pass the evening of her disappearance. Call it six or six thirty or so when a woman made a call from that phone during that time, to 911. As you will remember, she said she was inside the women's restroom at that rest stop. The dispatcher called her back for more info and got cut off, so the patrol headed up there pronto. They said the rest stop was totally empty, really dark by then, of course, and witch-tit cold. They looked around for quite a while and saw a few footprints and tire marks, not many, but nothing else. They combed the place. Nothin'."

"And then the phone is moving erratically."

"Well, it was at the rest area or in the vicinity after the woman's call, then it started moving west on 90 and then down all these county roads, all over the damn place, as you know. Get a bead on it, and off it went again. That's why it's been taking all this dad-blast time."

"And now?"

"Well, the Billings patrol apprehended an extremely drunk person of interest, the driver of a garbage removal truck. He's picking up garbage on Homestake Pass the evening of the day Viola Six disappears. His girlfriend texts him that she's taken off for parts unknown with his best friend from childhood that he was blood brothers with. Next stop for our boy is that shitty little road bar near Rocker, where he leaves with a couple fifths of Black Velvet and proceeds to drown his sorrows while driving a mammoth garbage truck all over the damn state for a couple of days, with Mrs. Viola Six's phone buried back there in all the crap. Not a pretty job, but they found it."

They both mulled silently for a few moments, then agreed to reconnoiter the next day and map out some potentials.

Before he went to bed, Maki checked his emails, knowing he shouldn't. He almost always found something that churned him up and kept him awake.

There was a very short one from Daphne, saying their mother was not doing so well, that she was leaving garbage all over their parents' living area, not noticing or caring about the mess, and putting weird things in the refrigerator, like her face cream, and that she kept repeating, with much laughter, a story in which her own mother had called her "too dang big for her boots."

Maki couldn't fashion this person from the image he retained of their mother's fastidiousness and propriety, her utter lack of joy. Age had produced an impersonation, it seemed to him. He had nothing to say, so he didn't respond.

Another email was from Professor Clovis to Mrs. Krepps, who had forwarded it with no comment.

Dear Mrs. Krepps,

Just a note to extend my support to someone who is doing a difficult job in difficult times, and to say (in all modesty) that I have become something of a "layperson/expert" on real estate finances and trends in this long wake of the 2008 slump and subsequent "corrective" legislation that impacts us all. Although the condo market has gained viability in certain areas, Pheasant Run suffers, as we all know, from certain issues regarding maintenance, occupancy rates, and so on. It's my belief that the long-term personal and financial interests of the owners might, at this point, be best served by being very open to the possibility of negotiating the sale of the building to a qualified buyer. You have suggested that such a buyer might exist, and we in the association hope to learn more about that very soon. Let me just say at this point that I believe the association should seriously entertain any credible offers that are forthcoming.

We are sitting on an uneasy condo market and facing expensive structural repairs to the building. Perhaps this is the time to negotiate a sale that is advantageous to all.

Let me know what you think, Mavis (if I may).
Very sincerely yours,
Rydell

Maki noticed that the email had been sent to her the day of the fire, late in the evening. *Busy, busy*, he thought.

There was a brief message from one of the geeks who had retrieved all the recent searches and all the messages sent or received or scrubbed on Herbie's iPad.

"One email Mr. Bonebright thought he'd scrubbed appears to be a threat. It is addressed to Felix Wingate, who is general manager of Longleap Enterprises. Bonebright threatens to reveal damaging information about Longleap unless he is paid a sufficient sum to stay quiet. Details at the morning meeting! P.S. The guy spells worst than my little neece whose 4."

"Well, well," Maki said to Rhonda, who was reading the newspaper in bed.

"They've found four new species of legless lizards in California," she announced. "A couple of famous reptile professors did. They thought there was only one spe-cies—I'm guessing Roscoe's—but they searched and searched and found some others. Guess where?"

Maki raised his eyebrows.

"At the end of a runway at LAX, in a vacant lot in downtown Bakersfield, on the edge of the Mojave Desert, and among some oil derricks in the lower San Joaquin Valley."

"You're not alone!" she called to Roscoe before returning to the newspaper. "'The biologists are trying to determine whether the lizards need protected status,'" she read.

"We all need protected status," Maki said.

Just after daylight, Maki and Hanrahan met in the basement of city hall to chat with the geeks. The technical staff, as they preferred to be called, were three exceedingly pale, round-shouldered young men who shared so many gestures and physical traits they could have been triplets. Even their voices, wry and singsongy, sounded alike.

The two rooms in which they labored were low-ceilinged and filled with computer equipment, cardboard boxes, reference manuals, cords, wires, and junk. The overhead neon buzzed faintly, and an enormous espresso machine on a corner table hissed and sputtered.

The one named Harley handed two printouts to Maki and Hanrahan and moved boxes and papers off a couple of chairs for them to sit on. The one named Charlie brought them espressos and stale powdered sugar doughnuts.

One printout was Herbie Bonebright's iPad email to Felix Wingate at Longleap. "You did not pay me when you said, and yet I have been doing my job as agreed. I suggest that you quit your threts and pay me imedialy with a bonus for my efforts or I will have to take some action."

The other printout was a record of recent searches on the iPad, the majority of them having to do with long-ago charges involving property destruction and criminal mischief in someplace called Bryan, Ohio.

One of the geeks brought forth a plastic bag containing the egg-shaped entity Maki had discovered on the floor of Herbie Bonebright's clothes closet.

"I know what that thing is," Hanrahan said. "I do my research."

"An amulet carried by a member of a lost space tribe?" Maki said.

"This," Hanrahan announced, "is a mindfulness and activity tracker. A hundred and twenty-four bucks at Amazon."

"And that buys me…what, exactly?"

"Mindfulness and productivity. You clip it to your waistband or whatever and head into your day, and every time your breathing gets tense, it emits a gentle little bleat." He bleated quietly. "It also tracks your steps, counts your calories, and monitors your heart rate and other sorts of respiration patterns besides the tension ones. Connect it to your phone and you can get some meditation sessions thrown in. Charges on a charging plate, which wasn't in the closet or anywhere else in Herbie's place. I checked that out."

"I don't know," Maki said. "My vision of Herbie Bonebright doesn't fit with the mindfulness part. Or with paying a bunch of money to track whatever mindfulness is. Or with keeping track of physical activity at all, for that matter. You know what I'm saying?"

Hanrahan bleated.

"But it does fit a little better with Professor Clovis, the fitness buff and fire extinguisher wielder. Yes?"

Another small bleat.

On their way to Pheasant Run, Hanrahan told Maki he'd contacted Longleap in hopes of getting Herbie Bonebright's work history, address history, emergency contacts, and recommendations prior to his employment at Longleap. The office administrator, an extremely thin and thin-voiced woman of an uncertain age, had reluctantly retrieved the file.

It was skimpy at best. Several previous jobs were mentioned: security guard, delivery driver for a beer company, manager of a bowling alley in another state, employee of a carpet cleaning company. He was forty-one years old. Born in Finch, Ontario, Canada. No felonies registered. No chauffeur's license. In case of emergency, contact a woman in Ontario named Edith Bonebright. Hanrahan had located her last residence and discovered she'd been dead for a decade.

He asked the office administrator whether Herbie had any previous property management experience, and whether Longleap had verified the "no felonies" information.

At that point, the woman had become quite huffy, he said, and had launched into a weird little speech—he imitated a high-pitched voice—in which she affirmed that she was not in charge of hiring, that she merely made sure the records were in good order, and that she left it up to her higher-ups, most particularly Mr. Felix Wingate, to handle personnel matters directly, which was his preference, those matters including all hiring, and that the idea that she would know, for instance, whether or not a criminal record had been investigated thoroughly was preposterous, as that was not her job, and was not a job she would want, whether it was offered to her or not, he could be sure of that.

None of it made much sense, and, in fact, Hanrahan had concluded that Longleap seemed to have more than its share of so-called eccentrics, to put it most kindly, and he wondered how they managed to stay in business, and why anyone would enlist their services. So he'd begun to poke around.

"For now, I'll just say that Felix Wingate and his associates seem to have done business under a few other corporate names in a few other states."

"Property management?" Maki asked.

"Well, yes, seemingly," Hanrahan said. "But the properties are always in prime locations and are always occupied by older people on fixed incomes. And, what do you know, those people start selling or moving out, and suddenly there is an empty building in a good location getting bought by a developer and turned into extremely high-end real estate. Luxury condominiums. Boutique memory care. Who knows what else?

"And you think Herbie was the hit man at Pheasant Run, so to speak. The enforcer. The terrorist."

"That might explain a mindfulness tracker in his closet," Hanrahan drawled. "Stressful work."

At Pheasant Run, they took the elevator up to the fourth floor. It thumped and shuddered before the doors opened. As they waited for Clovis to answer the door, Hanrahan adjusted his cuffs and whistled through his teeth. As usual, he wore a pressed white shirt, leather vest, and blue jeans with a crease ironed into them. Instead of the boots that would have completed the look, he preferred dazzling white running shoes because he felt they gave him that extra edge, should he ever have to run. It didn't happen often in his line of work, but it happened.

Clovis's greeting was curt. He looked disheveled in an unidentifiable way, nothing about him obviously out of place, but the whole package a little blurry at the seams. His face darkened when Maki introduced Hanrahan as a police detective, and he lifted his hands in fake surrender.

Hanrahan strolled across the living room and took a look out the window, his belt buckle glinting as he turned to survey the room. There was a photograph of a large ram on a precipice, its curled horns blaring. A wine-colored leather chair. An etching of Oxford in some previous century. Fewer books than you might expect for an English professor. A few odd ones. Secrets of various sorts of winners, biographies of athletes.

Clovis indicated the couch as if he were flicking an insect away. He emitted an ostentatious sigh.

"First off, remind me again what you were doing immediately before the fire alarm went off," Maki said, extracting a notebook from his shirt pocket.

"My daily routine, my exercise routine. It's a half hour and includes a program of racewalking, stairs up, racewalking backwards, stairs down—basically consistent cardio."

"Just keep on keeping on, eh?" Maki said. "Do you start the minute you leave your place?"

"No," Clovis snapped. "First I take a nap in the hall. Of course I start when I leave my place."

"And just keep on keeping on," Maki repeated like a machine. "Do you keep track of what it's all adding up to with some kind of gizmo? I don't know much about the latest gadgets, the really elaborate ones, but there are these Fitbits and chronometers and such, right, that can track everything to the minute."

"Right," Clovis said.

"In fact, don't they have things now that can test your mentality and also tell you when you should drink some water, maybe both at the same time? And then someone told me there is a computer app that can make your refrigerator also be a stereo and a photo album. Did you know that?"

"Why would a person want to do that?" Clovis asked.

"You tell me," Maki said. "But you use some kind of device to monitor your morning exertions, pure and simple, is that right?"

"That's right," Clovis said.

"And I suppose it keeps you moving pretty steadily, and at a darn fast pace," Maki said.

"That's the point."

"What's confusing me a little is that Mrs. Riddle down on the second floor said she saw you walking pretty slowly down the hall in the vicinity of Mr. Bonebright's apartment, shortly after seven on the morning of the fire. She thought she heard something at her door and looked through the peephole and saw you walking by, slow as mud."

Clovis took this in.

"Well, I am seventy." He held up his hand like a traffic cop. "Don't say it: I don't look it. But that's a fact, and very occasionally during my workout I have been known to take a breather."

Hanrahan walked over to the window. "Look at that cat on the very top of that steep roof over there," he said. "Good traction. Must have sticky stuff on its foot pads."

He appraised his large white shoes as if they were suddenly wanting.

He looked up quickly and drilled a look into Clovis.

"We've found evidence that Herbie might have had something on his employer, Longleap Enterprises, and wanted money to keep quiet about it. Do you have any idea what that might be?"

Clovis shook his head, as if he couldn't believe the stupidity he was forced to acknowledge. "I know you gentlemen might not believe it, but I have better things to do than to listen to speculative rubbish. I really do. In fact, I have a meeting at the university in less than an hour."

"Oh yes," Hanrahan said. "You're a finalist for a job over there. Some center for something or other, am I right?"

"For Ethics and the Digital Humanities," Clovis said slowly, as if he were spelling it out to a child.

"See?" Hanrahan announced to Maki. "I *do* do my homework." He sat down in the big leather chair. "Maybe you could enlighten us as to the mission of the place, or group, or whatever it is. Just for background and whatever."

"Let's just say in basic layman's terms that I—the new director, I should say—will supervise a series of initiatives aimed at exploring the potential interface of ethics studies and the digital zeitgeist, especially as it relates to what we used to call contemporary literature."

"Katie bar the door," Hanrahan said.

"Actually," Clovis said, taking the smaller visitor's chair, "we're talking about no less than a rebraining of the human universe, a process that is happening at such speed that the old intellectual fiefdoms, segregated from each other by walls they've enthusiastically built them-selves, simply aren't up to the task of offering anyone help in living their lives in a mindful sort of way."

"So when I want to make an appointment for a mind-ful rebraining, can I come to you?" Hanrahan said, slowly unwrapping a toothpick from its paper sleeve. He stuck it in his mouth and wiggled it up and down.

"I'm guessing it's too late," Clovis said airily, consulting his phone.

Maki extracted a printout from his vest pocket.

"You sent an email to the president of the condo as-sociation, Mrs. Mavis Krepps, suggesting that the group consider selling the building to an interested buyer, should one step forth." He handed the printout to Clovis, who read it slowly. The tips of his ears turned a faint pink. He coughed.

"We've asked Mrs. Krepps to forward to us any com-munications she gets regarding the building or its tenants," Maki said.

"Well, this place has its problems, in case you haven't noticed," Clovis said. "I think we'd all be smart to sell to some person or group with the money to make this build-ing what it could be."

"That's the thought that warranted an email to the association president late on the day of the fire? Couldn't it wait?"

Clovis shrugged.

"Our technical staff also discovered that Herbie was researching your early days and found that you were something short of an angel as a youth," Maki added. "A firebombed car was involved, if I remember right."

Clovis stood, then turned on his heel and walked to his little kitchen. He returned with a glass of water and set it down carefully on a side table.

"They found a search record?" Clovis asked.

"They did," Hanrahan said. "It took some doing, but the geeks finally unearthed it."

Hanrahan let the quiet come into the room and stay. Maki knew better than to say anything. No one was better than Stacy Hanrahan at sitting with the kind of silence that becomes so weighty it feels permanent.

"I did have a juvenile record of sorts," Clovis finally said. "Though for God's sake, that stuff happened when I was a very lost lad, what, some fifty-five years ago. A half century! And to my knowledge, my lawyer got it expunged from my record, and it was gone, done, buried."

"Not deep enough," Hanrahan said.

"Given Mr. Bonebright's extortionist tendencies, I'm wondering if he ever brought up the fact of your misspent youth with you," Maki said. "And if he did—just saying—I think I'd want to know just how far he'd gone with his own research. In fact, I'd almost be tempted to get a look at Herbie's iPad, just to see what all he'd been up to. That is, if I could get into his account by, I don't know, knowing his password or using some kind of all-purpose one? Do they have those? The geeks seem to be able to do it, eh, Hanrahan?"

"Geeks are geeks," Hanrahan pronounced. "The university has a pack of them, too."

Maki took the egg-shaped tracker from his pocket and put it on a coffee table in front of Clovis, who squinted as if it wouldn't come into focus. He yawned with his eyes open.

"OK," he said. "You can stop. I did go into Herbie's apartment, about ten or fifteen minutes after he left for breakfast the morning of the fire. His door was, not surprisingly, unlocked. I looked for the iPad just to check his search record. I found nothing." He looked hard at Hanrahan.

"Well, our geeks might be a step up from you in the cyber realm," Hanrahan said with an elaborate shrug.

"I heard someone coming, hid in the closet," Clovis said in a newly soft voice. "Waited. Fidgeted with my tracker because I was very tense and was afraid some beeping was about to go off, and it must have loosed from my waistband and dropped somewhere in that hellhole unbeknownst to me. Someone was in the kitchen doing something, and then they were gone, and I was out of there like a shot."

"Taking just a second or two to lock the door from the inside."

"If I saw someone in the hall, I wanted to be able to say I'd tried his door—wanted to talk to him about something, whatever, even though I was pretty sure he'd left for the Den—and it was locked. That way, I couldn't be placed inside the apartment at any time."

"Who did you think was going to try to place you inside the apartment?"

Clovis yawned widely. He stood up.

"Well, look," he said. "Whoever came in after me was up to something in the kitchen, and it wasn't baking cookies. I could hear whoever it was testing the burners, and there was a smell of some type of fuel, then some tapping and raspy swearing, and he was out of there. I wanted out of there, too, before the place blew up."

"But it didn't," Maki said. "There was something of a wait before the fire occurred."

"And I was ready for it, alert to the possibility shall we say, and I put the damn thing out," Clovis said, aggrieved. "And this is the thanks I get."

Hanrahan had been studying the photo of the ram on the precipice, focusing closely on the way its hooves were placed at the very edge.

"That whispered swearing, or however you described it," he said. "You ever heard that voice before? You remember the words?"

"Well, people sound different when they're whispering, so, no, I really couldn't say I recognized the voice or what it was saying."

They all considered this for a few moments.

"And you didn't bother to take a good look at the kitchen on your way out?"

"No."

"Well, OK," Hanrahan said. "Food for thought. Food for thought."

"Oh, please," Clovis said. "Just get out."

Without the plodding presence of Herbie Bonebright, Pheasant Run took on a suspended aspect. Whatever he was—fraudulent or just moody, inept or sinister, a doughy no-count or, as Viola Six would have it, an ex-con with an agenda—his duck-footed presence as he walked the halls in his beach clothes had grounded many of the Pheasant Run residents in the day at hand. It was difficult to drift into ethereal sadness or regret, or to stew in long-ago memories, or to dwell on the sinister nature of new aches and pains, or to tease out the tendrils of the circumstances that had left you utterly alone in a cackling and money-mad world when there was a figure like Herbie moving in all his dim corporeality across your line of sight. He was like a slow reptile in an old terrarium, unsavory but strangely absorbing.

Now that he was gone, vanished it seemed, some of the residents found themselves listening for his thumping walk or the roar of his leaf blower or the talk radio that emanated from his apartment door when he left it open a few inches to tend to something somewhere else in the building. Others found themselves rereading his ridiculously contorted missives—"Please! After garbage, binn lid is closed and window above lock tite!!"—simply to remind themselves again that their own diminishments and sagging fortunes didn't include outright illiteracy.

For a week now, Herbie's apartment door had opened only to admit or relinquish various investigators. There was a piece of yellow plastic ribbon across it ordering others to stay clear. A sign told anyone who needed assistance with repairs or lost keys to contact Longleap and to be aware that the cost for delivery of a replacement key would be twenty-five dollars. The investigators had walked out with plastic containers for a few days, and then they stopped arriving much at all.

This morning's mail contained a letter to all the residents from Mrs. Krepps, who had been fielding queries about the investigations into the whereabouts of Viola and Herbie, particularly whether any information had surfaced that suggested foul play.

Dear Pheasant Run Residents,

Regarding the whereabouts of our resident manager Mr. Herbie Bonebright and our long-time neighbor Mrs. Viola Six, may I suggest, as president of the Pheasant Run Condominium Association, that we take stock of our good fortunes in life and leave the authorities to their work? They have assured me that little has surfaced that sheds light on either disappearance, and that, when and if it does, we shall be informed promptly.

Meanwhile, we must remind ourselves as a group to keep our collective wits about us and proceed with our lives in a calm and regular manner.

To that end, I have appointed an interim building manager from among the building's tenants, Mrs. Lydia Wishcamper. She is the person you should see about any concerns relating to the maintenance and upkeep of your units. She has employed an on-call handyman to address small maintenance concerns, and will relay larger ones to our property management firm, Longleap Enterprises. Mrs. Wishcamper was more than generous to take on these duties for what amounts to a token salary, and it would behoove everyone to thank her in whatever way seems appropriate.

I also have new information about the potential purchase of the building. Be reassured that nothing is imminent, and that any purchase will, of course, depend upon a unanimous vote of the building's condo owners. I invite all owners to make appointments to meet with me separately regarding additional terms and details of the potential buyout.

Finally, I would remind all occupants of the building that any holiday decorations you wish to put on your doors or in the common lobby area must be flameproof according to the condo association regulations and, I believe, city ordinances. Also, any guests that you may be entertaining must be reminded that this is a smoke-free building and that any cigarette smoking they may wish to engage in must be done twenty feet or more from the building. And finally, the recent "thumping" of the elevator was investigated by the elevator company repair people, who extricated a foreign object from the shaft that was apparently causing the noise and represented no immediate danger to elevator users. I believe it was a stocking.

Kind regards,
Mavis Krepps

In her mail, Cassie also had a single thick letter with no return address, but with a handwritten order to "Open Immediately Upon Receipt." Cassie recognized Viola's writing. It had been mailed three days earlier in Los Angeles. The letter was dated November 12, two days before the fire. There it was: evidence that her friend was at least well enough, safe enough, to post a letter. She found herself trembling slightly as she opened it.

Dear Cassie,

I hope this doesn't sound to you like the ravings of someone who is "off her rocker." I continue to stay on my rocker, and, in fact, feel very calm and levelheaded at the moment, despite my awareness that something eerie and dangerous is going on at Pheasant Run. I hope to be able to have a cup of coffee with you soon and spell it out from A to Z, but I might have to leave the premises quite suddenly. In that case, I won't post this until I am so far away, and in such a populous locale, that I won't be easily found.

There are unscrupulous people out there who want to empty Pheasant Run of its owners and renters and buy it for a song. Then they will resell it for a handsome profit to purchasers who have deep pockets and special needs. That's the short and long of it. We are entirely expendable to these ruthless people in the wings who hope to profit from our gullibility and our fears. I alerted our property manager, Longleap, that I knew they were likely involved somehow, then realized, too late, that I may have put myself in considerable danger.

There are many dots that connect.

Meanwhile, dear Cassie, when you get this, I will be far far away from Pheasant Run. My son Rod won't know where I am, but my friend Rebecca Tweet has moved to Santa Barbara, California, and she will have heard from me and can confirm that I am safe. If you hear that I have moved (or been moved) because I can't live independently anymore, know that the facts are otherwise.

Your friend,
Viola

Cassie read the letter again. Though it seemed proof that Viola was alive, or had been several days ago, the contents seemed overheated in a way that made her worry. Was it possible Viola had fashioned this disappearance simply to insert drama into her life, the way she had perhaps concocted personal adventures that seemed unlikely at best? Had she really had a sojourn in Athens with a handsome businessman who was a secret gunrunner? A journey on a tramp steamer in the company of a bohemian crowd that included not one but three soon-to-be-famous poets, all sleeping with each other? Maybe the stories had become her antidote to a tedious marriage to a carpenter named Ollie and a subsequent alliance with a fool who let a con man erase her savings, not to mention the existence of her hapless and infuriating only child, skipping from surefire deal to surefire deal, everything a disaster, and then he was there again at his mother's door, whining about his fortunes and convincing her to hand over money she couldn't spare.

But there was also that ravishing photo of Viola in Italy. So who really knew?

And where was Viola now? Where could she possibly be?

Cassie called Inspector Maki to tell him she had heard from the missing woman. He was working closely now with the police and would know where to direct it. She left a message on his voice mail that he was welcome to pick up the letter at his convenience. And then she read it again, and folded it tenderly into the envelope, which she placed under a paperweight next to the photos of her husband and daughter.

Rereading the newspaper, she came across a tidbit she'd marked with a big check, and recorded the information on her little machine.

"Note from the larger world: it seems that large chunks of ice from melting glaciers are being airlifted to Antarctica for safekeeping because the glaciers are predicted to entirely disappear in the decades to come. Since bubbles in these ancient glaciers are frozen records of our past atmosphere, scientists have constructed an Antarctic ice bunker to keep them safe for future research.

"Time is kept safe. Time is transported. Time is melting."

Several mornings a week, Cassie walked from Pheasant Run to a coffee shop on the other side of the downtown river bridge. It was the most she could manage without feeling slightly weak-kneed, and she didn't attempt it when the sidewalks were wet or icy. This autumn, so dry and warm after the shocking October deep freeze, had delivered an unbroken sequence of walkable days. She liked to leave fairly early, and to proceed in such a way that all her senses were as fully engaged as she could make them. This required a certain slowness and a willingness to stop at times to let her sensations find a place to alight, deep within her. Her brain, yes, but also her fingertips, her nose, her retinas, the delicate hairs and bones of her inner ears.

When she got to the coffee shop, she found an inconspicuous corner table if she could, and she ordered Earl Grey and an oval cookie sprinkled with sugar crystals and orange zest. Then she took a small notebook from her purse, and her silver Eversharp, and pretended to write things down. This was a way to deflect the pity of strangers who might be tempted to see her as a frail isolate with nothing in her day that she really had to do. She could be making a grocery list, or a Christmas card list. She could be jotting down remembered lines from a lecture she had attended at the university the night before. She could be compiling a list of possible donors for a pressing cause in which she was involved. Or making an intricate little drawing because she was a brilliant, largely unrecognized artist who drew, who conjured, in a manner habitual and necessary, like breathing. And then, when her cookie and tea were over, she liked to replace the notebook and pencil in her purse with a tinge of regret, as if the contingencies of the unfolding day spared her only these brief islands of repose.

The morning that Viola's letter arrived, she walked downtown on a day that had quickly taken on an anemic cast and an unengaged gray. But the flatness seemed to push the river and the vegetation on its banks into sharper relief. Standing at the railing of the bridge, two stories above river level, she could make out bright-red berries on the bushes, clouds of them here and there, and, in between, some white ones that seemed almost translucent. From a half block away came the toasty smells of the bagel place.

Despite the pallid weather, she was feeling uncustomarily alive. Twenty years earlier, the feeling would have produced a spring in her steps. She thought about the boy in the laundry room, Clayton, and realized that her buoyancy had much to do with their conversation. How long had it been since she had conversed with someone who seemed to want, to need her company? And Viola's letter, too, wasn't making her sad now. It meant, she trusted, that her friend had been alive to mail it. She decided to believe in Viola Six's resilience.

The fact that Cassie had created a workable alibi for the boy was not bothering her as she had feared it might. He had his troubles, certainly, but she would stake her last dime on her belief that he was no arsonist—if, in fact, the fire did turn out to have been criminally ignited, as Lander Maki now seemed close to confirming. And the boy seemed so desperate in general, so fragile and hunted, that she had feared for his stability should he become, officially, a suspect.

Inspector Maki seemed to believe her. She saw no need to revisit the issue. And maybe, years down the road, Clayton Spooner would remember the lengths to which she had gone for him, and think of her, not for the first time, as the person who had halted a downward spiral that could have killed him. As the person who had reversed the course of his life.

The river was extraordinarily clear, clear and low, and she was reminded, as she watched it, of how pleasurable it is to see moving translucence atop a bed of rocks, the way the translucence keeps altering the colors of those rocks, just slightly, so that they become moving things themselves.

The ringing bell of the Catholic church over beyond the courthouse reached Cassie and the river and the river's bridge. That old sound. That measured, measuring, lovely old sound arrived, then fell gently to the river to be taken west. She hoped no one would get rid of the bell, or alter it in a terrible fashion, as with the electronic version she'd once heard in a strip mall, where it emerged from behind a big clock sounding as if it were a real bell that had been hit on the head and was staggering around, stunned. It had made her feel bleak, to the point that she decided against the shopping mission and went home.

A bicyclist whooshed past her on the street. She could feel his air. She passed a woman with a leashed dog, a big dog with a yellow bandanna around its neck, who looked up at Cassie without interest.

The bridge began to slope downward and extend beyond the river, over a grassy area and concrete lot that were the site of the Saturday morning markets, bright and clotted and jolly, but were empty now. The lot gave way to stairs that ascended to street level. Two willows and a large pine had been planted in a concrete balcony that bordered the stairs.

Cassie stopped to make sure she hadn't forgotten her wallet again. She seemed to be doing that too much lately. It was there, in its allotted corner of her purse. She retrieved her bills and counted them, to remind herself, then replaced the wallet and looked down at her feet to make sure she hadn't dropped any bills, though she was certain she hadn't.

Her feet were near the edge of the sidewalk. A small paper rectangle, damp-looking, seemed pasted to the walk near her right toe. It said "English Oriental," only that, which made Cassie wonder what it could possibly have been attached to. A piece of crockery? A can of tea? She bent closer to read it again. She could see the dirt beneath the willows and the plump pine, and below their branches she saw something else, quite close, on the ground, just six or eight feet below her feet.

It was a young man in a sleeping bag that was zipped to his chin. He was on his back. He wore glasses, and the hair on his forehead looked trimmed and clean, and his eyes were open and he was watching her. He blinked. His face wore no expression that she could discern. Not menace. Not fear.

She was so startled she didn't know what to do. She felt embarrassed, somehow, that she had intruded upon the cave he had discovered so near the traffic sounds, the footsteps, the dogs and bicycles of the bridge, the shadowed cave that perched above any danger coming at him from below.

He blinked and rubbed a finger across the lenses of his glasses. Then he looked up at her, still mild, still absent any expression.

"Aren't you cold at night?" Cassie blurted out.

He turned his head away and extricated an arm from the bag. He raised it as if to push her back.

Cassie stood up straight and fixed her gaze on the moving river.

"Are you hungry?" she said to the river, as a young mother wheeling a baby cart maneuvered around her.

The young woman stopped.

"Hungry?" she said, interested and incredulous.

"Go on," said Cassie. "I wasn't talking to you. I talk to other people when I feel like it, even if they don't answer. Don't worry about it. Go on."

The woman patted her carefully on the arm and rolled away slowly. "You take care," she called, picking up speed. "You have a good day."

The man in the sleeping bag had begun to mutter. She bent to hear him, hoping he might tell her how she could

help him. Sometimes a person just needed a listener. The
man clawed his glasses off his face and threw them toward her. He was hissing slightly now, as he talked, and
the words that came from him were vile, rapacious, wit's
end. He wanted her destroyed. He wanted her out of his
glasses. He began to bark, or hiccup, and she fled.

In the coffee shop, Cassie found herself crying. Just a little. Just enough that the girl who brought her tea gave her
a pat on the arm and asked if she couldn't bring Cassie
anything else. They were out of the lovely orange-zest
cookies, and this felt like a quick blow. The tears started
again. The waitress took some time to reassure her that
the cookies would be back in the morning, and they'd be
better than ever.

15

The door slammed and Carla Spooner's old Saab revved loudly, and then she was gone. Clayton took a long breath and hauled himself out of bed.

On the breakfast counter were a protein shake and his pills. He took a long drink and watched Foster run back and forth along the front yard fence, as silent and mechanical as a toy. Because the neighbors had complained about his morning frenzies, Carla had bought him a collar that emitted a burst of strong lemon scent every time he barked, and it was working. Clayton imagined the helpless stutter of the dog's little heart as it ran, terrified of the lemon blast, paws leaping forward on their own to pull the little beast behind them. He put his pills, as he had for the past few days, down the garbage disposal.

When he had showered and dressed, he retrieved the gun from beneath a pile of sweaters in the furthest reaches of his closet. He took it out and wrapped it in a sweater to place at the bottom of his backpack. He had come to love the grave weight of it against the small of his back.

The morning of the fire at Pheasant Run, he had returned to school with the gun. At lunchtime, smoking with Raven in the alley, he invited her to reach inside the pack and see what was at the bottom of it. Her reaction was amazing. For the first time since he had met her, she seemed fully alive to his presence. Her face dropped its mask of ennui and remove, and her black-rimmed eyes opened wide. She searched his face, then closed the backpack and placed it very slowly at Clayton's feet. He waited for her to say something. She took a couple of long drags on her cigarette and threw it abruptly onto the gravel.

"So," she said, her voice as airy and distant as ever. "So what's the story with that?"

The story was simple, Clayton told her. He'd found it. He intended to keep it.

"Why? Because of Chaser and his morons?"

"Call him Josh," Clayton said. "It's his name. I don't like the way he orders you around."

"So you come back with a gun," she said.

"Well, he might treat both of us different, with this. Anyway, I just wanted to show it to you. I think it looks awesome. Like from some other century. One of the cool centuries."

"Well, listen to me," she said. "Don't bring it to school. I've seen it. I'm impressed. Now take it home, and throw it away, and forget about it."

Clayton shrugged. He didn't know what he had expected, but this surprised him. He felt a little sick.

"Listen again," Raven said. "I'm going to get out of town in a few hours. I'm having some stupid and scary shit going on at home, and I have to get out of here for a while."

"Where?"

"I don't know. The Twin Cities. California, maybe. Someplace with a lot of people who don't give a shit about me one way or another. Just for a while."

Clayton wanted her to ask him to come along. They could strike out on an adventure together. They could get to know each other in the real world, beyond shared cigarettes and complaints about school, get to know each other in the minute sorts of ways Clayton had imagined for them, when the time was right. But he knew, almost as soon as the wish came to him, that there would be no asking. Her face was set. She was agitated in an exclusionary sort of way.

To recall her to him, he told her that the principal had called him into the office, about an hour after he got to school, and said the fire inspector was looking for a student in a Star Wars T-shirt. That he wanted to talk to him about why some people saw him outside the tall building down the block just after a kitchen fire in one of the apartments early that morning. He said he probably would tell the guy the honest truth: that he'd hidden inside the building to save his life and knew absolutely nothing about any criminal incidents. Raven simply shrugged.

"Why don't you get in touch when you get wherever you're going?" he said, hating the faint pleading in his voice. "Or not. Whatever." He wanted to give her a raincoat. He wanted to give her a bag of gold and her own jet.

"I will," she said. "I'm all organized about this. It's been coming for a while." They heard the bell inside the school building. She waved in that direction and started off in the other.

"Lose it!" she called over her shoulder.

A week later, and the gun still accompanied him to school. He had no bullets for it, but they'd be here soon. He had spent some time online determining what kind he would need and where he could get them, then scrubbed his search history and used a public computer at the library to order them, using a credit card he'd lifted from Carla's wallet. She always came home long after the mail arrived, so he'd intercept the bullets, and when the bill arrived, he would deny any knowledge, hoping she would conclude that someone at work had stolen and replaced the card. It had happened before.

With bullets, the effect of the hidden weapon would intensify, he knew. Because this was what had already happened in just a few days: Josh and his friends—clueless about the contents of his backpack—had begun to treat him in a slightly altered manner. The change wasn't dramatic—they still snickered and murmured when he passed; they still called and texted insults, and feigned accidental stumbles that pushed him off balance in the halls—but there was something distinctly different about their attentions now, a stylized, almost bored, aspect that made the pack of them seem brittle and light, when they had formerly seemed all meat and muscle and intention. Clayton suspected the change had to do with some new sheen of steadiness and power, some new armor, on him. Maybe it was the thrown-away pills. Maybe it was the presence of the gun in his backpack. Maybe his old shrink would have called it incipient bipolar grandiosity. Whatever it was, he liked it. It was getting him through the days feeling almost fine.

In the time since he had stopped playing video games with Steiner and Mack, Clayton had turned to his small, out-of-date, single-player stash. In one game, he exhausted himself by shooting many of the enemy in the far reaches of the Afghan desert, then pushed on to play a tier in which he had to figure out which of his buddies had betrayed him to the captain they all knew was an intelligence agent for the mujahideen. He clicked on the virtual envelope that had been slid under the floor mat of his Humvee and learned that torture of the betrayer might be involved and was he game for it? He was allowed a question. "Do the stakes warrant it?" he typed. "What do you think?" came the reply, which appeared against a collage background that contained exploding fireworks, photos of ordinary family-type people in sepia tones, and a huge American flag that billowed in languid time to the national anthem.

His next decision was to choose the soldier he would interrogate first. (There was a Hispanic, a Black man, and a carrot-topped Caucasian.) He chose the carrottop and got down to some fairly complicated business.

At the end of the game, the screen was blaring his victory, two former friends were dead, one was seriously and permanently maimed, and it was time for his avatar to drive his Humvee into the sunset, contemplating the next best use for his gifts. In the melee, the captain had been spirited away by a pair of infiltrators, then outed as a double agent, and he was presumably getting stoned to death at the moment. (He could click on that and make sure, but at this point in the game, he always felt it was time to turn his thoughts to the future.)

He drove slowly. He was alone, as all strong men are inevitably alone. The screen changed from a khaki-colored sky with some dust storm squiggles on the horizon into a clean, inscrutable blue. His vehicle threw a long shadow across the stern desert, and the sky morphed into lilac with a peach-colored blush at the horizon line. A drop-down gave him his choice of music to mull by. Everything was now aglow, including his perfect strong hand on the wheel, its soldierly square tips lined up just right. He felt his heart slow into a calm, intelligent rhythm. The world around him was its own entity, and it was impervious and gorgeous. Clayton felt as if he could drive forever, a man who had accomplished justice, who had risked his life and who drove forth boldly into the violet and the gold and the pink of alien terrain.

He thought about what he had summoned in himself to eliminate men who had been comrades, at least on the surface. He had the stuff, clearly. It would have been nothing to do the same to an enemy.

To relax from the rigors of killing, Clayton increasingly turned to *Call of Duty: Modern Warfare 2*, which had its share of firefights and swarming ambushes, but which also had its lulls, in which your avatar could simply explore buildings that had been inhabited but were empty now, except for the occasional body in a pool of old blood. One decrepit house, thought to be the periodic hideout of a terrorist, had books on a bedroom bookshelf: *The Jungle*

Book, a biography of Karl Marx, and *Atlas Shrugged*. Physical objects seemed designed to contain clues. There were suitcases and boxes and crates. You only had to shoot at them to see their contents fly out.

On the third story of that silvery old house, blushed by backlight, was a conservatory full of plants that seemed to be fueled by acid-green blood. They glowed; they grew and tendriled before your eyes, they drooped above velvet, jewel-toned furniture and baroquely framed portraits that hung on the old-gold walls. They seemed to be having a demented sort of fun.

There was a drop-down that could change the time of day. Clayton changed the scene from noon to dusk. The long shard of light that had arrowed into the room from the top of a mullioned window dropped lower and changed in color from wheat to old brass. The furniture threw shadows, and the plants took on various gradations of blue. A huge fern that canopied an entire corner of the room lost its predatory look and became a sheltering silver fan. Orchid blooms on metal-colored foliage became heirlooms instead of decor. Horizon gray. That was Carla's favorite color for staging rooms—the name an apt description because it was a gray that expanded instead of enclosed, soothed but didn't lull. The plants in the conservatory now were various shades of horizon gray.

The portraits, in heavy bronze frames, were three: one of a pair of children with a white, long-nosed dog on a bright sward of grass; one of a young woman with reddish hair falling in a profusion of wild ringlets down the thin white material of her blouse; the last of an elderly woman with large, beautiful green-gray eyes and a wreath of gauzy white hair. She had the kindest, most knowing face Clayton had ever seen. She seemed to look directly at him, and to like and admire what she saw. Next to her portrait, pale-yellow curtains billowed in the breeze from a tall window, open to admit a landscape of burnished hills and endless lavender sky. Clayton wanted to sit on that windowsill and rest his exhausted head against old bricks. The breeze sounded like feathers.

Someone must have offered the school administration a plausible explanation for Raven's absence, because, in the week she'd been gone, no one had remarked on it. At lunch, Clayton walked alone to the pizza place for a slice. He hoped he'd catch sight of Raven's only female friend, Courtney, so they could speculate together about where she might be. He knew she would call him soon, maybe with a report about California, the parts of it that seemed cool or uncool, or whatever, and there might be a hint of something in her voice that suggested she missed him, or that she had these ideas, maybe, about someplace down there where they could hang out together and plot their next moves.

He caught sight of Courtney standing by herself against a tree in the pocket park across from the school building. She was a tall, spectrally thin girl with stringy hair that she had somehow dyed in dots for a leopard look. Her snaky arms were wrapped around her torso. He crossed the street, trying to look nonchalant, and deposited the greasy paper from his pizza in the bin nearest her. She didn't move. Her eyes were closed and her face was clenched, drawn into itself, in a way that looked like fierce, blind concentration, or as if she had just heard terrible news.

He drew closer. He cleared his throat, summoned everything he had. "Wazzup?" he asked, as her eyes slowly opened. Suddenly, as if he had pressed a switch, tears fell down her face. She didn't wipe them away. She didn't close her eyes. She started to say something, and all that came out was a chirp of pain, as if she'd been poked in the ribs.

They heard the inside bell ring faintly behind the big doors. The park was empty.

"Raven called me," Courtney said in a near-whisper. "She isn't coming back, ever. I can't believe it. She wouldn't do this to me." She took a long, shuddering breath.

"Do what?" Clayton asked. He felt that he had walked into a movie that he'd never be able to describe, even to himself.

"Do what she's doing," Courtney said. "You don't know us. You don't know anything about us. You have a few smokes with her and you think maybe you have some kind of, I don't know, bond or something. Right?"

"I don't know. No. What am I supposed to say?"

"That you're sorry," she hissed. "That you're sorry I'm going through this."

"Through what?" Clayton asked. She shook her head at the impossibility of his very presence.

"She called from a pay phone so she couldn't be tracked," Courtney said. "You know the whole situation with the stepfather, right?" Clayton shrugged. He realized he and Raven had never made conversation a priority.

"She said she got down to California and had this vision of doing something really awful to him. Or getting someone else to. She hates his guts." The tears started again. She swiped at them as if they were insects.

"I would have," she wailed. "I would have done anything for her. But now she says she's going to put everything behind her." She fastened her wide wet eyes on Clayton. "Because she's met someone. This guy Ralph who is letting her stay in his house rent-free."

Clayton couldn't digest any of it. He felt as if he were listening to a story about someone he'd never met.

"He has a gardener and a cleaning woman who comes every day for four hours," Courtney said. "She called her mom and stepdad, and they told her she's making her bed and she can lie in it with the rest of the barnyard animals, or something. Whatever."

"How did she get there?" Clayton asked. The question seemed almost too big to voice.

"Stole a car," Courtney said. "It was parked and running outside Freddy's Market while the driver ran in for wine or something, and she just got behind the wheel and said adios and eat my shit. She dumped it somewhere near some beach after she met the guy with the gardener and shit."

There was a long silence. He touched her lightly on her shoulder.

"You should go home and get some rest," he said, like a doctor. "I'm going to Spanish."

She gathered up her book bag and ran distracted fingers through her wild hair.

"*Muchas gracias,*" she said bleakly. "Tell Señora Kirschenbalm *yo tengo catarro.*"

"Yo," said Clayton. It was the last word he could manage.

In his desk during fifth-period Spanish, he texted Carla and told her that, it being Friday, he wanted to chill at Steiner's house and probably spend the night, and it was OK with Steiner's mom. He hadn't actually spoken to Steiner in a couple of weeks, but Carla didn't know that, and she had been so frazzled this morning that he knew she would want, badly, some time alone with a dumb novel in an aromatherapeutic bath, and wouldn't be likely to check up on the arrangement. She had begun to cry softly in the bath sometimes—he heard her when he tiptoed past the door to his room to wall himself off from it all—and he couldn't bear the sound. There was something in it that seemed ongoing and biological, like breathing.

To his surprise, Clayton saw that he had a text from his dad. He was just "checking in." Another pinged its arrival, again from his dad, clearly about to propose some kind of bonding activity to ease his guilt. For a few seconds, Clayton couldn't decide whether to read it all, his throat so tight he couldn't take a real breath. It was the same way he'd felt in English when the teacher quoted some poet from three centuries ago writing about his dead son: "Farewell, thou child of my right hand, and joy; / My sin was too much hope of thee, lov'd boy."

He swiped the text away and tried to summon again the wild autonomy of his Humvee in the desert, the peace of the conservatory windowsill. He tried to see the sentences on Raven's hands, to remember some of the words. He tried to conjure her face, but it hurt too much to look.

After his last class, he decided to return to Pheasant Run. He could see no one in the lobby area, so he walked straight in through the unlocked front door. From there, it was just a few steps to the door that led down a flight of stairs to the basement and the storage cubicles.

No one had fixed the lock. His small space welcomed him back. He felt that he'd arrived from another era, another galaxy. All the smells and textures were redolent of a reality he seemed to have encountered only in his furthest dreams. There was the leather saddle tipped on its horn in a corner. Beneath it was a blanket made from sheepskin. The old patchwork quilt with its dusty, old-flower smell welcomed him back. He spread it on the floor and lay down on it, his head on the sheepskin blanket, the saddle propped behind it like a shallow enclosing shell. Its smell was ancient leather and what the boy presumed was horse. He had never seen a horse up close. The horse part was grassy and woody, like warm tree bark, with a little sweet salt on the edge. The ghost of a horse or horses dead now for many decades. And still the smell remained.

The saddle was heavy. Almost everything he discovered in the storage cubicle by the light of his phone was heavy. The soft herby quilt was filled with heavy cotton or wool. The Christmas lights in a large paper sack were as big as robins' eggs. The binoculars on a dusty shelf seemed to be made of iron. The phonograph records in a warped cardboard box were red and heavy and thick. The gun, now his, had left the other objects behind, but remained the heaviest object of all.

Raven would love this place. He would show it to her when she decided she was through with California and hated Ralph and his house and wanted to come home, for a while at least. At school, Josh and his friends would treat her with respect because the person at her side, Clayton Spooner, had a new look about him that said, *One* fucking *word, and you will pay dearly.*

His thoughts circled back to the old lady he'd encountered last week in the laundry room. She seemed to contain a deep calm, a kind of watchful stillness that he yearned to have for himself. She also seemed to be someone who had been through battles, the way he had been through battles. She felt like a fellow warrior. And it seemed her story about his alibi had been swallowed hook, line, and sinker by Maki, the fire investigator, because after that first brief interview, he hadn't heard a word from him.

Slowly he scrolled down his short contact list to Cassie McMackin's number. He wanted to see her. He wanted her to explain what needed explaining. He wanted to sit on her windowsill and listen to her talk.

Her voice when she answered was pale and kind. She hesitated only a moment or two.

"Well, yes," she said. "Let's have a chat. When you get to the building, take the elevator to the fourth floor and come to 412."

He waited and, in his mind, walked toward the building from several blocks away.

In the lobby, he hit the elevator button. Nothing happened. He hit it again, fast, faster.

16

He was pale, puffy, sloppily dressed, the way he had been when she met him in the laundry room on the day of the fire. He stood in the doorway, looking sleepy and ashamed and ill at ease. There was a long abrasion on his forehead.

Cassie had slept scarcely at all the night before—she'd had fire dreams and homeless dreams. She had a dream in which the Pheasant Run residents were being driven onto the street by fumigators who used things that looked like Fourth of July sparklers to do the trick, very dainty things that shot out thin streams of smoke—it seemed to be only smoke, but maybe it was mixed with some kind of drug or poison. They walked down the hallways in stocking feet, these fumigators (yes, there was something in the smoke that killed vermin or disease) and wafted, so daintily, the sparklers back and forth in front of the door locks, sending the very thin smoke through the mechanism to bloom on the other side. And they called out something innocuous. "Up and at 'em." As her mother had.

So she felt, as she greeted Clayton, a little dismantled still, a little ephemeral, from the rancid dream and the night of so little sleep.

"I'm glad you're here. Come, sit down."

He shuffled in and wrangled his overloaded backpack off his shoulders. It was in a camouflage print. Maybe he liked it because it seemed military, made him feel like a soldier. Though the rest of him—the grimy T-shirt, the low-slung cargo pants, the dirty sneakers—worked against the effect. He reeked of cigarette smoke. Or probably, Cassie corrected her impression, he smelled exactly as she and all her friends had smelled in high school, not to mention their parents, everyone on the bus, even some teachers who lit up before they embarked on the day's instruction. It was a smell that had been integral to the environment, and then it wasn't. It was gone. Cassie couldn't remember if she had even noticed it when it was there.

His head fell back against the couch and he closed his eyes. Cassie waited a few moments. She studied the skinned forehead.

"Are they still giving you a bad time?" she asked.

"One of them knocked me against a wall a few days ago," he said, touching his forehead lightly. "Now they are sort of backing off." He consulted his backpack. "At least they were today.

"There is really one main guy," he added. "And his sister is shacked up with my dad. I don't think I told you that." He glanced at her, then away.

"Is that what he's furious about? Your dad and his sister?"

"Oh no," Clayton said. "He likes it that his sister can wrap older guys around her little finger or whatever. Plus she gives him information about me, some of it a bunch of lies, that he uses against me."

He closed his eyes again. "Their mom had a different first husband. The sister is seven years older than Josh. Like, twenty-two, I think."

"An older woman," Cassie said. "What does your dad say about all this?"

A flush crept over the boy's face. He took a long breath that had a shudder at the edges, then squeezed his eyes tightly shut.

"Oh…fuck!" he said. "Nothing! Too much! Everything that comes out of his mouth sounds so lame and stupid, I want to hit him. He's like a snot-nosed little kid. I feel like his parent. And I wish he would just…get out of town. He keeps wanting to do something together so that he doesn't have to feel me hate him so much. Or, I don't know, so he can say he tried."

He lifted his stripped face. "Tried *what*?" he wailed. Then he was hunched over, face in his hands, shoulders shaking.

Cassie walked over to him and rested her palm on the top of his head. Then she stood by the window and looked out at the neighborhood roofs. It was a steely afternoon, the light already fading. Someone in an upper story of one of the houses turned on a lamp. Someone on her floor was cooking hamburger.

She wouldn't ask about the mother. What was there about her situation that Cassie couldn't guess? She had read somewhere about a group, a cult, something that demanded the strictest monogamy of its married members, with the exception of a six-week period every year when everyone was free—was encouraged—to fornicate to their fill, with as many partners as they wanted or could handle. Rules of hygiene and safety to be observed, of course. Or maybe it was some kind of sociosexual group experiment. She couldn't remember the details. What she did remember was that quite a few in the group went for it in the beginning, avidly and imaginatively, but that, in the end, six weeks was too long. They started drifting back earlier to their husbands and wives and children, often within a few days of their so-called freedom. They didn't deny that the hiatus was a good idea, but, because they had another shot at it in a year, they didn't feel obligated to follow through fully at the moment. Over time, the experiment basically ran itself out.

Was this another thing she thought she had concluded, somewhat gradually, over her long life? That the prospect of experimentation becomes not so alluring once it's condoned, codified, endorsed? Or that perhaps it's not sex at all, but transgression that forges the kinds of bonds that can obliterate the past?

Clayton got up and paced the room, shaking his hands as if they were covered with cobwebs or feathers. He slumped. He shook his greasy head. His shoelaces were untied, and he flipped each step almost imperceptibly to keep them off to the side.

He bent to examine the photos of Neil and Marian on the end table. Neil wore his Scotch-plaid driving hat, the brim tilted above his beautiful shaggy white eyebrows, his laugh-crinkled eyes. His smile was alert, knowing, wry, happy. There were two of Marian. In one she was a topknotted child planting a big kiss on the wooden ear

of a merry-go-round pony. In the other she was standing in front of a khaki-colored tent, a foot on the fender
of a Jeep, reporter's notebook on her knee, writing. She
had wild graying hair pulled into a haphazard ponytail.
Presumably she was interviewing someone, but that person wasn't in the photo. Or maybe she was amplifying
and clarifying notes she had taken fast, on the fly. Her
head was bent. She wore very dark sunglasses. Beyond
the tent, the little that was visible was glaring and empty
and white-hot.

At first, soon after she got the news, Cassie almost
banished that photo to a box or the trash, leaving only
the charming everything-is-funny image of the child
Marian. But every time she removed the war zone
photo, she put it back, the reason having something to
do with an obvious symmetry between that utterly engaged person and her fully present father that Cassie
could not bear to disrupt.

"Where is he?" Clayton asked, startling Cassie.

"Where is he?"

"Your husband. Is that him? Where is he?"

"Stop saying that," Cassie said. "He's dead."

"Oh," he said.

"But if I hadn't answered when you called, you would
have heard his voice on the machine," she said. "I've kept
it there. For quite a few years, actually. I like to think
that it sends a signal to callers with any bad intentions,
or even just something to sell. Back off. There is a man
in the house."

"Yeah. Totally."

"Your girlfriend with the bird name," Cassie began. "Does she feel that way? Does she feel safer in a man's company, or is that completely old-fashioned?"

"Raven," the boy said dully. "No. I don't think so. Not at all, actually. I think her stepdad, like, thinks she's hot. And she doesn't feel safe at all with him as the man of the house."

"The man of the house," Cassie echoed, her voice a little drifty. Ordinary turns of phrase were, more and more, sounding strained, even tortured, to her.

"She hasn't even texted me," Clayton said, his voice very quiet. "She said she would, if she didn't throw out her phone. I think she must have thrown out her phone. So no one could find her."

Maybe that's what Viola did, Cassie thought.

"Her friend Courtney told me Raven called her from a phone booth and told her she's staying with some guy in California. Courtney is actually sort of mentally ill. She says anything. Plus she's jealous of me and Raven, so she's just going to do anything to get to me."

"Are people looking for Raven, like perhaps her mother and the stepdad?" Cassie broached. "I mean, has an accident or something like that been ruled out? Are the authorities involved?"

"Like declaring her a missing person? I don't think so. Courtney says Raven called them and they said like, whatever. She has run away other times. It's like that boy that could have been in some kind of danger, like from a fox or a lion, but no one believed him because he had done it so many times before."

"Wolf," Cassie said, suddenly drained. "The boy who cried wolf."

"Whatever, yeah, that sounds right," Clayton said. "Some animal." He hoisted the backpack onto his soft shoulders.

"That looks heavy and awkward," Cassie said. "Like you're carrying tools around."

"I sort of am," he said, suddenly eager, as if he wanted her to press the issue.

"You're heading home?" Cassie asked, trying to mask her relief. All she wanted at the moment was her chair, her feet elevated, a cup of peppermint tea, herself to herself. She also wanted to feel as if she had provided something to this strange kid, but he seemed to drift beyond the range of possible contact.

"So that Maki guy believed you about being with me when that fire happened, must be," Clayton said. "He hasn't been back in touch with me."

"Good," Cassie said. "I'm going to trust that you had nothing to do with it."

"Oh yeah, no worries," he said. "I had plenty of reasons to be inside this building that didn't have anything to do with setting random fires. Like one reason was I'd get destroyed if Josh and those others caught me. Maybe almost killed. That would make them happier, almost killed. Because I'd feel it more."

At the door, he lifted his hand.

"See you around," he said.

"Take care," she said. "See you around."

He turned away.

"Come back sometime," she said, surprising herself. "Get some sleep. Don't do anything you haven't thought through."

The door shut and he was gone.

"OK?" she called.

Silence. Breathe. Breathe again.

She leafed through the small pile of newspaper clippings on her coffee table. So many strangenesses. Small strangenesses. This one felt worth recording, for what reason she didn't know. She pressed the button and leaned close.

"From the Earthweek column in today's paper:

"'One audible legacy of Ukraine's 1986 Chernobyl disaster is that the woods surrounding the derelict nuclear reactor are filled with songs of lonely male birds.

"'Very high levels of radioactive contamination have killed far more of the female birds, mainly due to the stressful combination of coping with the radiation while reproducing.

"'Writing in the journal *PLOS One*, biologist Timothy Mousseau of the University of South Carolina says that after counting the number of females to males around Chernobyl, researchers conclude that lonely bachelors are spending more time calling out for mates that just aren't there. The study also found more yearlings than mature birds, meaning the survival rate is relatively low in the contaminated zone.'"

17

During the evening shift change, Viola Six woke from a delicious nap to hear two nurses in the hall talking about arrangements to take her to something called "transitional living." It had a terrifying sound to it. Transition to what? Whom would she be living with? What kinds of new skills would she be expected to master?

Viola's head was swathed and throbbing, but she didn't have a fractured skull. In fact, the blow from her fall on rocky ground among the towering blue plants had done relatively little structural damage. The doctors speculated that she had gone down so fast and completely because of her age, possible exhaustion, and severe dehydration.

Viola hadn't been saying much to anyone. She assumed her driver's license was still where she'd put it before she got on the bus to Lotusland, under the inner sole of her right moccasin with Rebecca's phone number and the cash from Raven. Hospital staff popped into her room from time to time to ask who she was, where she lived, who were her next of kin, whether she knew anyone in Santa Barbara. She told them she couldn't remember much of anything.

She didn't want a single detail to change for a while. She wanted to stay in her white room and be tended to;

she wanted people to ask how she was feeling, whether her thoughts were becoming more clear. She wanted to rest in a safe place, to be anonymous, to be asked what sounded good for lunch. She pretended, at times, to be unresponsive or confused, so this swaddling twilight would continue.

Now, though, the reference to transitional living had spooked her, and she decided to come fully around. She told the night nurse, Devon, her full name, where she was from, and what her son's phone number was. She asked for her moccasins and retrieved the driver's license and Rebecca Tweet's phone number.

"My plans," she told the nurse as crisply as she could, "are to stay here in Santa Barbara with an old friend. I have no intention of returning to Montana. Certain conditions in Montana are quite dangerous to me." She could see his antennae go up.

"It's not paranoia," she reassured him. "It's a living situation in which I was likely to be injured. Rotten maintenance. Stairs. Ice…" She turned her hand in a vague circle that included many dangers too tedious to mention. "I have an old friend here in Santa Barbara, and I'd like to call her, if I may."

"Be my guest," Devon said.

The phone rang and it rang. Seven, eight…and then a woman's small voice.

"I told you to stop bothering me," it said, in a near-whisper. "I have no nephews needing bail money in Nigeria."

"Rebecca?"

"No Rebeccas at this number."

"Rebecca, it's Viola Six. Your friend from Seniors. You sent me all those postcards. I'm here."

There was a long silence.

"I need your help," Viola said. "I've been injured and I need someplace to go for a little while or they'll put me in transitional living."

"Take me off your list," came the shrunken voice. "You people are always bothering me. Don't call again. Take me right off your list." The phone clicked dead.

Devon stepped into the room with an armful of clean sheets.

"Was your friend glad to hear from you?" he urged.

Viola nodded. "But she's very hard of hearing," she said. "It makes conversation difficult."

She thought for a while. She called her son. He answered warily.

"Where are you?" she asked.

"Jackpot. Still here in Jackpot. Working things out."

"Why haven't you or anyone else come looking for me?" She realized, as she said it, how utterly abandoned she felt. "It's been days now since I've been in my apartment, and no one has come looking for me. Including you."

"Someone from your building called, but I didn't have anything to tell them. How could I know where to look? Where are you? Are you back home?"

"No! I'm in a hospital in Santa Barbara, California."

"Why?"

"Because I have a concussion and contusions!"

"Were you able to come up with your rent money? Or stall the landlord? I really needed it, and my business deal" went south, and I've pawned a few things so I hope I can get the cash to you pretty soon."

Viola answered with a long silence.

"Why would you be in Santa Barbara?" Rod asked.

She sighed as audibly as she could. "Because I was kidnapped. Abducted. That's why."

"In Santa Barbara?"

She didn't have the energy to keep answering stupid questions.

"You have to come and get me," she said. "You have to be helpful to me. Just once, you have to try to make my life a little better."

This time, the silence was so long that she thought he had disconnected.

"It sounds like a complicated story," Rod said. 'How did all this start?"

"Just get here, please," she said. "I will review it for you in detail."

Another long silence.

"I'll need you to cover the gas," he said.

Viola gave herself twenty-four hours to think about nothing connected to her next steps. She knew she had to recharge herself, and she knew they weren't going to discharge her for the next couple of days. So she could invest all her energy, temporarily, in the sweet routines of being attended to. What to order them to bring her on a lunch tray. Yes, good, time now for a pill and a nap. A brief, solemn assessment before she checked which face on the wall chart represented her level of pain. (She hated the one with the severely down-turned mouth, the drawn brows, the sweat drops flying off into the air, minuscule capsules of sheer pain.) The chatterings of the nurses and aides, the solemn Madonna face of the phlebotomist as she bent over the needle. The change of the bed. The solicitous arm on hers as she walked the hall. The waking up in the night to the sounds of purposeful steps, murmuring voices at the desk down the hall, knowing that she had only to press a button and someone would come to talk to her about any concern she might have.

It would be different, she knew, if she were lying there disoriented, in serious pain, or with a dreadful, or even iffy, prognosis. If she were just holding on, alone, in a hospital in a strange city, perched at the top of a non-negotiable, unequivocal descent—yes, then she would feel something like terror. But this was not that. She was going to recover, she'd been assured by the young professionals with tired eyes and untroubled brows who stopped by in the mornings. Her cognitive powers were now functioning pretty well, given her age. She was ready for transitional living, probably by the weekend.

After her twenty-four-hour reprieve from thinking, she asked for a pen and paper, and she wrote a note to Cassie McMackin. She had not been able to get out of her mind the possibility that Cassie, upon receipt of her first letter, which outlined the problems at Pheasant Run, might have taken it upon herself to register a complaint with Longleap, or to request that the owners' association investigate more closely the buyout offer and who might be behind it. If she had, then she, too, might be a target of violence. Herbie had his marching orders, and she was sure they weren't restricted to her.

She would, yes, write a note to Cassie, and she'd add the information about how she got taken away from her home. Cassie would pass on this information to the authorities. She would know what to do.

She would miss Santa Barbara, though she had been granted only a few hours to walk around and take it in. She would miss the celebratory wintertime birds, the benign light, and the flashing ocean. The pretty buildings and handsome houses she would miss. But none of it would miss her, she realized. Everything would stand back, arms folded, and watch her go.

Rod would arrive and Viola would be on her way back to Pheasant Run. He would want the details, the chronology, so she began to think about what she would tell him and how he would react.

For someone who didn't have the vaguest idea about how to order his own life, Rod was stunningly unhesitant about questioning the conduct of hers. Even as a child, he was constantly asking Viola why she had done this and not that, why she wore what she wore and drove how she drove and bought the food she bought.

As an adult, he only got worse. There had been her trip to Italy when he was stumbling through his first and only year of junior college, and did she get so much as a question from him about the experience? Not that she would have felt comfortable sharing the most memorable details, especially in the realm of romance, but you would think he could have summoned a sort of brute curiosity about people and places that were unfamiliar to him.

And her few years with Captain and the disaster that he'd turned out to be? Rod had professed permanent speechlessness at the scope and consequences of her mis-judgment—this all while he was trying to extricate him-self from his joke of a marriage to the Slovakian teenager who had convinced him that she was a wealthy young woman of virtue who needed only a green card to facili-tate Rod's access to the complicated monetary assets she wanted them to share as a couple.

She knew that none of that would stop him from be-rating her for landing, contused, in a California hospital 1,300 miles from her home. So she tried to mentally line up the circumstances in a way that seemed simple enough for him to comprehend and traumatic enough to encour-age a little empathy.

She had, that early morning a week ago, made preparations to flee her apartment in order to avoid harm that might befall her as a result of what she knew about skullduggery at Pheasant Run. (The details of it she would skip, be-cause Rod wouldn't care anyway.) And then came the hard knock at her door, and the sound of a key in the lock, and the voice of Herbie Bonebright in her living room.

She felt she should call out, but her voice wasn't working properly, and she could manage only a squeak. Footsteps now, and Herbie stood at the doorway to her bedroom. Her first thought was that evil intent comes, so often, in stupid-looking packages. No wonder so many children were afraid of clowns.

Herbie's Steelers cap was pulled low over his eyes, so she couldn't really see an expression. He stood with his legs spread like a football coach and wore the large plastic clogs that constituted his winter footwear.

He told her to get a coat, his voice pitched higher than usual. He said they were going for a drive.

She asked him why.

Just do it, he said, and don't bother about shoes. She wouldn't be taking any long walks that day.

He walked her to the elevator and they took it to the basement, where a door opened onto the alley. She recognized the parked car, his turquoise Honda Civic.

She asked him why he wasn't having breakfast at the Den, as he did every day at this time.

He didn't answer to her, he said, and now they would go for a little drive.

Viola's whole body became very quiet. He pushed her into the front passenger seat, where she struggled briefly with the seat belt before she realized the irony of self-protection. Nothing could protect her now. She felt quite sure she wouldn't see the end of the day, or maybe the next hour. Would Rod have the slightest comprehension of the terror in that?

Herbie drove slowly toward the interstate entrance, then gunned it when they were leaving town. The landscape flew by. Trees, glint of river, trees, tawny mountainside, billboard, fence, river. The sky was wide, silvery, impervious. As they traveled, it turned low and tired.

November and its short light, Viola thought. *My life and its short light.* Tears welled in her old eyes. What had it all amounted to? She felt the urgency of trying to answer that question in whatever time she had left—minutes, hours. And she felt, too, a slowly growing sense of something oddly like victory. Whatever else she had done or not done, whatever mistakes and misjudgments she had made along the way, whatever her death might feel like when it happened, she would know that she wasn't dying a victim. Near the likely end of her long life, she had stood her ground against some kind of evil afoot. She would like Rod to understand that.

She had been a force, a threat, her suspicions clearly expressed and clearly on the mark. And for that, she was going to pay the ultimate price.

Finally she had summoned the courage to try for some answers from Herbie. The moment returned to her, engraved.

"Why are you doing this?" she asked. "Not me. I don't mean taking me out on the road like this to terrorize me. I know that's what they expect you to do. But why are you doing the bidding of that sleazy company you work for? They must pay you a lot."

"Longleap Enterprises pays shit," Herbie said, his voice flat. "They need to clean up their act."

Viola looked at him sharply.

"What they need to do is make it worth my while to do my job, instead of threatening to terminate my employment."

"Have you told them that?" Viola asked carefully, as if they were confidantes.

"Shut up, Mrs. Six," Herbie said. "Shut. The. Fuck. Up."

He fished a plastic liter of Diet Pepsi from beneath the seat, clasped it between his legs, and twisted the top off with some difficulty. "Fucker!" he said to it. He took an oblong pill from his vest pocket and swallowed it with the Pepsi. He had a white-knuckle grasp of the wheel and had started huffing.

"Maybe we should just turn back and start the day over again," Viola suggested. "You're expected back at the building about now. People will wonder where you are. Or do you have to find someplace to knock me out and dump me in the river first?" She hoped she sounded calming and self-mocking.

"There's an idea," Herbie said, pulling into a rest stop near a river. He got out, locked her in the car, and paced the parking lot, checking his phone. She guessed he was checking in with Longleap, maybe reminding it that he was upping his terror campaign against the tenants of Pheasant Run, and she was the proof. She felt weariness, like a huge hand, pushing her into the seat back. She discovered that she was crying. She stared at her slippered feet and felt a wash of pity for them.

Herbie returned to the car hissing through his teeth. She asked to use the restroom. The only other people in the lot were a couple of stoned-looking teenagers at a picnic table, so he let her. After she peed, she removed her phone from her jacket pocket and stared at it. Was there one button to summon help, or did she just press 911?

"Out!" yelled Herbie, pounding on the restroom door.

She slipped the phone into the waistband of her underpants, opened the door, and walked with him back to the car. Herbie hissed again.

"Is there a reason you're making that sound?" she asked, trying to sound polite. He gaped at her, as if she were some wild creature who'd bounded in from the woods, panting and unpredictable.

"I'm making that sound because Longleap just fired me. There's been a fire in my apartment at Pheasant Run, and it's going to get me canned by the condo association anyway, they said. Well, it's going to get them canned, too, but maybe they didn't think of that yet."

Viola clenched her eyes and covered her face with her hands.

"Shut up!" Herbie said. "No one's hurt. No big deal. But I can tell you this, Mrs. Six. Both of us have gone missing, haven't we? They cleared the building, and we turned up missing, and now they are looking for us."

He stared at the phone in his hand. And he walked to the bank of the river and threw it in.

"Get out," he called. Then he thrust his hands in the pockets of Viola's ski jacket, a move that shocked her almost as much as if he had hit her.

"Phone check," he said, coming out empty-handed. "Good girl."

She returned to her seat and curled into its corner. For many miles they traveled an untrafficked state highway. The tawny foothill country was glazed with snow that began to take on shadows as the day moved into the light violet of late afternoon. They said nothing. Herbie appeared to be working out a very complicated puzzle in his head. His lips moved.

Eventually they circled back to the interstate, passed through Butte, its mine gallows etched black on the hills above town. Traveling east, the Civic labored up the long mountain pass, lurching as it geared down. It was dusk.

"We've been driving around all day," Viola said. "Aren't you starving?"

"Shut up," Herbie said.

Viola told him she was desperate again for a rest stop.

At the top of the pass, they pulled into one. A green sign said they were at 6,355 feet above sea level, and on the Continental Divide. A single semi idled on the far side of the otherwise empty lot.

"Get in there and make it quick," he said. "I don't want any accidents in my car. And remember, if anyone's in there and you say anything, they'll think you're batshit. I mean, look at you."

She ran her eyes down her ski jacket, her pajamas, to her slippered feet. In the restroom, she went to the farthest stall and locked herself inside. She retrieved the phone and stared at it. She poked at it and the screen lit up, so she swiped it as Rod had shown her. The keypad that came up had an "emergency call" square, so she pressed it. Her heart began to chatter. She pressed it again. "Go somewhere," she whispered. A voice came on.

She listened. She told it what it wanted to know, and then she pressed the red phone icon that stopped the call. She found the button that turned off the phone entirely, then returned it to her waistband, washed her hands, and opened the door.

Herbie's car was gone. The semi, too. Taillights were dropping down the steep slope to the east, fast. Something had made him leave in a hurry.

She was alone atop the Continental Divide under a sky that was partly scarved with clouds and partly clear, the blackness littered with stars. A chilly wind harried trash scraps across the lot. Herbie was gone. People were looking for her. She had to decide on her next steps.

The rest of the trip with the girl Raven, and her fall in the strange blue garden, she would summarize very briefly. Rod would just have to believe her about it all. She wondered if he would. She wondered, if he believed her, whether he'd care much at all about what she'd experienced.

For the first time in many years, her answer to that question felt like grief.

VERGES

18

Rhonda's confidence notwithstanding, Maki seriously doubted that the blue butterfly around his neck was doing much to mitigate his general unease, especially his guilt about his parents. But he did find that he was able to call his sister more frequently than he had in the past, in order to inquire about her circumstances and theirs. Before he called, he fortified himself with a smoke and a cup of steaming chai, sometimes enhanced with a shot of rum, though he had to watch the booze in his exchanges with Daphne because he sometimes found his voice turning hectoring or his eyes, amazingly, filming briefly with tears.

The information Daphne provided about her own life was comprised mostly of reported alterations, usually minimal, in her daily patterns. (Maki thought this might be a defining characteristic of a certain kind of aging: an iron-tight embrace of the usual, a suspicion of any break in the routine.) She was still driving the school bus, but she had a new route that required a dangerous U-turn at one point in the process of delivering her charges, and she was making no headway with management in getting this changed, though it was an unnecessary and stupid move on its face. And her cat Critter was no longer disgorging furballs with alarming frequency, having mysteriously resumed his previous hairball-less pattern, but he was now drinking more water than he used to, and she wondered if he might have some cat version of diabetes. And if so, then what? Daily monitoring? Shots?

Daphne had talked once about coming to Montana for Christmas—Rhonda had insisted on the invitation—but it developed that her habit of briefly visiting their parents every other day at five fifteen was so fixed that she feared any change would produce anxious behavior on everyone's part, and then the assisted-living company might jump on their parents' changed behavior as a reason to insist on a higher, costlier level of "amenities," such as a person to make sure they were both taking their five or seven daily medications.

There was no margin for an increase in their living costs, Daphne had pronounced. In fact, they had about two years' worth of assisted living at their current level of amenities, even with the sale of the house, and then they were looking at Medicaid and a nursing home, if there was space in any of the facilities nearby and if they would qualify for Medicaid under what she referred to as "the changing world order."

Certainly her own condo was far too small. So the parents might have to go further afield, to Montana maybe, or to Costa Rica, where she thought their younger brother the Christian wellness person was still living, though no one had heard a word from him in several years. Presumably someone had contact information, and they would have been notified if he were dead.

When Daphne was a young girl, she was so wiry and loud, skinny and wild. Their mother, especially, feared for her safety and her reputation well into her teenage years, with justifiable cause. At nineteen or twenty, however, something happened. She seemed to stop in place. There was a stab at community college courses in accounting, and another at being a recreation assistant at a girls' summer camp. And then she got a chauffeur's license and began to drive the bus, and embraced a solitary life that eventually left her heavy and humorless and utterly without spontaneity of any kind. What had happened? Their mother told Maki at one point that Daphne seemed to have had a serious "romantic reversal," but Daphne herself never alluded to anything of the sort, and their father declared that she was merely a female version of the bachelor uncle everyone seemed to have in their family—solitary and stoic—and that to investigate her life and her choices any further would be a fool's errand.

Maki swallowed the last of his unspiked chai, stubbed out his Kool, and contacted Daphne for the monthly update. The butterfly felt oddly warm against his chest, but maybe that was the chai.

She told him their mother was in the hospital. Several weeks earlier, she had been moved at the direction of Forest Glen's manager into the memory-care portion of their facility after a couple of episodes of nighttime wandering, including one that had resulted in a fall and a severely sprained knee. The director hadn't bothered to tell Daphne that the bill for this memory-care stint was going to be triple what the regular quarters cost. And Daphne hadn't bothered to tell Maki any of it because the arrangement seemed temporary and she wanted something solid to report. The so-called memory-care area, she added, was really no different from the regular assisted-living apartments—maybe a few more grab bars in the bathroom and along the hall—and the staff was sparse and included no real medical types that she could discern.

So Daphne had, a few days ago, brought their mother back to the couple's apartment in an adjacent building, and it was then that the bedsores were discovered. They were deep and on the verge of necrosis. And they meant that their mother, when Daphne wasn't there on a stop-by, had basically been left in a bed. Not once had she said anything to her daughter, though she must have been in extreme pain.

"Can you imagine," Daphne said, and it wasn't a question.

Maki felt sick. He quizzed her about who was ultimately responsible for this transfer decision, and why hadn't anyone been informed about the extra cost, and what was the nature of the company, ElderIntegrity, that owned Forest Glen, and how could it cause such neglect to occur? Had it ever been sued for negligence at Forest Glen or at any of the hundreds of other assisted-living facilities it owned? Daphne didn't know. She said the hospital expected their mother to heal up in a week or so, with luck, and she'd go back to the apartment she shared with her husband, and everyone would hope that their Medicare gap would cover the medical bill and that there would be no mental issues surging up again. Daphne sounded very tired.

"Care!" she scoffed.

When Maki hung up, he went to the computer and started poking around. He felt a white anger. He wanted to take ElderIntegrity to the cleaners. He *would* take them to the cleaners if it seemed they were engaged in systematic neglect of this kind.

Increasingly, he discovered, assisted-living companies were converting a portion of their facilities into higher-cost memory-care units. More income out of the same bed. They offered housing and "daily care," but rarely medical attention, to the occupants.

He also discovered online that ElderIntegrity, one of the giants in assisted-living facilities across the country, had been the defendant in several lawsuits charging that profits had taken precedence over care, resulting in death or injury to several elderly tenants. One jury had awarded a victim's family $19 million in punitive damages, a decision ElderIntegrity had immediately appealed.

Enough was enough. Maki tuned up Ravi Shankar on YouTube and played spider solitaire and tried as hard as he could to think about nothing at all.

An hour later, he drove to the Cabin to review the status of the Pheasant Run investigation with Hanrahan. It was late afternoon, and the day shift was wiping down tables and changing out the cash registers for the next crew. Weak, late-day sun filtered through the small, high windows on the building's west side, giving the interior a cloistered, intimate atmosphere. A few day drinkers murmured to each other up at the bar, but the place was otherwise empty, which was why Maki and Hanrahan liked to meet there on business from time to time.

Hanrahan texted Maki that he'd be a half hour late. Maki ordered a light beer and inhaled. The place smelled like tap beer, slightly dirty bar rags, peanuts, and bleach, with undertones of hair spray and hamburger wrappers.

The unruly jumble of smells reminded him that he had learned something important about Leo Uberti the minute he stepped into his apartment.

To all immediate appearances the apartment was cluttered and chaotic. An easel was set up near the window atop a paint-spattered cloth that covered half the small living room. On a rickety card table were a pile of old newspapers and an open can of turpentine. His paints, mineral spirits, and varnishes were stored on the shelves of an old wooden bookcase. The entire opposite wall was floor-to-ceiling bookcases filled with books. A single large chair next to a good reading lamp filled one corner, facing a hi-fi flanked by boxes of LPs.

As they spoke, Maki did what he always did in an interview: he split himself into an avid listener and a subtle but thorough noticer. And what he noticed was that everything Uberti might want to use—as a painter or a reader or a hi-fi user—was impeccably ordered. The books were arranged by subject matter, and, within those categories, alphabetically by author. Although he couldn't examine the LPs as closely, he suspected the raised markers in the boxes indicated a similar cataloguing technique. The boxes of paint supplies were arranged in their own categories—brush cleaners, paints, rags and gloves, framing materials—all of them labeled in small clear letters.

The range of book categories was broad and eclectic, and included World War II, World War II in Italy, three biographies of Houdini, magician's manuals, infamous criminals, battlefield strategies, a history of life insurance, European internment camps, American internment camps, Arthur Conan Doyle in three volumes, Maerz and Paul's *A Dictionary of Color*, illustrated biographies of the painter Bonnard and the photographer Leiter, and a collection of grave rubbings from small-town cemeteries in the West.

Uberti had answered the door in casual clothes and stocking feet. He struck Maki as exceptionally fit for his age, which he gave as eighty-nine. He confirmed that, yes, he owned a bicycle and rode it regularly around town and to the cemetery near the old fort, where he liked to sketch the old gravestones, sometimes as studies for paintings. He stored his finished paintings in his basement storage unit, he said, or he gave them away to anyone who would have them. He couldn't seem to summon what he called "an instinct for commerce" and painted mainly for himself because it helped him "see better" in his old age. Maki didn't ask what he meant, because he felt he knew.

Uberti had large, brown, slightly hooded eyes and a deep, resonant voice with just the barest trace of an accent. His manner was courtly, reserved, and, in some way Maki couldn't quite identify, calming. He understood instinctively why other Pheasant Run residents spoke so highly of him, of his reserve and kindness, his formality and quiet warmth.

Uberti offered coffee and brought a tray to the little table just off the galley kitchen where he and Maki could sit. On it he had arranged the cups and saucers as well as a small pitcher of cream, sugar, and two small spoons. He picked up Maki's spoon, examined it under the light, and returned it to the drawer for another. He washed his hands and dried them carefully before he poured the coffee, which was excellent.

Their talk yielded no helpful information. Uberti had seen Viola before the fire. He had no fond feelings for Herbie and wasn't sad that he'd gone missing. Beyond that, nothing.

When Maki rose to go, he asked to use the bathroom. This was something he'd done at the end of every interview.

He noticed nothing remarkable in the room, or in the medicine cabinet. A pair of tennis shoes had been placed on the edge of the tub, soles up, as if they'd been washed. Maki sniffed them and smelled the residue of grass, dirt, and some kind of pungent weed. Sage, perhaps.

He was thinking about that clean, weedy smell and trying to decide whether his beer glass had actually been washed when Hanrahan arrived and apologized. He ordered a Dr Pepper with a Dr Pepper back and slid his chair away from the table to give his big legs room to stretch.

Maki found himself reviewing the situation with his parents and what he'd dug up about ElderIntegrity without half trying.

"Scumbags," Hanrahan said. "Yellow-bellied snakes. And they're everywhere, it seems, especially now that the boomers are marching in massive battalions straight into their so-called golden years. You want to make a pile of dough? Let me count the ways." He spread thick fingers and jabbed at them, one by one. "Memory care! Boutique memory care! Luxury condos! Luxury condos in genteel and intellectually stimulating environments! Gated golf communities!" He clenched his fist, then fanned his fingers to count again. "Personal trainers! Rehab facilities! Plastic surgery! Joint replacements! Gourmet food-delivery services!"

He took a long swig of his drink.

"What I'm sure you've noticed, Maki, is that this consumer market is a very special one. Shall we call them the one percent? The five or ten percent? The elderly members themselves, or those who are responsible for them, are loaded. So there is big money to divest them of, and the so-called entrepreneurs are going to make sure they do. And if they have to pull the rug out from the rest of the old people to do it, that's, by golly, what they will do."

Hanrahan held up his Dr Pepper to the dim light. "Dangerous stuff," he said. "Makes me into a screamin' preacher."

They sat with their own thoughts for a while.

"So, Longleap," Maki said. "They're in the business of ousting old people from their homes, perhaps to make way for other old people who will pay some developer a fortune to live in a retooled version of said home?"

"That's one scenario," Hanrahan said. "Basically the Longleaps of the world are in the business of delivering real estate empty and unencumbered. But you or I will have all kinds of trouble proving that agenda. Because, hey! People move out of buildings all the time for every kind of reason. People sell their places for every kind of reason. So what you're looking at is a conspiracy, if that is in fact what's going on, and conspiracies are notoriously difficult to prove because they are crimes of the mind, not the deed. Maybe Herbie Bonebright made the folks at Pheasant Run feel afraid enough, in some cases, to move out. But what did he do that constitutes a chargeable crime? And maybe our Professor Clovis, who very much wants a job at the university, sees that it's to his advantage in some way to encourage the sale of the building to the university or someone connected to it. But maybe he really believes it's a good idea."

"And what benefit would the university see in an emptied-out Pheasant Run?"

"Research dollars," Hanrahan said flatly. "There are certain so-called educational enterprises that require a certain kind of cover, so to speak. Someplace near the campus, preferably, but masked to the general public. Animal experiments. Cybersecurity labs. And if the institution can deliver it, the research money follows. So hell, maybe the center for ethics and whatever would be housed on the bottom floor as a front, and the dirty work would take place upstairs." He shrugged elaborately. "Or maybe they just want to obtain it cheap and sell it high. To support the higher education enterprise.

"Actually," he added, "Mrs. Krepps says that, though she's aware of a possible buyout offer, the so-called new information she mentioned to the residents is that she still doesn't have concrete information about who that buyer might be. Longleap simply presents itself as a generous-minded broker of any deal that would be to the advantage of all parties. Not exactly property management in the strictest sense of the word, but oh well. They assure her that any potential purchaser would be honest and credible and all that hoo-ha, but none of the owners really knows squat, at this point."

Hanrahan got up to use the restroom, making his way doggedly across the dance floor, white shoes aglow even in the far dim recesses of the big room.

When he returned, he was listening to his phone. He looked disgusted. He wanted a where. He wanted a when. He wanted the names of the lead investigator and the highway patrol at the scene. He wanted to know exactly where to look on a topographical map. He wanted a callback when someone knew anything more. He grunted, swore, disconnected.

"Well for fuck's sake," he said. "Herbie Bonebright's been stone dead for the past week."

Maki experienced a ruffle of shock. He quickly realized that he hadn't believed that Bonebright—what he knew of him—was important enough to be dead. The thought made no sense whatsoever, but he couldn't shake it. He also felt a trickle of something like dread. That, too, made no sense.

Hanrahan told him he'd been talking to a sheriff named Bang Scofield over in the eastern end of the state in Rosebud County. A couple of fishermen on the Yellowstone River had hooked themselves a turquoise Civic, and when it was hauled out of the water, a bloated male body took up most of the front seat. The license was run, and Herbie's name and address came up. Because

Hanrahan and Scofield had done some investigatory work together a few years earlier, Hanrahan got the call.

Tire marks showed that the car left the interstate just short of flyspeck Forsyth. There were brake marks on the concrete for a short stretch, then wavery tire lines off the shoulder in the dirt and grass, but the vehicle had apparently been traveling at such a high speed that Bonebright sailed right off the riverbank and landed well away from shore. Anyone passing by on the interstate would have been unable to see the car, which had floated a way downstream, then nosed down in deeper waters.

"Time of death is a guesstimate at the moment," Hanrahan told Maki. "But it probably was six, seven days ago. Not so long after the fire in his apartment."

"Huh," Maki said.

"My sentiments, to a T," Hanrahan said.

That evening, Maki got a call from Hanrahan, who said Herbie's body and the car were on their way back to town.

He had another piece of news: Viola Six had been located in Santa Barbara, hospitalized for a fall and some temporary memory problems but otherwise OK.

"She says Herbie Bonebright forced her into his car and drove her all over hell and gone before stopping on Homestake Pass to let her use the facilities. When she came out, he was gone. This was the day of the fire, but she says neither of them had any awareness of any fire when they started their journey, and Herbie only found out about it from a text he got from Longleap sometime that afternoon when they were wandering around the highways and byways. Or so he said."

"Lots to talk about with Mrs. Six," Maki said. "But first: Did she just spread her wings and fly from a Montana mountain pass to lovely Santa-Barbara-by-the-sea?"

"In her pj's, yet. Well, she says a young gal in a big old-fashioned Buick or something pulled into the rest stop and they sort of decided to be road warriors together and get themselves to California where they could think about something other than their troubles for a while. That's the short version."

"And do we know who the young gal is?"

"Yes. Her name is Beth-Ann Felska but she goes by Raven, and she ran away from home a week ago. That's a longer story, too, but, bottom line, after some interviews with the cops and lawyers about what exactly happened when she got to LA, she will be coming back here, too."

"And that goofball Bonebright will get autopsied here, and the car examined for any problems," Maki said.

Hanrahan nodded. "Former goofball," he said. "Mrs. Six said he talked to Longleap when they were on the road, and then he seemed to be fleeing the dogs of war. Or maybe it was the hounds of hell. Something extremely unfun."

19

Carla still got the morning newspaper, though she never had time to read it until she got home from work, and by then the news might as well have been last week's. She liked that about it. She told Clayton she liked to thumb through large sheets of paper and find everything in its place, like a table set for a holiday: her horoscope, the funnies, the car ads, the national news, the local news. It calmed her down to be in the presence of information that didn't come to her sounding telegraphed, breathless, and pursued.

The front page of this morning's paper had a story about the Pit over in Butte, seven hundred acres filled with fifty billion gallons of acid and heavy-metal runoff from defunct copper mines, growing by the year and now, these past few days, a death lake for hundreds of migrating snow geese that had landed there in the face of an impending winter storm. Landed there to die, to get their throats burned out, though most of the story was given over to the sound of company officials sputtering about all the efforts they'd made to keep this from happening once again. (Several hundred geese had died years earlier in a similar scenario.) Loud noises were employed, they said. Gunshots were fired and drones buzzed the cough syrup-colored water because, during the past two decades, the banks of the lake had become so eroded that it was impossible to lower crews in rowboats onto the toxic stew to haze the birds away.

"Is this real?" Clayton whispered. "Fifty billion gallons?"

He sat down heavily and read the entire story, then put his head in his arms and tried to make his mind go numb. He felt personally attacked, personally targeted, because the birds hadn't done anything wrong except try to get some rest so they could keep going, and they got tortured and killed for it. And that was how he felt every day when he tried to get himself together to go to school, when he counseled himself to stay calm and not expect the worst, because hadn't they seemed for a while to be backing off? And then he would get there and they were waiting for him. And if they weren't waiting for him, they had left poisonous messages on his phone, to the point that he felt he carried, in his pocket, a small bomb.

There was another story in the newspaper. It pointed out that Montana's suicide rate was nearly the highest in the nation, and some expert said it was the fault of guns and alcohol and untreated depression. *Like if you didn't acquire a weapon, or drink alcohol, or let yourself get miserable, you'd live happily ever after. Like what about conditions outside yourself that might lead you to the conclusion that the world was a pit and a terror, and no place for anyone to want to live?* Clayton thought. *How about seven hundred acres of pure poison waiting to trap and kill innocent birds? What about being terrified to look at your phone messages because some of them would tell you you were already dead, even if*

*you didn't know it, and where was your bodyguard? Or that
every girl in school believed you had an STD that was transmitted by your putrid breath alone, and they'd be advised to
keep their distance? Or that a photo was going around of a
cock with huge dripping warts on it, and the message said it
was yours?*

Every day a new surprise, to the point that when
the text ping went off now, he felt as if he'd been shot.
And what was there about going on with life, then, that
seemed so great? It was an exhausting and cruel business,
all of it, and now Raven was gone, on top of it all—could
she really be staying with some guy named Ralph?—and
he kept looking at his messages to see if she had checked
in, as promised, and there was nothing from her but
screaming silence.

If he casually took the gun out of his knapsack, and
just stood there in the hall with it when Josh and his posse
walked up, what then? Would they back off very, very
slowly, faces drained of color, all respectful murmurs,
and when he lifted the weapon a few inches, whimpers
and pleas? And then down goes the gun, and relief floods
their faces and then—whoops!—up it is again and they
are ready to grovel and apologize until they have no more
words in them.

Meanwhile: adult observers in the shadows and furtive skitterings, like rats in a basement, and whispered,
choked calls to 911 to make the next thing happen. And
would the next thing be the gun in his mouth and his decision to remove himself from the whole sordid setup and
their stupid pleas banging on his eardrums until everything was alarm and cymbal and clamor and end-stage

everything? No, better some dignity. Let them come in their jungle camo and automatics. Let them find him slowly swiveling, small smile on inevitable face, weapon ready for business, the off-screen clatter of terrified running, the sun a wound in the sky, the surging triumphal trumpets. Let them be the murderers.

Let Clayton Spooner lift off from the poisoned waters, the hissing of snakes, the faithless woman, the smashed home, the threat-chants, lift off to popping noises and overhead shadows of scrutinizing drones, lift off with a burning throat and a horizon that stretched in a silver line, magnetized and pulling, until he was across it and safely delivered to nothingness.

20

For two Mondays in a row, Rhonda had behaved in ways that worried Maki. Because her communicator sessions sometimes left her feeling exhausted, she tried to schedule them early in the workweek, after a weekend of rest and exercise. Mondays were typically high-energy and productive for her.

Maki arrived home, the first odd Monday, to find her finishing a conversation with a troubled cat whose human companions were trying to figure out why she had started yowling every night. As it turned out, Rhonda told Maki, she was warning her sleeping humans that a black bear had come down off the mountainside and passed through their yard, and that he intended trouble. The cat told Rhonda she'd watched the bear from her perch on a high windowsill, and that when he caught sight of her up there, he sat back on his haunches and did the most strange and chilling thing. He laughed. And then he reminded the cat, Trinket, that he could polish her off in one enthusiastic gulp and that he would have no problem inflicting serious wounds on any humans who tried to come to her rescue.

"Did she stay up there on the windowsill to be verbally abused?" Maki asked.

"She did not," Rhonda said. "She jumped down and went into the bedroom to make sure the humans were aware of an antagonistic animal walking around in their yard, having murder and revenge fantasies. Thus her yowling, which the humans think is about nothing. Dementia maybe. Deafness maybe. They say those things as if she isn't even in the room. But the bear could be back anytime, is Trinket's reasoning, so she does this warning ritual every night, and now the humans have about had it with her. The wife even jokes in a very unfunny way about sending her to the happy yowling grounds. I've tried to reassure her that she's done all that could be expected of her in terms of warning the humans, and that she should try very hard now to let them sleep. She's thinking about it."

Rhonda closed her eyes and shook her head. She looked pained and exhausted.

"You did what you could," Maki said. "Yes?"

Rhonda's mouth moved, but no words came out. A look of confusion swept her face.

"Rhonda?" Maki said, sharply.

She waved vaguely and shielded her eyes with her hand, as if he'd shone a flashlight on her.

She mumbled something, then cleared her throat and blinked. "What?" she said.

"What's wrong?" Maki asked.

"Wrong?"

"You stay out there with the critters too long," he said. "Sometimes I feel that you don't quite know your way back."

"Back?" she said, as if she was trying to place the meaning of the word.

"Yes," he said, scared and angry. "Stop it, please."

She searched his face. "I just feel spacey," she said. "And I have a headache. I think I'll take a shower, then maybe we can find something with a laugh track on TV."

"You hate laugh tracks," he said, tapping her lightly on the head.

"Very rarely, I like to watch them to remember how much I hate them," she said. "Find something truly awful, OK?"

Maki put the episode in a corner of his mind, but kept a sharp eye on her and was relieved to see, as the week progressed, that she was again the Rhonda who rose briskly and made her chai and joked with the creatures, even poor Roscoe, and fed them and kissed Maki and either sat down at her computer or drove out to the Humane Society for her six hours that paid almost nothing. On the weekend, she took several long walks, did no work, read, watched a movie, slept in.

She was reading *Fools Crow* by James Welch, a distant cousin on her mother's side. On Monday morning, she stayed in bed to reread the scenes in which Mik-api, the frail old Pikuni who tends to the tribe's sick, performs his healing ceremonies, sitting with the unresponsive person for many hours, singing, calling on the animal spirits. Her lips moved as she read. When Maki, on his way to work, appeared at the bedroom door, she motioned to him to sit for a moment on the side of the bed and read to him the last lines of the book. Winter was over. Spring rains had come to the Pikunis. The life-giving buffalo were out there in the dark.

"'Far from the fires of the camps, out on the rain-dark prairies, in the swales and washes, on the rolling hills, the rivers of great animals moved,'" Rhonda read, her voice almost a whisper. "'Their backs were dark with rain and the rain gathered and trickled down their shaggy heads. Some grazed, some slept. Some had begun to molt. Their dark horns glistened in the rain as they stood guard over the sleeping calves. The blackhorns had returned and, all around, it was as it should be.'"

When she put the book down, she clenched her eyes as if trying to block any tears. "Go," she said. "I have things to do." And so he did.

When he returned at the end of the day, she was studying a photo of a German shepherd whose head was cocked quizzically. Rhonda had dressed, but her hair was uncombed and she looked pale and worried.

Maki didn't want to know the dog's story. He had spent much of the day thinking about his interviews with Leo Uberti and Rydell Clovis, and he was depleted.

The fire had been deliberately set—he was sure of that now—and it had been set to be contained. There had been just enough fuel in the kitchen for it to burn itself out relatively rapidly. A meticulous calibration, actually. And of the two men who kept surfacing as suspects for Maki, the surprise was that Uberti was the stickler for detail. His place was a mess on the surface but there were those rabidly catalogued books and LPs; there was the coffee preparation that approached a laboratory procedure. And, of course, he had all the accelerants he could have wanted, right out there in plain sight: thinners, turpentines, paints, mineral spirits. Maybe he'd made a mixture that was a near-match for the smell of Coleman fuel. Or maybe he had obtained Coleman fuel somewhere else, then gotten rid of the container somehow.

Clovis, on the other hand, arranged his books haphazardly, and his bathroom, which of course Maki had visited at the end of his interview, was a warren of used towels and capless containers. To scare Herbie or warn him against blackmail, would he have been capable of setting a very precise fire, which he himself would then put out? Perhaps. Perhaps not.

At dinner, Rhonda took a long sniff of the gelatinous chicken soup he'd made and delicately spooned up enokis and chicken chunks from the bottom of the bowl. He stood above her like a solicitous waiter, trickling chopped chives through his fingertips, then moved to his own bowl and did the same. He sat down with a long sigh.

They ate in silence for a few minutes. Rhonda asked him if the Pheasant Run case looked to be on the home run. Her head was bent over her soup. Maki tipped her chin up so she had to look at him.

"Run?" he said.

"What?" she said.

"Did you hear what you said?"

She seemed for a moment to be listening to a replay in her head.

"Run," she said. "To home."

Rhonda tore off a chunk of baguette and dabbed at the dregs of the soup. She seemed confused and embarrassed.

"Home stretch," she said.

Maki decided to move on.

"Hanrahan has discovered that one of Wingate's previous enterprises got into tax trouble a few years ago because it wouldn't disclose the names and assets of its investors, who had incorporated as an entity called Sunset Inc. with business headquarters in the Cayman Islands," he said. "He says Sunset buys cheap properties and retools them into boutique memory-care facilities. In a couple of instances, they also made deals with quasi-government entities that needed the memory-care units to function as a front for other activities on the premises, like cyber-security facilities that needed to be very much out of sight."

"Who better than the memoryless to not ask questions?" Rhonda said. She was back in the room.

If it was someone like Sunset who had designs on Pheasant Run, and someone like Herbie crossed or threatened their agent, Longleap, they would likely want no muss, no fuss, Maki thought. Just pay him off or threaten him or maybe even run him off a road, make it look like an accident. It wasn't beyond the pale, he thought.

He held out his arms to Rhonda. She sat on his lap, an arm around his shoulders, her right temple pressed to his left. He could almost feel her in there, among his thoughts. The only sound in the room was a scritching in the lizard's cage.

"How long do you think it will take for Roscoe's tail to grow back?" Rhonda asked wistfully.

She got up and removed the cloth that covered the cage. The segments of the former tail jumped and shivered when she toed the enclosure, while the rest of Roscoe huddled in a corner, frozen.

"His enemies are supposed to be distracted by the

moving tail chunks while he—most of him anyway—slips away," she reminded Maki. "But he can't slip away, so I wonder what he thinks is going on."

"He's just trying to stay out of sight until he gets his chance to get the hell out of there," Maki said. "What does he think is going on? I'm not even going to hazard a guess. That's your department."

"It can't be enjoyable to see parts of yourself looking so ugly and desperate," Rhonda said. "Even from the wings."

The phrase reminded Maki that Hanrahan had suggested that the shadow developers might be waiting in the wings for events to play out at Pheasant Run. Longleap would be expected to watch and wait while things cooled down after the fire and Herbie's death. Then they might make another effort to empty the building while Sunset or something like it identified the "special-needs" purchasers who had, in the past, also included animal experimentation operations that didn't want to draw any attention to themselves.

He gave Rhonda the outlines of the conversation.

"The vulnerable!" she said. "Always the vulnerable. Scare old people out of their homes. Torture animals. Extort millions from the guilty relatives of the memoryless. Will these people ever stop? Money, money, nothing but money. Pretty soon we'll look up and see the flag waving in the breeze, and it will be nothing but a huge gold dollar sign."

She blinked rapidly and, to Maki's surprise, began to weep into her hands.

"Something is wrong," she wailed. "Something is off. The animals are upset; they are telling me they don't know why, but they are very upset. That cat on the roof talked to me again, and she said she is especially upset about me. She wouldn't give me specifics, but she was very concerned. She is sensing something huge, on the move, but doesn't know yet exactly what it is."

"Rhonda, please," Maki said, rubbing her neck with small, furious motions. "These thoughts are taking you nowhere. They're bringing you down. They're based on nothing."

Rhonda closed her eyes and removed his hand from her neck. "Nothing to you," she whispered. She tried and failed to smile, then shook her head with energy.

"That was good soup," she said briskly. "No surprise."

"Don't be angry at me," Maki pleaded.

"I'm not," she said. "I'm really not. I just need to lie down for a bit." She replaced the cloth over the lizard's cage. "I shall lie down for a bit and return transformed. Transformed, reset, recalibrated. And then we move on, into the dizzying future, into the who-knows-what."

21

The kid, Clayton, was sleeping on Cassie's couch. He'd arrived after school, and they'd spoken a little, and then he did what he'd done the last several times: he fell asleep.

He slept as if he were refueling, taking long, needy breaths. His body stretched the full length of the couch; his arms were flung over his head in a position of frozen exasperation. He'd removed his shoes, and his socks looked as if he'd worn them for weeks.

Except for the boy's breathing, the apartment, the building, were quiet. It was the late-afternoon hour before TV news and preparations for dinner, most of them minimal, as no one was that interested in putting together a meal anymore. They had made many thousands of meals in their lifetimes, the women especially, and had found that the appeal was gone when the food was only for yourself.

Cassie stood over the boy, studying him. His eyelashes quivered as he dreamed. His rib cage rose and fell. His hands were folded on his sternum, as if someone had arranged them that way. It was remarkable: something seemed to have been decided between them in the last week or so. He arrived, without notice, at the door. She let him in. They talked briefly. And then, at her bidding, he slept as he was sleeping now: dead to the world. This was the third time.

On the floor by the couch was his lumpy backpack. He always removed it in a careful sort of way, as if it were both heavy and fragile. And he never opened it in her presence. She touched it with the tip of her shoe. Whatever was inside was heavy.

He moaned a little in his sleep. It's all right, she wanted to say to him. There was a deep furrow between his eyes. He looked like the oldest fifteen-year-old in the world, and, not for the first time, she tried to think what she could say to him to restore him to his youth.

This, too, shall pass? Could she say that to him and be believed? Could she remind him of how much a life could change in the span of a day, weeks, a very few years? Anything she said along those lines presupposed in him a sense of context, of breadth; an acceptance of, a belief in, vicissitude. And she simply did not believe that he possessed such a thing. He felt consigned to ongoing desperation.

And what about you? Her advice, her perspective and wisdom, had turned into a question that pivoted and addressed her. And shamed her, now.

She walked slowly to the back room, to the closet, and lifted the cover of the old printer. The bottles were lined up like soldiers where the cartridge had once been. Her pills, her stash. And though she did not see them as the product, in any way, of an impulse, an unexamined impulse, they embarrassed her. For the first time, she looked at them and felt the heat climb up her face.

No, she thought. *No. You can't advise the boy against this when you are reserving the option for yourself.* You can't urge a kind of fortitude, or forbearance, that you aren't willing to enact for yourself.

In the living room, she once again assessed the boy, the depth of his unconsciousness, and she picked up the backpack and took it to the back room. She slid out the sweater and whatever was inside it and placed it on the bed. She opened the sweater and flinched. Very carefully, she lifted the gun out and held it in two hands. And she carried it that way to the closet, where she placed it on the floor, next to the printer, and covered it with a spare blanket.

Since Neil's death, she had used the room for a study. On the desk were several paperweights, one of them a heavy brass elephant that Marian had picked up at a street bazaar in Beirut. She placed the paperweight inside the sweater and returned them to the backpack. And, in her stocking feet now, she returned the pack to its place at the foot of the couch.

She found the mystery she was reading and stretched out on her single bed. The boy moaned again, and she began to drift, herself, toward sleep.

The voice was excited, inquiring, and she thought it was the residue of a dream until she fully woke and realized it was Clayton and he was speaking to someone on his phone.

"Where are you?" he asked. "Why didn't you call? Are you coming home?"

Then he laughed, a sound Cassie had never heard from him. It was adolescent and squeaky on the edges.

"Two hours?" he said, incredulous. "Cops? Real cops?" He listened.

"Awesome," he said. And then, more carefully, "Courtney said you wanted to hang there for a while. That you were cool. That there was a swimming pool and shit."

Cassie turned on the teapot and got her cup and saucer from the cupboard. The boy never wanted anything to eat or drink.

"Wild!" he said, and then, almost reverently, "Totally." His voice cracked on the word.

"I'll be there," he said.

He bent to retrieve his old sneakers from under the coffee table, then folded his arms on his knees and buried his head in them. His back moved as if he were gasping. Cassie made her tea.

He lifted his head and stood. Then he shook himself all over, head to toe, like a dog shaking off water.

"Oh," he said. "Oh, man."

He turned to Cassie and told her that his girlfriend, Raven, would be back from California in two hours or less. She was being escorted by some cops or the highway patrol, or some other kind of authorities, and they were bringing her home because she had been living in the house of a guy who had a reputation for dealing badly with girls he found on the street.

She would move back in with her mom and step-dad, it looked like, but they were going to have some major group counseling about inappropriate behavior and anger management. They'd had second thoughts about letting her make her bed and lie in it after they saw a documentary on TV about sex slave rings, and they had alerted the authorities, who found Raven and were returning her.

"You must feel relieved," Cassie said. She heard the sorrow in her voice and hoped he hadn't. "Maybe you'll stop by pretty soon and give me an update on everything, especially Raven." She knew he would be leaving her. Leaving her. She couldn't offer him the consolation, the company, the hope that Raven would bring by simply being present again in his life. Present a little. Present a lot. It might not matter.

In the laundry room tonight, Neil's handkerchiefs would fly through the humid heat and she would complete the ritual by ironing them and placing them in two white piles in his dresser. She would leaf through magazines while she waited for the laundry to dry, and there would not have been a fire, earlier in the day, to think about—all that threat and ruckus and, yes, excitement—and there would not be a wild-eyed boy bursting in on her, desperate to the point that she would make an outlandish promise of protection from scrutiny.

Something about him on that night had told her he would not survive an assumption of possible guilt, the leading questions, the probing, and so she'd made the boy and the fire disappear from the radar of the investigators, most especially Lander Maki.

And Maki had never pressed the issue, never questioned her version. These weeks later, she had decided that the reason was probably very simple: he knew who had set the fire, and why. And he wasn't, for some reason, willing or able to say.

Clayton picked up his backpack and prepared to leave. He was headed for the park across from the high school to wait for Raven. Whoever was bringing her home had agreed that she could talk a bit with an old friend before walking back into the cauldron of her family, where things were likely to get complicated and fractious pretty fast. They could have a quiet chat.

Clayton shifted the backpack to his other shoulder.

"I wonder if there will ever be another fire in this building," he said. "It seems so weird, that it even happened."

"Don't say things like that," she said. "Nobody needs another fire." But even as she said it, she knew that part of her was nothing but grateful that it had occurred.

After he'd left, she retrieved the gun, rubbed it all over with a cloth to remove any fingerprints, wrapped it in a scarf, and put it in her largest purse. She would take it to the river tomorrow, early, just after daylight. She would walk along the bridge. Just before she got to the spot where she had seen the man in the sleeping bag, she would lean on the railing, put the wrapped weapon at her feet, and casually, very casually, fix her eyes on the rising sun and kick it into the silver, moving water.

22

What had Leo Uberti said about seeing Viola Six when most of the Pheasant Run residents still slept and the fire was ten, fifteen minutes away from ignition? Maki leafed through his notebook. Yes, Uberti said he'd seen her "not long" after seven when she was "getting into the elevator." What he didn't say, and what Maki had neglected to ask, was where he had been at the time. Because the Six and Uberti apartments were near each other on the fourth floor, both within sight of the elevator, he realized that he'd pictured Uberti looking out his door, perhaps to check if the newspaper had arrived, when he caught sight of Viola entering the elevator.

Viola had a different version when she spoke with Maki after her return from California. Uberti, she said, had been getting off the elevator as she prepared to get on. He looked upset or ill, she said. He seemed distracted. He said he had been about to knock on her door and borrow some coffee, both of them being early birds.

Her son had driven Viola home from Santa Barbara, and Maki interviewed her the next day. He realized he had expected to find a wavery, flighty sort of woman given to extravagant speculations, theories and digressions.

But the residents who had encouraged that image got it wrong. Despite the trauma of being hauled off in her pajamas by the demented Herbie, and despite a fall that had landed her nearly comatose in the ICU before she came around, Viola struck him as steady, relieved, cogent, and somehow happy. As they spoke in her living room, she rose from time to time to adjust a photo, straighten a pillow, and her movements were sure and tender. It was as if the surviving of her ordeals had given her a new fuel.

Hanrahan had already taken her account of her time with Herbie, but Maki wanted to be clear on one point. Did Herbie seem genuinely surprised when he got word that Longleap had fired him?

"Yes," Viola said. "And then he just jabbered nonstop, saying all kinds of things about contracts and agreements and betrayal and leaving him out to dry in the wind or flap on the clothesline, something along those lines. All I could see in my mind's eye was a shark flopping around on a golf course. Did you hear about that?"

Maki said he hadn't, though the story sounded vaguely familiar.

"Fell out of the sky," Viola pronounced. "Landed on a putting green. That is the sum total of what I know."

Maki was in his thinking shed reviewing all the notes he'd assembled in the two weeks since the fire. The afternoon was bright, crisp on the edges, and a breeze pushed children's-book clouds across the wide sky and made the long dry grasses shiver and bend. Rhonda was inside the house, communicating and typing. They had been shy with each other all day, because the previous night in bed had left them racked and exultant. "Who are you?" Rhonda had whispered afterward, and Maki had felt amazed again that the ordinary could sometimes, so flagrantly, rip wide open and throw itself away.

He studied the most recent of his notes, made during this morning's breakfast visit with Hanrahan at Herbie's old haunt, the Den. They didn't have much luck adding to the sketchy profile of the late Herbie—the guy on duty remembered that he liked Polish sausages and kept to himself and sometimes seemed twitchy—but they hadn't really expected to.

Hanrahan had more interesting things to talk about, namely the fact that a Coleman stove and an almost-empty can of Coleman fuel had been found, along with two bald tires and a broken TV, in Herbie's storage unit in Pheasant Run's basement.

The autopsy had established that Herbie died by drowning and that he had dextroamphetamine in his system. Attempts to locate any next of kin had been futile so far, and Longleap's Wingate professed utter ignorance about the man. Beyond what Herbie had told the company about his background, Felix Wingate knew nothing, he said. Nada. "'These people come along and you trust that they are who they say they are, and sometimes your faith is simply misplaced,'" Hanrahan said in his mincing and pious Wingate voice.

Hanrahan's final nugget concerned Professor Rydell Clovis, who had seemed genuinely shocked, even horrified, when Hanrahan told him about Herbie's death. A few hours after their talk, Clovis texted Hanrahan that he'd pulled out of the search for a new director of ethics and the digital humanities, was putting his Pheasant Run properties up for sale, and planned to decamp to greener pastures where he wouldn't have to deal with "'fires, blackmail, kidnappings, criminals, murky university agendas, and deferred building maintenance,'" Hanrahan said, reading from his notes.

"What a wimp," Maki said. "He still could have stayed in town."

"I think the professor wants to put as much distance as he can between himself and both the university and Pheasant Run," Hanrahan said. "I mean, look: he might have almost made himself a party to some kind of arrangement that was going to make a dog's dinner of his blood pressure and mindfulness. That tracker would have bleated itself crazy."

Maki put aside his notes and stretched. He decided to take a long walk before dinner. A beef bourguignon was thawing in the refrigerator, and if he put it in a very low oven, it would be scenting the entire house when he returned.

He did that, then washed his face and put on his jacket. Sid had already taken a long walk with Rhonda and dozed, now, by the pellet stove, so Maki decided to leave him. Rhonda wore her intent listening look and typed as she gazed at a photograph of a beautiful gray cat with lemon-yellow eyes. Maki put a hand on her head and bent to kiss the back of her neck. She didn't turn, but reached for his hand and held it for a few moments, tightly. He kissed her neck again and left.

—–—

As he walked through the neighborhood park toward the university area, he tried to listen to whatever it was that tugged at him, demanding that he pay attention.

The discovery of the Coleman fuel made Herbie a definite suspect in the arson. He could have learned about setting a delayed-ignition blaze with a candle and balloon, giving him time to be far from the building when a fire broke out. But why set it at all? To further unsettle the building's residents and speed up the process of getting them to leave? And would he really have been so stupid as to put the fuel back where it would be linked to him? Wasn't it more likely that the actual arsonist picked a padlock and planted it there?

And why would Herbie bother terrorizing Viola Six in such a dramatic fashion? Could it have been one last lame-brained attempt to curry favor with the employer he had tried to blackmail? Maybe that was Herbie's version of logic.

There was something else, and he wanted to check it now.

When Maki had first met Leo Uberti, he had smelled something vegetal on him, something that reminded him of a house fire he'd investigated out by the fort. And when he examined Uberti's bathroom at the end of his interview with him, there had been those wet tennis shoes drying on the rim of the tub, their soles still saturated with sage.

Where would Uberti have been walking through sage? He couldn't picture it anywhere in town. What he was smelling was wild, uncultivated sage, a weed really, and it had been present in profusion near that burned house on the edge of town, next to the cemetery for the old fort. And Uberti had said he liked to visit the cemetery, because of its ungroomed quality, those interesting old slabs, and the way the nearby sheep reminded him of his childhood home in a village overlooking the Adriatic.

The late-afternoon sun warmed Maki's bare head as he walked slowly, across the bridge, to Pheasant Run. It was just after five. He texted Rhonda that he would be home by six.

As he approached the building, he saw Leo Uberti on his bicycle, rounding a corner to ride out of sight. *Not a good idea for the old guy to pick the going-home hour to join the traffic*, Maki thought.

Inside the building, he ducked under the yellow barrier and unlocked Herbie's apartment door. Most of the smoke smell had dissipated. The furniture and Herbie's personal items had been cleared out a few days after his body was found, but the cleaning company hadn't yet come to shampoo the rugs and do whatever else it needed to do.

Maki walked slowly through the carpeted, empty rooms. He slitted his eyes and summoned his nose. The hallway door opened on a short corridor. Through a door to the left was the kitchen. Straight ahead was the living room, with a short hall off it that led to the bedroom and bath. He started again at the hallway door, walked a few steps, and got down on his knees to sniff the carpet. He proceeded through the apartment in the same manner, finishing with the kitchen.

He stood and smiled. He'd learned what he had expected to learn. Only a very small area of the carpet that lay just beyond the hallway door smelled different from the rest. Its smell was absent in the living room, absent in the bedroom and the bedroom closet. The smell belonged to someone who had entered the apartment and turned immediately into the kitchen, and had never ventured into the rest of the place.

Leaving the unmistakable smell of sage.

He walked home in near-twilight. The solstice was just two weeks away, and then the days would begin to creep forward into greenness and light. A chill hit him, and he wished he'd worn his hat. The breeze had died down and the mountains were colored lavender and charcoal. Food smells came from several houses he passed, and the lights inside were soft and gold. The leaves of the maples had finally begun to let go, and he kicked at them like a kid as he walked briskly toward his little red house and Rhonda, down there at the end of the block.

In the distance he heard a sound, a thin wail, that he thought, at first, came from someone's TV. As he walked, it grew louder. It sounded pleading, mournful, unstinting. The lights in the little red house were not on. The sound was Sid.

Maki began to run.

FEBRUARY 23,

2020

23

Fourteen months later, and Maki still felt blindsided by the sight of Rhonda on her knees beside the couch, her upper body stretched onto it in supplication, Siddhartha frozen at her side, howling. Those headaches, those few short blip-outs, and the next day was her appointment to get it all checked out. But now, inside that beautiful curly-haired head, wreckage, a clot, and Rhonda gone from him forever.

Maki could scarcely remember the person he had felt himself to be before that discovery. He had lost the kind of life he had thought he was going to live out. He had been hollowed. He could no longer summon much interest in the puzzles of his profession. He had different eyes, and they felt very old.

He drove very slowly in the dark toward Pheasant Run, where he would briefly attend a gathering he dreaded in a muted sort of way. The residents had fashioned a tribute to Leo Uberti, who had been killed just a week after Rhonda's death when a florist's truck hit him on his bicycle near a downtown intersection. His estate had finally been settled, and Pheasant Run was the major beneficiary of a large life insurance payment, earmarked for the building's maintenance fund.

Maki didn't know why the residents wanted him there, except perhaps for his advice on fire-prevention upgrades, but he took it as a chance to put the place and its people behind him forever, linked as they were to Rhonda's evaporation.

He was accompanied by Sid, who pushed his head farther out the open passenger window as they approached Pheasant Run, then yawned hugely and shivered in an uninvested way.

Siddhartha, it occurred to Maki now, was the moral obverse of whatever entities might have hoped to acquire Pheasant Run on the cheap. After Herbie's death, Longleap Enterprises had relocated to someplace in the Sun Belt. And any interest the university might once have had seemed to flicker out with Clovis's abrupt departure. The Center for Ethics and the Digital Humanities was no longer on anyone's agenda, it seemed. The university had mentioned a financial reassessment.

Snow was falling now, in veils, falling and rising in the February night. Pheasant Run, just ahead, stood tall and bored and pale. The circular drive was lit, and human shapes moved behind the gauzy curtains of a big window on the ground floor.

Maki parked and lit another cigarette, then fished in the glove compartment for a meal-bone for Sid, who snapped it into his mouth and chewed with contemplative attention. When their small pleasures had been consumed, they both drew long breaths. Maki put Sid in the back seat atop a woolen poncho that smelled, still, of Rhonda.

He found that he couldn't move toward the building. The people inside were milling and clumping, and off to one side was something that looked like a long table topped with platters and bowls. There would be Crock-Pot meatballs, he guessed, and celery sticks and a sheet cake or two. He would be expected to greet and mingle. And then, he hoped, he could slip away and drive to the motel where he sometimes stayed when he couldn't bear to return in the empty night to his own small home.

His house was for sale, and Maki was investigating placements for the creatures—the mynah bird, the ancient turtle, the cat, and the glass snake. Sid he would keep because he sometimes couldn't imagine staying upright without the dog's steadiness. For more than a year, he had worked on automatic, going through the motions only. He had refused to talk further with Hanrahan about the Pheasant Run case, because he simply didn't care. Hanrahan ultimately told the residents that Herbie Bonebright, an unhinged loner, had regrettably been hired by Longleap without an adequate background check, and had very likely set the kitchen fire for reasons unknown.

He had completed the paperwork for his resignation as fire inspector, and had a meeting tomorrow with someone at the regional Forest Service office about openings that might be available for a seasonal fire lookout. He saw it clearly: A small wooden room on a mountaintop; good binoculars and a transmitting radio; empty, pine-smelling days and not another person except the supply guy with his pack mule, trudging upward on the first day of the month. Some books, just a few. Forested mountains sternly arranged between himself and the far curve of the earth. Bird sounds and chattery squirrels. A light and steady breeze rippling the treetops below. And below the trees, at the invisible bases of the mountains, on the valley floors littered with roads and houses, all the humans, going about their human business.

A fibrillating ache in his throat had intensified, but now he was sensing, also, the presence of a threat that had been sneaking around but hadn't, until now, fully announced itself.

The danger registered in the fine hairs of his ears. It wasn't the gluey pull of depression and loss, the familiar brute extraction of all feelings except itself. It wasn't his sense of banishment from all the humming little agendas and hopes of the healthy. It was, this new thing, some kind of unassailable information, which told him that the humming of the healthy was the equivalent of light from a long-dead star. It was flotsam, the detritus of something long and forever gone. Gone to him, at any rate. There was a trickle of terror in the idea, which he adamantly counteracted by conjuring the mundane. Had Sid gotten a drink of water before Maki put him in the car? Had he fed all the creatures at home? Had he made an appointment for the Volvo to get its oil changed?

He returned to the driver's seat and started the car, needing to mimic momentum, at least, before he was stuck indoors at the gathering. He was early anyway, so he could drive around for a few more minutes to try to uproot the tendrils of panic. He pointed the car down the empty street, gunning it a little. The bony branches of the tall maples arched overhead, creating a tunnel. Its floor was dusted with the light new snow and illuminated in vague, widely spaced circles by ineffectual streetlights. The dread stayed with him. He punched the wooden dashboard, hard, to banish it, then examined his knuckles and saw that he'd broken the skin, and, in the few moments that his eyes left the street, a large creature landed on the hood of his car, hooves aimed at the sky.

He slammed on the brakes and the Volvo lurched and sashayed as the animal flew off into the dark. He threw the car into park and ran to the unmoving thing. A deer, a doe, lay on her side and panted in a resigned way, like a spent marathoner. There was a long bloody scrape on her shoulder, but her legs looked unbroken. Her ears shivered. She raised her preposterous long eyelashes to look up at him. He touched her shoulder and she flinched.

The closest houses were dark; the street remained empty of moving vehicles. Somewhere a dog yipped metronomically. And then a woman in a long Cossack coat rounded a street corner and came to stand beside him. She wore glowing old-leather boots, and her straight black hair fell from beneath a beret. Her face was handsome, lightly lined. She said nothing, just sank into a graceful squat and placed the tips of her gloved fingers on the deer's neck as if feeling for a pulse. She closed her eyes.

Maki waited. Time elapsed. "What are you doing?" he finally asked.

"I'm trying to give her some energy," the woman said. "She needs energy for living, at this particular moment." Her voice was low and lovely. The trees had become walls and a roof. The smoky snow cavorted outside the fissures in those walls, and the space he and the woman occupied became extremely quiet. He could hear her light breathing, the rhythm and purpose of it.

The doe's right front hoof scraped at the scrim of snow. Some long moments passed. The woman hummed very softly, off-key. Maki felt a strange urge to sleep. The animal closed her eyes. Then she took a long shuddering breath, and in one fluid scramble was on her feet.

Maki backed away. The woman stood and stepped backward as well. The deer swayed her neck and head slowly, then flicked her tail and emitted a delicate, jagged sigh, the emissary of her rebounding breath. She took a few steps, scraped at the snow again. As if testing each movement, she slowly disappeared behind a dense black hedge.

They peered through the shrubbery and watched her gain momentum, lope across a large lawn, and leap a low fence on the other side.

"Oh, good," said the woman.

They faced each other, not knowing what to do or say next.

How long had it been since he hit the deer? Maki found it impossible to guess. He felt he'd stepped out of time altogether.

He extended his hand and she shook it. Then she gave him a slow, comradely pat on the forearm and set off down the sidewalk. He watched her turn the corner and go away.

He made his way shakily back to his car. His entire body buzzed. His big dog was asleep, his nose deep in the folds of Rhonda's poncho. Maki roused him and he clambered onto the curb, where he sniffed the air and gave two deep warning barks before climbing into the front seat. Maki drove slowly around the block and made for Pheasant Run. A block away, he yielded at an intersection for another car, resting his hand on Sid's haunch. Sid threw him a quick look and barked again. Not at the car. Not at scurrying danger. Not a warning this time, just pure canine eagerness for the next new thing.

And it was that bark, snatching at every pleasure to be retrieved from the wide dark beyond the headlights' reach, that Maki would later remember as the first small jolt of his long pivot in the direction, again, of *yes,* a *yes* that would persist in the face of all that was soon to come.

24

Inside Pheasant Run, there was a hum of voices coming from the large room off the modest lobby. There was a smell of Crock-Pot concoctions and sheet cakes. Sid lifted his head, nose quivering anxiously. Maki, too, felt bombarded by the complexity of the odors coming at him. Beyond the food, beyond that mélange of sauced beef and baked sugar and the cool vegetal presence of chopped carrots and celery for dipping, the human smells trickled forward in thready and intersecting vapors. Someone wore a cologne that had been Maki's grandmother's in the previous century. A woolen suit, somewhere behind him, had been retrieved from a closet containing mothballs. And the candles on the tables, he saw, were battery powered. The absent smell of pooling wax was palpable. This was a relatively recent turn in Maki's hyperosmia: he could smell, with acuity, what should have been there and wasn't. His olfactory sensitivity had become so intimately intertwined with memory that the smell of a remembered presence arrived in tandem with the smell of its absence.

Maki had changed his mind about leaving Sid in the car because a number of the building's residents knew and liked him. He did have to watch him, though, as his size and amiability made him something of a hazard for the bird-boned. Just yesterday the dog had leaned affectionately against a wizened octogenarian in the Albertsons parking lot, tipping him softly into the row of emptied carts. The man flailed but didn't fall, and appeared to shake it off. Then his adrenaline kicked in and he informed Maki, in a plaintive shout, that his dog was a walking death trap. Maki had a brief urge to respond that the man's age and frailty made him his own death trap, but he summoned a little empathy and apologized, while Sid fastidiously sniffed the man's shoes.

There were several dozen people in the room, most of them quite old and looking, in their dress clothes, like extras in a country-house drama. Several, however, had invited grandchildren or nieces and nephews, and the young ones were huddled in a corner giggling at something one of them had summoned on his phone.

Mavis Krepps, the president of the condominium owners' association, usually wore a sturdy knit pantsuit in a neutral color. Tonight she billowed forth in a long shiny skirt and a poet's blouse, her reading glasses dangling from thin rhinestone ropes. She greeted Maki in her deep lecturer's voice and begged him to shake the snow off his jacket before it melted through and soaked him to the bone.

"You're hurt!" she said when she saw the blood on his jacket sleeve.

He noticed for the first time an oblong splotch of the deer's blood.

"I'm late," he said. "I hit a deer and had to see if it was going to be all right. A doe. She had a big scrape on her shoulder and just lay there for a while, then sprang away."

"But you're all right, too, yes?" Mrs. Krepps asked.

For a long moment, Maki couldn't make himself say anything. He blinked back a ridiculous film of tears and nodded.

Mrs. Krepps grew brisk and urged him to eat, to mingle.

Sid ambled across the room and lay down at the feet of Viola Six and Cassie McMackin, who sat on a striped settee. Viola waved Maki over. She wanted to tell him about how she planned to incorporate her abduction by Herbie into a memoir she'd been working on for years. It would, she said, give her account the "fizz" she felt had been missing, and she'd already signed up for a local writers' conference to "try out" some excerpts on truly discerning readers.

Because of the dog at their feet, she couldn't rise to tell him more, so he reached over and shook her soft and bony hand, and that of Cassie as well. The room felt very hot.

Cassie smiled at Maki. Since the day he met her, Maki had felt in her presence something akin to infatuation. Though it had drastically receded in the wake of Rhonda's death, as all his feelings had in a dark rush, he could still remember it and approve of his discernment. She had the lovely facial structure and lit-up smile of a true beauty, though the beginnings of a dowager's hump and the arthritic nodules on her delicate long fingers confirmed that she was well into her eighties. But it was more, far more, than the way she looked. Avidity. That was all he had been able to come up with. Though he knew she was basically alone—that she'd lost both her only child and her husband—she seemed to have retained a remarkable level of interest in the peculiarities of human behavior, the human life span, the physical universe.

He and she had several long conversations immediately after the fire in Herbie's apartment, and a single long one just two weeks after Rhonda's death. Shattered, he had blamed himself for not recognizing the precursor ministrokes; for spending a full hour in Herbie's apartment before he walked slowly home that terrible day, lingering for a while by the river. He had come by to tell her he was finished with the investigation, satisfied that he'd taken it as far as it could go, and he'd appreciate it if she told the others. She listened, agreed to do that, and said nothing else. When she said goodbye, he felt he was leaving someone who knew something he never would about the secret of ongoingness.

At one end of the settee, a modest memorial had been assembled for Leo Uberti. There was a blurry photo of him, white hair springing from the bottom of his stocking cap, squinting into the sun. It leaned against a painting that rested in an easel.

"Beautiful, I think," said Cassie, as Maki studied the painting.

"What is it supposed to be?" he asked.

"I don't know," she said. "What it's supposed to be might be the least of it."

The painting foregrounded a window, fogged and seeping with rain. It was beautifully and precisely watery, so that the window seemed both alight and obscuring. Beyond it were the vague shapes of a white streetlight and a large tree with brown leaves. The composition directed the eye to the space between their tallnesses. In it floated three blurred images: a ship, a young woman's face, and a candle alight. Across the bottom was a line of tiny rough letters: "Don't tell me about time; it is all now."

Cassie told Maki that there had been much discussion in the building about what Leo meant to convey in the painting. Most of the residents knew the outlines of his experience on the Italian ship and his time interned on the edge of town. But who was the young woman? And why a burning candle?

Maki knew the answer to the last question, and he also knew, quite suddenly, that he was never going to share it with anyone at Pheasant Run. He had explained some of the technical details that suggested arson, but they never had to know that their gentle and courtly neighbor had been the one to set it. That could remain a mystery. The world was full of mysteries.

Leo's mistake in setting the fire was one that he couldn't have known he was making. He had worn shoes that carried on their bottoms a smell that was unique to him and that was not evident anywhere in Herbie's apartment except that short strip of carpet between the hallway door and the kitchen. Maki remembered the sound of Leo's voice when he mentioned Herbie, the restrained vehemence in it, and it seemed reasonable to conclude that the arsonist's motive was simply to get Herbie fired. Get him gone.

He had used Coleman fuel because it was an accelerant that would not have been immediately tied to a painter, the way turpentine and other thinners would. Maybe it was something he'd kept in his own storage unit, long after any camp-stove days. And he had placed the container in Herbie's storage unit as a kind of joke, Maki supposed. Certainly Leo seemed the kind of person who would know how to pick a lock.

Leo must have known that he was quite ill, and must have known as well that he could not go to a doctor for a diagnosis, not if he wanted to renew his term life insurance policy for the last time. And when he found out that Herbie was dead and that the condo association had voted unanimously to cancel all ties with Longleap and reject any buyout offer, he knew it was time to act. And so one day he unchained his old Schwinn and set out along the streets, knowing he wouldn't chain it up again. Maki felt quite sure about that.

He had specified in a recent handwritten, notarized will that proceeds from his estate—which turned out to be handsome—were to be applied to pressing maintenance issues at Pheasant Run, including fire-danger mitigation measures, and to structural improvements that would allow the building's residents to use a large grassy area behind the building.

The insurance company tried for months to fight the award, arguing that Leo had seemed to ride directly into the path of the flower truck, and that the case was a probable suicide, making any benefits moot. But a hardworking rookie investigator for the police discovered during a second interview with the truck driver that he hadn't slept for twenty hours at the time of the crash and had been texting his estranged boyfriend virtually nonstop, the last text coinciding almost to the minute with his unsuccessful swerve to avoid Leo.

The grassy space was the ceiling of Pheasant Run's underground parking garage, and structural engineers had long ago pronounced it not weight-worthy. No one was supposed to walk on it, much less place lawn furniture there or in any way use it as a public space. So it stared back at them, green and blank, when they looked out their windows or sat cramped on their tiny concrete balconies, a parody, a virtual vision, of a grassy park. All that was soon to change.

Now the basement area would be suitably buttressed, thanks to Leo Umberto's largesse. *He taketh away and he giveth*, Maki thought. *And that's the short and long of it.* Next to the photograph of Leo, someone had placed a potted yellow chrysanthemum with a miniature plastic bicycle stuck into the soil.

The wind had picked up—light snow had turned to a full blizzard—and the windows in the room rattled. February this year felt like a return to the real winter that had been so eerily in abeyance last year, and it was a relief. Maki was suddenly exhausted. He beckoned Sid to his side and began to make his apologies for leaving.

Across the room, someone at the door caught Mrs. Krepps's eye, and she buoyantly waved her inside. Maki blinked hard. The woman's hat and her long coat were heavily dusted with snow. She had clearly continued to walk after the deer disappeared. *A pale ghost*, Maki thought.

Mrs. Krepps introduced the woman in the long coat as Tessa Whetstone, the newest resident of Pheasant Run and "the very youngest." She was not subject to the over-sixty-five rule because she was caring for her great-aunt, Mrs. Rideout, in #115.

"We're so pleased she is here," Mrs. Krepps said, and invited Maki to stay just a little longer.

25

Perhaps a dozen people still occupied the room, which had taken on a low glow because the overhead fluorescents had been turned off in favor of table lamps alone. A few who were preparing to leave made final, slow passes to say good night, to take another look at the Leo shrine, to give Sid a pat on the head and their fellow tenants pats on their backs, a kiss on a cheek. A number of women had gathered around the food table to pick up the remains of the dishes they'd brought, and to make dinner plates for those in the building who had felt too old or weak or disinclined to leave their rooms.

One of them, Mrs. Rideout, had recently returned from a cruise that took her to picturesque ports along the coast of Mexico, and she had come down with a particularly concerning cough, and now, according to her niece Tessa, a fever.

There was a brief discussion about what to do if the recipients didn't answer the knocks at their doors because they were asleep or too deaf to hear them, and the consensus was that the bearers of the food, in those cases, would wrap it up and keep it in their own refrigerators overnight, to be offered again the next day.

Snow was falling in heavy waves, making the night beyond the large sheer-curtained windows silver and dark, in motion, indecipherable. Sprays of frozen moisture hit the window like fine gravel, and the wind moaned and huffed. Even those residents who drove cars would be changing their minds about going anywhere at all the next day, even to the nearby grocery for a few Lean Cuisines and a quart of milk. It was the sort of enveloping storm that had the effect of making it difficult to imagine easy locomotion on dry pathways, sun, the trill of a bird.

Cassie McMackin listened to the storm and tried to think about a summer day and herself in a lawn chair on the grassy green commons. About her would be her little mountain city in the light of June, the trees looking so drenched and pleased, the mountains vaulting toward the horizons. Yes, it might happen that she would be present. The thought gave her a small start, as it seemed to confirm that she had decided, absolutely, against a new date for a self-imposed exit.

At first, she had put it off because she wanted to find out what had happened to Viola Six and Herbie Bonebright. Then she had become curious about the cause of the fire, and the motive for it, and what the intimations of some larger potential crime would yield. And then she had come to know Lander Maki and Clayton Spooner, and it was only then that her pills, that stash in her printer, had come to seem silly, and worse.

So yes, she might be present when summer rolled around. And, equally likely, she might not. Because that was one of the quiet dramas of old age: ordinary-sounding expectations could not be treated as assumptions when you were in your eighties. Eleven residents had died since she moved into Pheasant Run, four of them somewhat precipitously, all of them well past their threescore and ten. "And if by reason of strength they be fourscore years, yet is their strength labor and sorrow; for it is soon cut off, and we fly away."

We fly away. She looked around her at the old lined faces, at the long table, soon to be clear of everything but its long white cloth.

Almost everyone had worn going-to-church clothes, pressed and decorous. She knew it would have taken some of them most of the day to get their clothes in order, get themselves clean if not showered, make a dish to bring and share, fasten a circle pin to a sweater. The world outside this world was cold, snowy, restless. But today it was well past the solstice, and the season would climb, now, toward thawing and light.

It's all borders, she thought. *All the way, all the time.*

Gone from the gathering now was Tessa Whetstone, the newest resident of Pheasant Run, who had talked for some time with Maki. They stood near the food table, and when Cassie helped herself to another sugar cookie, she caught shards of their conversation. It seemed to be about Maki's plans to quit his inspector's job and move to a fire lookout come summer. Tessa wanted details of the lookout—where it might be, how far it was from any other people, the attraction of a place that seemed the ultimate in solitude. Her voice was lovely, soothing. The questions were surrounded by a lot of room. Maki seemed to be weighing what she said, what she asked.

When she left to go to her great-aunt, worried about the new fever, Maki walked her to the elevator and Cassie watched them. They shook hands gravely. Tessa's hair, dark auburn in an old-fashioned twist, gleamed as she inclined her head.

Now, across the emptying room, Maki studied Leo's painting. He stood by himself, head tilted slightly to one side. He had acquired a stoop in the past year, as if he'd sustained a blow to his sternum. His hand rested on the head of his tall and patient dog.

He seemed to be listening to the painting in addition to seeing it. His head made minute adjustments as if to catch what was coming at him through the air. But when his nose twitched, minutely, Cassie saw that he was smelling, as well. Smelling now or remembering a smell.

From the first time she'd met him, she sensed (why, she wasn't sure) that he might be someone who shifted constantly between thought and memory, present and past, the past being incorporated always in a hybrid present that anticipated the future. Maybe it all stemmed from the conversation they'd had once about his fire-investigation methods, in which he had so memorably described the necessity of mentally reconstituting what the fire might have destroyed. Only when that very pragmatic act of the imagination had occurred could speculations begin about how the former presences had been removed. His olfactory gifts, he'd told her, were key to his successes.

She thought about the lonely male birds of Chernobyl

calling, calling for the absent females, responding so ardently to the before but unable to know how it had been taken away.

Leo's painting certainly encouraged a sense of blended time, or, more accurately perhaps, a sense that memory is as real as the present-time portals to it, in Leo's case that rain-smeared window, beyond which existed the streetlight, the tree, the ship, the face, the candle. Perhaps, for Maki, his young, gone wife remained as present to him as whatever, in the day at hand, could conjure her. She hoped that might be the case.

She wanted to walk over to him and place an arm around his waist, in solidarity. She wanted to rest her head against his shoulder, his chest, the way she had loved to rest against Neil. But, of course, that was inappropriate, would be misunderstood.

A few weeks earlier, walking under her umbrella in the almost-sleet rain, Cassie had passed a young couple who made her happy simply by their presence. The boy: thick red-brown hair combed forward to frame his face under a backward baseball cap. And that face: dark eyebrows, dark eyes, smooth-skinned with an olive cast, but, no, it wasn't so much the face itself (and his beautiful loping walk, smooth calves under long shorts) but his expression as he looked at the girl beside him (also slim and young and in some way physically perfect, their bodies still children's bodies, smooth and light and springy, but on the verge, on the very verge...).

Inexplicably, she wore gray mouse ears on a headband and painted-on mouse whiskers, done with a light touch, and she was a little taller than the boy and talked in an animated and happy fashion. And the boy? Lit up with interest and bliss and hope. Lit up.

She hadn't seen Clayton Spooner lately, but he stopped by every now and then, and he'd told her during his last visit that he was in "a better place." He and Raven had started a dog-walking business that was doing surprisingly well, and both of them had transferred to the alternative high school, where they hoped to focus on subjects that interested them, not people who judged them or tormented them in random fashions. Clayton thought he might become a "veteran," because of his newfound affinity for dogs, and Cassie didn't have the heart to correct him.

Never had either Cassie or Clayton mentioned her confiscation of the gun, though Cassie opened her apartment door one morning to find the brass elephant she'd put in his backpack to replace it.

All she wanted, finally, for Clayton Spooner was that his path forward take him far beyond the troubles that had dropped him into her life. Beyond any fists and phone threats and weeping mothers. Beyond the clashing drugs, the sleepy and terrified brain, the craving for vengeance and for attention, for love. Beyond, maybe, eventually, the fiercely inscribed bird-girl with the ancient kohl-rimmed eyes.

Cassie turned out the last table lamp and sat on the settee in the dark. Maki had been the last to leave. The snow had lightened to a granular haze, and she watched his car, low and running, at the curb. Exhaust vapors climbed lazily into the trees. Sid had his head out the open passenger window, and his breath, too, was visible in the frigid air. Maki smoked a cigarette and flicked it out his own open window. His headlights were on and they arrowed fuzzily into the dark. It all seemed to swirl and exhale, as if the car and its occupants might levitate or vanish.

Watching him, she felt she was witnessing a decision on his part. She guessed that it involved the fire lookout plan, and that he might be altering or abandoning it. Just a guess.

She closed her eyes and lifted a hand to let it drift. It came to rest in her lap. She was as vaporous as Maki and his big dog. *I sit here*, she thought, *on a winter's eve that caps a year of events no one could have divined: arson and abduction, premature death, a too-convenient accident, perhaps a murder. And beyond those shocks, the insidious undercurrent of plain old venality and a willingness to visit it upon those most easily damaged by it. Greed. Plain old dead-eyed greed.*

And yet here we are, still, in our fair house. My old neighbors above my head are removing their good clothes and propping their aching feet. They are taking their pills, their countdown markers, finding sleep, or seeking it. Suspended in white air between sky and ground, they are rounding the last lap.

The table with its long white cloth glowed faintly in the dark room. Maki's car engaged and pulled away. Cassie listened to the whispered thoughts of all her neighbors, and, beyond the wall, the snow crystals colliding, the night animals murmuring. They sounded restless, agitated, prescient.

She heard the earth's battered but stalwart heartbeat shaking the branches of the winter trees, shaking them hard, as if the last leaves had reappeared and, once again, refused to fall.

ACKNOWLEDGMENTS
my thanks and appreciation go to:

Sarah Chalfant, my gifted and constant agent

Daniel Slager, who welcomed this book
and saw what it needed

Connie Poten, perceptive reader, dearest of friends

Lee Oglesby, Joanna Demkiewicz, Mary Austin Speaker,
Claire Laine, and the entire, exceptional
Milkweed community

Dana Boussard, for her haunting cover image
and her friendship of many years

Bob Rajala, fire expert (any factual errors are my own)

Carol Van Valkenburg, for her impressively researched
*An Alien Place: The Fort Missoula, Montana,
Detention Camp 1941-44*

April Bernard for the line about time
at the bottom of Leo's painting, borrowed from
the opening to her lovely poem "Wheeling"

Lois Welch for permission to use the passage
about the return of the blackhorns
from James Welch's Fools Crow

The faculty, students and staff of the Bennington
Writing Seminars, for support, inspiration
and enjoyment

Mark Bryant

DEIRDRE MCNAMER is the author of four previous novels: *Rima in the Weeds*, *One Sweet Quarrel*, *My Russian*, and *Red Rover*, which was a winner of the Montana Book Award and was named a best book of the year by *Artforum*, the *Washington Post*, and the *Los Angeles Times*. Her essays, short fiction, and reviews have appeared in the *New Yorker*, *Ploughshares*, the *New York Times*, and *Outside*, among other venues. McNamer chaired the fiction panel of the National Book Awards in 2011 and was a judge for the 2015 PEN/Faulkner Award.

She has taught writing at Cornell University, Williams College, the University of Ohio, the University of Oregon, the University of Alabama, the University of Montana, and the Bennington Writing Seminars, where she currently holds a faculty position in the low-residency MFA program. She lives in Missoula, Montana.

THE
Eye OF
Zoltar

JASPER FFORDE

THE CHRONICLES OF KAZAM • BOOK THREE

THE Eye OF Zoltar

HOUGHTON MIFFLIN HARCOURT
Boston   New York

Originally published by Hodder & Stoughton

www.hmhco.com

Text set in Garamond 3 Lt Std.

LIBRARY OF CONGRESS CATALOGING-IN-PUBLICATION DATA
Fforde, Jasper.
The Eye of Zoltar / by Jasper Fforde.
pages cm. — (The chronicles of Kazam ; book 3)
Summary: Sixteen-year-old Jennifer Strange faces the impossible when the Mighty Shandar emerges from his preserved state and presents her with a task that sends her and her companions on a journey from which they may never return.
ISBN 978-0-547-73849-9 (hardback)
[1. Magic — Fiction. 2. Voyages and travels — Fiction.
3. Fantasy — Fiction.] I. Title.
PZ7.F4443Eye 2014
[Fic] — dc23

Manufactured in the United States of America
DOC 10 9 8 7 6 5 4 3 2 1
4500491909

I don't do refunds.

—The Mighty Shandar

ONE

Where We Are Now

The first thing we had to do was catch the Tralfamosaur. The obvious question, other than "What's a Tralfamosaur?" was "Why us?" The answer to the first question
was that this was a *magical* beast, created by some long-
forgotten wizard when conjuring up weird and exotic
creatures had been briefly fashionable. The Tralfamosaur
is about the size and weight of an elephant, has a brain no
bigger than a Ping-Pong ball, and can outrun a human.
More relevant to anyone trying to catch one, Tralfamosaurs aren't particularly fussy about what they eat. And
when they are hungry—which is much of the time—
they are even *less* fussy. A sheep, cow, rubber tire, garden
shed, antelope, smallish automobile, or human would go

down equally well. In short, the Tralfamosaur is a lot like a *Tyrannosaurus rex,* but without the sunny disposition.

And we had to capture it. Oh, and the answer to the "Why us?" question was that it was our fault the rotten thing had escaped.

In case you're new to my life, I'm sixteen, a girl, and an orphan — hey, no biggie; lots of kids don't have parents here in the Ununited Kingdoms, because so many people have been lost in the endless Troll Wars these past sixty years. With lots of orphans around, there's plenty of cheap labor. I got lucky. Instead of being sold into the garment, fast food, or hotel industry, I get to spend my six years of indentured servitude at Kazam Mystical Arts Management, a registered House of Enchantment run by the Great Zambini. Kazam does what all Houses of Enchantment used to do: rent out wizards to perform magical feats. The problem is that in the past half century, magic has faded, so we are really down to finding lost shoes, rewiring houses, unblocking drains, and getting cats out of trees. It's a bit demeaning for the once-mighty sorcerers who work for us, but at least it's paid work.

At Kazam I found out that magic has not much to do with black cats, cauldrons, wands, pointy hats, and broomsticks. No, those are only in the movies. Real magic is weird and mysterious, a fusion between science and faith. The practical way of looking at it is this: Magic swirls about us like an invisible fog of emotional energy that can be tapped by those skilled in the mystical arts, and then channeled into a concentrated burst of energy from the tips of the index fingers. The technical name for magic is variable electro-gravitational mutable sub-atomic force, but the usual term is wizidrical energy, or, simply, crackle.

So there I was, assistant to the Great Zambini, learning well and working hard, when Zambini disappeared, quite literally, in a puff of smoke. He didn't return, or at least not for anything but a few minutes at a time and often in random locations, so I took over the running of the company at age fifteen. Okay, that *was* a biggie, but I coped and, long story short, I saved dragons from extinction, averted war between the nations of Snodd and Brecon, and helped the power of magic begin to reestablish itself.

And that's when the trouble *really* started. King Snodd thought using the power of magic for corporate profit would be a seriously good scam, something we at Kazam weren't that happy about. Even longer story short, we held a magic contest to decide who controls magic, and after a lot of cheating by the king to try to make us lose, he failed — and we are now a House of Enchantment free from royal meddling and can concentrate on rebuilding magic into a noble craft.

I now manage forty-five barely sane sorcerers at Kazam, only eight of whom have a legal permit to perform magic. If you think wizards are all wise purveyors of the mystical arts and have sparkling wizidrical energy streaming from their fingertips, think again. They are for the most part undisciplined, infantile, argumentative, and infuriating; their magic only works when they *really* concentrate, which isn't that often, and misspellings are common. But when it works, a well-spelled feat of magic is the most wondrous thing to behold, like your favorite book, painting, music, and movie all at the same time, with chocolate and a meaningful hug from someone you love thrown in for good measure. So despite everything, it's a good business in which to work. Besides, there's rarely a dull moment.

So that's me. I have an orphaned assistant named Tiger Prawns, I am now Dragon Ambassador to the World, and I have a pet Quarkbeast at least nine times as frightening as the most frightening thing you've ever seen.

My name is Jennifer Strange. Welcome to my world.

Now, let's find that Tralfamosaur.

Zambini Towers

Those forty-five sorcerers, Tiger, and I all lived in a large, eleven-story, ornate ex-hotel called Zambini Towers. It was in a bad state of repair, and even though we had some spare magic to restore it to glory, we had decided we wouldn't, other than expanding the Kazam offices after business picked up. There was a certain charm about the faded wallpaper, warped wood, missing windowpanes, and leaky roof. Some argued that the surroundings were peculiarly suitable for the Mystical Arts, others argued that the place was a fetid dump suitable only for demolition, and I sat somewhere between the two.

When the call came in, Perkins and I were in the shabby, wood-paneled lobby.

"There's a Tralfamosaur loose somewhere between here and Ross," said Tiger, waving a report forwarded by the police.

"Anyone eaten?" I asked.

"All of two railroad workers and part of a fisherman." Tiger was twelve and, like me, a foundling. He was stuck at Kazam for four years and after that could apply for citizenship or earn it fighting in the next Troll War, which probably wouldn't be far off. Troll Wars were like Batman movies: both were repeated at regular intervals, featured expensive hardware, and were broadly predictable. The difference was that during the Troll Wars, humans always lost—and badly. In Troll War IV, eight years ago, sixty thousand troops were lost before General Snood had even finished giving the order to advance. The final death toll was six times higher.

"Three eaten already?" I said. "We need to get Big T back to the zoo before he gets hungry again."

"How long will that be?" asked Tiger, who was small in stature but big on questions.

I swiftly estimated how much calorific value there was in a railway worker, matched that to what I knew of a Tralfamosaur's metabolism, and added a rough guess of how much of the fisherman had been consumed. "Three hours," I said. "Four, tops. Which sorcerers are on duty right now?"

Tiger consulted his clipboard. "Lady Mawgon and the Wizard Moobin."

"I'll help out," said Perkins. He smiled and added, "As long as I'm not eaten."

I told him I couldn't really offer many guarantees as far as Tralfamosaurs were concerned. "Still in?" I asked.

"Why not?" he said with a chuckle. "I haven't been terrified for — ooh — at least a couple of days."

Perkins was Kazam's youngest and newest legal sorcerer, licensed for less than a week. He was eighteen and, while not yet very powerful, showed good promise; most sorcerers didn't start doing any really useful magic until their thirties. Perkins and I had been about to go on our first date when the Tralfamosaur call came in, but that would have to wait.

"Okay," I said to Tiger. "Fetch Mawgon and Moobin, and you should also call Once Magnificent Boo."

"Got it," said Tiger.

I turned to Perkins. "Okay if we go on that date later? You know how it is in the magic industry: spell first, fun second."

"I kind of figured that," he replied, "so why don't we make *this* assignment the date? I could bring some food and a thermos of hot chocolate."

Considering that neither of us had any experience in romance whatsoever, a working date would surely be easier than an actual date. "Okay," I said, "you're on. But no dressing up, and we split the cost."

"Game on. I'll go and make sandwiches and conjure up that thermos."

While I waited for the other sorcerers to arrive, I read what I could about Tralfamosaurs in the *Codex Magicalis,* which wasn't much. The creature had been created magically in the 1780s on the order of the Cambrian Empire's Emperor Tharv I, because he wanted "a challenging beast to hunt for sport," a role it played with all due savagery. Two hundred years later, people still pay good money to try to hunt them, usually with fatal consequences for the hunter. Oddly, this made Tralfamosaur hunting *more* popular; it seemed that citizens were becoming increasingly fond of danger in these modern, safety-conscious times. The Cambrian Empire now made good money out of what it called jeopardy tourism: vacations for those seeking life-threatening situations.

The first to arrive in the lobby was Wizard Moobin, who, unlike all the other sorcerers, was barely insane at all. Aside from his usual magical duties, he worked in magic research and development. Last month, Moobin's team had been working on spells for turning oneself temporarily to rubber to survive a fall, as well as a method of reliable communication using snails. He was good company, aged a little over forty, and was at least polite and gave me due respect for my efforts.

"The Tralfamosaur escaped," I told him. "When you and Patrick surged this afternoon during the bridge re-building, two quarter-ton blocks of stone were catapulted into the sky."

"I wondered what had happened to them," said Moobin thoughtfully.

"One fell to earth in an orchard near Belmont, and the other landed on the Ross-to-Hereford branch line, derailing a train that was transporting the Tralfamosaur to Woburn Safari Park for some sort of dangerous animal exchange deal."

"Ah," said Moobin, "so we're kind of responsible for this, aren't we?"

"I'm afraid so," I replied, "and it's already eaten three people."

"Whoops," said Moobin.

"Whoops nothing," said Lady Mawgon, who had arrived with Tiger close behind. "Civilians have to take their risks with the rest of us."

Unlike Moobin, Lady Mawgon was *not* our favorite sorcerer but was undeniably good at what she did. She had been the official sorcerer of the Kingdom of Kent before the downturn of magical power, and her fall from that lofty status had made her frosty and ill-tempered.

She had recently turned seventy, scowled constantly, and had the unsettling habit of gliding everywhere, as though she wore roller skates beneath the folds of her large black dress.

"Even so," I said diplomatically, "it's probably not a good idea to let the Tralfamosaur eat people."

"I suppose not," conceded Lady Mawgon. "What about Once Magnificent Boo?"

"Already in hand," I replied, indicating to where Tiger was speaking on the phone.

Once Magnificent Boo had, as her name suggested, once been magnificent. She could have been as powerful as the Mighty Shandar himself, but was long retired and saddled with a dark personality that made Lady Mawgon seem almost sunny. The reason was simple: Boo had been robbed of her dazzling career in sorcery by the removal of her index fingers, the conduit of a sorcerer's power. Lost for over three decades, the fingers had been recently recovered by us — but even when Boo was reunited with the dry bones, the only magic she could do was wayward and unfocused. These days she studied Quarkbeasts and was the world's leading authority on Tralfamosaurs, which was the reason we needed her.

"She'll meet you there," said Tiger, replacing the receiver. "I'll stay here and man the phones in case you need anything sent over."

Once Perkins had returned with the sandwiches, we trooped outside to my Volkswagen Beetle. There were better cars in the basement at Zambini Towers, but the VW had huge sentimental value: I had been found wrapped in a blanket on the back seat outside the Ladies of the Lobster orphanage one windswept night sixteen years earlier. There was a note stuffed under one windshield wiper:

> Please look after this poor dear child,
> as her parents died in the Troll Wars.
> PS: I think the engine may need some oil
> and the tire pressure checked.
> PPS: We think her name should be Jennifer.
> PPPS: The child, not the car.
> PPPPS: For her surname,
> choose something strange.

The car had been kept—all items found with a foundling were, by royal decree—and was presented to me when the Blessed Ladies of the Lobster sold me to Kazam. After checking the tire pressure and adding some oil, the engine had started the first time, and I drove to my first job in my own car. If you think fourteen is too young to start driving, think again. The Kingdom of Snodd grants driver's licenses on the basis of *responsibility*, not age, which can frustrate forty-something guys no end when they fail their responsibility test for the umpteenth time.

"Shotgun!" yelled Lady Mawgon as she plunked herself in the passenger seat. Everyone groaned. Being in the back of the Volkswagen meant sitting next to the Quarkbeast, a creature often described as a cross between a Labrador and an open knife drawer, with a bit of velociraptor and scaly pangolin thrown in for good measure. Despite its terrifying appearance and an odd habit of eating metal, the Quarkbeast was a loyal and intelligent companion.

"Right," I said as we drove off, "does anyone have a plan for how we're going to recapture the Tralfamosaur?"

There was silence.

"How about this," I said. "We modify our plans with regard to ongoing facts as they become known to us, then re-modify them as the situation unfolds."

"You mean make it all up as we go along?" asked Perkins.

"Right."

"It's worked before," said Lady Mawgon.

"Many times," replied Moobin.

"Quark," said the Quarkbeast.

THREE

Tralfamosaur Hunt Part 1: Bait and Lure

The cargo train that had transported the Tralfamosaur had been derailed about four miles outside Hereford. The locomotive had stayed upright, but most of the cars were lying in an untidy zigzag along the track. There was a huge number of police cars, ambulances, and fire engines, and the night was lit by floodlights on towers. A willowy officer introduced himself as Detective Corbett and then escorted us up the tracks, past the shattered remnants of the train.

"The engine driver was the first eaten," said Corbett as we stared at the wreckage. "See these footprints?" He pointed his flashlight at the ground, where a Tralfamosaur footprint was clearly visible.

"The creature headed northeast," said Moobin after looking at several other footprints. "Any reports from the public?"

"Nothing so far," said Corbett.

"A Tralfamosaur can be surprisingly stealthy," said Lady Mawgon. "Discovering one near you and being eaten often happen at pretty much the same time."

Corbett looked around nervously. "The roads are locked down for a fifty-mile perimeter," he said in a hasty *I'm leaving pretty soon* sort of voice, "and everyone has been advised to stay indoors or in a cellar if they have one. Artillery batteries have been set up in case it goes in the direction of Hereford, and if you are unsuccessful by first light, King Snodd has agreed to send in the landships."

"What about——" began Moobin, but Corbett had already gone.

It was a dark night, and a light breeze stirred the branches of the trees. Of the Tralfamosaur, there was no sign. Sending in the landships would be a last resort: little could withstand these immensely powerful four-story armored tracked vehicles, except trolls, who impertinently called them Meals on Wheels.

"I'm not sure a squadron of landships chasing after a single Tralfamosaur would do anything but cause a huge amount of damage," said Perkins. "What's the next step?"

"Search me," said Lady Mawgon. "Moobin?"

"Not a clue. Let's face it; recapturing nine tons of

pea-brained enraged carnivore isn't something we do every day. How was it captured last time?"

"Licorice," came a loud voice behind us, and we jumped.

"I'm sorry?" said Lady Mawgon.

"Licorice," repeated Once Magnificent Boo, who had just arrived on her moped. We fell silent. Boo never used more words than absolutely necessary, rarely smiled, and had eyes so dark they seemed like black snooker balls floating in a bowl of cream. "If you listen very carefully to my plan and follow it to the letter, we have a reasonable chance of catching the Tralfamosaur without anyone being eaten."

"Define 'reasonable chance,'" said Lady Mawgon, but Boo ignored her and continued.

"We require only a grenade launcher, six pounds of industrial-strength licorice, two spells of Class VIII complexity, a shipping container, a side of bacon, an automobile, several homing snails, a ladder, and two people to act as bait."

Perkins leaned across to me and whispered, "Boo was kind of looking at us when the 'two people as bait' thing came up."

"I know," I whispered back. "It's possible to refuse, but the thing is, who are you more frightened of: Once Magnificent Boo or a Tralfamosaur?"

* * *

An hour later Perkins and I were in my Volkswagen, parked near a crossroads on high ground a mile or two from the damaged train. We had watched the lights that dotted the countryside gradually wink out as residents were told to extinguish their house lights, a lure for the Tralfamosaur. Soon we could see nothing but the stars through the open sunroof and the pinkish glow of the Quarkbeast sitting on a wall close by, sniffing the air cautiously. The Quarkbeast had been created magically as a sort of bloodhound to track other magical beasts, so it would be able to sense the Tralfamosaur at a distance of at least five hundred yards.

"Enjoying the date so far?" I asked cheerily.

"It could be improved," Perkins replied.

"In what way?"

"Not being used as Tralfamosaur bait, for one thing."

"Oh, come on," I said. "It's a lovely night to be eaten by nine tons of hunger-crazed monster."

Perkins looked up through the open sunroof at the broad swath of stars above our heads. As if on cue, a shooting star flashed across the sky.

"You're half right," he said with a smile. "It's a lovely night. Crazy or nothing, right?"

I returned his smile. "Right. Crazy or nothing. Let's check everything again."

I flicked the two glowworms above the dashboard with my finger. A faint glimmer illuminated the SpellGo buttons that Moobin and Lady Mawgon had placed on the dash. Spells could be cast in advance and lie dormant until activated by something as easy to use as the two large buttons. One was labeled BOGEYS and the other FLOAT.

"Got the rocket-propelled licorice launcher handy?" I asked.

"Check." Perkins patted the weapon, which instead of an explosive warhead contained a lump of industrial-grade licorice about the size of a melon. It smelled so strongly we had to poke the launcher out the sunroof to stop our eyes from watering. Tralfamosaurs could smell licorice from at least a mile away if the wind was strong enough.

We jumped as a snail shot in through the open window and skidded to a halt inside the windshield, leaving a slippery trail across the glass. Homing snails were one of Wizard Moobin's recent discoveries. He had found that all snails have the capacity to do over one hundred miles per hour and find a location with pinpoint accuracy, but didn't because they were horribly lazy and couldn't be bothered. By rewriting a motivating spell commonly used by TV fitness instructors, communication by homing snail was entirely possible—and snails were more reliable than pigeons, which were easily distracted.

The snail was steaming with exertion and smelled faintly of scorched rubber, but seemed pleased with itself.

I gave it a lettuce leaf and popped it in its box while Perkins opened the note that had been stuck to its shell. It was from Lady Mawgon.

"Reports from worried citizens place the Tralfamosaur three miles down the road at Woolhope." Woolhope was the Kingdom's sixth-largest town and home to twelve thousand people and a marzoleum processing plant.

I had a sudden thought. "It's heading for the flare."

Marzoleum refineries always had a gas flare lit on a tall tower, and it was this, I guessed, that would attract the Tralfamosaur. It might have a brain the size of a Ping-Pong ball, but when it came to looking for food at night, it was no slouch. Fire and light, after all, generally led to humans.

"There," I said, stabbing my finger on the map near a place called Broadmoor Common, just downwind of Woolhope. "He'll be able to smell us easily from there."

I whistled to the Quarkbeast, who jumped into the back seat of the car, and we were soon hurtling along the narrow roads. It was about three a.m. by now, and I admit that I drove recklessly. The police had locked down the area tight and told everyone to stay in their homes, but even so, I was half expecting to run into a tractor or something. I didn't. I ran into something much worse.

The Quarkbeast cried out first, a sort of *quarky-quark-quarky* noise that spelled danger, and as I braked, my headlights illuminated something nasty and large and reptilian on the road ahead. The Tralfamosaur's small eyes glinted as it looked up. It was bigger than I remembered from my occasional visits to the zoo, and it looked more dangerous out in the open.

There were about fifty yards between it and us. We sat there for a moment, the engine of the Beetle idling. The creature stared at us blankly until I realized we were upwind, so it probably wasn't aware of the licorice. I slowly backed the car up, but the Tralfamosaur didn't follow. Against my better judgment I stopped, and then inched slowly forward again. Still it didn't seem that interested.

"Better show yourself," I said to Perkins, "and try to look appetizing."

"Yes," he said sarcastically, "I'm well known for my pie impersonations."

Perkins took a deep breath, undid his seat belt, stood up through the sunroof, and waved his arms. The Tralfamosaur gave out a deafening bellow and charged.

I slammed the car into reverse and swiftly backed away, then pulled the wheel around, thumped the gearshift into first, and drove off with the Tralfamosaur in close pursuit.

Part one of the plan was now in operation.

FOUR

Tralfamosaur Hunt Part 2: Chase and Capture

The Tralfamosaur could smell the licorice now, and it made a wild bite at the car as we accelerated away. We felt the jerk as a tooth caught in the bodywork, then the metal split, releasing us. I glanced into the rearview mirror as we took off the way we had come, and could see the Tralfamosaur glowing red in the taillights as it chased us with a heavy, lumbering gait. A Volkswagen is speedier than a Tralfamosaur, and we maintained a safe distance.

We took a left at Mordford, then a right over the River Wye, where the Tralfamosaur stopped to sniff at the ironically named Tasty Drinker Inn. It was so distracted by the smell of citizens hiding inside that we had to reverse almost to within reach of it before the creature changed its mind. Overcome by the sheer succulence of the licorice, it came after us, knocking over two parked cars and demolishing both bridge parapets as it lumbered across.

"Wow!" said Perkins, hanging out the window to watch the spectacle. "I think I've seen everything now."

"I sincerely wish that were the case," I said, "but I doubt it. We're new to the magic industry. Pretty soon, stuff like this will be *routine.*"

After another ten minutes I took a tight left turn into a field. I had left the gate open and hung an oil lamp on the gatepost so I wouldn't miss it. I had to slow down to take the corner, however, and the Tralfamosaur caught up and closed its teeth around the rear bumper.

The car was lifted high in the air, held there . . . and then, with a tearing noise, the bumper ripped off. The car fell back onto the grassy slope with a crash and bounced back into the air. The Quarkbeast was catapulted off the rear seat and stuck fast when its scales became embedded in the roof.

Undeterred, I put my foot down and aimed the car toward a second oil lamp, positioned where we had removed a length of fencing between the field and the railroad.

"Stand by for SpellGo One!" I yelled as we drove up

the stone ballast and onto the railroad track, the tires bumping noisily. Perkins's hand hovered over the first of the two spell activation buttons.

"*Now!*" I shouted, and Perkins thumped the one marked BOGEYS. With a bright flash and a buzzing sensation, the Volkswagen's wheels were transformed into rail bogeys — that is, train wheels. They slotted onto the rails, and the ride smoothed out. We were now, technically, a train. Now that I didn't need to steer, I let go of the wheel, pressed the accelerator, and looked out the window behind us.

The Tralfamosaur was close — and even angrier. It was snapping at us wildly, driven on by the overpowering smell of licorice.

And that was pretty much when we entered the Kidley Hill railroad tunnel. The engine sound and the Tralfamosaur's bellows bounced off the tunnel walls to create a noise that I would be happy to never hear again.

"Right!" I yelled. "Timing is everything for this one! I'm on the SpellGo button, you're on the grenade launcher!"

"Right-o," replied Perkins, and shouldered the weapon. He stood up through the sunroof and faced not the beast, but the other direction — toward the far tunnel opening.

I accelerated to give us some distance from the creature, then came to a halt alongside a single green lamp

I had left earlier. I switched off the engine and flashed my headlights. In the distance a light flashed back at us, then stayed steady. Perkins took aim at the light with the grenade launcher and flicked off the safety. Citizens of the Kingdom of Snodd are expected to fight and perhaps die gloriously and pointlessly in a Troll War or two at some point, so all receive military training from an early age.

I placed my hand over the SpellGo button marked FLOAT and stared out the broken rear window. I could hear the footfalls of the Tralfamosaur and its panting, but could not see it, and after a few moments everything went quiet.

"Now?" asked Perkins, finger hovering on the trigger.

"When I say."

"How about now?"

"When I say."

"Has it gone?"

"It's moved back to stealth mode," I whispered. "It's there all right, somewhere in the darkness."

I peered into the inky blackness but could still see nothing, then had an idea and stamped on the brake pedal. The brake lights popped on, bringing extra luminance to the brick-lined tunnel. It was good I did. The creature was less than ten feet from the rear bumper, and in the warm glow I could see its small black eyes staring at us hungrily.

"Now."

There was an explosive detonation as Perkins pulled the trigger, and the licorice rocket flew down the tunnel, illuminating the sides as it went. There was a metallic *thang* as the rocket hit something.

I thumped the SpellGo button marked FLOAT. There was another buzzing noise, and the car lurched up into one of three ventilation shafts that connected the railroad tunnel to the world outside. The Volkswagen bumped against the walls as it rose, eventually pitching nose-down. The headlights illuminated a confused-looking Tralfamosaur below us on the shiny tracks. It pondered us for a moment, then followed the licorice scent left by the grenade launcher. As soon as the creature vanished, we looked at each other and smiled. We were, for the moment, safe.

The car bumped and scraped up the ventilation shaft to emerge into the early morning light. Moobin was waiting for us as planned, and a dozen men deputized from the nearest town placed hooks onto the now lighter-than-air Volkswagen. The men heaved on the ropes as the car swung around in the breeze, and after a lot of grunting, the floating car was tied to two heavy tractors.

I breathed a sigh of relief. It had been an exciting and dangerous night. As we sat there, the Quarkbeast fell from the roof of the car onto the back seat with a thump.

"Umm — are all our dates going to be like that?" said Perkins.

"I hope not," I replied with a grin, "but it was fun, wasn't it? I mean, it's not like we were killed or eaten or anything, right?"

"If your idea of a good date is not to be killed and eaten, you're unlikely to ever be disappointed."

And he leaned toward me. I think I may even have leaned toward him, but then a voice rang out from below.

"Are you coming down from there?" It was Moobin.

A ladder was placed against the car, and we climbed down to join him; he congratulated us before we walked down the hill to find Mawgon and Boo waiting at the mouth of the tunnel. Before our chase, a shipping container had been reversed up to the portal; the Tralfamosaur, urged on by the licorice grenade fired into the back of its new prison, had swiftly been contained. We could hear contented chewing through the thick steel wall; we had left several slabs of bacon in there, as well as half a bison.

The dawn was well established as the last part of the plan was completed: the floating Beetle was hauled down the hill and anchored to the shipping container with self-tying string. The Tralfamosaur was soon snoring, pretty much worn out after the night's excitement, which could be said for most of us.

"A fine job," said Once Magnificent Boo in a rare moment of congratulations, although you wouldn't know it from looking at her — her mood seemed as dark as usual. She climbed the ladder to the Volkswagen, gauged the speed of the wind, slammed the door, and ordered the ladder away.

"Ahoy, Moobin and Lady Mawgon!" she called out the window. "I need Jenny's car to be twelve tons lighter."

The two sorcerers complied, and with a straining of wires, the Volkswagen lifted the container into the air. Within a few seconds the breeze had caught the strange flying machine and it was drifting away over the treetops in an easterly direction.

"She's a bit high for just going to the zoo," I said.

Moobin and Lady Mawgon said nothing, and I figured out what was happening.

"She's not going back to the zoo, is she?"

"No," said Moobin quietly. "She's carrying the Tralfamosaur across the border to the Cambrian Empire. They have wild Tralfamosaurs there, and it can do . . . whatever it is Tralfamosaurs do."

"I'm not sure the king will be pleased," said Perkins. "The Tralfamosaur was a valuable tourist attraction for the kingdom and one of his personal favorites, even after the queen insisted he stop feeding his enemies to it."

"The queen was very wise to do that," Moobin replied, "but I don't believe Once Magnificent Boo gives two buttons what the king thinks."

And with the dawn sky lightening, we watched the Volkswagen with the shipping container slung below drift off into the early morning. Soon it was high enough to catch the sun, and my car was suddenly a blaze of orange.

"I'm going to miss the Volkswagen," I said.

"Don't be so sentimental," said Lady Mawgon. "It's only a car."

But it wasn't just a car. It was my *parents'* car. The one I had been abandoned in. It was part of me, and it was hard to see it go.

Wizard Moobin turned to Perkins and me and smiled at us each in turn. "Good work, you two. Come on. Breakfast is on me."

FIVE

Angel Traps

Prince Nasil was already up when I walked into the converted dining room we now used as the nerve center of Kazam. It was from here that the day's work was arranged, and where all sorcery-related meetings took place. It had been two weeks since the Tralfamosaur escapade, and the company had returned to what we called normality.

"Hello, Jennifer," said Prince Nasil cheerily. "Any news of Boo?"

"Nothing yet," I replied, "but we know she got there. She released a homing snail that told us she and the Tralfamosaur were safe in Cambrianopolis."

"If my carpet hadn't been damaged so much on that

trip up to the Troll Wall," said the prince wistfully, "I might have been able to help."

He was referring to a recent high-speed flight to Trollvania. The trip had further damaged an already-worn-out magic carpet, and Nasil would need it rebuilt if he were to resume any sort of aerial work.

"Look at that," said the prince, holding up a tatty and threadbare excuse for a rug, "already ten thousand hours and two centuries past rebuild."

"What can we do?" I asked.

"We need more angel feathers," he announced, much as you might ask for an oil change on a car.

"Okay . . ." I replied slowly. Angel feathers were by their very definition somewhat tricky to obtain. "And where would we find angels?"

"Oh, they're everywhere," he said in a matter-of-fact tone, "keeping an eye on stuff. But they're fleet of wing, and catching them is the devil's own job. Here." He handed me a wire-mesh box that had a hinged flap on a tensioned spring.

"It's possible we might be able to catch one if we bait the trap with marshmallows," he said without a shred of shame.

I looked at the trap dubiously as Tiger walked in. The prince handed him an angel trap too, explaining what it was and that the first person to trap an angel would win a Mars bar.

"Should we be trapping angels?" Tiger, despite his youth, knew right from wrong when he saw it. "I mean, is that ethical?"

"I very much doubt it," replied the prince cheerfully, "but it's a lot better than running intensive angel farms like they used to in the old days—that was the real reason behind the dissolution of the monasteries."

"I didn't know that."

"Not many people do."

"Where's the best place to leave an angel trap?" asked Tiger as soon as the prince had gone.

"Angels are everywhere," I said, "but usually only intervene during times of adversity."

"You should have had one of these when you were chased by the Tralfamosaur," said Tiger, and I nodded.

"Have you seen this?" asked Wizard Moobin as he walked into the offices holding a newspaper. "The Un-united Kingdoms are gearing up for Troll War V. The landship foundries have been working overtime—the orphan workforce is receiving extra gruel allowances."

"I can't think there's much appetite for another Troll War," I said. "Most nations in the Ununited Kingdoms are still bankrupt from the last one. The only one who really benefits is King Snodd, making money off those rotten landships." We all fell silent, sadly contemplating a potential Troll War V. This would produce only three things: profit for the king, more orphans—and Troll War VI.

"Speaking of kings," I added, "I have an audience with His Majesty at eleven."

"Any idea what he wants to see you about?" asked Moobin. "If he was going to have us executed for losing the Tralfamosaur, he would already have done it."

"I think he blames Boo for that. Besides, given our recent triumph, even he would think twice about any monkey business."

The recent triumph was about the appointment of the royal advisory position known as the Court Mystician. The only reason the king had wanted a Court Mystician was so he could bully that person into doing moneymaking enchantments, and he'd wanted to award the job to a corrupt sorcerer named Blix. Kazam had fought and won a magic competition over it, and Blix's House of Enchantment had been absorbed into ours. The Court Mystician position was now mine, and Blix had been transformed to granite—bad for him but good for Hereford museum, which had him as their chief exhibit.

"Even so," said Moobin, "be careful of the king. Ah! Customers!"

The bell had just sounded in the offices, and we got to work. The morning was spent discussing jobs with potential clients who had heard about our triumph in the magic competition, and were waking up to the idea that home improvements could be done by magic. We discussed realigning houses to face the sun better, and moving entire trees. We agreed to find some lost keys, animals, and grannies, and then, inevitably, had to turn down the usual half dozen who wanted us to do what we couldn't: make people fall in love, bring someone back from the dead, and, in one case, both.

The most interesting client was a man who proposed that we send him into orbit within a steel ball so he could watch the sunset upon the earth and "muse upon immortality" until his air ran out. It was a ridiculous idea, of course, but ridiculous was never treated with much scorn at Kazam — most of magic is far, far beyond ridiculous. Magnetic worms, for instance, or removing the moles from Toledo, or giving memory to coiled cables on telephones, or echoes, or bicycles staying upright — or, most strangely, the once-serious proposition to magic a third ear onto the earth's four billion rabbits in order to "lessen pain when lifting."

"Right," I said, checking my watch as soon as we had told our low-earth-orbit client to return with a doctor's note that declared him sane. "Time for a trip to the palace."

I'd had to find another car the morning after my Volkswagen floated away. Luckily, there were many forgotten cars lying dormant under dust sheets in the basement of Zambini Towers. I'd chosen a massive vintage car called a Bugatti Royale. Inside, it was sumptuously comfortable; outside, the hood was so long that in misty weather it was hard to see the radiator ornament. I chose the car partly because it started pretty much the first time, partly because it looked nice, but mostly because it was the biggest.

The Bugatti Royale, however, had one major drawback: the steering was unbelievably heavy. Lady Mawgon dealt with the problem by spelling me a Helping Hand™, which looks more or less like a severed hand but can do all manner of useful hand-related work, such as kneading bread, copying letters, or even taking the Quarkbeast for a walk. Although helpful, a disembodied hand on the Bugatti's steering wheel was a bit creepy, especially because this one was hairy and had *No More Pies* tattooed on the back.

"So," said Tiger as we drove away from Zambini Towers, "do I get to meet the king this time? I am, after all, the faithful assistant of the Court Mystician."

"It's probably best to stay in the car," I replied, knowing full well how foundlings were regarded in the palace. "You'd be ordered to polish the silver or clean the chimney or something. You can keep the Quarkbeast company. The last time I took him in with me, five knights fainted, and then he licked all the nickel plating off the door hinges. The lord chief advisor said it was okay, but I think he was just being polite."

"All right, then," said Tiger, who had long ago become used to a life of third-class citizenry.

"Quark," said the Quarkbeast, who hadn't much liked the taste of the hinges anyway.

SIX

Audience with the King

The castle at Snodd Hill was outside the kingdom's capital, not far from where the nation shared a long border with the Duchy of Brecon and a short one with the Cambrian Empire. The sun had enveloped the castle with its warm embrace, which made the dark stone structure less dreary than usual. The Medieval Chic fashion was still very much the rage, which is okay if you don't mind lots of weather-beaten stone, mud, funny smells, poor sanitation, and beggars dressed in blankets.

I left the car in the reserved Court Mystician parking space with Tiger and the Quarkbeast settling down to a game of chess, then trotted past an ornate front entrance guarded by two sentries holding halberds polished to a high sheen. I gave my name to a nearby footman, who looked at me disparagingly, consulted a large ledger, sniffed, and then led me down a corridor to a pair of large double doors. He rapped twice, the doors opened, and he indicated that I should enter.

The doors closed behind me. At each end of the room, a log fire crackled in a hearth the size of a bed. Instead of courtiers, military men, and advisors milling about, there were maids, servants, and other domestic staff. This wasn't so much business at court, but home life. The king's spectacularly beautiful wife, Mimosa, was present, as were their Royal Spoiltnesses, Prince Steve and Princess Shazza. The princess was engaged in her studies, which meant that a university lecturer was nearby doing her schoolwork for her. The whole scene looked suspiciously relaxed and informal. The king, I think, wanted me to see his softer side.

"Ah!" said the king as he spotted me. "Welcome, Court Mystician!"

King Snodd was neither tall nor good-looking, nor had any obvious attributes that might make him even the tiniest bit likable. Of the many awards he'd won at the annual Ununited Kingdoms Despot Awards, the high points were Most Hated Tyrant (twice), Most Corrupt King of a Medium-Sized Kingdom (once), Best Original Act of Despotism Adapted from an Otherwise Fair Law (three times), Worst Teeth (once), and Despot Most

Likely to Be Killed by an Enraged Mob with Agricultural Tools. He was, in short, an ill-tempered, conniving little weasel obsessed with military conquests and cash. But weasel notwithstanding, he *was* the king, and today he seemed to be in a good mood.

I approached and bowed low, and he permitted me to kiss his large gold signet ring.

"Your Majesty," I said with all due solemnity.

"Greetings, Miss Strange," he said cheerfully, spreading an arm wide to indicate the hall. "Welcome to our little oasis of domestic normality."

Normality was not a word I would have chosen. I didn't know anyone whose food taster had a food taster, nor anyone who had made mice illegal, taxed nose hairs, or changed their curtains hourly "so as not to afford good hiding places for assassins."

"And an apology may be due for that regrettable incident two weeks ago," the king added, "when it might have appeared that I used the power of the state to attempt to win the magic contest."

"Water under the bridge," I said diplomatically.

"Your forgiving air does you credit," came a melodious voice. It was Queen Mimosa, as elegant a figure as I had seen anywhere. She held herself with poise and quiet dignity, and she moved as though walking on silk.

"Your Majesty," I said, bowing again.

"Tish to protocol, Jennifer," said the queen with a

smile. "I am glad to see you well, and" — she glared at the king — "I was most glad to see you and not Mr. Blix appointed Court Mystician."

The king and the queen could not have been more different. Rumor said she had agreed to marry him and bear his children in order to give a better life to his subjects; if true, this would be a very noble sacrifice indeed. Before, she had been just plain Mimosa Jones, a medium-ranked sorceress, and it was rumored that the queen was a Troll War orphan herself, which might explain the charity work she did for the orphan cause. The reason the Kingdom of Snodd enjoyed a better-than-normal reputation these days was solely due to Queen Mimosa's guiding hand.

"Now, then," said the king, eager to get down to business; he had, apparently, an execution to witness at midday, and didn't want them to start without him. "Since you and the rest of those irritatingly disobedient enchanters have the odd notion that magic should be for the good of many, I am coming to terms with the fact that my relationship with sorcerers cannot be as one-sided as I might wish. Wife? Translate."

"He means," said Queen Mimosa, "that he knows he can't boss you around."

"Exactly," said the king. "But there is a matter of extreme delicacy that we need to speak about." He turned to the princess, waiting for her homework to be completed for her. "Peaches, would you come over here, please?"

"What now?" The princess rolled her eyes in a *whatever* sort of way.

"If it's not too much trouble, sweetness."

The princess huffed again, and walked over in a sulky manner. We were the same age, but we could not have had more different upbringings. While I had spent my first twelve years eating gruel and sharing a dormitory with sixty other girls, Princess Shazza had been indulged in every possible way. She wore clothes cut from the very finest cloth, bathed in rainwater imported at huge expense from Bali, and had her food prepared by Michelin-starred chefs. She was undeniably pretty, with glossy raven-black hair, fine features, and large, inquisitive eyes. We had never met, yet she was very familiar. She could barely catch a cold or be seen with an inappropriate prince without it becoming front-page news.

"This is Her Royal Highness the Crown Princess Shazza Blossom Hadridd Snodd," announced the king, "heiress to the Kingdom of Snodd."

She looked me up and down as though I were considerably less important than garbage, but did not make eye contact with me.

"I hope this interruption to my valuable time has a purpose," said the princess in a pouty voice, arms folded.

"Pay attention, Princess," said the queen in the sort of voice that makes one take notice. "This young lady is Jennifer Strange. She is the Court Mystician."

"Like, totally big yawn," replied the princess. "Magic is so last week."

"She is also Dragon Ambassador to the World," continued the queen, "manager of Kazam Mystical Arts Management, and a young lady of considerable daring, moral worth, and resourcefulness. Everything, in fact, that you are not."

The princess looked shocked. *"What?"*

"You heard me," replied the queen. "Soft living has rendered you spoiled beyond measure — a state of affairs for which I admit I am partly responsible."

"Nonsense, Mother!" said the princess haughtily. "Everyone loves me because I am so beautiful and charming and witty. You there." She pointed to a servant whose job it was to clean up after the royal poodles, who were numerous, unruly, and not at all housetrained.

"Yes, my lady?" The servant looked no older than the princess and me. She was pale, had plain mousy hair, and was dressed in the neat, starched dress of the lowest-ranked house servants; she also looked tired, worn, and old before her time. But she somehow held herself upright, with the last vestiges of human dignity.

"Do you love your princess, girl?"

"Begging your pardon, yes, I do, my lady," she said with a small curtsey, "and am surely grateful for the career opportunities your family's benevolence has brung to me."

"Well said," said the princess happily. "There will be an extra shiny penny in your retirement fund. It will await you on your seventy-fifth birthday."

"Her Ladyship is most generous." Clearly knowing when an audience had ended, the girl went back to cleaning up after the royal poodles.

The princess turned to her mother. "You see?"

"A character reference from a Royal Dog Mess Removal Operative Third Class is hardly compelling, darling. Our minds are made up. If Miss Strange agrees, you shall take counsel from her and try to improve yourself."

The princess gaped inelegantly, like a fish, for several moments. "Take counsel from an *orphan?*" she said incredulously.

I could have taken offense, I suppose, but I didn't. You kind of get used to it. In fact, I was getting a bit bored, and was instead wondering whether Once Magnificent Boo was safe in the Cambrian Empire and if my Volkswagen had floated up into a tree or something.

"You may shake hands with Miss Strange," continued the queen, "and then we will discuss your education. Is this acceptable to you, Miss Strange?"

"Only too happy to help," I said, not believing for one second that the princess would allow anything like this to happen.

"Good," said Queen Mimosa. "Shake her hand and say good afternoon, Princess."

"I'd rather not," retorted the princess, glancing at me directly for the first time. "I might catch something."

"It won't be humility," I replied as I stared at her evenly, figuring that this was probably what they thought the princess needed. If my head were off my shoulders in under ten minutes, that meant I'd been wrong.

The princess went almost purple with rage. "I have been *impertinenced!*" she said. "I insist that this orphan be executed!"

"I'm not sure 'impertinenced' is a word," I said.

"It is if I say it is," said the princess, "and Daddy, you did say for my sixteenth birthday I could order someone executed. Well, I choose her." She pointed at me.

The king looked at Queen Mimosa.

"I *did* sort of promise her she could do that, my dear. What sort of lesson is it if I don't keep my word?"

"What sort of lesson is it to a child that she can have someone executed?" retorted the queen, and glared at him. Not an ordinary glare, but one of those hard stares that leaves your neck hot, causes you to fluff your words, and makes you prickly inside your clothes.

"You're right, my dear," replied the king in a small voice. Updating his style of medieval violent monarchy to Queen Mimosa's benevolent dictatorship was a bitter pill to swallow, but the king, to his credit, was trying.

"I will not be talked to like this —" began the princess, but the queen cut her short.

"You *will* shake Miss Strange's hand, my daughter," she said, "or you will regret it."

"Come, come, my dear," said the king, attempting to defuse the situation. "She is only a child."

"A child who is vain, spoiled, and unworthy to rule. We will not leave this kingdom in safe hands if the princess is allowed to continue her ways. So," concluded the queen, "are you prepared to greet Miss Strange, Princess?"

The princess looked at her parents in turn. "I would sooner eat dog's vomit than —"

"ENOUGH!" yelled the queen in a voice so loud that everyone jumped. "Leave us," she said to the people in the room, and the royal retinue, used to making themselves scarce at a moment's notice, all headed for the door.

"Not you," the queen said to the royal poodle cleaner-upper who had been quizzed by the princess.

"My dear . . ." began the king when the servants had left, but his entreaties fell upon deaf ears. The queen's fury was up, and instead of holding his ground, he cowered in front of her.

And that was when I felt a buzzing in the air. It was subtle, like a distant bee in fog, but it meant only one thing: a spell was cooking. And if that were so, it could only be from the ex-sorcerer, Queen Mimosa.

The princess crossed her arms and stared at her mother.

"You will do as you are told, young lady," said the queen in a measured tone, "or you will not be in a position to do anything at all."

"Do your very worst!" spat the princess with an ugly sneer. "I will not be ordered about like a handmaiden!"

The queen slowly and deliberately pointed her index fingers at the princess. These were the conduits of a sorcerer's power, and if pointed anywhere near you, it was time to run, beg, or duck for cover. The king must have seen this before, for he winced as a powerful surge of wizidrical energy coursed from Queen Mimosa's fingers. There was a thunderclap. Then several drapes fell from the walls and the window glass decreased in size by a tenth and collapsed out of the frames with an angry clatter.

This wasn't the spell, of course, just the secondary effect. When the peal of thunder had receded into the distance, I tried to figure out what spell had been cast, but nothing seemed to have changed.

SEVEN

The Princess Changed

I looked at the king, who seemed as confused as I, then at the queen, who was blowing on her fingers as sorcerers often do after a particularly heavy spelling bout. Something *had* happened; I just wasn't sure what.

That was when I noticed the princess, who had a look of confusion that was hard to describe. She stared at her hands as though they were entirely alien. The king had noticed her odd behavior too.

"My little pooplemouse," he said, "are you quite well?"

The princess opened her mouth, but nothing came out. She looked as though she were going to cough up a toad or something, which is not as odd as it might sound, as that punishment is often bestowed upon disobedient children by their mother-sorcerers.

The princess opened her mouth again and found her voice. "Begging your pardon, Your Majesties, but I don't half feel peculiar."

"My dear," said the king to the queen, "you have given our daughter the voice and manners of a common person."

"My nails!" came a voice behind us. "And these clothes! I would not be seen dead in them!"

We turned around. The servant who had been ordered to remain had broken strict protocol and spoken without being spoken to first, one in a very long list of sackable offenses. The queen caught her eye and pointed to a mirror; the servant looked, then shrieked and brought her raw hands up to her face.

"Oh!" she said. "I'm so plain and ugly and common! What have you done, Mother?"

"Yes," said the king, "what have you done?"

"A lesson to show our daughter the value of something when you have lost it."

"That's our daughter?" asked the king, staring first at the servant, then at the princess, who had started to pirouette in a mildly clumsy fashion, listening joyfully to the faint rustle of her pink crinoline dress.

"You haven't—?" said the king.

"I most certainly have," replied Queen Mimosa. "The

princess has swapped bodies with the lowliest servant in the household."

The princess in the servant's body looked aghast. "I've learned my lesson!" she shrieked. "Turn me back, please! I will do anything — even shake hands with that hideous orphan person."

She couldn't even remember my name. I turned to the queen, impressed by her technical skill. "Remarkable, ma'am. Where did you learn to do that?"

"I studied under Sister Organza of Rhodes," she said. "The good sister was big on the transfer of minds between bodies."

"Please turn me back!" pleaded the princess again, throwing herself at her mother's feet. "I will *never* again blame the footmen for my own stealing or demand that people be put to death. I won't ever make fun of our poor royal cousins for only having two castles."

"I may have to insist you change her back," the king told the queen with uncharacteristic firmness. "I can't have a daughter with lank hair and a pallid complexion. It might attract the wrong sort of prince."

"Our daughter needs to be taught a lesson," said the queen, "for the good of the kingdom."

"There are other ways to punish her," said the king, "and in this matter I will be firm. Return my daughter this instant!"

"Yes!" howled the princess. "And I promise never to

pour weed killer in the moat again — I'll even restock the ornamental fish with my own servant's pocket money!"

"That was *you?*" said the king. "My prized collection of rare and wonderful koi carp, all stone dead at a stroke? I had my fish-keeper stripped of all honors and sent to work in the refineries — and you said nothing?" He turned to his wife. "I suppose it might be for the best," he said wearily.

"What?!?" yelled the princess.

"Right," said the queen, clapping her hands. "Miss Strange, I am entrusting you with our daughter's further education. I hope she will learn from the experience of having and being less than nothing."

"I won't go," said the princess. "I shan't be made to wear old clothes and eat nothing but potatoes and do my own scratching and share toilets with other people and have no servants. I shall savagely bite anyone who tries to take me away."

"Then we shall have you muzzled and sent to the orphanage," said the queen, "and they will allocate you work in the refineries. It's either that or going quietly with Miss Strange."

These words seemed to have an effect. "I shall hate you forever, Mother," the princess said quietly.

"You will thank me," the queen replied evenly, "and the kingdom shall thank your father and me for delivering them a just and wise ruler when we die."

The princess said nothing. The servant-now-princess spoke next.

"This is a very beautiful room, like," she said. "I'd not real noticed before what with not being allowed to raise my eyes from the floor and all. Is that a painting of a great battle?"

"That one?" said the king, always eager to show off his knowledge. "It is of one of our ancestors' greatest triumphs against the Snowdonian Welsh. The odds were astounding: five thousand against six. It was a hard, hand-to-hand battle over two days with every inch won in blood and sinew, but thank Snodd we were victorious. Despite everything, we were impressed by the fighting spirit of the Welsh — those six certainly put up a terrific fight."

"Look after her, won't you?" said the queen to me in a more concerned tone. "I trust your judgment in how you educate my daughter, and whatever happens, you will not find the kingdom or me ungrateful. Bring her back when you think she is ready and I will restore their minds to the correct bodies. Protect her, Miss Strange, but don't cosset her. The future of the kingdom may very well be in your hands."

The princess had quieted down when she realized that her mother meant it, and we were shown from the hall.

"No one is curtseying to me," she said in shocked

wonderment as we walked unobserved down a bustling corridor. "Is this what being common is like?"

"It's a small part of what being common is like," I told her.

"Do you think that horrible servant will get my body pregnant?" she asked as we trotted down the steps. "I've heard about you girl orphans having no morals and having babies for fun and selling them to buy bicycles and fashion accessories and onions and stuff."

"We think of nothing else," I said with a smile.

Tiger and the Quarkbeast were still playing chess when we got back to the car.

"Who's she?" said Tiger.

"Guess."

"From the look of her," said Tiger, "an orphan, probably bought for indentured servitude within the palace and used for menial scrubbing duties or worse. Here." He fished in his pocket. "I've got some nougat somewhere that I was keeping for emergencies—and you look as though you could do with a bit of energy."

He held out the nougat, mildly dusty from where it had sat in his pocket. The princess ignored it.

"I smell of dog poo, carbolic soap, and mildew," she said, sniffing a sleeve of her maid's uniform in disgust, "and I can feel a booger in my left nostril. Remove it for me, boy."

"Holy cow!" said Tiger. "It's the princess."

"How did you know that?" she asked.

"Wild stab in the dark," he said sarcastically.

"Hold your tongue!" said the princess.

"Hold it yourself," said Tiger, sticking out his tongue.

"I dislike that redheaded nitwit already," said the princess. "I'm going to start a list of people who have annoyed me so they can be duly punished when I am back in my own body." She rummaged in her pockets for a piece of paper and a stub of pencil. "So, nitwit: Name?"

"Tiger . . . Spartacus."

"*Spart-a-cus,*" The princess wrote it down carefully.

"If anyone finds out you're the princess," I said after a worrisome thought, "I'd give it about an hour before we have to fight off bandits, cutthroats, and agents of foreign powers. For now, you'll take the handmaiden's name. What is it, by the way?"

The princess seemed to see the sense in this. "She doesn't have a name. We called her 'poo-girl' if we called her anything at all."

I told her to take the orphan ID card out of her top pocket.

"Well, how about that," said the princess, reading the card, "she does have a name after all, but it's awful: Laura Scrubb, Royal Dog Mess Removal Operative Third Class, age seventeen. Laura *Scrubb?* I can't be called that!"

"You are and you will be," I said. "And that's the Quarkbeast."

"It's hideous," said the princess. "In fact, you all are. And why is there a disembodied hand on the steering wheel?"

"It's a Helping Hand™," explained Tiger, "like power steering, only run by magic."

"Magic? How vulgar. I am so *very* glad I inherited no powers from my mother."

We climbed into the Bugatti Royale, I reversed out of the parking space, and we headed back toward town. The princess, once past her fit of indignation at how hideously unsophisticated we all were, spent the time staring out the window.

"I don't usually see much beyond the castle walls," she said in a quiet voice. "What's that?"

"It's a billboard, advertising toothpaste."

"Doesn't it come already squeezed onto your toothbrush every morning and evening?"

"No, it doesn't."

"Really? So how does it get from the tube to the toothbrush?"

I didn't have time to answer; I stamped on the brakes as a car swerved in front of us. It was a six-wheeled Phantom Twelve Rolls-Royce, with paint work so perfectly black it looked as though one could fall into it. Only one person was driven around in the super-exclusive Phantom Twelve, and I knew that this was not a chance encounter.

An impeccably dressed manservant in a dark suit, white gloves, and dark glasses climbed out of the Phantom Twelve, walked across, and tapped on my window.

"Miss Strange?" he said. "My employer would like to discuss a matter that concerns you both."

We were stuck in the middle of an intersection.

"What, here?"

"No, miss. At Madley International Airport. Follow us, please."

The Rolls-Royce pulled away and we followed. The car would contain Miss D'Argento; like me, she was an agent. But she wasn't just any agent — she didn't look after movie stars, singers, writers, or even ordinary sorcerers. She didn't even look after careless kings who found themselves temporarily without a kingdom and needing a public relations boost.

Miss D'Argento was the agent for the most powerful wizard living, dead, or, in his case, otherwise: the Mighty Shandar.

EIGHT

The Mighty Shandar

The trip to the kingdom's international airport did not take long. Instead of going to the main departures terminal, we were led into a large maintenance hangar that contained a Skybus 646 cargo aircraft emblazoned with Shandar's logo: a footprint on fire. The rear cargo hold was open, and a large wooden crate was being unloaded by a forklift. I parked the Bugatti and watched as Miss D'Argento alighted elegantly from the Rolls-Royce's rear door, held open by the manservant.

The D'Argentos had been looking after the business interests of the Mighty Shandar ever since his appearance as a featured Sorcerer to Watch in the July 1572 edition of *Popular Wizarding*. As far as anyone can tell, there have been eleven D'Argentos in the employ of the Mighty Shandar, and all but one female. Miss D'Argento was about eighteen and dressed as perfectly as a socialite twice her age.

I told Tiger and the princess to stay in the car. Body-swaps leave little residual post-spell echo, so Shandar was unlikely to divine who the princess really was, but it was always better to be safe than sorry.

I walked across to Miss D'Argento and waited for the forklift truck to deliver the crate in front of us. Several other henchmen were dotted around the hangar, each dressed in a black suit, dark hat, white gloves, and large sunglasses. I peered at the one closest to us. There was no flesh in the small gap between where his glove ended and his shirt cuff began. It was an empty suit, animated by magic. You can usually identify a drone by its jerky and decidedly unhuman movements, but these were top class — at a distance you'd think they were human.

"Good afternoon, Miss Strange," said Miss D'Argento in a cultivated voice, her high heels *click-click*ing on the concrete floor as she approached us. "Congratulations on being made Court Mystician. I reported it to the Mighty Shandar, who expressed admiration for your fortitude."

I nodded toward the closest drone. "They move well for the nonliving."

"Thank you," said D'Argento. "Shandar does us all proud."

"And from a purely professional interest," I added, "are you running them on an Ankh-XVII RUNIX core?"

"You know your spells," said Miss D'Argento with a smile. "We run them with the Mandrake Sentience Emulation Protocols disabled to make them less independent. Make no mistake, they are twice as dangerous as real bodyguards, for they fear no death."

She wasn't kidding. Pharaoh Amenemhat V of the Middle Kingdom was said to have attempted to expand Egypt along the Mediterranean with an unstoppable drone army of sixty thousand. They got as far as what is now Benghazi until Amenemhat V was killed in battle.

The forklift placed the crate in front of me and reversed away. Several of the lifeless drones unlatched the crate and wheeled the two sections apart to reveal the Mighty Shandar himself.

But it wasn't a flesh-and-blood Shandar. It was Shandar as he spent most of his time these days: stone. Every fold in his clothes, every pore in his skin, every eyelash was perfectly preserved in glassy obsidian. This was how the Mighty Shandar could still be a serious player in the world of magic four centuries after his birth. In stone, you don't age.

But spending time *in petra* was not without dangers. The world is littered with sorcerers who had turned to stone for some reason, only to have an arm, leg, or head get knocked or sawn off. Those who return to life generally bleed to death before they can be saved. But with the right storage facilities and barring erosion, accidental damage, or mischief, a sorcerer in stone could live hundreds of thousands of years without losing a second of his or her own life.

"The Mighty Shandar celebrates his four hundred and forty-fourth birthday next year," said Miss D'Argento, "yet in his own personal life he is only fifty-eight. He doesn't get out of stone for anything less than a million an hour, and at current life-usage rates will live until 9356." She looked carefully at Shandar's features, unclipped a feather duster from inside the crate, and flicked some dust from the statue.

"He spent the entire seventeenth and eighteenth centuries turned to stone," continued Miss D'Argento proudly, "but that was mainly for tax purposes. Four generations of my family never spoke to him at all."

"You must be very dedicated."

"Dedication does not even begin to describe our commitment to the Mighty Shandar," said D'Argento, "but enough chitchat. Read this."

She passed me a sheet of paper. I scanned the contents, and my heart fell. It was a letter from Representatives of the Ununited Kingdoms to the Mighty Shandar, outlining a breach of contract they had filed with the UnUK's highest court.

"The thing is," said D'Argento in a half-apologetic

tone as I read the lawsuit, "the Mighty Shandar doesn't do refunds."

The problem was this: The Mighty Shandar had been contracted to rid the kingdoms of dragons four centuries before, and was paid a lot of money to do so. His plan had required the last dragon to die of old age, a plan in which I had personally intervened to spoil. There were now two dragons left, and that was two more dragons than the contract stipulated. Unless Shandar rid the kingdoms of every dragon, he'd have to return the cash. And it was a *lot* of cash. Paid to him four centuries ago, the interest alone would fund at least half a Troll War.

"We have the money," said D'Argento. "The Mighty Shandar's share in Skybus Aeronautics would cover the debt pretty much on its own. No, it's the *principle* of the matter. A job was left unfinished, and we're not keen to make a habit of it. Clients might lose confidence, and in business, confidence counts."

"I agree with that," I replied, "but this is a job that doesn't need finishing. Dragons aren't much into eating people anymore—it's probably the last thing on Feldspar's and Colin's minds."

"They have names?"

"Certainly. In the first month of their new life, they did a goodwill tour around the world to promote their Not Eating People or Burning Stuff agenda, and they are now in Washington, D.C., reading the entire contents of the Library of Congress in order to understand a little more about humans."

"Admirable, I'm sure," said Miss D'Argento, "but the refund issue still stands. Don't take my word for it, for you are to be honored: the Mighty Shandar wants to speak to you personally."

Miss D'Argento checked her watch. As a clock struck two, the statue of Shandar turned from black to gray to a sort of off-white. There was a pause, and then Shandar took a deep breath as life returned to his body. The off-white coating burst off his skin and clothes like dry skin. He staggered for a moment, shook himself, and looked around.

"Welcome back, O Mighty Shandar." Miss D'Argento beamed and clicked a stopwatch. "It's two o'clock on the afternoon of the fourteenth of October. You've been *in petra* for sixty-two days. We're currently at Madley International Airport in the Kingdom of Snodd." She handed him a damp towel so he could refresh himself, then a clipboard and pen. "Ongoing progress reports, sir."

His eyes scanned the text. "I'll take two minutes." His voice was a deep baritone that transmitted confidence, awe, and leadership in equal measure.

"This is Jennifer Strange," said D'Argento, gesturing in my direction, "as you requested."

He looked across at me. He was a handsome man,

tanned and imposingly large. His eyes were of the brightest green, like a cat's, and seemed to regard everything in unblinking detail.

"Miss D'Argento? Make that four minutes." He shook my hand. "I'm *very* pleased to meet you at last, Jennifer Strange. A worthy opponent is the only opponent worth opposing." His hand was firm, yet cold, which was hardly surprising; a few seconds ago he had been stone.

"You assisted the dragons in destroying my carefully laid plans," he added in a quieter voice, "plans four centuries in the making. All that work for nothing, and now they're asking for a refund. Worse, you have damaged my one hundred percent wizidrical success rate and bruised my credibility as a sorcerer of considerable power. For any one of those reasons, I should banish you to the icy wastes of outer Finlandia."

"If that was your plan, you would already have done so."

"Very true," he said with a half smile, "but I'm not into revenge. It has a nasty habit of biting you back when you least expect it. I have a feeling that punishing you would upset the delicate good-bad balance."

Most sorcerers believed in what they called "the balance." Simply put, all life requires equilibrium to survive. For every death there is birth, for every light there is dark, for every ugliness something else shines with greater luster. And for every truly heinous act, there are multiple good acts to compensate. It's why evil despots are ultimately defeated, and why a truly awful reality TV show can never go on forever.

Shandar looked at the clipboard, signed something, then continued to read while he spoke to me. Someone as powerful as Shandar would be able to read two books and converse with three people at the same time, even in different languages.

"You seem a resourceful young lady, Jennifer. I'm not often beaten, and the experience has renewed a sense of excitement that I have not felt for a long time. You appreciate that I have almost unlimited power at my disposal?"

"I know that, sir, yes."

The Mighty Shandar pointed to a clause in one of the notes he was looking at. "Are we sure about this?"

"Yes, sir," replied D'Argento. "They want the state of Hawaii moved to the middle of the Pacific."

"I thought it was fine between Montana and North Dakota."

"The venerable Lord Jack of Hawaii requested the move on account of the climate—and they want to retrofit the collective memory so everyone thinks it's always been there."

"Standard stuff," said Shandar. "They didn't quibble over the price?"

"Not a murmur."

He sighed and shook his head. "Where *have* all the good negotiators gone?"

"Two minutes gone," said Miss D'Argento, consulting her stopwatch.

"So with my power at almost unimaginably high levels right now," Shandar continued, turning back to me, "your friends the dragons are easily exterminated. I could—and would—destroy them in a heartbeat, thus completing the contract and avoiding a refund."

"Then you will battle with the combined power of everyone at Kazam as well, Mighty Shandar," I said, "for we will do *anything* to prevent your harming a single scale of a dragon." It was a bold speech, and I shivered in anticipation of his reaction.

He appeared not to hear me at first and spoke again to his agent. "We're not doing this," he said quietly as he handed an unsigned contract back to Miss D'Argento. "There are quite enough boy bands on the planet as it is." He turned back to me. "The combined power of your sorcerers would not equal one-thousandth of my power."

"I know that," I replied, "and so do they. But it would not stop them. They would all die defending one of their own, and the dragons are one of us."

The Mighty Shandar regarded me thoughtfully. I'd not consulted Kazam's sorcerers on any of this, but I knew them well enough, and so did he.

"Then I have a proposition for you, Miss Strange. Are you listening?"

"I'm listening."

"As you can see, my time is strictly rationed. I have no spare time to search for rare and exotic trinkets to add to my collection of Wonderful Things. Miss D'Argento is too busy managing my affairs, and drones are all very well for heavy lifting and the odd senseless act of violence, but they have no finesse. So. If you find something for me, I will leave the dragons alone and take the indignity on the chin."

"I'm still listening," I said. "What do you want me to find?"

"A magnificent pink ruby the size of a goose's egg. It belonged to a wizard I admire greatly. You may find me . . . the Eye of Zoltar."

"That's a tall order." I had absolutely no idea what he was talking about, but it didn't pay to look like an idiot in Shandar's presence.

"One minute to go," said Miss D'Argento.

"Do we have a deal?" asked Shandar.

I didn't need to think for long. If I didn't agree to find this Eye of Zoltar, then Shandar would attempt to kill the dragons, and I would be honor bound to try to stop him, and that would end in collective annihilation.

"I'll find you the Eye of Zoltar," I said, "whatever it takes."

"Good choice," said Shandar with a grin. "I knew you'd agree."

"Any clue as to where it is?" I asked. "The world is a big place."

"If I knew where it was," snapped Shandar, "I'd get it myself."

Since the meeting was clearly at an end, I returned to the car, where the princess, Tiger, and the Quarkbeast were waiting. From the Bugatti Royale we watched as Shandar talked quietly with D'Argento, signed some more forms, and, when his four minutes were up, changed rapidly back into obsidian.

The drones quickly crated him up; the forklift re-appeared and placed the crate back into the rear of the cargo aircraft. Once that was done, the drones approached a clothes rack standing to one side and deftly jumped back onto their coat hangers, the empty suits return-ing to what they had been — creatures given life only by the will of Shandar. The human manservant wheeled the clothes rack into the back of the cargo hold, swiftly fol-lowed by Miss D'Argento at the wheel of the Phantom Twelve. A minute later the cargo door was closed, and the engines started up. By this time tomorrow, Shandar and his cohort could be anywhere on the planet.

I tapped the Helping Hand™ to bring it out of sleep

mode; it dutifully pulled the steering wheel around, and we drove out of the hangar. We paused on the perimeter track as Shandar's aircraft lumbered into the sky, which seemed almost impossible, given the plane's disproportionately tiny wings. Then we headed toward Zambini Towers.

"The Eye of Zoltar?" said Tiger when I'd finished relating what Shandar had said.

"What on earth's that?" asked the princess.

"I've no idea," I said. "The person to consult is someone with a clearer idea of what the future might bring."

"I'm no clairvoyant," said Tiger, "but I think I know who you mean."

NINE

The Remarkable Kevin Zipp

The Remarkable Kevin Zipp was one of Kazam's most accomplished clairvoyants. When we walked back into the offices at Zambini Towers, he was checking out baby futures. Not in a stocks-and-shares kind of way, but what a baby's life had in store. It was a good way to earn ready cash, as Kazam was constantly short of money. Two mothers had their tots with them, and Kevin was checking by holding on to the left foot of each baby in turn.

"If she wants to go out with someone named Geoff when she's sixteen," he said as the first mother stared at him anxiously, "try to get her to go out with Nigel instead."

"There's a problem with Geoff?"

"No, there's a problem with Nigel. Ban Geoff from her life and he'll become unbelievably attractive and she'll forget all about Nigel, and believe me, she needs to. Nigel is big trouble."

"How big?"

"*Really* big."

"Okay. Anything else?"

"Not really — although you might consider joining the National Trust and vacationing in Wales. It's quite nice, I'm told, and not always raining."

"Oh. Well, thank you very much." The mother handed Kevin a ten-moolah note and moved away. The second mother presented her baby. Kevin closed his eyes and rocked slowly in his chair as he held the baby's foot.

"This is preposterous," said the princess. "I've never seen a more ridiculous load of mumbo-jumbo in my entire life!"

"This is nothing," I said. "Lots of time to see some gold-standard mumbo-jumbo, and quite frankly, Kazam is the place to see it."

"Concert pianist," Kevin murmured thoughtfully, still holding the baby's foot, "and make sure he likes boiled cabbage, tasteless stew, and runny porridge."

"He'll be a pianist?" asked the mother excitedly.

"No, he's going to murder one at age twenty-six, so better get him used to prison food from an early age . . . hence the boiled cabbage."

The mother glared at him, slapped the money on the table, and left. Kevin looked confused. "Did I say something wrong?"

"Perhaps you should temper the bad news with good," I suggested.

"I couldn't tell either of them the really bad news," he replied. "The 'concert pianist' thing was the minority timeline; the senior timeline—the most likely one—has them both not lasting the week."

I picked up the mail on my desk and opened a letter that was postmarked from Cambrianopolis, the capital city of the Cambrian Empire. It looked official.

"Oh, dear," I said as I read the letter. "Once Magnificent Boo's been arrested for 'illegal importation of a Tralfamosaur.'"

"That's a trumped-up charge," said Tiger. "The Cambrian Empire has herds and herds of the things—people pay good money to hunt them, for goodness' sake."

"There's a reason," I added. "She's been transferred to Emperor Tharv's state-owned Ransom Clearance House, ready for negotiations."

"The Cambrian Empire is *still* kidnapping people?" said Tiger. "When are they going to enter the twenty-first century?"

"I think they have to consider entering the nineteenth century first," said Kevin.

Traditionally, it was princes and kings and knights

and stuff who were ransomed because they were worth a lot of money, but in the Cambrian Empire, pretty much anyone was fair game. If you weren't royal, the release fees could actually be fairly modest — people cost less to release than a parking ticket, which was both kind of depressing and very welcome. But the long and short of it was that if we wanted Boo back, we would have to pay. And that would mean going over there with a letter of credit and doing a deal.

Kevin nodded toward the princess. "Who's that?"

I put the letter down. "This is Laura Scrubb. She'll be with us awhile." I nodded to the princess, who reluctantly shook hands with Kevin, then made a point of smelling her hand with obvious distaste before wiping it on her uniform.

"She's the princess, isn't she?" said Kevin with interest, peering at what might appear at first glance to be an undernourished handmaiden.

"I'm afraid so," I replied, "but keep it under your hat. If she's kidnapped by agents of a foreign power, we'll have to waste a lot of time and energy getting her back."

"Probably do her the power of good," said Kevin, "and knock some sense into her thick, overprivileged head."

"You are *so* disrespectful," announced the princess haughtily, getting out her list and pencil again. "Name?"

"Kevin Spartacus."

"Related to this nitwit here?" She pointed at Tiger. "That figures, and I don't know who to pity more."

She scribbled the name on the piece of paper while Kevin peered at her as one might gaze at a particularly intriguing variety of beetle. I was suddenly worried — I'd seen that look before. He was seeing something, or had seen something. Something in the future, and about the princess.

"This is very interesting," Kevin said at length. "Yes, very interesting indeed. *Definitely* keep her identity a secret." He prodded the princess with a bony finger. "Fascinating."

"Okay," said the princess, "let's get this straight right now. No one is to prod the Royal Personage."

We all ignored her. Technically speaking, she was an orphan, nothing more.

"You will almost die several times in the next week," said Kevin Zipp thoughtfully, "but will be saved by people who do not like you, nor are like you, nor whom you like."

"That'll be you two, then," said the princess, looking at Tiger and me.

"It might help if you were to invest in a bit of warmth," said Kevin.

"If you have foreseen I am to be saved, then it doesn't much matter what I do, now, does it?"

"I only foresee a version of the future," said Kevin. "How it unfolds is up to you."

The princess didn't make any retort, and instead asked where the lavatory was. I told her and she stomped off.

"Was that true?" asked Tiger. "The near-death thing, I mean?"

"Oh, yes," said Kevin with a shrug. "She'll come within a hairsbreadth of death—may even meet it. It's all a bit fuzzy, to be honest. But I'll tell you this: the princess will be involved in the next Troll War, which will start when least expected. It will be bloody, short—and the aggressors will be victorious."

"We will?" I asked in surprise, for past Troll Wars had been noted only for the swift manner in which humans had been utterly defeated.

"Yes. Strange, isn't it? Then again," Kevin added cheerfully, "I've been wrong before. And don't forget that what I see is only a *possible* version of events—and sometimes it's a knotted jumble of potential futures all seen as one."

This, unfortunately, was true. Fate can never be precisely determined. All of us are somewhat clairvoyant; any future you can dream up, no matter how bizarre, retains the faint possibility of coming true. Kevin's skill was of dreaming up future events that were not just possible, but likely. He once said, "Being a clairvoyant is ten percent guesswork and ninety percent probability mathematics."

"So," said Kevin, "aside from princesses looking like handmaidens, what news?"

"Lots. I need to find something called the Eye of Zoltar. Heard of it?"

"Sure. It's had Legendary Grade III status for centuries."

A Legendary Grade III status meant that the Eye was "really not very likely at all," which wasn't helpful, but better than Grade II: "no proof of existence" or Grade I: "proven nonexistence."

"Grade III, eh?" I said. "That doesn't sound good."

"Unicorns were Grade III at one time," said Kevin, "and the coelacanth. And we all know they exist." He then frowned deeply, looked at me again, and a cloud of consternation crossed his face. "Who *precisely* wants you to look for the Eye of Zoltar?"

I told him about the meeting with the Mighty Shandar and the options regarding the refund. Kevin thought for a moment, then said, "I need to make some inquiries. Call a Sorcerer's Conclave for an hour from now."

I told him I would, and he dashed off without another word.

"Kevin's seen something in the future," said Tiger, "and I don't think he likes it."

"Yes," I said. "I noticed it too. And when clairvoyants get nervous, so do I."

The princess came back in, holding a roll of toilet paper. "Do I fold it or crumple it before I . . . you know?"

Tiger and I looked at each other.

"Don't give me your silent-pity nonsense," said the princess crossly. "It is a *huge* sacrifice to live without servants, a burden that you pinheads know nothing about. What's more, this body I'm trapped in is covered with unsightly red rashes and I think I may be dying. My stomach has a sort of gnawing feeling inside."

"You're hungry," I said simply. "Never felt that before?"

"Me, a princess? Don't be ridiculous."

"You're going to have to trust that body when it starts telling you things. Let me have a look at the rash. Growing up in an orphanage tends to make you an expert on skin complaints."

She made a *harrumph* noise and I led her off in the direction of the lavatory.

Fortunately for the princess and for Laura Scrubb, the rash was not bad and likely the result of sleeping on damp hay. After instructing her — not assisting her — on the toilet paper problem, I took her down to the Kazam kitchens and introduced her to our cook, known by everyone as Unstable Mabel, but not called that to her face.

"Where did you find this poor wee bairn?" said

Mabel, ladling out a large portion of leftover stew and handing it to the princess. "She looks as though she has been half starved and treated with uncommon brutality. From the palace, is she?"

"That's an outrageous slur against a fine employer," said the princess, shoveling down the stew. "I'll have you know that the royal family are warm and generous people who treat their servants with the greatest respect and rarely leave them out in the rain for fun."

Unstable Mabel, who was not totally without lucid moments, looked at me and arched an eyebrow. "She's the princess, isn't she?"

"I'm afraid so."

The princess stopped mid-gulp, her manners apparently forgotten in her hunger. "How does everyone know it's me?"

"Because," said Mabel, always direct in speech and manner, "you're well known in the kingdom as a spoiled, conniving, cruel, bullying little brat."

"Right," said the princess, getting out her piece of paper. "You're going on the list too. Everyone on it will be flogged for disrespect. Name?"

"Mabel . . . Spartacus."

The princess started to write, then clued in to the ongoing Spartacus gag.

"You're only making it worse for yourself," scolded the princess. "When I'm in my own body again, none of you will be laughing, I can tell you." And she gave us both a pouty glare and folded her arms.

Mabel turned to me. "Can I make a suggestion?"

"Yes, please."

"Take her down to the orphan labor pool and have her allocated to sewer-cleaning duties for twenty-four hours. She'll have to live outside for a couple of days afterward due to the stench that no amount of scrubbing will remove, but it might teach her some humility."

"I hate all of you," said the princess. "I hate your lack of compassion and the meager respect you show your obvious betters. If you don't take me home *right now* I will hold my breath until I turn blue, and then you'll be sorry."

I stared at her for a moment. "No need for that," I said with a sigh, taking my car keys from my pocket. "I'll just apologize to the king and the queen and tell them their daughter is beyond my help, and probably anyone else's. You can live out your spoiled life without effort, secure in the depths of your own supreme ignorance, and die as you lived: without purpose, true fulfillment, or any discernibly useful function."

She opened her mouth only to shut it again.

I continued. "You don't need me to drive you home, Princess. You know where the door is and you can walk out any time you want. But I'd like you to appreciate that Laura Scrubb, the orphan with whom you are not even worthy to share skin disorders, cannot walk out a door to anywhere until she's eighteen, and even then it's to a life of grinding poverty, disappointment, backbreaking toil, and an early death, if she's lucky."

The princess was silent for a moment, then pulled up a sleeve and looked at Laura's rash.

"Okay," she said, "I'm staying. But only because I choose to do so for educational reasons and not because any of your words meant anything to me, which they didn't."

"Good," I said, "and you'll *choose* to do what I tell you rather than endlessly complaining and putting people on your list?"

The princess shrugged. "I might *choose* to do that, yes."

I stared at her and she lowered her eyes, took the list out of her pocket, and tore it into tiny pieces. "Pointless anyway," she grumbled, "what with everyone called 'Spartacus.'"

And she chuckled at the joke. It showed she had a sense of humor. Perhaps she might become bearable in time.

"Okay, then," I said. "Let's get you into some clean clothes and out of that terrible maid's outfit."

"Thank you," she said with a resigned sigh. "I'd like that."

I led her up to my bedroom, found some clothes

about the right size, and told her not to come down until she had showered and washed her hair. She fumbled with the buttons on her blouse until I helped her.

"Hell's teeth, Princess, did you not do *anything* for yourself at the palace?"

"I did my own sleeping," she said after a moment's thought. "Usually."

I gathered up her tattered clothes as she took them off, then chucked them into the recycling. As I left to alert everyone about the Sorcerer's Conclave, I heard her scream as she mishandled the temperature dial on the shower.

TEN

Sorcerer's Conclave

Along with Tiger and me, in the Kazam offices an hour later were Wizard Moobin, Lady Mawgon, Full and Half Price, Perkins, Prince Nasil, Dame "She Whom the Ants Obey" Corby, and Kevin Zipp, who was busy scribbling notes on the back of an envelope.

They all listened to what I had to say, from D'Argento's appearance to Shandar's offer of a deal. Find the Eye of Zoltar, or he'd kill the dragons and us too if we tried to stop him. I didn't tell them about the princess, as they would all guess soon enough.

"Zoltar?" said Perkins. "Anyone we know?"

"Zoltar was the sorcerer to His Tyrannical Majesty Amenemhat V," said Moobin, "and was ranked about third-most powerful on the planet at the time. He turned to the dark Mystical Arts for cash, as we understand it, and was killed in an unspeakably unpleasant way not long after Amenemhat V himself."

"And the Eye?" I asked.

"It was a jewel," said Dame Corby, reading the *Codex Magicalis.* "It says that Zoltar liked to use a staff, the top of which was adorned with 'a mighty ruby the size of a goose egg. Cut with over a thousand facets and said to dance with inner fire, the ruby was always warm to the touch, even on the coldest night.' It says that the Eye worked as a lens to magnify Zoltar's power. After Zoltar's death, the Eye changed hands many times but not without mishap—lesser wizards were changed into lead when they attempted to harness its vast power."

"Changed into *what?*" said Perkins.

"Lead," said Dame Corby. "You know, the heavy metal?"

"Does it say what happened to the Eye?" I asked.

Dame Corby turned the page. "Changed hands many times—traditional reports of a curse, death to all who beheld it, ba-da-boom-ba-da-bing usual stuff. It was definitely known to be in the possession of Suleiman the Magnificent in 1552, and was said to be instrumental in maintaining the might and power of the Ottoman Empire. It was thought to have been on one of the trains that T. E. Lawrence derailed on the Hejaz Railway in 1916.

Lawrence may have owned the Eye until he died in a motorcycle accident in 1935 but nothing was found in his effects. No one's heard about the Eye since then."

"I'm not so sure," said Kevin Zipp. "And I'll relate a conversation I had a few years back with an ex-sorcerer named Able Quizzler."

Everyone leaned closer.

"Quizzler was part of the team that did the early spelling work for levitating railroads," said Kevin, "but when I met him he was scratching out a living doing voiceover work for I Speak Your Weight machines. He told me that he had spent the last forty years attempting to find the Eye of Zoltar, hoping it would restart his sorcery career. He had almost given up when he heard stories of a vast, multifaceted ruby that seemed to dance with inner fire, was warm to the touch, and gave inexplicable powers to those skilled enough to tame it. A ruby that changed the unworthy to lead."

"The metal lead?" said Perkins, who was having trouble grasping this.

"Yes, the metal lead."

"And where was this?" asked Lady Mawgon.

"The Eye of Zoltar had apparently been seen around . . . the neck of Sky Pirate Wolff."

Everyone sighed and threw up their arms in exasperation.

"Oh, for goodness' sake," said Moobin skeptically. "If

there is a tall tale kicking around, then Pirate Wolff will be at the bottom of it."

I knew of Sky Pirate Bunty Wolff, of course — everyone did. She was a mythical figure, also of Grade III "really not very likely at all" status, with more wild stories attached to her than almost anyone on the planet. Blamed for many acts of aerial piracy but never caught, she inspired sightings that were sporadic, sketchy, and prone to exaggeration.

It was said that she had tamed a Cloud Leviathan, which is a bit like saying you caught a Zebricorn to ride into battle. The Leviathan, a creature of obscure origins and as large as an aircraft, was seen only rarely and had been photographed just once, about eight years before. The photograph had been front-page news in the world's newspapers and downgraded the Leviathan's legendary status from Grade IV: "not very likely, to be honest" to a Grade V: "okay, some basis in fact, but still partly unexplained."

It was speculated that Sky Pirate Wolff's hideout was in the Leviathans' Graveyard, which has Legendary Grade III status and is reputedly located somewhere in the misty heights of the mountain known as Cadir Idris. It's where Cloud Leviathans go to die. The facts were all a bit hazy, but if Wolff were somehow real, this would be how she'd want it. And if Wolff really had tamed a Leviathan, perhaps she had actually captured entire jetliners on the wing. That could explain the loss of the liner *Ty-rannic* and even account for the capture and destruction of Cloud City Nimbus III, where every man and woman had been made to walk the plank — it had rained Cloud City citizens for weeks, some say.

"Sky Pirate Wolff doesn't exist," said Moobin. "It's more likely the *Tyrannic* was lost at sea. No one knows what happened to Nimbus III, and as for pirates boarding jetliners, it's more probable that the scallywags stowed away aboard inside the wheel wells before takeoff."

That sparked an argument about whether the legendary pirate existed or not, whether it was safe or even possible to hide oneself in wheel wells, and the wisdom of chasing after Grade IV legends and half truths told by Able Quizzler, an old man driven insane by a quest that had dominated his life.

"Okay, okay!" I yelled above the arguing. "Let's all just calm down. Kevin, finish your story, please."

"Last time we spoke, Able Quizzler told me that the Eye of Zoltar was within his grasp. He was in Llangurig at the time. I think it's worth pursuing."

"When was this?" asked Lady Mawgon.

"Six years ago. But I trust Able. We go back awhile."

Everyone went quiet.

"If Quizzler and the Eye were in Llangurig, that's well inside the Cambrian Empire," observed Moobin, "in a region notorious for bandits, wild beasts, emulating slime mold, and other perils. It's too dangerous."

"So is fighting Shandar," I said. "What's the harm in traveling to Llangurig to see if I can find Quizzler? After all, the refund isn't due for another month — and I could negotiate for Boo's release at the same time."

This got a reaction from the gathering, but before we could discuss it further, there was a *whoosh*ing of wings and some brief bickering as two dark shapes flew by the window.

"That's just what we need," said Lady Mawgon. "A couple of infants."

And with a clatter, two dragons attempted to enter through the window at the same time. They elbowed each other petulantly, breaking the window frame and several panes of glass.

"Hey!" I said in my loudest voice, and they went silent. I was about the only one who could control them. "Cut it out, you two — what happened to dragons being creatures of great dignity, learning, and wisdom?"

"Sorry, what did you say?" said Colin, removing one of his iPod earbuds. "I was listening to the Doobie Brothers."

ELEVEN

The Dragons

The two dragons I found myself vaguely responsible for were called Feldspar Axiom Firebreath IV and Colin. They were each the size of a pony and decidedly reptilian in appearance, manner, and gait. They each had long jaws with serrated teeth, ornate head frills, long barbed tails, and explosively flammable breath. Their wings were a triumph of design. Unfolded, they took up the entire room and were as translucent as tissue paper; folded, they fit neatly into dimples on their backs. They had muscular arms and legs, with sharp talons that needed to be clipped often to avoid damaging the hotel's parquet flooring.

But despite their appearance, which was both elegant and terrifying, they acted like particularly dumb teenage brothers, only with immeasurably higher IQs and better taste in clothes and friends. They had spent the past two months in Washington, D.C., reading the contents of the entire Library of Congress so they could better understand the human mind.

"Welcome home," I said. "Were you impressed by all that learning?"

"Good in parts," said Colin thoughtfully, "but generally inclined to repetition."

"That's it?" said Wizard Moobin. "Our entire intellectual output dismissed in a sentence?"

"We can discuss human literary output further if you'd like," said Feldspar, "but we'd only get round to Aristotle before you'd do that thing where you stop working and fall apart. What's it called again?"

"Dying?"

"That's it. But your output isn't *all* boring. We thought a few humans were really smart, but they seem too rare to be of any real use, and rarely become leaders who can actually change things."

"And," added Colin, "I was a little disappointed about all that killing." He was a strict pacifist, and as much a vegan as any dragon could be.

"There is quite a lot of it in our history," I conceded.

"I knew how much before I went," said Colin. "I was just unprepared for the range of ridiculous excuses. It's somewhat bizarre to learn that many of you think other humans are somehow different enough to be killed, when you're all tiresomely similar in outlook, needs, and motivation, and differ only in peculiar habits, generally shaped by geographical circumstance."

"We're not *all* bad," I said, suddenly finding myself defending my own species.

"No," agreed Colin, "some of you are hardly rubbish at all, and a few — there are always a few — are quite exceptional. Mind you, you can always take solace in the fact that humans are generally better than trolls."

"Better than trolls?" said Lady Mawgon scornfully. "Praise indeed."

"Generally better," repeated Colin.

We fell silent, and Feldspar looked around the room carefully. "Is this a Sorcerer's Conclave?" he asked, and I nodded.

"It's about the Mighty Shandar," said Moobin, and he outlined the refund issue and how finding the Eye of Zoltar might help.

"I thought he might want to kill us," said Colin in a matter-of-fact manner. "Most do. We'll defend ourselves as well as we can, but it won't be much of a fight — neither of us will be full-grown and at peak magic for at least another century, perhaps two."

"Which is why we need to find the Eye," I said. "Heard of it?"

"Nope," said Colin, "but then our dragon transdeath

memory is weak at present. If you want to give us thirty years or so for our forefathers' memories to settle and co-alesce, we'd be happy to help then."

"That might be too long," said Moobin.

"Humans!" said Feldspar. "Always in such a hurry. Well, I must be off. There's a princess down in the West Country who needs me for a guarding gig, and the venue needs my approval for suitability. Tall tower, abandoned castle, island, that sort of thing."

"You never mentioned this," said Colin, mildly an-noyed.

"I don't have to tell you everything, brother. Besides, it's only for thirty years or until successful abduction of said princess by said brave knight."

"You wouldn't catch me doing any princess guard-ing," said Colin grumpily. "It's so depressingly medi-eval. Guarding princesses and vaporizing knights with a white-hot ball of fire is not the publicity we dragons need right now."

"How about guarding without the ball of fire thing?" asked Moobin.

"It's an idea," replied Feldspar thoughtfully, "al-though I'm not sure you *can* guard princesses without roasting a few knights. It'll be fine. I get to meet the princess in advance, and if we don't hit it off, I can al-ways turn the job down." And with that, he flew out the window.

"Okay," I said in my most authoritative voice, the one I use when I make some sort of wise or portentous pronouncement. "It looks like I'm going into the Cambrian Empire on a dual mission. First, I'll head for Llangurig to find Able Quizzler and see if there is any truth in his claim that the Eye of Zoltar is in Pirate Wolff's possession."

"And second?" asked Lady Mawgon.

"I'll see if I can negotiate for Once Magnificent Boo's release. I'll be gone for two days, three at most."

There was a mild grumbling of discomfort; whenever I went away or had a day off, things generally became a bit chaotic at Kazam. But there were no major objections, because everyone understood this was important.

"Okay, then," I said, eager to move on, "who's coming with me? Not you, Tiger; you're staying here to look after things in my absence."

"I can be tactical air support," said Colin. "I might not be large enough to carry anyone, but I can manage reconnaissance duties."

"Thank you," I said. "Anyone else?"

There was silence, and for good reason.

"I'm not sure *any* of us can come with you," said Moobin apologetically, "with the passage of licensed sorcerers across borders so strictly controlled. Travel permits would take six months or more."

"If we sneaked across the border and were caught, we'd end up no better off than Once Magnificent Boo," added Lady Mawgon.

"My carpet and I aren't going anywhere until I get some more angel feathers," said the prince gloomily, "but if you shout, I'll come running and do what I can."

"I'm too lazy," admitted Kevin Zipp, "and can foresee more terrors than will be helpful for you to know."

This was worrying. I could go on my own, but I'd prefer company.

"I'm in," said Perkins. "Officialdom moves slowly in both the Kingdom of Snodd and the Cambrian Empire. It's doubtful that my licensed-sorcerer status has even left the outbox of the Ministry of Infernal Affairs. The worst that can happen is that I'm refused entry."

"Thank you, Perkins."

"My pleasure. Never been on a quest before."

"Hang on a second," I said. "Let's all get this perfectly clear — this is not a quest. All we're doing is traveling into the Cambrian Empire to find evidence that Able Quizzler chanced across the Eye of Zoltar."

"Besides," said Moobin, "all quests need to be approved by the Questing Federation."

"Exactly," I said, "and we don't want *them* involved."

"So what if we do find evidence of the Eye of Zoltar?" asked Perkins.

"Then we continue, I guess, and see what we can find."

"It will be dangerous," said Dame Corby. "The Cambrian Empire always is. My uncle Herbert went there to do some mild megapike fishing and was stuffed and mounted by the Hotax."

"I'm thinking I shouldn't ask this, but what's a Hotax?" asked Perkins.

"A sort of cannibalistic savage with an unhealthy enthusiasm for taxidermy."

"I knew I shouldn't have asked."

"Don't forget to keep your angel traps on you at all times," said Prince Nasil, "especially when imminent death is close by. Did I tell you they like marshmallows?"

"Yes," Perkins and I said in unison.

"Take this with you," said Moobin as he scribbled on some *Kazam!* notepaper. Once done, he sealed it with red wax and handed it over.

"It's a letter of credit to the Ransom Clearance House," he explained, "for twenty thousand. We'd like to go higher, but that's all our life savings."

I looked around at the other sorcerers, who sagely nodded their agreement. It seemed that Boo was more valuable to them than I'd thought.

"Try to negotiate them down, won't you?" said Lady Mawgon.

I said I'd do my best, and put the note in my pocket.

"Right, then," I said to the group. "The duty roster is posted on the board, and don't forget to fill out your paperwork. Tiger will help you."

"Thanks for agreeing to come with me," I said to Perkins as the meeting broke up.

"I don't like the thought of you going on your own," he replied. "Besides, Kevin once let it slip that I would grow old in the Cambrian Empire. If I'm eventually going to retire there, it makes sense to at least visit the place. What's the plan, by the way?"

"We drive to the border in the Bugatti, posing as a couple going on vacation."

"And then what?"

I had to think quickly. "We . . . modify our plans as events unfold in front of us."

"You mean make it up as we go along?"

"Pretty much."

Perkins smiled. "Sounds like an excellent plan."

"Can I come?" asked the princess. I'd forgotten about her, but she must have slipped into the room and heard everything.

"It's too risky," I said. "Besides, we can't take a princess into the Cambrian Empire without an import license."

"But I'm not the princess right now. I'm an under-nourished orphan named Laura Scrubb with unsightly red rashes on my arms and legs."

"She's got a point," said Perkins.

I thought for a moment. The king and queen had told me she needed educating, and a fact-finding mission to the wildly unpredictable Cambrian Empire might be just the thing.

"Okay, Princess," I said, "you're in — but if you blow your cover and get kidnapped, your father will have to mortgage the kingdom to get you out. And think of what that will do to your inheritance."

"I'll take that risk," she said with a toss of her head. "Now, shall I be a Tralfamosaur research student from a wellborn family who has fallen on hard times but is otherwise treated as her high station befits?"

"No, you're to be my handmaiden."

Her face fell. "Will I have to do any ironing?"

"*Can* you do ironing?"

"No."

"Then probably not."

"Okay," she said with the first real smile I'd seen. "Game on."

TWELVE

To the Border by Royale

As soon as our local gas station was open in the morning, I checked the oil level and topped off the fuel on the Bugatti Royale. Just in case, I added a couple of cans of spare gasoline to the cavernous trunk, then drove back to Zambini Towers, where I packed a camp stove and a billycan for tea. I fetched several cases of one-meal expanding biscuits from Mabel and an enchanted tent that swore angrily to itself when self-pitching, thus saving you the effort.

Perkins was the first of the travelers to appear, dragging a leather suitcase behind him.

"A few things Moobin and Mawgon put together for

me," he explained. "Potions, spells, temporary newting compound, anticurse cream, that sort of stuff."

"Keep it well hidden," I said. "I don't want to spend the next week in prison, trying to convince a judge we're not dangerous magical extremists or something."

"Promise," said Perkins, and with a clever use of perspective manipulation, tucked his heavy suitcase into the Royale's glove compartment.

Tiger appeared. "This is the best guide I could find," he said, handing me a copy of *Enjoy the Unspoiled Charms of the Cambrian Empire Without Death or Serious Injury.*

"Not exactly a confidence-inspiring title, is it?"

"Not really. I got you this one, too."

He handed me *Death and Injury Avoidance Techniques for the Discerning Traveler in the Western Kingdoms.* I put both guides in the door pocket of the Royale, then briefed Tiger as best as I could while we waited for the others.

"Okay," I said, "Lady Mawgon and Moobin will be working on the spell for getting the mobile phone network running again. Keep Patrick of Ludlow confined to earthmoving, tree transplanting, and other lifting; let Dame Corby and the Prices do the subtle work. The Instant Camera Project will need testing once Mrs. Pola Roidenstock has finished perfecting the 'develop before your eyes' spelling. She'll need help thinking up a good name to sell it under, too. The rest you'll find on the board, but, well, you know pretty much how it works by now."

"I can contact you if I have any questions, right?"

"Not by the usual channels. Do you have your communi-conch?" Emperor Tharv had decreed that the Cambrian Empire should be isolated from the outside world; there were no phone lines, and all TV and radio channels were jammed. *Magic* communication, however, was still possible.

Tiger held up his conch shell, I showed him mine, and we touched them together to reinforce the twinning. They were a left and right pair, ideal for long-distance communication. We could have used winkles, which fit easily into the ear, but the reception would have been poor because limpets used the same bandwidth for their inane chitchat.

"I'll call every night at seven to check in," I told him. "If you don't hear from us for forty-eight hours, alert the king. And Tiger, would you take care of the Quarkbeast? They hunt them for fun in the Cambrian Empire, so there's no way he can come along."

"Sorry I'm late." With a *whoosh*ing of wings and a flurry of dust, Colin alighted on the pavement beside us, startling some passersby who ran away screaming in terror. "I'm the honored guest at a supermarket opening this morning, so I'll meet you inside the Cambrian Empire later on. It'll be easier for me to get across the border on my own anyway."

"Good luck with that. What news from Feldspar and the princess-guarding gig?"

"To be honest," said Colin, "I'm jealous I'm not doing it. Lots of grub, comfy digs, and a superb castle — just the right amount of ruined, and it's off the coast of Cornwall with angry seas all around."

"Is there a volcano?" I asked, knowing how such things go in and out of fashion.

"No, but Feldspar gets Wednesdays off, so we'll be seeing him from time to time, and the princess he's guarding has a relaxed attitude about being a prisoner; she often nips into Truro to meet friends. Better go now — see you in the Cambrian Empire!" And with another *whooshing* of wings, he was gone.

"Speaking of princesses," said Perkins, "I thought ours was coming with us?"

"I thought so too."

We waited another five minutes as I rechecked that everything was in the car.

"I left my angel trap behind," said Perkins. "No matter how much Nasil needs feathers for his carpet repair, entrapment just doesn't seem right."

"I left mine behind too."

The princess kept us waiting for a half hour. Partly because it was customary for princesses to never be on time for anything, and partly because she'd been fussing over her clothes. She had to dress as a handmaiden, of course, but insisted on being an upmarket one. She had been out shopping with Unstable Mabel, an expert in this particular field.

We headed west once she turned up, toward the six miles of frontier the Kingdom of Snodd shared with the Cambrian Empire. The route took us past Clifford, where my old orphanage stood gaunt and dark against the sky, tiles missing from the roof, broken glass in the windows, the shutters askew. One of the gable ends had collapsed into a pile of rubble, exposing the interior to rain. Not much different from when I lived there, in fact. I thought of dropping in to see Mother Zenobia, but we had work to do.

We crossed the border post leading out of the Kingdom of Snodd without a problem, then drove slowly across the bridge that spanned the River Wye, which marked the divide between the nations. On the Cambrian riverbank were tank traps, minefields, and razor wire, and beyond this were batteries of anti-aircraft guns. Behind *them* were obsolete landships manned by a ragtag collection of Cambrian Army irregulars.

"Are the fortifications there to keep people in or out?" asked Perkins as we drove past several Cambrian border guards who eyed us suspiciously.

"Probably a bit of both."

We stopped behind a line of vehicles once we were off the bridge and waited to be called forward to the customs post. To our left was a large board listing the many items that were illegal to import. Some were quite straightforward, like weapons, aircraft, record players, and "magical paraphernalia," but others were quite bizarre, such as spinning wheels, peanuts, flatworms, Bunsen burners, and anything "overtly red in color."

The Cambrian Empire was a large, ramshackle, and lawless nation composed almost entirely of competing warlords, warring tribes, and family fiefdoms, all of whom squabbled constantly. Despite the constant small fights, the citizens of Cambria were fiercely loyal to Emperor Tharv, who lived in a magnificent palace within the fashionably war-torn and picturesquely ruined capital city of Cambrianopolis.

Despite its being one of the largest nations in the UnUK, occupying half of what was once Wales, very few people lived there, possibly due to the aforementioned bickering. Most visitors entered to explore or hunt in the Empty Quarter, a twelve-hundred-square-mile tract of ex-Dragonlands that had moved seamlessly into the Cambrian Wildlife Trust upon the death of a dragon fifty years earlier. Many had asked why Emperor Tharv would do something so sensible, but his madness, it seemed, was unpredictable. He once claimed to have trained a thousand killer elephants to lay waste to the Ununited Kingdoms, and also bragged about a plan to destabilize the yogurt market by flooding the industry with cheap imports. But he had also instigated the best national health system in the kingdoms, along with a robust childcare program that allowed women to go out marauding, thieving, and kidnapping with their husbands.

"It says here that most foreign currency in the empire is earned through jeopardy tourism," said Perkins, reading from *Enjoy the Unspoiled Charms of the Cambrian Empire Without Death or Serious Injury*. "Such tourists are after excitement and adventure, even if it means possible loss of life."

"I guess that's where this bunch is going." I indicated the steady stream of men and women eagerly waiting to cross into the nation.

"For some it will be for the last time," said Perkins. "It says here tourism mortality rates haven't dropped below eighteen percent in the past nine decades."

I looked again at the line of tourists. If Perkins was correct, eighteen of every hundred people wouldn't be coming back.

"My father sold Emperor Tharv an option on my daughter for his grandson," said the princess absently.

"You don't have any children," said Perkins, "and neither does Emperor Tharv. How could Tharv offer the hand of a grandson he doesn't yet have?"

"It's called 'dabbling in the princess options market,'"

she replied, "and it's not uncommon. In fact, a third of the emperor's private income is earned on marriage-trading options. Last year he paid fifty thousand moolah for an option on the hand in marriage of my second daughter *if* I ever have one, for his grandson, *if* he has one. His grandson doesn't have to accept the option, but if he does, it'll cost the empire another million. Nice little earner for the Kingdom of Snodd's coffers. For Emperor Tharv, he has now gambled on not only securing a good marriage for his grandson at a competitive price, but also gained a tradable asset—he can sell that option to anyone he pleases. If I actually *have* a second daughter, the option jumps in value, and if she turns out to be beautiful, clever, and witty, Tharv can make even more money from selling the option. Conversely, if my second daughter turns out to be a vapid, air-headed little dingbat without the traditional beauty with which princesses are associated, his option value sinks to nothing."

"So *that's* how the options market works," said Perkins. "And there was I, thinking it was complex."

"Is that why some queens have so many children?" I asked. "For the option rights?"

"Exactly," said the princess. "The King of Shropshire managed to fund most of his highway network via the trading options on his twenty-nine children."

There was a pause.

"I don't suppose," began Perkins, "you know anything about collateralized debt obligations, do you?"

"Of course," said the princess, who seemed oddly at ease with complex financial transactions. "First you must understand that loss-making financial mechanisms can be sold to offset—"

Luckily we were saved from that explanation when a Skybus Aeronautics delivery truck in front of us was allowed through, and the guards waved us into the border post of the Cambrian Empire.

THIRTEEN

The Cambrian Empire

I pulled forward and rolled down the window as the border guard came toward us. It was only then that I noticed that the Helping Hand™ was still firmly attached to the steering wheel. As illegal magical contraband, it was likely to be confiscated. There was no time to remove it, so I hid my own hand high in my cuff and slipped my sleeve over the Helping Hand™, pretending it was my own. The border guard stopped at the driver's-side window and looked at me suspiciously.

"Hello!" I said brightly.

"Good afternoon." He looked at me, then at the car. "Is this . . . a Bugatti Royale?"

"Yes."

"What's the chassis number?"

"It's 41.151," I replied promptly. Everyone asked me for this number and the body type, and added a stiff admonishment for using the Bugatti as my daily vehicle. Apparently the Bugatti Royale is quite rare, but we needed a car, and it *was* a car, first and foremost.

"I see," said the guard, "and why is one of your hands really hairy and like a man's?"

I lifted my arm and the Helping Hand™ did what it was meant to do—help. The hand moved with my arm and looked eerily as though it were attached to me.

"I lost my own hand in a car accident," I said, thinking quickly. "This one belonged to a landship engineer who was accidentally dragged into the number three engine. All they could salvage of him was an ear, this hand, and a left leg that is currently doing useful service attached to a bus conductor somewhere in Sheffield. I've not heard where the ear is these days."

"And the tattoo about pies?" he asked, gesturing toward the *No More Pies* tattoo on the back of the Hand.

"You know, we never did find out."

"Okay." The guard seemed to have fallen for my capacity for invention. "Papers?"

I handed him our IDs and personal-injury waivers, mandatory for all visitors to the risk-desirable nation.

He stared at them for a moment. "Purpose of visit?"

"Negotiation for the safe release of a friend," I said,

showing him the letter from the Cambrian Empire's Ransom Clearance House, "but before that, my companion and I will enjoy a day or two of vacation in the Empty Quarter, accompanied by my handmaiden. Who knows? We might even indulge in some mild jeopardy."

He looked at us all and then saluted smartly. "Welcome to the Cambrian Empire. There's a tourist information office down the road where you can decide which particularly perilous pursuit you'd like to attempt first."

The small border town of Whitney was doing a brisk trade preparing tourists for their excursions. The shops sold supplies, maps, guidebooks, and Get Me Out of Here emergency escape package deals at grossly inflated prices. Parked on the street was a parade of armored four-wheel-drive trucks, ready to take visitors into the interior. I parked the Bugatti and turned off the engine.

"Keep an eye on the car, one of you," I said. "I'm going to find a guide."

I climbed out and headed for the tourist information office. I hadn't gone five steps when I was accosted by young backpacker carrying a guitar. He was wearing a baggy shirt open at the chest, flip-flops, fashionably ripped jeans, and had beads woven into his blond hair.

"Hey, Dragonslayer babe."

"I'm on vacation," I said, used to being recognized in public.

"The name's Curtis," said Curtis. "Want to hang out, play some guitar, talk about the latest fashions and the best places to be seen, and just generally chill?"

"You must be mistaking me for someone who is shallow and indifferent," I said. "Goodbye."

"Wait, wait." Curtis clearly did not take *no* for an answer. "The full name is Rupert Curtis Osbert Chippenworth III. From the nation of Financia. *Chippenworth,* yes?"

He said it as though I was expected to know who he was, and yes, I had heard of the Chippenworths — a family of huge wealth and privilege in the financial center of the kingdoms.

"Let me guess," I said. "You're here to have a few dangerous scrapes so once you have been shoehorned into your cushy and undemanding job, you'll have something interesting in your past to brighten an otherwise unremarkable life?"

"Pretty much," Curtis said, apparently unfazed by my assessment. "So listen, I know you run Kazam, so got any *S*? Y'know, something to while away the dull evenings between bouts of excitement and terror?"

"*S?*"

"*Spells,*" he said in a low voice. "The weirder the better, but none of that 'changing into animals' stuff because it can totally mess with your head."

He laughed in a clumsy attempt to charm me. The

use of magic for recreational purposes was stupid, dangerous, and irresponsible. Supplying mind- or body-altering spells to idiots like Curtis would also have you drummed out of the magic industry quicker than you could say *zork*.

"No," I said, "and here's why: You'll start with something simple like a Pollyanna Stone that tells you what you want to hear. Pretty soon you'll move on to stronger and heavier spells that promote unrealistic levels of optimism and self-delusion. After that you'll be always looking for the next spell, and when the spells lose their power you'll be lost, frightened, and bewildered, and your life will tip into a downward spiral of recrimination and despair."

"Okay, okay," he said, backing away from my icy stare. "I only asked. Boy, some people are so square."

He returned to where his friends were waiting and they went into a huddle, throwing the occasional dirty look in my direction. I ignored them and entered the tourist information office.

The woman behind the desk was middle-aged and dressed in the traditional Cambrian badger skins. A tattoo on the left side of her face denoted her clan and status, and she wore an ABTA Silver Star medal on her left breast to denote tour guide valor, which probably had something to do with her missing left arm.

"Welcome, noble traveler and adventurer," said

the woman in a long-rehearsed patter, "to the land that health and safety forgot. In these risk-averse times, the Cambrian Empire is one of the few places where danger is actually dangerous. The possibility of actual death brings fear and excitement to even the most mundane pastimes; the adrenaline surge that comes by cheating death is a wild ride you will wish to repeat time and time again. Now, what do you fancy?"

She indicated a board behind her, with each activity listed next to a price; its level of danger was marked by way of a Calculated Fatality Index. The most dangerous was a six-day Wrestling with Flesh-Eating Slugs trip at fifty-eight percent, which I took to mean that for every hundred tourists willing to risk the dangers, fifty-eight would end up as semi-digested gloop. Below that was Tralfamosaur Hunting, with a fatality index of forty-two percent. The list went down in danger from there, past Prodding a Hotax with a Stick, to Searching for the Source of the River Wye, and then to Watching Tralfamosaur from a Distance before the least dangerous activity of all, a shopping trip to Cambrianopolis. While relatively risk-free by Cambrian standards, this could still lose one visitor out of a hundred.

"Mostly to crush injury, holdups, and food poisoning," explained the tourist officer when I asked, "and the fatality index does rise to two-point-two percent during the January sales. Now, what are you after?"

I had to think carefully. If I just said we were going to Llangurig, I wouldn't even need a guide. But if Quizzler had been right and the Eye of Zoltar was with Sky Pirate Wolff, I'd need the best guide there was. I decided to opt for the most adventurous scenario.

"Party of three to discover the legendary Leviathans' Graveyard, please," I replied, "and there to meet up with Sky Pirate Wolff. And we'd like to go by way of Llangurig to visit a friend."

The woman looked more amused than shocked. "Yes, yes, very funny," she said. "Seriously, what would you like to do?"

"As I said."

"Listen," she said, lowering her voice and beckoning me closer, "the reason we don't list excursions to search for the not-very-likely Leviathans' Graveyard is *because* of Sky Pirate Wolff. The last two expeditions suffered an eighty-six percent fatality index. Risk of death is our selling point; almost certain death is not. Dead tourists don't come back and spend more money."

"I'll be okay," I said. "I'm big into peril."

"Oh, yeah?" She sounded unconvinced. "How big?"

"I . . . sleep in the same room as a Quarkbeast."

The tourist woman blinked twice. The Quarkbeast's fearsome reputation was known all over the kingdoms. "Leviathans' Graveyard and Pirate Wolff, eh?"

"If it's not too much trouble."

"Okay, then," said the woman. "There *is* one guide who might be willing to help you search for the Leviathans' Graveyard, but it won't be cheap and comes with an eighty-six percent fatality index. Is that acceptable?"

I told her it was, and she asked me to wait outside while she made arrangements. I thanked her and walked back out into the autumn sunshine.

The Bugatti was gone. Our luggage was sitting in the dust by the roadside, and sitting on top of our luggage was Perkins.

"Where's the car?"

"Requisitioned by agents acting for Emperor Tharv," said Perkins meekly. "I tried to stop them, but there were eight of them, and they all had very sharp swords."

"Couldn't you have done a simple occluding spell or something?"

"Yes, well, I could have, but it all happened so fast. They did say thank you very politely and issued a receipt."

Crime in the Cambrian Empire was always business, never personal. You would not be a victim of crime here without an apology, an explanation of why you were being robbed, and a receipt to facilitate an insurance claim. Perkins passed me the receipt, which conveyed in very official-sounding language that the car had been claimed by the emperor, as anything in the nation could be. I would be compensated to the value of one Bugatti Royale.

"That's a blow," I said, looking around. "What about the princess? Don't tell me they requisitioned her as well?"

"No, she went shopping."

The princess returned a few moments later. "I had ID tags made so our bodies can be identified, just in case," she said cheerfully, handing us each a disc of metal. "The man in the shop said they were Tralfamosaur-gastric-juice– and flesh-eating-slug-ooze–resistant. Where's the car?"

I showed her the receipt.

"Oh," she said, studying the piece of paper, "how interesting. Since it's issued on Emperor Tharv's order, technically it's a one Bugatti banknote."

"And how would we redeem it?" asked Perkins. "Go and ask Tharv for the equivalent in sports cars and take the change in motorcycles and hubcaps?"

The princess shrugged. "I don't know. Shall I go and see if I can find a rental car?"

"Make sure it's good on all terrain," I replied, "and armored."

The princess trotted off, enjoying the newfound freedom her handmaiden disguise offered her.

While we waited, Perkins and I checked our budget. I hadn't thought we would need to rent a car, and a specialist guide was going to cost. We had enough, I figured, as long as we didn't eat out too often and didn't buy any tourist knickknacks.

"Almost like a vacation, isn't it?" said Perkins, watching tourists move here and there, organizing their jeopardy gleefully.

"If you say so," I replied absently, since I'd never been on a vacation and wouldn't know what to do if one chanced along.

"Sort of peaceful," said Perkins. "Tranquil, even."

At that precise moment, there was a tremendous explosion close by, then another and another. The air was soon filled with a sound like rolling thunder, so loud and heavy it seemed directionless. I looked up and saw that the anti-aircraft guns less than a hundred yards away were firing into the sky. I had once been on the receiving end of anti-aircraft fire while attempting to escape on a flying carpet, and it is most unpleasant. My heart froze as a distinctive silhouette in the sky jerked and twisted while the anti-aircraft shells exploded around it.

"Oh, dear," said Perkins. "That's Colin."

FOURTEEN

Colin's Fall

And so it was. Colin, obviously finished with his supermarket opening, had flown over the border to join us and had been mistaken, we supposed, for a trespassing aircraft. We could do little but watch anxiously as Colin attempted to turn and head back the way he had come. Disoriented by the smoke, noise, and hot shrapnel, he wandered farther into the Cambrian Empire's airspace.

Eventually there was a puff of black smoke, and Colin rolled onto his back and began to fall toward the earth. We could see that one wing was tattered and frayed, and the other beat the air ferociously in a vain attempt to control his descent.

I looked at Perkins; his index fingers were already

pointing at the dragon as he mumbled a few words under his breath.

"Looking good," I said. Colin had stopped struggling as Perkins transformed him — sadly, not into anything usefully energy absorbing, but glass. The impact upon hitting the ground would be catastrophic.

"Try again," I said, as quietly and as relaxed as I could.

Perkins did try again, and suddenly Colin became an ornate decorative dragon carved from marble. The impact would have the same fatal effect, and possibly leave a large hole, too.

"Okay, okay, I've got it," said Perkins, and let fly again.

Colin was less than a thousand feet from the ground and still whirling as the air rushed past his now-rigid wings. Gravity, never a close friend of dragons, would surely raise the historical score to dragons: nil, gravity: sixty-three.

Perkins tried again. Colin changed to bronze, then to alabaster, then became a shiny metallic lucky Chinese dragon with a waving front leg. All of these feats, while powerful and complex in themselves, helped us not one bit. As Colin passed the three-hundred-foot mark and was changed by Perkins into a delicate ice sculpture, I took the last resort. I punched Perkins hard on the arm with the Helping Hand™. It was a risky undertaking and

could have gone either way: he could get the spell right
or fail utterly.

"What the——?"

"Get it together," I snapped, "or we're done."

Actually, Perkins and I were not yet really a couple,
but I had to think that the possibility might be something he valued in order to give him an emotional surge
and get the spell right. With only two hundred feet and
a few seconds until a nasty, shattered end, Perkins tried
again and Colin changed abruptly to a dark matte black
substance.

I held my breath.

Colin hit the road with the loudest, deepest, and
densest-sounding *thud* I had ever heard. He narrowly
missed two backpackers and a car as he quickly spread
out into a flat disc about six inches thick. In an instant
the elasticity in the rubber molecules that now made up
his body sprang back into shape and Colin was catapulted
high into the air. He went so high that the anti-aircraft
guns opened up again, but this time none of the shell
bursts came close. Colin was soon on his way back down,
this time five hundred yards or so farther away, and a
second later catapulted back up. We watched with growing dismay as Rubber Colin bounced off into the distance
and vanished behind a low hill to the north.

"Blast," said Perkins, lowering his now-steaming
fingers. Magic was strictly forbidden in the empire, but

fortunately no one seemed to have noticed that he was responsible. Perkins suddenly looked tired and sat on our luggage, head in hands.

"You okay?" I asked.

"I think so," he said. "I've not spelled that strongly before. Do I look okay?"

He looked drained and somehow . . . different. More world-weary. I told him he probably needed an early night, and he nodded in agreement.

"How far do you think he went?" I stared at the horizon.

Perkins looked at his watch. "He'll be bouncing for the next ten minutes or so. Best guess, thirty or forty miles."

"How much wizidrical energy would it take to change him back?"

"Bucketloads if you want it done immediately," replied Perkins thoughtfully, "but the spell will wear off on its own within a week or two. Either way, he's not flying out of here on his own—not with a wing like that."

"But he's safe as a rubber dragon until he turns back?"

"Sure—as long as no one tries to make car tires or doorstops or rain boots out of him. But it's not all bad," he added. "At least he'll be waterproof if it rains."

I sighed. This was a bad start to our search. I pulled my compass out of my bag and took a bearing on the hill behind which Colin had bounced, then drew a line on my map. It was, luckily enough, pretty much in the same direction we had to travel. If our calculations were correct, Colin would run out of bounce not far from Llangurig.

The princess returned five minutes later. "The rental car agency had run out of armored cars," she said, "so I persuaded them to upgrade us to a military half-track at the same rate. I can't drive, so they'll deliver it to us here." She looked at Perkins, who was still sitting with head in hands. "Problems?"

I told her about Rubber Colin.

"Ah," she said. "I wondered what that was that bounced past. Do you think we should upgrade this to a quest, what with searching for rubber dragons as well as the Eye and Pirate Wolff and stuff?"

"It is *not* a quest," I said emphatically. "If it was, we'd need to register with the International Questing Federation, adhere by their code of conduct, and pay them two thousand moolah into the bargain."

The Questing Federation was powerful and would insist on a minimum staffing requirement: at least one strong-and-silent warrior, a sagelike old man, and quite possibly a giant and a dwarf, too. All of them would cost bundles, not just in salary but hotel bills. A quest these days needed serious financial backing.

"No," I said even more emphatically. "This is a search, plain and simple."

"Jenny?" said Perkins, still with his eyes closed.

"Yes?"

"Why *were* they shooting at Colin? At barely the size of a pony and with fiery breath no more powerful than a blow lamp, he's not exactly dangerous."

A voice chirped behind us. "They shot him down because all aerial traffic in the Cambrian Empire is banned."

I turned to see who was speaking, and that was when we met Addie Powell.

FIFTEEN

Addie Powell

Her face was dirty, she wore no shoes, and she was dressed in a loose, poncho-style jacket tied at the waist with a leather belt, from which hung a dagger. It was the costume favored by the Silurians, a tribe on the lower slopes of the Cambrian Mountains. The three small stars tattooed on the left side of her face told me she was a daughter of middle rank, a braid in the left side of her hair denoted that she had no parents, and a ring on the third toe of her left foot indicated that she held financial responsibility for someone, probably a younger sibling or a grandmother. I guessed she was about twelve or thirteen, but it was hard to tell. Children grow up fast in the empire. She could have been as young as ten.

"Hungry?" I asked, for Silurians value hospitality above everything. The girl nodded, and I dug some cheese out of my bag and offered it to her. She paused, approached warily with one hand resting on the hilt of her dagger, then took the cheese and sniffed it.

"Extra-mature Hereford Old Contemptible," she said expertly, "with chives. My favorite. Thank you."

She sat on a rock beside us, took a bite of the cheese, chewed for a moment, then said, "New in the empire?"

"About an hour ago."

"Was that rubber dragon anything to do with you?"

"Um — no."

"Ah-ha. Did I just see your Bugatti being towed away?"

I nodded.

"Not unusual," said the child. "Our glorious emperor is a bit car crazy. He sees a car he likes, he takes. But at least he's willing to pay for it. He's odd like that. He cries bitterly when he signs an execution order and always pardons the victim after it's been carried out."

"There's a lot to be said for not holding a grudge."

"I suppose so. Why do you have *No More Pies* tattooed on the back of your hand?"

"Actually," I replied, "it's not mine at all."

I took the Helping Hand™ out of my cuff and tweaked the second knuckle for two seconds to put the Hand into sleep mode. The Helping Hand™ made some rapid hand signals as pre-shutdown diagnostics, then went limp. The girl did not seem taken aback, but if you were brought up in the strife-torn Cambrian Empire, a hand without a body attached probably wasn't such a big deal.

"You're a sorcerer?" she asked.

"I *know* sorcerers," I told her. "The Hand is enchanted, but not by me."

"I see," said the girl, "and why do you want to find Pirate Wolff?"

I raised an eyebrow. "News travels fast."

"Gossip has been clocked at 47.26 mph out here," explained the child. "Gossip is so fast, in fact, that we have no need for newspapers or a postal service. The only place where news does not travel is across the border. I know nothing of your culture other than you seem mostly well-meaning, are ridiculously wealthy, and regard anything dangerous as somehow fun."

She was right. Little information crossed between our borders. If you were visiting across the border, a war might be raging in your own country and the first you'd know about it was when you returned home to find your house a smoking ruin, with armed militia eating the contents of your pantry and *Viva el Presidente* painted on the walls.

"So," said Addie, "what do you want with the pirate captain?"

"We're curious," I said, not wanting to give too much away, "and we like an adventure. We hear Wolff rides the Cloud Leviathans, and we'd like to see a Leviathan up close."

She stared at us for a moment, head cocked, sizing us up.

"You're right," she said at last. "The best place to start is the legendary Leviathans' Graveyard, where the huge beasts go to die. Many have sought the ivory in the dead animals' jaws, and many have been lost in the attempt. Actually, *all* have been lost in the attempt, which is why it's kind of off the tourist trail. When can you leave?"

"As soon as our transport arrives, and our guide."

"Your guide is here," said the girl with a smile. "My name is Addie Powell, and I will take you to Cadir Idris as long as we can agree on the terms."

"Don't take this the wrong way," I said, "but you seem quite young for a guide."

Addie narrowed her eyes. "Don't take *this* the wrong way, but the last person who said that ignored my advice and is now carrion up on the Empty Quarter. If they'd done what I'd said, they'd be inheriting a kingdom about now. Besides, it's not the age, it's the mileage that counts."

She definitely looked as though she had seen the mileage. Her eyes had a hard look in them, and I noticed a scar on one cheek and that one of her fingers was missing.

I apologized, told her that I had complete confidence in her abilities, and we all shook hands. I introduced everyone, even the princess, who made an awkward half curtsey in order to remain convincing in her handmaiden role.

"Will it be risky?" I asked as we sat down to negotiate the fee.

"Risky?" said Addie. "Put it this way: Statistically speaking, you're dead already, your bones gnawed by wild animals and bleached in the sun, your life nothing more than fractured lost moments and memories for those who knew you best."

"Very . . . jolly," I said.

Addie shrugged. "There are many dangers, and I don't want you to start whining when someone gets eaten or drowned or something. But here's the deal: A golden moolarine per person for wherever you want to go for the next week, and for that I can promise you a fifty percent survival rate."

"The woman in the tourist office said the fatality index was eighty-six percent."

Addie smiled. "I can offer better odds than the official rate. It is a gift passed down from one tour operator to the next—a sixth sense that tells me how many we will lose. I am never wrong. But let's be clear on this:

Half of your party will die, get lost, or be eaten. Are you sure you want to shoulder that responsibility?"

I looked at Perkins, who nodded.

"Yes," I said.

"Then we have a deal," said Addie, and we shook on it.

At that moment an ex-military half-track turned up in a cloud of yellow marzoleum fumes. I'd not seen one up close before. The front two wheels were for steering, and at the rear were caterpillar tracks, like on a landship. The vehicle was protected by a quarter-inch of armored plate on the sides and bottom. The top was open to the air but could be covered with a canvas tarpaulin. Perkins and I looked at the half-track doubtfully.

"Where we're going, the roads are bad," said Addie. "This was a good call. We leave in half an hour. Wait here."

"Fifty percent casualties?" said Perkins as soon as Addie had gone and we had signed the half-track's rental agreement. "That's —"

"One and a half of us, plus two and a half fingers if you count the Helping Hand™," said the princess. "I better not be the one half dead, especially in Laura's body."

"You should be more serious, Princess," said Perkins.

"And you should hold your tongue when talking impertinently to royalty, Mr. Porkins."

"It's *Perkins.*"

"Perkins, Porkins, Twitkins—like I give a monkey's—"

"No one is dying or losing fingers," I interrupted, "and we've got a few magical moves that should help us get home safely. And Princess, hold your tongue. You're Laura Scrubb right now, and will be until we get you back to the palace."

We chucked our baggage inside the half-track and I climbed in to figure out how to drive the vehicle. It didn't seem much different than the Bugatti, in fact, and I was just reading the part in the instruction manual about track maintenance procedures when a voice made me look up.

"Hey!" It was Curtis and two others—all young, all dressed kind of hip, all looking a bit smug, confident, and stupid.

"Hey, Dragonslayer dude," said Curtis, grinning at me, "heard you were heading off through the Empty Quarter toward Cadir Idris to do some Cloud Leviathan spotting. Sounds dangerous, and, well, we're like totally up for it."

"This is a private expedition," I said sharply. "You're not coming."

"Too late," he said. "We've already okayed it with your tour guide, and she's taken our money."

"Is that true?" I asked Addie, who had just walked up with a bedroll on her shoulder.

"Yes, indeed," she said. "If it comes to a scrap, seven people are better than four."

"I really don't think —"

"I'd like you to trust my judgment on this one, Miss Strange."

We stared at each other. There was something she wasn't telling me, but I had to trust her — only a fool ignores a local guide.

"Okay, welcome aboard," I said, and indicated the others. "This is Perkins, and this is my maid, Laura Scrubb."

"Awesome," said Curtis. "These are my buddies. Meet Ignatius Catflap."

He indicated the shorter of the two. Ignatius had a shock of black hair and seemed to be trying a little too hard to grow a beard. He was chewing gum and his red-rimmed hung-over eyes blinked stupidly.

"Hi," he said. "This is just like going on a trip to some weird and awesome dangerous place."

"It's not *like* it, you dope," said the princess. "It is."

Ignatius stared at her. "A little bit forward for a handmaiden, aren't you?"

"She's kind of a bodyguard as well," I said. "Try to be nice to the morons, Laura."

"Yes, ma'am."

"Ignatius's family owns the Catflap Corporation," piped up Curtis, as though this were exciting and relevant. "They make novelty placemats."

"They do what?" I asked.

"Placemats," said Ignatius. "Mats to put your plates on at mealtimes. I'm here doing research into our planned Extreme Jeopardy line. Each mat will depict a frightful end suffered by someone here in the Cambrian Empire. What do you think?"

"I'll tell you what I think: *Tasteless* is a word invented just for you."

"And over here is Ralph," said Curtis, eager to move on, "another of my old school friends."

The third traveler was tall and slender, and rubbed his hands together nervously when he spoke. He seemed to be the least idiotic of the trio and looked to be here against his better judgment.

"Hello," he said quietly. "Ralph D. Nalor. Pleased to meet you. I'm—um—twenty in June."

"Anything else?" I asked.

He thought for a moment. "Nothing springs to mind."

After shaking hands—it was best to at least attempt to get along, I thought—and after they'd stored their baggage in the back of the half-track, Addie called for our attention.

"Right," she said, climbing onto the half-track's hood. "The first thing to remember is there is only one rule: Do as I tell you, no matter how insane or idiotic it sounds. If we are held up by armed bandits, I do the talking. If we are all kidnapped, I do the talking. If *you* are kidnapped, then make polite conversation and have tea with your captors until I come to bargain for your release. That might take up to a year, *but I will come.* Trying to escape is considered unspeakably rude, as are wailing, crying, and pleading for your life, and these are the quickest and easiest ways to get yourself killed. The tribes who populate the Cambrian Empire are a murderous bunch of cutthroats, bandits, and ne'er-do-wells, but they are polite, hospitable, and won't tolerate bad manners. Does everyone understand?"

"Yeah, little girl, anything you say," said Curtis with a smirk.

Addie looked at him, and in a moment her dagger had punctured Curtis's collar and pinned him to a tree.

"Sorry," said Addie, "did you say something?"

"I said," replied Curtis, clearly rattled, "that you're totally the boss-dude."

"Okay. Now, all together: What's the one rule?"

"Do as you say," we said in unison.

"Good," said Addie, and five minutes later we pulled the half-track into the road and headed for the interior of the Cambrian Empire.

SIXTEEN

Addie Explains

We headed north along the main Cambrianopolis road. I was driving, with the Helping Hand™ making easy work of the half-track's ridiculously heavy steering. Perkins was in the passenger seat with Addie between us, and the princess just behind. The fields we drove past contained cultivated almond tree groves, from which refined marzoleum was derived; the syrupy oil was used for fondant icing, sunblock, window putty, aviation spirit, and pretty much anything in between.

Curtis and his friends had been standing in the back of the vehicle because they thought they looked cool and manly, at least until the dust, flies, and road debris got in their eyes and mouths. With eyes streaming and throats sore, they bravely sat in the rear instead.

I looked back to make sure they weren't within earshot, then said to Addie, "Why were you so eager for Curtis and his dopey friends to come along?"

"Simple. We need those three to make up the fifty percent fatalities."

This made me uneasy. "That's not a great thing to hear."

"Perhaps not, but this is: You'll go home safely, and Curtis and his losers get to be the honored dead. What's not great about that?"

"A lot," I replied. "Everyone matters, even those three."

"I don't think they do," said the princess. "If they never came back, it wouldn't change much. Their families would be a bit glum, but they'd get over it. Besides, you don't come to Cambria without accepting at least the possibility of tragedy."

"I know you're not actually a handmaiden," said Addie astutely, "what with your un-servantlike manner and all, but you speak my language."

"Well, I don't," I replied. "I'm not having those three used as cannon fodder."

"They knew the risks," said Addie, "and so did you when you agreed to the trip. I offered you a fifty percent fatality index, and you accepted it. No point getting all precious about it now."

"We were taking the responsibility for ourselves," I said, "not other people."

"And you still are," said Addie with a shrug. "I can only guarantee the fifty percent. I can't say for certain who will live and who will die."

Addie's logic was strange, but did ring true—sort of. We fell silent for a few moments.

"Have you lost many tourists?" asked Perkins.

"Hundreds," said Addie nonchalantly. "I used to keep count, but after a while there were just too many. You always remember the first and the youngest and the one you liked most, but after that they're simply a blur."

"Wait a moment," said the princess. "Jennifer, me, Porkins, you, Ignatius, Ralph, and Curtis only make up seven. If you expect a fifty percent casualty rate, how does that work?"

"We'll pick up someone on the trip," said Addie. "We always do. It'll pan out, you'll see. I have a gift."

"I'll believe that when I see it," said the princess. "What's that up ahead?"

On the road someone had painted SORRY in large letters.

"Hunker down!" shouted Addie, and we all did as she said. The half-track had an armored flap that could be swung down in front of the windshield in case of attack.

Addie reached up and released the catch; the flap swung down with a bang, leaving the driver a small slot to see through. A second or two later, the first bullet hit the vehicle, followed by a second, then a third.

"Don't stop," Addie told me.

The air was suddenly heavy with the crack of rifle fire and the metallic *spang* of bullets as they bounced off the half-track.

"Okay," said Addie as if we were doing nothing more unusual than driving through heavy hail. "Here's the plan: We'll enter the Empty Quarter soon and stay at the Claerwin Reservoir tonight; they have some pod-poles. Tomorrow afternoon we'll reach Llangurig and visit your friend. We'll stay the night there and then head off into Mountain Silurian territory to get to the foot of Cadir Idris. We'll search for the Leviathans' Graveyard on its rocky slopes until you give up—which you will, because the graveyard doesn't exist—and then return."

"Good plan," I said, "although our plans really depend on what my friend in Llangurig says—I'm not keen on going any farther than we have to."

I wasn't wild about the idea of climbing the mountain. Cadir Idris was known not just for its stark beauty—a soaring pinnacle of sheer rock almost six thousand feet high, it was the highest in the Cambrian Range—but for the number of people who had vanished on its rocky slopes. Despite numerous expeditions, no one in modern times had reached the summit, or if anyone had, they had not returned to tell about it. I'd risk our lives if there was a chance of finding the Eye of Zoltar, but not if there wasn't.

"Don't worry," said Addie, mistaking my silence for nervousness. "Cadir Idris will be fun."

"Ever been there?"

"No. That's why it will be fun."

As we drove on, the rifle fire slowly diminished until it stopped completely, and Addie gave us the all clear to raise our heads above the armored body of the half-track.

"What was that?" Perkins asked her.

"What was what?"

"The rifle fire?"

"Oh, *that*. I don't know. The local warlord could be annoyed that they built the bypass around his village. It's cut travel time by a third and reduced congestion, but it also means he can't extract money from travelers — so he fires on any car that passes. It's nothing really serious."

"Unless you're not in an armored car," said Perkins.

"But everyone is," said Addie simply. "Take the next left and continue on for about twenty miles."

The half-track was neither fast nor quiet, so to conserve fuel and our eardrums I drove as slowly as practical. We spent the time taking in the spectacular local countryside. It was utterly unspoiled. There were few modern buildings, no shopping malls or fast food joints, and no billboards, electricity poles, or other modern contrivances. Away from the almond groves, broadleaf forests covered much of the lowlands; the small houses dotted haphazardly about were constructed of stone with riveted steel roofs, and all were fortified in some way.

"What's a somnubuvorus?" asked the princess, who had been reading *Enjoy the Unspoiled Charms of the Cambrian Empire Without Death or Serious Injury.*

"It looks like a cross between a baobab and a turnip," explained Addie, "and it's about the size of a phone booth. It's actually not a plant at all, but a fungus that releases puffs of hallucinogenic spores into the breeze. If you inhale them, you become suddenly convinced that being near the somnubuvorus will enlighten you with devastatingly relevant social and political commentary. Once there, of course, you are soon overcome with a sense of listlessness and torpidity, and fall fast asleep."

"It sounds like what would happen if you weaponized French cinema," I observed.

"Pretty much, if French cinema secretes enzymes from its roots and dissolves you while you sleep."

"Yag," said the princess, and returned to the book.

I had a thought. "Why did the gunners shoot down Col—I mean, that dragon just before we left?"

"That's easily explained," said Addie. "Emperor Tharv deplores mankind's need to defy gravity, so he's banned all aerial traffic above his empire. Because he wants to be equitable and just, he thinks that it would be unfair if birds, bats, insects, and so forth were allowed to fly — so he banned them, too."

"And that includes dragons?"

"Right."

"But that's absurd," said Perkins. "Are you saying that geese and pigeons and bees and bats and dragons and stuff can't fly at all in the empire?"

"That's exactly what I'm saying."

"And how does the emperor expect to enforce that?"

Addie shrugged. "He can't, obviously, except —"

"Except what?"

"Have you seen anything that flies since you arrived?"

Now that she mentioned it, I didn't think I had.

"If there are no airplanes in Cambria," said Perkins, pointing toward two trucks stopped in the road while their drivers chatted, "what about them?"

The trucks were painted with the pale blue logo of Skybus Aeronautics. As we watched, the one heading into the empire lumbered forward with a grinding of gears while the one heading out accelerated away.

"Aircraft components," said Addie. "Emperor Tharv may not support flying, but he does apparently have an aircraft component factory somewhere in the empire."

"It doesn't sound like a very consistent policy, does it?"

Addie shrugged. "Perhaps not. But as insane as he is, he does okay for us. Do you get free health care and child support in your country?"

"No."

"We do. And even though the Cambrian Empire boasts the lowest life expectancy in the kingdoms, at least we get to live our short lives in a way that is full of interest, fun, and adventure. Which would you prefer? A short life as a tiger or a long one as a rabbit? I'm with the tiger."

"The only place where we don't agree," I replied after some thought, "is that I think everyone should have the *choice* to be a tiger or a rabbit — or anything in-between."

SEVENTEEN

Flesh-Eating Slugs

We stopped for lunch at one of the many tearooms along the road, each designated a neutral area where even rival warlords could stop and have a cup of tea and a currant bun without risking a dagger between the shoulder blades. The lunch was simple yet tasty, but marred by Curtis's and Ignatius's behavior, as they thought it amusing to talk loudly, flick food at each other, and generally act like the complete idiots they were. We apologized as we left, and were told cheerily that youthful high spirits were generally tolerated, but if we set foot inside the café again, Curtis and Ignatius would be tied inside a sack and beaten with sticks.

After we were back on the road, Ignatius clambered to the front of the half-track.

"I'm not listening to anything but an apology," I said.

"It was only a *little* food fight," he said with a grin, "barely worthy of the name."

"What do you want?" I asked.

"There's a slug farm coming up." He pointed to his copy of *Ten Animals to Generally Avoid in the Cambrian Empire.* "I thought we should stop and have a look."

I looked at Addie, and she nodded. "You should all see firsthand the sort of dangers we may encounter," she said, "and we have the time. Besides, they're quite amusing in a gooey kind of way, and who knows? With a bit of luck, he'll be eaten by one."

"Oh, come on!" said Ignatius. "I'm not *that* bad."

Addie stared at him until he smiled sheepishly and rejoined his friends in the back. We took the next right turn and parked in a dusty parking lot alongside a half dozen armored tour buses. Addie told us to go on ahead, as she'd seen flesh-eating slugs many times. Ralph said he wouldn't come either, as he had a peculiar allergy to "anything without legs, such as cats."

"Cats have legs," said the princess.

"They do, don't they?" agreed Ralph, looking confused, but he declined to join us anyway. So Perkins, the princess, Curtis, Ignatius, and I trooped into the farm.

After paying the entry fee, we walked down between circular concrete pits, each containing about a dozen slugs the size of piglets. They were the color of double cream, had grooves along their bodies, and were covered with a slimy gel that smelled of rotting flesh. The slugs had no eyes, mouths with razor-sharp fangs, and atop each small head was an array of antennae that waved excitedly as we walked past. If any creature had AVOID stamped all over it, the flesh-eating slug was it.

"Whoa," said the princess, "that is *so* gross."

"It's about the only placemat design we have already agreed upon," said Ignatius excitedly, producing a camera from his bag. "You may be interested to know that we only ever do six designs in a set of placemats."

"Is that a fact?" I said.

"Yes. Although the average seated meal is only 3.76 persons, you might think that four designs would be enough, but no. What about a dinner of six? With focus groups and market research, we have discovered that while repetition of placemat design is acceptable in a group larger than six, in any group smaller than six, it is not. So we do six designs. Clever, right?"

"Where's the nearest somnubuvorus?" said the princess. "I want to throw myself into it."

"The nearest what?"

"Never mind," I said. "Laura, stop antagonizing the nitwits."

"Yes, ma'am," said the princess, doing her best curtsey yet. We joined the crowd milling around one of the feeding troughs, where the slug farmers were giving a talk.

". . . the slug's mucus—or slime—can be used in products from meat tenderizer to skin exfoliant to paint stripper to battery acid, and an adult slug can ooze almost a gallon a day, if kept moist. Any questions before feeding time?"

One of the tourists raised his hand. "Is it true that enriched slug slime is part of Emperor Tharv's secret chemical weapons stockpile?"

"That was never proved," said the farmer, "but knowing Tharv, almost certainly."

"Can we wrestle them?" asked a stupid-looking young man who turned out to be Curtis.

"This is a *farm*," said the slug farmer testily, "not a circus. If you want to fight one, go to an official slug-wrestling salon, or even easier, find a slug. They sleep until midday, usually in the damp shade of limestone outcrops. Any more questions? No? Okay, then let's feed them."

The farmer explained that keeping intelligent slugs in captivity denied them the stimulation of hunting prey, so the slugs had to do tricks for their supper. For the next five minutes we watched the slugs balance balls on their antennae, play a passable rendition of the "Beer Barrel Polka" on a descant recorder, and do synchronized back-flips, to sporadic applause. The show finished with an entire pig carcass being chucked into a trough of a dozen slugs. The pig was devoured in a little under thirty seconds and with such uncontrolled ferocity that when there was nothing left of it but bones, there were only ten slugs remaining.

"That often happens," said the farmer sadly.

We walked back out through the gift shop once the show was over. I bought Mother Zenobia some skin exfoliant for her feet, while the princess wrote a postcard to her parents, even though it would never be delivered across the border.

"I was disappointed not to see someone being devoured," said Ignatius as we returned to the parking lot, "or lose a foot at the very least."

"If you cover yourself in lard first, you can wrestle them quite easily," remarked Curtis, reading from a leaflet, "and make a fortune in prize money."

"Anyone eaten?" asked Addie as we rejoined her and Ralph in the half-track.

"No one even got nibbled," grumbled Ignatius. "Are you okay, Ralph? You look a little . . . strange."

"It's nothing, dude," said Ralph. He did look unusual—drunk, almost. "Probably the altitude. I'll be fine."

"Did you do anything to him?" I asked Addie once I'd climbed into the driver's seat.

"Not me," she said. "I went to the bathroom, and when I got back he was sweating and muttering something about anchovies."

"Mule fever?" I asked.

"No, probably just Empty Quarter nerves."

I looked at Ralph again; he seemed to have relaxed somewhat, although I could see his pupils contract and dilate several times a second.

We drove for a half hour and came across the dormant marker stones that indicated what had once been the Dragonlands but was now the Empty Quarter. There was a large and very chewed sign that read:

DANGER
Empty Quarter
Remain Vigilant or Remain Here

EIGHTEEN

The Empty Quarter

The Empty Quarter was exceptionally well named. It took up almost exactly one-quarter of the Cambrian Empire and was, well, empty: an unspoiled tract of rolling upland, squarish in shape and forty miles across. No one was crazy enough to live there, so for the most part the Quarter was simply thousands of acres of scrubby grass, hog marsh, stunted oak, and the occasional bubbling tar pit.

We entered full of expectation, but after half an hour of driving had seen nothing more exciting than a distant herd of Buzonjis and the fleeting glimpse of a snork badger's corkscrew tail. We passed several armored cars returning from a failed Tralfamosaur shoot, and were then overtaken by two off-road motorcycles we reencountered three miles up the road, the bikes twisted and mangled and with no sign of the riders.

When Curtis asked Addie what had happened, she replied, "We'll probably never know. Only half the missing are ever accounted for. Death certificates here in the empire have a box for 'Nonspecific peril-related fatality,' and it gets checked off a lot."

"It would be a good place to kill someone you don't like and get away with it," said Curtis thoughtfully.

"We think that happens too," said Addie, "but natural justice has a way of making good."

We drove on, and twice met armed road bandits about whom Addie seemed curiously unconcerned. She took one look at their clothes and general demeanor, and told me to ignore them and drive on, which I did without incident. The third roadblock was somehow different, and Addie instructed me to stop.

"These kidnappers are Oldivicians," explained Addie. "*Much* more dangerous. Our tribe and theirs had a brief misunderstanding recently, and things are still a little tender."

"How recently?" asked Perkins.

"Three centuries. Let me do the talking."

We pulled to the side of the road, and Addie climbed

out to meet three armed men who walked up with an arrogant swagger. They were dressed in the traditional wool tweed suits of the Oldivicians, with leather boots and flat caps. Like Addie, they displayed a complex series of tattoos on their faces to denote kinship, position, and allegiance. They were armed with ancient-looking weapons, and wore twin bandoliers of cartridges crisscrossed across their torsos. They had already done some business that day: A downcast-looking prisoner sat on a rock close to where their Buzonjis tramped the soil impatiently.

"Hello, Addie," said the first bandit cheerfully. "Tour work good these days?"

"Haven't lost anyone for almost a month now, Gareth," she replied, "so not bad. How's the kidnapping business?"

"It's terrible, to be honest with you, Addie," he said. "No real celebrities attempt to cross the Empty Quarter except with bodyguards and loaded with heavy weaponry."

"We live in sorry, untrusting times. You going to let me pass?"

"Perhaps. Have a look, Rhys."

One of the other bandits stared at us through the window of the half-track, then consulted a well-thumbed copy of *Miller's Guide to Kidnappable Personages,* which I noticed was more than three years old. I'd probably make next year's edition. Luckily, he wouldn't recognize the one person in our group who was definitely in *Miller's:* the princess. Rhys stared at us in turn, looked back at Gareth, and shook his head. But Gareth, it seemed, wasn't convinced.

"Anyone in there we should know about?" he asked.

Addie shifted her stance to rest her hand on her dagger. Gareth changed his stance too, followed by his compatriots. I heard a safety catch release. The tension seemed to have risen tenfold. Addie spoke next, and her voice was menacing in its softness.

"The thing is, Gareth, if you ask me if there's anyone kidnappable with me, then I'm honor bound to answer, and then you'll ask me to turn them over, and I'll tell you that you'll have to kill me before I'd do that, and my tribe and your tribe are in a blood feud but it's our turn to kill one of yours, and if you kill me then an Oldivician will have killed two Silurians in a row, and that's all-out war. You want that?"

As Addie and Gareth stared at each other danger-ously, I saw the attention of the kidnappers shift toward the top of the half-track. Suddenly everyone's eyes were on Ralph, glowing with a pale yellow light and floating a couple of feet out of the vehicle.

"Well, what do you know?" said Gareth with a smile. "You've got a sorcerer. They're worth bundles. Grab him, lads."

Perkins and I looked at each other as the bandits moved forward.

"Ralph can't be a sorcerer," I whispered. "We would have spotted it."

Gareth's men pulled the glowing Ralph out of the back of the half-track, holding him by his shoelaces as if he were a helium balloon in a breeze. He was giggling stupidly and mumbling something about camels, and as we watched, bright sparks started to fizz out of his ears. He turned blue, then red, then green, then burped out a large iridescent bubble that produced a flock of brightly colored butterflies when it burst.

I glanced at Ignatius and Curtis, who were giggling stupidly at Ralph's predicament, and I suddenly had a terrible thought. "Perkins," I whispered, "did you leave your spell bag in the half-track when we went to look at the slugs?"

Perkins hurriedly retrieved and opened the leather suitcase that contained his potions, balms, and one-shot spells written on rice paper. It was, predictably enough, empty. Ralph, like Curtis, must have had a fondness for abusing magic, and finding some spells unattended, had consumed them all.

Ralph was beginning to stretch and flex, as though a pony were inside him trying to get out. I'd not seen anyone have a magic overdose, but I'd heard about it. The lucky ones turn themselves inside out and die a horribly painful death. The unlucky ones turn themselves inside out over and over, forever.

"Fun's over," said Gareth to Ralph, who was still floating and now doing some rapid transformations between a piano, a walrus, a wardrobe, and back again. "Give it a rest and come down here immediately."

Ralph, predictably enough, ignored him.

"Blast," said Perkins, thumping the seat of the half-track with his fist. "I'm responsible for this."

"No, if the idiot what's-his-name is stupid enough to consume a bagful of unknown spell," said the princess, "then he can deal with the consequences."

I looked at Perkins, and he looked back at me and sighed. With the skill of Mystical Arts comes a certain responsibility.

Perkins got out of the half-track. "It's me you want," he told Gareth the bandit. "That bloody fool is suffering the symptoms of acute magic poisoning. Do what you want with me, but I need to help him before he bursts."

Ralph responded by wrenching his shoelaces free of his captors and doing three somersaults in midair, braying like a donkey, and then turning into a tiger and back again, all the time giggling uncontrollably. Ignatius and Curtis were laughing and cheering him on, and even some of the bandits seemed to find it amusing.

But just then Ralph's foot expanded explosively to four times its normal size, shredding his boot into scraps of tongue, laces, leather lowers, and man-made uppers. No one was laughing anymore.

"Go on, then," said Gareth.

Perkins outstretched an index finger and began to concentrate. A standard Magnaflux Spell Reversal was tricky, but I knew he wasn't planning that — it would be too complex now that there were thirty or forty spells coursing through Ralph's body. No, he'd be trying the grandmaster of all reversals: the rarely tried, personally draining, and supremely risky Genetic Master Reset.

Ralph stopped giggling as his head swelled to twice its size and shrank again, followed by a curious rippling of his skin that morphed his front into his back and into his front again, which is a lot more unpleasant to behold than it is to describe. Even Ignatius and Curtis grimaced.

Ralph started to scream in pain. Not a stubbed-toe sort of pain, but more a detached-kneecap kind of pain, along with seven simultaneous childbirths, neuralgia, and a tooth abscess mixed in for good luck. The sort of pain you hope you will never experience.

While Ralph screamed, his ear migrated across his face with a sound like tearing cloth. The tips of his fingers shot off and ricocheted dangerously around the small group, smashing a side mirror and making two of the bandits duck for cover.

And that was when Perkins let fly.

There was a burst of energy from his fingertips. A

cold fireball burst out from Ralph and then expanded to a sphere about thirty feet wide. It paused in a wonderful display of crackling light, then collapsed rapidly into a glowing ball that enveloped the still-screaming Ralph before vanishing in a twinkling. There was a distant rumble, and all was quiet.

Ralph, such as we'd known him, was gone.

NINETEEN

It's an Australopithecine

Where's Ralph?" said Ignatius. "And who's that?"

He pointed at a small, hairy, and very primitive-looking man about four feet tall, with a flattish face and protruding upper and lower jaws. He had a mild stoop, long arms and legs, and was completely naked. He stared at us all in a furtive manner as Perkins sat down heavily, exhausted. I jumped out of the half-track.

"That's Ralph as an Australopithecine," I said. "What Perkins did was a Genetic Master Reset. The only way to release Ralph from the spells was a complete scouring of anything that made him Ralph. And since Ralph *was* human, a Master Reset brought him back to the first thing that would eventually turn out to be Ralph that wasn't *quite* human."

"You turned Ralph into a caveman?" said Curtis, staring accusingly at Perkins.

"It was either that," murmured Perkins, his eyes still closed after the effort, "or resetting him to Standard Rabbit. Believe me, Australopithecine is better. At least this way he can evolve back into a human. A rabbit, well, that just stays a rabbit."

"Evolve back? That's a relief," said Ignatius. "I promised his mother I'd have him home in a week."

Perkins and I exchanged looks.

"It'll take a little longer than a week," I said.

"I suppose we could keep him in a spare room or something," said Ignatius. "How much longer?"

"About 1.6 million years. I'm sorry to say that Ralph will spend the rest of his days as a primitive version of a human. He'll still be Ralph, only with one-third brain capacity, some peculiar habits, and a mostly obsolete skill set. Despite this, he'll pick up a few words and may even learn how to use a spoon."

"Ook," said Ralph, staring at us all with his small dark eyes. He still looked a lot like Ralph, just shorter and hairier and more extinct.

"Turn him back, you sorcery piece of scum," said Curtis menacingly. "I don't believe this. You turned my best friend into a caveman!"

It was Perkins's turn to get angry now, but he wasn't going to. First, he was exhausted, and second, it wasn't in his nature. But it was in mine.

"Listen here," I said, taking a step forward and pressing a finger against Curtis's chest. "Ralph as you know him isn't coming back. And just so you know, Perkins didn't *have* to help him. But when he did, he gave up some of his own life to do so. That's right, idiot. Notice anything different about Perkins? He's aged a decade. He gave those years to save your dumb friend's life, so the next time you open your stupid mouth it will be to say 'Thank you, Mr. Perkins, we are not worthy of your generosity.' Understand?"

Curtis and Ignatius frowned and looked at Perkins curiously. He *was* older. A few minutes ago he had been a spotty-faced eighteen-year-old, but now he was a handsomish man in his late twenties. A Genetic Master Reset takes a lot of wizidrical energy, and if there's not enough energy in the air around you, there is only one place you can go to get it: your own life spirit. Magic is a form of emotional energy bound up inside everything that lives, and we are all part of that same magical energy — *Life is magic, and magic is life.* And Perkins had given ten years of his life to help Ralph, whom he neither knew well nor liked.

Ignatius and Curtis went silent and stared at each other with, I hoped, a sense of shame. Gareth and his bandits, who had been watching the spectacle with appalled curiosity, had seen enough.

"We're done," said Gareth. "Lower the finger, wizard, and do exactly what we say."

Perkins was too tired to do anything other than what he was told. Within a few minutes, Gareth had gone through Perkins's papers and soon ascertained that he was totally kidnappable.

While this was going on, Addie moved across to me. "You might have told me you had a wizard with you," she whispered.

"There's lots of things I haven't told you."

"Like what?"

"Like we're actually looking for the Eye of Zoltar. The guy in Llangurig we need to visit is called Able Quizzler, and he's the link between the Eye and Pirate Wolff."

Addie sighed. "I can't speak for Able Quizzler, but Pirate Wolff hasn't been seen for years, if she was ever seen at all. The legendary Leviathans' Graveyard is exactly that: legendary."

"Even so," I said, "I still need to search."

Addie looked at my face and seemed to realize just how serious I was. "If you're chasing dreams and legends across Cambria, Jenny, you must want the Eye of Zoltar pretty badly."

"If we don't find it, then our two dragons are to be

killed by the most powerful wizard in the land, and we will be honor bound to die attempting to save them."

"And would one of those dragons be rubber right now, the same one you denied knowing anything about?"

"Something like that."

"Terrific. Anything else? Surprises, I mean?"

I thought about the princess. "There might be more . . . It's an installment kind of thing. Will you still be our tour guide?"

"Of course," said Addie. "Deluded tourists chasing after barely credible legends is not just our bread and butter, but also quite entertaining. I think you're mistaken, but I'll still help you."

I thanked her, and then my attention was caught by a comment from the bandit named Rhys. "How much can we ransom him for?"

"We're not going to ransom him," announced Gareth. "We're going to give this sorcerer away."

The other bandits stared at Gareth suspiciously.

"To the emperor," continued Gareth. "His Tyrannical Majesty will look favorably upon such a valuable gift."

The bandits nodded enthusiastically, and my heart fell. Emperor Tharv needed sorcerers, and for one reason: to help him develop a powerful thermo-wizidrical device with which to threaten his neighboring kingdoms. Needless to say, this would not be a good thing.

"It's time we left," said Addie in a low voice, "before Gareth starts wanting the half-track as well."

"No way," I said. "I can't leave without Perkins."

"You don't have a choice, unless you think you can kill those three and get out of the country before the rest of his tribe catches up with you."

"I have . . . a dragon," I said. "Okay, he's rubber right now, but he'll be turning back pretty soon."

"And *if* he does, and *if* he can get here, will he be willing to kill the bandits to get Perkins back?"

I thought about Colin's strictly pacifist nature. "Actually, probably not. But he can be seriously scary—talons, teeth, barbed tail, fiery breath, that sort of thing."

"I'm sure that's very scary from where you come from, but considering the loathsome creatures that either squirm, squelch, drift, or creep around this country, a dragon has a terror rating of two. And to put that into context, a Tralfamosaur is a five, and my gran is an eight."

"Your grandmother must be very scary," I said.

"She ate a live whippet once," said Addie, "which *is* pretty scary, especially during a wedding."

"What did the bride and groom say?"

"She *was* the bride. I think she wanted to make a statement to her in-laws."

"That would be quite a statement," I said. "But there must be something we can do about Perkins. He's a good friend, and I really like him."

Addie shrugged. "It's not like he's dead. You'll meet him again sometime, I'm sure."

"True. But I also think Emperor Tharv might reopen research into thermo-wizidrical weapons if he had access to a sorcerer."

Addie thought for a moment. "You're right, and that would be a screaming disaster. Wait here."

She patted me on the arm and approached the three bandits, who were congratulating themselves about their good fortune.

"How much for him?" she asked Gareth, pointing not at Perkins but at the man sitting nearby, the previous kidnap victim of the bandits.

"Getting into the kidnap business, Addie?"

"Tour guide pay is not what it used to be. We'll give up Perkins without a fight if you give us him."

Gareth thought for a moment, then agreed. They went into a huddle for some bargaining, and two minutes later Addie returned with the previous victim. He was in his mid-sixties and dressed in a tweed jacket and golf knickers. He had a genial demeanor, an impressive mustache, and looked as though he hadn't slept in a proper bed for a week.

"This is Mr. Wilson," said Addie, "and we're leaving."

"Why did you buy him?" I said to her in a low voice.

"I have a plan to get your Perkins back," she said, "and there can't be any witnesses."

I stared at her to see if she was pulling my leg, but she seemed dead serious. She nodded toward the bandits, who were readying to leave.

"Better say your goodbyes."

I walked across to Perkins. "Hey," I said, "how are you feeling?"

"Not great," he said. "They want to present me to Emperor Tharv as a gift. I've never been a gift before."

I leaned forward to kiss him on the cheek, and took the opportunity to whisper, "Trust us. You'll be fine."

The bandits mounted Perkins on a spare Buzonji and were soon lost to view in a swirl of dust. I watched them go and returned to the half-track with a heavy heart. Perkins was the closest thing to a boyfriend I had, and despite our recently increased difference in age, I didn't want to lose him.

I looked at my watch. At seven I would contact Tiger using the conch and report what had happened. Moobin or Lady Mawgon would know what to do.

TWENTY

At the Claerwin

H ello, everyone," said our new traveling companion as soon as we were on the move. "You don't have to call me Mr. Wilson. Wilson is just dandy. I'm an ornithologist."

"A what?" asked Curtis.

"It's someone who studies birds," said the princess.

"Hadn't you heard?" said Curtis with an impertinent laugh. "Birds have all but vanished in the empire."

"Which makes the sport of bird watching quintriply fascinating," said Wilson. "Think of the thrill of finding a bird where there aren't any. Marvelous."

"You're nuts," said Curtis.

"Bit rude," said Wilson cheerfully. "Who's the hairy chap, and does he know that his thing is showing?"

"That's Ralph," I said, "and I don't think he cares if it's showing or not."

"Ook," said Ralph, sort of in agreement.

"An ornithologist?" I said.

"It's how I managed to negotiate his release so easily," said Addie. "Gareth mistook *ornithologist* for *anthologist*. Practitioners skilled in the art of collecting works of poetry are sound, tradable commodities out here, while bird watchers just eat your food and say, 'Ooh, stop the car a minute; I think I see a painted dillbury.'"

"Where?" asked Wilson excitedly, before realizing it was simply an example. "The funny thing," he added, "is that I am also an anthologist. I didn't tell them because they never asked. I'm very grateful, by the way. As a special treat, I'll tell you all about the cloud pippit. The sparrow-size bird has a density only slightly greater than helium and nests upon rising columns of air—"

"Bored now," said Curtis.

"Still rude," said Wilson.

"Where are you heading?" I asked him.

"This way now," he said, pointing in the direction we were going. "I have no plans. You?"

"Llangurig," I answered, "and then perhaps to Cadir Idris."

"To watch Leviathans?" he asked, sounding excited.

"It's possible."

"Not *exactly* birds, but they do fly and have as-yet-unobserved mating rituals. I'm in."

"It's on a fifty percent fatality index," I said, "and we've not lost anyone yet, so mathematically speaking, you could still be fair game."

"I'm still in," said Wilson with a grin. "I've heard Leviathans are a total blast."

There were no other incidents for the next hour. After driving through a narrow gorge where we had to pay two subquality bandits an insultingly low fee for the privilege to pass, we came upon the Claerwin Reservoir, a large body of water that nestled quietly about twenty miles inside the Quarter. We drove along the banks of the lake and arrived at one of the many campsites dotted about the countryside, reserved for travelers eager to spend a safe and unmolested night.

"Okay," said Addie as we pulled into the deserted campsite and parked next to the shattered remains of long-abandoned armored vehicles, "I know it's not late, but we'll camp here for the night. It'll be a long day tomorrow if we're to make Llangurig before nightfall."

We climbed out of the half-track and stared at the lake, which was about a mile across.

"It looks almost perfectly circular," said Curtis.

"I read in *Conspiracy Theorist* magazine that the lakes around here are craters created by top-secret thermo-wizidrical weapons tests back in the eighties," said Ignatius.

"Thermo-wizidrical . . . what?" asked Curtis.

"Using magic to cause explosions," I said. "Usually two contradicting spells draw increasing power as they attempt to cancel each other out. If left unchecked, the spell will break down and either fizzle out or go super-critical and violently explode."

"There was magical fallout for years following the testing," said Addie, "resulting in all sorts of odd occurrences: balls of light, strange apparitions, levitations. We think it's how Buzonjis were created. A pony and an okapi were too close to each other while drinking at the lake and bingo—fused by a wayward spell."

"Wow," said Ignatius, "it's like we're standing near a massive weapons-test area or something."

"It's not *like* we are," said the princess. "We *are* standing on the site of a weapons-test area."

"Is it still dangerous?" asked Wilson.

"Not if we don't stay too long," said Addie. "Forty-eight hours, max. If anyone notices any weirdness, raise the alarm."

"What sort of weirdness?" asked Curtis.

"Metal corroding too quickly, sand changing into glass, growing extra toes. You'll definitely know it when you see it."

"Like that?" Curtis said, pointing. A jetty had been built out into the lake, and several rowboats were tied to it. All three boats were floating in the air like balloons, held only by the ropes that attached them to the jetty. Two boats bumped gently in the breeze like inverted wind chimes.

"Yes," I said, "kind of like that."

We had a look around. There were several camping tables, barbecues, and what looked like old leather sofas. I was about to sit on one when Addie stopped me. She kicked the sofa a couple of times, and it eventually rose in a very fed-up manner and waddled off into the brush.

"Physarum emeffeye metamorphica," said Addie, "a sort of furniture-emulating slime mold. More annoying than dangerous. Ten hours of sleep on one of those and it would digest all the stitching out of your clothes. I've seen them transform into Regency card tables, futons, and barstools. One that had disguised itself as an Eames lounge chair got to the first round of bidding at an auction of contemporary furniture."

"More magical fallout?" asked the princess.

"Exactly," said Addie. "It's why we can't stop here for more than forty-eight hours. These will be your home tonight." She indicated one of the more obvious features of the campsite: the pod-poles.

To guard against night predation by Tralfamosaur, Hotax, snork badger, or Variant-N flesh-eating slug, it was wise to sleep inside a small pod situated atop a shiny steel thirty-foot pole anchored firmly into the ground. There was a ladder for access, which could be hauled up out of reach.

While Curtis and Ignatius went off to find some fireberries for heat and light and Wilson and the princess went on a hunt for any abandoned food supplies, Addie and I went to check that the perimeter fence was intact.

"Do you think Curtis and Ignatius are safe digging up fireberries?" I asked, knowing how easily the large, volatile, radish-like vegetable could ignite when handled roughly.

"Who cares?" said Addie. "Hang the wire back on the post, will you?"

I did as Addie asked, and before long we had the perimeter fence back up, though the fence was basically no more than lots of tin cans hanging on a wire.

"So what do we do if we hear the cans clinking?" I asked.

"It's not a question of if, but when," said Addie, "and hopefully it'll be when we're safe up our pod-poles. I only hope the Tralfamosaurs don't come. They can't reach us, but the hungry smacky noises could keep us awake for hours."

We heard a mild *whompa* noise as the first fireberry ignited, followed by several more dull concussions as other fireberries were lit and placed in baskets on high poles, for light. When we got back to the camp, we found that Ignatius had set up an awning attached to the half-track, held up with two tent poles, and that several pieces of non–slime mold furniture had been gathered together for us to sit on.

Once supper was cooking, Addie beckoned me aside and lowered her voice. "I have an . . . errand to run. Don't wait up for me, and make sure everyone is up their poles the moment the fence jangles."

I told her I'd be a lot happier if she didn't take the half-track, but she just smiled, put two fingers into her mouth, and gave out a silent whistle that made Ralph wince. There was a patter of hooves nearby, and an Appaloosa Buzonji approached rapidly from the southwest, where, I presumed, it had been tailing us all day. It trotted up and tossed its head happily as Addie gave it a carrot. She released the stirrups from the finely tooled saddle and expertly mounted up.

"If I don't come back, I'm dead and you're on your own," she told me.

"I wish you wouldn't say things like that. What are you going to do?"

"You don't want to know. See you in the morning." And she galloped off like a bullet into the evening light, back the way we had come.

"She's very tough, isn't she?" said the princess, who had come up behind me. "Do you think she'd want to be my bodyguard when I'm a princess again?"

"Please don't tell her you're a princess," I replied. "What with rubber dragons, Grade III Legend–status amulets, pirates, Leviathans, and a missing boyfriend whose age difference is now a teensy-weensy bit inappropriate, I've got about all the drama I need."

We sat down to wait while Wilson made supper over an extra-large fireberry. Unlike the smaller, brighter ones, it burned slowly, with a dull red glow.

Ralph, newly Australopithecine, was fascinated. "Ook?" he said as I held one of the light-giving fireberries in my cupped hands, the light spilling past my fingers. "Ook?" he said again as I placed the fireberry in his small, nut-brown hands.

Curtis and Ignatius stared at their friend with a mixture of dread and disgust.

"We can't take him back to his family like that," said Curtis, "primitive, barely housetrained, and with his thing showing."

"I agree," said Ignatius. "It would be kinder to just turn him loose and let nature take its course. We can tell Ralph's family he fell into a swamp or got eaten by slugs or something."

"Or we could just put it to *s-l-e-e-p*," suggested Curtis.

"That would be the humane thing, I suppose."

"Ook?" said Ralph, listening with a confused expression.

"Wow," said Curtis, "it's like it almost understands us."

"Can you sit farther away?" I said to Curtis and Ignatius.

"Any particular reason?"

"How about 'Your lack of compassion disgusts me'?"

"Whatever you say, boss-girl," said Curtis sarcastically.

"And," I added, "if you so much as touch a hair on the head of the Australopithecine, you'll have me to reckon with."

"We were just joking," said Curtis in a tone that suggested they weren't. But they moved away. Ralph watched them leave but stayed with us.

"I don't like that Curtis fellow one bit," said the princess. "He keeps on staring at my whatnots. I mean, I know they're not the royal whatnots, which are protected from prolonged staring by a death sentence, but even so, Laura's whatnots are whatnots nonetheless, and he shouldn't stare at them."

I told her I was in firm agreement, having experienced something similar from Curtis myself.

"Shall I kill him?" said the princess after a pause. "My father insisted that I be trained in the art of silent assassination just in case."

"Just in case of what?"

"Lots of things," said the princess. "Doing away with a dopey royal husband in order to take over a kingdom, for one. It happens more than you think, believe me."

"Wouldn't going to marriage counseling be safer?"

"What, and discuss our marriage problems with a stranger? Don't be ridiculous. So, shall I kill him?"

"Absolutely not. You can't kill someone for staring at whatnots, royal or otherwise—even if you are a princess." I looked at my watch. "Hold down the fort. I'm going to call home."

TWENTY-ONE

Speaking on the Conch

Communication conches work best with a relatively clear line of sight, so I climbed a low hill to the west where the bleached bones of a long-dead Tralfamosaur were lying in the grass. I sat on the massive skull, waited until precisely seven o'clock, and then spoke quietly into the conch.

"Kazam base from Jennifer mobile, come in, please."

There was a whistling from the large shell, then several clicks and a buzzing sound, but nothing intelligible.

"Kazam base from Jennifer mobile, come in, please."

There was only static, so I said, "Tiger, can you hear me?"

There was more buzzing and a gentle warbling sound, then the conch sprang abruptly into life.

"Testing, testing, one two three . . . Is this thing working?" It was Moobin. I responded, gave him a position report, and asked how things were.

"Hello?" said Moobin again. "Jennifer, can you hear me?"

"I can hear you."

"Jennifer, are you there?"

"I'm here."

It was clear that Moobin couldn't hear me, probably because the communication spell was being disrupted by the thermo-wizidrical fallout. Moobin realized this too.

"Hello, Jennifer, it's possible that you can hear me and I can't hear you. I'll be brief because there have been a few developments and we're kind of busy. Nothing too serious, so no need to come home. Keep looking for the Eye of Zoltar and take special care of the princess. If you're getting this message, send us your first homing snail to confirm. But remember: Defend the princess and find out what you can about the Eye of Zoltar."

He repeated the message, but didn't elaborate on what developments had occurred, and after a while the conch went silent. It seemed odd that Moobin was urging me to find the Eye when he had been the one against it, but wizards were unpredictable.

I took out my notebook and pen:

Received your message but due to interference can't transmit. Claerwin tonight, Llangurig tomorrow, Perkins kidnapped, Colin rubber, Bugatti confiscated, have employed excellent guide. Request more information on "developments." Handmaiden well. Weather good.

— Jennifer

I checked the spelling, folded the note up small, and then stuck it to the side of the homing snail. I removed the snail's head-cozy, tapped the shell twice, and it was gone in a puff of dust. We were about fifty miles from home, so at homing-snail cruise speed it would be there in about twenty minutes, assuming it could negotiate the heavily fortified border. I'd never heard of a snail being defeated by a tank trap, a river, or a minefield, but you never know.

"All well?" I said as I walked back into camp.

"We thought we heard a snork badger sniffing outside the perimeter," said the princess, "and Ignatius spotted a Hotax encampment."

"Where?"

"Over there." She pointed to the lake, where I could

see a floating island of logs and hogbrush and a small wisp of pink smoke rising from a fireberry. Hotax often used drifting homesteads to keep them clear from danger, although what they might regard as dangerous, given that they were very dangerous themselves, was never clear.

"What exactly *is* a Hotax?" asked the princess as Wilson doled out omni-rice, a sort of camping rice meal with everything in it.

"It's a primitive and barbaric tribe of humans," I said, "who have only a rudimentary language and little understanding of the modern world. They're cannibalistic, with a curious habit of preserving their victims after death."

"To assist them on their long journey through the afterlife?" asked the princess.

"That would be vaguely honorable," I replied, "but no, it's thought they do it for fun. They'd have all been exterminated long ago, but Emperor Tharv thinks they're good for jeopardy tourism and reputedly has a pet Hotax called Nigel."

"I wish I hadn't asked," said the princess, looking around nervously.

The omni-rice was actually quite good; the inclusion of custard and sardines helped it enormously. We ate in silence for a while, then had marshmallows for dessert. The conversation became quite animated between Wilson, me, and the princess. Curtis and Ignatius kept to themselves, but their conversation was not hard to follow.

"I'm thinking we just tell his parents it was mule fever," said Ignatius.

"Agreed," replied Curtis, "but we'll need to find somewhere for him to stay in case he does go home. I wonder if we can sell him to a circus freak show or something? At least that way we can recoup some cash."

"Good idea," said Ignatius.

"Ook," said Ralph.

The thought of the dangers that lurked beyond the perimeter increased as the light faded, and by the time it was dark, we were all talking less for fun than to stave off nervousness.

Ignatius brought out two packs of cards and suggested canasta, but we couldn't agree on the rules. We eventually agreed that someone should tell a story, but no one volunteered, so we all sat in a circle and I spun a bottle. When it stopped, it pointed at Wilson.

TWENTY-TWO

The Naval Officer's Tale

O oh," said Wilson, "let's see now. I could tell you more about the yellow helium pippit, but I can see some of you find ornithological matters of less than passing interest. So I will tell you of a time forty-one years ago when I was barely twenty-two and a communications officer in the port rudder control tower of the S.P.I. Isle of Wight, during Troll War I."

I could sense the small party settling in to listen. Of all the nations in the Ununited Kingdoms, the steam-powered Isle of Wight was the only one that was movable, unless you count some of the marshier sections of the Duchy of Norfolk. While usually moored off the south of England, the Isle of Wight was fully seaworthy, and in times of peace used to cruise off the Azores to avoid the long, damp winters of the British archipelago.

Wilson began. "I went through naval college, and at the time that Troll War I began, I was communications officer in the port rudder control room. This was when the island's engines and rudders were controlled not by the command center at the front of the island, but by a series of secondary control centers that took orders from the admiral via telephone. My job was to answer the command telephone when it rang and relay the orders to Rudder Captain Roberts, who was one of those implacable naval officers who had made the Isle of Wight such an efficient movable island in peacetime and war."

Wilson gathered his thoughts, then continued. "It was the morning of the first push of Troll War I, and we'd steamed up the coast to Borderlandia the week before. The plan was that as soon as the war began, we were to cruise up and down the coast firing broadsides to divert the trolls from the main landship advance.

"So there we were, making good headway up the west coast of Trollvania at eighteen knots, shelling the trolls from about two miles offshore. There was a bit of retaliation from the trolls, but nothing spectacular. A few of their siege engines fired boulders at us, but all fell woefully short — we were well out of range.

"As we were turning about for the third run up the

coast, the order was given to move within 750 yards off the coast so we could more accurately rake the trolls' positions with high-explosive shells.

"We had some initial success shelling their positions, with the main observation tower reporting direct hits. Our rejoicing was short-lived, of course, for the trolls had tricked us: They had been firing their boulders purposefully short to make us *think* we were out of range, so now that we had been enticed closer, the trolls opened up with everything they had. Large rocks the size of cars and buses rained down upon the island, taking out shore batteries, centers of communication, and eventually the main observation tower."

Everyone was silent, so Wilson took a sip of water and continued. "Naturally, as soon as the bombardment started, we felt the engines increase in power, and the order 'Full hard starboard rudders both!' came through the telephone. We complied, but as the combination of full hard rudder and full power came in, the island began to tip. Anything loose in the control room slid across the floor. Charts fell, and the teacart was upended near the stairwell.

"The tilt increased as the rudders bit, decreasing the depth beneath the port side of the island—and the port propeller hit a reef. The propeller stopped dead, but with the engine still at full power, the prop shaft was twisted like a tube of damp cardboard, putting one engine out of action."

"Did you know this?" asked Ignatius.

"We pretty much guessed," said Wilson, "and a fearful shudder ran through the entire island. The island rapidly fell back onto an even keel and slowed, while the *thump thump thump* of incoming boulders punctuated the deathly silence in the rudder control room. We all stared, horrified at what was happening.

"Things were just about to get worse. We had one engine out, only one rudder, and the troll strategy was apparent — the course we were taking would run us aground off the coast of Trollvania, and we could be boarded and overrun by trolls, never anything but savagely murderous in their treatment of humans. Putting the engine full astern wouldn't help us, as the island would run aground backwards, destroying the second engine, and also placing us at the mercy of the trolls. The only course of action was to get the rudders to starboard, but both had to be moved — one to port and one to starboard would do nothing at all.

"Rudder Captain Roberts told us all to stand fast at our posts despite the boulders falling closer and closer to the control room, then called his second-in-command to his side, a career petty officer named Trubshaw.

"'Listen here, Trubshaw,' said Captain Roberts,

'you've got to get over to the other rudder control room and bring the starboard rudder hard over, no matter what. Drive like the wind, old girl.'

"It was a good plan, the *only* plan, and if it wasn't completed in half an hour, the island would run aground and the trolls would board us, and all would be lost. Trubshaw just had time to salute when a massive boulder ripped through our control room and I was knocked off my feet. When I stood, there was nothing left of Trubshaw, the other officers and men, or even the control room, which was a ragged mass of tangled steel and broken glass. I called in to report the damage, but all communications were down. I crossed over to the rudder captain, who was barely alive; his body was half crushed beneath a steel stanchion.

"'It's up to you now,' he told me, 'and this one's from the admiral: Hard a-starboard both, *all other considerations secondary.*'"

"What does that mean exactly?" asked the princess in the pause that followed. "'All other considerations secondary'?"

"Exactly as it sounds," replied Wilson. "I was to undertake my orders with no consideration of anything else. This was the most important order I was to carry out — that *anyone* on the Isle of Wight was to ever carry out, and nothing could stand in my way. Everything and everybody was expendable in the execution of this one order. If the trolls boarded the island, a hundred thousand inhabitants would be eaten or enslaved."

"Wow," said Ignatius, "it's like you could do anything."

"It's not *like* I could do anything, my muddle-headed friend, I *could* do anything. I took my car and drove like the wind to the starboard rudder control center on the other side of the island. Twice the road was blocked by rubble, and twice I had to abandon my vehicle, climb across the rubble, and find another car. When I got there, I found Rudder Captain Gregg on duty. I told him my orders were from the admiral himself, and he told me to calm down, leave, and only return 'when I was acceptable to be presented to a superior officer.'"

"What did that mean?" I asked.

"I had lost my cap," said Wilson, "so was not technically in uniform. I didn't know it at the time, but my ear was half hanging off and my face was covered with blood. I must have looked quite a sight.

"I told Rudder Captain Gregg that if he did not get the rudder hard over to starboard, the island would be lost, but the rudder captain insisted that he would only accept orders direct from the admiral or the admiral's staff—and that if I didn't leave, he would have me arrested."

"What an idiot!" said Curtis. "What did you do?"

"I took out my service revolver and shot him dead right there. His second-in-command made a move to stop me, so I shot him, too." Wilson stopped again, and I saw his eyes glisten.

"To be fair to Rudder Captain Gregg," he continued, "I think he was probably in shock, and his number two was just being loyal. In any event, I was now the ranking officer. I called 'Rudder hard a-starboard expedite!' and with a groaning and shouting from below, the order was executed. The island swung around, and within an hour we were heading back to the safety of the open sea. Communications with both rudder command posts were restored, and we limped back to port for extensive repairs.

"The Isle of Wight, once the finest seaborne island in the world, was a shadow of its former self. We lost seventeen hundred men and women and three-fifths of all buildings. We didn't set sail for another nineteen years, and haven't participated in a Troll War since."

"What happened to you?" asked Curtis after a pause. "I mean, you shot two officers."

Wilson sighed, and I saw his shoulders sag. "I'll let you in on a secret," he said quietly, "although I was there on that fateful day, I'm *not* the officer who saved the island. I told it first-person to make it more exciting. No, the young man who saved the day was Brent, an officer of considerable resource, resolve, and steely-eyed adherence to duty. He's now Admiral Lord Brent of Cowes, the most decorated officer we have ever honored."

We were all quiet.

"So what were you doing on that day?" I asked finally.

"I was the second officer in the starboard rudder control room, the one who was shot by Communications Officer Brent. I should have assumed command from Rudder Captain Gregg and solved the crisis myself, but I didn't. I was tested and found wanting. I failed not just myself and the service, but everyone on that island. Consumed by shame, I left the Isle of Wight soon after, never to return."

Wilson fell silent, deep in thought, and after we all agreed that it had been a good story even if it wasn't his own, we spun the bottle again.

TWENTY-THREE

A Deal with Curtis

The bottle pointed at the princess.

"Goody," she exclaimed, clapping her hands. "I'll use this opportunity to explain precisely how the financial futures market works."

"This should be a bundle of laughs," grumbled Curtis, but the princess ignored him.

"The first thing to remember about futures is that they are a contract for the supply of *specific* goods at a *specific* price at a *specific* time in the future—"

"What was that?" said Ignatius, staring into the darkness.

"Oh, no, you don't," said the princess crossly. "I'm

not going to have my fascinating account of financial derivatives sidelined by the old *what was that?* trick."

"I thought I heard something too," I said, "a clinking of tin cans."

Then we were on our feet, staring into the darkness. Something was either trying to get through the fence, or was already through and was now inside, staring at us from the darkness.

"What do we do?" whispered Curtis.

"We get ready to scoot up our pod-poles," said Wilson. "Better to be safe than eaten, as the saying goes."

We started to back off toward our pre-allocated pod-poles. And while pre-allocation might seem a bit nerdy and controlling, it can save lives; just imagine sixteen panicked tourists all trying to climb up the same pole. As soon as we were each fifteen feet up the pole, a lever could be tripped and the first section of ladder would be drawn upward. The terrors of the Cambrian Empire had been well accommodated over the years.

As we crept slowly toward our poles, there was a faint crack and a rustle in a nearby hedge. With images of snork badgers, Hotax, and flesh-eating slugs on our minds, everyone ran for it. There was a scream from the princess, and I looked back to see her rolling on the ground.

"Get it off me!" she yelled.

I jumped down and ran back to where she lay clutching her face. There seemed to be a trail of glistening slime on her arm, but if there *was* a flesh-eating slug, it was a very small one — no bigger than a pickle.

"Hold still, for admiral's sake," said Wilson, who had reached her first, "and we'll get it off—"

"Wait!" I yelled, and they stopped struggling. I pulled the princess's hands away and plucked a homing snail from her face.

"There's no panic," I said. "I think this was meant for me. But you know, it's really time to turn in before something genuinely nasty finds us."

There were mutterings of agreement, and those already halfway up their pod-poles continued on, leaving Wilson, the princess, and me on the ground.

"If you're okay," said Wilson, "I'll be off to bed."

"Thank you," said the princess, and clasped his hand for a moment.

"It was only a snail," replied Wilson, "barely dangerous at all."

"But you didn't know that when you came to my aid," replied the princess.

Wilson looked at us both, and I detected a resigned look in his eyes. "I am bound to help wherever possible," he said sadly. "I was found wanting once. It won't happen again."

"Is that why you're out here?" I asked, realizing that Wilson probably wasn't here just for the bird watching and the scenery.

"Back home, my name is forever linked with cowards and ditherers. I am here looking for a second chance — some extreme jeopardy where my intervention can make a difference."

"That can't be too difficult out here, surely?" I asked.

"You'd be surprised," said Wilson. "Simply saving a life is not enough. My act of contrition must have far-reaching consequences, so that years from now, someone will say, 'Without Wilson, all would have been lost.'"

He sighed, then bid us good night. We wished him the same, and he scooted nimbly up his pod-pole.

"I feel like a fool to have been frightened," said the princess, wiping the snail slime off her face with a handkerchief. "Most unregal. A princess should be resolute and unflinching in the face of danger. I'd be a rotten queen."

"Queenliness is a skill that must be learned," I told her, "and this is the place to do it."

"I hope so," she said with a sigh, then added after a pause, "I was so obnoxious to you back at the palace. You must think I'm a complete arse."

"Don't even think about it," I replied. "We are both victims of a random chance of birth: you a princess, me an orphan. But we're both working against it to improve ourselves."

"I suppose technically speaking I'm an orphan too," said the princess, "or I will be until I get my body back."

"It's the mind that defines the person," I said, "not the body."

"Oh," she said, "looks like I am a princess after all. What does the note say?"

I unfolded the message stuck to the shell of the homing snail, and let the princess read it over my shoulder by the light of the nearest fireberry.

Received your msg, contents noted. use EVERY EFFORT to secure return of Perkins, then find Rubber Colin. will be waiting at the conch seven tomorrow if possible, much happening and not any of it good, take no risks with yourself or the handmaiden and carry on search for E of Z with all determination. Raining here in Hereford, Tiger says hi.

— Moobin

I read the note twice. There seemed to be something going on that didn't sound good, and a sense of urgency about our task.

"He underlined 'every effort' and capitalized it," said

the princess. "Do you think that's an 'all other considerations secondary' kind of deal?"

"I think so," I replied, "and if I know Addie, that's
what she'll do to get Perkins back. What's worse, I think
I asked her to do it, which makes me responsible."

"How does that feel?"

"Not good. I'll see you tomorrow, Princess"

"Laura," said the princess. "Just call me Laura."

We climbed our pod-poles, but I got quite a shock when I
clambered into mine, for I wasn't alone. Curtis was there,
and he smiled in that *I'm so cute* manner that I found so
utterly odious.

"You better have a good reason for being up my pod-
pole."

"Oh," he said with a chuckle, "is it yours?"

"You know it is. Out."

The smile dropped from his face. "I thought we could
be friendly over this, but never mind. Although today
I'm a tourist, I'm also a businessman, and a businessman
is always on the lookout for new business opportunities."

"You said 'business' three times in that sentence."

"So?"

"It's bad syntax."

"No, it isn't."

"Yes, it is. It's like me saying, 'You're the dumbest
dumb person I've ever had the dumb luck to meet.'"

"You're very impertinent for an orphan."

"You noticed?"

Curtis scowled. "Fun's over," he said. "This is why I'm here: I thought at first that you were out here for a holiday too, but then I got to thinking. You're Jennifer Strange, the Last Dragonslayer. You run Kazam, recently established as the only licensed House of Enchantment in the world. You are Court Mystician to King Snodd as well as Dragon Ambassador. You look like just a kid, but you are probably the most powerful and influential person working in magic today."

This was worrying. Idiots like Curtis I can handle as long as they stay idiots — I have a terrible temper and can fight dirty, if pushed. But when idiots stop being idiots and start sounding smart, that's another matter entirely.

"So what are you saying? You want to write my resume?"

"I'm saying that it's a little suspicious: You're heading off toward Cadir Idris Mountain with a half-track loaded with fuel and the most experienced guide in the empire, supposedly to look for Leviathans."

"So?" I said. "Everyone needs a vacation."

"With a handmaiden who I suspect isn't a handmaiden, an illegally imported sorcerer, and a rubber dragon? This is a quest, isn't it?"

"It's a *search*."

"No way. This smacks of an arduous journey to

greater spiritual understanding of oneself and a greater truth."

Blast. He'd rumbled us.

"If the International Questing Federation finds out you're questing without a license, you'll be in serious trouble, and not just with them — the Cambrian authorities don't like anyone questing out here without a permit. A call from me and you'd be in custody quicker than you can say 'blackmail', and you can kiss goodbye whatever it is you're after."

We stared at each other until Curtis spoke again. "What I want to know is what you're looking for. It's something of extraordinary value, isn't it?"

I had to think quickly. "I'm not telling you anything," I told him. "Go on, call the Questing Federation. I'd die before I'd tell you anything."

Curtis drew a flick-knife from his pocket. A second or two later he had me in an armlock with the knife at my throat.

"Let's try again," he said. "What are you looking for?"

I stamped hard on his foot and struggled. He held the knife so close I could feel the coldness of the blade; his hands gripped me tightly and I could smell his breath against my ear. This was good news, as I now had Curtis precisely where I wanted him: convinced he was stronger and smarter. And now that he was an idiot again, I could act.

"Okay, okay," I said in a strained *please don't hurt me* voice. "It's no big deal. We need Leviathans' teeth. They're useful in spells. In particular, we're trying to re-animate the mobile phone network, which will require a couple of dozen."

"Leviathans' teeth?"

"Yes; we usually extract them from the Leviathan bites we find on the tails of jetliners, but the attacks have dropped off these past six years."

The Leviathan tooth story was nonsense, of course. No one had used them in potions for years due to the whole growing antlers side-effect controversy of the 1720s, and we certainly didn't need them to spell mobile phones into existence. Only one part was true: Leviathans did chase jetliners, like dogs chase cars, some say.

"So without Leviathan teeth, the mobile phone network won't work?"

"And a lot of other spells, too," I said, "and here's the deal: Keep quiet about the quest and help us to find the Leviathans' Graveyard. It's where the creatures go to die, and if we can find it, there will be hundreds of tons of dry bones for us to search through. Your silence and assistance will be rewarded: five Leviathan teeth for you to trade as you see fit. Deal?"

"I'll stay quiet and help you," said Curtis, "but for twenty teeth."

"I can go as high as ten."

"Fifteen."

"Okay," I said, "you've got a deal."

He relaxed his grip and took the knife from my throat. "Well now, *partner*," he said with a greedy smile, "this sounds so much better. And this Leviathans' Graveyard is somewhere near the top of Cadir Idris, yes?"

"So legend has it. And now that you know where we're heading, you can get your objectionable carcass out of my pod."

"Only too happy to oblige, Jennifer. See you tomorrow."

I closed the door after he had gone and bolted it, then took a deep breath. Curtis was out of my hair for a while, but now that I knew he would use violence to get what he wanted, I'd have to keep a careful eye on him. If Addie was right and he was along only to make up the fifty percent casualty rate, I half hoped he would hurry up and become a statistic. I then felt guilty for half hoping he would die, then felt stupid for feeling guilty about half hoping he would die. This could have gone on for a while, so I pinched myself out of the emotional-guilt feedback loop and set out my bedroll.

I lay on my back and stared out at the night sky through the skylight, listening to the jangling of the perimeter fence as the night creatures stalked through our camp. Moobin was suggesting I use EVERY EFFORT to rescue Perkins, and despite the fact that Moobin had been against looking for the Eye of Zoltar, he was now asking me to carry on with all determination. Something wasn't right.

I was still trying to figure it out when I fell fast asleep.

TWENTY-FOUR

Slow Boat to the
Land of Snodd

When I awoke, the sun was up, by not by much. I had been disturbed twice in the night, once as a Tralfamosaur herd moved through noisily and again when Ignatius found that a cucumber-size flesh-eating slug had been sucking on his toe as he lay asleep. He screamed and dislodged it, which was a relief to the rest of us who might have had to help him.

I unbolted the door of my pod and looked cautiously out. A ground fog had crept in; it would offer good cover for a Hotax attack, so we would need to remain vigilant until the fog cleared. I folded up my bedroll, tidied the pod, collected my belongings, and then signed my name in the visitor's book before descending the pole to get breakfast going, all the while keeping a wary eye out.

The half-track had been shoved a few feet sideways, presumably by a clumsy Tralfamosaur, but aside from a small piece of bent armor plate, no damage had been done. There were snork badger footprints aplenty, and here and there were the shiny trails of flesh-eating slugs. If we wanted to earn a few moolah, we could have scraped up the trails and sold them to any glue supplier, as slug slime is that gooey substance you find in glue guns.

"Ook?" Ralph appeared from the brush seemingly unharmed by his night out in the open. He would have been used to sleeping with dangerous creatures all around him, even though most of the nasty creatures he could have known would have died out by the end of the Pleistocene.

"Sleep well?" I asked, and he stared at me.

"G-ook," he said. I think he was trying to learn to speak. Or relearn, at any rate. "L-ook." He showed me the flint knife he had been making.

"May I hold it?" I asked, putting out my hand. After looking at me suspiciously for a moment, Ralph gave me the knife. It was well balanced, with a carved bone grip in the shape of the half-track. The blade was finely curved, dangerously serrated, and so thin it was almost translucent. I smiled appreciatively and handed it back. He gave an odd half smile and placed the knife in a large ladies' handbag he must have found somewhere, then hung the bag over the crook of his arm.

"Jennifer," I said, pointing at myself.

"J-ookff," he said, then pointed at himself and said, "R-ooff."

"You're getting it," I said with a smile, then nodded as he pointed at various things around the campsite and tried to name them. A small part of what had once been Ralph's brain was attempting to speak through an Australopithecine voice box.

"Hfff t-Ook," he said, pointing at the half-track. After a while he settled down by himself, practicing pronunciations and eating some beetles he'd collected.

I had noticed with dismay that Perkins's and Addie's pod ladders were still down, indicating that they'd not returned during the night. Ignatius's ladder was also down, so I checked his pod—it was empty. I found a few slime trails and oddly shaped footprints at the base of his pod-pole, but no evidence of Ignatius. It was not until I went to search for a fireberry to cook breakfast that I found him. He was huddled—*wedged* might be a better word—in one of the wooden rowboats we had seen dangling straight up due to thermo-wizidrical fallout, tethered to earth only by a frayed rope tied to the jetty. Ignatius was alive, awake, and staring at me with a shocked expression.

"Are you okay?" I called.

"No, I am *not* okay," he said. "Several large creatures, two small ones, and a slimy thing tried to eat me in the night."

"That's an uneventful night in the Empty Quarter," I said. "Didn't anyone explain the dangers before you came out here?"

"No, they did not," said Ignatius in an aggrieved tone. "They said this experience would be like the most amazing and enjoyable danger-fest known to man."

"And—?"

"They said it would be *like* it—not *actually* it. You all must be stark staring bonkers to want to be out here. I'm going home."

"Fair enough," I said, glad to be rid of him. "You can pick up a G'mooh when we get to Llangurig tonight."

"I'm not going a step farther. You can call me a G'mooh as soon as you find a pay phone. It can come and get me."

G'mooh was an acronym for Get Me Out of Here, the universally accepted name for a fast-exit taxi, which guarantees those who have lost their nerve a speedy way out of the empire. The G'mooh drivers are usually battle-damaged ex–tour guides who stop at nothing to return their passengers to safety. It's expensive, but few haggle.

"Okay," I said, "if you want to stay out here on your own, but I'd not . . ."

I was distracted by Ralph lolloping up the jetty; when he reached us, he stared up at Ignatius huddling in the vertically moored boat.

"Go away, monkey boy," said Ignatius. "Go on, shoo."

But Ralph did not shoo, and instead flicked the taut rope that anchored the rowboat with an inquisitive forefinger. He looked up at Ignatius. "No mmnk . . . *boy.*"

"What did he say?" asked Ignatius.

"I think he said he wasn't a monkey boy."

Ignatius laughed. "Well he *is* — that much is obvious — and a nasty piece of genetic throwback to boot."

Ralph frowned, rummaged in his handbag, and brought out the razor-sharp flint knife. Without pausing, he sliced cleanly through the rope that tethered Ignatius to the ground. The rowboat, with Ignatius in it, began to rise gently in the morning air.

"Ralph!" yelled Ignatius, suddenly panicking. "What in —!"

"Wait there!" I said. "I'll throw you a line!"

I ran to the half-track and rummaged in the toolbox for a length of cord. By the time I found one, Ignatius was about twenty feet above me, drifting east. I tied a wrench to the end of the line and readied myself to throw it to him.

"It's okay!" he yelled excitedly. "The wind is taking

me toward the border. Cancel the taxi; I'll be home and safe in an hour or two!"

"Hang on, Ignatius!" I had seen civilians try to use magic for their own ends enough times to know it could go horribly wrong. "I don't think this is a good idea."

"Nonsense!" called Ignatius happily. "By the time the magic wears off, I'll be home and dry."

"Wait!"

But I was too late. The rowboat was drifting faster as the breeze caught it, even bumping against Curtis's pod-pole as it went past. Curtis popped his head out to see what was going on, and was surprised to see Ignatius drifting by.

"I'm off for home," said Ignatius. "Join me?"

Curtis said he wouldn't but wished him well; they agreed to meet up at a bar in London sometime when all of this was over. Their voices roused the princess and Wilson, who also wished Ignatius well but probably, like me, were fed up with him. The rowboat rose until it met its maximum levitation of about six hundred feet, and continued to drift in the direction of the Cambrian border.

Now that everyone was awake, they came down their pod-poles. The fog had dispersed and the risk of Hotax attack lessened, so we all washed in the lake while we swapped notes about the night's noises, terrors, and close calls, then sat down to a breakfast of coffee and bacon and eggs. By the time we finished, Ignatius and his rowboat were a distant dot in the morning sky.

"I've just had a thought," said the princess. "I mean, aren't there anti-aircraft batteries along the border?"

"That's just for aircraft coming in," said Wilson. "They'd have to be either crazy or vindictive to shoot at anyone leaving. Wouldn't they?"

And as if to prove that Emperor Tharv's orders to his military were just that — crazy *and* vindictive — we saw puffs of anti-aircraft fire explode around the small dot. It was a slow-moving target, and Ignatius didn't stand a chance. There was a large explosion, and we saw a few bits fall to earth, trailing smoke.

"That was bad luck," remarked Curtis without a shred of compassion. "Should have stuck with us — or taken a parachute."

"I trained in the navy," said Wilson, "and the first thing you learn is that parachutes are not generally required while boating."

"Ook-ook-ook," said Ralph, with a slight curling of the lip that I took to be an early-hominid smile.

"Do you think Ralph planned all that?" asked the princess.

"I'm not sure Australopithecines *can* plan," I said, "but you never know."

As soon as we had given Ignatius a minute's silence

as a vague sort of respect, I said, "Okay. This is where we are: Addie went to rescue Perkins last night and told me that if she didn't return, she was dead. It's now nine o'clock. I say we wait until midday before assuming the worst. After that, we head off toward Llangurig. Any objections?"

There weren't, of course, and we settled down to wait.

TWENTY-FIVE

Leviathans Explained
and Some Tourists

I t rained for about half an hour, so we sheltered under the awning attached to the half-track. At eleven o'clock two Tralfamosaurs moved through the camp, so we climbed the pod-poles until they were safely past.

The morale of the small group was not high. Despite the fact that none of us had liked Ignatius, and his demise tipped Addie's guaranteed fifty percent survival rate in our favor, a member of our group had still died, and somewhere he would be mourned. Curtis was being unbearably smug, thinking he had one over on me, so I avoided him. I'd told the princess about his visit to my pod the previous evening; she again suggested that she kill him, which I again refused. So with neither of us talking to Curtis and with Ralph not talking very well, Wilson was about the only person we could all turn to for a chat. He spent the time writing up his bird-watching notes in a blue exercise book.

I looked over his shoulder and noticed that the *Birds I've Seen This Week* page was almost completely blank.

"Not much luck seeing birds?" I asked. "Tharv's ban must be working."

"The absence of birds has nothing to do with him," said Wilson. "Birds have a hard time living out here. The successful ones either learn how to burrow, like sand martins, puffins, or blind mole sparrows, or have a huge turn of speed, like the swift or falcon X-1. Anything else that flaps is devoured."

"By what?"

"The Cloud Leviathans, of course," said Wilson. "The beasts swoop low across the land, ingesting huge volumes of air, along with everything that's in it. The air is compressed in a Leviathan's muscular chambers, and when the run is over, the beast swallows the flying creatures and vents the compressed air through pressure ducts on its underside, adding lift at the end of a feeding run."

"Sort of like whales in the ocean?" asked Curtis.

"Absolutely," said Wilson. "Leviathans have been known to swallow flocks of starlings more than ten thousand strong, and are thought to be the reason behind the passenger-pigeon extinction in North America. They're the reason birds migrate, too — to avoid being eaten. I'm not surprised at the lack of birds here. Cloud Leviathans are about the size of a smallish passenger jet, so they can get pretty hungry."

"How does it fly with such ridiculously small wings?" asked the princess, holding up a blurry photograph on a page of *Creatures of Cambria and Which to Avoid.* The creature looked sort of like a stubby plesiosaur, with four tiny paddle-shaped wings and a large mouth on the underside of a broad, flat head.

"No one's ever been able to study Cloud Leviathans in depth," said Wilson, "first because they are rare — less than five in existence, it's believed — and second because they have chameleonlike skin that allows them limited invisibility. No one has ever found a corpse, far less a skeleton, which leads us to the theory of a legendary graveyard — a hidden place they all go to die."

"Do you think it likely Sky Pirate Wolff trained one?" I asked.

Wilson thought for a moment. "It's always possible, of course, and I've heard the stories about aerial piracy, but I'm fairly skeptical. As Laura noted, the Leviathan doesn't look like a good flyer, so how could it support the weight of a team of pirates?"

I considered the possibility of Sky Pirate Wolff and whether she even existed. If she didn't, then the Eye of Zoltar might not exist either. I reminded myself that I was not necessarily here to *find* the Eye, but simply to ask Able Quizzler what he knew. I could still do that, even with our current difficulties.

On the strike of twelve and with no sign of Addie and Perkins, I decided that we should go on ahead. I wrote what we were doing on a sheet of paper and left it taped to the bottom of Addie's pod-pole. Wilson suggested that he take the wheel, and after some grinding of gears, we departed along the compacted dirt road marked LLAN-GURIG AND THE NORTH, to which the Cambrian tourist board had helpfully added *32% chance of being devoured, but good scenery with ample picnic spots.*

We hadn't gone more than two miles when we came across a dusty Range Rover parked by the side of the road. We slowed down as we passed and looked in at the driver and passenger, who were staring at the view. They didn't look at us, and sensing that something might be wrong, I instructed Wilson to stop the half-track a little farther down the road.

"Wait for us here," I said to the princess and Curtis, then walked cautiously back to the Range Rover, accompanied by Wilson. Ralph, who didn't seem to want to stray too far from my side, followed along.

"Everything okay?" I asked the driver, but he didn't reply. A well-dressed middle-aged man, he held a camera in one hand while the other rested lightly on the steering wheel. His brow was wrinkled as though he had just seen something puzzling, but he made no movement. Something definitely wasn't right.

"Hello?" I said, and waved a hand in front of his face. He didn't even blink.

"Mine's unresponsive," I said. "What about yours?"

"Same," said Wilson, staring uneasily at the passenger. She seemed frozen in midstretch, her mouth open as though just finishing a yawn.

"Mule fever?" I suggested.

"If it was, they'd have grown mule ears long before the paralysis set in," replied Wilson.

"I can't feel a pulse," I remarked, holding the driver's wrist, "and the skin feels hard and waxy."

"Hotax did this," said Wilson.

I looked at the motionless people. "What are you saying?"

"I'm saying," said Wilson, "that the Hotax are not just murderously cannibalistic but big into conservation. They retain the skin, hair, and bones and preserve them perfectly. Look."

He lifted the hair from the back of the passenger's neck to reveal a row of fine cross-stitching in the skin, then reached over and tapped the eyeball of the driver. The eye seemed not human at all, but skillfully made of glass.

I peered closer. It was as realistic as anything I had

ever seen, and ten times better than the garbage you find at the wax museum.

"Amazingly lifelike, aren't they?" said Wilson. "The families of Hotax victims often elect not to bury their relatives but to use them as hat stands in the hall. Mind you, the good thing about a Hotax attack is that you don't know anything about it—there's just a slight prick in the neck as the poisoned dart hits home. Then you're like this, preserved at the moment of death, forever."

"I . . . suppose I could think of worse ways to go," I said.

"I could definitely think of worse ways to go," agreed Wilson thoughtfully. "Knowing Hotax, they would have stripped the car for anything tradable, too. Look." He lifted the hood to reveal an empty engine bay.

We stood musing on the Hotax's odd mix of utter savagery, skilled artistry, and business sense when the roar of an engine punctuated the silence. It was the half-track. We turned as it clunked swiftly into gear and lurched off.

"Hey!" I yelled, and ran after it. As it drove away, I could see the driver: Curtis. The half-track was not fast, but Curtis had a head start. I couldn't catch him.

"Tell me you didn't leave the keys in the ignition," I said to Wilson as he joined me.

"Whoops," he said. "Sorry."

"Ook," said Ralph.

"This is bad," I said, looking around at the empty

moorland and wondering what horrors lay hidden just out of sight. "*Really* bad."

"He's probably doing it as a stupid joke," said Wilson without much conviction. "He'll be back soon."

"He's gone for good," I said, realizing what was happening, "on a journey to the Leviathans' Graveyard."

"Why?"

"Because he thinks Leviathan teeth are key to the magic industry and wants them all for himself, I imagine."

"Are they?"

"Not at all. And I don't know why he took my handmaiden with him and didn't just dump her by the side of the road."

"I have a theory about that," said Wilson. "The Cambrian Empire has suffered a servant shortage for the past three decades, and it's not just handmaidens. Footmen, cooks, pastry chefs, and even boot boys are in short supply. He probably wants to sell her in Llangurig, and I daresay he'd get a good price."

I sat on a boulder and rubbed my face with my hands. "This trip is getting worse and worse."

"We might be able to buy her back," said Wilson, "unless she's good at ironing—a well-ironed shirt out here is as valuable as gold."

"I've got a feeling the prin—I mean, Laura's not that good at ironing," I said, guessing that she'd be unable to identify an iron in a lineup of fruit. "How far is it to Llangurig?"

"By road, about thirty miles," replied Wilson. "Half that if we cut across country. But one thing's for certain—"

"We don't want to spend a night in the open."

"Right."

I walked to the other side of the road, picked up a stone, and in a pointless display of anger and frustration, chucked it as far into the Empty Quarter as I could. I had entrusted the care of the expedition to a twelve-year-old who had lost Perkins to a gang of bandits and then failed to rescue him, leaving Perkins at the mercy of Emperor Tharv and a possible—no, probable—restarting of his thermo-wizidrical device project. I had lost the princess entrusted to my care by woefully underestimating Curtis's greed, giving him a reason to abandon us to our deaths in the Empty Quarter, the most dangerous place in the Cambrian Empire, which is the most dangerous place in the Ununited Kingdoms.

Terrific.

I think Ralph and Wilson sensed my anger, for they held back across the road for five minutes, then walked over to join me.

"Well, now," said Wilson, who seemed to have an overwhelming capacity for optimism in the face of unrelenting failure. "I expect that a lift may be along soon."

"Between when we stopped last night and right now," I asked, "how many vehicles have passed us?"

"Well, none," said Wilson, "but that's not to say they won't. And although the Empty Quarter is the most dangerous region, we're not actually in the most dangerous place in the Quarter. Or at least, not quite. And we should count our blessings that we're still alive."

"Whoop-de-doo," I replied, staring at the ground. "Happy days."

"Dan-jer!" said Ralph in a sharp, urgent tone. I looked around and could not see where the danger lay. But Wilson could.

"Don't move," he whispered.

"Hotax?"

"Sadly, no. Something much worse. Remember a second ago when I said we should count our blessings that we're still alive?"

"I remember that, yes."

"I—I might have spoken too early."

TWENTY-SIX

A Brush with Death

I stared in the direction that Ralph and Wilson were looking, but could see nothing. The Empty Quarter was living up to its name surprisingly well.

"I can't see anything," I whispered.

"*Moribundus carnivorum,*" said Wilson in a low voice, "moving in from the northwest."

"*Mori* — what?" I whispered back.

"*Moribundus carnivorum.* A Lifesucker. Nourished not by the proteins, fats, and starches *within* life forms, but by the very essence of life itself."

I looked again. There was nothing visible except a rabbit, nibbling the grass about thirty feet away and steadfastly ignoring us.

"You mean the rabbit?"

"The rabbit? No, of course not the rabbit. *Behind* the rabbit."

"I can't see anything behind the rabbit. Except . . ."

My voice trailed off. I didn't actually see the Lifesucker, but I saw the effect as it slowly crept up on the rabbit. All around us the grass was bright and green and lush, but a trail of brown, withered grass was advancing slowly toward the rabbit like gravy on a tablecloth. The brown stain of death was no more than six inches wide, and as the rabbit stopped nibbling and looked around cautiously, the encroaching dead grass stopped and waited.

"I see it now," I whispered. "It's stalking the rabbit."

"It usually takes bigger prey than that," Wilson whispered back. "Must be hungry. It will take one of us if it picks up on our scent."

"We can outrun it, can't we?"

"Outrun death?" said Wilson, eyebrows raised. "I think not."

When the Lifesucker was about a foot away from the unwitting rabbit, it pounced. The rabbit seemed shocked and tried to run, but then faltered, convulsed, tipped on its side, and twitched a few times before lying still.

"Sh-*ook,*" said Ralph, as we all stared intently at the dead rabbit. But it wasn't yet over. The Lifesucker stole not only life itself but stripped away many of life's functions: warmth, moisture, beauty. In less than a minute the rabbit had aged and withered until it was nothing more than a dry husk of patchy fur stretched tautly across a brittle skeleton.

"I've not seen anything like —"

"Shh!" whispered Wilson. "It's strongest when freshly nourished. It will be hunting for more prey — I've seen one take an entire herd of sheep before collapsing into a gorged stupor. If you can push anything charismatic and life confirming to the back of your mind and fill your head with utter banality, now's the time to do it."

"How do I do that?"

"I usually start with daytime TV, and then work my way down through celebrity biographies to international road aggregate trade agreements."

It's hard to think boring thoughts when death is lurking nearby, so I just attempted to relax, and I could see Wilson and Ralph do the same. The dead grass moved at a slow walking pace in our direction, then stopped a few feet from Ralph. The Australopithecine held utterly still and stared absently into the middle distance, his mind apparently blank. The dead patch of grass remained in one place for what seemed like an age, then moved past Ralph, past Wilson, and headed toward me in a slow, purposeful manner. I'd faced down death a couple of times, but never like this.

I stayed as still as I dared until the Lifesucker was

barely a yard away, and that's when Wilson stamped his feet.

"Hey ho!" he yelled in a forced voice tinged with fear. "Boy, am I feeling terrific today! So full of *life*. So much to do, so much to see! Everything in the world is out there, and I am the one to breathe in its many varied splendors!"

For a moment, the dead patch of grass paused, but then continued in my direction.

"Ook, ook!" Ralph joined Wilson and did an odd dance while making a strange trilling noise that was not exactly musical, but might become so in a few hundred millennia.

I hurried to get away, stumbled on a rock, and fell heavily to the ground.

"Ha, hoo!" yelled Wilson as he moved closer, trying to draw the Lifesucker away from me. Ralph joined him, but it wasn't working. Death was after me. A small frog died instantly as the patch of dead grass moved under it. In my panic, still on my back, I found myself attempting to flee in an undignified backwards floundering movement.

Just as Wilson looked like he was about to put himself between the Lifesucker and me, a bellow rent the air. "HOLD!"

I stopped. Wilson and Ralph stopped. Death, ever

the opportunist, stopped as well — perhaps a tastier snack was suddenly within easier reach.

The newcomer was standing less than a dozen paces away. He wore walking breeches, stout boots, a checked shirt rolled up to the elbows, and carried a large rucksack. He could have been in his thirties, though he had an agreeably boyish face, and his thick brown hair was tied up with a red bandanna. He regarded me with the most piercing green eyes I had ever seen; they didn't so much look *at* me but *into* me.

He was weighing a stone up and down in his hand, as though to ensure accuracy when he threw it. I wondered if you could kill death with a stone, until I realized the stone wasn't for death. It was for me. He swung his arm around, there was a sudden blaze of light, and everything went black.

TWENTY-SEVEN

The Name's Gabby

H er life force positively glows," came an unfamiliar voice out of a darkness punctuated by flashing stars. "I can see why the Lifesucker homed in on her. Have you known her long?"

"Since yesterday," said a second voice, more familiar. "Her party rescued me from some kidnappers. I think she's something big in the magic industry."

"No kidding?" The unfamiliar voice sounded impressed. There was a pause, then: "Where did you find the Australopithecine?"

"His name's Ralph. He had a Genetic Master Reset."

"I'm not sure what that means."

"To be honest," said Wilson—for that was the familiar voice, I realized—"I'm not really sure myself. I think it's a kind of magic."

"There's not much round here that isn't. Does it trouble you that his thing is showing?"

"No, we're kind of used to it by now."

"Ook."

I opened my eyes to find Wilson, Ralph, and the stranger staring at me. Wilson was holding a damp handkerchief to my head.

"Am I dead?" I asked.

"If you were," said the stranger with a smile, "would you choose this place as heaven?"

I looked around. I was still in the Empty Quarter, leaning up against the Range Rover. If this had all been a bad dream, I was still in it.

"Sorry I had to knock you out," said the stranger, "but your heart was belting out a funeral march so loud every Lifesucker on the planet could hear you."

I looked at the handkerchief in Wilson's hand. There was only a smallish spot of blood.

"Thank you—?"

"The name's Gabby," said the stranger amiably, "a traveler like yourselves."

"Jennifer," I said, shaking his outstretched hand, "and this is Wilson."

"I've heard of you," said Gabby to Wilson. "Been here awhile. A lot of close scrapes, but you always got away."

"I *will* die out here," said Wilson. "I'm choosing my moment — and I've been lucky."

"I'm not so sure luck has much to do with it out here."

"What does, then?" I asked.

"Fate," Gabby said, "and chosen moments winning out over lost moments. But we don't choose the moments — the moments choose us."

"I'm not sure I understood that," said Wilson slowly. "Jennifer?"

"Not really, no."

Gabby shrugged. "Actually, me neither. I heard it from a smarter guy. Was this your transport?"

He nodded toward the Range Rover, and I explained that up until an hour ago we'd had a half-track but it had been stolen, along with all of our luggage and a handmaiden.

"Llangurig, eh?" said Gabby after Wilson had explained where we were heading, but not why we were heading there. "Me too. We better get going if we're to have even a hope of finding a safe place to spend the night."

"The Lifesucker," I said with a start, suddenly remembering. "Is it still around?"

"It'll always be around," he said, "and will eventually return for you, as it will for us all. Death cannot be avoided forever, but it can be postponed—it's very much like doing the dishes. Now, we must leave before the batteries run down."

"Batteries?"

It turned out that the reason for death's sudden disinterest in me was that Gabby had coaxed it away by playing a small tape recorder with the sound of a party in full swing. The joyous laughter and unrelentingly upbeat chatter of happy humans was considerably more attractive to death than unconscious me. Gabby had placed the tape recorder in the branches of an oak, and the patch of dying grass was currently circling beneath the tree the way a dog might pace angrily when seeking a squirrel. The tree was now quite dead, of course, as was the ground beneath—but better it than me, I figured.

The four of us began to walk along the empty road to Llangurig, keeping a watchful eye out for peril. Ralph moved about like a spaniel on a walk, sniffing a plant here, scrabbling under a stone for a beetle or two there.

"What are you doing out here?" I asked Gabby. "You don't look as though you're on vacation."

"I collect information on death likelihood for a major player in the risk-management industry."

"Can you explain that in simple terms?"

"Everything has an element of risk," he said, "and

by identifying the potential risk factor of everything humans do, we can decide where best to deploy our assets to avert that risk."

"You work for an insurance company?"

"Our data is used in the insurance industry," he said, "but we also freelance. As you can imagine, a place as dangerous as the Cambrian Empire offers unique opportunities for studying risk. For example, if a group of people are confronted by a Tralfamosaur, which is more likely to be eaten first? The one who panics, the one who runs, the one who looks most dangerous, or the one who looks juiciest? There are many factors."

"I'm guessing juiciest."

"Yes, me too — it's not a good example."

"You must know the Empty Quarter very well."

"I can't stay away from this place," he confessed with a smile, "and studying people as they weigh the risks of their decisions is fascinating. Did you know that you are statistically more likely to die driving to the airport than you are on the flight?"

"You've never flown by JunkAir, clearly."

"There are always exceptions to the rule," conceded Gabby.

No traffic appeared in the next hour, except two Skybus trucks, presumably taking aircraft parts out of the empire. The trucks swept past and were soon lost to sight.

The day grew warmer, and we spoke less as we walked. Wilson, usually voluble and optimistic, fell silent, and even Ralph seemed to have calmed down and was keeping a closer lookout. With Llangurig still twenty-five miles or so away, it would not be possible to get there before dark, and a night in the open seemed inevitable.

"I think we should turn back," said Wilson when we stopped for a rest. "At least the pod-poles would be a safe place to stay for the night. We could wait there until a tourist party comes along with transportation to give us a lift out." He took off one of his boots and stared sadly at a blister, one of several.

"That might not be for a week or more," I said, "and I've got Perkins, a half-track, and a handmaiden to retrieve." There was a rubber dragon, Once Magnificent Boo, and the Eye of Zoltar to consider too.

"We could leave the road and cut *across* the Empty Quarter," said Gabby thoughtfully. "I know a Hotax trail that would take us directly to Llangurig past the lair of Antagonista, the dragon who once ruled these Dragonlands."

"Cut across the Empty Quarter on foot?" Wilson sounded incredulous.

"Sure," replied Gabby. "The dragon lived here for so long that local animal memory evolved to include it — the dragon's been dead for almost half a century, and still nothing goes near the lair. I calculate the risk factor of sleeping near the old dragon's lair at no more than four percent."

"Sounds good to me," I said, since dragons held no real fear for me. "Ralph? What do you say?"

"Yoof," said Ralph, staring at me curiously, still holding the ladies' handbag in the crook of his arm. His response might have meant yes or no or almost anything between, but I'd felt I should ask him anyway.

Wilson shrugged. "Lead on and let's get it over with."

And so it was agreed. After about half a mile we left the road to take a narrow path close to a roadside memorial to an Unnamed Tourist who was "dissolved but not forgotten," but judging from the state of the half-buried headstone, probably had been.

After a deep breath and an exchange of nervous glances, we struck off across the open country of the Empty Quarter.

TWENTY-EIGHT

The Old Dragonlands

The Hotax path was easy to follow between the tussocks of grass, but the going was slow. We encountered a jumble of boulders that had been carved by the wind into curious and frightening shapes, then gaping sinkholes, marshes, and the occasional flaming tar pit littered with the charred bones of large herbivores.

We passed a herd of elephino staring thoughtfully at their feet, as was their habit, then came across a giggle beetle migration, where a line of yellow-spotted carapaces stretched into the distance in both directions, chuckling constantly. We stepped across, walked through a long-deserted village, then found an abandoned road paved with large, flat stones etched with curious markings.

We picked up the pace over the grass-fringed flag-stones. "This would have been the dragon's route to his lair," said Gabby, "in the pre-Dragonpact days, when dragons roamed freely and were of the same prestige as kings and emperors."

We followed the ancient roadway in a stop-start fashion all afternoon. We had to wait a half hour while a herd of Tralfamosaur moved through, and another time we paused due to a strange noise, only to discover it was a small herd of honking gazelle, so named because their call is indistinguishable from a car horn. A herd honking in unison sounds exactly like a traffic jam in Turin.

We stopped for a break near a spring of fresh water that bubbled out of the ground and tasted of licorice; there was probably a seam of it somewhere underfoot.

"Anyone got anything to eat?" I asked. I had left everything—food, drink, conch, Helping Hand™, cash, Boo's twenty-grand letter of credit—in the half-track.

No one had anything, although Gabby was carrying a full backpack, which he didn't remove as he sat on a grassy bank.

Ralph disappeared and returned five minutes later with a dead slug the size of a rat and about as appetizing. I knew slugs *could* be eaten if one were desperate, but desperate in this context meant "perilously close to death," and we weren't quite there yet. Because the flesh-dissolving enzyme was on the outside of the slug, it would have to be turned inside out like a rubber sock and then eaten like corn on the cob. After our polite refusal, Ralph ate it himself.

We followed the trail up a hill, crested the ridge, and looked down upon a huge, bowl-shaped depression about a mile in diameter. At the center was a large grass-covered dome, surrounded by a high wall that had partly collapsed. This, said Gabby, was the abandoned lair of the dragon. Nothing seemed to be growing around the lair, and even from this far away we sensed a dark, oppressive feeling. The breeze seemed to grow chillier, and high above, despite the gray overcast, a circle of clear blue sky could be seen directly above the grass-covered dome.

"Okay," I said, "we should be cautious. Long-unused spells may have recombined in unusual ways."

As we walked into the valley, the strangeness of the redundant strands of magic manifested itself. The grass in the cracks between the paving stones seemed to shift underfoot as we walked, and when once I looked back, the grass we had trodden upon had become nourished by our life force. Stranger still, partially hidden by the scrubby grassland were what appeared to be statues carved from reddish sandstone. One was human and three were Ho-tax—like humans, only stockier and with broader, flatter heads. Most were animals: several Buzonjis, a snork badger, a pair of ground sloth, and even an elephino, some honking gazelle, and a juvenile Tralfamosaur. They weren't true statues, but real creatures enchanted into stone, and one factor linked them all: Each had been caught in an expansive yawn.

"Don't yawn, anyone." I pointed to the victims. "A Turning to Stone defensive enchantment has recombined with a spell activated by yawning. The combination is potentially fatal if you become tired or bored."

They nodded sagely and we quickened our pace out of the danger zone.

We reached the outer wall around the lair, which had once been ten or fifteen feet high and made of interlocking blocks like a three-dimensional puzzle. The lair itself had been a neat truncated dome, much like a cake, with the vertical edge supported by a twenty-foot-high wall of river stones interspersed with jewels.

We walked partway around the paved circular courtyard, and that's when we came across the dragon — or at least the remains of it. His massive bones were lying in a heap where he had fallen. The jewel was missing from the forehead of his great skull. We could see the evidence of ax marks around his jaws where the teeth had been removed long ago; a dragon's tooth has a sharp edge that never blunts and is prized as a weapon or in manufacturing, and with a price to match.

"Treasure hunters," said Gabby, "eager to find the gold, silver, and jewels known to line a dragon's lair." He was right. The fine tiles that had once decorated the floor were broken and scattered.

"What a mess," muttered Wilson.

"What about the books?" I asked, indicating the remnants of bindings also scattered around. "From the dragon's library?"

Gabby nodded. "It's like vandals stripped anything of value away."

"Sham-ook," said Ralph in a soft voice.

"I know," I said. "This place must have been spectacular once."

As the whole sorry scene unfolded before us, I thought of the Mighty Shandar's role in the dragon's destruction, and how the powerful and mysterious lair of this beast had been stripped, like so many others, for nothing more than souvenirs and cash. Multi-millennia of wisdom simply lost. If Shandar's threat to destroy all dragons had been wrong before, it was triply wrong now. Colin and Feldspar must survive, must thrive, and must one day inhabit a lair such as this, where they could think deep thoughts and live a life in the pursuit of greater knowledge.

"This place has sadness stitched into its very fabric," said Wilson. "Can you feel it?"

"I can," said Gabby, "like a heavy, damp chill. I think we should pick up the pace."

"I agree," I said, and with Ralph leading the way, we skirted past the massive bones and headed toward the route beyond.

As we stepped from behind some fallen masonry, Ralph stopped dead. We stopped too. There, bathed in the warm orange light of the setting sun and looking every bit as dangerous as its eight-ton bulk would suggest, was a Tralfamosaur. It was barely fifteen feet away and was crouched, ready to spring. It cocked its head, regarding us in a dinner-y sort of way.

I'd been this close to a Tralfamosaur before. I'd seen the tiny red eyes and the saliva glistening on the razor-sharp teeth, but last time the Volkswagen's windshield had been between us, and there had been a plan. Here there was no plan, nothing between us, and the only possible thing in my favor was that Ralph was closer and probably tastier.

Ralph realized it too, and apparently unwilling to become an appetizer without a fight, quietly reached into his handbag and drew out his flint knife. The Tralfamosaur blinked at us all and flexed its front claws menacingly. I moved slightly as a precursor to darting right, hoping that Ralph and the others might dart left and then one or two of us might have a chance.

But as I moved, the Tralfamosaur moved with me. It had zeroed in on me, and it wasn't a pleasant feeling. As I was about to make my leap to a boulder a dozen paces away, a hand rested lightly on my shoulder. The Tralfamosaur cocked its head again, perhaps wondering if it could take two of us at the same time.

I looked over and saw Gabby at my side. He had opened his mouth wide, displaying two perfect rows of fine white teeth. It took me a moment to figure out what he was up to. He was pretending to yawn, and I did likewise; Ralph and Wilson joined in.

Yawns are, oddly enough, infectious. Once one person yawns, others are likely to follow. And since we were only *pretending* to yawn, I figured the spell would not affect us. The question was: Would the Tralfamosaur join in the yawn we had started?

The answer was: Not really. As we pantomimed yawns that would win no amateur drama prizes but could win gold in the Desperate Measures Challenge Cup, the Tralfamosaur peered at us hungrily and rose on its toes, ready to lunge. Faking yawns had been a long shot, obviously, and it looked like we would need to instigate Plan B, which was along the lines of "run like stink and hope for the best." It is always prudent — and I give you this information for free, as it might come in handy one day — when you are attacked by a hunger-crazed carnivore the size of a bus to remind yourself that it has immeasurably higher mass and cannot speed up, slow down, or change direction as quickly as something smaller. It was said that lively jumping, dodging, and jinking could postpone the inevitable for a minute — tops — until brute force would finally end the sorry spectacle. But even for the unskilled, the first bite could usually be avoided if you kept your eye on the beast.

So I fixed my eyes on the Tralfamosaur's, and as I watched, its jaws opened as a precursor to a lunge. I paused, wavered, then shifted my weight as I waited for it to make the first move.

But the move never came. The open mouth had actually been a vast yawn, accompanied by the foul stench of rotting carcasses, and the Tralfamosaur changed instantly to a dark granite statue that shimmered subtly in the last dying rays of the sun.

"Ook," said Ralph.

We looked at one another and burst out laughing — out of relief, I think — and then moved past the silent beast without talking.

We set up camp in an abandoned armored scout car. While Ralph went off somewhere, the rest of us found some fireberries and ignited them by twisting the stalks sharply to the left.

"Anything to eat?" I asked, as hunger was beginning to gnaw.

"Ralph had a hunting look in his eyes," said Gabby, "but if he comes back empty-handed or fails to come back at all, I have a Snickers somewhere."

Ralph did return, and with a skinned swamp rat. Using some scrap steel as a frying pan, we soon had it cooked, and the rat was about as welcome as any food could be. Huddled in the wreckage of the armored car with dried grass and heather pulled over us, Wilson and I soon settled down for the night. It wasn't easy. There were snuffles, scratches, clicks, and whistles as the night-life of the Empty Quarter went about its nocturnal business — thankfully, at some distance away.

Gabby sat nearby, filling in a report in a leather-bound ledger. "Paperwork," he explained when I asked. "The top floor wants to know everything we get up to here."

"I know the feeling," I said, as the magic industry was a stickler for paperwork.

As I stared up at the stars, bright and clear in the night sky, there was a screeching noise, and a homing snail arrived hot and sweaty on my chest. It was muddy and bruised, one of its antennae was missing, and several scratches on its shell spoke of a narrow escape from a predator. It was well past seven, and since my evening attempt at communication with Kazam hadn't happened — the conch was still in the half-track — Moobin and the others had sent a snail. I sat up, plucked off the message, and read it by the light of the fireberry.

The previous evening's message had been written in a neat hand, but this one seemed more hurried.

Couldn't raise you on the conch so hoping all
well. Eye of Zoltar and Perkins now imperative.
Tell Perkins from me that all other considerations
are now secondary, and Kevin says that if you
ever find yourself on the shoulders of giants and
need to take a leap of faith, go for it. weather
irrelevant, Moobin

I considered the message carefully. Did Moobin mean "all other considerations secondary" in the way that Wilson had described it in his story? "To use whatever means available to carry out his task"? And Kevin had said to take a leap of faith from the shoulders of giants? What was that all about? Giants had died out years ago and were long ago consigned to Grade VI Legend status, the same as dodos: "once existed, but now proven to be extinct."

By the light of the fireberries, I could see Ralph sitting sentry on a rock, flint knife at the ready. I tied my handkerchief around my head to guard against yawning, then tried to get comfortable against the remains of the seats in the abandoned scout car. After the day's events, I thought sleep would be impossible. In less than five minutes I was proven wrong.

TWENTY-NINE

The Morning Feeding

I awoke with a chill in my joints. The air was cold, and a thick layer of fog had draped the land in a soft, milky blanket. Sounds were muted, I could see barely twenty feet ahead, and the light was broad and directionless. It was early, and Wilson was still fast asleep close by. Ralph was perched on the rock where I had seen him the previous night, now hunched over, also fast asleep. Gabby was nowhere to be seen. As I looked around and stretched, I was suddenly aware of a distant whistling, like the wind that sings through the tassels of a fast-moving flying carpet.

The noise seemed to be coming from the north and was getting louder. In another second a worried-looking

Gabby came running into the campsite while wrestling to put on his backpack.

"Hang on to something!" he yelled. "Leviathan on a feeding run!"

Wilson had not awakened, so I flung myself on top of him and wedged myself—and him—with both feet into a corner of the vehicle and wrapped my arms around the bent steering wheel. Gabby, seemingly used to this, also held tight to the vehicle.

The whistling increased and a breeze stirred up. A moment later the air was flooded with birds eager to outrun the predator. I saw gulls tear past us, then sparrows, a hawk, three herons, a pelican, and two dozen starlings grouped together for protection. Many alighted in the wreckage of the vehicle and, ignoring us, tucked themselves into any crevice they could find. Three puffins snuggled inside my coat, and assorted sparrows, choughs, curlews, and a woodpecker desperately attempted to wedge themselves beneath the armored car's hull.

The whistling got louder and the wind increased. My ears popped, and suddenly a cloud of insects moved past, tumbling and fluttering. Butterflies and bees, wasps, ladybugs, and myriad others gathered in a confused and erratic swarm. The ground fog was blown away, and dust and dirt and small stones and clumps of grass were lifted and whipped and whirled into the air.

That's when I noticed Ralph. He was standing on his

rock, flint blade in hand, peering at the colossus that was fast approaching. I could see the Cloud Leviathan now, or at least its mouth—an oval gaping maw twenty feet wide and ringed with pearly-white teeth the size of artillery shells. The rest of the Leviathan was indistinct, more like a wobbly pattern in the air.

In another few seconds it was upon us, and as it went thundering overhead with the sound of a gigantic vacuum cleaner, I caught a glimpse of Ralph jumping into an attack.

Perhaps he thought a lone Australopithecine could bring down a Leviathan. Perhaps he wanted to be the first one to try. Perhaps deep down, the risk-averse loner who had once been Ralph D. Nalor wanted to end it all with the most daring endeavor of all. Whichever was true, Ralph managed to sink his dagger into the leathery hide of the beast as it moved past. He did not let go, and was carried away as the Leviathan continued on its feeding run, seemingly untroubled by its passenger.

The armored car in which we'd sought refuge lurched as the Leviathan went over us, and then all was still. The wind subsided and the birds hopped from their hiding places, rubbed their beaks, and flew off, apparently unperturbed. Gabby and I watched as the shimmering shape of the Cloud Leviathan reared vertically upward, venting air from the twin rows of vectored nostrils on its underbelly.

"Isn't that Ralph?" I asked.

It was. Ralph was clinging to the belly of the beast as it rose high into the air, streaming dust, feathers, dirt, and grass as it went. Ralph was tenacious; that was clear — he even had his large ladies' handbag still in the crook of his arm.

"Did I miss something?" asked Wilson, blinking and getting up.

"Kind of." I pointed toward the tiny dot that was Ralph, clearly visible on the shimmering outline of the translucent Leviathan. It looked almost as if Ralph were rising unsupported by anything at all. After a moment or two, the Leviathan rolled onto its side to head north, and Ralph was lost to sight.

"Do you think he's okay?" I asked.

"He'll be fine for about as long as he can hang on," replied Gabby.

We stared into the empty sky in silence.

"He was a loyal companion to us all," I said sadly.

"And will be missed," added Wilson.

"You always lose friends here in the empire," said Gabby philosophically, "and you'll lose more before the trip is over, I wager."

"Mathematically speaking, you may be right," I said, thinking of Addie's predicted fifty percent fatality index, "but I hope not."

"That Leviathan was low," mused Gabby as he unhooked a leathery scrap from the jagged edge of the armored car's shattered body. He laid the material across his arm, where it changed color to match his skin.

"Scraps of Leviathan skin fetch a good price on the Cambrianopolis black market, I've heard," said Wilson.

"If the emperor's men find you with this remnant, your head will be off," said Gabby. "It's better to let it go." And he released the scrap, which floated up like a helium balloon.

"Leviathans are lighter than air?" I said, amazed at what I was seeing.

"How else do you think something so large could fly?" asked Gabby. "We better get going. With luck we can get to the edge of the Empty Quarter before something considers that we'd make a fine breakfast. And Jennifer?"

"Yes?"

"I think you've still got some puffins inside your jacket."

It was true. They seemed to have taken a liking to the pockets, and had to be politely evicted.

Gabby, Wilson, and I walked in silence for the next three hours, now and then pausing to hide from danger, drink from a mountain stream, or nibble on some wild radishes. Eventually we came across the dormant marker stones that marked the edge of the Dragonlands and the northern edge of the Empty Quarter. The stones were covered with a thick crust of lichen, and appeared forlorn and forgotten. Llangurig would be only a few miles away.

Gabby called a halt.

"Any particular reason?" I asked.

"Breakfast."

"You have some?"

"No," said Gabby with a smile, "but they will."

He pointed toward a stunted oak. The roots had grasped one of the marker stones tightly, and the over-hanging branches partially hid a small group of people. A quick leg count told me there were five people, and I was apprehensive until I realized that six of the legs belonged to one creature—a Buzonji.

The other legs belonged to Perkins and Addie. I blinked away tears. I had convinced myself that I would never see them again.

THIRTY

Friends Reunited

H ey ho!" said Addie cheerfully as she came out from under the tree. "How are my tourists?"

I have rarely been so glad to see someone safe and well. Perkins, that is, and Addie a close second.

"Hey, Jenny," said Perkins, and he gave me a long hug, whispering in my ear that he'd missed me. I returned the compliment gladly and unconditionally, but I must confess that his increased age—he'd put on ten years with Ralph's Genetic Master Reset, remember— was not something I would get used to quickly.

"Are you okay?" I asked. "Not harmed in any way, I mean?"

"I'm fine," he said, "but I can't say the same for the kidnappers."

"Dead?"

He just looked at me and raised his eyebrows.

"Hail, fellow," said Addie to Gabby, grasping his hand and shaking it warmly. "Good to see you again."

"You know each other?" I asked, surprised.

"He's my secret weapon," said Addie. "Everyone should have a Gabby to look after them."

"You sent Gabby to keep an eye on us?" I asked.

"Only to remain on standby in case anything happened."

I looked at Gabby, who shrugged. "I should have said something, I suppose," he said, "but I didn't know until now that Addie was okay, and, well, I'm only in this for the rescuing."

I thanked him anyway, and Addie quizzed him further.

"I found them two clicks northwest of the podpoles," replied Gabby. "They'd lost their transport and were about to be emptied by a Lifesucker. I brought them here by way of the dragon's lair."

"Was that wise?" asked Addie.

"Perhaps; perhaps not," said Gabby, "but we made it without loss."

"Except Ralph," I said, "who tried to attack a Cloud

Leviathan on a low-level feeding run. I think he had an exciting ride while it lasted."

"And the others?"

I explained that Curtis had stolen the half-track with my handmaiden on board, and Addie agreed that Curtis would be heading toward Llangurig "almost certainly to sell Laura," as Wilson had thought. She didn't know, of course, that Laura was anything but a handmaiden—an odd one, but a handmaiden nonetheless.

"Laura sold?" said Perkins, who *did* know the princess was a princess. "That's not good."

"We'll get her back," I said, "whatever it takes. That's about it. No, wait, we lost Ignatius."

"Flesh-eating slugs?" asked Addie. "He never was a fast mover."

"He tried to escape to the border in a rowboat and was shot down by anti-aircraft fire."

"Wow," said Addie. "I would never have seen *that* coming."

"Neither did he."

"If you don't need me for anything more," said Gabby, "I'll be off. I've got some raw recruits to train in the risk-management business. Staff turnover is savagely high these days."

We all shook hands, I thanked him again, and after

politely refusing an offer of breakfast, Gabby was off at a brisk walk and soon lost to view over a rise.

We sat on the warm grass, and a picnic breakfast never tasted so good. Addie made tea in a billycan too, boiled over the residual thermo-wizidrical energy emanating from the runic markings on the fallen marker stones.

"So what's the deal with Gabby?" I asked.

"He's exactly what you see. Someone who assesses risk of death and steps in to intervene if the right conditions prevail."

"Why didn't he save Ralph?"

"Ralph wasn't human," said Addie, "and Gabby's instructions are clear. If he had to rescue nonhumans, where would he draw the line? Tralfamosaurs? Rabbits? Ladybugs?"

"He was definitely a bit strange," said Wilson thoughtfully. "He never ate or drank, and I didn't see him sleep last night. He was still awake as I nodded off, and awake before me."

"And me," I added. "And he never took off his backpack. I saw him struggling to put it on just once, when he returned to camp this morning."

"Listen," said Addie. "Gabby is what Gabby does, and it's best not to ask too many questions. There are some things out here that defy explanation, and Gabby —

well, he's one of them. Have you ever fully explained your Quarkbeast?"

"No," I replied.

"He's like that. Well, not exactly like a Quarkbeast, obviously, but you get my point. Don't look too close. He may not like what you find."

"Don't you mean *I* might not like what I find?"

"I know what I mean," said Addie, shooting me a look.

"So . . . what about the kidnappers?" I helped myself to another roll, this time with peanut butter. I saw Perkins and Addie exchange looks.

"If you'd rather not —" began Wilson.

"No, we should tell you," said Addie, taking a sip of tea. "I tracked them to about five miles from Cambrianopolis, and then waited until dawn before walking into their camp. I told them my word of death was in the steel I carried, and that they could stay there alive if they relinquished Perkins or stay there dead if they did not. I knew they wouldn't give him up, but it's traditional to offer some sort of deal."

"Three against one?" I said. "No offense or anything, Addie, but you're not even half their size. Did you think you had a chance?"

"What I lack in weight, I make up for in savagery," she said, "and no offense taken. I weighed my chances at about seventy-thirty in my favor. It would have been a hard hand-to-hand struggle, but I would have won eventually. I would have left them to the flesh-eating slugs, set free their Buzonjis, and returned with Perkins. When they took him, they would have expected me to do this."

"Did it pan out that way?" I asked.

"It would have," said Addie, "but for your friend here."

I turned to Perkins. "What did you do?"

"She turned up and, yes, did the whole dopey tribal honor speech," replied Perkins, "which was quite stirring in a simplistic, barbaric, and pointless-death kind of way, and I said that if she killed them, I wouldn't come with her."

"I told him he didn't have a choice," said Addie, staring into her teacup. "I would bind him like a hog and return him whether he liked it or not."

Wilson and I looked at Perkins expectantly.

"So," said Perkins, "I told her I would pop myself if she laid so much as a finger on any of them."

I raised my eyebrows. Popping was the last resort for a wizard, a simple spell that caused a hemorrhage in the brain. Unconsciousness would be instantaneous, and death would follow.

"That put me in a quandary," said Addie, "for it would be a triple failure. I would still have to kill the bandits, the Silurians and the Oldivicians would go to war, and the trophy in the argument—Perkins—would be lost anyway. There were no winners. So I did something I've never done before. I told them that I would not kill them, as there was no good reason for it, and that I would lose my honor to keep the peace between our tribes."

"I'm getting really confused over this whole honor thing," I said. "Isn't a willingness to die and to kill for an abstract concept of dubious relevance a bit nuts?"

"I'd be the first to admit that," said Addie. "Honor is kind of what you get when you weaponize manners, but if you're brought up in a system where honor is valued more than life itself, it makes a lot more sense. Some. A bit. Anyway—they attacked me as they were honor bound to do, and I defended myself as I was bound to do, but killed them in *self-defense*. I think it was what Gareth had planned. He had dishonored himself by kidnapping Perkins in the first place and causing conflict between our tribes, then being the cause of me dishonoring myself, which brought dishonor upon himself. By attacking me, he allowed me to restore my lost honor by killing him, and, odd as it might seem, his honor as well. He thus died with honor, and I thank and respect him for it. We didn't leave them to the slugs at all, and instead buried them with tribal honors, which is why we were kind of delayed getting back to you. The ground was hard, and we had to ride for miles to find a shovel."

"I'm totally lost," I said.

"Me too," said Wilson.

"And me," said Perkins, "and I was actually there witnessing it."

"Okay," I said, "what happened then?"

Addie continued. "We got to the pod-poles long after you had left, found your note, and followed your trail as far as the Hotax-attacked Range Rover. By that time it was late afternoon, and since Trigger wouldn't follow, we decided to find a hotel in Llanidloes."

"Who's Trigger?"

Addie nodded in the direction of her Buzonji, which tossed its head impatiently.

"So the plan is now —?" I asked.

"Same as before, pretty much," said Addie. "We'll head into Llangurig and see if we can retrieve your hand-maiden and the half-track and get some payback on that idiot Curtis."

"And then?"

"You can see what Able Quizzler has to say for himself, I guess — and take it from there."

This seemed the best plan, and after Addie had instructed Trigger to head on home, she led us toward a downhill path.

"Any news?" Perkins asked me. I showed him the latest note from the homing snail, and watched his reaction to "all other considerations secondary." A look of consternation crossed his face, but was soon gone.

"They're eager to keep the princess safe," he said, "and the Eye is still our number one priority."

"Maybe so," I said, "but if Able Quizzler has no information about the Eye of Zoltar, I'm pulling the plug. We've lost two people already, and hunting Leviathans and a legendary pirate across Cadir Idris sounds like a fool's errand."

"Fair enough," said Perkins. He pointed at Moobin's note again. "What's all this about a leap of faith?"

"No idea," I said, "and why did Moobin want to tell you that all other considerations are secondary? Are we in some kind of trouble?"

"I'm not sure," said Perkins. "Perhaps he just wanted to impress upon me the importance of this mission."

We came to a thin line of beech trees on a ridge, and Addie pointed toward a town on the valley floor. "Behold," she said dramatically. "Llangurig."

THIRTY-ONE

Llangurig

The town of Llangurig was situated on a bend in the river. It was surrounded by a high wall with a curved overhang at the top to protect against attack by Tralfamosaur and other terrors, and looked clean and tidy. The open countryside outside the walls was churned up and shattered by recent conflict. And I mean *really* recent — several armored vehicles were still smoldering from a battle.

"What are they?" I pointed to what looked like two encampments, one a half mile east of Llangurig and one the same distance to the west. Each encampment had its own system of trenches and earthworks, within which I could see troops at readiness.

"Two conflicting sides," said Addie, "have fought violently over Llangurig's territory for more than a century. The leaders of these two factions will stop at nothing to defeat the other, while between them, the target of their endless battle awaits the outcome with bated breath."

"Are they warlords?" I asked.

"If only," replied Addie. "At least power-hungry nut jobs eventually know when to call a truce. No, these two factions are fueled by greed, and are utterly ruthless in their pursuit of power, influence, and territory."

"You mean—?" said Perkins.

"Right," said Addie. "Railroad companies."

I looked again. The two encampments did appear to have cranes, piles of building materials, coal, and even a locomotive or two. Behind each fortified area was a railroad track, snaking away and soon lost to view in the endless green folds of the countryside. The churned soil and shattered earth were confined, I noticed, solely to the area around Llangurig.

As we watched, a salvo of artillery was fired from the encampment to the east, and a few moments later several shells burst close to the camp in the west, which returned fire and felled an ancient oak that looked as though it had survived several near misses in the past. While the barrage continued, engineers and armored fighting vehicles on the western side attempted to lay some track in the direction of Llangurig. This was soon noticed by those to the east, who sent some skirmishers to stop the engineers. Just three sleepers were laid, in exchange for a body count of five, as far as I could tell.

While this was going on, the engineers in the east used a steam crane to deliver a completed section of track about thirty feet in length, which was met with a fusillade of small-arms fire from the west. Welders in heavy body armor ran out to affix the new section of track, and although they welded with incredible bravery, the new track was apparently condemned by the Inspector of Works, dressed in a striped umpire's outfit.

"Not enough ballast under the track," said Wilson expertly. "It would never have taken the weight of a locomotive, let alone fully loaded coal wagons."

It all seemed very strange indeed, even by Cambrian Empire standards. The two factions seemed to be fighting over nothing more than the mile of empty ground between their tracks.

"Okay," I said slowly, "and they are fighting because . . . ?"

"I'll tell you as we walk down," said Addie, glancing at the sun to gauge the time. "We want to get to town in time for the 12:07 ceasefire."

"That seems very precise."

"Railroad militia are notorious sticklers for punctuality. They are sometimes late, but always apologize and let you know why, and if the ceasefire is really late, you can apply for a refund."

"A refund of what?"

She shrugged. "No one really knows."

As we climbed down the hill, the story unfolded by way of Addie's spirited storytelling. The conflict had begun with Emperor Tharv's grandfather, who was eager to bring modernity and riches to the empire via then-new railroad technology. A flurry of rail companies sprang up to bid on the lucrative contracts, but due to a misunderstanding, two rail companies were mistakenly awarded the line from Cambrianopolis to the deep-water anchorages at Aberystwyth.

"After some wrangling," concluded Addie, "the emperor decreed that whoever got to Llangurig first would control the line, so a flurry of building ensued. The Cambrian Railway Company built from the east, and the Trans-Wales-Rails Corporation from the west. The companies met on either side of Llangurig, and one thing led to another — angry words, a bloody nose, someone shot someone, and before you knew it, there was a war."

"Since when?"

"Almost one hundred and forty years. There are goods stacked high at the docks and in Cambrianopolis waiting to be transported by rail. If your great-grandfather ordered a Cambrian piano, it'll be in a warehouse somewhere, still waiting to be shipped."

We stopped within sight of the town's south gate as the warring companies exchanged another artillery salvo and several brave railroad militiamen were cut down by machine-gun fire.

"How many people have died over this mile of railroad track during that century and a half?" asked Perkins.

"Eight thousand," said Addie, "give or take."

"Working for the railroad is quite dangerous out here," said Wilson.

"True," said Addie, "and each of those soldiers is fighting not for glory, but a share of the profits. If the company you fight for builds the track to Llangurig and you survive, you'll be rich beyond your wildest dreams."

"What if you're killed?"

"You get a cardboard box to be buried in, and a fifty-plotnik Target gift card goes to the widow."

"Do they have any trouble recruiting?" asked Wilson.

"People are lining up."

"Someone should put a stop to this," growled Perkins.

"The battle has been going on for so long and the profits to be made from the line are so huge that whoever wins bankrupts the other," said Addie, "so it really is a matter of corporate life and death."

"What if it's a tie?" I asked. "Couldn't they share the line?"

"They would have to drive in the final two spikes at precisely the same time," she said, "and that's not likely to happen."

We waited until the 12:07 ceasefire, and the guns fell silent. Immediately each company came out to remove its wounded and dead, and the gates of the city opened. A torrent of traders, walkers, vehicles, railroad enthusiasts, TV crews, goatherds, and other assorted townsfolk spewed forth, eager to get out and back again before the battle recommenced at 14:38.

We walked to the gates and entered the town. It was busy. *Very* busy. Llangurig wasn't just a railroad trophy town, but a frontier town. All the land north of here was unexplored and uncharted. Llangurig was a good starting point for tours into the rarely traveled and mostly inhospitable Plynlimon and Berwyn Mountains.

"But the tours tend not to go to Cadir Idris," said Addie. "Even jeopardy tourism has its limits."

As we headed toward the nearest hostel for something to eat, I noted numerous street traders buying and selling railroad shares. With signs naming them Honest Bob and Rock-Steady Eddie and so forth, each trader had set up a blackboard with an up-to-date report of the current worth of the companies. After the morning's battle, the shares of the Cambrian Railway Company were slightly higher than the shares of the Trans-Wales-Rails Corporation, but from the look of all the hastily scrubbed and rewritten chalk on the board, this was a state of affairs that was constantly changing.

"The value of shares can go up as well as down!" came a cheery voice behind me. I turned to find the princess beaming at me.

"Oh, boy," I said, "am I glad to see you."

"Likewise," said the princess, giving me a very unprincess-y hug. "Hullo, Wilson; hullo, Addie and Mr. Perkins. Hang on, my goat shares have taken a dive."

She pointed at another trader dealing in commodities—things you can consume, like orange juice, beef, and goats. It seemed that the price of goats had suddenly dropped.

"Princess Someone must be dumping cheap goats on the already-saturated goat market," she mused. "I thought the price couldn't go any lower, but what a fool I was."

"Is that what you've been doing here for the past twenty-four hours?" I asked. "Dabbling in goat shares at the Llangurig commodities market?"

"I've not had so much fun in years," she said happily.

"The smallest thing can set prices tumbling. Shall I demonstrate?"

"No, please don't. What happened to Curtis and the half-track?"

"Gone, and not soon enough. Why not come over to the Bluebell Railway Inn? I can explain it over lunch."

This seemed a good idea, and we trooped across to the inn and ordered some food.

THIRTY-TWO

The Handmaiden's Tale

Once large tankards of tea had been placed in front of us by a burly barmaid with a pair of Star Class locomotives tattooed on her forearms, I said, "So, what's been going on?"

The princess turned her chair toward the window so she could see if the stock traders changed any prices, then began. "I was watching you examine the Range Rover on the road yesterday morning — what was it, by the way?"

"Hotax attack. Two tourists stuffed."

"Ah. Well, all of a sudden there's this colossal bang, and when I wake up, I'm rattling around on the floor of the half-track, bound and gagged and with a shocking headache. I figure Curtis must have whacked me on the head with a tire iron or something. We get to Llangurig during the afternoon battle, then enter the town at teatime. Curtis immediately sells me to a local kingpin named Gripper O'Rourke, then stays the night at the Llangurig Ritz and heads out first thing this morning in the half-track. I don't know where."

"Did he take any goats with him?" asked Addie.

"Four."

"He'll be heading north to Cadir Idris," said Addie. "The goats are payment to cross the Mountain Silurian territory."

"Why Cadir Idris?" asked the princess.

"To find the Leviathans' Graveyard," I said. "I told him Leviathan teeth were highly valuable to sorcerers."

"Are they?"

"No, although they might have some novelty value. Where's this Gripper fellow? I've got to buy you back."

The princess chuckled. "You won't have to. Let me explain: Since handmaidens are extremely valuable out here, Gripper didn't quite have enough cash to pay Curtis outright, and Curtis didn't trust that Gripper would send him the rest of the money, so I suggested that I float myself on the Llangurig Stock Exchange."

"You did *what?*" asked Perkins.

"Floated myself. It's very simple. If you consider that I have a value for doing handmaiden-y things, then I could incorporate myself as a company named Laura

Scrubb (Handmaiden) Ltd. I could then sell — or float — myself to buyers with my value split into one hundred shares. If you bought ten shares in Laura Scrubb (Handmaiden) Ltd., I would give ten percent of my sixty-hour working week to you, or six hours of labor."

"Wouldn't just selling your time for hourly pay work better?" I asked.

"No, this is much better," said the princess with a grin, "because those Laura Scrubb (Handmaiden) Ltd. shares are tradable. Gripper had a sixty percent share, but Curtis retained thirty percent, which he immediately sold for seventy plotniks a share. Not a great price, but for an unknown commodity — me — it was the best price he could get."

"So then what happened?"

"Okay, so to raise the value of Laura Scrubb (Handmaiden) Ltd. stock, I spent two hours being useful: making beds, walking dogs, doing dishes, polishing shoes, that sort of thing. I've been watching people work for years, so I figured out how to do it myself. Anyway, pretty soon everyone wanted a piece of Laura Scrubb to do their menial tasks, and my shares rose in value to two hundred plotniks a share. So the value of Laura Scrub (Handmaiden) Ltd. went from seventy to two hundred plotniks a share in just two hours. Are you following me?"

"Kind of. Gripper's shareholding is now worth almost three times what he paid for it?"

"That's pretty much it. Okay, now this is where it gets good. See that woman behind the bar?" We turned to see a kindly-looking woman with long black hair and a red face, chatting with another customer. "That's Madge Ryerson. She's a lovely lady but the worst gossip imaginable. Whisper something to her, and it's all over town in a matter of minutes. I *suggested* to her that I can do ironing as part of my handmaiden duties."

"No one likes ironing," said Wilson. "Out here, a well-ironed shirt is hugely prestigious."

"Exactly," said the princess. "Within twenty minutes Laura Scrubb (Handmaiden) Ltd. was trading at almost a thousand plotniks a share. In fact, shares in the Cambrian Railway Company fell because people sold those shares to buy into Laura Scrubb. And those who couldn't buy shares bought options to buy shares if they became available later. I then had Madge spread the news that I can make a cracking apple-and-blackberry crumble, and an hour later, shares in Laura Scrubb had peaked at three and a half thousand plotniks, the highest climb ever recorded on the Llangurig Stock Exchange."

"But listen," I said as the sandwiches arrived, "you don't know the first thing about ironing. Hardly anyone does. The Guild of Master Ironers keeps that secret arcane knowledge well guarded."

"I know, so this is the clever part, and you have to pay attention. I had kept ten percent of myself as payment for setting up Laura Scrubb (Handmaiden) Ltd. At that peak value, my ten shares were worth thirty-five thousand plotniks, so I sold them."

"Wouldn't people worry about why you were selling all your own shares?" asked Wilson. "I mean, it's a bit suspicious, don't you think?"

"You're right," said the princess, "so I set up a series of bogus companies so no one would know I was just selling my own shares. I had the butcher's boy and the blacksmith's apprentice sell my shares for me a few minutes before trading ended. Then, the next morning — today, in fact — I denied I knew anything about ironing or apple-and-blackberry crumble, then spread the rumor that I was catching the mumps and would be unable to work for a month."

"In order to lower the value of your shares?" I asked.

"Bingo. By ten o'clock, the share price of Laura Scrubb (Handmaiden) Ltd. had bottomed out at one plotnik a share, and I then used the profit I'd gained last night to buy back all the shares. Once everyone had been paid off — Madge, the butcher's boy, a few dodgy accountants, and several ratings agencies I didn't bother to tell you about for simplicity — I was twenty thousand better off and Laura Scrubb is a free woman. Admittedly," the princess concluded, "I lost half the profit on my ill-conceived goat-commodities speculation. But I'm still flush. The sandwiches are on me."

"You like economics, don't you?" I asked.

"Everyone should know the basics," said the princess. "Lasting peace will only be brought about through economic means. We should be trading with the trolls rather than fighting them."

"Good luck with that one," I said, "but listen, Laura, wasn't any of that trading a teensy-weensy bit illegal? I mean, Gripper O'Rourke lost almost everything he put in, and all those people who bought shares in you are now broke."

"That's the stock market, buster," she replied cheerfully. "Win some, lose some. Yes, maybe it was technically a *bit* illegal, but who's going to find out? By the time they realize they've been ripped off, I'll be long gone. The Llanguriganeans are all a bunch of unsophisticated dullards who wouldn't know an illegal stock-market manipulation if it fell on them."

"Laura Scrubb?" A man in a tweed suit had just approached our table, followed by two constables.

"Yes?"

"My name is Brian Lloyd. I work for the Llangurig Financial Services Commission. I have to inform you that all trading in Laura Scrubb (Handmaiden) Ltd. has been suspended, and we are arresting you for eighteen counts of illegal manipulation of the stock market, nine counts of fraudulent accounting, and six counts of misrepresentation and corporate fraud."

"That's an outrageous suggestion," said the princess haughtily, "but since I have neither time nor inclination to defend your clearly bogus charges, I'd be more than happy to deal with this here and now. Shall we say two thousand, cash?"

"And one count of attempting to bribe a public official."

"Whoops," said the princess, and a constable snapped some handcuffs on her.

"Dear, oh, dear," said Mr. Lloyd, shaking his head sadly, "you must think we're all a bunch of unsophisticated dullards who wouldn't know an illegal stock-market manipulation if it fell on us."

The princess put on a good show of looking shocked. "The thought . . . never crossed my mind."

"Sure it didn't," said Mr. Lloyd. "You rogue traders are all the same. You think it's just business and not stealing. It is. One question: Did you have anything to do with the falling goat prices?"

"I noticed that too," said the princess. "Weird, huh?"

"But nothing to do with you?"

"Nothing."

"Very well. Constable? Take her away."

"Here, Jennifer," said the princess, tossing me a bag stuffed with share certificates and the remains of her ill-gotten gains. "Better try to get me a good lawyer, a bent lawyer, or, failing that, any lawyer. Oh, and buy Trans-

Wales stock when it drops below a hundred and twenty plotniks a share. If goats go above half a plotnik a head, sell them all."

The two constables took the princess by the elbows and marched her swiftly to the door, followed by Mr. Lloyd. I jumped to my feet and followed them outside.

"What's going to happen to her?" I asked as we crossed the street to the law courts, which doubled as a bakery named, appropriately enough, All Rise.

"This is a railroad town, so she'll be tried using the fast-track method," replied Mr. Lloyd. "The trial will begin after the 18:24 ceasefire but before the railroad militia night raiding parties begin at 20:15. She'll be found guilty, of course, and will receive the penalty demanded by law."

"Which is?"

Mr. Lloyd turned and stared at me. "For a first offense, execution."

"Execution?" I echoed. "Isn't that a *little* severe?"

"If we didn't execute bankers and rogue traders found guilty of financial mischief, it might give them a clear signal that it's actually okay, and then where would we be?"

"The judge may show mercy," I said.

"I doubt it," said Mr. Lloyd with something of a cruel smile. "Judge Gripper O'Rourke has taken a special interest in this case."

"Oh, dear," I said. "Sir, I wonder if you can direct me to the best lawyer in town?"

"We have one lawyer in town, miss, and it's me. I will be prosecuting this case. You may engage me to conduct the defense as well, if you wish—I will make every endeavor to be just and fair."

"I'm not sure that's allowed," I replied.

"Me neither," said Mr. Lloyd, "but it saves a lot of time. Oh, and in case you're thinking of bringing in a lawyer from elsewhere, only Llangurig lawyers can speak at Llangurig trials. Good day, miss." And with a tip of his hat, he was gone.

I returned to the others at the inn. "She's going to be executed," I said desperately. "Tonight, and there's not a lawyer to be found in town. We have to rescue her!"

"She did break the law," said Addie. "What do you think they should have done? Given her a bonus for her daring and ingenuity?"

I took a deep breath. It was time to tell them who she was.

"Okay, listen up: She's not Laura Scrubb at all. She's actually Princess Shazza, the heir apparent to the Kingdom of Snodd, and I swore to her mother, the queen, I'd look after her."

There was a shocked pause from Addie and Wilson. Wilson then said that he doubted this very much, as Laura's teeth, nails, and skin complaints were hardly princess-y. So I told them all about the king and the queen wanting me to educate the princess, and how Queen Mimosa had used the Sister Organza mind switcheroo to put her daughter into a handmaiden's body.

"Any more surprises?" asked Addie sullenly. "Another two dozen rubber dragons or a few wizards or spells or you're actually Princess Tharvina in disguise or something?"

"No," I said, after thinking hard. "You've got it all."

"We'll just tell the judge she's a princess," said Wilson. "They're not going to execute royalty. Not even Tharv does that, and he's as crazy as a barrel of skunks."

"Who will believe us?" said Perkins. "She's in Laura Scrubb's body right now, so we can't prove it's not Laura—and she did say she was Laura as soon as she got here."

"We could contact King Snodd," suggested Wilson.

"With what?" I said. "There are no public cross-border phone lines, and my conch and the last homing snail are with Curtis in the half-track. Besides, knowing the king, he'd go way over the top and invade the Cambrian Empire or something."

We lapsed into silence, our appetites lost.

"Okay," I said, taking out the cash that the princess had handed me. "I don't know how we're going to rescue her, but rescue her we will. I need ideas. Here."

I gave most of the cash to Wilson and Addie, then

told Wilson to see if there was anyone to bribe to postpone the trial, and asked Addie to find us some transportation.

"To where?" she asked.

"I'm not sure," I said, realizing that I needed to find Able Quizzler before we left Llangurig. He was our only link to the Eye. "Just get me some wheels, and I'll let you know."

Wilson and Addie left the pub, leaving Perkins and me at the table. I beckoned the barmaid over and asked if she knew where I could find Able Quizzler.

"Able?" she said. "Are you friends of his?"

"Yes."

"Then you can pay his unpaid bar bill."

"More colleagues, actually," I added quickly. "Do you know where he is?"

"That I do," she said. "In fact, I can tell you precisely where he is right now."

"A man of habits?" asked Perkins.

"*Very* fixed in his ways," said the barmaid. "You'll find him in the cemetery."

"A gravedigger, is he?"

"No, he's dead—and has been these past six years."

THIRTY-THREE

Trouble with Gravediggers

L langurig's cemetery was on the north side of town. It was a dismal place, the grass patchy and the stones stained with streaks from the rain. Even the fresh flowers on the graves looked tired; the clouds were dark, the wind chill. Row upon row of headstones charted the history of Llangurig's railroad conflict, from the first death in 1862 to the most recent only forty-seven minutes before. The latest had already been buried, due to a hyperefficient funeral service that could have someone in the ground before they were cold. Ten graves had been dug in preparation for the inevitable casualties that evening, and the cemetery's eight thousand inhabitants outnumbered the Llangurig living five to one. The graveyard was twice the size of the town itself.

"This is grim," said Perkins as we walked past the headstones, each commemorating a young man or woman's life cut short.

"The loss seems even more when you see them laid out like this," I said.

"It doesn't make much sense," added Perkins. "If Quizzler had died, wouldn't Kevin have foreseen it?"

"Kevin doesn't see everything," I replied, "but I agree it's annoying. We'll find out what we can, grab the princess, and get out of town. Without any evidence that the Eye of Zoltar even exists, we're not going any farther."

Perkins hailed a passing gravedigger. His clothes were worn but respectfully neat, his hands were leathery, and his shovel had been worn shiny by constant use. The man introduced himself as something that sounded like Dirk, and Perkins explained who we were looking for.

"Kin?" asked Dirk, staring at us suspiciously.

"A distant cousin," I said, "on my mother's side."

"Ar," said the gravedigger, "follow I."

He led us past hundreds of headstones carved with a name, date, and a short epitaph in a typical Railwayese style. They ranged from the direct—*Ran out of Steam* or

Hit the Buffers—to the more polite—*Shunted to a Quiet Corner of the Yard* or *Withdrawn from Service.*

We turned left at a crossroads and followed another avenue of headstones.

"You must be kept busy," I said to the gravedigger.

"Busier than a turkey neck–breaker at Christmas."

"Nice simile," said Perkins, "full of charm."

"Jus' thar," said Dirk as he pointed at a simple cross marked *Quizzler* and a date six years back.

"Ever meet him?" I asked.

"Only once." He chuckled. "But he were in no mood for talkin'."

"You know how he died?"

"Some say it were the grass what killed him."

I sighed. Gravediggers always spoke in dark riddles. As a student at gravedigger college, you had to master the art of random quirky banter before they'd even let you touch a shovel.

"The grass?" I asked.

"Aye. Was all grass around here when he arrived. He wasn't brought here by the undertaker, and we didn't dig his grave, neither."

"Then who did?"

"He done dig it hisself. He done everythin' hisself 'cept read the sermon. Delivered hisself alive he did, then dug his own grave while he was a-dyin'."

Perkins and I looked at each other.

"So what you're saying," I said slowly, "is that he walked in alive, dug his own grave while dying, and was then laid into it?"

"Sort of," said the gravedigger, "only he didn't walk in here, and wasn't put into the grave. Came in fast, he did, and buried hisself quicker than a sneeze. Heard him the other side of the yard."

Perkins was becoming exasperated too. "If I give you some money," he said, speaking very slowly and firmly, "would you tell us what in the blue blazes you're talking about?"

Dirk wagged his finger and laughed again.

"Okay," I said. "I've almost got this. He arrived in a hurry but not through the entrance, and buried himself while he was dying in almost no time at all while making a loud noise?"

"Aye," said the gravedigger, sounding disappointed at our failure to understand him. "And you'll get nothing further from me, not till you've learned some smarts."

He turned to walk away, but Perkins called after him.

"Did you just . . . backfill over him after he landed?"

Dirk stopped, then turned slowly to face us. His eyes twinkled and he very purposefully looked up. I didn't need to follow his gaze; I knew what he meant. Able

Quizzler had arrived in the graveyard not by walking, but by falling. And if he had hit the grass hard enough to bury himself, he had fallen from a great height.

"From a Leviathan, do you suppose?" I asked Perkins.

"No other explanation," he said. "And Leviathans lead us to Pirate Wolff, and from there we get to the Eye of Zoltar. Or do we?"

"Sadly, no," I said after a moment's thought. "We just get to Able Quizzler hitching a ride on a Leviathan. Ralph would have suffered the same fate—only I don't think he had the good luck to fall into a graveyard."

I stood there, unsure of what to do. I would risk all our lives if there were evidence of the Eye of Zoltar, but not for evidence of a Leviathan. This was a magic expedition, not one in pursuit of an endangered species, fascinating as that might have been.

"Right," I said, coming to a decision. "Once we've got the princess back, we're moving on to Cambrianopolis to negotiate for Boo's release. My goal was to find evidence of the Eye. We don't have any, so I'm pulling the plug."

"Shame," said Perkins. "I was looking forward to climbing Cadir Idris and facing all those terrors. Jeopardy tourism has kind of grown on me."

"Well, it's not growing on me," I said. "Come on."

We walked back through the graveyard after giving Dirk a tip. We had almost reached the entrance when Perkins stopped.

"Jenny?" he said. "I was just thinking. I mean, is it even *possible* for someone to bury himself by falling from a great height?"

"What's your point?" I asked.

"I'm thinking that perhaps you'd only leave a dent in the ground, if that. Unless—"

"Unless what?"

"Unless you were made of something much, much heavier."

It dawned on me. "Like . . . lead?"

Able Quizzler must have come into contact with the Eye of Zoltar. But it had not given him the power he craved—it had changed him to lead, the fate of anyone unskilled who tried to tap its massive powers. Quizzler would have been riding on a Leviathan when it happened, and if he'd become too heavy to be carried aloft, they— Pirate Wolff, probably—would have dumped him over the side.

We stood in silence for several moments. This changed everything.

"Well," I said, "Kevin was right about the Eye. Looks like we're heading farther north after all."

THIRTY-FOUR

The Fast-Track Trial

We had agreed to reconvene at Mrs. Timpson's Battlement Viewing Tearoom atop the town wall near the south gate, which afforded the many rail and military enthusiasts drawn to Llangurig a clear view of the battles below. But we were there for a more culinary reason: Mrs. Timpson's was reputedly the best tearoom in Llangurig. I wanted to savor one last excellent scone with jam and clotted cream before we headed north.

"Even if this news about Quizzler shows only that the Eye of Zoltar was here six years ago, I'm for going on," I concluded, "but if anyone wants out now, I understand."

"I've got something to add before you all get too

excited," said Addie. "I made a few inquiries, and everyone who has ventured toward Cadir Idris to look for Pirate Wolff or the Leviathans' Graveyard has vanished without a trace."

"How many?"

"Fifteen expeditions, two hundred sixty people," said Addie. "A one hundred percent fatality rate, and that's weird. Even the most hideously dangerous undertaking leaves *someone*."

"The Mountain Silurians?" I asked. "They're pretty unpleasant."

"Unpleasant but not gratuitously murderous," replied Addie. "They let people travel across their territory as long as they get paid in goats. No, I think there's something else. Something we don't know about—a hidden menace waiting for us at the mountain."

"Still want to go there?" I asked.

"You can only be talking to me," said Wilson with a smile, "because Addie, we know, would sooner accept death than dishonor her profession by bailing out, and Perkins is as loyal and as unswerving as any man I have ever known."

Addie and Perkins nodded in agreement.

"As for me," continued Wilson, "that brush with the Cloud Leviathan really got my ornithological blood racing. Okay, it's not a bird, but lighter-than-air flight in the animal kingdom is the scientific discovery of the century. I'll be on the cover of *National Geographic,* as long as that woman with the gorillas hasn't done anything exciting that month. Listen, wild Buzonjis wouldn't keep me from this expedition."

I thanked them all, and asked Addie and Wilson how they had done since we last met. The short answer was: Not very well. Addie had found us a battered Jeep that was now waiting for us, fueled and oiled, at the north gate.

"The Jeep is worn out," said Addie, "but it should get us to Cadir Idris. I've also got eight goats in a trailer so we can barter safe passage with the Mountain Silurians."

"Good. Mr. Wilson?"

Wilson explained that he had tried giving a small test bribe to the clerk of the court but was met with stony defiance. "I then went and told Judge Gripper O'Rourke that Laura was a princess."

"How did that work out?"

"The judge laughed and told me everyone tries that and to come up with something a little more imaginative."

"I could try magic to spring her," said Perkins, "but this is a tricky one. I've never used magic against the accepted rule of law, and that might cause some morality blowback."

"Some what?" asked Wilson.

"Morality blowback. Using magic to go against the natural order of justice can do serious damage. To use magic for wrong, you have to believe the wrong is correct, and I'm kind of thinking that because the princess was trading fraudulently, somewhere in all this is a form of justice — even if execution itself is unjustified."

"Morality and magic are a minefield," I said. "That's why wizards never spell death — just newting or stone transformations and stuff. It's why an evil sorcerer genius always employs minions to do the dirty work. Even someone like Shandar would risk everything if he tried to kill someone or something *directly* using magic. Perkins is right. It's too risky."

We all fell silent for a while. We heard the gates of the town swing shut, and a second or two later the warring railroad companies commenced their 18:02 Teatime Express Battle special.

We had a good view as the two armies locked in combat once more, this time with tanks and flamethrowers. Two Trans-Wales-Rails armored bulldozers advanced to lay ballast for the tracks. They might have succeeded, had the earth not collapsed beneath them as a result of secret tunneling by Cambrian sappers. As the battle intensified, the Cambrian railroad men brought out a completed sixty-yard section of track under cover of a diversionary pincer movement to the south.

As we watched the proceedings, the assistants of

Honest Pete and Rock-Steady Eddie stood nearby on the town wall and communicated by a series of bizarre hand signals to their masters in the street below about how the battle was faring. With every sleeper or length of track that was added or removed, each company's share value rose or fell accordingly. By the time a short volley of mortars heralded the destruction of any small gains twenty-two minutes later, the shares had settled at about the same price as when the battle started. The railroad tracks had not progressed even an inch.

The rail enthusiasts in the tearoom made notes in their books as the dead and wounded were carried off, the town gates opened again, and everything returned to Llangurig's version of normal.

"Senseless waste of time, effort, and life," said Perkins.

"So," I said, checking my watch, "any ideas on how to spring the princess?"

There weren't, which was discouraging.

"Okay, then," I said, "we'll just have to improvise."

We paid for the tea and scones and made our way toward All Rise, the combined bakery/courthouse, to take our seats for the trial. It was hot in the courthouse, as the bread ovens had only just completed the afternoon bake, and the public was busy fanning themselves.

"Where's Perkins?" I said to Wilson; I'd lost sight of him as we went in. Wilson offered to find him, but I said not to worry. I wanted the princess to see at least three of us there.

The princess was escorted in by the two officers who had arrested her earlier. Mr. Lloyd, prosecuting, was sitting at his bench surrounded by a mountain of paperwork. In the Cambrian Empire, lawyers were paid not by number of hours worked, but by a complex algorithm that took into account the weight of the paperwork, the age and height differential between counsel and defendant, recent rainfall, and the brevity of the trial. It was said that the best way to make a profit as a Cambrian lawyer was to be a tall octogenarian who could generate three tons of paperwork, conduct cases in the rain for no more than three minutes, and prosecute only those under twelve.

"All rise!" said the clerk, and we all rose dutifully as the judge walked in and took his seat. He rummaged for his glasses, and had the court sit before he read the charges. While he did so, the public — there were at least thirty people there — tutted and went *ooh* and *aah*. The princess watched impassively, but did not look in our direction. She might have been in the body of Laura, but she clearly wanted to show us she could face the music like a princess if necessary.

"How do you plead?" asked the judge.

"Not guilty," said the princess, and there were more muted whisperings in the courthouse.

"Nonsense," said the judge. "I've seen the evidence, and it's highly compelling. Guilty as charged, to which the sentence is death. Anything to say before the punishment is carried out?"

"Yes," said the princess, "actually, I do—"

"Fascinating," interrupted the judge. "Thank you, Mr. Lloyd, for such a well-tried case. The legal profession may be justly proud of you. What was that? Nineteen seconds?"

Mr. Lloyd bowed deferentially after consulting a stopwatch. "Eighteen and a quarter, my lord, a new regional judicial speed record."

"Good show," said the judge, signing a docket the clerk had handed him. The scrap of paper was then passed to a bony old man sitting half asleep in a chair, who awoke with a start when prodded.

"Executioner?" said the judge. "Do your work, but make sure it's a clean cut—not like the messy job you did last time."

"Yes, my lord," said the executioner.

I jumped up.

"Objection!" I shouted, and several people in the courtroom gasped at my audacity. "This trial makes a mockery of the high levels of judicial excellence that we have come to expect from the great nation that is the Cambrian Empire. I counter that everyone has the right to be represented by counsel, to be judged by their peers, and to have all evidence scrutinized before any decision is reached. I move that this farce be declared a mistrial and the prisoner released forthwith!"

There was silence in the court. It wasn't a great speech. To be honest, it wasn't even a *good* speech, but several of the public were moved to tears and shook me by the hand. I even heard a sob from someone in the front row.

"Your impassioned appeal has moved me, miss," said the judge, dabbing his eyes with a handkerchief, "and I accede to your wishes. The trial will be declared void, the prisoner will be pardoned and released, and her criminal record expunged, with our apologies." He gestured to the clerk, who swiftly drafted a pardon for the princess.

"Th-thank you, my lord," I said, surprised by the results.

The judge signed the pardon with a flourish.

"There," he said, handing the document to the princess.

"Thank you, my lord," she said, then read it. "Wait a moment, this is postdated. I'm not pardoned for another hour — until after the execution."

"How . . . ironically tragic," said the judge. "Executioner? Get on with it."

"That's not fair!" I shouted.

"You shouldn't confuse justice with the law, my

dear," said the judge. "I have done everything that the law and you have asked: I have been both resolute and merciful. Now, stay your hand, or you shall be arrested for contempt."

I felt myself grow hot. The veins in my temples began to thump as a prickly heat ran down my back. This would end badly if I went into a rage, and I battled to keep my anger down. I squeezed the chair in front of me until the wooden back exploded into fragments in my hands. I felt a howling in my ears, which became a whistling, then a high-pitched squeal that sounded like a train whistle.

Everyone in the courtroom had heard it too — because it had come not from me, but from outside. My temper subsided as the judge, the executioner, Mr. Lloyd, and the public all rushed out to see what was going on. I took a deep breath and beckoned to the princess, who hopped over the barrier between the combined witness box and flour bin.

"All we have to do is keep you hidden for a half hour," I said, taking her hand and heading for the door.

Wilson and Addie followed as we made our way to the town square. With whoops of joy and resounding cheers, everyone was streaming out of the gates. Hats were thrown in the air, old women were crying, and a brass band had struck up a triumphant tune. Just beyond the gates I could see a shiny locomotive, big and bold and hissing with steam, where less than an hour ago there had been a battlefield.

"Go with Wilson and Addie," I said to the princess. "I'll meet you at the Jeep outside the north gate as soon as I can. Something's . . . not right. You two, use force to protect her if necessary."

"All other considerations secondary?" said Wilson.

"Exactly."

I ran beyond the town wall to find that a mile of shiny new track connected the depots of Trans-Wales-Rails and Cambrian Railway. The rails were dead straight, the sleepers perfectly aligned, and the ballast looked as though it had been laid carefully by hand. The jubilant townsfolk and equally jubilant (and now very wealthy) railroad troops were dancing in the dust by the short connecting piece of rail while the railroad militia generals shook hands in an annoyed but relieved fashion. The line would be shared; profits would be equal, and better yet, there would be no more senseless loss of life over an insignificant mile of railroad track somewhere in the forgotten wilds of the Cambrian Empire.

"In less than ten minutes!" said one man, dancing past me.

"It is a miracle!" shouted another.

"It's nothing of the sort," I muttered through gritted teeth. "It's Perkins frittering his life away."

I looked around, knowing he would still be nearby. Such a feat would have exhausted him, and he would need help getting back through town to the north gate. I eventually found him sitting on a bench.

"That was quite something," I said, my voice trembling. His face was obscured by his hands, and I dreaded what price his magic had exacted this time around.

"It was a win-win," he said in a tired voice. "The princess lives, yes?"

"Yes."

"And the Llangurig Railroad War is over?"

"It is."

Perkins looked up at me. A mile of track in under ten minutes was a fearfully large spell. By my best estimate he was now in his fifties. His hair was streaked with gray and there were lines around his mouth and eyes. A small mole on his cheek was now more prominent, and he wore reading glasses.

"I thought it would only take six years from me," he said with a smile, "but it took more than twenty. But then, I'm not as young as I was."

"It's not funny," I said. "Here, take my arm. We'll go through the town. It'll be quicker."

I pulled him to his feet and we stumbled back through the south gate and into the town, which was already emptying out. Now that the railroad had arrived, the reason for the frontier town had vanished. For Sale signs had sprung up, and townsfolk were loading hand-carts with their possessions.

We were passing a row of shops when I stopped outside an antique store and stared through the window. I moved closer. This was *not* what I had expected.

"Will you look at that," said Perkins as he followed my gaze. "He'll never live this down."

THIRTY-FIVE

A Rubber Dragon
Named Colin

Sitting in the shop window, surrounded by several pieces of furniture, a moose's head, and various items of bric-a-brac, was a large rubber dragon—its scales perfect, its mouth open, and a large array of black teeth on display.

"I can turn him back instantly if you want," said Perkins. "It'll only take ten years off me."

"Absolutely not. Your spelling days are over until we get you back to Kazam. I'll go make inquiries while you sit down and rest."

A bell rang above my head as I opened the door, and a few seconds later a middle-aged woman appeared from the back room and stared at me over her half-moon glasses. She didn't look like the type to take any nonsense, nor give any.

"I'm interested in the rubber dragon," I said, touching Colin's rubber scales with my index finger. In life they would have been hard and unyielding, but now they felt soft and pliable, like a marshmallow. "Is it for sale?"

"Everything's for sale," she said. "Make me an offer."

I emptied the contents of my pockets onto the counter. I had a shade over eight hundred plotniks. The woman looked at the money, then chuckled derisively.

"The rubber scrap value is worth fifteen hundred alone. Give me two thousand and it's yours."

"I don't have two thousand," I told her. "Eight hundred and an IOU for the rest."

"I don't take IOUs."

"It's all I have."

"Then you aren't going to own a rubber dragon today, and given that Llangurig is being abandoned, he'll be sold to the recyclers tomorrow and made into bicycle inner tubes and pencil erasers."

It wouldn't be a dignified end for such a magnificent beast. I had an idea; it wasn't a good one, and may even have been one of my worst. But I needed to buy Rubber Colin before anyone figured out who or what he really was.

"Then I'll trade," I said. "You give me the rubber dragon, and I'll give you . . . me."

I took my indentured servitude papers out of my pocket. I had two years longer at Kazam and after that I was free — or free to sell myself for another year or two, or whatever I wanted.

"I'll give you a year of me," I said. "I work hard and learn quick. That's got to be worth two thousand any day of the week."

The shopkeeper looked at my orphan papers and stared at me suspiciously. "There's something I'm missing here," she said. "No one in their right mind would swap a year of themselves for a rubber dragon — unless . . ."

Her voice trailed off. All of a sudden, she *knew.* A dragon — any dragon, in any condition, transformed or otherwise, would be worth a thousand orphan years. I'd let the cat out of the bag, and I wasn't sure what to do. I could have tried to grab Rubber Colin and run, but I wasn't sure how far I'd get with something I could barely lift. Besides, this was Llangurig, where it was perfectly legal to have a weapon hidden beneath the counter, and doubly legal — encouraged, even — to use it on shoplifters.

I took back my indentured papers and pushed the eight hundred plotniks and an IOU for another twelve hundred across the counter. We weren't bargaining any longer. I was going to tell her how it was.

"This for the rubber dragon. Agree or we take him and you get nothing."

"And how do you propose to take him?" she asked, her hand reaching under the counter.

"I have a sorcerer outside who can transform him back to a living, breathing, and very angry dragon in a twinkling," I said. "I know Colin personally, and believe me, he won't be happy to have been made into rubber. Take the money. It's the best you're going to get."

"You can't threaten me," she replied defiantly. "The law is on my side."

I leaned forward and lowered my voice. "And magic is on mine. Which do you think is more powerful?"

We stared at each other until, finally, she saw sense.

"Looks like you're the owner of a rubber dragon," she said, taking the money and the IOU.

"A wise choice," I said in a quiet voice, "but there's one other thing: I need a handcart."

A few minutes later I had loaded Rubber Colin onto the cart and was wheeling him along the street, Perkins at my side steadying the rubber creature, which wobbled all over the place in a very undignified manner. It was about the size of a pony, but weighed, fortunately, only about a tenth as much.

We found Addie, Wilson, and the princess at the

north gate, waiting next to a battered Jeep attached to a trailer that contained eight barter-quality goats.

"I'm not going to ask where you found that," said Addie, pointing at Rubber Colin, "but it's going to be a tight fit."

It *was* a tight fit. Ridiculously so. But with Rubber Colin in the back of the open Jeep, Wilson and Perkins on either side of him, and the princess and I sharing the front passenger seat, we could just about fit. Addie coaxed the Jeep into life.

"Is Perkins okay?" asked Addie. "He looks kind of . . . old."

"He's fine," I said, even though he wasn't, really. "Let's drive. The princess's pardon is still twenty minutes away."

So we did, taking the rough road north toward Cadir Idris. Although we breathed a sigh of relief when the princess's pardon came into effect, we didn't stop, and drove on in almost unparalleled discomfort for two hours until we reached a waterfall where Addie said a dry cave was hidden behind some rhododendron bushes.

The eight goats bleated plaintively, as they weren't used to being in a trailer and could sense the water nearby. We ignored each other for the forty minutes it took to set up camp in the cave; it had been a worrying afternoon, and despite the positive outcome of the trial, we could all feel the stress within our small group. I chased out a boogaloo that had taken refuge in the cave while Addie and the princess went to tether the goats near the river, and Perkins and Wilson wandered off to look for fireberries. Colin stayed in the back of the Jeep, his lifeless rubber eyes staring into the gathering gloom.

We reconvened when the fireberries were ignited, the daylight had gone, and supper was about ready. It was Spam, but everyone was too tired to complain.

The princess finally broke the silence. "Thank you," she said, "all of you. I knew you wouldn't let me down."

"You should thank Perkins," said Addie, pointing to where he sat on a stone farther back in the cave. He looked preoccupied.

"Did he give more of himself?" asked the princess anxiously. "In years, I mean?"

I nodded. "Over twenty."

"Oh." She went over and spoke to him in a quiet voice. She took his hand in hers, and I saw him shrug, then smile, then nod some thanks of his own.

We opened some tins of rice pudding, which along with the Spam and some pickled eggs were the only provisions Addie had found on short notice, and washed it all down with tea.

Conversation after dinner was muted. We had come a long way, and each of us had dodged death at least twice. The search had suddenly become more dangerous, more real. Despite Addie's promise of only a fifty percent fatality index, the fact that no one had ever returned from Cadir Idris was at the front of our minds. The princess kindly offered to tell us how hedge funds operated, but I could tell her heart wasn't in it, and there were no takers. There would be no stories tonight.

We ate, washed up, prepared for bed. Seven o'clock passed. I had no way to call Kazam, and no homing snail had arrived. I suddenly felt very isolated.

The princess placed her bedroll next to mine.

"I'm not doing very well, am I?" she said once we'd settled down and were staring at the roof of the cave. "I mean, this adventure is meant to make me less bratty and more wise and thoughtful and stuff, but all that's happened is that you've put all your lives on the line to save me and I've done little except need to be rescued. I feel like the worst princess cliché."

"It could be worse," I said. "You could be screaming and swooning and demanding a bath in rabbit's milk or something."

"That is certainly possible," she conceded, "but I just want to say thank you for rescuing me, in case there isn't a chance to say it later."

I hadn't cared much for her at the beginning, but I'd be sorry to lose her now. And not just because there was a hint of a fine queen about her, but because I actually

289

liked her. None of us had saved the princess from the executioner because she was the princess. We had saved her because she was part of whatever made us *us*.

"We'd have done the same if you were Laura Scrubb," I said. "We don't abandon our friends."

"I'm glad," said the princess. "Your friendship means more to me than everything I have, or everything I will ever be."

There was no answer to this, so I just nodded and asked, "What did you say to Perkins?"

"I conferred upon him the dukedom of Bredwardine in recognition of his sacrifices in the service of the crown. I know the honor system is a farce, but a Snodd dukedom also allows the holder a twenty-five percent discount at the co-op, free bus and train travel, and two free seats at the Wimbledon finals every year."

"He deserves it," I said, then added so everyone else could hear, "Don't tell the Federation, but I'm upgrading this search to quest status."

The flickering light of the fireberry played upon the roof.

"About time, too," came Addie's voice in the darkness.

To the Foot of the Mountain

That night, I dreamed again about the parents I had never known. They were scolding me for leaving my conch in the half-track and telling me that I couldn't marry Perkins because he was old enough to be my father. Then I was dreaming of Kevin Zipp, who said he had come to say goodbye and to tell me to not lose sight of all that is good. After that, I was chasing after Curtis and the half-track, and when I stopped and turned around, five Hotax were staring at me with their small piglike eyes; one was holding a surgeon's saw and another, a bag of kapok stuffing and a sewing needle. I turned to run but found I couldn't, and that's when I was shaken awake.

It was Addie. She put her finger to her lips and

beckoned me to the rhododendrons that hid the entrance to the cave. She gently pushed the branches apart to reveal two pale blue Skybus trucks stopped on the road next to the waterfall. The drivers seemed to be comparing notes about the journey, and from the way in which their large four-wheel-drive trucks were parked, one seemed to be heading off toward the Cadir range, and the other, mud-spattered and dusty, seemed to be returning.

As we watched, they shook hands, climbed into the cabs of their trucks, and drove off in the directions I had predicted. I looked at Addie and raised an eyebrow. She shrugged. She had no idea what they were doing here either.

"There are no manufacturing facilities out here," she said, "or at least, nothing that I know about."

"Smuggling?" I said.

"It's possible," said Addie, striding across to the tire tracks. "The Mountain Silurians used to illegally export spices, but if they are still doing it, why use Skybus vehicles?"

"I've counted at least six while I've been in the empire," I said, "all heading to and from the border. Aviation parts, you say?"

"So I'm told," said Addie, squatting down to study the tracks, "but I've never looked inside the trucks, so don't know for sure. Notice anything odd?"

We were at a muddy section of the road, and Addie

was pointing at the tracks. Those from one truck were deep and well defined, while the others hardly made an imprint.

"One truck is heavily loaded and the other not," I said. "So what?"

"Because," said Addie, "the one that's heavy is going toward the mountains—and the lighter of the two is coming out."

"These vehicles are delivering something to the Idris Mountains," I said slowly, "but it doesn't make sense that the cargo would be airplane parts. What could it be?"

"I don't know," said Addie, "but I'd like to find out."

"What about Curtis and the half-track?" I asked.

"Just there," said Addie, pointing at a ghost of an imprint on the dusty roadway, "and by the look of it, he passed through here yesterday afternoon about midday. If he stopped for the night, he may be only six or seven hours' drive ahead."

"It's not so much his capture or punishment I'm interested in," I said, "even though such a thing would be welcome. I'm really after the half-track, or to be more exact, my bag and what's in it."

It was the conch, of course, the Helping Hand™— I'd get hell from Lady Mawgon for losing it—and the letter of credit to negotiate for Boo's release.

"We better get a move on, then," said Addie.

* * *

Perkins rubbed his head when I woke him. His increased age had established itself more firmly overnight. His voice was deeper, his face more lined, his hair grayer — and he was painfully stiff after the cold night in the cave.

"Welcome to the club," said Wilson, "and don't worry if you start forgetting the names of things or are less sharp than you once were. You may even have trouble . . . have trouble, um —"

" — finishing your sentences?" put in Perkins.

"Exactly so. All entirely normal. But with age comes wisdom."

"I think wisdom comes with years, not age," replied Perkins sadly. "I've managed to separate the two. I think I'm going to be old *without* wisdom."

"If that is the case," said Wilson, "you won't be alone."

Addie suggested we let the Skybus trucks have a half-hour start so we would not be observed, but it took that long to get the goats herded into the trailer anyway. They had a certain bounciness about them that didn't permit easy herding.

"They're called ISGs," explained Addie once we had finally rounded up the goats and coaxed the ancient Jeep's engine into life, "for International Standard Goat. They're a sort of one-size-fits-all goat that does everything pretty well: lots of milk, soft fur, and excellent meat. The ISG was the legacy of Emperor Tharv's father, who was convinced that what the world needed was animal standard-ization. He managed to standardize the goat, honeybee, badger, and hamster, and was working on the entire class of birds when he died."

"It's why so many birds are small and brown," explained Wilson, "so he had moderate success."

We drove for two hours, stopping to fill the Jeep's leaky radiator three times, and climbed steadily up the rough, winding trail. Once we were on the high Plynlimon pass, we stopped to stretch our legs, change drivers, and make a short devotion to the shrine dedicated to the once-popular but now little-known Saint Aosbczkcs, the Patron Saint of Fading Relevance. This done, we surveyed the scene before us.

Below us the road slowly wound down through bumpy foothills toward the fertile valley floor, a random patchwork of natural woodland and open grassland. But beyond this valley and dominating our view was the place where the Leviathans' Graveyard and Sky Pirate Wolff's hideout were most likely to be hidden: Cadir Idris.

The mountain was more spectacular in real life than in any picture. Sheer walls towered vertically from the valley floor, presenting a dizzying pinnacle of gray rock that was both awe-inspiring and terrifying. Waterfalls cascaded out into space from high on the sheer rock walls; the water dispersed into clouds that clung to the lower reaches of the mountain. Although believed to be the second-highest mountain in the Ununited Kingdoms, after the peak named T4 in the Trollvanian range, the exact height of Cadir Idris had never been determined. The summit was always surrounded by clouds, making a triangulation survey impossible. Between six and seven thousand feet was a pretty good guess. At sunrise, the shadow of the rock extended across three kingdoms.

"From here on in, we're in Mountain Silurian territory," said Addie.

Perkins spelled himself a hand telescope by creating two O shapes with his index fingers and thumbs and conjuring up a glass lens in each. Early versions of the spell had required an operator to focus the telescope manually, but later releases had autofocus as standard, with a zoom feature and auto-stabilization a useful add-on.

"I can see the half-track. Looks like it's a couple of miles from the base of the mountain. Think he's still got your conch?"

"He didn't try to sell the Helping Hand™ in Llangurig," I said, for if he had, he'd have made several times the price of a handmaiden, "so I'm hoping."

Perkins scanned the parts of the road that were visible among the low hills and wooded areas. "The Skybus truck is not far behind him."

Because the vehicles were still moving, apparently neither of them had encountered the Mountain Silurians, or if they had, goats had been successfully bartered and passage had been allowed.

We moved on soon after, and as we descended into the dense woodlands of the Mountain Silurians' land, we could see how the increased rainfall made everything lush and moist. Bottle-green moss grew in abundance on the rocks and trees, lichen clung doggedly to anything it could find, and we were constantly fording small streams and rivers.

All this time, the overwhelming size of the bleak pinnacle of rock that was Cadir Idris loomed over us menacingly. A better place for a pirate hideout would be impossible to imagine.

"Where are the Mountain Silurians?" asked the princess. "I thought you said they were fearless tribespeople who would kill us all for amusement unless we gave them goats."

"I was wondering that myself," said Addie. "To get this far into their territory without being threatened with dismemberment and asked to pay tribute is unusual. I hope nothing's happened to them."

"I'm hoping something *has* happened to them," said the princess. "Any jeopardy we can avoid is one more step toward survival."

"I'll just be glad to sit quietly somewhere with my pipe and slippers," said Perkins, coming across a bit fiftyish, "and read the paper."

"You don't have a pipe," I pointed out, "or slippers."

"Or a paper — but there's a first time for everything."

"Slow down, Addie," I said. We had nearly caught up to the Skybus truck, which was stopped in a clearing ahead of us. Addie pulled the Jeep off the road and parked behind an oak tree. The Skybus driver had climbed out and was stretching his legs, then reached into his cab, took out a roll of toilet paper, and walked off into the forest.

"Stay here," said Addie. She jumped out of the jeep and darted forward noiselessly, stopped, looked around, and then moved forward again. Within a moment she was at the back of the truck, had opened the rear doors, and looked inside. Just as quickly, she shut the doors and slipped into the undergrowth. The driver returned and then drove off toward the mountain. Half a minute later Addie rejoined us. She didn't look too happy.

"Everything okay?" I asked.

"Not really," she said, pointing behind us, "and we've got company."

I turned to find that a dozen or more warriors astride Buzonjis had crept up on us silently, and were now fewer than twenty paces away. Each warrior was large, tanned, and amply but not skillfully covered in blue war paint. Every one was armed with a short sword and a lance, its steel tip piercing the top of a human skull. Traditionally, heads were harvested by lance in battle, and remained there as a trophy. The warriors were scowling at us in the most unpleasant and unwelcoming way I had ever witnessed. I heard Wilson swallow nervously.

We didn't need to guess who they might be. These were the feared Mountain Silurians.

THIRTY-SEVEN

The Mountain Silurians

ll hail Glorious Geraint the Great," said Addie, bowing low, "the gutsy, gallant, and gracious gatekeeper of the great green grassy northern grounds."

It seemed, from Addie's flowery and overblown greetings, that the Silurian chief himself had graced us with his presence. We all bowed as Geraint the Great looked on imperiously and the Buzonjis stamped their feet impatiently. After a pause that felt like ten minutes but was probably less than twenty seconds, Geraint the Great looked at one of his advisors, a giant of a woman dressed in the skin of a Welsh leopard, who nodded in reply.

"Your alliteration is acceptable, if mildly simplistic,"

said Geraint. "What do you seek, Addie the Tour Guide, champion of the blade, younger daughter of Owen the Dead, holder of the Tourist Good Conduct Medal?"

"Our lives are in your hands." Addie bowed again and continued the long-winded formal greeting. "We wish only peace and goodwill, and are merely travelers seeking to pass your sacred grounds."

"To where?" asked Geraint.

"To seek the Legendary Grade III Leviathans' Graveyard on Cadir Idris, Your Greatness. We wish to venture there and return safely and without hindrance."

"The Rock Goddess shall not be defiled," the chief intoned angrily while the rest of the warriors muttered darkly. "You shall be sacrificed to the mountain, your blood splashed about the rocks and your rotting carcasses picked apart by the condor. The mountain shall be appeased. You will die. I, Geraint the Great, have spoken."

"We have brought gifts," said Addie.

There was a pause.

"The mountain may be appeased . . . in other ways," said Geraint the Great. "We accept your gifts . . . as long as it's not more of those stupid goats. All we're ever given are goats, and let me tell you, we're sick of them. Sick of the sight of them, sick of the smell of them, and sick of the taste of them. Isn't that right, lads?"

The warriors gave out a hearty *Uuh!* sort of noise and waved their spears in the air.

"We have so many goats," continued Geraint the Great in an exasperated tone, "that we have to sell them at below market value to those milksops in Llangurig. If anyone were ever to try to offload those same goats back to us, our anger would be great, our violence most savage."

"Okay . . . " said Addie. "Please wait, Your Greatness, while I consult with my fellow travelers." She turned to us. "Looks like I was misinformed about the whole goat thing," she whispered.

"It explains why cheap goats are flooding the Llangurig commodities market," murmured the princess thoughtfully. "How fascinating."

"Not *really* important right now, ma'am," said Addie. "Has anyone got anything else we can barter?"

"I have two thousand plotniks," said Wilson, opening his wallet. "It's all I have in the world, but you are welcome to it."

"Any good?" I said to Addie.

"They're not fond of cash," she replied, "but I'll try."

"Gorgeous Geraint the Great," said Addie, turning back to the warriors, "as weary travelers of limited means, we can offer only two thousand plotniks."

The warriors all laughed uproariously.

"We despise your abstract monetary concepts. Value should lie in the commodity, and not be assigned arbitrarily to a device of no intrinsic value in itself."

"I like this bunch," whispered the princess. "They *totally* talk my language."

"So we only barter," continued Geraint the Great, "but no more goats. We want washing machines, food mixers, toasters, and other consumer durables. That nice man in the half-track gave us his iPod."

That explained how Curtis got past, at least. We told the chief we had none of those things, nor a reasonable chance of finding any at short notice.

"Very well," replied Geraint. "You will return the way you came and we will take the novelty rubber dragon in exchange for your lives." He pointed at Rubber Colin, who was still sitting, very much made of rubber, in the back of the Jeep.

"The . . . novelty rubber dragon is not for trade," I said.

The chief rolled off his horse in a less-than-expert fashion and drew his sword.

"Then you will die," he said, "and painfully — except for the Silurian, who will be enslaved, and the handmaiden, who will do our washing and cleaning for the rest of her natural life."

Addie drew out her dagger and glared at the warriors. "I will die protecting my friends." They were fine words and I knew she was good in a fight, but a dozen Mountain Silurians armed to the teeth against a twelve-year-old wasn't a fight I'd be betting on any time soon.

"Wait!" said the princess. "I can help you."

"You can iron?" said the chief. "That would indeed be a game changer."

"No, no," said the princess. "I'll help you change your financially crippling goat surplus into a valuable trading commodity."

Geraint looked at the princess and narrowed his eyes. "It's an attractive idea," he said. "We have thousands of the blasted things. How?"

"Well," said the princess, taking a deep breath, "we would first form a goat-trading corporation and use this to bring together all the other goat-producing tribes in order to control the number of goats moving onto the market. Instead of buyers dictating goat prices based on free supply, the goat-producing tribes can limit production and peg their value to an agreed 'minimum goat price' so that all producers get a fair deal. We can couple this with an advertising strategy to increase goat-use awareness among the public, and even develop a breeding program to generate expensive limited-edition goats for collectors. I think we can increase the value of goats tenfold in as little as six months, as long as all the other goat-producing tribes agree to join us."

"What's she talking about?" whispered Addie.

"I have absolutely no idea," I whispered back.

Geraint the Great stared at the princess for a long time, then replaced his sword in its scabbard.

"It shall be so," he said. "You will consult with our accountant, Pugh the Numbers."

One of the neater warriors climbed off his Buzonji as Geraint remounted his, and after Geraint had told us we were "the guests of the Siluri," the warriors were soon gone, leaving the princess to explain her complex goat-marketing plans in detail to Pugh the Numbers.

It was almost an hour before we were back on the road again.

THIRTY-EIGHT

Cavi homini

That's kind of weird," said the princess after we had driven a mile or two in silence. We had freed the goats and dumped the trailer, so although still cramped in the Jeep, we were at least a little faster.

"What's weird?" I asked. "There are a lot of options out here."

"The quantity of goats. Pugh the accountant said that Skybus Aeronautics gave them two thousand goats a month as payment for mining rights at Cadir Idris."

"What was Skybus mining?"

The princess shrugged. "He didn't say. But because the contract was well drafted, they couldn't convert the goats into something more usable. At least, not until now. I think the Goat Marketing Board will be a serious earner for the Mountain Silurians. It might even civilize them."

"You did say that peace would be brought about only through economic means," I observed.

"I did, didn't I?"

We reached the far end of the woods a half hour later, and Addie pulled into the shade of a large lime tree. We climbed out to consider our next move.

"There's at least a mile or two of open country before we reach the base of the mountain," said Addie, peering at the landscape through binoculars, "and we must be cautious. There's no way to know why every person who's traveled this way recently has vanished."

I took Addie's binoculars and looked up at the sheer gray mass of Cadir Idris, the top swathed in clouds. I saw now that one side of the rocky pinnacle seemed to have the remnants of a stairway cut into the stone. The road upon which we were parked led to the mountain, then branched off beneath the almost-vertical southern face. It appeared that some buildings had been constructed there, and they seemed quite new. I nudged Perkins and pointed. He spelled himself a hand telescope again and stared for a moment at the distant structures.

"Several large buildings," he said, "and a barbed-wire perimeter with lots of people milling about. Looks like a manufacturing facility of some sort. The Skybus truck has just arrived and the gates are being opened to allow it to enter."

"Manufacturing?" I said. "Out here?"

"Looks like it. With a sizable workforce, too, but they're too far away to see details."

"Not subject to the one hundred percent fatality index, at any rate," I said.

"Pugh the Numbers called them *Cavi homini*," said the princess.

Addie laughed, and I asked her what was so funny. "It's like Cloud Leviathan graveyards and Pirate Wolff and the Eye of Zoltar: all myths. The *Cavi homini* are spooks, bogles, mysterious men without morals or form. They take what they want, and nothing can kill them. It is said they are no more than empty walking clothes, with nothing inside. The translation from Latin is —"

"'Hollow Men,'" I said with a shiver.

"Yes," said Addie with a frown. "You have these fairy tales in the Kingdom of Snodd as well?"

"No," I said, "we've got them for real, as have you. We call them drones. They are used by . . ."

I paused as several pieces of the puzzle locked into place. The Mighty Shandar used drones and owned a large portion of Skybus Aeronautics. Here in the empty land near Cadir Idris, Hollow Men were manufacturing something for Skybus and shipping it out in the pale blue trucks. These things had to be connected somehow.

"Addie," I said, "just what did you see in the back of the Skybus truck?"

"Nothing," she said. "It was completely empty."

"It couldn't have been," I said. "They come in heavy and go out light—you said so yourself when we were examining the tracks."

"I did say that, yes. The empty truck I saw was one of the heavy ones being driven in."

"But if the light ones are going out, they contain *less than nothing?*"

Addie shrugged.

"I don't get it," said the princess.

"Sometimes when magic and the Mighty Shandar are involved," I said, "it's better not to know the truth."

"Jenny, I've spotted the half-track again," said Perkins, who had focused his fingerscope on the side of the mountain.

"And?"

"The vehicle looks abandoned, but on the stone steps I can see—what looks like Curtis. I'd recognize that arrogant swagger anywhere."

"What do we do?" asked Wilson.

"Do what we planned and climb Cadir Idris in search of the Eye," I said, "by way of the steps, preferably."

"And the Skybus facility and the Hollow Men?" asked Addie.

I shrugged. "They're what — two miles away? I say we worry about them if they start heading toward us."

So that's what we did. We got back in the Jeep and headed into the open land toward the mountain. It was open in that there were no trees, but it was not flat; the road rose and fell with the contours, then tipped into a shallow ravine where the river crossed our path.

Addie slowed to a stop when we reached the river, and we looked around silently at the morbid sight that met us. "Holy cow," said Perkins finally.

Addie switched off the engine and we climbed out. It was a medium-size river, stony and fast moving and no more than a couple of feet deep. But it wasn't the river that stopped us; it was the bones. There were thousands of them, all human, piled so thick in places that they clogged the river and raised the water level. There were vehicles, too, some overturned by winter floods, others corroded to nothing, and a few that looked as though they had been there less than a year.

"I'm thinking we've just discovered what happened to everyone who headed this way," said Addie. "Ambushed and massacred."

"By the Mountain Silurians?" asked Wilson. "They aim to kill us anyway?"

"After all my financial advice," said the princess, "that would be a pretty dismal thing to do."

Addie had approached the river and knelt down to inspect the bones. "It wouldn't be the Siluri," she said. "They're honorable people, if a little violent and not very sophisticated." She held up a cleanly sliced ulna, then a lower jaw cleaved neatly sideways. "No, these are random wounds by a swiftly wielded long sword. These people were overcome not by skill, but by numbers."

"Drones," I said. "Hollow Men."

We looked around nervously, but there was nothing except the gurgle of water through rocks.

"Over here!" Wilson was looking into a Land Rover half submerged in the river. The canvas top was sliced away and the keys were still in the ignition. In the back seat were rain-stained, mildewed sketchbooks filled with illustrations of the Cloud Leviathan, as well as notebooks packed with notes, observations, discoveries.

"A scientific expedition," said Wilson. "All that learning for nothing."

Addie drew her dagger and looked around. This low spot in the ground was a bad place to stop and a good place to attack, depending on your perspective.

"These were all attacked *returning*," I said quietly. "Look at the direction the vehicles were going."

Every vehicle was pointed toward the road we had

just come in on. All these travelers had discovered secrets out here — Leviathans, Hollow Men, even Pirate
Wolff and possibly the Eye of Zoltar — but the secrets
had stayed secrets. Dead men and women tell no tales.

"You were right, Addie," said Perkins. "There is a
hidden menace waiting for us. But even Hollow Men
have to come from somewhere, and the closest place is
that facility. Even if they started to march right now,
we'd still have time to get away."

"I think not," said the princess, who had moved away
from the group and was staring at the ground near a small
grassy hollow. "We're surrounded."

We joined her, and she pointed to four swords buried
up to their hilts. Positioned around them were four neat
stacks of clothing tied up with string: trousers, shirt,
shoes, gloves, jacket, tie, and hat, all identical, all carefully folded and waiting to be conjured into life to do
their master's bidding.

"All these people were killed by a small drone army
designed to do one thing and one thing only," I said.
"Stop anyone returning from Cadir Idris."

"It would explain why Geraint the Great wanted my
entire plan for the Goat Marketing Board up front," said
the princess. "He knew that people never return."

"But why?" asked Perkins. "What's the secret?"

"I'm only guessing here," I said, "but perhaps the

facility is manufacturing hollow suits for the drones to wear. Perhaps the magic is in the weave."

"If that were so," said Addie, "the trucks would come out heavier than they go in, but they don't. They're *lighter* on the way out."

"And yet the truck you saw coming in, the heavy one, was empty," said Wilson.

"I know," said Addie. "It doesn't make any sense."

"I've got a feeling the secret won't just be about Cloud Leviathans and Sky Pirate Wolff," I said. "It will be about drones, the Mighty Shandar, and Skybus Aeronautics."

Perkins looked around at the scene of the massacre. "And I've a nasty feeling that our enlightenment may be short-lived."

"You say the jolliest things," said Wilson, "but we're not dead yet. Let's get going."

THIRTY-NINE

Cadir Idris

I instructed the others to pick up half a dozen discarded swords just in case, and we climbed back aboard the Jeep in a subdued mood. We drove out of the shallow ravine and across the empty grassland. As we neared the mountain, it seemed to loom over us even more oppressively.

We parked next to the vacated half-track, and I rummaged through our baggage. Fortunately for us, Curtis was as lazy as he was unpleasant, and aside from taking all the cash, he had left everything else untouched. My Helping Hand™ was still there, as was the letter of credit with which to negotiate for Boo's release. More important for now, there was my last homing snail and the conch. I immediately tried to reach Tiger, but there was nothing but static and sounds of the sea from the conch. I'd not heard from Kazam for more than twenty-four hours—not even a homing snail—and I was nervous.

"What are you doing?" I called to Perkins, who was twenty yards away, treading stealthily back in the direction we had come.

"See that bundle of drone clothes over there?" he called. "Watch."

He took another six steps, and the bundle of clothes sprang into life like a jack-in-the-box. Stacked in the vertical order they hung on the body, the clothes moved with a slick liquidity: pile of empty clothes one moment, lethal killing machine the next. The drone drew a sword that had been buried up to its hilt in the ground and brandished it menacingly.

Perkins backed away, and the drone dropped back into a pile of clothes again, the string retying itself neatly, the sword sliding into the ground.

We had all watched, and the display was chilling. There were dozens of drone clothes packs dotted around, blocking our passage back toward Llangurig and safety.

"Any ideas?" asked Wilson as soon as Perkins had rejoined us.

"Not a single one," said Perkins, "but we're alive as long as we don't try to leave the mountain."

"I'm not staying here my entire life," said the princess. "I've a kingdom to inherit."

"And I've booked a group to go elephino watching next month," said Addie.

"Drat," said Wilson, "and I was so hoping for a heroic end to my life."

"I've an idea," I said, and brought out the last homing snail. It was strange to think that our lives might rely on a snail going for help, but it was pretty much our best and only hope. Even if we returned from our climb up the mountain to seek the Eye, we would be trapped here by the Hollow Men. A dragon on our side would be handy, but we would have to wait for Colin to de-rubberize, and then we'd need six months more for his wing to heal from the anti-aircraft shell. Six months would be a long time to scratch out a living stuck at the base of Cadir Idris. The rations in the half-track would last us a week tops, and I had no idea where we'd find enough food to feed Colin during the winter while his wing healed — or even if he would fly again. Rescue seemed the best hope, assuming Moobin and the rest could reach us and get us out.

I opened a can of Spam and fed it to the homing snail, who guzzled it down greedily. He'd need every bit of energy for his escape. I wrote out a note.

Moobin:

Surrounded by Hollow Men, little chance of escape. Have Rubber Colin, aim to climb Cadir Idris, Shandar up to no good, need help soonest, listening on the conch at all times. URGENT.

— Jennifer

I double-taped the message to the shell, then put the snail on the ground and removed its hood. It looked around for a moment, tasted the air, and was off like a bullet across the open ground.

A drone sprang to life and made a wild running dive. It missed the snail, but suddenly another drone made a grab. The snail, no slouch itself, swerved. Within a second, two dozen drones popped up, each making a grab for the escapee. The snail dodged another three, but that was it. I heard a squeal as it was caught, and then a sickening crunch. Their job done, the drones collapsed into piles of clothing again and all was quiet.

I felt Perkins put his hand on my shoulder. "Come on," he said, "we've still got the conch. We'll monitor it constantly. Moobin and Tiger and the others must be as anxious to contact us as we are them."

I agreed, and after loading as much food as we could from the half-track into our knapsacks, I taped a note to Colin's hand. If we didn't ever return, when he de-rubberized he would need to know what had happened and be warned about the drones. With nothing else to delay us, we began the long climb up the mountain.

The steps were finely hewn, but annoyingly large—twice as high as those in a house. It made me think the steps had been cut for giants, which would bear out the legend that the mountain was not a mountain at all, but an ancient viewing platform used by the giant Idris, who would have climbed these stairs to study the heavens and philosophize about existence.

I wasn't the only person who found the climb hard going.

"This would make Idris about twelve feet tall," panted Wilson, "a good size."

"But still one-third the size of a troll," said Perkins.

"Is an ogre bigger or smaller than a giant?" asked the princess.

"Human, ogre, giant, troll," I said, reciting the increasing order of magnitude of the bipedal species, "but there's sometimes a bit of overlap."

"Ah," said the princess, "good. That always puzzled me."

In several places the steps had broken away, forcing us to scramble across an empty patch near a precipitous drop to the ground far below. The path took us up in a zigzag fashion, so our view of the manufacturing facility came in and out of view as we climbed. From our lofty view, the facility's purpose was no easier to detect, and after a while we had climbed so high that the buildings looked like a few small boxes and we paid it no more heed. There was plenty of fresh water streaming out of the rock, which we all agreed was the best any of us had tasted. Even though the long drop alongside the path was vertiginous in the extreme, none of us felt nervous and instead experienced a sense of mountain elation, a sort of magic that glowed from the rock, a lingering aftereffect of the giant Idris.

There were two rockfalls as we climbed. One was a small torrent of rocks dislodged by a stream that cascaded down with gravel and weeds, but the second was larger and potentially fatal. A large chunk of rock dislodged and came bouncing down the mountain, so we pressed ourselves flat against the rock face as the boulders tumbled above us and bounced farther out, leaving us unscathed. The path did not fare so well, and another large chunk was torn out of the stairway.

When the rocks stopped falling, I looked up, and for a fleeting moment saw a figure that looked like Curtis peering down; none of us were in any doubt that it was he who had deliberately caused the rockfall. We spent the rest of the journey with at least one person keeping an eye out for any other skullduggery, but there were no more attempts on our lives.

We stopped for a bite at two o'clock, and then struck

off with renewed vigor, moving into the clouds near the summit at about four in the afternoon. The air felt damp and clammy, and fine droplets of water formed on our clothes. There was not a shred of vegetation anywhere, and soon the rocks themselves seemed to ooze water like leaky sponges.

Eventually large stone gateposts loomed out of the cloud, with a pair of ornate and very rusty gates collapsed between them. We climbed over, our small group now subdued and quiet. Although visibility was poor within the cloud, we knew this entrance must mark the summit.

We walked under an archway and entered a paved semicircular area about a hundred yards in diameter. Around the semicircle were delicately carved reliefs of strange creatures battling men in ancient armor, and in the center, next to the cliff edge, where a slip would send one tumbling into space, was a chair carved from solid rock. The seat was at least five feet from the ground — the chair for a giant.

"The Chair of Idris," said Addie, "where he would have sat and considered questions of existence, and stared into the heavens."

"This would once have been a full circle," said Wilson, looking around. "Half of this area has already fallen away."

"In a few years the chair will go too," came a familiar

voice, "so count your blessings that you have witnessed even this."

Curtis walked out of the gray fog toward us, grinning. He had shown little remorse when Ignatius died, treated Ralph like an animal, and left us to die in the Empty Quarter. He had kidnapped the princess, sold her in Llangurig, and then tried to kill us with a rockfall. I should have hated him, but somehow I hardly felt anything at all. He would not escape back to civilization either; the drones would cut him down before he'd gone twenty paces. It struck me as ironic that he knew nothing of his fate, but was the only one of us who vaguely deserved it.

"I've been up here two hours," Curtis said. "The top of the mountain extends for not much farther than you can see in every direction. I've checked the whole place, and there is nothing up here but damp rock, ancient history, and disappointment. There are a few human bones but nothing from a Leviathan, let alone a tooth. It was a wild-goose chase, Jenny. Addie was right—it's all legends, hearsay, old wives' tales. I should despise you for wasting my time, but hey, at least I got to climb Cadir Idris and see the giant's chair."

"Yes," I agreed, "there is that."

"Hello, Laura," said Curtis as the princess stepped out from behind the chair. "No hard feelings, eh?"

"None," said the princess. "I've never been kid-napped, knocked unconscious, or sold before. It was very . . . educational."

"Well," said Curtis, checking his watch, "you're all being very cool about this. I thought you'd be mad at me — but hey, I guess that's the rough and tumble of the Cambrian Empire. The big adventure, y'know? We should meet up when this is all over. Have a few laughs."

"Perhaps we will," I said, "but not together. Good-bye, Curtis."

He suddenly looked uneasy. "Okay, then," he said, his voice cracking with the briefest tremor. "I'll get go-ing. I should make it back to Llangurig by nightfall. So long."

"One more thing," I said. "I've taken the keys to the half-track, so you're in the Jeep."

"And if you touch our belongings," added Addie, "or try to sabotage the half-track or anything, I will make it my sworn life's duty to hunt you down."

He looked at us all in turn. I think he got the mes-sage. "Jeep it is, then," he said.

He turned hesitantly, paused, glanced at us again, and then walked away and was lost to view in the swirl-ing fog. We listened to his footsteps retreat, and heard a rusty clang as he climbed back over the fallen gates. We heard a few steps as he began the long descent, then no more.

"So," said the princess, "any ideas about this Eye of Zoltar thingy? I can't see a Leviathan graveyard anywhere."

"Nor a pirate hideout," added Wilson.

"Me neither," I said, "but the answer is up here somewhere. I can feel it."

I asked everyone to search the mountaintop to see if Curtis had missed anything. They fanned out, and I was left by Idris's chair to think. Something didn't add up: If the Mighty Shandar had gone to the trouble of protecting the area with hundreds of drones, then there had to be a secret up here that needed protecting. A seriously good secret.

All we had to do was find it.

FORTY

Perkins's Secret

Perkins was the first to return. He had found nothing except a shelter cut into the rock, presumably to offer meager comfort to any travelers caught up here in bad weather. I had no doubt that weather here could be very bad indeed.

"Bones and gristle and a few IDs," he said when I asked if there was anything inside, "and tattered remnants of luggage, a corroded radio, and some water bottles. I also noticed that every surface slopes gently toward the edge of the cliff. A few good rainstorms and this place would be hosed down—almost like it's self-cleaning."

"And the magic?" I asked. "Can you feel it?"

324

It wasn't the buzz of modern wizidrical energy, which is like the humming of power lines, but the low, almost inaudible rumble of old magic.

"I can feel it," he said, "but I can't pinpoint its source. Almost like it's all around us."

Addie returned next, then Wilson, followed ten minutes later by the princess. They, too, had found nothing but damp rock and a few buttons, coins, and shards of bone.

"Are we done?" asked the princess. "This place gives me the willies."

I looked at each in turn. Their fate was my responsibility. It was my expedition, my wish to come up here, my need to see what lay hidden at Cadir Idris. Now we were here—and there was nothing.

"Look," I said, "I'm really sorry. I was sure there was an explanation for all this—something that linked the Mighty Shandar, the facility down below, the drones, Able Quizzler, the Eye of Zoltar, everything. Even the reason Kevin sent us out here. Problem is, I just can't see it. Quizzler must have found the Eye of Zoltar elsewhere, which isn't so unbelievable; it was a legend that linked the Eye with Pirate Wolff, and only a half legend that linked Wolff with the Leviathans' Graveyard. And with all clues amounting to nothing, we're done. We'll head back as soon as we've had a break. You go below the cloud and dry out. I'm staying up here a few more minutes."

"I'm going to make some tea," said Wilson, practical as ever.

"I'll help you," said Addie. "I don't like it up here. It all feels wrong. Princess? Come and help. I think Jenny and Perkins need to talk out our options for our return."

They left, and Perkins and I sat on a lump of carved stone. We said nothing for several minutes.

"Addie was right," he said finally. "We need to talk. I'm your best and only chance to get home. I can't unspell the entire drone army, but I can probably disrupt them long enough to cover your retreat across the open grass-land. I think."

"Absolutely not," I replied. "We leave as one, or leave as none."

"If you had my powers, you wouldn't hesitate to use them," he said. "You'd give your life without batting an eyelid."

"This isn't negotiable, Perkins. This is about us. Promise me?"

He bit his lip and sighed, then rested his hand on mine. "I'm not what you think I am, Jenny, and there was never going to be an *us*. Not for long, anyway. I didn't tell you earlier, but Ralph's Genetic Master Reset wasn't the only spell for which I had to burn some of my own life spirit. The rubberizing spell took four years out of me. In fact," he said, dropping his gaze, "*all* spelling takes time off me. Every scrap of magic I've ever done has exacted a cost measured in weeks, months, and years. I'm a fraud, Jenny. I can't do magic—at least, not without shortening my life. I'm a Burner. A throwaway, and like all Burners, here for only one reason: to shine brightly for a fleeting moment to help others in their time of need."

I'd never met a Burner, but had heard of them: Detectable only once the aging became obvious, they typically lasted two or three big spells before they'd mined their own life spirit to nothing. Some of the finest magicians on the planet had been Burners, who did one fantastic, game-changing feat of magic, then were gone.

"No," I said, tears springing to my eyes. "No more magic. We can put you on other duties when we get back to Kazam."

Perkins shook his head sadly. "All I've ever wanted is to be magically useful. Jenny, we have been charged to find the Eye of Zoltar and protect the princess at all costs. Moobin told me to undertake my duties with 'all other considerations secondary.' He wouldn't have told me that if this quest weren't of vital importance."

He was right. Moobin wouldn't have made the decision on his own, either.

"The greatest sorcerers give everything to their craft,

and at least this way I get to spend the rest of my life with you. My mind is made up, Jenny. It's time you started treating me for what I really am: a useful yet limited resource to be expended wisely."

I looked up at him and gave him a wan smile. I think I realized that I loved him at that moment. Whatever happened in the future, my heart — my true heart — would always belong to Perkins.

"They always say you can't keep relationships within the magic industry," I said, wiping my eyes, "and some say that magic works to prevent it."

"Yeah," said Perkins. "That's how I see it too."

There was a pause.

"'A resource to be expended wisely'?" I repeated. "That's really how you see yourself?"

He smiled. "A bit harsh, yes, but I was trying to make a point. Remember that Kevin foresaw I would grow old in the Cambrian Empire? He was right — I just got there quicker than I thought."

I sighed, pulled out my hair tie, and rubbed my fingers through my hair. It was knotted and matted from three days without a bath. I'd been an idiot to think that this journey was anything but a quest. Searches were nice and soft and cuddly and no one needed to be killed. A quest *always* demanded the death of a trusted friend and one or more ethical dilemmas. I'd put us all in jeopardy, and now, as likely as not, I was going to lose the one person I cared for most.

"I'm so sorry," I said, "for dragging you into this."

"I came of my own free will," replied Perkins. "Okay, it's a serious downer that the Eye of Zoltar isn't here, but at least now we know that for sure. Ten minutes ago we didn't even know that."

"Perhaps, but it's useless if we can't get back to tell anyone. And what happens to Shandar's deal now? The dragons will die."

"Defeatist talk," said Perkins, jumping to his feet. "We can figure out the Shandar problem when we get home. Let's kick those drones where it hurts."

"I'm not sure that metaphor works with drones, who have no parts to hurt, but yes, let's go. What's your plan for disrupting the Hollow Men?"

"I'm working on something," he said with a smile.

As we walked toward the archway that led to the gates and the stairway back down, I turned to take one last look at the spot where the giant Idris would once have considered the cosmos.

"He wouldn't have seen much in this low cloud," said Perkins.

And that was when we heard the rattle of several things striking the ground behind us. We turned back, and there were a few human finger bones rolling on the ground. They hadn't been there before. Perkins and I frowned at each other, puzzled, as an ulna dropped out of the foggy murk above us; a wristwatch was still attached with some dried gristle.

I picked it up. It wasn't a watch — it was a wrist altimeter, as a parachutist or aerialist might wear. There was something engraved on the back.

"'To Shipmate Fly-Low Milo, the finest aerialist that ever there was,'" I read.

"Sounds like pirate grammar to me," said Perkins. "Everything but the 'Argh!'"

"No, that's engraved on the strap; look here."

"Oh. Right. But what does it mean?"

We looked up at the tendrils of fog. "Perhaps the old magic we sense is the cloud itself," I said. "Maybe there's a reason the top of Cadir Idris is constantly swathed in fog. The mountain is hiding something."

I picked up a stone and threw it up into the cloud as high as I could. I heard the rock hit something, and a second later we jumped aside as a small section of rotted aircraft wing complete with tattered canvas came wheeling out of the fog and crashed to the ground.

There was something hidden above us. We hadn't found Pirate Wolff's hideout for the very simple reason that it wasn't meant to be found. That's the thing about pirates. It's not wise to underestimate their cunning.

"If there's something up there, there must be a way of accessing it," I said, looking around. "We need to find the highest point."

After a brief scout around in the damp fog, we found it: the high seat back of Idris's chair. One side rose twenty feet above the hard stone ground, and the other was near a precipitous drop through the fog to the valley floor below.

"Give me a hand," I said, and Perkins helped me climb onto the large stone seat. I looked around and found a useful handhold, then a foothold, and then another. The holds were nearly impossible to see against the wet stone, but had been definitely cut for a purpose. I had soon climbed atop the seat back, a narrow rock edge less than six inches wide. I made a mental note that if I were to fall, I should try to land on the safe side of the chair—and by "safe" I mean a painful drop twenty feet onto wet rock rather than a seven-thousand-foot fall to certain death.

I cautiously stayed low and reached above my head into the cloud, which seemed to be thicker and distinctly un-cloudlike, more like smoke. My fingers touched nothing. Fortune favors the bold, so I stood upright on the narrow ledge, everything around me vanishing as my upper body was enveloped by the fog. I was mildly disorientated and my foot slipped on the wet rock; my heart beating fast, I regained my footing. I stood up straighter and reached above my head, straining to touch something. Even on tiptoes, nothing.

I was about to give up and return to firm ground when Kevin's last message rang out in my head: *If you ever find yourself on the shoulders of giants and need to take a leap of faith, go for it.*

I was standing on Idris's chair, as close to his long-dead shoulders as I was ever likely to be. If this wasn't a leap of faith, I wasn't sure what was.

I made a tentative jump as I reached above my head, but felt nothing, and when I landed, my feet slipped. For a moment I thought I would fall, but then caught my balance.

Come on, Jenny, I said to myself, *that was nothing like a leap.*

"Perkins?" I called out.

"Yes?" came a disembodied voice from below.

"I'm going to leap."

"And trust in providence?"

"No," I said, "something better. I'm going to trust in . . . Kevin."

And I jumped. Leaped, actually. Later I couldn't remember whether I jumped on the cliff side or the summit side, but it must have been the cliff side. Without the certainty of death, the leap wouldn't have worked.

I leaped as high and as far as I could and put out my

hands, hoping to grab hold of something, and I did. But it wasn't the rung of a ladder, or a rope. It was a human hand, and it grabbed me tightly around the wrist, held me for a moment, and then hauled me up until I was safe. I looked around and blinked, open-mouthed.

I had not expected to see what I saw, nor who had just saved me.

FORTY-ONE

The Sky Pirate's Tale

S urprised?"

"Just a little," I said, looking around. I was still enveloped in cloud but found myself sitting on a small, gently undulating platform that I soon realized was the distinctively broad, flat skull of a Leviathan. What's more, it was floating in midair. I knew a Leviathan was lighter than air, but I had not realized that the bones would remain so after death. To one side was a spiral staircase made of Leviathan bones, which vanished up into the gloom, and on the other side was the man who had hauled me to this strange new world within the clouds. It was Gabby, looking just as I had seen him last: youthful, sleeves rolled up, still wearing his backpack.

"What are you doing here?" I asked.

"Hiding. I'm not always in the mood to be found. But when you took that leap, well, I wasn't going to let you die."

"For the second time."

"Fourth, actually, but who's counting?"

"You are."

"Agreed. But you didn't see me the other times. In my line of work, being seen can raise difficulties."

"I don't understand."

"No, few do. Let me show you around."

Gabby led the way up the creaking spiral bone-staircase. We didn't have to go far before we broke cloud and came into the sunlight. I looked around. My mouth, I think, had permanently dropped open.

We were standing on a floating platform of massive Leviathan bones, lashed together and constructed of several different levels. There were walkways, stairways, and even rooms, passageways, and a main hall, the framework of each built solely of lighter-than-air Leviathan bones.

"The legendary Leviathans' Graveyard," I breathed, for here indeed were the remains of hundreds of Leviathans, their bones used to make a pirate hideout of crude beauty. There was elegance in the haphazard structure, and a certain recycled charm, for among the framework of bones was the booty of the aerial pirate — parts of aircraft stolen on the wing and adapted to make the hideout more like home. Wings became roofs, aluminum fuselage panels became walkways, aero engines were generator sets and winches. We were standing at what appeared to be a dock, ready to accept a Cloud Leviathan; a large leather harness was poised to strap a wicker balloonist's gondola on the creature's back, with mounted harpoon guns, grappling hooks, and cutlasses at the ready.

But for all this apparent readiness, the hideout was long abandoned. Everything was old, worn, and weathered. Exposed metal was corroded, and the leather strips that held the bones together had begun to rot.

There were human bodies too, or rather, partial bodies. A pirate close to us had died in a fight, his arm still holding a cutlass embedded in the handrail. Although most of him was now little more than a skeleton held together with dried gristle, his arm, half his chest, and his head had been preserved at the moment of death — as a dull gray metal.

I tapped the metal and stared uneasily at the grim determination stuck permanently on the dead pirate's features, then tested the metal for softness with my fingernail. There was no mistake: He had been changed partially to lead.

"The Eye of Zoltar," I breathed. "It's here — or *was* here."

I looked around to see if there were other bodies,

and there were, all partially or completely turned to lead. There had been a battle, and the pirates had lost.

"However did this place come about?" I asked as we followed the trail of dead pirates toward the main hall, the walkway flexing beneath our feet.

"The Cambrian species of Leviathan has always lived on Cadir Idris," explained Gabby. "It is hatched here, breeds here, roosts here, and eventually returns here to die. Once dead, it floats in the air until it rots away, and its bones rise to form a jumbled floating mass about twenty thousand feet above the summit. Usefully, that becomes the place where Leviathan eggs are laid. It's thought the first sky pirate tamed a Leviathan and then established a base in what was once the Leviathan's nest."

"We're not as high as twenty thousand feet." We walked past another pirate, lead from the waist down.

"Right," said Gabby, "and it would be too cold to live up there. We think that much of this aircraft scrap—the engines and undercarriage and whatnot—is for ballast, to weigh down the bones and keep them hovering just above the mountain's summit. One of the first acts of piracy was to kidnap a sorcerer to ensure that the nest—now built into pretty much what you see here—was permanently obscured by cloud."

"Which explains why the summit can never be seen, no matter the weather."

"Precisely. As the years went by, the pirating business moved from captain to captain but was always fairly low-key — until Sky Pirate Bunty Wolff took over. She had no qualms about plundering the biggest airliners literally on the wing. She would attack anything if there was rich booty to be had."

"So was the attack on Cloud City Nimbus III and the loss of the *Tyrannic* her after all?"

"Absolutely. She always made sure there were no witnesses."

"She sounds like a monster."

We had arrived at the main hall. We stepped across a half-lead pirate holding a musket, and Gabby opened two doors that appeared to have been salvaged from an aircraft. The hall had been constructed of an entire Cloud Leviathan rib cage, with walls made of a patchwork of aircraft fabric, still showing registration numbers and the names of every airline I could think of.

"Three out of four missing aircraft can be attributed to Pirate Wolff," said Gabby as we walked across the creaking floorboards, some of which were missing, revealing the swirling clouds below, "and she did very well out of pirating. Murderous thug, of course. Nothing glamorous in pirates — they're criminals, pure and simple."

"Have you heard of something called the Eye of Zoltar?" I asked.

"No, but I presume it's related to Zoltar the sorcerer?"

"It's a pink ruby about the size of a goose egg," I said, "which seems to dance with an inner fire. It can be used as a conduit — a concentrator of wizidrical energy. But it's dangerous. In the wrong hands, it will —"

"Turn a person partially to lead?" asked Gabby.

"Wholly, sometimes," I said, recalling Able Quizzler, who must have been turned entirely lead to have enough weight to bury himself when he hit the ground.

"Nasty way to go," said Gabby, "but in pirating, an unpleasant death is very much an occupational hazard. You seek this jewel?"

"That we do," I said, "and all the clues point toward Pirate Wolff."

"Then you'd better meet her," said Gabby. "She's in here."

FORTY-TWO

Sky Pirate Bunty Wolff

Gabby opened an inner door, and we entered Pirate Wolff's private cabin. The room was paneled with an interior stolen from the first-class lounge of a flying boat somewhere and must have once looked supremely elegant — before the rain had managed to gain access, turning parts of the paneling black with mold.

Sky Pirate Bunty Wolff sat before us. She had been completely turned to lead. It was not unlike being transformed into stone. Every pore, sinew, scar, blemish, and hair was perfectly preserved. She was dressed in traditional pirate uniform, although with a battered flying helmet in place of the tricorn hat. Her clothes were rotting around her — her body, like those of most of the other pirates', looked like a lead statue draped with tattered garments. One of her lead hands rested on a tabletop, and the other was empty and held aloft, her fingers open as though she had been showing off an apple or something. She wore a look of shocked surprise. Her enleadening moment had not been expected.

"Is your Eye of Zoltar anywhere here?" asked Gabby.

"It once was," I replied with a sigh. An open safe behind Pirate Wolff was stashed with jewels, but none the size of a goose's egg.

"Do you know when all this happened?" I asked.

"Six years ago," said Gabby, "give or take. We rarely intervene when it comes to pirates."

I looked at the hand Sky Pirate Wolff held aloft. Looking closer, I saw that her soft lead fingers had been bent apart. When she had been turned to base metal, she had been holding something—and it wasn't an apple.

"This is where the Eye of Zoltar was. Pirate Wolff was holding it. She was talking to someone seated right here." I dropped into the seat opposite the lead statue, and the pirate's dead eyes stared into mine. "They were talking. The person sitting here used the Eye to change Pirate Wolff to lead, then made a run for it. The People into Lead spell must be the Eye's default, or a gatekeeper or something."

"It would explain the trail of partially leaded pirates all the way out," observed Gabby. "Whoever took the jewel used the lead transformation spell to stop anyone from following."

He was right, and I swore softly to myself. The trail, then, had long ago turned cold. After six years, the Eye could be anywhere on the planet. I searched Pirate Wolff's room, then the main hall, but could find nothing that might have told us who took the Eye or where it was now. Kevin Zipp had been right about the Eye's whereabouts, but his timeframe had been way off.

We walked back the way we had come.

"Do you know who took it?" I asked.

"Sadly, I do not," said Gabby, "but it would have to be a sorcerer of some sort."

"The Mighty Shandar is skilled enough to tap the Eye's power," I murmured, "but sending me to find something he already has doesn't make much sense."

"There's a good reason why Shandar wouldn't want you poking around out here," said Gabby, "and it has nothing to do with the Eye of Zoltar."

I frowned and thought for a moment. "The Skybus facility below?"

Gabby nodded.

"What are they making?" I asked. "And why do the empty trucks coming in weigh more than the heavy ones coming out?"

"Because . . . they'd have to be."

I stared at Gabby, trying to figure it out. We had by

now arrived at the top of the bone-spiral staircase. A few steps down and we'd be in the all-obscuring cloud again. I reached out to one of the Leviathan bones and scratched off a small amount of bone that, once released, drifted up.

"Shandar is harvesting Cloud Leviathans?" I said, and Gabby smiled.

"Ever wonder how those huge jetliners seem to hang in the air on those tiny wings?" he asked. "How Skybus leads the world in efficient aircraft that can fly twice as far on half the fuel? Ever wonder why Shandar has made so much money through Skybus, and how Tharv can afford to give all his citizens free health care?"

"Tharv and Shandar are partners?"

"Very much so. The whole jeopardy-tourism thing might sound like a long and very complex joke, but without it, Tharv and Shandar would not be as stupendously rich as they are. All those tourists in the Cambrian Empire are snatched from the jaws of certain death, hundreds of times a day, month in, month out."

And that was when it hit me. The Cloud Leviathans' lighter-than-air capability was not by magic, nor by some natural process. Prince Nasil had even mentioned it back at Kazam before we left: The same thing that keeps a flying carpet in the air also keeps up a Leviathan.

"Angel feathers," I said in a soft whisper. "We were nearly vacuumed up by the Leviathan the night before last. They do that feeding run every morning, sucking up not just the birds and bugs, but also many of the Variant-G angels who are constantly employed in the Cambrian Empire. They are then digested to make the Leviathan lighter than air. Jeopardy tourism is there for a purpose. High risk of death, high concentration of angels."

I paused and looked at Gabby, who nodded.

"But," I added, "that's not the end of it, is it?"

"No, indeed," said Gabby. "The higher-than-normal concentration of ingested angel feathers leads to excess, which are then expelled by the Leviathans as all animal waste is expelled. The drones working in the facility below gather up the Leviathans' droppings with nothing more complicated than shovels, then extract the angel feathers using Shandar-supplied magic. The refined material is known in the aeronautical industry as Guanolite, and is stuffed inside aircraft wings to assist with lift. That's what's going out in those Skybus trucks. "

"Which must explain," I said slowly, "why the Skybus trucks are lighter on the way out."

"Of course. Fill a two-ton truck with concentrated Guanolite, and the upward force will ensure it weighs no more than a golf cart."

I digested this new information as we began the climb down the staircase. As I entered the cloud, I felt the clamminess, and soon we were standing on the Leviathan skull, the place where I first entered this strange place.

"*Who are you?*" I asked. "You travel around the Cambrian Empire with ease, and are easily able to avoid its dangers."

"You might say I have a version of Access All Areas," Gabby said with a chuckle. "As I explained, I collect information on death likelihood for a major player in the risk-management industry."

"I remember," I said, "and by identifying the potential risk factor of everything anyone does, you decide where best to deploy your assets to avert those risks."

"That's pretty much it," said Gabby. "We save lives . . . when lives need to be saved."

"It's not an insurance company, is it?"

"Not really, no. It's sort of . . . fate management. It's of vital importance that you — or anyone, in fact — will not die until you have achieved your function in the G-SOT."

"G-SOT?"

"The Grand Scheme of Things. Bigger than me, bigger than you, and everyone plays a part. It might be something simple like opening a door, encouraging somebody to take action, or even, as in Curtis's case, simply giving people a focus of someone to dislike. But sometimes it's for the greater good, like bringing a tyrant to his knees and leading an enslaved nation to freedom."

"Then my function in the Grand Scheme is still ahead of me?" I asked.

"It is. And Perkins's, too."

"He's going to burn himself out battling the drones on our return, isn't he?"

"To have a purpose is the right of all sentient beings," said Gabby, touching my shoulder. "To have a *vitally important* purpose is an honor not often bestowed." He smiled, then added, "For operational reasons we like to maintain our Legendary Grade II status: 'no proof of existence.' I can rely on your discretion?"

"Yes."

"Good. Time to go, but I calculate that the jump from here back to the top of the stone chair has a 99.23 percent fatality likelihood. Here."

Gabby tossed a rope over the side, and I heard it fall onto the damp stone below. I thanked him, then slid down the rope. My feet touched the damp stone of the semicircle around Idris's chair, and there I found a very astonished-looking Perkins.

"Okay," he said, "that was kind of strange, and I'm a sorcerer, so I should be used to it. You jump into the cloud, vanish for half an hour, and then return down a rope. What did you find?"

"Answers," I said, "but not the ones we're looking for. Let's find the others."

He started to move toward the gates, but I caught his arm and kissed him. It was my first, and I think his, too. I'd been meaning to for a while, but only after Gabby's words did it all seem more urgent. Perkins kissed me back, and it felt good—even better than I'd expected.

"What was that for?" he whispered as I held him tight.

"Because."

"Because what?"

"Just because."

We both knew he'd be burned out soon. This was our only chance for a lifetime's worth of hugs.

"Okay, then," I said, and we avoided each other's gaze as we separated. "Now let's find the others."

We walked down from the summit and out of the cloud to where Addie, the princess, and Wilson had made some tea. We rested for an hour while I told everyone what I had found, without mentioning Gabby. I told them about Sky Pirate Wolff's hideout and her leaden fate, that someone else had beaten us to the Eye of Zoltar years ago, and that now the Eye could be pretty much anywhere. I told them that the facility far below us was strategically positioned where the few remaining Cloud Leviathans roosted at night, and that the workers scraped up the droppings each morning to process into Guanolite.

"I can see why they have drones do the job," said Wilson. "It must be rotten work."

"I'd say the drones have more to do with secrecy,"

I replied, "which also might explain the Cambrian Empire's no-fly zone. The surviving Leviathans are worth so much to Tharv and Shandar's moneymaking scheme that they can't risk the creature being injured in a collision with anything—or to even be discovered at all."

"So all our careers in jeopardy tourism were simply there to facilitate the manufacture of angel feather–fortified Leviathan droppings?" asked Addie. "Hell's teeth, you just couldn't make this stuff up, could you?"

"Magic's like that," I said.

There was a pause.

"So what now?" asked Perkins.

I sighed. "We came out here to find the Eye, and we failed. So we're going home."

"Past the Hollow Men?" asked Wilson.

"Yes," I said, swallowing hard and avoiding Perkins's gaze. "We'll think of something, I'm sure."

So after packing up and trying the conch for the umpteenth time without any reply, we turned to leave. It was with a heavy heart that I descended the steep steps, but at least I had it on good authority that Perkins's life would not be in vain—and I now had a pretty good idea what Gabby kept hidden in the rucksack on his back.

FORTY-THREE

The Plan

The first thing we noticed at the base of the mountain was Curtis. He had apparently decided not to head back to Llangurig right away, and was instead standing at the edge of the empty grassland that separated us from the safety of the forest a mile away. He had a deep frown etched on his features.

I walked over to him. "Did you see them?" I asked.

Curtis said nothing, just stared off toward the safety of the woods.

"They're called Hollow Men or drones," I explained. "*Cavi homini.* Nothing more than the personified evil will of the Mighty Shandar: empty vessels bidden to kill us, without thought, malice, or guilt. It's why no one ever comes back from Cadir Idris."

Curtis still said nothing, so I continued. "I'm telling you this because we need to be a team to survive. Are you any good with a sword?"

"You're wasting your time." That sounded like something Curtis would say, but he hadn't spoken. Addie had come up behind me.

"Asking Curtis to help?" I said.

"Asking Curtis for anything."

I looked quizzically at her, and she nodded toward him. Now that I looked closer, he wasn't standing there looking thoughtfully out at the scenery, but simply standing there. I could even see the fine stitching down the back of his neck.

"Hotax," I said, waving a hand in front of his blank eyes. Curtis had been paralyzed, captured, boned, eaten, and stuffed. It wasn't a pleasant way to go, but would at least have been painless, and ornamentally he was now quite impressive.

"The Hollow Men don't see the Hotax as a threat," said Addie, "the same as Tralfamosaur and snork badger and all the rest. Leave him. He had it coming."

"No one deserves this," I said.

"Perhaps not," said Addie, "but he was only ever with us to make up the fifty percent fatality rate I'd promised, and you agreed to him coming along."

"That's true," I conceded. "How are we doing on that?"

Addie counted the casualty rate on her fingers. "Out of the eight on the team, we've now lost three: Ignatius, Ralph, and Curtis, which is pretty much what I'd planned. If I'm right, we only need lose one more."

"It's a nice mathematical theory," I said, "but I'm not sure the fifty percent thing is valid anymore."

"You're right," Addie said sadly, "but it helps to have something hopeful to cling to, no matter how slender. Some people have a lucky Gonk or a deity. I have statistics." She gave me a smile and offered her hand for me to shake. "Listen, it's been a lot of fun. Most tourists just moan about the food and the weather and the transportation and the hotels and stuff and then think of devious ways they can fleece me for a refund. You were different, and I'd like you to know that whatever happens, I'd tour guide for you anywhere, anytime — and with a generous discount."

"Thank you," I said, knowing that such a compliment was not often given, and a discount even less so. "And on my part, you've been amazing. If we survive this final push, I'll be giving you the best feedback I can." We shook hands again.

I walked across to where the rest were preparing the

half-track for the return journey. The tracks had been tensioned, and as soon as Rubber Colin was lashed down, I asked Perkins about his plan.

"I'm not sure."

"That's not helpful," I said. "We're kind of counting on you."

"No, I mean, I'm not sure *yet*. I won't be able to come up with a countermeasure until I get an idea of the spell the Hollow Men are running. I can't defeat a hundred drones, obviously, but there may be some way I can disable them long enough for you to get away."

With me driving, the princess no good with a sword, and Perkins concentrating on a countermeasure, that left only Addie and Wilson wielding swords against the Hollow Men. And while the drones were easily dispatched with a sharp sword — they were hollow, after all, and needed their clothes to move and fight — the sheer numbers might prove too much. Not knowing how many there were didn't help, either.

"Is it worth de-rubberizing Colin?" I asked. "I know his fiery breath is not fully developed at his age, but at close quarters it might do some damage."

"I thought of that too," said Perkins, "but I read the laundry label on those Hollow Men clothes we found earlier, and they're made of fire-retardant synthetic material. I'm going to keep the power I have for the countermeasure."

"Whatever that might be."

"Yes," said Perkins, "whatever that might be."

"These swords are a bit rusty," said Addie, showing me one of the weapons we had retrieved from the river earlier, "but I've managed to get an edge back on them."

"What do I do?" asked the princess.

"You keep your head down."

She looked at me petulantly. "Like hell I will. If we're going to die, I'm going to go down fighting, even if I'm terrible with a weapon."

"Fair enough," I said, and handed her a cutlass. She swished it around.

"Pointy end toward the bad guy, right?"

"Right."

I gathered everyone around. "Okay," I said, "this is the plan. The Hollow Men are tireless, violent fighters, but we have one advantage: they can't run faster than a half-track. We're going to charge across as quick as we can. Addie, Princess, and Wilson, you're on defense. Perkins here will let fly with whatever he can as soon as he figures out a weakness."

"How long will that be?" asked Addie.

"I don't know," said Perkins, "but the closer they get, the better I can sense the weave of their spell."

"Terrific," replied Wilson, "so *let* them get close?"

"If you can."

"Any more questions?" I asked. There weren't. "Okay. Good luck, everyone."

We shook hands in silence, and as I looked from face to face I could see that none of us rated our chances very high, yet there was no hesitation from anyone. Truly, I was in the very finest company.

Addie positioned herself on the hood of the half-track, with Wilson perched on the rear left and the princess on the rear right. Rubber Colin had been laid flat and covered with blankets, the note I'd taped in his hand amended to describe what we were attempting right now. If worse came to worst, he would revert naturally and find himself in a deserted half-track in the middle of nowhere, and it was important he be able to tell Moobin and the others what had happened to us.

Once we were all positioned, I started the engine. Perkins sat next to me and concentrated hard. I depressed the clutch and selected first gear in low range. I figured there was about a mile to go before we were safe. At thirty miles an hour, it would take us two minutes — assuming we could get to that speed. I put out my hand, and Perkins squeezed it.

"Crazy or nothing," he said, and smiled.

"Crazy or nothing," I replied.

I placed both hands on the wheel, gunned the throttle, and released the clutch. The tracks bit into the soft earth, and we were away. Instantly a pile of clothes popped into the air ahead of us and took the shape of a human. In a few seconds six more had joined it.

I yelled "Hold on!" and floored the accelerator.

FORTY-FOUR

Battle of the Hollow Men

Since we had a decent run-up, the first three drones were easily dispatched under the front wheels, and Addie expertly sliced another in half and Wilson two more. The Hollow Men were surprisingly easy to bring down, as they were only as strong as their clothes. They remained animated when cut in two, but the top half was dangerous only if it could reach you, and the bottom half not dangerous at all unless it gave you a kick.

But I couldn't much focus on this, as my view through the windshield was filled by more Hollow Men popping into life. I was relieved that they didn't seem to be in huge numbers, and I steered into them, the lifeless husks disappearing under the heavy treads and into the mud.

"Anything yet?" I shouted to Perkins.

"Not yet," he said, concentrating hard, fingers on temples. "I think they've been spelled in ARAMAIC-2."

I turned the wheel and accelerated toward a group of three; they vanished under the front wheels.

"They're getting up again!" shouted Wilson as he fought off two drones that had popped back into life after the tracks had passed over them. One managed to climb aboard, but was soon dispatched by the princess, who had discovered that if a drone's right sword arm was sliced through, it had to stop to find the sword with its left before continuing.

I steered near several to help Addie slice through two at once, then positioned the vehicle to run over two more. All seemed to be going well — until I noticed three drones run *toward* the half-track and dive under the front wheels, which suddenly made me wary.

"This is too easy!" shouted Addie.

"I'm not complaining!" yelled Wilson, hacking a drone diagonally from the shoulder to the waist. I changed gear to speed up, and the half-track lurched aggressively to the left. Addie was caught off balance and fell off the hood. I accelerated, but this made the swing to the left worse, and in a few more seconds we had spun around and were pointing not at the forest and safety, but back toward the mountain.

I clutched in the vehicle and came to a halt as Addie eliminated another approaching drone, one of ten or twelve still out there. The Hollow Men seemed to be walking toward us in a relaxed manner, and I didn't like the look of it.

I thumped the wheel. "I think we've lost a track! Addie? Damage report!"

While Wilson jumped off to engage the closest drones, Addie ran around to the right of the vehicle to have a look, then yelled, "Reverse, but easy does it!"

I clunked the half-track into gear and reversed slowly. It seemed to move correctly, but then lurched in the opposite direction, and Addie yelled at me to stop. "Three swords are jammed in the right-hand track!"

"Let me see." I left the engine running and jumped out as Wilson and the princess stood by defensively against the slow-approaching drones. The swords were bent around the drive sprocket, jamming it completely. Also jammed into the tracks were several Hollow Men, or at least their clothes. Those that had run under the vehicle hadn't been fighting at all, just searching for a weakness, and they'd found it. The Achilles' heel on a tracked vehicle is the same as its advantage: the tracks.

I looked around. We had covered barely four hundred yards and had not even reached the river. We might have to abandon the disabled half-track and go back for the Jeep—but when I looked back to where we had left it, six more drones popped up from the earth.

"They're cutting off the retreat," said Wilson.

"Perkins!" I shouted. "We're going to need something from you pretty soon!"

"Working on it!" he replied.

I grabbed a sword from the back of the half-track and faced the drones alongside the others.

"Hang on," said the princess. "They're stopping."

She was right. We were surrounded by at least thirty Hollow Men, standing at readiness about twenty yards out, the gap between each drone and its neighbor precisely the same.

"They're waiting," said Wilson.

"They're waiting because they have time in their favor," said Addie. "Look behind them."

Behind the circle of drones, other Hollow Men were popping into malevolent being all over the scrubby land and walking closer. Reinforcements. I looked again at the jammed track, swore to myself, and climbed into the half-track to switch off the engine.

"Okay, the half-track is dead. We need a new plan."

Worryingly, there were no suggestions, and Perkins climbed out to join us.

"They're like a conjoined military mind," he babbled excitedly. "They don't need a chain of command because each one is a general and a soldier combined. They will study their enemy, exploit its weakness, and neutralize its strengths. The reason they've stopped is because they don't yet know how to neutralize ours."

"We have a strength?" asked Addie.

"It's me," said Perkins. "They know I'm reading them. And since they've stopped at a distance, I'm sure they do have a weakness we can exploit. Watch this."

Perkins took three strides toward the line of drones, and they all withdrew. When he returned to us, they moved back in again.

"They're waiting until they have overwhelmingly superior numbers," said Addie as more drones arrived, "and waiting is something we can't do."

"They might be made of nothing but drip-dry polyester," said Wilson, "but if they charge us, we won't stand a chance."

He was right. The drones were now three deep, and more were arriving by the second. Just then, one of the Hollow Men wrapped around the track tried to grab me with an empty arm attached to a muddy empty glove. We had needed a break, and we got one.

"Bingo," I said. "Perkins?"

Perkins looked at the drone's gloved hand as it felt around, the rest of the drone still jammed in the drive sprocket. The other drone costumes wedged into the track, I noted, were lifeless, just empty clothes.

"Ah," said Perkins, "wounded. Spellcode probably disrupted. Here goes." He held the glove for a moment, then said excitedly, "Now *that's* something I can use. Sickeningly simple, when you think of it. They were right to be nervous. Wait a moment."

And he squatted down to prepare himself as the crowd of drones grew to five deep. There were now about a hundred and fifty of them less than ten steps away.

"Blast," said Perkins.

"What?"

"I need forty years of life-spirit to make this spell work, and I wouldn't have made it past age seventy-six, so I've not got enough years to trade. I need a dozen more to figure out a countermeasure *and* to clear the swords out of the half-track."

"Take it off me," I said. "I'll still be only twenty-eight."

"No," said Wilson, "use me. This way I get the value-added death I've always wanted. Dying to protect you all. It is poetic. It is *heroic.* I insist."

"I'm only twelve," countered Addie, "so I'm the most qualified to surrender any years. I'll be in my early twenties, and I feel twice that old already. Perkins, do your thing."

The drones, now six deep and numbering at least three hundred, began to tramp the ground as though ready for attack.

"Okay," said Perkins, holding out his hand to Addie. "Repeat the count of three. One."

She took his hand. "One."

There was no time for any goodbyes or pithy final speeches. I didn't have time to even think before the Hollow Men drew their swords in unison — a sound, like the Song of the Quarkbeast, that I hoped never to hear again.

"Two," said Perkins, eyes tightly closed, concentrating hard.

"Two."

The Hollow Men advanced a step. I could see nothing but black suits and white shirts in every direction.

"Three."

But Addie Powell didn't get to say three. With surprising agility, Wilson jumped forward, knocked their hands apart, and replaced Addie's hand with his own.

"Three," said Wilson, and Perkins summoned every second of his life and let fly. There was a high-pitched wail, a bright flash, and a pulse of blue light that moved rapidly outward as Perkins and Wilson vaporized, the spell squeezing every vestige of mortality from their souls.

A moment later, Addie, the princess, and I were left standing alone, the Hollow Men every bit as alive as before.

"This isn't good," I said.

The drones charged, and the three of us, our tempers high, met the first wave head-on with an angry clatter of swords. I had expected to meet a swift end, but a second later the first rank of Hollow Men seemed to falter and collapse, quickly followed by the second and the third. Swords fell to the ground as Hollow Men collapsed like deflating parachutes, their clothes literally falling apart around them.

Perkins had not had the power to defeat drones outright, but he did have the power to turn the nylon stitching to its component parts: gaseous nitrogen, carbon dioxide, and quite a lot of hydrogen. If I'd had nylon stitching, my clothes would have fallen off too, but I was sensibly dressed in cotton.

Addie and I looked around at the hundreds of pieces of fabric blowing in the wind. They were twitching as the drones attempted to recover and develop a counter-measure of their own. But Hollow Men don't *do* magic— they *are* magic. And unless they came up with several hundred seamstresses in the next ten minutes, we had won.

FORTY-FIVE

The Last Stand

Correction: We'd sort of won. Perkins and Wilson were no longer with us. On the ground where they had been standing were their ID tags, the change in their pockets, and a few zippers, gold fillings, and Wilson's gallstones. The swords stuck into the tracks had been transformed into ice and were melting.

Perkins had outdone himself. We were back in the game.

But there was no time to reflect. "I'm thinking we shouldn't be hanging around," said Addie, pointing to where the Hollow Men on the distant ranks of the surrounding army were not quite as dismantled as the rest. They didn't seem dangerous, but already we could see more Hollow Men popping into life and heading our way.

I jumped into the driver's seat and fired up the engine while Addie joined me in the passenger seat. We looked at each other. Someone was missing.

We found the princess crouched on the ground behind the half-track, cradling her arm. She looked up at us with an apologetic smile.

"I took a hit the second before Perkins did his stuff," she said. Her right hand was severed cleanly at the wrist. If we didn't do something soon, we'd lose her to blood loss.

Addie had dealt with this sort of thing before on the tourist trail, and pulled a bandage kit from one of her pouches. "This will hurt," she said.

"It already hurts," said the princess. "Go ahead."

Addie bound the stump tightly, which slowed the bleeding though didn't lessen the pain. We quite literally threw the princess into the back of the half-track next to Rubber Colin, and I jumped into the driver's seat.

"Hurry," said Addie. "There are more, and they're redeploying." She grabbed her sword and returned to her place on the hood.

The princess climbed in next to me and stared forlornly at her stump. "Laura Scrubb will be pissed when she finds I've lost one of her hands. Before I was useless but *with* a sword. Now I'm double-useless without one."

"Maybe not," I said. I rummaged in my bag and passed her the Helping Hand™. A Helping Hand™ is Memory Pre-Loaded with every dexterous act imaginable, from mending barometers to building box-girder bridges. With a pair of them, you could play Rachmaninoff's third piano concerto, which is seriously hard. More relevant now, a Helping Hand™ can wield a sword as expertly as if it were conducting open-heart surgery — which are not as unrelated as one might think.

"There's some duct tape in the toolbox." I gestured toward the back. "Get a couple of lengths and I'll tape it on."

She did, and soon the princess had two hands again, even if her new one was too large, four decades older than her, hairy, and had *No More Pies* tattooed on the back. The Helping Hand™ grabbed a sword, and the princess joined Addie on the hood.

We covered the next four hundred yards in less than a minute, the engine laboring to overcome the drag of the clothes still stuck in the tracks. We plunged down the slope into the shallow ravine and forded the river, barely glancing at the decaying bones of the massacred. We made it another hundred yards, and just as the engine temperature was nudging into the red, the Hollow Men closed ranks into an unbroken wall in front of us. There were fewer — Perkins had depleted their numbers by at least two-thirds — but more were streaming from Shandar's Guanolite facility, quite literally dropping their droppings to assist in this most important task: protect the secret.

Overheating, the half-track slowed to a walking pace, then stopped with a clatter.

The Hollow Men were standing between us and the safety of the forest. As their ranks swelled with identical compatriots, they began walking slowly toward us, the outer edges of the long line curving around to attack on all sides.

I grabbed a sword and joined the others on the hood for what was now a last-stand defense. The Hollow Men would be upon us in thirty seconds, and unless we could each take down seventy drones before succumbing ourselves, the end would not be long in coming.

"It's funny what runs through your mind when the end is near," said Addie. "All I can think about is how annoyed I am that my numbers didn't add up. With Perkins and Wilson, we've lost five out of eight, and that's one more than the fifty percent I'd calculated."

"I was thinking of odd stuff too," I replied with a half smile, "like who will look after the Quarkbeast. Tiger, I guess."

"I was thinking about walking one more time in the palace gardens," mused the princess. "The fountains are very cooling in the summer."

I looked behind us at Cadir Idris. I could see the Jeep

and the rock-hewn stairway. We'd be safe there, but only to die of starvation, or be attacked if we again attempted escape.

"We'd never reach it in time," said Addie, "and I don't run. Not from anything."

"Me neither," said the princess. "Fleeing for one's life is so very . . . unregal."

So we stood together on the hood of the half-track, swords at the ready, awaiting our fate. I wasn't thinking only about the Quarkbeast. I was thinking about the Eye of Zoltar, and where it might be. I was thinking that I had failed to find the Eye, and that the dragons would die. And I was thinking about Perkins.

Then I had no more time to think, for the Hollow Men had charged.

With her new old hand, the princess was now the most skilled with her sword, and Addie was not far behind. They dispatched three each in quick order, keeping the drones from climbing upon the half-track. I simply swiped where I could with my sword in both hands.

It was desperate, but we were not so much fighting as postponing the inevitable. I sliced through a drone that had jumped on the hood, then ducked as Addie cut down another behind me. I could feel my muscles begin to tire. When I could no longer swing a sword, it would be over.

And that was when we heard a loud rushing noise. It was like a distant express train, but ahead of the noise was a call, like the sharp bark of a seal. The noise increased to a thunderous roar, and a moment later the Hollow Men in front of us scattered like playing cards, disrupted by a foe whose form was wobbly and indistinct.

Almost instantly the drones regrouped to fight the new, larger, mysterious enemy, and we were once more on our own. I had a cut on my thigh, had lost part of my boot, and I think my little toe. I could also feel the salty taste of blood in my mouth from a cut lip, but we were still alive.

We heard the *whooshing* noise again, mixed with a faint *Ook, ook!,* and then saw the indistinct outline of a Cloud Leviathan as it executed a steep hammerhead turn in the air and dived down for the second attack, its large mouth open. As the rushing sound increased again, we could see that the Leviathan was not alone — he was being ridden.

But the rider was not a pirate — it was Ralph, standing on the Leviathan's back, surfing the creature without any apparent fear.

The second pass was more devastating than the first. The drones not gathered up in the Leviathan's massive mouth were blown apart by the high-pressure air venting out of its underbelly. We jumped off the half-track after the second pass to lend a hand with slicing the lingering Hollow Men to ribbons. But there was no need; it was an enemy in rout.

Ralph and his new friend conducted six passes before the Hollow Men had fully retreated or simply collapsed back into parcels of clothes. The drones were powerful, but even they knew when to call it a day. This time the battle was truly over.

We looked at one another, a picture of exhaustion, stress, and relief. I wasn't the only one who had taken some damage. The princess had two nasty cuts on her arm and chest, and Addie was wrapping her arm with a bandage.

The Leviathan parked itself nearby in a low hover and Ralph jumped down to join us, still carrying his large ladies' handbag in the crook of his arm. Smiling in his odd Australopithecine way, he greeted us with clasping of our hands and a soft chuckle. We had not been enamored with Ralph when we first met, but after Perkins devolved him, it was we who had cared for him. Clearly, friendship and loyalty went back a long way, before we were truly human. We'd looked after Ralph, and he'd looked after us.

"Thank you, Ralph," I said.

"No *Ralph,*" he said, his mouth contorting as though chewing the words together before he spoke. "Name . . . *Pirate 'aptain Ralph.*"

"Ralph . . . Wolff?" Why not? "But a pirate?"

"Only f'good," said Sky Pirate Ralph with another semi-grin, before looking around. "Others?"

"All gone, Captain."

"Sorrow f'all," said the Australopithecine, "'cept Curtis. Glad dead, 'natius too. Wilson, 'erkins — liked. Sorry."

"We're sorry too," I said. "Who's your friend?" I nodded toward the Leviathan, whose chameleonic skin blended in with the scrubby grassland he was hovering above. Pirate Ralph looked at the Leviathan, smiled one of his ancient smiles, and touched all our hands again.

"Friend," he said, and rummaged in his oversized handbag before handing me a small object carved out of Leviathan tooth and attached to a gold chain. It looked like a whistle. The pirate captain pointed at it, made a blowing gesture, then pointed at himself, the Leviathan, and me.

"I understand," I said, and he smiled again, snapped the clasp of his handbag shut, climbed back upon the body of the beast, and they moved off and up as one. By the time they were a thousand feet up, the Leviathan's underbelly looked like the clouds, and a second later we couldn't see it at all.

We stood there for some moments in silence.

"Well, Addie," said the princess at last, "looks like your fifty percent fatality rate was correct after all."

Addie frowned as she counted up the numbers in her head. Eight had come out, and four had survived.

"Yes," she said sadly, "but I wish I'd been wrong. Without Perkins and without Wilson, all would have been lost. Jenny, I'm truly sorry."

And we hugged, spontaneously and in silence, while the tattered remnants of the Hollow Men were blown by the breeze across the scrubby grassland.

FORTY-SIX

We Become Sisters

The half-track had cooled down enough to be started once we'd cut the clothes from the tracks, so we moved off and didn't stop until we reached the cave where we'd spent the night before. It was late when we arrived, and, too tired to bother hiding the half-track or posting one of us as sentry, we all fell fast asleep.

I was awakened by a faint noise from outside the cave. I looked at my watch only to discover that a sword cut had removed its face and hands. I nudged the princess, who mumbled something like "No, no, nursey, a pedicure at ten, I said," before turning over and going back to sleep. Addie's bedroll was empty, and I found her crouching silently at the cave entrance, watching. It was painful to move, as all my cuts and nicks stung horribly.

I crouched near Addie. "Who's outside?" I whispered.

"The Mountain Silurians," she whispered back.

"Let's see what they want," I said, standing up. "They know we're here, and after yesterday, I'm not sure much really scares me anymore."

We stepped out from behind the rhododendrons to find three warriors astride Buzonjis silently waiting for us.

"Greetings on this day," I said, "and all respects be upon you. But if you mean to kill us, then be quick about it. We have faced more death in the past twenty-four hours than we would care to see in a lifetime, so do it now or go about your business and leave us to ours."

"We're not here to kill you," said the middle warrior and the largest of the three. "We are here to bring Geraint the Great's word of congratulations. He salutes the brave warriors who have faced the *Cavi homini* and returned, and also thanks you for the goat thing, which looks like sound financial advice. He deems you worthy of calling you his sisters, and grants you free access upon our lands and the full protection of the Mountain Silurians, wherever you might be."

"Oh," I said, "good."

"Then you accept?" asked the warrior.

"Do we?" I asked Addie.

"Hell, yes!" said Addie enthusiastically. "An honorary sister of Geraint the Great? You'll never have to line up at the grocery store again. And that's just for starters. Never mind all the other fringe benefits of being affiliated with the most terrifying warrior tribe in the whole of the kingdoms."

"I don't shop at the grocery store," said the princess, who had come up behind us. "In fact, I don't think I shop at all."

"Laura Scrubb will have all the benefits when you return her body," I said. "Perhaps it might make up for the lost hand."

"You're right," said the princess. "I'm totally in."

The warrior on the left slipped expertly from his Buzonji and asked us to sit down. An induction into the Mountain Silurians' affiliation was designated by a tattoo of a small blue star on the right temple. It took about twenty minutes each, and after presenting us with an elegantly bound book of eligible bachelors within the tribe and three offers of marriage for the Fearless Tour Guide Addie Powell, the warriors remounted their Buzonjis and were gone.

"Mother will be furious I got a tattoo," said the princess, looking at the livid mark in the half-track's side mirror. "Yes, I *know* it's technically not on me. It's just that I've become so used to this body, I'm not really sensing much of a difference. In a strange way, I'm actually enjoying being Laura Scrubb."

We had a good wash in the waterfall, then took a half hour to tension the half-track's tracks, as was insisted upon in the rental agreement. I even checked the oil and refilled the radiator with water.

We repacked, climbed in, checked that Rubber Colin's straps were still secure, and headed off down the Llangurig road.

"Do you think Laura has had as interesting a time in my body as I have in hers?" said the princess, who had been thoughtful for some time.

"I'm thinking almost certainly," I replied.

"I'm going to free her," she said, "with a generous pension. In fact, I'm going to free all the orphans working in the palace. And when I become queen, I'm abolishing this whole ridiculous orphan-based economy. The trade in orphans ends under me. The fast food joints and hotel industry will just have to figure it out another way."

I smiled. Things were looking good for the Kingdom of Snodd, and for orphans in general. Queen Mimosa had been right to send her daughter out with us, even if by every other measure, the trip had been an abject failure.

"Maybe that's why we have the Troll Wars," mused the princess, "to supply the orphan-based economy with orphans."

"It's crossed my mind many times," I said.

We came within sight of Llangurig, and I was suddenly aware that the past few days, adventurous as they were, had not helped us one atom in our fight against the Mighty Shandar. In fact, since we'd lost Perkins and Colin was still rubber, we were worse off. The only upside of the not-finding-the-Eye issue was that things hadn't gotten worse—just stayed the same.

We found Llangurig a ghost town. The arrival of the railroad had made it irrelevant; the handful of residents who remained were there only because they loved it, and none of us had any issue with that.

We had lunch at the Bluebell and each ate two main courses, with sponge pudding for dessert. Cadir Idris had given us an appetite.

"So who did take the Eye of Zoltar?" asked Addie, calling for more custard.

"I don't know," I replied, "but whoever did has had six years to unlock its power, and I'm figuring they haven't. We'd certainly have heard about it."

"Tell me if I'm pointing out the obvious," said the princess, "but when did Able Quizzler die from that fall?"

"It was . . . six years ago," I murmured.

"And when did Pirate Wolff get changed to lead, did you say?"

"Six years ago."

"Is that important?" asked Addie.

The princess didn't need to answer. I knew precisely what she was getting at. I got up and placed some money on the table.

"Where are we going?" asked Addie.

"We're going to find some shovels," I said, "because the princess just picked up on something we all missed."

"And then," added the princess, "we're going to the cemetery."

I had no difficulty finding Able Quizzler's grave again, and started to dig immediately, much to the outrage of Dirk the gravedigger.

"You can't be doing tha'!" he said. "We only 'cept deposits, not withdrawals!"

We ignored him, so after waving his arms at us for a while, he shambled off about as fast as he could go.

The ground was waterlogged and heavy, but we eventually unearthed a leaden foot, twisted and mildly flattened by the impact, about two feet beneath the surface.

"Kevin Zipp might have been right after all," I said as we continued to dig, "and this is my theory: Able

Quizzler found his way to Pirate Wolff's lair, and as soon as the Eye was shown to him, he used the most easily accessible magic within the Eye to make his escape, in this case, a Turning to Lead Gatekeeper. He pried the Eye from Pirate Wolff's hand, then killed every pirate in his way using the Eye's magic before escaping on a Leviathan. But the Eye's Gatekeeper spell did what Gate-keeper spells are meant to do: protect the jewel. Quizzler himself was turned to lead soon after, and fell from the Leviathan."

"And landed here, while still — we hope — clutch-ing the Eye," said the princess.

"Fingers crossed."

We uncovered Quizzler's torso, also deformed with the impact, and then finally his leaden face, still fixed with the triumphant grin he'd worn six years before and ten thousand feet up. I knew then that my theory was sound. Quizzler had been killed by the Eye's malevolence just as he had achieved his lifelong quest.

"There!" said Addie as we brushed more dirt off the body.

Able Quizzler's leaden hand was clenched around a large, pink jewel. Despite the ground being wet and muddy, the jewel seemed to repel the dirt and shone with a brightness that almost invited avariciousness. It was ac-tually, I think, even bigger than a goose's egg, and from somewhere deep inside the jewel, there was a light—a pulsating glow, like that of a human pulse. It seemed that Zoltar's evil will, the guiding force of the gem's power, was still in residence.

We'd found the Eye of Zoltar. But we were going to have to be very, very careful unless we wanted to end up like Quizzler—lead, and very dead.

We all stared at the jewel, hardly daring to breathe.

"I've got no magic in me," said the princess, "but even I can feel it—a sort of dark wickedness."

"I feel it too," said Addie, "and I'm also thinking that no one should touch it."

I agreed with this, and after a brief discussion I had the princess go into town to buy an iron cooking pot, several large balls of twine, and as many candles as she could carry. And then, without touching the massive jewel, we pried it from Quizzler's grasp and placed it in the pot surrounded by clay we had dug up from the grave. We bound the lid of the pot closed with twine, then poured molten candle wax over the string to seal it tight.

We carried our treasure gently to the half-track, where we lashed it securely to the floor in the back of the vehicle next to Rubber Colin. It was the most dangerous magical artifact that I had ever handled, and I wondered then about the wisdom of giving it to Shandar, even if it would save the lives of the dragons. But I would consult with Moobin and the others at Kazam about that.

"Okay, then," I said, "just one more thing to do and we're heading home."

"I really hope it doesn't involve going back into the Empty Quarter," said the princess.

"No, we're going to Cambrianopolis — to negotiate for Once Magnificent Boo's release."

FORTY-SEVEN

Negotiations in Cambrianopolis

Cambrianopolis was close to the border with Midlandia and still a good hour's drive north of the Kingdom of Snodd. It was a sprawling city built in the "shabby war-torn chic" style so popular in the empire. Most of the city seemed made up of piles of rubble interspersed with roofless houses and half-dilapidated apartment buildings, leaning dangerously and blackened by smoke. It was all contrived, of course, like a theme park to mankind's warmongery. Most of the apparently empty buildings were fully occupied and not actually unsafe. The overall effect was of a nation in constant civil war, which was not the case at all; the Tharv dynasty had ruled unopposed for more than three centuries.

We found our way to Emperor Tharv's state-owned Ransom Clearance House, a large building that, despite bars on the windows, was run like a five-star hotel: it had an extensive menu, reliable room service, and a health spa and pool. If you were going to be kidnapped anywhere, Cambrianopolis was the place. Some even tried deliberately to be kidnapped, as the Clearance House was full of interesting people. One might, for instance, have breakfast with the Duke of Ipswich, a long-term resident, and be invited to buy tea for the deposed and penniless King Zsigsmund VIII in the afternoon.

Addie said she'd wait for us by the half-track. I showed my credentials at the door, took a number, and then sat with the princess on a bench and waited to be called. The Clearance House was designed to make negotiations as quick and easy as possible: agree on a price, pay the money, release. Nevertheless, negotiations *could* drag on for decades. The Duke of Ipswich had been here sixteen years while everyone tried to come to an agreement. The ransom was the easy part; the argument was over who would pay the duke's food and laundry expenses.

Our number was eventually called, and we entered a small, cheerless room furnished with a shabby table and chairs, dusty gray filing cabinets, and a dead potted plant. Our negotiator was a young, tidily dressed woman with an intriguing scar running vertically down her cheek and across to her lower lip.

"Hello," she said pleasantly, rising to greet us. "Welcome to the Cambrian Empire's Ransom Clearance House. My name is Hilda, and I will be negotiating on behalf of the nation. Offers made in this room are legally binding, and negotiations may be recorded for training purposes."

I asked if my handmaiden could sit in, which was okay, and then said who I was and who I wanted to release. Hilda's eyebrows rose, but whether that was because of me or Boo, I wasn't sure. I'd like to think both.

Hilda picked up a phone and asked to have Boo's file sent up, and then made small talk about the weather and any news from the Kingdom of Snodd. I tried to fill her in about politics, but she was really only interested in the kingdom's most famous stunt performer, Jimmy "Daredevil" Nuttjob.

"On fire, last I heard," I told her.

"Oh," she said. "News doesn't really cross the border. There could be a war going on, and we'd be the last to hear about it. Ah, the file. Thank you, Brigitte."

Hilda opened the file and scanned the contents.

"So," she said after a while, "Miss Boolean Champernowne Waseed Mitford Smith, aka Once Magnificent Boo. Occupation: Sorcerer. Condition: Healthy but lacking her spelling fingers so deemed 'damaged goods.' Charges: Unauthorized importation of a Tralfamosaur, illegal flight over the border, and using magic to avoid detection. Charges dropped by the intervention of the emperor, but after refusing to do any sorcery for him and threatening to 'punch him painfully in the eye,' Miss Smith was transferred to the Clearance House for disposal. We've had two best offers for her, both of which are currently on hold. But since you are a recognized negotiator for Kazam Mystical Arts Management and have the prior claim, we will transfer her to you if we can agree on terms. If you don't buy her release, we'll accept the highest best offer. Okay?"

"Not really," I said.

"Splendid. Here we go: We're looking to get thirty back for her."

Thirty grand was a lot of cash, and actually a little lower than I thought they would ask. But she was, as they said, damaged goods, so her value was limited.

"Ridiculous," I said. "She's not even on staff at Kazam. I'm here as a friend, and will ask Boo to pay me back once we get her home."

"But she *is* a sorcerer," said Hilda, "and even though her power might be diminished, we understand she can still spell, just with limited accuracy and duration. Give us twenty-five, and you can take her away now; I'll throw in some Home Depot vouchers and two tickets to the Nolan Sisters concert next month."

"Twenty-five?" I echoed. "Out of the question. Houses of Enchantment don't have that kind of cash, and you well know it."

The negotiations went on like this for about twenty minutes. We were both polite but firm, and I finally agreed on eighteen, which I thought quite reasonable. It was always possible Boo might contribute a few thousand, although somehow I doubted it.

"Excellent," said Hilda, filling out a form. "How will you be paying?"

I placed the twenty-thousand-moolah letter of credit that Moobin had given me on the table and slid it across. Hilda glanced at it.

"That'll do for her room service and bar bills. What about the rest?"

"Eighteen, you said," I told her. "This is good for twenty."

"Oh," she said. "I meant eighteen million."

"Eighteen *million?*"

"Of course. Miss Smith was once one of the world's greatest sorcerers. The highest best offer was for eight million. Do you want to go away and raise the funds and come back? I'll have to warn you that if we don't see the cash by Sunday, we withdraw our terms and take the best offer."

"Hang on——" I began, but the princess interrupted me.

"We'll pay now," she said, rummaging in my knapsack. "You do take all forms of currency, don't you?"

Hilda nodded, and said that they took everything except goats, as there was "something of a glut at present." The princess presented her with the receipt I had received for the Bugatti Royale.

"There," said the princess, "this should cover it."

Hilda looked at the note, which stated that we were owed the value of the Royale, signed by Emperor Tharv himself.

"We don't take receipts," said Hilda.

"It's not a receipt," said the princess. "Technically speaking, what you have there is currency. Any currency is merely a promissory note issued by a government against its assets to enable the citizenry to more easily trade commodities. By 'assets' one might usually mean gold, although you could choose mice, turnips, or tulip bulbs. Often you don't need any assets at all — if the citizenry believes that their national bank will remain solvent come what may, a simple promise is enough, backed by nothing more tangible than . . . confidence."

Hilda looked at the princess blankly, then at me.

"Yes, I know," I said. "We've had to endure her for a while now, but the funny thing is, she's usually right."

Heartened by this, the princess continued. "And since that receipt is signed by Emperor Tharv, who is the

Cambrian head of state, that note is legal tender for the value of one Bugatti Royale."

"But it's a car," I said. "It's not worth eighteen million."

The princess smiled. "Not *quite* correct. There were only seven Bugatti Royales made, and the last one sold at auction for over twenty million. The Bugatti is not so much a car as an exquisite work of art you can take to the shops. You've been driving a Van Gogh."

"You like economics, don't you, handmaiden?" said Hilda, picking up the telephone. "Hello? I need to speak to the Master of the Sums."

We waited while Hilda explained the situation, and after a minute or two she put her hand over the receiver. "The Bugatti Royale exchange rate stands at 19.2 million Cambrian washers," she said. "Would you like to take the deposed and penniless King Zsigsmund VIII in lieu of change?"

"No, I'll take a Volkswagen Beetle, please," I said, "one in particular. Orange — the one Boo arrived in. The rest can be cash."

FORTY-EIGHT

Heading Home

We stayed overnight in Cambrianopolis while Boo's paperwork was processed. We each had a good meal, took a much-welcome bath, and slept in clean sheets for the first time in what seemed like an age.

Talk between the three of us had been sparse, with each of us lost in our own thoughts. We'd all be returning to our usual lives over the next few days. The princess would go back to being a princess, I would return to Kazam, and Addie would deal with her usual bread-and-butter tour work: taking eager and dopey tourists into high jeopardy, then attempting to stop them from being eaten.

We were waiting outside the Clearance House twenty minutes before it was due to open. I'd tried to reach Kazam on the conch again, but still nothing. The good news was that my Volkswagen had been found, repaired, filled with fuel, and returned the previous evening. We had spent an amusing half hour trying to squeeze Rubber Colin inside the car, only to give up and lash him onto the roof rack. Addie had returned the half-track to the Cambrianopolis branch of the rental company; we were very glad we'd taken the additional collision waiver, as the vehicle was in a far worse state than when we'd rented it.

Boo stepped blinking into the daylight as soon as I had signed the paperwork. She did not seem particularly happy to see us.

"You shouldn't have paid the ransom," she said. "If no one paid, the kidnapping business would collapse in an afternoon. You're all fools."

"It's good to see you again too, Boo," I said. "This is Addie Powell, our friend and guide, and this is Princess Shazza of Snodd."

"A Sister Organza switcheroo?" asked Boo, staring at the princess and prodding her with an inquisitive middle finger.

"My mother did it," said the princess.

"Once, I knew the queen very well," said Boo, raising an inquisitive eyebrow at the princess. "A good woman until she married that idiot, your father. Ask her if she remembers the incident with the squid."

"I will," said the princess, who seemed to have become immune to the insults her father's name attracted.

"Right," I said as soon as we were in the VW, where Once Magnificent Boo deferentially allowed the princess to sit up front. "Let's get out of Cambrianopolis before someone changes their mind."

Luckily, no one did, and soon we were heading back toward the border. Barring bad traffic or a breakdown, we'd be back at the palace by lunchtime and the princess and the handmaiden could be switched back.

"I used to think Laura Scrubb was the ugliest girl I'd ever see," said the princess, staring in the visor mirror at the face she'd been using, "but I've come to like the snub nose, shortness of stature, and lack of any agreeable bone structure."

"You'll soon be yourself again," I said, with mixed feelings. The princess in Laura's body and I had gotten along really well, but I wasn't sure how that would translate once she was back to being beautiful and rich and influential once more.

As we drove toward the border, I related everything that had happened over the past four days. I told Boo all that I could recall—leaving out the part about Gabby, to keep my promise of discretion—and expected her to make comments, ask questions, or say, "Ah-ha" or "Really?" or "Gosh" or something. But she didn't say anything until I'd finished.

"That explains why there's a rubber dragon strapped to the roof," she said at last. "I was wondering about that. Where's the Eye of Zoltar right now?"

I told her it was in the cooking pot on the floor of the back seat, and she drew her feet away.

"It'll be nothing but trouble. If I were you, I'd drop it down the first abandoned mine shaft you come across."

I reiterated that we needed it to save the dragons, and that we'd hold a Sorcerer's Conclave to discuss everything when we got home. Boo merely shrugged and muttered darkly about "meddling with powers you could not possibly hope to comprehend."

We passed a road sign alerting us that the border to the Kingdom of Snodd was ahead.

"Thirty minutes," said Addie, who would be picking up her next group from the tourist office, where we'd first met her.

"About time," said the princess. "I'm really beginning to miss being me."

I ran over my speech to Queen Mimosa as we drove along. About how I felt that the princess had progressed from being a spoiled brat of the highest order to someone who could, and would, think of others. On second thought, I probably wouldn't need to say anything at all; the princess would simply open her mouth and speak, and the queen in her wisdom would know.

We spotted the smoke when we were still some distance from the border.

Boo leaned forward in her seat. "That's not the border," she said. "It's farther away."

"Hereford?" I asked.

"Closer than that," said Boo. "Perhaps the palace."

"The palace?" echoed the princess, and urged me to drive faster. The palace was ten miles beyond the border, and as we crested the last rise and the kingdom was spread before us, the princess's home came into view. What we saw was neither expected nor welcome.

"No!" cried the princess, and put her hand to her mouth. I stopped the car at a lookout spot where several other people were watching, and we climbed out.

The royal palace was on fire, and a long pall of black smoke drifted across the land. As we stood, there was a small explosion in the castle, then another.

"My lovely palace," said the princess. "I do hope Mother and Father got out okay."

"The powder magazine must have blown up or something," I said.

"Don't be a clot," said Boo. "The palace is under attack. See there, landships on the move."

She was right. Far in the distance we could see the unmistakable rhomboid shape of King Snodd's defensive landships moving across the land; one exploded into fragments as we watched. Beyond the palace, another distant smudge of smoke drifted into the sky. They — whoever they were — had attacked Hereford as well. I felt anger rather than fear, and concern over my friends and colleagues.

"Who would dare attack us?" said the princess. "A sneak attack by what, Midlandia? But why? My cousin is the crown prince and the one I was most likely to marry. Our kingdoms would have been joined peacefully in the fullness of time."

"It's not Midlandia," said Boo in a dark tone. "Look down there." She pointed toward the Cambrian-Snodd border. The Cambrian artillery, pointed toward the sky when we entered the country several days earlier, was now pointing across the River Wye toward the Kingdom of Snodd. Tharv had mobilized his troops to defend his nation, although how well they could do this wasn't clear. As we watched, a single Snoddian landship headed toward the border with Cambria.

"Boo," I said, "can you do a fingerscope?"

"Of a sort." She made two circles with her middle fingers and thumbs and then uttered a spell. In an instant, there was a lens within each of her encircled fingers, and we crowded around her shoulders to see the Snoddian landship close up. It was badly battle damaged, and from the forward hatch fluttered a white flag of truce. Whoever was in the landship was attempting to escape across the border into the empire. This was a defeated army on the run.

There was another explosion at the castle.

"Oh!" said the princess, clutching her chest in pain. "Oh, oh, oh!" She dropped to her knees and tried desperately to regain her breath. "She's frightened. I can feel her."

"Feel who?" asked Addie.

"Me—her—Laura, the princess. She's running. Running for her life!"

I held her hand and squeezed it, and she looked up at me with the same confused realization I had seen when her body was swapped.

"This is bad," said Boo. "Whoever the aggressors are, I think this war is all but lost."

As if to punctuate her words, another huge explosion tore through the castle, flinging masonry and rubble in all directions. We watched in shock as the castle collapsed in on itself in a massive ball of dust and debris.

I looked at the princess silently sobbing on the ground, and then at Boo, who shook her head sadly.

"It's over," she said. "I can feel it in the air. A collective sadness, a negative emotion disrupting the background wizidrical energy. I'm sorry, ma'am, but your parents, the king and queen, are both dead."

"Oh, no," the princess said in a quiet voice. "And my little brother, Stevie?"

"Of this, I know nothing."

"What about Laura Scrubb?" she asked. "And my beautiful and elegant body?"

Boo shook her head, and the princess nodded, accepting that she could never truly be herself again. But with the king and queen dead, her real body destroyed, and the whereabouts of the prince unknown, this could mean only one thing.

"Your Gracious Majesty," I said to the princess, bowing my head, "rightful ruler of the Kingdom of Snodd, you have my loyalty above everything. I wish only to serve, and serve well."

"And I," said Addie, giving a low bow, "humbly request leave to be your personal bodyguard."

"I, too, am at your disposal, Your Majesty," said Once Magnificent Boo, "in matters magical, wherever I can serve. Loyal, like us all, until death."

"Loyal," we affirmed in unison, "until death."

The new queen stared up at us from where she was still sitting on the ground. We'd had no confirmation that Laura Scrubb was gone, but it seemed that something inside the princess knew it was true. Perhaps a small part of her had stayed with the real Laura.

"Okay, then," she said, taking a deep breath and wiping away her tears. "I accept all the responsibilities of my birthright, and will not rest until the perpetrator of this foul deed is brought to justice. But I will not be calling myself queen until I am once more in full command of my lands and people. Help me up, will you? I think I've got a cramp."

We helped her up and sat on a bench, all four of us, and watched the black smoke drift across the distant countryside. The princess broke the silence.

"Jennifer," she said, "I should like you to be Royal Counsel."

"With respect, ma'am," I said, "I'm only sixteen. That's a job usually reserved for gray hair—someone with experience."

"Nonsense," said the princess, "you have plenty of experience, and what's more, I trust you completely and know you will always do the right thing. You accept?"

"I accept, ma'am."

She thanked me, smiled, and looked at her hands. The left was still raw and calloused from the previous owner's years of toil, and the other was still the Helping Hand™, held on with duct tape and with its *No More Pies* tattoo. It wasn't an ideal look, and as far as we knew, it was a first for royalty.

"This is my body now, isn't it?"

"Yes, I think it is."

"Then I better start looking after it. Tell me, Jenny, am I horribly plain?"

I looked at her pale, sun-starved face, her brown hair still lank with undernourishment, and her tired eyes.

"It's not the outside that counts, ma'am."

FORTY-NINE

Aftermath

Ｉt was too dangerous to cross the border until we knew more about what was happening, so we stayed put. I tried over and over again to reach Kazam on the conch, but with no success. The road out of the kingdom was soon packed full of refugees, vehicles, and medical personnel tending to any wounded who had managed to escape. Tharv, true to his cherished principles of unpredictability, welcomed the refugees from the Kingdom of Snodd, and from the garbled reports from displaced citizens, we managed to piece together what had happened — yet it took us a while to realize who the enemy was.

The Snoddian royal family was, as we had feared,

killed when the palace was destroyed. We also learned that the war had not been solely against the Kingdom of Snodd. Of the twenty-eight nations within the Un-united Kingdoms, all but nine were now overrun, or had surrendered. Information was scarce, but it seemed that Financia had been spared because it was a center of banking, the Duchy of Portland had been defended successfully due to its deep moat, and the seagoing nation of the Isle of Wight had been away conducting sea trials in the North Atlantic.

It was hard to describe the chaos in which we found ourselves as we walked up to the border. Homeless people had grabbed what they could before fleeing, and mothers desperately searched for husbands, their children clinging on tightly with a look of numb terror upon their faces. There were casualties, too; soldiers with appalling wounds were being treated as best they could be. Amidst all this, the Cambrian gunners lay waiting, their weapons trained upon the invaders, poised to return fire if attacked.

For the invaders *were* there, sitting outside the Snoddian customs post on the other side of the River Wye, doing nothing, awaiting orders. The larger members totaled six and were each twenty-five feet tall, dressed only in a loincloth and heavy battle-bootees. Their skin was covered in elaborate tattoos, each had a dead goat decorating a copper war helmet, and their small, cruel eyes stared greedily.

"Trolls," hissed the princess when we saw them. "I hate trolls."

"And not alone," said Addie. "Look."

The other members of the group she indicated were fewer in number and stature, and looked like nothing more than businessmen in dark suits and sunglasses. The group had planted two flags in the ground denoting their allegiance and the extent of their new territories. The Trollvanian flag was obvious, but the second standard gave me a shock. It had the sign of the flaming footprint: the Mighty Shandar.

"I can't see from this distance," said Addie, "but I'll bet good money there's nothing in those suits."

"Hollow Men," said the princess, "presumably there to relay orders from their master to the troll warriors."

"The Mighty Shandar," said Boo, "as treacherous as he is arrogant. Despite all that he has done, I never trusted him. Not one inch."

"But Kevin Zipp was right," I said. "The next Troll War was going to be when it was least expected. It would be bloody, short, and the aggressors would be victorious. Sadly, the victorious aggressors weren't us—they were the trolls."

"It explains why Tiger and Moobin were so keen for us to find the Eye of Zoltar," said the princess. "To defeat Shandar, we're going to need some serious magical power of our own."

"It also explains why Moobin was telling you that the princess needed to be protected at all costs," said Addie. "A defeated nation needs leadership."

"I think they would have fought bravely," said the princess, "my parents, the army, everyone at Kazam."

"They'd have fought to the death," I said, "even the really strange ones."

"They could be still alive," said the princess. "We don't know anything yet."

"I hope so," I replied, "but —"

"Jenny?"

I started. It was Tiger's voice. Very faint, but unmistakable.

"I can hear Tiger's voice now," I said. "It must be a last shout from the astral plane before he passed to the other side or something."

"I don't think so," said Addie, "because I can hear it too."

It was the conch.

"Tiger?" I said after hurriedly removing the large shell from my bag. "Where are you?"

"Thank goodness," he said in a relieved tone. "Shandar has finally stopped jamming the conchways, probably because he thinks we're all dead. I'm in the basement of Zambini Towers along with the Quarkbeast, Mabel, the Mysterious X, and Monty Vanguard."

I heard a *quark* in the background.

"Okay," I said, "if it's safe to do so, stay right there. I'll be there as soon as I can."

"We don't really have a choice," said Tiger. "We're trapped. I think the building has collapsed above us."

Tiger explained as much as he knew. Shandar had returned to the Kingdom of Snodd, and he had brought the trolls with him. He was clearly not worried about the dragon refund, because no one would be there to demand one. It seemed he had been biding his time all these years, remaining in stone for centuries until the moment was right to strike and strike hard. The previous four Troll Wars had not been wars at all, but a series of warm-ups, preparing the trolls for the ultimate invasion.

"Shandar targeted Kazam before the war began," said Tiger. "Kevin Zipp was kidnapped so we couldn't see it coming, and Kazam was hit first on the morning of the invasion. Feldspar came back from princess duty to rescue us, but could only carry away one at a time. Moobin was first. I don't know if anyone else made it out."

"Any idea why Shandar had me look for the Eye of Zoltar?"

"To get you out of the way, Lady Mawgon thought. You've bested him once before, and we think he's actually quite frightened of you."

"I'm going to make sure of that," I said. "What about you guys?"

Tiger explained that there was ample food and water,

as they were in the basement kitchens. He thought they were safe for the time being; they had heard trolls up above searching through the rubble, but the trolls had moved on. I told him to sit tight, to not use the conch in case Shandar decided to listen in, and that I'd organize a rescue party as soon as I could.

"At least we know Moobin is safe," said Once Magnificent Boo. "We will need many people to retake the kingdoms."

"I hate to be a downer," I said, "but how are we going to retake the kingdoms? We are a vanquished nation without an army, weapons, and, at present, ideas."

"We have hope," said Addie, "and a sense of moral outrage and natural justice. We will retake the kingdoms, no matter what it takes."

"I second that," said Boo. "Dark Magic never triumphs. We will rally what sorcerers we can, and build up an army from scratch if we have to. We have my limited powers, your leadership, the princess as a figurehead, and Addie's unique survival skills. Moobin is still around somewhere. And remember that we have the terrifying possibility of harnessing the awesome power of the Eye of Zoltar."

We were silent for a moment. Things didn't seem so bleak after all.

"Holy smoke," came a voice behind us. "I feel like I've slept with a spare tire in my mouth."

It was Colin. He had returned to normal, still strapped to the roof of the Volkswagen. That might have seemed unusual, but in the surrounding chaos, no one was paying any attention to us at all.

"Oh, yes," said Once Magnificent Boo. "We also have two dragons."

The Chronicles of Kazam will continue . . .